A Novel

The
Kitchen
Mistress

D1711698

KATHLEEN SHOOP

Other Books by Kathleen Shoop

Historical Fiction:
The Letter Series:
The Last Letter—Book One
The Road Home—Book Two

Donora Story Series:
After the Fog—Book One

Romance:
Endless Love Series:
Home Again—Book One
Return to Love—Book Two
Tending Her Heart—Book Three

Women's Fiction:
Love and Other Subjects

kathleenshoop@gmail.com
kshoop.com
Twitter: @kathieshoop
Facebook: Kathleen Shoop

ISBN-13: 978-1519301413
ISBN-10: 1519301413

Cover design: Jenny Toney Quinlin –Historical Editorial and
http://historicalfictionbookcovers.com

To all the patient and generous readers… thank you.

Part I

Chapter 1

The Gift
Katherine

1892
Des Moines, Iowa

I'm a liar. I hate that I am, but the truth put me in suffocating straits. There's no alternative but to keep my truths secret, tucked away where no one can reach them and use them against me. Fear of being accused of lunacy or evil sits deep in my bones and courses through my blood. Sometimes a lie is the only way to survive.

I'm lying right now. To Mama. There's no other choice. She's standing right there in front of me, my secrets alive between us. She doesn't see them, though. I can't tell her that I parcel pieces of who I am, that I fence off sections to protect me inside, that doing so keeps those I love even safer on the outside.

So when I saw the deceased Mrs. Mellet walk right into the room that morning, I almost told Mama the truth. I should have told her the first time I saw her, but I simply couldn't untangle my words from the binding fear that noosed them in my mouth.

"What is it?" Mama asked. "You look like you've seen a ghost."

And so I had. I nearly blurted out that dead Mrs. Mellet was standing there, her spirit, along with what I could only think was an angel, coppery light shimmering in the corner of the room, watching over us. I hoped it was an angel. I thought of the Christoffs and the church elders, the people who had caused my suffering because of things just like this, and I wanted to tell Mama everything.

Trust might be suitable in this case. This was my mother after all. She loved me, I knew that. Yet when I started to explain, the words came against a rush of my own uncertainty. I couldn't trust that love would overcome everything the world brought forth. I wanted to tell the truth. But more than that, I wanted Mama's grace raining down over me like summer sunshine. I wanted her to know me again. But all I could do was swallow my words, let my heart hold my truth, and hope that someday I could reveal everything, let her see the parts of me that made people fear me as though I entered the room with the devil himself.

I inhaled deeply. *Was* I even sane? For I had come to understand that, if not a liar, I was unhinged or possessed. None of these possible truths were suitable for my mother or anyone with sense. I called up the words again, but their sour taste made me stuff them back down. How could I tell Mama that dead Mrs. Mellet was here, in the room, her presence sulfurous, as real as the two of us?

Was it really her? Wispy gray hair, pillowed in a loose updo. Limping toward me, crooked-eyed, twisted-limbed, kinked hands, and curled bare toes. She wore a black sateen high-necked shirtwaist with a belled skirt, far out of fashion in cut. Mrs. Mellet's movement brought the sound of her skirt rustling to my ears as it might have if the woman had been alive in the room. Mama had told me of Mrs. Mellet's twisted toes and fallen arches, and her movements were plodding as if her spirit still suffered her earthly pain.

At first, I thought she appeared angry, hostile. A chill pricked over my skin like a million spiders marching. *Was* she there? I squeezed my eyes shut and wished with all my being that when I opened them the old woman would be gone. When I did, she remained, but the angel had disappeared. A metallic taste gathered in my mouth, saliva rushing, my body wanting the cold sensation gone before my mind even decided the same.

I felt my mouth gaping and saw Mama out of the corner of my eye. She had turned and stopped talking at the sight of me struck dumb, as though she could see my heart pounding in my chest, could feel the same presence that I did.

She moved toward me, a cloudy haze coming with her, bringing the chill closer. I dropped the hairbrush and closed my eyes. I forced an exhale, hoping to clear the room of Mrs. Mellet's spirit with one breath.

At the age of fifteen, I'd already been visited by plenty of spirits, especially in recent times, even by bodies I believed to be angels—even by my own dead brother. But this time, this appearance left me unsure of what I was seeing and why.

"Katherine?"

I shot a look at Mama, who appeared perplexed as she fussed with her sewing box. I looked past her. "Do you see . . . ?"

She followed my gaze, pausing for a moment and then reaffixed it on me, her expression questioning. "What?"

A burst of air rushed past us. She rubbed her arms and looked around. "Storm must be coming with that cold breeze. I'll get the window."

I looked beyond my mother as she gripped the handles on the window and pushed it down. Outside, the oak, the maples, even the massive walnut tree, stood stock-still. No wind at all. The chill had materialized right inside the walls of the boardinghouse bedroom.

"You felt that? The cold?" I said.

Mama turned and squinted at me. "Well, yes. That's why . . . are you coming down with the grippe?"

I looked at Mrs. Mellet, standing near the dresser. She seemed confused. She was trying to tell me something, but I could not make sense of her message. With her death, Mrs.

Mellet had bequeathed a gift to us. Perhaps she was just here to say her final goodbye to Mama, to thank her for the work she had done for her before she died.

"You look nervous," Mama said. "We should only be cheered on this very wonderful day."

I forced a nod, trying to swallow. I bent down for the brush, hoping that when I stood Mrs. Mellet would be gone.

"Let's try the dress again," my mother lifted her voice to match her happy mood.

I stood, and Mrs. Mellet was smiling, nodding, reaching toward me. My initial feeling of being threatened had passed. Mama smiled, her face a blend of pride and optimism—an expression I hadn't seen in years. Chills lifted the hair on my arms again.

"We can't be late for Mr. Halsey," Mama said. "I'm sure he's elated to finish his business with us." She exhaled deeply. "And I'm surely glad to be finished with him and the Mellet family."

Had Mrs. Mellet been alive, I might have said the woman's eyes were welling from regret for what she'd done to our family. I wanted to confide in Mama. But I couldn't.

Mama lifted the dress and shook it. The summer-sky-blue cotton billowed, making the sound of wind in sails as she shook out any lint or dust that might have gathered on it. The neckline was round, and the front of the skirt was straight and would be draped as was the fashion. Mama's attempt to create an illusion of being well-to-do was good, but we both knew anyone who was the type to follow fashion would recognize her effort to fool the eye for what it was.

"It's nearly ready."

My feet wouldn't move, the brush heavy in my quaking hand.

"What is it?" Mama said over her shoulder. "You feeling faint?"

I shook my head as Mama set the dress over the cane-backed chair. She came to me, gripping my arms.

"You're scaring me."

My insides quivered. I wanted her to understand what I was experiencing, but I couldn't form the words. Dizzy thoughts of the Christoff family tangled my tongue. Memories swarmed like bees. Images of the church elders, their faces going bloodless upon learning of my ability to communicate with the dead. They sought to punish and hide me away—their fear and beliefs compelling them to believe I was evil. I couldn't risk Mama reacting the same way.

Mrs. Mellet had told me she was sorry. I already knew that much. Part of her making amends led to Mama, Tommy, and me all coming back together after years boarding apart. She'd told Mama that she was sorry for being part of the investment failure that led us to flee Des Moines to the prairie in 1887. We knew she wanted to pay us back money that was owed us. Her death one year ago should have meant we were given our due right then, as was written in the will. But Mrs. Mellet's heirs clogged up the works, and time ticked away until this very day, which would allow us finally to make our way back to some measure of respectability. That was the business we were to put to rest this very morning at the lawyer's office. I knew she'd apologized to Mama before she died. And leaving us money and restoring our name was how she was to apologize going forward.

I pressed my hand over the pocket in my skirt where I normally hid the crystal pendant that had fallen from a decrepit chandelier. But I hadn't put it there that morning. Fear shook me again. *Think clearly.* What if I *wasn't* really seeing anything at all? I thought of the newspaper articles I'd read about the insane, the people they locked away for believing they could see such things. What if I *had* turned lunatic? What if it *was* the devil slithering up through the earth's crust just to tempt me?

There was no denying I had been saved. Not saved at a revival, not by God in the way that the church members experienced it. But I had been rescued. The appearance of generous spirits just when dangerous people or perilous

situations threatened had saved me many times. It was my
sweet brother James who appeared to me in the fields with
the Christoffs just in time for us to take shelter from the
tornado. And then I convinced the man sent to haul me back
to the Christoffs' to let me leave, assisted by the arrival of his
deceased mother who offered just the right words to
convince him I was not the devil or a thief. I gave him
comfort in conveying her words and then he gave me my
freedom from the Christoffs. I could not deny those things.
And yet, it all still confused me, frightened me at times. Like
this time, with Mrs. Mellet arriving, giving me a sense that
her apology was not for what was in the past, but something
pending.

Mama cupped my cheeks. "Katherine?"

I grabbed her wrist.

"What is it?"

"I just," I said. "I hope that . . ."

"We've *all* been hoping for a long, long time," Mama
said, her voice soft and comforting. "It's all right now."

I nodded.

Mama's brow creased with confusion. She pressed the
back of her hand to my forehead. "You're white as perfect
lace. Clammy."

I gripped her wrist tight and struggled to organize my
thoughts.

Mama brushed her rough thumbs over my skin. "The
time for worrying has passed. Allow yourself a moment's
peace. I'm here now. We're together for good."

Mama's expectant words were a relief, and as she spoke,
her sentiments seemed to usher Mrs. Mellet from the room
as if satisfied Mama understood what I could not. I watched
Mrs. Mellet's form dissolve into the air like sugar in warm
tea. Perhaps Mama's strong will had returned to her and was
enough to send this negative energy on its way.

I would confide in Mama. Not yet, not without knowing
what she would think of me, how to show her not to be

afraid of me. The warmth in the room returned, enveloping me with the promise Mama's words carried.

She squeezed me and kissed my cheek. "One more thing to fix on the dress," she said as she waltzed past.

The chill was gone, but the fear lingered. A tangible undercurrent ran inside my veins, mixed with my very blood. I wanted to ignore it. Mama's strong words seemed to have cleared the woman's gloomy spirit, and relief spiked. But I had learned that Mama could not always be with me, could not always keep me safe. Luckily, I'd also learned what would help me at those times.

I went to my case and fished inside, fingertips grazing the little pouch that housed my treasure. With muslin scraps, I'd created a pouch the size of my palm with plain hemp drawstrings to close the bag. For a firmer purse, I'd flattened newspaper in the bottom and added fabric over that.

I glanced at Mama, her eyes narrowed on the collar she was stitching. One lesson learned good and hard at the Christoffs' was that people didn't like what I could do. Communicating with spirits wasn't something I could tell anyone about, not even Mama.

Inside the simple bag, I had tucked away my most precious possession. I turned my back to my mother and loosened the pouch's strings. The puckered maw gaped, and I peered inside. My ragged heartbeat steadied. I drew a deep breath, and a calm emerged from my soul and filled me outward.

The sun shifted and streamed through the window, the rays reaching inside the pouch, licking at the crystal facets that reflected a purple wash of light. I looked back at Mama, still engrossed in her stitches. I pulled out the plum-sized ball, rubbed my thumb over the hexagon faces of the chandelier pendant, and was soothed by the sensation. I slipped it into one of the pockets I'd sewn in my underskirt and patted it, pressing it against my leg, secure in the knowledge that it was back where it belonged. *I had finally* been put back exactly where I belonged. At least for that one moment it felt that way. And I told myself it would be so.

**

An hour later we trundled through Des Moines, Yale in my arms, her cheek soft on my shoulder, lips parted slightly in sleep. My stomach growled, and I thought I heard my sister's rumbling as well. I had grown accustomed to hunger, to squirreling away morsels of food for when I was desperate, but it broke my heart to think of Yale learning the same lessons.

Someone bumped my arm, jarring Yale, but not stirring her from her nap. The population of Des Moines had grown in the years since we Arthurs were forced to the prairie, running from my grandfather's bad investment deals. In the time we were gone, the growth of the city brought filth and overcrowding while simultaneously providing us with cover from our former life. I wished we could have just slunk away to a dark corner of town when it all went bad instead of lighting out for the prairie. Maybe then James would not have died in the blizzard, my father wouldn't have been faced with his own weakness in dealing with the loss, and we would not have all been separated like a shattered china teacup on the floor, pieces scattering everywhere, some never to be seen again.

Like a young man who outgrew his clothes every few months, Des Moines outgrew itself, and the result was a raggedy sense of making do. Every few minutes a breeze would rush past us, raising the odor of horse, making me turn away from a clutch of wagons and carriages in the street to our left. Traffic intermittently stopped and started on the mud roads, iron wheels turning over cedar-block paving, loosening and breaking pieces as they went. The sidewalks were jammed tight, people causing us to stop and start again, giving me a chance to glance into the shops.

The storefronts of Hartley's Haberdashery, Cobbler Luke's, and Jenny's Dry Goods were eyebrowed in pine green awnings meant to hide the soot, dust and age, but they had turned more gray than green. Their windows bore circles and ribbons of gray where the shop owners had wiped down the glass only to have the wetness capture the swirling grime that rushed by before the moisture could evaporate.

One lone pure white awning stood against the gunmetal scene, drawing me in—La Reine's Fine French Couture. The windowpanes gleamed like sheets of diamonds, and the dresses in the window were every shade of sorbet. All manner of decadent silk ruffles, summer wool bustles and soft cotton sleeves graced the shop, and I knew that business would profit this season as women who had money to spare would enjoy the sense that this dress shop with the whitest awning meant the store was the best in French fashion. Mama would have thought so way back when.

Mama patted my back and kissed Yale's cheek, causing her to open her eyes for a short second before dozing off again. "You'll have beautiful things again someday, I promise," she said.

Tommy, Yale, Mama, and I passed smiles back and forth as the knot of pedestrians unfurled and we surged with the crowd toward our future.

"Remember that?" Tommy said as he stepped onto the broken cobblestones to let a set of ladies pass. "It used to be Miller's Haberdashery," he shouted before hopping back up onto the sidewalk with us.

"And that," Mama pointed. "Lilly DeMare's dress shop. All boarded up. Shame."

Their mindless conversation comforted me, made me think that I must have been wrong to intuit anything dark from Mrs. Mellet's presence earlier. Surely, the mere cheerfulness of my family would not erase the sense of foreboding she'd brought with her if something awful was soon to happen. Yet my sense of knowing when it came to events that affected me were not as accurate as they seemed to be when I was reading for others. That kept a seed of discomfort firmly planted in my gut. I wished I had a better handle on what I could "do" with this ability I saw partly as a gift and partly as trouble simply waiting to visit.

As we turned the corner to head down Locust Street, it became even more crowded. The sidewalks teemed with smartly dressed folks headed to offices, men in tattered shirts pushed toward warehouses, soot-covered men dragged home from coal mines and riverboats, and fashionable ladies floated past, heading to shops.

A wash of odors filled my nose—floral perfumes, hair pomade, body odor, manure—an olfactory tapestry woven with the scents of city life.

A cramp gripped my forearm. Four-year-old Yale was heavy, feeling more like one hundred pounds than the thirty she probably weighed. A man stopped short, and I almost smacked right into his back. Yale moaned. "Just a little ways more. Almost there." I heard Yale's stomach growl. "You're hungry, aren't you?"

I popped Yale onto my other hip, fished an apple slice out of my pocket and pressed it to Yale's lips, wanting to quell the burn in my stomach but wanting her to feel the hunger less than I.

Tommy came up behind me. "Mama stopped at the flowers back there. Checking her list."

My twin brother swept Yale from my arms and plopped her onto his shoulders. He moved through the crowd toward Mama and the flowers but stopped to talk to a thin redheaded girl, who I recognized as Pearl, the girl from the post office. He waved me over to them.

When I reached them, I caught her words.

"Hey, Prince Charming," she said, her voice thick, her words staccato.

Prince Charming?

The girl slapped her hands with the blackened nails over her mouth and moved closer, putting her face into Yale's.

Awe took over her features, and she appeared to have never seen a child before.

"Oh, Pearl, don't start," Tommy said.

"Well, if you ain't Prince Charming, I can't say who is."

"No such thing. You know better."

"A girl can dream, Tommy."

She turned her bright smile on me and pushed her hand out forcefully. "Big day today, right?"

Her dirty nails, ragged hem, and graying shirtwaist did nothing to dull her spirit. Her cheeks were splotchy with grime she never seemed to be able to remove, but her bottle-green eyes were lit like a lamp, her red hair shining under the little bit of sun that snuck through two buildings behind us.

I smiled; the ease of this clearly rough-hewn girl always took me by surprise and warmed me all over. She glowed with goodness in a way I didn't remember ever seeing a person radiate.

I took Pearl's hand. The firm and overzealous handshake made me burst out with a laugh. "It is a big day."

"You folks'll still speak to me once you get all that money owed you, right?"

"Jeez, Pearl," Tommy said. "Of course." Tommy and Pearl continued to tease and banter while the image of Mrs. Mellet came to mind again. A chill scrambled through me, and I forced my focus back on Pearl and her endless optimism that she wore like skin.

We couldn't be late to the lawyer. I glanced at my mother, who was studying a piece of paper.

"Have to run," Pearl said. She bounced away, weaving through the crowd, a glimpse of her hair coming and going until she disappeared for good. Tommy shook his head. "There she goes. There she goes again." He pulled the brim of his hat down, telling me he was done with the subject of Pearl.

**

Before we reached the attorney's office, Mama stopped and pulled us into an alley. She removed Tommy's hat and swatted it against the wall. "Dust and street all over it."

She dug her handkerchief from her sleeve and licked it. Tommy pulled away, knowing what was coming next. "I'm fifteen, Mama."

As Tommy tried to dodge Mama's attempt at mothering, a wagon rattled to a stop near the alley. The clatter of voices and tins clanging against each other drew my attention. The passenger sitting in the front of the wagon spat into the road, for some reason bringing cheers of triumph from the batch of young men in the back.

From the corner of my eye, I saw an enormous man bolting down the street, chasing down the wagon. His massive size belied his grace as he hurdled a barrel that rolled in his path and wove in and out of the giant holes that had yet to be filled. He finally reached the rig and dove over the back hatch, kicking as he wiggled his way between the others.

The wagon heaved and groaned as it began to move again. Some of the boys sat atop a pile of stone and another perched on the wooden side while the remaining ones seemed to be forced to sit on the floor of the wagon. One stout fellow got to his knees and leaned over the edge of the wagon, reaching his blackened hand toward me. "Come here, little chickadee," he said.

I looked away, but in my peripheral vision I saw the wagon had stopped moving. A group of people passed in front of it, and the clump of men now stretching over the edge of the wagon, hands waving, called to me. "Have a ride with us, beautiful," one said. I glimpsed the rig one last time and saw the big fella, the one who'd been running, stand in the back. I looked past all the other faces, all the outstretched arms; something lured my gaze to him, and the world went silent. He spread his thick arms out, trying to balance himself as the wagon began to move again, bobbing and quivering with each turn of the wheels.

I shaded my eyes to see him better. His blue irises pierced mine, riveting me. His hat covered most of his golden hair, and as the wagon pulled away, the big blond one rubbed his chin, silent as the others continued to chirp. I leaned forward, still drawn to him. The rig jerked forward, all the cargo lurching back and forth, causing all but the big one to jostle into each other. I could see them all laughing, but their voices had all fallen away as though I were absorbed into some parallel space with one man and me, just staring. And as the wagon began to turn the corner down the way, the giant blond one shuffled around the others, around the stones, to keep his gaze on me, to keep mine latched to him.

And then they were gone.

I was left frozen in place for the second time that day. A name came to me, skittering through my mind. *Aleksey. Aleksey Zurchenko.* Flutter, flutter, flutter, like a butterfly, the name flounced through my head.

A gust of wind pulled at the bonnet tied around my neck. A lock of hair whipped against my eye. I tucked it back into the knot at the nape of my neck. I exhaled deeply and pressed the orb in my skirt pocket against my leg, bringing me a measure of calm.

What would Aleksey Zurchenko be doing in a wagon in Des Moines? The next thought chilled me. Was it possible he was deceased, his spirit finding me so far from where we first met so many years ago? I hoped that was not the case, that Aleksey was alive and well with his wonderful family, where he belonged.

Mama came behind me, putting her hand at the small of my back. "Let's move along."

I nodded as we ambled onward. "Did you see that wagon full of boys—the one hauling stone?"

Mama craned to see up one end of the street and then the other. "Boys? No, darling. I didn't."

I shook my head. Perhaps my mind *was* slipping toward lunacy. My solace in this was that no one I loved knew of my ability, and that would keep them safe.

We continued on, heading to claim the money that Mrs. Mellet had promised to repay my family after all these years of having none. Aleksey's name came to me again. I imagined what would have happened if that had been him in the wagon. Would he have jumped out to say hello? Shouted and waved?

The thought of him being near warmed me. And I decided that once we were settled, I would write him. No matter that we hadn't exchanged letters since shortly after I left the prairie, that I had no idea what I would say to him. Suddenly, I needed to know that he was safe and sound and happy.

Chapter 2

Two Girls
Aleksey

Late again. I bolted through the streets of Des Moines, my breath pulsing deep in my ears. I couldn't miss the wagon, not today. Palmer had threatened extra work in return for another tardy. That meant Fat Joe would scarf down my share of meat and gravy at supper. And my study time would erode like rain dissolved a sugar cone.

"Late is worse than absent. I can plan for absent." Palmer's gravel voice had ground at my eardrums with that same tune a thousand times. I certainly understood responsibility, but I'd been honest with him when he took me on for room and board. My studies came first. And I did twice the work the others did to make up for any time I missed.

My feet pounded over the cobblestones, books underarm, one suspender letting go. I caught it before the metal clasp struck my eye. My pace slowed, but I kept running as I reattached the catch to my waistband.

My legs burned as I picked up my pace. I scarpered past meandering townspeople, irritation coiling inside me. Palmer could wait five extra minutes for me, but he never did. I couldn't afford to spend what little money I made on a driver to return me to the farm. Just one more year before I would take my law exams and start my real life, the one that would change the way my family lived.

A stitch stabbed the side of my torso as I ran. I gritted my teeth, now angry that a farmer could not—no, *would* not—forgive a young man for being late because he had been studying the law. Certainly, the wall I was to patch today could wait a few minutes. It had stood with hardly any trouble for the last hundred years.

I rounded the corner and an elderly man and his wife appeared before me. I sucked in my breath, sliding to the side like a circus performer to avoid plowing them over. "'Scuse me, sir, ma'am." It was then I focused up ahead, where the wagon always waited. My breath hitched at the sight. The wagon lurched forward, away from the curb, where it had been waiting for me.

I stuck my free hand in the air. "Wait! I'm here!"

The passel of young men, fellow boarders whom I'd come to know well, were standing in the back of the wagon and waved when they saw me running full-steam. All but Fat Joe cheered me on. Palmer kept on, not turning back or stopping.

I pressed into the sharp winds kicking dirt up off the road. Twenty more yards. I churned my feet faster. One of my books began to slip. The strap holding the four of them together had loosened. I reached across my body to pull the stack back into place, slowing my pace just enough that the fellas in the rig cheered and groaned all over again. I dug down as the wagon took a corner. After that, it was one more block and it would move out of town, making it impossible for me to overtake.

Pound, pound, pound. The ball of my foot pressed through the hole in my leather sole. Almost there. I reached for the hatch, my fingertips catching it. Fat Joe cackled and brushed my hand away. Harold jostled Joe to the side and leaned over the back, reaching toward me so far I thought he would tumble out.

I stretched toward him, focusing on his fingers as I inclined forward while keeping up my pace. Our fingertips brushed. I pressed hard and lurched. We clasped hands, old Harold yanked his arm back, and I lifted my foot onto the step, pushed upward and flopped into the wagon, rolling onto my back, sucking in air. I closed my eyes while hands gave me playful punches, merry greetings mixed in with Fat Joe's boos and his harder blows.

"Glad you could join us, Counselor," Palmer said.

A coating of road dirt in the back of my throat made me cough. This sensation always made me miss my home back on the prairie. "Me, too, Mr. Palmer. Me, too." Gravel and rocks that had been shoveled into the wagon bed along with the thick, neatly stacked stones stuck to my backside. I sat up to gather my scattered books and dusted myself clean. The wagon came to a jerking stop. A swarm of people crossed in front of the wagon, earning them Palmer's icy stare. "Take your time," he said. "It's not as if I have a farm to run."

I was still catching my breath when the fellas began to call to a girl standing near an alleyway.

I gave her a passing glance, my thoughts on the juicy roast, tasty potatoes and greens that Mabel was preparing for us back at the farm. The fellas spilled out over the side of the wagon, vying for the girl's attention. I paid her very little mind since they called to every female they saw from the safety of the wagon. I was ready to lie back down and finish catching my breath when something made me look toward her again. No. It was as though *she'd* called my name, as though a woman's voice just materialized in my mind.

I got to my knees to get a better look. She stepped out of the alley, her brown hair shining like glass, the sunrays splashing through the chestnut strands. She looked away, but I could tell she knew we were watching her. She glanced back, her chin pushed up, posture graceful and straight. Something familiar in her expression gripped me. The wagon jerked forward. Her expression—bothered, proud, irritated by the ridiculous young men in the back of the rig—brought to mind someone I once knew so well.

Katherine.

I drew back. Could it be?

I stretched to get a better look, but I couldn't see past Fat Joe. I grasped his shoulder and shoved him aside. The wagon veered around the corner, and the girl lifted her hand to shield her eyes from the sun. And there it was. Her hand. The pinkie finger was missing. *Wasn't it?* She stared at me. Our eyes met, and I felt as though my breath was gone all over again.

The wagon disappeared behind the building and I couldn't see her anymore. It couldn't have been her. But the finger. Katherine. Without thinking, I was moving again. I straddled the back hatch, preparing to leap out of the wagon. I reached back for my stack of books.

Fat Joe snatched the bundle away from me. "Oh, no you don't. She's mine. You can have Mabel and all her extra helpings of supper, but you can't have that one."

I swiped at the books. He snatched them away.

Harold wrenched them from him but wouldn't hand them over to me. "You can't be late. Use your head."

I nodded and looked back over my shoulder. She was gone. I tried to will the girl to come around the corner. Maybe she recognized me. Maybe she would run after the rig. Maybe it wasn't really her. I swung my leg back into the wagon and sat down.

Harold tossed me the books. "What's got into you?" He studied me as his body swayed with the motion of the wagon, an amused look on his face. The others fell into conversation about all the yellow-haired, sable-haired, freckle-faced girls with tight-laced waists who had held their interest in the last week.

I shook my head. "I think I know that girl." I'd told them the story of Katherine a hundred times. It was too fantastical that it might have been her so I kept that part to myself.

I leaned forward and pulled one of the stray rocks that was bouncing around the bed toward me, wanting to steer the conversation away from the girl who may have been a long-lost friend. I held up the dusty, misshapen geode that fit in my fist as though made for it. "Wonder if this one has those dazzling ice-crystals inside."

Harold snorted. "I never saw your gaze follow a girl who didn't have her arms loaded with a roasted turkey and a dozen buttered rolls."

I tucked the rock into my shirt pocket and my mind went back to her, her face, those eyes I'd seen so many times before, but not in years. "I do know her," I said, not realizing the fellas were looking right at me.

"Ah, yeah, righto," Joe said. "Zurchenko knows that beauty by the alley. Righto. Because one woman isn't enough, he has to collect as many as possible."

"He does have a raging appetite," Sledgehammer said. And as the wagon picked up speed, the fellas began their merry punching, like my brothers used to do. I was the big one, the one who did the most work, got the most praise, and then at dinner, the most food.

**

I sat at the table with six fellas and Mr. Palmer. Mabel served us with a smile that turned her face from plain to pretty. She was shy of five feet tall, a wisp in a dark, heavy dress, but she had the lightness of a sprite and the strength of a man. She kept Palmer's house, cooked, baked, and even helped in the fields when needed. Just eighteen, same age as me. Her parents had died when she was sixteen, and Palmer, who had looked after them while they were ill with the flu, offered Mabel room and board until she married or moved back east with her extended family. "It's what we Grangers do," he had said the first day we stayed with him.

"Leastways, until one of 'em decides he wants what's yours. Then even a Granger is revealed to be just another man."

He shook his fork at us, like he always did when he talked about the Grangers. He wore his pride and passion in his association with them like a Union army uniform. He taught us as though we were on the path to becoming them as well, but he had yet to clarify what he meant by another Granger wanting something that had obviously been his. He had yet to explain why he was no longer an active member of the group if he was so proud of them. "I keep my vows," he said, "and I said I'd care for Mabel until she was safely married off or back east with her aunt and uncle. I keep my vows."

That first day we'd all nodded, agreeing with the dedication of the men and women who belonged to the farmers' organization known as the Grange. We even took our own oaths to be honest and hardworking for Mr. Palmer. In exchange, we got a bed, our meals, and lessons in how tending the land and each other would teach us what we needed to do to make our way in the world.

Sometimes it was hard to listen to Mr. Palmer's lessons on how clearing the land would instruct us on how to deal with life's obstacles. Periodically, my mind was too overwhelmed by Mabel's scrumptious meals to pay attention. She roasted meat, stewed it, boiled it. Even her chicken dishes tasted like something dropped down from heaven, with just the right taste of sweet and savory, so tender it melted on my tongue. She served us all, smiling, humming along, always a nice word for each of us, even for Fat Joe.

"And here *you* are, Aleksey Zurchenko." She slid a heaping plate of food under my nose as though I were a king. "I just love to say Zurchenko." She would sing my name and smile as she moved around the table checking on each of us. Other times, I couldn't focus on Palmer's lessons because my mind was focused more on my law studies and the obstacles I'd already faced—losing my sister to the Great Plains and some brothers and friends to a blizzard, watching Ma nearly die from sorrow, seeing Father withdraw under the weight of it all.

We were halfway through the meal when Mr. Palmer clinked his glass with his knife. "I'm not satisfied with the output I'm seeing. You're lacking teamwork. On the face of it, Zurchenko should have me in the black with the amount of work he does for the farm. But he eats his profits—hell, he eats Harold's and Sledgehammer's, too. Fat Joe does too little. The rest of you do mediocre work. I'm losing money on the lot of you and considering letting one of you go."

I stopped chewing and met his gaze, trying to discern if it would be me who he let go. I contemplated eating less and passed a hunk of my bread to Harold. He pushed it back to me and smiled, knowing how my belly nearly always ached for more.

Mr. Palmer stabbed his meat and stuffed it into his mouth. He leaned onto his forearms and turned his plate while swallowing. "It's as though you boys think I'm speaking to hear myself talk. You can't move on to the next phase of becoming Grangers if you don't do the work at the first level and so forth."

I slowed my chewing. Maybe if I ate slower, I would at least appear to eat less. I couldn't afford the upheaval of moving and finding another farm to work with a farmer who would let me split my time with studying.

"We'll step it up, sir," Harold said. "You just watch."

Mr. Palmer narrowed his gaze on Harold and nodded.

"I can, too," Sledgehammer said. "The grippe had me, but I'm feeling spry again."

The other fellas chimed in with their oaths to work harder, faster, and longer and to eat less. I promised along with them.

Mr. Palmer put his elbows on the table and clasped his hands. "I'll take you at your word for now. Engaging with that frivolity at the river might not help with your ailing health and sorry output, boys."

We exchanged looks, hesitant to agree to relinquish our one diversion, the dances held twice a week at the riverside, but everyone nodded and acquiesced. Certainly, I could fill my time with more studying rather than dancing, even if I'd become fond of seeing an occasional female smile turned my direction, the feel of a pretty woman in my arms.

Mr. Palmer dug back into his roast and, after wiping his plate clean with his bread, pushed it away and sat back in his chair. He picked the newspaper off the floor and snapped it open. "Shortcuts in life normally lead nowhere good. Look at this." He flicked the paper to a photo of a woman with the headline "Madame Smalley Arrested Again." He sneered as though the person was right there in the room. "Laziness, conning others, just leads to jail time. It always does eventually. What you're doing on this farm will help you learn skills that allow a good, honest life."

"Yes, sir," we said. I'd heard about this case at the courthouse. This Madame Smalley wasn't the only person being accused of conning people in Des Moines.

"Now," Mr. Palmer cleared his throat. "The wall along the east field, the one nearly to the river, the one by the walnut—"

"The dead walnut tree?" Harold asked. "The Medusa tree?"

We all nodded.

"Yes, that one," Palmer said. "The wall's a mess. And Mr. Sterling nearly killed the tree by shoveling into its roots a few years back. Swears he didn't. But I saw him there one day, shovel in hand . . ." He shook his head. "Very next day my wife's favorite tree began wilting like lettuce in the sun. But it's the wall next to it that needs attention."

"We could cut it down if it's dead," I said. "Extra firewood."

"It's *not* dead." Mr. Palmer slammed his fist on the table, making everything on the table shudder, and we froze.

He clenched his jaw and after a few moments took a long swig of water.

"There're several branches budding every year," he said. "Don't touch that tree."

We all nodded. We passed the wall and tree when we went to the dances at the river. It was spindly but enormous. Its branches recalled images of Medusa, with snakes bending and twisting up and out like a storybook illustration come to life right in that clearing near the wall.

"Fat Joe," Mr. Palmer said, "I'm doing your father a favor keeping you here. Work harder or I'll send you back postage paid. That goes for all of you."

"Yes, sir," we all said in turn.

"Aleksey. I'll need you on that wall. Mr. Stevens said you're allowed the day off tomorrow to work it. Livestock wandered through that section, and I can't have my cows trampling Mr. Sterling's fields again, giving him the excuse to take advantage just because something I own finds its way onto his property. He told me, 'Possession's nine-tenths of the law.' Is that right? That thing about possession, Aleksey? Finders, keepers?"

I swallowed, unsure what he was rambling about. It was as though he'd taken to drink or laudanum. Something I'd never seen him do, but his babbling sure sounded odd. "No, sir. Well, yes, sir. It depends, actually," I said, knowing that the answer depended upon specific circumstances. I wasn't sure he was really asking me for an answer as there appeared to be an entire conversation happening in the privacy of his own mind. Still, I needed some clarity.

"But you're sure it's all right if I don't go into Des Moines tomorrow? I'm supposed to finish two briefs and turn them in."

Palmer raised his hand. "Mr. Stevens said a day late is *not* a dollar short if you bring the work late. Something about a stay or staying or . . . leaving? Oh hell, I dunno. I'm not a lawyer."

A stay. Good for Mr. Stevens. He was helping with a case in front of Judge Calder, and this news was good if it was accurate. "I don't want to let him down."

Mr. Palmer nodded. "Let's just not let *me* down. How about that?"

I wasn't sure what he was talking about. I understood that we needed to contribute to the farm, not detract from it, but the idea that we might let him down didn't quite fit with our role here. I reassured myself that if I worked harder than the rest and did all my work for Mr. Stevens, then it would not be long before I was on my own, making money, perhaps hiring boys to help me with my land. The thought of such a thing brought a smile to my face. Yes, someday I would do something to help others. Someday I'd be in the position to matter.

Chapter 3

Again
Katherine

Cool, leaden clouds had rolled in, as though God were stirring the sky. With the sun masked and wind brushing past, goose pimples rose on my arms. Springtime was unpredictable in Des Moines, like life, I supposed.

From the covered porch of the Halsey Law Offices, I watched raindrops fall, slow and fat. The first dribbles plunked down, blasting into the earth like tiny meteors. The wetness transformed the dusty road to thick mud, releasing the smell of fragrant earth. The porch banister was lined with baskets of ivy, lilacs, and massive, bowed heads of white peonies—their scent mixing with fresh rain. Several wagons passed, and I found myself searching the back of each for a clutch of boys, boys that included Aleksey Zurchenko.

Aleksey? An apparition? Someone who looked like him? The wagon had disappeared so quickly, as though it had never been there at all. The rainy chill made me think of Mrs. Mellet. *Maybe I have gone mad.*

We stepped inside the office, my sister's legs warm around my waist. Yale stretched and let out a small cry. I patted her back. "Be still," I said. She gave me a sleepy smile, and Mama disappeared behind a hulking carved door, leaving us to wait. I strained to hear through it while Tommy sat across the room, taking a pen to the newspaper ads listing homes for sale. He and Mama were eager to leave this proceeding and find a home to buy with the tidy fortune of fifty thousand dollars we were inheriting today.

Over the year that we had been waiting for this matter to be resolved, Tommy had made a case for finding a place that was regal, reminiscent of the home we once owned on Grand Avenue. Mama entertained his ideas until just the other day when she had looked to the sky, pensive, a shroud dropping over her hopeful expression, as I'd seen happen so many times since we'd been reunited. "No, no, Tommy," she'd said. "We aren't *that* family anymore."

"We'll need the space, and when Father returns, for—"

Mama cut him off. "A small cottage can be made to feel grand if it's ours alone." She had leaned toward him and cupped his cheek, stopping him from pressing. "We'll look at a few types. Remember, the home we had in Des Moines before required staff. Even if our purse is fat enough to afford a twenty-two-room house, we don't have steady income to pay for help."

Tommy drew up. "But I'm working at the Savery. Word is I may be promoted to desk clerk soon. I've been there a year now."

I knew what Mama was thinking. As hard as Tommy had been working, his bellboy salary, even with room and board, was hardly the kind of income that kept a staff paid and fed. Not to mention Mama and I had learned that money and homes with servants meant nothing after we'd lost three lifetimes of savings and holdings when Grandfather's investments went bad. Much better to find a cozy abode that could be managed with our own hands and maybe hire one girl to help out while Tommy and I were at school. Mama had brushed her hand down Tommy's arm, placating him as she used to do to our father when he started to dig his heels into one side of an argument. "You and Katherine have school, too. Just two more years and you will graduate. Don't lose sight of that."

Each time Mama and Tommy burrowed deeper into the ins and outs of hiring staff, my mind would lift out of it, their words receding into the background. *What if Father was still with us, if Mama had not divorced him?* Life might not have been harmonious, but we wouldn't have all lived apart for several years.

Tommy and Mama had come to some sort of agreement on how to approach the housing matter. Whatever it was, I knew my mother would be practical. It was who she was, perhaps even to a fault.

I rubbed the back of my neck as worry pulled my shoulders. Murmurs came from behind the closed door, muffled words rising and falling.

And so as Tommy sat, circling listings and giggling with glee at the budding day, I rubbed Yale's back. At one point, the murmuring in the office stopped. The air thickened, my breath stuck in my throat. A surge of anger and fear shuddered through me. I jerked away from the door, protecting the back of Yale's head with my hand.

"Hogwash!" the man's voice came booming from inside the room.

Garbled shouts stirred in the room again, and Tommy joined me at the door.

"What? What is it?" he said, paper at his side. He pushed his pen behind his ear.

"Something's wrong."

"That son of hers," Tommy said. "Maxwell Mellet's probably hot over us getting some of his fortune. As though he wasn't getting enough. Two hundred thousand big ones. As if that's not enough for a fella to live on."

"He is her son," I said.

"He accused Mama of creating fake documents at the original reading of the will," Tommy said, putting his ear against the door.

"Must have been awful for Mama," I said.

"Yeah, well. Grandfather and Mrs. Mellet took us and most of the town to the river and back with nothing to show for it. Mrs. Mellet hid her part in it and was one of those who made us suffer for our grandfather's sins. It makes sense that she wanted to apologize by paying us something for our trouble. And we deserve the money, whether Maxwell thinks so or not."

I couldn't shake my unease. If the will had been clearly written, I thought this matter would have been settled long ago.

Tommy took my elbow. "I know you and Mama think I'm wretched wanting a big house and that money. But it's not what you think. I want you both happy and settled again. When Father gets here, I want him to see that we set up house for him, that we are strong and loyal."

My heart tugged at the anticipation I saw in Tommy's eyes, the way they lit up at the thought of something big, something wonderful. "I know, Tommy." I gave him a kiss on the cheek and stepped closer to the door again, straining to untangle the stream of voices, only the occasional burst of Maxwell Mellet's protestations rising over the din.

"You keep looking for places to buy," I said, not wanting to see his face cloud over with disappointment or worry. Another wave of quiet came from the other side of the door. Mrs. Mellet's family must have been processing the news. What was the news? I put my palm on the door, my fingertips tracing the thick fleur-de-lis carvings.

"That's it," Tommy said. "I'm going in."

He stormed toward me, but the door swung open before he could turn the handle. Maxwell Mellet, his wife, and his sister barreled past us. They charged the front door, exiting so fast that when they slammed the door the windows shivered in their frames. I looked back into the office. I couldn't see Mama.

I stepped inside and could now see her seated across from Mr. Halsey's desk. Straight and still as starched collars she sat, only her hands, nested in her lap moved, quivering. Mr. Halsey came around his desk and leaned back against it, his arms crossed over his silken vest.

"I'm sorry it came to this, Mrs. Arthur. I did my best to find every penny."

Mama shifted in her seat and met his gaze.

"I hope you have a measure of peace," he said, "that you were indeed included in the will as Mrs. Mellet had promised, that she stated you and your children were not at fault for the investment scandal."

Mama nodded.

He crossed his legs at the ankle. "The state of her home should have hinted that she didn't have access to the money she promised all of you."

Mama coughed into her hand and squeezed her eyes closed before meeting his gaze again. "Yes."

"I advanced you four dollars over the course of the past year," Mr. Halsey said. "I was optimistic the stock and notes were legitimate, that we'd find the bank account that once held her fortune."

It was then I noticed that Mama had opened her hand and that she was staring at a dollar and some coins in it. He leaned forward and closed her fingers over the money. "That's yours. I wish it was more. I hope that helps."

The cold chill that had crept up my back when Mrs. Mellet's spirit appeared to me that morning came back as I watched Mama. Mrs. Mellet had been trying to tell me that we weren't getting any money. I'd had trouble discerning her message, but her dark presence should have been enough. My stomach clenched at the thought of what one dollar and some change might buy us—it would keep us for a short while if we had already been settled with income. But Mama's sewing and my housekeeping took more from us than they gave.

Tommy had room, board, and salary. But it was time for Mama, Yale, and me to find somewhere more permanent. My heart beat so hard at the thought we might be separated yet again. I shivered and looked around. *Mrs. Mellet?* Lightning flashed and lit the dark room. No sign of her. Had she come to apologize earlier? Mock us? Perhaps I couldn't summon spirits on demand, but that morning set the realization in my bones that spirits would walk with me and that I needed to listen when they came. I thought about the boy I'd seen in the wagon. Had it been Aleksey Zurchenko? Or was the spirit of the deceased Aleksey roaming this earthen world, locked out of heaven? The year I'd been back in Des Moines hadn't brought many exchanges with the dead, as though the spirits who had helped me in the past saw me safe with Mama and didn't need to visit often.

Why did you do this, Mrs. Mellet?

Tommy grumbled and went to the bank of windows. He pushed his hand through his hair. *Please let him be able to handle this.*

Mama went to speak but ended up coughing, one slender hand at her mouth, the other at her throat, as though it were closing in on itself, strangling her.

"Tommy, take Yale." I handed her to him and went to the cut-glass water set on the credenza and poured a glass of water.

Fear coursed through me as I remembered Mama's melancholy when James died, the black sadness on her face when she handed me off to the first family I had to board with in Yankton four years ago. I could hear my own shrill scream in my head as I begged Mama to change her mind. I had reached for her. But she had turned away, practical to the end, promising it would just be for a few days.

I would not let that happen again. I was older now, and I would make sure Mama knew it was better to have me around than not. I thought of our father's letters to Tommy. Perhaps he was going to come back. Perhaps I could convince Mama that Tommy was right—that we needed Father despite his weaknesses. Anything to keep her from handing us off again. I felt this great swell of fear and strength rise in me all at once, like steam rising off hot wood in a summer storm. There was nothing more I wanted than to have my mother, perhaps even my father, protect and care for us again. But if that could not be, I would at least make certain we were all together. Even if I was the one who did the protecting.

I knelt in front of Mama and held the tumbler toward her. She stared, motionless. I put her hand to the glass, curving her fingers around it. "It's all right, Mama. We'll make do. We'll work hard and save money and buy that little cottage with the garden you were telling Tommy about earlier. We can put off high school until we save money."

I pushed the glass to her lips. It clinked against her teeth, causing her eyes to focus finally, to notice me. She nodded and sipped the water. She nodded again. "And so we will, sweet Katherine. So we will."

But as she spoke the optimistic words, as I watched her force a smile that dissolved as the tendons in her neck pulled her lips back straight, I couldn't say for sure Mama believed what she'd just said.

I stood and looked toward the windows, where the rain battered the glass, trailing down the panes like great tears as if someone had sliced open the sky to weep alongside of us.

I smoothed my hair back, adjusted the knot at the nape of my neck. I called up the images of Mama when she'd been strong and ran our lives, when every bit of it was under her control. But I'd seen her fragility since the days on the prairie. I understood how she could never be the same after that. Still. Her strength, that full flame that used to fuel her, lived in me even if it was just a flicker inside her now. I knew right then that if Mama could no longer believe, I would believe for all of us. I would make everything better.

Chapter 4

Midwife's Assistant
Violet

New York City
Spring, 1872

It was a dreary Easter Sunday. Icy pinpricks of half-rain, half-snow dropped from the sky. She came down the boulevard, watching, dreaming, wanting. Her gaze caught every flash of purple, pink and silvery blue satin that beribboned the other girls' shiny, tube-curled hair. Their mothers' fashionable spring coats hugged small waists and cascaded over voluminous skirts in the same bright hues as their daughters' ribbons, sweeping the tops of gleaming boots at just the right height to avoid dusting up the dirt under their feet.

The little girl with the quick eyes and sturdy legs watched all this as she darted down Fifth Avenue, her graying coat too big, hanging too long but too small in the shoulders, and pinching at her every step. At ten years old, Violet looked younger, more like seven or eight, maneuvering around the pedestrians. She was late for church due to assisting the midwife. Violet had given herself the title of midwife's assistant because her responsibilities were far more valuable than the midwife had thought. Violet's work running, schlepping, watching, fetching, and cleaning was vital to a healthy birth. Violet knew life would be what she made of it, and so she named her position accordingly. She ducked between finely dressed couples and families with children scrubbed clean, even their kid gloves glowing white, as she rushed toward her heart's yearning, church.

God's house was the one place Violet could slip into the world of the wealthy and indulgent, the world where families smiled at one another and mothers doted on children, even the worst behaved of them. It was the one place where the affluent people softened their sneers as they listened to the word of God, just enough that Violet could pretend she was one of them and that the mother in the pew who offered her a crescent-moon smile was her own. Violet revered them all. She harbored no jealousy for she knew that someday she'd have all that they did and more.

Violet stopped at the corner, the great spires on the Presbyterian church at Fifth Avenue and the corner of Nineteenth Street looming overhead, giving her a sense of Godly protection. She looked over her shoulder, searching for her father, who often joined her in the back row. No sign of him. She patted the pocket on the coat that the midwife had found for her at the beginning of winter. Inside were the few pennies she'd earned for assisting at the birth of Mrs. Colgate's seventh son. Violet would donate two of those pennies to the church's collection basket passed during the middle of the service. There was always someone who needed it more than she did, and she felt good in giving to the poor—the gesture lending her power she felt in few other ways.

She tapped her toe while she waited with the crowd at the street corner. Carriages groaned to a stop in front of them, blocking their progress. A horse defecated. Violet covered her nose with her bare hand while the folks around her dug into pocketbooks and trousers for lacy, starched handkerchiefs. A woman to her right scowled at Violet's dirty hand and turned her back.

Violet was accustomed to such actions. It was only when these people entered the hallowed church confines that their demeanor softened toward her. It didn't matter how they treated her; it would never color her view of herself.

Her father had taught her about one's standing in the world and promised her that when she worked her way to a higher social level, she will have deserved the position. Violet knew when she was educated and swathed in fine clothes and married off to a proper man, the sneering woman-type would smile instead. Someday Violet would offer kindness to those less fortunate, far beyond the walls of church.

The carriages moved on, and the crowd adjusted themselves, gentlemen offering arms to wives, mothers scolding sons to help their sisters over horse manure, quietly trailing to where the church sidewalk gleamed for Sunday service.

Violet stepped toe first off the walk, dodging shit, staying with the group, pretending she was with one particular affectionate couple and their two young children. Oh, what a wonderful big sister she would have been. At the stairs to the church, she hugged one side, ascending the steps to the doors, waiting for just the right time to enter the church. Up ahead, the line stopped moving.

Violet couldn't wait to enter the sanctuary, smell its cleanliness, see the shiny marble floors, rest her bottom on the warm, carved wooden pew, feel its smoothness under her bare hands. She'd asked the minister if she could dust and clean the church during the week, even for free, but he had declined the offer the year before. She wanted so much to be allowed extra access to the place that for one hour a week, during the service, had let her assume what she dreamed was her future standing in society.

The bottleneck inside the doors gave way, and the crowd parted for a couple ascending the stairs, several children trailing behind. Violet stood on her toes, craning, wondering who they were. The husband turned to say hello to someone near Violet, and suddenly she knew. Congressman Tierney. Before Violet could stop herself, before she thought it through, she lifted her hand in the air.

"Sir! Sir! How's your little one?"

He stopped and stared at Violet but then glanced away as though he had not understood her words.

She pushed through the crowd, remembering the way the baby girl had struggled to breathe at first, the way the congressman had wept when he thought the infant had died, the way his tears turned joyous when he saw the child was pink with a perfectly shaped skull. She tugged on his sleeve. "The baby? How is she?"

He looked down at Violet and yanked his arm away as though she'd seared it with a branding iron. "I don't know you."

Violet squinted. "Sure you do. I was there when your wife had the . . ."

It was then Violet saw the perfectly coiffed woman with the small waist on the congressman's arm. She was glaring. Finally, Violet's mind began to work. If this woman gave birth a week ago, she would not be at church today. The woman who'd given birth was not his wife. Violet covered her mouth and stepped back, mortified.

And as the congressman and his family disappeared inside the church, Violet's stomach balled tight. What had she done? She thought of how she could change the story. She'd been told over and over that her job was just running for linens and delivering news, calling for the doctor, but above all, she was to be discreet, silent as snow.

She thought of all the ways she could apologize to the man and his wife. She reassured herself that she had the entirety of a church service to clear her mind and make right the wrong she'd done. The midwife had warned her repeatedly not to disclose who it was she aided in birth, not to approach patients at any time. Now Violet understood why.

Finally, she made her way into the lobby of the church and inhaled its sweet scent, its rich, loving atmosphere. She was home.

A hand clamped her arm. She pulled away, but the hand didn't release her. She looked up into the face of a grim-mouthed man. "You're not welcome anymore," he said.

She shook her head in protest. But the man simply yanked her toward the door, lifting her over the threshold, and closed the set of doors right on her.

With one sentence to someone in charge at the church, the congressman had shut her out of her church, a place where everyone was welcome. Everyone but Violet.

Outside, she laid both hands on the massive mahogany doors, brushing her fingers against the grain. She thought she might fall over from her shallow breathing, the sadness that swept her. The Easter sun's rays finally shot through the dark clouds, illuminating her hands, and she rested her head against the warmth.

Please let me back in, God. Please let me in.

A hand warmed her back, and she startled. She turned and looked up to her father, smiling, his face ruddy where it wasn't splotchy with soot. He took her chin and lifted it.

"Don't weep, my sweet flower. Someday you'll find your way into their world. I believe that to the tips of my toes."

Violet took his hand and looked at his feet. He wiggled his toes through the hole in the leather, like he always did when he wanted to make her laugh. And she fell into him, clinging to his stinking coat, for the first time ever thinking there was no way he could possibly be right.

Chapter 5

Searching
Katherine

Des Moines
1892

Harlot. Thief. Ne'er-do-wells. The words stung as we stood under an elm, rain plucking at the leaves before dropping onto us. Drenched, we plotted our next move. I shuddered and stared at the house where the woman with the acid words sneered through her front window.

Frankly, I was relieved the hag who lived there wouldn't rent us rooms. The broken-down place filled me with an eerie dread even before Mrs. Ashbaugh had lashed out at us. When she had opened the door, it was as though great sprays of misery splashed over us, coming like waves running atop the Des Moines River on a blustery day.

"Let's go, Mama," I'd said before we even inquired about the rooms. "I don't think this is the place for us."

Mama had lifted her eyebrows, questioning.

"Just a feeling. Let's try another."

"There is no other," Mama had said.

So, we had approached the home. When that malicious Mrs. Ashbaugh recognized Mama and declared us to be poison rattlesnakes due to her family having been ruined by Grandfather, due to the divorce that made Mama a questionable woman, I wished I'd been strident about avoiding this home.

I could not stop my mind from reeling. True, Grandfather's investments had caused many Des Moines families, both rich and struggling to begin with, to lose all or much of what they owned. No one knew that more than me. But why would they make Mama pay for it over and over and all these years later?

She'd been a writer, not a banker. She hadn't convinced one person to invest with Grandfather. Mama had lost her home, her jewels, the life she knew, her son James. She'd paid for her father's sins already, and I didn't think she owed more.

As Mrs. Ashbaugh had continued to hurl insults and Mama froze, I thought of my escape from the Christoffs', the last family I'd been forced to live with. The parents were hateful. I could've turned on Mama for not being strong enough to keep us together, for subjecting me to abuse in other people's homes. But in that moment with Mrs. Ashbaugh, seeing her treat Mama with venom, I felt for the second time that day that I had the strength that was required to be sure our family stayed together. I touched the place where the orb that I had hidden in my pocket lay and pressed it against my leg. The crystal had fallen into my hands, and it provided me with a vessel to absorb my fears and then reflect back my strength. Like a baby with a swatch of blanket she needed to feel safe, I had this pendant.

You'll be all right.

I jumped at the voice. *James.* I'd heard him clear. I'd looked at Mama to see if she had. No. Tommy? No. Mama's shoulders had been slumped. Her face paler than it had been that morning, even with all the walking. Her voice had been thinner. I thought again back to that day when she had given us away just so we could survive. This time survival would be different.

"Katherine the Great," James's voice had come again.

I'd felt a joyful giggle rise in me. I'd stifled it, though I reveled in it. James.

And as my mother had begun to explain to the wretched woman why none of her characterizations that stemmed from being divorced were accurate, I could not bother with this home or the woman who lived in it. I'd repeated James's words. *I'll be all right.* And then, just like I had known something dark was looming when Mrs. Mellet appeared, I knew there had to be something better for us. Instead of begging Mrs. Ashbaugh to have mercy on us, or explaining why she was wrong about us, I'd grabbed Mama's wrist and pulled, first gently but then with my nails digging into her skin. "Let's go."

"Where you gonna go?" Mrs. Ashbaugh had said.

"You don't know a thing about us," I'd told her.

"Know what I need to," the woman had hissed. "God smites evil. Not surprised you're back here broken and sopping wet, mud-caked. Look atcha. God won't help you none."

I'd bitten my tongue. I'd held my fist at my side. I'd told myself to let the anger go before I got us into trouble. I'd turned to Mama. She looked as though Mrs. Ashbaugh's words had physically landed on her, pushing her back a step, posture slackened. Finally, she'd lifted her eyes to me. She'd stared, fear flashing over her face. I'd slid my hand into hers and squeezed it three times to say, "I love you." Mama's eyes had widened with life that at one time had always lit her gaze. She'd smiled and squeezed back.

"You're repulsive," I'd said, pulling Mama away, the woman shouting insults at us. "Don't listen to that, Mama. She's despicable."

And so we'd hauled our things a few homes down the street and gathered ourselves under those dripping branches of the leafy elm. Mama fussed over Yale's dress, her hair, her sodden shoes, while I paced, attempting to dispel the anger that swelled inside me. No, not anger. Something solid. Determination. Not a hot anger that would drag me down or turn me bitter and woeful. No. This feeling left me knowing something was different this time.

"Tommy. When did Father say he was coming? In your letter?"

His face lit up, and he dug an envelope from his pocket. He pulled out a paper reading back through it. "Says here, 'Soon.'"

"No date?"

Mama grasped his wrist. "Let's not start down that road again."

"But if it's the only way?" I said. With this new surge of power I felt, I knew I could fend for us right now, but long-term? I wondered if it was better to invite my father back. I couldn't believe I was suggesting it. I knew my mother had not sent my father away for no reason. But perhaps it was time to move past that and work together as a whole family again.

"Impossible, Katherine," Mama said.

I wanted to tell her that James had visited me and told me anything was possible.

Tommy patted her back. "It's all right, Mama. Look," he said, pointing to the newspaper. "I found another listing. On the last page. We missed it before."

Mama straightened and exhaled deeply. "Let's have a look."

He handed her the paper.

Mama's hand went to her chest, fingers splayed at her graceful collarbone. "A woman, Miss Violet M. Pendergrass, is looking to let one room in her home. One room."

I stepped around her and read the listing over Mama's shoulder. "We could make do in one room after all we've been through; even a small room would be manageable."

Mama looked back down the street at the Ashbaugh home. "Yes. Let's do it."

As we headed farther down Mulberry Street, I felt a mix of comfort and distance all at once. There was so much familiar about Mama, the things that years living separately hadn't erased: she looked haggard, ashen, but still exuded an elegant, sinewy carriage. Even after looking beaten by Mrs. Ashbaugh, eventually her chin pushed squarely up, defiant, even, against the searing words of an uneducated, poor woman who by simply *not* being divorced occupied a social standing better than Mama.

"I'm sorry if I hurt your wrist," I said. "I just had to—"

Mama patted my arm. "I know. I was simply, well, stunned for a moment. I didn't know how to respond. I hadn't really thought it through—that anyone we were asking for room and board in this neighborhood would have known us at all or might've lost money to your grandfather." Mama choked on the words. I knew how difficult it still was for her to accept her father's betrayal. "I didn't think anyone would know us in this neighborhood, not after all this time."

We crossed Thirteenth Street, which had once boasted home after stately home of prominent, leading Des Moines citizens. But now most homes and storefronts were peeling and blackened, any whitewash long gone as the fancy class moved farther out with the expanding city. Farther down Mulberry, Tommy stopped and whistled loud and long.

I gasped at the sight. Out of the summer morning fog rose a shock of salmon and green.

"Look at *that*," I said barely above a whisper. A smile came slow and satisfied at the sight of such a beautiful jewel amidst all the sooty brokenness of the rest of this part of town. "That was the McCarthy house, wasn't it?"

Completely transformed by paint, but yes, it was the same house.

Tommy snapped the paper open and drew his finger along the listing. He looked back up, staring again.

"What's the address we're looking for?" I elbowed him.

"That's it," Tommy said. "The one listed here in the paper."

"I hope we're not too late to get the room." I moved toward the house. Three stories stood under gabled rooflines except for the turret with its bell-shaped lid. Scalloped siding, alternating lily orange, pink, and magenta, made the large house feel happy and welcoming. Spring-green pillars lined the front porch, and a yellow sun was painted into the point of the foremost gable. Ox-eye windows were trimmed in pine-tree green, and I could imagine the inglenook hideaways inside, all the places to curl up with a book or share a secret with a girlfriend, or, better yet, with Mama.

"Sure is colorful." Mama caught up to me. "I wonder what Mrs. McCarthy would think of her once stately white-and-deep green-shuttered home."

"I like it better now," I said, remembering the parties we attended there. They were formal, boring affairs, a perfect fit for the plain exterior. "Pale pink and dark pink and mauve and green and yellow, oh, how . . . well, alive it is now. I *love* it!"

Mama drew a deep breath and smoothed her hair back. That morning she had fastened it into a coiled bun at the nape of her neck. Her grace and poise evident even in the face of losing our promised fortune. Yale's dirty fingerprints had marked Mama's sunken cheeks.

Mama began to walk toward the house.

I grabbed her arm. "Wait. Let me . . ."

She turned, her brow furrowed, head cocked. "What?"

I drew my hanky from my bodice and licked it, taking Mama's chin. "Just a little, here."

Mama nodded but appeared hesitant to allow me to care for her that way. I dabbed at the planes and dips of her face. Though Mama wasn't beautiful in the way that artists painted women, or advertisers drew them, she was stunning in a way that was even better.

When Jeanie Arthur entered a room, people stared, sometimes even gaped at her, with all her strength and determination and smarts somehow on display even when they lived inside her. Her dark eyes hid deep thoughts and quiet dreams that had been dashed repeatedly. Strength. Intelligence. Those were the words I thought of most that had marked Mama for so long.

I drew away and studied her. "There. Now you can meet this Miss Violet M. Pendergrass with confidence."

Oh, please let there be a room for us.

Mama smiled and looked at her feet for a moment, a flash of humility—no, shyness—dropped over her expression, surprising me again. Oh, how we all had changed.

Mama drew a breath and smoothed her skirts. We grasped hands and swung them for a moment.

"This is it," I said.

Mama nodded. "Yes."

We dropped hands. Mama edged closer to the house.

I pushed my bonnet off my head and studied the looming structure in front of us. Off to the left side of the freshly painted home lay pitted, broken wood that must have been removed and replaced.

I wished people could discard their pitted souls like old wood and start again as though there was no past. If only we Arthurs could make ourselves over with a splash of salmon paint and deep green trim. All the other homes on this street were ragged or in the process of being redone. Miss Pendergrass's home was a polished gem among rough stone.

The sun broke though thinning clouds, lighting the house with golden rays. I smiled. Yes, I knew the good feeling that came with seeing the house meant this was the right place. It was different than others we'd seen that day. Violet M. Pendergrass was the answer. She had to be.

Chapter 6

Women
Aleksey

I spooned the last of the gravy from my plate and wished for a third serving. But I'd already eaten more than the rest of the fellas. Palmer pushed away from the table. "Let's finish the chores and get some shut-eye. Need every speck of daylight out of Zurchenko we can get."

I rose and picked up my plate, reaching for Harold's in order to help Mabel. She entered the dining room bearing a large white cake. Mr. Palmer's eyes widened.

"It's your favorite," she said.

He was enthralled with the sight. His reaction made the rest of us stare at it as well. It looked scrumptious, but I couldn't see what was special beyond the obvious, well, cake.

"But how?" Palmer said, looking as if he'd seen a ghost.

She set the cake at his seat. "I was rearranging the pantry and behind the coffee canister was a paper with this recipe. The note said, *Andrew's cake*. I assumed that meant . . ."

Palmer put his hand up to stop her from talking. He sank back into his seat and nodded. "Eat, eat."

We watched as he bit into the cake, smiling as though he was enjoying an experience well beyond the sweet taste of a white angel cake.

The surprise had made Palmer quiet, but not in the dark, moody way that he often got into. It melted in my mouth, sweet and light.

Mabel refilled Harold's coffee cup and slid behind me. She swept her hand over my back, from one shoulder to the other. Shivers ran through my body, making me smile. She grinned. She took Fat Joe's empty plate and passed behind me again. This time she stopped. I couldn't see her, but I felt her warmth against my back. The sensation of her fingers coming through my shirt, warm against my skin, startled me.

I straightened and looked over my shoulder, trying to see how she'd done that.

"Looks like I'll need my sewing kit tonight."

Palmer cleared his throat. Harold gave me a wicked smirk.

"Oh, that Aleksey," Fat Joe said. "Ripping through his seams like the great Adonis himself."

"Again?" Palmer said. "Mabel loses hours a week on stitching your clothes. Money down the privy."

I rubbed my shoulder and shrugged. "I come from big stock."

"Well, stop growing," Palmer said. "You're eating us out of house and home as it is."

"And still hungry at night," Fat Joe said.

"Yeah, I barely get a minute of sleep," Howard said, "with his belly growling like the 'Jack and the Beanstalk' giant."

"And that lamp always burning away," Matty said, pointing his knife at me. "We should limit his study time so we can sleep better. That's why we don't work hard enough, Mr. Palmer."

"At least give us law papers too when you get yours," Fat Joe said. "We should get something for being up with you, even if we never cracked a book."

"What's a book?" Sledgehammer said, mocking himself. The whole table roared with laughter, recalling when they witnessed the very first time Sledgehammer had ever seen a book. None of us believed it was possible. Even Fat Joe had read several books. But old Sledgehammer swore it was so.

Born in the middle of a lakeside wood in a place where snow lashed high, crisp, and tight until June, Sledgehammer heard stories by the ton from his family, but he'd never written a single word nor read anything that had been written on more than one sheet of paper.

"Heck," Sledgehammer said, "I ain't even seen more than half a page of writing ever. Can't fathom how you manage all that decoding. Two books in a day sometimes? It's like a puzzle your eyes unlock, but mine can't, Aleksey. A miracle."

"Yeah, tell us about that house dug right from the earth where you learned to read," Matty said.

I laughed along with their friendly banter and leaned forward, remembering the girl near the alley. Could that have been her? Was she the same girl who taught me to read? The feel of my story was completely different knowing it was possible she was right here in Des Moines, just waiting for me to find her. "Well, you see, I've told you before. Katherine Arthur was her name. And they had a house dug right from a hillside as well, one homestead over. She was a wonderful friend."

"But younger," Matty said.

"Three years," I said.

"And smarter," Harold said.

"So much smarter. And quick and so . . . confident, I suppose," I said. "Worldly, philosophical."

"Unless those words mean she was sweet to look at, you can move right along with the tale," Sledgehammer said, drawing laughter.

"Fancy," I said. "She was fancy."

"On account of how she grew up here in Des Moines," Matty said.

"In a mansion on Grand," Harold said.

I nodded as we all formed the pictures in our minds. "With servants and breakfasts of something called quiche and French crepes and syrup that she said made her mouth water just coming down the front staircase in the morning."

"And then they lost it all," Harold said.

"And her family ended up on the prairie. With almost nothing but the clothes on their backs," Matty added.

"And some fancy fabric," I said.

"And her mother made dresses for all the ladies nearby."

"And she brought her books and her paints," I said.

"But they couldn't farm a lick," Matty said.

"Not to save their lives." I looked down. The sadness in that fact always hit me hard.

"Go on," Harold said.

"It was instant—my desire to learn to read. Once I came to understand there were whole worlds closed up inside those compact covers." I sat back, remembering Katherine's face when she'd handed me my first book. She was formal and serious at first, rehearsed. She explained it was a collection of stories; silly tales with moral lessons. The brim of her hat had hidden her eyes, but as she talked she grew bolder, more animated and her head lifted, the sun lighting her eyes.

Every single color of the earth right there in her irises. Every shade of blue and gold and green. But I didn't tell the boys any of this. "All it took was one time of her reading Aesop's tales to me," I said, "and I wanted to be able to read like her."

"But she was a taskmaster," Harold said.

They all laughed.

"Oh yes. Once she saw I had an interest, she made it her mission to make me a reader." I took a bite of cake and swallowed. "No. She made me a *thinker.*"

"Only took a little while," Matty said.

"I was a quick study."

Thinking of Katherine teaching me made my sister's face leapt to mind. "Anzhela had died that year. Awful thing for us," I said. It was hard remembering now how she had wandered off into the tall grasses that day when Katherine and I were watching her. We had just turned to watch a hawk circling above, just for a moment. Seeing that girl today was bringing all these images back to me, fast and hard as a train.

"And then her brother died in the Children's Blizzard," Harold said softly.

"Her brother James." I looked at my plate, the sense of loss from my own brothers, Artem and Anton, dying in the same storm filled me.

"And you survived. You and your Katherine curling up with a cow that barely fit into the house built into a hillside," Sledgehammer said.

"With her baby sister between you," Harold said. "Dripping melted snow into the baby's mouth to keep her alive."

I kept the information regarding Katherine having to have part of her finger amputated later to myself. I don't even know why, but I never said it aloud to them.

"And her family fell apart, and she left all her books behind when they fled," Sledgehammer said.

"And you read every book several times over," Fat Joe added, rolling his eyes. "And wrote your own."

"Yes," I said.

We were quiet for a moment. And before I could stop myself, the words flew out of my mouth.

"I saw her today."

"Today?" Fat Joe said.

"Near the alley," I said.

"Oh heavens, Aleksey." Palmer tossed his napkin onto the table. "That's impossible."

"Couldn't have been," Matty said.

Fat Joe leaned forward, elbows on the table. "Of all the parts of that story you tell us nearly every other day, the least that I believe is that you think *your* Katherine was that girl near the alley."

"The alley girl was a beauty." Sledgehammer stretched and then laced his hands behind his head.

"Beauty ain't everything. Beauty complicates things," Palmer said, surprising us with his thinking aloud. He'd never said a word about my stories in the past.

"The alley girl shone like the sun," Fat Joe said.

"She wouldn't give you two words, Fat Joe," Harold said.

"She was staring at me," Fat Joe said. "She even stepped out of the shadow just to get a better look at me. Didn't you see?"

"No," Harold said.

I sighed. "She'd be older now. But something about that girl . . ."

"And you never said your Katherine was a beauty," Fat Joe said. "Couldn't have been her. If yours had been a beauty, you would have mentioned it first thing with the very first telling. The story would have started with 'I learned to read from the most beautiful girl in the world.'"

"She was a kid, then, fellas."

Everyone turned to me at once, staring, questioning. I certainly knew these fellas started half of their stories with the words, "The most beautiful girl in the world . . ."

I called up the image of Katherine from years back. The memory of her, the way she squared her shoulders and lifted her hand just before giving me a lesson on vowels in the middle of words, her finger and thumb slightly apart as though she were holding the middles of words for me to see, explaining that they were the trickiest parts to sound out. The way she would show me the correct way to bow and ask a lady to dance, bending at the waist, her eyes looking up at me, the incredible mischief in them, in everything she did. The way she took my hand and showed me how to dance properly. It had all been clinical, official. Beauty never entered into it.

I shrugged. "She was a friend, someone who knew so much more than me and was willing to give it all to me." I held up my hands like I was holding a box. "Like she had this treasure and could have kept it to herself, but didn't. Her family lost everything. Imagine that; jewels, artwork, homes, their reputations, all of it gone in an instant. But she still had this magic, this way into the world that I thought I might never have the chance to share. And now look at me."

We grew silent. "I suppose her education was all she had, and I saw that it mattered, this invisible thing she could do to turn black squiggles on a page into rousing stories and wondrous information about parts of the world I'd never even heard of."

"So she *wasn't* pretty," Fat Joe said.

Palmer put down his fork. "This ceaseless talk about girls. How about you spend as much energy on laying the walls straight and strong, with the stones set so the water dribbles out of the wall instead of to the bottom, where it will start everything crumbling from the ground up?"

"Yes, sir," we all answered.

Palmer shifted in his seat. "Some women stay by your side. Others don't. And you don't know which is which until it's too late. So, I suggest you take a lesson from Aleksey here and worry about something more than the next tight-laced, curly topped girl you see standing at the edge of an alley. With that said, I'll thank you, Aleksey Zurchenko, to make it your business to be on time. Your work is noble, but the law is no more so than farming. I hired you for a reason."

"Yes, sir," I said. I thought of my parents and the way they worked the land, bringing forth a harvest even in the worst of times. I didn't know what had Palmer in this mood, why the cake set him off, why he decided to share this knowledge about women all of a sudden. I knew his wife had died, that she had been struck by lightning. Perhaps grief for her loss left him bitter still. I could understand that.

"Now, back to assignments and learning. Each of you has your pouch containing a pencil, a notebook, and a knife.

Aleksey makes fine use of all his items. Harold does the same. Sledge is merely tracing his letters at this point, as he's illiterate. Matty's good with the knife. Fat Joe, you bring to each of us an obstacle. As field labor teaches us to deal with life's obstacles, I am left to wonder if you're learning any of that at all or are you simply just becoming acquainted with all manner of obstacles, not overcoming any of them?"

Fat Joe flinched. "I'm doing my best, sir."

Palmer grimaced. "Working the land is noble. Did I wrongly gather that you understood that, Fat Joe?"

"No, sir."

"I'll remind you—the ax prepares the land and teaches you how to work through roadblocks in life. The plow grinds through the dirt like your . . ."

We nodded along. He reminded us about the harrow and the spade and their connection to how we would develop as men. "So, Fat Joe. You're the biggest offender, and I've seen several other boys who take on your habit for napping at times. Laziness spreads like poison ivy, like spring rains flooding the roots of that walnut tree near the wall."

Everyone turned to Fat Joe. His face reddened. I felt sorry for his difficulty, but so much of it was his own making.

"I," Palmer said, "had to redo your part of the wall in the field by Cherry Run the other day."

I felt for Fat Joe despite his bitterness toward me. "Mr. Palmer, we'll make sure Fat Joe works up to standard."

Palmer rubbed his chin, staring at me. Fat Joe's face showed some relief that I had taken up for him.

"Then tomorrow, Zurchenko, after all the morning chores and cleaning the wheat are finished, you take Fat Joe down to the river bend and work that wall. And do it right first time around. Let's use our ox, Aleksey, best we can while we got him or before he bursts through another set of clothes and Mabel has to spend an entire day sewing."

The fellas groaned and fell back against their chairs in mock despair. Fat Joe glared at me, then softened into a smile.

"Oh, Aleksey," Fat Joe said, "your bones must hurt from all that *growing*. Your brain must sting from all that *knowing*. Toiling away . . ." He shook his head but didn't appear angry at me, like he usually did.

"Oh, poor Aleksey." Sledgehammer winked at me.

"Poor, poor, rabbit," Harold said, laughing.

Mabel sauntered into the room, needle and thread in hand, all eyes on her as she approached me. There was nothing I could do about my growing and nothing I could do about Mabel's attention. So, I was sure to work doubly hard as any of them. I knew one day I would live a high life. Harold would, too. He was plenty driven and smart enough. He just needed to hear from Drake University about when he would start his studies.

"When you study to be a Granger, they ask if you literally took care of the fences," Palmer said. "It's a double meaning, but I want to be able to say yes. Fat Joe here needs to learn all of this. He doesn't have a career in law to fall back on."

"Yes, sir," we all said.

Palmer was right about that. The Grange would be useful to Joe and Sledgehammer if they kept progressing along. Palmer talked often about the crew who had been with him before his wife died. Now each of those men ate in their own homes with their own wives, and this was his evidence of how hard work could enrich a man's life. Fat Joe was cut out to work a field. Or maybe a coal mine or steel mill. I imagined him moving from farm to farm, his gaze forever following girls he couldn't have. He did more moaning than working, but as far as I could see there was plenty he could do to remedy that if he decided to. So, I didn't worry myself about him. He chose poorly, and he had no one to blame but himself.

"Well, at least we got the sight of Aleksey's Katherine in our minds for later," Fat Joe said. "Katherine Arthur is for all of us now."

My stomach tightened. I responded by staring him down until he could not bear to meet my gaze any longer. I once had to sock him in the stomach, and the threat of that was enough to keep him in line most of the time.

Besides, any thoughts, even those of the alley girl, would get lost inside Fat Joe's empty brain before he could ever imagine what it might be like to have one conversation with her, let alone have the chance to hold her hand.

"Well, wasn't her anyway. Like Mr. Palmer said," I told them, "that's the least believable part of my tale, now isn't it?"

And as they nodded along with me, something stirred inside. Katherine was here in Des Moines, and I knew it like I knew my name.

**

That night, I sat at the table made from a slab of found oak I had sanded flat. I'd built the desk legs from rocks gathered around the farm. Mr. Stevens had been trusting enough to allow me to take some of his law books home—his extras. I was afraid of not returning them in perfect condition and would not allow myself sleep until I took the notes I needed and read each book to completion. I could revisit them in his office if I needed to, but it was important for me to get through them once and have notes for home.

The lamp was low on oil, and I went to the kitchen to refill it. Knowing I had hours more of reading, I put the kettle on to make coffee. I'd be tired the next morning when the roosters called, but I could do physical labor still half-asleep.

I sat at the table waiting for the water to boil, and Mabel entered. She should have long been asleep. But she always knew when I was in the kitchen alone. Said she could smell me, feel my presence.

Just like always, Mabel floated into the kitchen under the cover of dim lighting. And this time, like each time before, I would at least begin by averting my gaze. She was always fully covered but outfitted in a billowing, gauzy gown meant for sleep, not for my eyes. She smelled of violet-scented water. From my peripheral vision, I saw her hair was loose, streaming over her shoulders. She pulled a chair next to me and sat. "I've been thinking."

No longer backlit, I could look at her without seeing the outline of her body through her gown.

She walked her fingers toward my hand and rubbed the back of it. I glanced toward the kitchen entry and strained to listen for the sound of Palmer or one of the fellas stirring. The hush was tight around my ears as her touch sped up my heartbeat.

"I need to go back east," she said.

I felt a stab of disappointment. But I knew her life had turned lonely since her parents died, and she'd mentioned having to care for elderly relatives in Philadelphia.

I nodded. "Yes."

She drew back, her face devoid of her typical pleasant expression.

Had I done something wrong? "I understand that you need to go," I said. "That's the right thing."

Her mouth dropped open. She crossed her arms.

"What is it?" I said.

She gripped my hand. Her fingers tiny vices. *"That's it?"*

I put my hand over hers and patted it. "That's it, *what?*"

She drew deep breaths, her shoulders trembling.

Her cheeks pinked.

"Are you ill?" I said.

She inhaled sharply, putting her hands to her chest.

I got to the edge of my seat. "Mabel? What is it?"

"You confided in me. Said you were lonely."

I recalled our conversation about how much I missed my mother and sister. I slumped back in my seat. I had told her how I carried the death of my other siblings heavy in my heart. "Yes. Sometimes I'm lonely."

She shook her head. "I gave you all that food."

I didn't know how she leapt to this topic, but it was true. "You did."

"And you *ate* it."

"Of course. You're a talented cook. I told you so many times."

She balled her dainty hands into fists on the table. "I *mean* you gobbled my food like a starving beast. You couldn't get enough."

Had I offended her with how quickly I ate? Were my manners worse than I thought? Still, I was more confused about what all of this meant in relation to when I'd said, "That's it?"

She leaned forward and grasped my hand again. "Last time we talked you agreed that me going home to start a life, to return to family was a good thing."

"It *is* a good thing."

"Then we kissed. Like so many other times. You enjoyed it, I know." She looked down at my lap. "I could tell."

I exhaled. We certainly had kissed. I envisioned it often. I could feel it, especially the last time. Soft lips, a lingering taste of strawberries. The memory of *how* she had eaten the berries while looking at me, licking the juice from her lips, moving toward me, her hand trailing up my shirtsleeve, her fingers buried in the hair at the nape of my neck as she had bent into me, brushed her lips over mine before pressing harder, her tongue warm and expert in her teasing explorations. She'd lowered onto my lap, causing every bit of my body to harden, every nerve shuddering, and at that moment I wanted her warm body against mine forever.

And then, as I was tumbling farther into her kiss, imagining all the ways it could go on and on, her hand had moved from the back of my neck to my cheek. She'd pulled out of the kiss and traced my lips with her finger, making me nearly fall over with pleasure, a puddle of a man, unable to do anything but wait for her lips to settle on mine all over again.

It was then the kettle had screeched, Palmer's feet had hit the floor, and he dashed down the stairs. We'd leapt apart just as he raced into the kitchen, his hair wild around the top of his head.

Gasping for air, he'd stared at us. He'd run his hand through his hair, smoothing it out, and looked down at his bare chest, shuffling his feet. "Enough with the books!" he'd said. "There's wheat to clean in the morning. Get to bed. Both of you."

And he'd stood there until Mabel and I left the kitchen, each of us going our own way, me to the bunkroom with the boys and Mabel to the back of the house by herself.

She gripped my hand harder now, bringing me back to the discussion at hand.

"Did you hear me?" she asked.

I nodded.

"Well?"

Well, well, well. "Well, what?" I asked as gently as I could.

"What's your answer?"

I squinted at her.

"You didn't hear a word I said."

"About the kiss?"

Her face went red, her eyes widened, taking on a crazed appearance "About *us*," she said. "About how I was inviting you to my aunt's home in Philadelphia. I told her that you and I were very, very close."

About then, the gravity of what she'd been thinking, saying, assuming began to settle in. I pushed my chair back from the table to put space between us. "Listen," I said, "you're so lovely, Mabel. You really are." I wanted her to know that my sincerity was clear on the matter.

"And so?"

"And so . . ." I scoured my mind for how to express what the "and so" was supposed to be without hurting her feelings.

"And so you want to spend the rest of your life with me," she said.

I stopped breathing.

She gripped my knees, her nails pushing through my trousers. "You'll finish your law studies in Philadelphia. We'll have a late summer wedding and—"

My heart raced. Panic swirled in my mind. "When did I say all of *this*?" I shouted with a whisper not to waken Palmer.

Had I lost all my senses? Been talking in my sleep, loudly, so she heard it two floors down? I stood and paced near the stove, watching to be sure the water didn't boil and whistle and call Palmer.

She stood and held out one hand. She pressed her pinkie down. "You said you were lonely. I said I was, too." She pressed her ring finger down. "I said I should consider going back east, and you said that sounded like the right thing." She pressed her middle finger down. "I piled your plate higher than anyone else's. Mountains higher. You ate every bit, devoured it."

I waved my hands at her. "Wait, wait. This doesn't make sense. None of that is a conversation about marriage and my moving to Philadelphia. I miss *my* family, not yours."

She cast her eyes down, dropping her hands to her sides. "It was the way you said it."

My insides felt heavy. I couldn't imagine that I'd conveyed anything of the sort.

"Every word you spoke filled with the love I plainly saw in your eyes." She opened her arms to me.

I drew back, hands up. *"Love?"*

She nodded, a pout forming on her face. Had I led her on? There *was* kissing. I could not deny that. Was that all it took? No. She was the one confused, not me. I thought of my parents, how they loved each other. I'd always been too busy to think about that kind of affection. "I think a person has to say the words 'I love you' for it be so."

"Not true for men like you—the strong, silent type."

Strong and silent. I'd heard those words before. Spoken about my father by my mother. But my father had adored my mother. He showed her with his entire being. He even said so, silent most of the time or not, he spoke those words often.

I didn't want to hurt her feelings, but to lie about my true feelings would be unkind. It might hurt now, but in the long run it was better. "But I promise you I wasn't trying to silently indicate love. When the time comes that I love someone, I will state my love and intentions loud and clear."

Now she stepped back from me. She put her hand on her stomach, as though I'd struck her. I hated seeing her appear injured.

"Well then, your kiss," her voice was airy, pleading. She stepped closer, and I stepped back. The heat of the cooktop at my back caused sweat to form at my brow. "*That* kiss said all I needed to know."

Oh no. I wasn't the only one replaying our kisses, I suppose. "I shouldn't have kissed you. It was wrong of me, and I apologize."

"*I* kissed *you*, Aleksey. Every time, I started it. But it wasn't one-sided. I feel like I'm talking to a thirteen-year-old rather than an eighteen-year-old man. You're playing naïve to draw me in, aren't you?"

"No . . ." Now my voice was thin.

She moved closer and put her hand on my shoulder. I moved away, getting the coffee tin down from the shelf near the sink.

She came up behind me and wrapped her hands around my waist. "I've tested men with kisses before." She began to caress my stomach above my waistband. I pushed her hand away and slipped out of her embrace, and she loped after me.

"Some men kiss as though they're settling an account at the grocer's," she said. "Some press into me as though they'll eat me alive. But you. You kissed me with sweet, gentle love. So different than how you ate my cooking. I just knew that meant there was more to our relationship than met the eye."

None of this made sense, and I hadn't intended this outcome. I certainly didn't know I was part of a relationship. Could I be in love and not even know it? The kettle let out the beginning of a whistle, and I spun around to remove it from the heat before it grew louder. Love? I shook my head at the thought. I closed my eyes and let the question settle inside me. Had I missed my own somersault into love? Lust, yes. Anything else? I waited for a feeling I could say was true affection to show itself. But nothing came. Nothing like it. I was far too busy for love.

When I opened my eyes, I saw tears at the corners of Mabel's eyes. Her lips quivered. And all I wanted was for her to stop crying. I couldn't stand to see someone sad, anyone, but especially, it turns out, a woman. I'd seen my mother cry too many times, and the sight of weeping just shook me from the inside out.

I reached out, and she grabbed my hand.

"I'm so sorry," I said.

She rested her head on my chest, her tears wetting my shirt. I patted her back, tapping in a way that I might do to my sister or even my mother—decidedly unromantic.

She looked up at me. "So you'll come back east with me? You do love me?"

I held my breath, stepped back into the heat of the stove. I took her shoulders, and with soft but direct wording I told her I couldn't entertain the idea of heading back east with her for any length of time, for any reason. "You're lovely. As was your kiss. But I can't love you, simply because I don't."

She let out a guttural gasp and covered her mouth.

"But I offer my friendship for as long as you will have it," I told her. "And sometimes that's so much better, isn't it?"

She swallowed hard and stepped away, and I released her shoulders and watched her disappear into the hallway, leaving me to breathe again.

**

Morning broke, and we gathered at Palmer's table for hotcakes, sausage, potatoes, and milk. Mabel moved quickly, fresh-faced and tear-free. I sighed at the sight of the smile she turned on me. Relieved, I was satisfied she had no more loved me than I had her. It appeared to be the same type of morning it always was. I took my spot and was served last, as usual.

But instead of my plate piled high with salty bacon and five sweet maple syrup-covered hotcakes, I had one. I looked at her to see if she was going to add more to my plate, but she was already leaving the room with nothing more than a wink at the beaming Fat Joe. It turned out symbolism was Mabel's preferred mode of communication, and my sparse breakfast said everything her lips would not.

I didn't mind that she had spoken this way. I wouldn't have to feel guilty about inhaling my food, worrying that it meant something more than I was simply ravenous.

And that I was. Starving. That entire morning, while redoing the portion of the wall that Fat Joe had done wrong the other day, all I could think about was my next meal. I grew so hungry that the thought entered my mind, the philosophical question arose—did the way a man gobble his food say anything at all about love that may or may not have been in a man's heart? At one point, I became so hungry that I foraged for berries in the brush on hands and knees. I thought perhaps this was why men led women along. Sometimes a man's stomach got in the way of everything else, including his good sense.

**

Noon supper left me with only a chicken wing the size of one of my fingers, a small potato, and one dry biscuit. While the fellows worked the harrow and the spade that morning, they must have come upon some information in regard to why my portions were suddenly infinitesimal. I figured this to be the case when they sent sympathetic gazes my way, and Harold distracted Fat Joe (who now received enormous portions), and Sledgehammer swiped a biscuit from his plate and shuttled it to me under the table.

Stomach still empty and wanting, I left the table frustrated and headed to the privy by way of the kitchen. I should have paid more attention to where Mabel kept the bread. I searched the upper cupboards, the lower doors of the pie safe, and finally located a half loaf of bread in a tin container near the sink.

I cut some slices and began to butter it.

"Stealing, are we?"

I jumped at the sound of Mabel's voice and turned to see her tapping her spatula in the palm of her hand.

"Hardly." I took the softened butter and swiped it over one side of three pieces of bread.

"You can have another chance. Seeing now what you've lost in giving me away."

I shook my head. "You deserve someone who can give you all that you want—someone who will go east, marry you, and live at your aunt's home."

"You could."

I bit into a piece of bread, the butter sweet on my tongue. Could I? I could recall my lips on Mabel's. I could certainly imagine my hands on her waist, her skin against mine. The pleasure that came with those thoughts was undeniable. But when I imagined reading with her by the fire, talking about the law, the troubles of the world, having children with her?

"I can't, Mabel. I am sorry to hurt you, but I can't say that we should be together."

With the spatula, she smacked her palm and a crack released into the air. "Then I can't say that you'll get enough food to fill your belly, Aleksey Zurchenko."

"Suit yourself," I said and started toward the back door.

"I'll tell Mr. Palmer you ate more than your fill."

"He knows that," I said.

"Well, just don't come back for me in a few days. I'm no longer yours for the taking."

I nodded as the door slammed behind me. I plodded to the outhouse, jamming sweet, thick bread down my throat. My hunger toyed with my mental state, creating doubts that I'd not had since I began this journey. After a relaxing stop on the pot, I scrubbed up my hands and started back to my place at the wall.

**

It took about thirty minutes for me to walk back to the wall. As I rose over the hill, the arthritic walnut tree near the stone hedge I was to fix came into view. Medusa. Other healthy walnut trees formed a path to the river just beyond my sightline.

Fat Joe had been assigned the job of hauling rock to me so that I could get started on assessing how much of the wall needed to be rebuilt. The sun was high and hot, a stiff northwest wind pushing through clouds. I studied Medusa, sunrays pouring through its crooked, swaying, bare limbs. Small sections of the tree bore soft green walnut leaves, creating the look of a leafy crown braided through the writhing locks, making me wonder if it was coming back to life more than it was dying as Palmer had said.

He'd never given many details in regard to his deceased wife, but his reaction sure let me know there'd been unfinished business between them when she died. I knew she'd been struck by lightning near this tree, a tree she apparently loved. Maybe that was why Palmer didn't want to see Medusa go—it had witnessed his wife's last breath. Maybe he and his wife had carved their names into the trunk. Perhaps Palmer had proposed to her here or they'd shared weekly picnic lunches under it.

I looked behind me, craning for the sight of Fat Joe leading in the stone. He'd made one deposit of stone the day before, all shapes and sizes trailing along the wall where I could easily reach while repairing it.

But instead of beginning to work, I went to Medusa. I stepped into marshy mud that spread out from the base of the trunk, my shoe nearly suctioned right off. I thought of Palmer saying that solid land and good fences were part of the duties of first-degree laborers seeking to become Grangers of the fourth degree.

I stepped around the base of the tree, wanting to see the whole thing despite the wet soil. I ran my hands around the ropy bark, its thickness belying its thinning mane. On the side nearest the river, there was a hole in the trunk. I stepped back and studied it. It looked like the profile of a woman watching over the land beneath her, as though the face had been carved by an artist, and it made the snake-like limbs even more Medusa than tree.

Part of the hole reached through to the other side, sunlight shining through the face, giving it an eerie appearance. I stuck my head inside it, trying to see into the bottom of the trunk, but the light didn't illuminate more than a few inches down.

I wondered what had caused the hole, if the deadly lightning bolt had wounded it on the way to hitting Mrs. Palmer, somehow leaving this depiction of an angel's face with demon hair as though half Pomona and half Medusa. I thought of all the goddesses depicted in the Grange manual, how beautiful and good they were. Pomona was the goddess of fruit and nuts—and this dying tree with its ugly hair and comely face made me think Medusa had stolen away the beauty of Pomona's work. Suddenly, I thought the tree should never be cut down.

"Aleksey!" Fat Joe's voice startled me. I moved around the tree and saw he was nearing the wall, hauling his load. I waved and walked the opposite way around the tree, where the ground was less marshy. I found the areas of the wall that were falling apart. Mr. Palmer had been adamant that the border between his and Mr. Sterling's property never be broached. The odd thing was the cows could wander past the stand of walnut trees, down to the river and then over to Mr. Sterling's property even if we shored up the wall. But it was clear to me now that this particular wall and the tree stood for more than Palmer had indicated to us.

I bent down and felt along the face of the wall, finding that some of it had been last repaired with splintering slate and lumpy granite while other sections were comprised of perfect limestone that would last another hundred years. Fat Joe hopped out of the wagon and followed behind me, filling in the center of the wall with smaller rocks and debris so that we could plant the hedging along the top.

"Cornish hedging. That's what Palmer wants," Fat Joe said as he pulled up next to me. "Said it looks nicer. Nice greenery right on top, less of a sightline to Sterling's property."

I nodded, having heard that clearly from the man himself. I got down on my knees and pulled away the broken pieces that easily gave way. I picked up two stones, holding one in each hand, getting a feel for their weight, discerning the slope of the stones, determining which would fit best into the crumbling section of wall.

"That's how I played with Mabel's tits last night," Fat Joe said.

I dropped the heavier stone, and it crashed to the ground with a thud, roll, and clank into the wall in front of me.

I stared at Fat Joe, dark clouds forming behind him.

"She came to me all weepy about this or that. Wouldn't say what, but she climbed right under my covers and did the damnedest things. Let me play around with her tits. That was it, but that's enough. Then I got that breakfast the size of your big giant self. Must have done something right. You must have done something wrong."

I couldn't speak. This made Fat Joe grin widely. I rubbed my chest. Was that jealousy? I reached down for the stone. No. It was sorrow for the girl, that my rejection had sent her to Fat Joe, that he might think I had my hands on her body that way.

"I never touched her like that," I said. "And you better not do that again. She's a nice girl who doesn't need to be used."

Fat Joe swiped a sprig of grass from the earth and popped it into his mouth. "Oh, but you worked her over with your eyes and all that intellectual talk, always got her attention. Everything you did got you something from her. You used her. What'd you do wrong to make her come running to me?"

I shook my head. "Being nice to a person doesn't mean I used her. She gave me extra food upon her own volition. And I never touched her like that."

I thought of the kiss. I wouldn't shame her by explaining how she'd approached me, how she'd found her way into my lap without any direction from me at all, how I revisited her kisses nearly every night.

"She fancies me," Fat Joe said. "What can I say? And she showed me loud and clear."

I thought of my conversation with Mabel the night before. And with my studies and work on the farm, I had no time to explore whether I wanted more from Mabel than a kiss, no matter how enchanting it had been. No, Fat Joe was the better choice for Mabel. "Well, Joe, if you like her and she likes you, well then, that's a good thing."

"Oh, you Mr. Brightside."

"Nothing wrong with seeing the sunshine through the clouds," I said, "but you better be good to Mabel. She's nice."

"She's gold, I know."

I nodded, oddly convinced he was sincere. "Now get on unloading that haul so we don't get docked pay or get the boot by Palmer."

I put my hands against the rocks that were still standing strong on the weakest part of the wall, trying to determine which stones beside me might be best for patching, both in appearance and utility. It was then a glint in the space right above the foundation of the wall caught my attention.

I scooted on my knees, moisture seeping through my trousers. Fat Joe babbled away about how Mabel pulled her nightgown up, how her skin lit him afire, how his hardness surprised and shocked even him, who was apparently used to exploring his hardness multiple times a day, his breath nearly disappearing from the room as her hand swept up his leg, her fingers passing right over the part of him he wanted her to touch the most.

"I settled for a mess of kissing and her beautiful soft tits in my hands. Oh my god." He dropped his head back, eyes shut. "Like heaven. She let me kiss them even. For a second and then she made me stop. Next time, I figure I'll pay all my attention right there."

"Sounds good, Joe." I got down on my belly and peered between two stones. I dug my fingers into the crumbling sections. "Last guy who fixed this sure didn't pay good attention to how he laid these. Didn't even lay the stones so they crossed the seams. What a dummy." I looked up at Medusa to the left of the wall. "Or it's the walnut tree's roots. Maybe they're pushing the foundation up, cracking it."

Joe leaned against the wall, gazing up at the tree and its woody canopy, and I brushed away some of the fill coming between the crumbling stones. It was then I realized I had been wrong. The stonemason fixing this wall hadn't done a poor job at all. Whoever did this work had made sure this portion of the wall was loose in order to stow something away.

"Whatcha got there, big fella?" Fat Joe asked.

"Not sure."

I knelt and quickly brushed away the crumbling rocks. The dark soil out of the way, the glint I'd seen earlier became clear. A box. I dug into the stubborn fill that surrounded the back end of it.

Fat Joe stood behind me. I wiggled and gently tugged on the box, trying not to damage it. Fat Joe dropped to his knees and let out a long whistle. "Well, I'll be. I've hit the jackpot twice in less than twenty-four hours—a girl and some treasure. I should head to town and play saloon keno today, don't you think?"

The tin was rusted shut. I felt for a sharp stone and began to tap around the lip. "Not yours, Joe."

"Well, it ain't yours neither."

"Didn't say it was."

A few more slugs with the rock and its corroded mouth popped, then whined open. Joe shouldered me over so he could see. "A sack," I said. I ran my fingers over burlap and pulled it up by strings that puckered the top like a woman's collar.

Joe pulled it away from me. "Let me see."

He cradled it in his hands, hefting the sack up and down as though weighing it. "Stacks and stacks of paper money. Has to be." He looked to the sky as though imagining it were true. "Wonder how many one hundred-dollar banknotes make up two pounds of weight."

"Can't even imagine," I said.

He set it between us. We stared at it. "I almost don't want to find out what's in it. Make a wish, Aleksey."

"Why, Joe, you're practically a romantic."

He squinted at me, then his features softened in a way I'd never seen before. "Suppose at heart that's what I am. Got myself a girl and all."

I thought of Mabel. One interlude with her and Fat Joe was soft as spring down.

He narrowed his eyes on the sack. "I wish it to be stacks and stacks of cash. How about you?"

I considered all the things I wanted and needed. To be finished with my law studies. To be with my parents. To see my brothers and sisters again—nothing that would take thousands and thousands of dollars. A home, though. A place to work and read into the night without anyone bothering me.

A fine but small library with a soft leather divan like the one in Mr. Stevens's office would be all a man would want— that I would want. "Well, cash is always nice, for sure." I thought of my mother toiling on the prairie, how wonderful it would be if I could provide a soft bed for her tired bones. Fat Joe's enthusiasm was contagious. "I'd like a nice home, latched up tight and warm. Brick, maybe. Yes, I can dream." Perhaps an enormous sum of money sounded as if it wouldn't be so bad. Suddenly, the idea of treasure buried in the heart of a wall thrilled me.

I grabbed the bag, dug my fingers into the neck, and loosened the strings. Rotted burlap fell away, floating like dandelion seed. I reached inside, felt around, and stopped.

"Well, go on." Fat Joe's eyes were wide.

My shoulders slumped. I knew what it was without seeing it. I pulled the object out and held it up.

Fat Joe's face dropped, and he flopped onto his back, clasping his hand over his heart as though he'd been shot. "Crap! A book!" He doubled over, rolling around as though the disappointing treasure actually hurt him.

It wasn't a book like you'd find in the library, with a fine linen and leather cover, with embossed letters on the front and spine. A sapphire-blue velvet ribbon held this weathered burlap cover with a leather spine closed. I remembered a story I'd heard at the courthouse the first day I started to work with Mr. Stevens. A man had hidden all his money in his books because he knew his son could not read and would never open a book and find it there. When the man died, the son gave away all the books, scoffing at them until he caught the rumor the volumes had held his father's life savings. He'd stuffed it between the pages of some books and cut out sections in other books where he stowed great stacks of greenbacks.

"It could be inside," I said. I set the book on the ground and dug into the knot in the ribbon.

"What?"

"Money."

Joe shot to sitting. "Yes! Like that story you told us."

"Yes, yes, yes," I said while undoing the velvet knot, swept up in the thought of treasure being so close at hand. I unwound the ribbon from the book and exhaled, pausing before pulling back the leather flap and opening the book.

"Well, come on," Joe said.

I opened the book and several stones fell from inside the flap onto my lap. We both examined them—small cornflower-blue stones, some darker blue, hued with bumps and smooth spots, several sparkly purple crystals, and several clear stones that caught the cloudy light of the day.

Fat Joe inhaled, his eyes wide. "Diamonds? What are these others? Sapphires? We're rich! We're rich." He leapt to his feet and did a jig. I couldn't help but agree treasure had been found. My heart pounded as I ran my finger over each stone, imagining a jeweler might pay a lot for these items.

I opened the book and paged through it. Certain pages bulged, showing me they hid items between them. I flipped through, my fingers flying, excited at the possibility of treasure. As pages fell open, the treasures were revealed— dried roses, honeysuckle, and herbs scented the pages. No hundred-dollar bills or coins. Only recipes for dinners, vegetables, desserts, and medicines inside. And on some pages there were drawings of stones like the ones that had fallen out when I opened it. In rolling, pretty handwriting it said, "Clear quartz," clarity for discerning solutions in the midst of problems. Blue flourite—creativity. Selenite—angel wing—opens mind to knowledge and the unseen. Meteor stones—luck, wealth, sorrow, always sorrow. Agate . . .

"What's all that? Jewels?" Joe said over my shoulder.

"I don't know, actually. Not that I've seen a lot of jewels in my life, but I think they're just rocks."

"I've had enough of rocks." Fat Joe fell to his knees beside me. "Sure are pretty, though. But to me, unless those pages are made of banknotes, I say let's get this back to Palmer so he can reward us for our finding it. No—it's ours, right? Finders, keepers."

I shook my head, wondering who owned the book. I flipped back to the front where it said, *To Winnie P., Book One, Cures and Cautions.*

A chill crept through me. Winnie Palmer? "Did Palmer ever say what his wife's name was?"

Joe stopped. "What? It's her book?"

I scooped up the stones and put them back in the flap. "I assume so. It says *Winnie P.* Full of recipes and notes about people." I shrugged, looking over the stones one last time before folding the flap back over. "And the list of stones corresponds with these little ones that were inside. At least I think so. No selenite here, but I've seen it before. All of these stones must have come from clearing the land. Like those geodes with the purple crystals inside. We find those every day."

"Well, let's get them back to Palmer. He'll tell us. Why would he bury them here?"

"It's this *Winnie's* book, not his. I imagine whoever Winnie is buried it here."

"Well, what does it say inside?"

"Says way too much for us to read in one sitting. Full of notes and things. And it feels personal. If Palmer doesn't even speak his wife's name, I can't imagine he'd want us reading her personal thoughts—if it's hers."

"I dunno," Fat Joe said. "Those blue stones look pretty valuable to me."

I shook my head. Thunder rumbled overhead, coming from the northwest with sharp gusts of wind. The scent of rain suddenly filled my nose. Thick drops pelted the ground, releasing a grassy scent.

"You're not just saying that book is nothing because you want to keep it for yourself?"

"No, Joe."

I packed it back in the tin and set the box on the floor of the wagon under the driver's seat. "Let's get something done before the rain gets too heavy. We'll both be fired for having nothing to show for our labor than a woman's book of recipes."

Fat Joe nodded. "Sure went from feeling high as a kite to low as a snake."

"Losing a treasure'll do that to a man, I suppose."

And I went back to the wall, thinking maybe there was more hidden where we'd found the book. I cleared away more of the crumbling stone and ran my fingers through the fill, making sure we weren't passing up something valuable. I reached for a final scoop of dirt, dragging it toward me when my hand hit something hard. I dug into the dirt and pulled it out.

It was caked with dirt, and I brushed as much off as I could, then spit on it to wipe it clean. I cleared away the filth to reveal a clear crystal. Selenite. I thought of the drawing in the book. Angel's wing, the notation had said. I spit on it again and wiped at it with my shirt.

It looked like a chunk of rough ice, cloudy in some spots, diamond-clear in others, catching daylight in its stacked layers with a thinner center, creating a look of a butterfly made of silken ice threads and moonlight all at once.

I knew it wasn't valuable—nothing treated this way could be, but something made me want it. I put it into the tin with the book and closed it tight.

**

Fat Joe and I got about two hours of work in when the rains came so hard that we had no choice but to get the horses back to shelter. Trying to build a dry wall in blinding rain didn't make for useful work. I knew this would irritate Palmer, but at least I could use the time to study, if nothing else.

Fat Joe and I hoped that even if Palmer was disappointed that the rains ruined our workday that we could surprise him with this book and the stones, a treasure for him, even it hadn't been for us.

When we arrived back, after sheltering the horses and drying off, we found Palmer laying a fire in the keeping room near the kitchen. We waited for him to finish his chore, and when he turned to us, we held the box toward him.

He narrowed his eyes on it. His jaw tightened, then he met my gaze.

"We think it was your wife's. Maybe?"

He flinched.

"Was her name Winnie?"

He nodded almost imperceptibly.

I lifted it higher, closer to him. "There's a book inside. We didn't read it, just looked to see whose it was. And there're some stones inside and—" I stopped talking when he put his hand up. His body seemed to shrink as though it were folding into itself.

Then he took the book from the box and flipped it open. He turned the pages, slowly absorbing the words, but not revealing his thoughts to us. He ran his finger down one page and chuckled. "That damned hair dye. My whole head and face swelled up like a pumpkin when she used it on me." He choked back a sob and stared at the book before he slammed it shut.

"Get rid of it."

"But there're some stones," I said. "I think some are meteor fragments, and there are purple stones and selenite and clear quartz and—"

"Get rid of it. Burn the whole thing or bury it again, I don't care, but don't mention it to me or anyone again."

I flinched.

He stalked out of the room, leaving Fat Joe and me standing there looking at the box in my hands.

"He can't be serious," I said.

Joe shrugged and began to say something when Mabel sauntered into the room with a wooden spoon hovering over her palm. "I bet Joe would like to sample my stew for dinner."

Joe's face reddened, and he followed her into the kitchen, sniffing along as if he were a dog after a treat.

Alone in the keeping room, fire blazing, I wrenched open the box again. A stale odor filled my nose. I pulled out the bag that the book had been in when we found it and walked to the fire. The selenite angel stone and others were in the tin, where I'd put them earlier after finding them.

Burn it.

I sighed. I didn't want to. But he'd told me to. I tossed the burlap sack into the fire and watched it burn. I opened the book again, paging through it, not really reading it but wanting to keep it. I didn't know why I was drawn to it, why I would risk disobeying Palmer for some old book and rocks that I could find while clearing any Iowa land.

Something made me want to keep the items, and so I set the tin next to the fireplace and took the book and stones with me. In our bunkroom, I opened my travel chest full of my books and clothing. I shuffled sweaters and shirts and books around, burying Winnie Palmer's halfway down under a dictionary and the two law books I'd found at a secondhand store in town.

Next I took the selenite angel wing stone and wrapped it in a handkerchief, tying it with twine to make a small satchel. I'd no idea what made me do that, why I wanted any of it. But I did, and all I could do was hope that the boys stayed as disinterested in my books as they'd been all along. Palmer, too, as I didn't know what his aversion to his wife's book was all about, but I knew ignoring his orders, if he found out, would only bring me trouble.

Chapter 7

The Financier
Katherine

Tommy, Yale, and I trailed behind Mama, breath held, hoping this house, Miss Violet M. Pendergrass's home, would be the house for us. We approached the picket fence around the pink home, and a woman with thick sandy-blonde hair tied into several knots at the nape of her neck stuck her head out her door and peered at us. She stretched this way then that as though she needed to take in all of what was happening around her.

"You've come about my ad?"

Violet M. Pendergrass. She was magnificent.

Her voice carried, deep and rich like a man's, though still feminine.

We nodded. "Yes," Mama said.

Miss Pendergrass emerged from the doorway and flounced across the porch, her silk skirts pushing forward and sweeping back. With a rush of energy, Miss Pendergrass filled the porch space as though performing on stage. I could not take my eyes away.

Her dress was pale green silk and embroidered with an evergreen thread covering the bodice and thinning out as it streamed down the skirt and ended in curlicues that turned up at the hem as if it were water poured from a pitcher. It was a still life on a skirt. The bustle draped the dress in such a way that the woman appeared petite yet powerful in a way that made even Mama ordinary by comparison.

But it wasn't just the clothing that captured my attention; it was the woman—dynamic and compelling looking, even though she was quite short and wiry under all that fabric.

"Well," she said. "Come on through the gate and up on the porch with me." Miss Pendergrass swung her hand up over her shoulder. "I need to have a look at things."

We followed orders except for Tommy who hung back on one of the lower stairs. When the rest of us reached Miss Pendergrass she plunked her fists on her hips and pierced Mama then me with her gaze. The wind kicked up and blew the scent of rose perfume past us. I inhaled it, wanting to step into the aroma and let it settle on my skin.

Miss Pendergrass glanced down the stairs at Tommy before focusing on Yale. "I don't like that I'm staring at a baby." She wiggled her finger. "The older two—hardy enough. But then again, this isn't a farm. I'm looking for grace and discretion more than brute strength." She gestured at Tommy. "He's a big boy. That's for sure."

"And educated," Mama said. She began to tout our schooling history, and my eyes rested on what was in front of me.

I couldn't remember the last time I'd seen such a beautiful gown close up, even longer since I'd worn one. The blue dress the Christoffs had put on me may have been decent at one time, but it had been plain and stolen off a corpse because they could not bear to clothe me in something that was clean and new. The odor of the sweat-stained armpits came back to me as though I were wearing that dress again. My stomach churned. *Don't think about it. That's over.*

I looked again to Miss Pendergrass. She stood a little over five feet tall—a full seven inches shorter than I. But the woman's voice was crisp, deep, demanding, a person who didn't have time for nonsense. Like a man who went around saying, "I've had enough of this," or "Be at my office at nine. Don't be late."

Mama shifted Yale on one hip and shoved the advertisement from the paper toward Miss Pendergrass. "So you see, we're educated, well-read, and we appreciate discretion. We'd like to see this room, please."

Miss Pendergrass pushed the paper back, her small close-set eyes darting from one of us to the other as if she were intuiting information that we weren't offering. Up close now, I saw the woman was more handsome than beautiful, her freckled face with all its sharp angles and planes was off just enough to make her unbecoming, but in a pretty way, with all the trappings of her dress.

She flicked her fingers at us. "Ad doesn't say a thing about children. I'm looking for work to be done."

"We can work." I stepped forward. "All of us." I couldn't bear the thought that we'd be turned away from this impressive and decadent-looking home. I steadied my voice, proud that I was so forward for the second time.

Mama stole a look at Yale. I had to concede that one caveat. "Except the baby, of course. She can't work. But she's no trouble. Doesn't make a peep. We promise that."

Miss Pendergrass threw her head back and crossed her arms, resetting her attention on Mama. "Now I heard it all. A baby who doesn't make a peep."

"She doesn't," Tommy blurted from the bottom of the stairs. I whipped around and shushed him with my finger to my lips.

Miss Pendergrass stomped her foot and threw her hands toward Yale like a joker on All Hallows' Eve. "Boo!" Yale looked at the woman, eyes wide, grinning.

The woman stepped back, hands on hips, her nails smooth, shiny moons, and leaned into Yale, twirling a lock of my sister's hair around her finger. "Well, darn if she doesn't just smile like she's backward or something. This little one's backward, right? That's worse than a normal, squealing—"

Now this shut me up completely. I'd never heard anyone speak of Yale this way.

Mama thrust the ad forward once more. "Please." Her voice was tight, the way it used to be before. "We won't bring trouble nor look for it. We'll toil as needed, then we'll be off to greener pastures before you know it."

Pursing her lips, Miss Pendergrass raised her eyebrows. "Greener pastures? *That* I understand. So that's your story, Mrs. . . .?"

"Arthur. Jeanie Arthur. And this is Katherine." Mama looked over her shoulder at Tommy, leaning against the bottom of the banister. "That's Tommy. And this is Yale. And yes, that's our story." Mama smoothed Yale's hair.

I held my breath. *Oh, please say yes.*

Miss Pendergrass lifted her skirts and descended the steps with the click, click, click of silken shoes. At the foot of the stairs, she raised her hands above her head.

"Well, come on down with me," she said to us and shrugged. "I'm still considering."

We exchanged perplexed glances and joined her at the walkway that led to the sidewalk and the freshly painted picket fence.

"Take a look at my property," Miss Pendergrass said, sweeping her hands wide, and we faced her house.

"I own this happy pink-and-green home," she said, "but I also own that house." She swung her hand in the direction of the smaller boxy house to the left.

It was still painted the original white and green that the main house had once been. Its white siding was darkened with soot, its deep green shutters faded and peeling.

"Why, yes," Mama said, "that's the old summer kitchen to this home. Then it became the servants' quarters. Back when . . . well. Yes, we see it."

"You're familiar with this property, then. Hmm. Well, that part of the property hasn't been addressed yet. A fire destroyed the breezeway between the big house and the old kitchen house. So far, I've recovered all of the rooms in the big house. But haven't managed a thing with this one."

I nodded, optimistic. Surely Miss Pendergrass wouldn't tell us all of this and then turn us away.

Miss Pendergrass plunked her fists on her hips again and faced us. "I arrived from New York a few months back. As you can see, I own a business"—she pointed to the plaque bearing her name— "I've accomplished a lot to set things up so far."

She motioned to the smaller house again. A strip of grass about twenty feet wide lay between the homes where the breezeway had been destroyed. "Perhaps it would be wise to give you room and board in that home if you're willing to work on it as part of the deal? Might take you a bit longer to find your greener pasture, but you could be together and eventually put away savings."

I held my breath. I wanted to scream. "Yes! We'll take it." I slipped my arm into the crook of Mama's.

Miss Pendergrass pointed to me. "Can you cook and bake? Wash?" I thought of the endless hours spent baking at the Christoff home. I lifted my chin like I'd seen my mother do a million times and nodded in the self-assured way I knew so well. "Of course, yes."

"What about him?" Miss Pendergrass peered at Tommy, who was juggling stones. "He handy around the house?"

"I am."

"He can paint the siding on this house," Miss Pendergrass said, "repair that banister, run errands, and do chores for me?"

He dropped one of the stones he was juggling with a thud. I glared at him, wishing he'd not jeopardize our chance to live near this fine woman.

"Tommy's father was a fine carpenter," Mama said. "Taught him all he knew."

Miss Pendergrass crossed her arms and tapped her foot. "And you?"

Mama straightened. "Anything. Sewing, washing, gardening."

"Gardening?" Tommy and I blurted out. In the year we'd been together, Mama had mentioned gardening at some homes she stayed in, but not in the way she announced it as being expert. Certainly, our garden on the prairie had been a disaster.

"Yes, darlings, I know gardening."

Miss Violet appeared confused.

"We've lived apart for a while," Mama said. "Things have changed, and we're together now. I haven't had a chance to garden since we returned to Des Moines."

"And she can *write*," I blurted out. Somewhere in the back of mind, I surmised it might make up for us giggling over Mama's gardening skills. "She was the *Quintessential Housewife* before, well, *before*. She had a newspaper column, had—"

"That's not important." Mama waved her hand through the air.

Miss Pendergrass nodded. *"Quintessential Housewife."* She paused, studying them all again. "So where's the husband?"

Harlot. Thief. Ne'er-do-wells. Mrs. Ashbaugh's words came to mind, causing the air in my lungs to solidify, stopping my breath.

"Well, at the time that I wrote that column, I was . . . the *Quintessential Housewife*, I had, well, of course the title implies it . . . a husband. But now, no. No husband."

Harlot. Thief. Ne'er-do-wells.

Unlike earlier at Mrs. Ashbaugh's, Mama stood in front of Miss Pendergrass appearing confident even as her unusual stuttering over the facts ensured the negative consequences of the truth. Even as I knew a reputable businesswoman wouldn't want a scandalous divorcee and her family living right next door, I was proud of Mama.

I patted her hand. No matter what, I felt the comfort of knowing we were going to be together this time.

Miss Pendergrass studied us again, rubbing the back of her neck, and after a long stare she pointed down the street in the direction from which we'd just come. "No luck with other listings? You tried Mrs. McQueen?"

"Yes."

"And the Ashbaugh woman? Turned you down on account of divorce?"

Mama hesitated but didn't break Miss Pendergrass's gaze. She straightened and gripped Yale tighter. "Divorce. Yes."

Oh no. My stomach clenched. Divorce was not something polite society entertained on any level.

I couldn't keep my thoughts inside any longer. "Don't ostracize us on account of the dissolution of our family. It's unfair."

"Katherine," Mama hissed.

"No, Mama. I've had it with this day full of rejection and—well, it's simply unfair."

Miss Pendergrass nodded. Her expression softened as she stepped closer and brushed Yale's hair back from her face. "I've certainly come to see that even the poor like Mrs. McQueen and Mrs. Ashbaugh will hold desperately tight, lovingly even, to their self-righteousness in exchange for a slimmer purse." She shrugged. "As though it were possible to eat their self-appointed honor."

"I agree," I said, my heart thumping against my chest wall. Mama stared at me, mouth open. "I think—"

"Katherine." Mama gently took me by the arm. "Decorum, please."

Miss Pendergrass waved Mama off. "Divorce doesn't matter to me. People have needs. I don't judge. I'm unmarried. Some men are useful, some are majestic, but in the world of finance, which is my business, I see the value of *not* being married. Running a business will do that. I'm sure you understand how unusual it is for a woman to be involved in finance. Very, very few women have managed to do it. New York was my training ground, and I learned from the few women who ran businesses. Like Victoria Woodhull."

I gasped at hearing her name.

"Yes," Mama said.

Miss Pendergrass looked hard at Mama again. "But you're educated, cultured, aren't you, Mrs. Arthur? I can see that a mile away. It's the only reason I allowed you on my porch with those children in the first place. I know value when I see it."

I stole a glance at Mama, feeling as though this woman might actually understand our predicament somehow. I'd heard all about women's rights from the time I was young. Mama and I had many conversations regarding the matter. I'd read about Elizabeth Cady Stanton, Lucy Stone, Susan B. Anthony, Victoria Woodhull, and Amelia Bloomer. I knew those women were both powerful and at the same time still small, depending on how you measured them and their lives. Their independence was alluring for many reasons, and now here was one of their kind right in front of me.

Miss Pendergrass tapped her nails against her hips, one finger after the other, creating rhythm against the fabric. "My mind's all about numbers, not emotion or the heart. For instance"—she held up her finger—"when I picked Des Moines for my destination, I knew there were opportunities here for me as a woman. People who come west are a certain sort. Hardy. Open-minded. Practical. As a matter of fact, I employ several women. With a few well-placed letters from my New York City colleagues—male, of course—why, I've managed to get my investment business running. I'd like for it to really hum, like the town with the railroad just built through." Her gaze slipped away as she seemed to be recalling something before setting her attention back on Mama.

"With me crunching and twisting and wringing out numbers all day, why, I haven't even had time to hire someone to clear out the mess of dead vines and useless weeds in the back. Both my home and the servants' quarters' rear properties are divided by an old fence and some hedging. There's a shed, a barn way back, some cows, hens. Nothing's organized or growing besides the weeds. I'm told it was once magnificent. I'd like the area directly behind my half to be suitable for entertaining and the three quarters remaining for a garden, and I'd like it to be just as stunning but—"

"Useful."

Miss Violet smiled broadly, sweetly, for the first time since we'd met her. "Yes."

"I was once very familiar with the gardens here. How they looked anyway," Mama said.

Miss Pendergrass's eyes slipped over Mama's un-bustled dress and too-small sleeves. "Back when you were the *Quintessential Housewife*?" Her words mocked, just a bit, just noticeable enough to me. I opened my mouth, wanting to yell, "Mama owned a home four times the size of yours, and it burst with all the help a woman could want. She *wasn't* the help." But I caught my mother's nod, and I sealed my lips.

Miss Pendergrass ran her hand over her shiny hair, keeping her gaze on Mama. "Yes. I've been missing a kitchen garden, herbs, and flowers. None of the hens will lay. If not for so many very demanding clients, I'd do it myself." She closed her eyes and drew a deep breath as though the very garden she desired had come to life and was under her nose for the smelling.

Miss Pendergrass fixed her gaze on Mama. "So. You're a gardener, Jeanie Arthur?"

"Yes, I am."

I flinched at the way Mama's words flew out of her mouth like bullets, as though ludicrous that she might have a black thumb—the killing touch she'd had my entire life. Still, I smiled, wanting Mama to take the chance.

"You can manage with the baby?" Miss Pendergrass said.

"She's four now." I grabbed Miss Violet's wrist, and when I realized my grasp made me look desperate, I released it, putting my hand behind my back.

Miss Violet cocked her head again, studying us.

Tommy raced up the porch stairs and held out an iris to Miss Pendergrass. He presented the periwinkle bloom like he'd sprouted it right out of his palm, producing a smile from his target.

"Whatever you need," Mama said, "we can do. I admire that you keep full reign of your life. I'd like to get back on my feet in the company of someone who shares the underpinnings of self-worth, strength, and independence."

Mama locked her gaze on Miss Pendergrass, conveying as hard as she could that she'd do a good job for her in every way. I silently cheered her. *This* was the mother I remembered.

"I worked for a woman in Sioux Falls and I kept a journal with fine examples of blooms and seeds and the process by which her gardens fed multiple households. Her gardens were exquisite. And, well . . ."

Miss Pendergrass sniffed the iris, then pointed it at Mama. "Useful."

Mama turned her palm up and out to Miss Pendergrass for emphasis. "Yes."

"You understand that, being from New York, I have high standards." Miss Violet tapped her nose with the flower.

Mama cocked her head. "I find that smart women everywhere have the ability to understand the quest for elegant independence. I can see that only the best, the highest quality, will suit you. Why, it's as if I were born and raised in New York City, that vision is so clear to me."

"Yes, well," Miss Pendergrass said.

Oh please. I wanted to ask Miss Pendergrass how she started her business. How'd she get investors to take a chance on her?

She was breathtaking in a way I'd never seen. Despite the manly cut of her square jaw, Miss Pendergrass's power and grace shone like a fallen star dropped into my very hand. The woman reminded me of the way Mama used to stand in front of her help, doling out orders. Everything about her had been magnetic, and it was the kind of charisma that drew people in even when they wanted to go the other way. This was Miss Pendergrass. And immediately, she felt special to me.

Miss Pendergrass's shoulders relaxed, and she sighed. "Well. It seems as though you understand my reproductive organs don't prohibit my brain from operating."

"Of course," Mama said.

"And I understand divorce doesn't render a woman evil or stupid," she said.

I bounced on my toes, marveling at the idea that she was completely independent, relying on her own sharp mind.

"If your brood can keep quiet, and if the children work for room and board as well as you—"

Tommy stuck his hand in the air. "I have a job at the Savery Hotel, but I can do things like start the furnace in the morning or milk the cow."

Miss Pendergrass stepped toward him. "I need someone reliable to run messages to my clients, to send telegrams, to haul rainwater, other small things."

Tommy looked at his mother and nodded.

"And that little one there, as long as she keeps quiet and doesn't mess." I could see Miss Pendergrass was still busy calculating the benefits and costs of boarding the Arthurs. "You're in dire straits right now," she said, "but I can also see your breeding as clear as day. You're just what this section of town needs in its resurgence."

I grabbed my mother's hand and squeezed, trying to tamp down my excitement.

"As long as you don't cost me time, trouble, or money in damages of any sort, this may work. There are rules."

"Of course," Mama said.

"I have regular meetings. The best and the brightest gentlemen come to me. So, no noise. Anyone working in my home or yard must do so with all the racket of a church mouse."

My shoulders released their tension.

"If you want to talk to me, you knock at the kitchen door. I like a neat porch out front here, and you can see that the porch that fronts the home you will board in needs to be repaired. I don't want your side to resemble a poorhouse or bear any sign of children whatsoever. Understand?"

We all nodded.

"Good. And since you're boarding at my property, the children may refer to me as Miss Violet."

I could barely contain myself. The idea of living with my family again, going to school, putting our past behind us made me dizzy with happiness.

"That one, the young man," Miss Violet said, "I'll need him to paint the front porch, probably another shade of pink to complement mine. Why, I think the universe or God or someone like that surely saw to it that we meet today, that the self-righteous woman down the way was too blinded by her Bible to see your strengths. I believe that sure as I'm standing here drawing breath."

And in those few words at the end, I fell under what I decided was Miss Violet M. Pendergrass's spell. I quietly agreed. We'd been meant to meet that day, and this meeting would change the course of our lives. I touched the orb where it lay hidden in my skirt pocket. The calming was stronger than it had ever been. I knew the moment we saw Miss Violet's house that it was calling us. It scared me to finally begin to recognize these feelings of revulsion or calm as certainties, to trust these feelings would be risky, but this day had shown me that I needed to take that chance.

Chapter 8

The Kitchen Mistress
Violet

Des Moines
1892

Remove the ashes, set the kindling, adjust the flue, light the fire. All before dawn and a single scrap of food is made. Soak and scrub the clothes, hang them to dry, and afterward iron shirtwaists until collars stand like petals on a blooming rose. Violet groaned at the thought. She bent in close to her dressing-table mirror and pinched her cheeks to redden them. She lifted her bustled skirt and perched on the tufted stool, studying her face, turning it right and then left.

She was full of gratitude that she had the kind of mind that allowed her to run a business and hire girls to perform all the awful housework. Technology may have brought the water to some households in America, but it didn't reduce the amount of work a woman had to do each day. No, it even increased when men, as the heads of households, decided their wives needed less and less help with the invention of a sweeper.

From the far southern shores of Florida to the farthest corner of Washington State, women were noting change in their world. Not all appreciated the movement, the line of what they saw as decency being breached as transformation unfolded. Some disliked the agitating women's rights advocates who demanded wives be treated as equal marriage partners, who pushed for the right to vote, the desire to wear trousers and ride bicycles. Others were scared nearly to death of them.

There had been a time when Violet Pendergrass strove for the opportunity to surrender herself along with her bank accounts to a man who'd vow to love her through all the best and worst that came in life. Not anymore.

She reread the headline in *The Des Moines Register*: "Miss Violet Pendergrass Doubles Investors' Money." The article in front of her was flattering for the most part, but like anyone writing about a woman who stepped out of the kitchen and into a world not intended for her, the reporter interviewed other females for their ideas on the subject: *She should find herself a man who will take care of her accounts. Everyone is lucky once in a while. She will be sorry if she loses her looks before finding a husband. She should tuck away her bicycle bloomers before it's too late.*

Stupid, stupid, stupid women. Think of all the money she could make them if they thought for themselves. Violet was accustomed to these female assertions quoted in the papers as they chronicled the increasing hand-wringing that came with changes in women's rights.

Violet laughed to herself. She wished she could be honest with reporters and disclose her disdain for the unattractive bloomers that she had no intention of wearing. She dusted her nose with powder, obscuring her freckles only a bit, and chuckled. She wasn't opposed to riding a bike but had done so just fine in her dress and had even ridden nude on occasion. Holly Springs, a progressive resort for those searching for optimal health and happiness, welcomed guests to capture the sunrays without a stitch of clothing.

Even still, Violet had to admit she had taken that allowance too far when she'd gathered several men and women to join her on bicycles. It was all for health, she'd reminded them as attendants rushed after them, shaking robes and sheets, screaming that they were to keep their nakedness to the women's and men's lounge areas only.

She pushed the paper aside and splashed the last of her rose water onto her cleavage and considered how far she'd come since she was a little girl, the midwife's assistant.

She glanced over the rest of the business page, noting that Madame Smalley's business had opened again in an old jewelry store in town. Violet exhaled, relieved that she'd smelled the woman's fraud from down the street and had turned down her offer to work together. Violet's business was based in numbers and data. She didn't need anyone sullying that, even someone who'd managed to make her own fortune before being tossed in and out of jail, accused of conning the good citizens of Des Moines. She folded the paper and set it aside.

Piano music wafted up the stairs, making Violet smile. "Moonlight Sonata," Olivia's favorite to play. She must have finished her studies for the day. Violet found Olivia useful in her business sense but less so in the kitchen. A gifted pianist who'd fled her hometown due to scandal with her teacher's husband, Olivia's graceful appearance and ability to quietly charm men into taking a closer look at Violet's financial services was well worth having her in the business, even though she wasn't tremendously smart, not like Violet was.

Now that Katherine was working the kitchen, Olivia's skills could be better put to use along with the other girls. Surveying herself in the mirror once more, she was satisfied her appearance was alluring but tasteful, having a robust glow, not looking at all painted. Yes, she wished she'd been born without freckles, but she'd learned to love them. She'd learned none of that mattered with the skills she'd developed to wield in the world.

She scanned the bathroom, stood, and wiped out the inside of the gilded slipper tub. She pressed the switch that lit the crystal chandelier in the middle of the room, appreciating every glittering inch of the room her hard work had earned. At her dressing table, she ran her hand over her ledgers and her notebook, the secret to her success. Thirty years old. Violet was considered attractive, seductive, electric, but not beautiful, not even pretty in a plain sort of way.

No matter, she'd managed without trading on her appearance, and the result was something she could hold in her hands, something she could share, something she could use to make even more money. A final glance at the newspaper and the sliver of an article about the success of her investments made her heart pound. This was just the beginning. She'd been frustrated by Judge Calder's unwillingness to invest or even show much interest in her business. He reigned over far more than a courtroom in Des Moines, and she needed him in order to proceed as she'd planned. *Be patient. He'll come around.*

The music stopped, reminding Violet she had work to do. She swept the leather-embossed books into her arm and glided into the adjoining room, her boudoir, and squatted down to the floorboards. She slid a planter aside, pressed firmly on one end of a floorboard, and the other end rose. She jiggled the board next to it and patted the stack of cash hidden there before guiding the two ledgers into place. More important than the cash was what was written on the pages of the leather books, notes delineating the money coming in and going out of her business. Two sets, just in case. She replaced the planks and the plant, adjusted her bustle, and took a final assessment of herself.

Colt Churchill was arriving within minutes. He was a valued customer for some of her services and a partner in others. But now it was time to grow her business, to create the kind of security that would last a lifetime.

She descended the stairs to the foyer, thinking she'd see Olivia in the parlor, but she was gone, probably enjoying the last hours of her time off. A bang coming from outside startled Violet, questioning again her decision to allow Jeanie Arthur and her children to board in the old servants' quarters. She remembered Tommy was working on the porch of the old servants' home where the Arthurs were staying. No doubt there would be some noise until he finished the work.

Voices from the kitchen made Violet pause in the hallway. Colt Churchill. He'd arrived without her knowing it and was in the kitchen, of all things? She neared the kitchen, and the tone and lilt of another voice rang clear. Olivia? She'd been working with Colt, but she would never invite him to the kitchen. "Miss Violet will be down soon," the female voice said.

Katherine Arthur. Not Olivia. When Violet thought of the girl, seeing the girl's beauty and skill in the kitchen, her mind was torn between wanting to work her to the bone and wanting to protect her. From what? Violet didn't know. But there was something engaging about Katherine in a way that was quiet but powerful, and there was something inside Violet when they were together that she could only say was oddly maternal.

Violet peeked around the corner. Colt was not a shy man, sometimes even unpleasant, but something made her stop from going into the kitchen.

Katherine's back was to Colt. He leaned against the worktable in the center of the kitchen, watching her, his hands in his pockets, the clock ticking above his head. His black hair was longer in the back and neatly combed. Spats as white as fresh cotton wrapped his sparkling shoes, and his blue suit was perfectly tailored, instantly conveying wealth. Violet thrilled at the sight of this man, what he brought to her business, her future.

He brushed the face of his pocket watch with his finger and shoved it back into his pocket. "You're Violet's new girl." He rocked on his heels.

Violet almost stepped into the kitchen to make a proper introduction, but instead she studied Katherine, knowing this interaction would tell her much about the girl she had hired. Katherine casually stepped around the worktable, putting it between her and Colt.

Very interesting. The girl was beautiful and young, but she was not utterly green. Violet narrowed her eyes on Katherine, waiting for the girl to either embrace his seduction or weep at his overtures.

"You're new in town?"

"I am." Katherine pulled a large wooden bowl of apples off the countertop and set it on the table. A short answer—a lie, in fact, as Katherine was not completely new to Des Moines, but she didn't leave it open for discussion. Her body language was matter-of-fact. She didn't gaze at him through her eyelashes or offer a flirtatious word, no half smile or provocative movements that promised something untoward.

He moved around the table toward her, and she held the bowl of apples against her stomach, between them. He stepped closer, and she tossed him an apple and moved to the other side of the table.

Well, well.

This was a girl who had practice diverting a man's advances and had no interest in falling prey to one now. This was good. Violet could trust that Katherine would not be distracted from her work, not even for the wealthiest of men who came to conduct business.

Violet remembered Jeanie's mention of her divorce. Was it possible her mother brought men home who fancied the daughter more than the mother?

Colt bit into the apple.

"May I get you something?" Katherine asked him, her voice steady. "Besides the apple? I'm not completely accustomed to this kitchen yet, but I could put on some hot water."

"Thank you," he said after swallowing a bite of apple.

Katherine looked around, putting the bowl back on the table. "I'm sure the tea is here somewhere." She opened the pantry, turning her back to Colt again.

She lifted onto her toes to reach for the tea canister. Colt moved toward her.

"Tea sounds wonderful," he said.

Katherine turned and pushed the canister into his chest before scooting away, sliding behind the table again. She took a rag and began to scrub at something on the table.

Violet covered her mouth to stifle a laugh. *Very good, dear Katherine.* Violet felt a swell of inexplicable pride at Katherine's skill at eluding a man many years older. Violet had been such a quick study, though she could not know how many times Katherine had been put in this position, how many times she'd been successful.

"Miss Violet sure went light on the compliments regarding you."

Katherine stopped scrubbing just long enough that Violet could see from her expression his comment unnerved her. "I just started," Katherine said.

This was enough of a test for now. Violet squared her shoulders and entered the kitchen. "Colt Churchill. I see you've met Katherine Arthur." She stood beside Katherine. "Our new baker."

Katherine smiled, head held high.

"No," Violet said. "'Kitchen mistress.' That's the title befitting the baker and manager of domestic affairs that I require."

"Kitchen mistress," Colt said, his gaze on Katherine. "I like that."

"She's boarding next door with her family. Her mother will do some plain sewing, gardening, odds and ends. I told you about them."

Colt nodded, his face softening. "Why, yes, you did, but you didn't indicate Katherine's beauty. You left that part out."

Violet tipped her chin up. "Now, now, I don't think the kitchen help, even a kitchen mistress, is worthy of a mention when it's finance that's our calling, right, Mr. Churchill? You brought the papers, I presume?"

Violet saw a smile pull at one side of Katherine's lips. She patted the nape of her neck. And with that, Colt Churchill seemed to grasp Miss Violet's hint.

He stalked across the floor and extended his hand to Violet, shaking it firmly. "Why, yes, Miss Pendergrass, I did. Why don't we take a look at what I've come up with and finish what we started the other day? The judge is coming at one o' clock and we want him quite satisfied with our plans, don't you agree?"

"Yes, I do," Violet said, and she led Colt into the hall. She glanced back to see Katherine reading her list of things to do.

Oh, how you surprised me, pretty Katherine, very, very much.

Chapter 9

The Promise
Katherine

I looked up from my list of things to do to observe Miss Violet and Colt Churchill stroll into the hallway. As they disappeared, I heard the two exchange phrases like *projected value, return on investment,* and *strategic planning* until their voices dissolved in the distance. I admired my boss more each time I saw her.

Miss Violet was at complete ease with him, even while issuing orders and discussing whatever the projected values were. And me, a *kitchen mistress*. The way Miss Violet said the title lent an air of French accent and importance. She'd said how important it was for a young lady to characterize her position in the world in a way that demonstrated its significance. I appreciated this subtle, uplifting nod to what was menial work no matter what you called it. I'd seen Mama manage our lives back before it all crumbled away, yet the dynamic was different than what I'd just witnessed in Miss Violet's kitchen.

Mr. Churchill had succumbed to Miss Violet's suggestion to get busy with their meeting without a whimper or power-struggle, like my father would have done to Mama. And when Mr. Churchill crossed the kitchen to greet Miss Violet, he didn't put her delicate hand to his lips, no flirtation lit his expression; it was as though the two of them were friends, partners, noble peers.

The thought that this businesswoman from New York City might be treated as though she was just another person instead of a fragile flower waiting to be given an order, or a shrew demanding orders be fulfilled, exhilarated me. I'd do my best to please Miss Violet and learn everything I could from her. Perhaps she'd even let me learn about finances and investments—*projected values*—along with the other girls she employed.

Miss Violet had given me a tour the day I started, mentioning that she created a kitchen reminiscent of the French homes she stayed in while overseas two years before. She introduced me to the other girls who worked and studied with her. Some helped with the laundry, but they mostly worked with numbers, like Miss Violet.

One girl in particular, Olivia, seemed relieved I was there to assume the kitchen duties. They were all polite, but not very interested in being friends. It was during the tour, when Miss Violet allowed Olivia to introduce me to the kitchen equipment, that I realized I knew far more than she about cooking and baking.

Olivia hadn't seemed to appreciate the beauty and efficiency of Miss Violet's space. Blue-and-white tiles covered each wall, even the hood protruding over the large range. I retraced the path we'd taken on the tour. I walked toward the mustard-colored door leading into the butler's pantry and to a butter-yellow dining room. A large oil painting of a field of red flowers hung over the fireplace.

"France, oh how I love her," Miss Violet had said during the tour. "I brought some of France home with me—the colors, the art, the life." Olivia and the other girls had nodded along as though they'd lived there with Miss Violet.

Miss Violet had swept her gloved finger around the gilded frame of the center painting, vibrant sunflowers against a shocking blue sky. The soft look of the petals, a blurring effect, even with their bright colors—the painting reminded me of the portraits John Singer Sargent had done of my family back before we lost everything we owned. One portrait of my parents and siblings sitting on silken settees in the middle of a field had hung over the fireplace in the dining room. The other portraits, one of each of us, were placed in the drawing room and foyer. Grandfather's portrait was above our mantel in the parlor. Each had disappeared when we had to sell off everything we owned, and I could not even imagine where they'd ended up. I didn't mention any of that, knowing none of them would care, knowing they shouldn't.

Miss Violet had straightened the sunflower painting. "This one had been part of a very famous collection in France. *Le Francais.*" She spoke with an accent and looked as though she was somewhere else, somewhere that turned her soft and wistful with one gaze at the regal yellow flower.

"Girls," Miss Violet had said to the others. "I'll finish acquainting Katherine with my home. You go on and prepare for your clients. There's news to report, and I want you sounding professional and knowledgeable."

"Yes, Miss Violet." They'd left the room, excitedly chatting about whatever it was they were about to prepare.

Miss Violet had looked back at the painting. "Oh, he was passionate, this artist. He was about to burn this set when I stopped him. Exquisite man but . . . distant." She'd shaken her head as she stared in awe at her own belongings. "I admired his quest for perfection. But I suppose perfection in art is a silly quest."

I'd agreed. I'd been critical of most of my drawings and paintings, but I couldn't imagine burning any of them.

"Just beautiful," Miss Violet had said, barely above a whisper.

Seeing her reaction reminded me that I had wanted to draw and paint for Mama. This reaction, the way art could transport someone, might be just what Mama needed. I felt sure I could give her that gift with the right painting or drawing.

Violet had pulled at the tips of her gloves, tugging them off and fixing her attention back on me. "The French have exquisite taste and manners, and much of their lifestyle pairs well with my goals for business and pleasure. You can see I'm fastidious about my home. Every surface, each corner of my home, my work, of myself, should gleam."

"Of course," I'd told her, but I could not take my gaze from the lively paintings.

Now, alone in the dining room, I stared at their beauty again, always excited to visit them each time I came to work. Work! What was I doing loitering as though a lady of leisure on a day at the museum?

Back in the kitchen, I read my list. Dutch oven. Where would that be stored? I spun in a circle and finally opened one cupboard. Nothing but mixing bowls. I took in the kitchen's unusual artistry. Even our grand old twenty-five-room mansion had been outfitted with a bland kitchen. Surely this attention to detail was a testament to Miss Violet's success as much as the articles that were written about her in all the papers. My mother had read aloud to us the three that had been published about her since we'd met her.

The brass pulls on drawers and cupboards gleamed, and rows of delicate china lined the breakfront, like a china flower garden, cheering even the darkest days. Besides the table in the center of the kitchen there was another taller worktable, half-marble and half-wood, near the back door and under the bank of wide windows letting in fresh air. The windows stretched across the entire twenty feet of space, overlooking what would become Miss Violet's garden for entertaining once Mama cleaned it out.

Also under the windows was a wet sink with a lemon-colored apron and a dry sink beside it. A large clock hung above the doorway that led into the back hall. Along one wall of the kitchen was the pantry that stood between the kitchen and dining room. Between the pantry and one set of windows was a range built into the mouth of the six-foot-wide fireplace. On the back wall of the kitchen, there was also a pie safe. Beside it hung a coffee grinder, an eggbeater and molds, and under those there was a refrigerator.

Adjacent to the refrigerator was another small thin table with a potato parer that looked pristine, and I was sure it had never been used. I opened the pantry door to a coffeepot, plates, glasses and mugs, pitchers, buckets, and along the bottom shelf, a neat stack of preserves. There was also a sugar cone and flour canisters. And a Dutch oven.

I wrenched it out of the back corner, and I imagined that all the blue, white, and yellow in the space would light even the darkest winter day's work. The thought made it easier to deal with my chores ahead. I would go to school when it opened in the fall, but until then, it had been made clear there was lots of work to do.

I opened the firebox of the range and saw the coals were weak. I adjusted the damper until the red heat caught the black coals, the temperature strong again, and closed the door. There was a stack of apple crates and potatoes waiting for me. The two recipes at the top of Miss Violet's list for me—potato puffs and applesauce.

I leaned over the apples and inhaled the sweet scent. My fingers brushed over one, then another, then back to the first, a nice small one. I sniffed its honey sweetness, tempted to eat it right there. I strained to listen for the sound of Miss Violet, still having her meeting, and the other girls working for her, who were busy upstairs. Nothing. My mouth watered. I felt the pocket sewn into my underskirt that held the crystal pendant and glanced over my shoulder again.

No one will know.

I lifted the skirt and slipped the apple into the second hidden pocket. I couldn't wait to be alone, when I would slowly relish each bite.

I took a colander from the pantry and hauled one of the apple crates to the sink. I located a slop pail behind the blue-

and-white checked cloth concealing the sink's plumbing and turned the stubborn handles; water came rushing out of the faucet. I leaned down to get a whiff. No odor. It ran diamond-clear and frigid. I cupped my hand for a taste. Wonderful. It had been so long since I had running water in a kitchen. Our house had a pump inside, which was better than having to go to a well, but this, at Miss Violet's, was decadent. I filled a pot for the apples and put it on the beautiful new range to boil and then stoked the fire.

I rechecked the list—wash and peel the apples—they'll be more tender. So I did. Tossing the cores into the slop bucket, I patted my hidden cache, then went to work on peeling and slicing the apples, creating spirals of apple skin that sprang like a debutante's curls. My mouth watered as I inhaled the luscious apple scent. I could hear Violet's voice at a distance, her laughter stabbing at the quiet in the kitchen.

No one will know.

I spun one apple, looking for just the right spot to bite, and sank my teeth into the skin, eyes closed. I relished the first bite and swallowed, wiping my chin with the back of my hand, and ate the rest so fast I nearly choked. Leaning on the table, I drew deep, long breaths, telling myself the apple I'd eaten, and the one I'd tucked into my pocket, were part of the board I was earning in working for Miss Violet.

No one will know.

When I opened my eyes, I startled, dropping the core right onto the table. Seated across from me was a man. Dark-haired, he wore a stubbly salt-and-pepper beard. He shook his finger and laughed. I covered my mouth, forcing the last of the stolen apple down my throat, nearly choking.

He smiled and steepled his fingers. "She'll know you did that. Nothing gets past my Violet."

Fear paralyzed me, froze my tongue. Fear of being punished, of my family being asked to leave, turned my insides cold. This man must be charged with watching over the household inventory for Miss Violet.

I swiped the core from the table and began to apologize, ready to beg for a pardon. But the sizzling sound of water boiling over made me turn to the range. Water pushed through the spout, spitting and hissing.

I bolted to the pot and grabbed the handle, the heat burning my palm. I yanked my hand away, blowing on it. The water spurted and hissed as it hit the range-top. I twisted to the dry sink area and pulled open drawers, finally finding small towels to use to remove the pot from the hot surface. I slid the pot to the left, to the cooler part of the range.

My hand was smarting from the pain, but it was not burned badly. I turned back to the man, but he was gone. Instead, standing next to where the man had been, Miss Violet was there, her hand on the chair where he had been sitting.

I fought to settle my breath to rid myself of the fear coursing through me. "Miss," I said, clearing my throat. "Miss Violet." The man must have already told Miss Violet that I'd eaten something I shouldn't have. I walked to the table, prepared to explain that I missed breakfast that day and was so hungry I couldn't stop myself, that it would never happen again.

But when I looked toward the pantry, the back door, everywhere for a sign of him, the man was nowhere to be seen. Violet was busy reconstructing the slices of apple with a corresponding core. I hadn't considered that she might keep track. I should have cut the slices into chunks. My heart raced at the thought of being caught stealing, at the thought of having to face Mama and confess that we were being put out on the street because of my dishonesty.

But the man? Where was he?

Miss Violet stopped her work and waved her hand through the air. "This is silly. We both know you ate one of my apples." She held up the core that I had dropped on the table when the man appeared in the kitchen. "I want to trust you, but now, I just don't know."

My eyes stung as I imagined the man telling her I was a thief. "I'm sorry. I was just so hungry."

I suddenly thought of the apple in my skirt. What if she searched me? Another lie? No, she would have no idea I had the hidden pockets. She stared at me, and her eyes penetrated me. Perhaps the man had seen me hide that one away. I felt as though she were pulling the thoughts right out of my head. She knew. I could feel it.

I slowly pulled up my skirt, rolling the fabric upward. When I exposed the pocket, I dug into it and pulled out the tiny apple I'd hidden away. I placed it on the table.

She stared at it, then back at me with her hard gaze.

"Please, please forgive me," I told her. "You can count it against my food for the day."

Her eyes went to my skirt where the apple had been.

"I went hungry for so long, so many times, that I just wanted to keep the apple in case . . ."

She crossed her arms, holding my gaze. I swallowed my panic.

Miss Violet looked away. I waited for her next words, my firing. But she just stared out the window. She turned back to me, and her eyes went to my shaking hands, still holding my skirt up.

"What's that other lump?"

I flinched

"That there." She wiggled her finger at the pocket that I thought had been off to the side of my skirt far enough that she wouldn't have noticed a bulge.

Run. Just go.

She stepped closer, her perfume filling my nose. I drew a shallow breath, reached into the small pocket, and pulled out my crystal pendant. It sat in my palm, light from the window catching its facets, radiating a rainbow of color on the ceiling. "This is mine."

Violet tapped her chin with one finger. "But it was someone else's first."

I shook my head. How could I explain this in a way that sounded sane?

"Tell me the truth or you're out, and so is your family."

My hands shook. I threaded them together in order to stop them from quaking. "I earned the pendant. A family I boarded with couldn't pay me. They gave me that instead."

She studied my face. "Why would they pay with such a thing?"

I shook my head. "They were redecorating and didn't want the chandelier. They thought the pedant suited me."

Truth. Lie. Lie. The pendant had sought me out, falling right into my hand after shuddering right off the chain that held it to the dusty chandelier.

She crossed her arms and widened her stance, as if to prevent me from running away as I'd wanted to. "This family was good to you?"

They were awful. Except for Hannah, their daughter. She saved me so I could save myself. That was the truth. "Yes, good."

Violet nodded. "That explains why you keep the ball with you."

I nodded, exhaling.

"My father always said trust is a gift given freely, but when abused, it disappears like feathers in the wind. Always said I have a knack for trusting the right people."

I swallowed hard. *Her father always said?* Could that have been him who had seen me stealing?

"I can see how you might have counted the apples toward your board. But I keep track of everything, everyone coming in and out of here. I can't have skimming of any sort."

"No," I said. "Skimming's always trouble." I felt faint at the thought that I might still be dismissed. The urge to bolt remained. I squeezed my eyes shut for a moment, willing away the wooziness.

Miss Violet drew back, eyebrows raised. "What?"

I cleared my throat.

Miss Violet glanced over her left shoulder, then the right. "What are you staring at?"

I put my hand to my churning belly. "Nothing. I just felt woozy for a moment."

Miss Violet uncrossed her arms, relaxed her shoulders. She squeezed my forearm. "You are hungry, aren't you?" Her face softened. "You can always have a meal here, Katherine. As part of your earnings. I just want to know exactly what's coming and going in every area of my business. It's the only way."

My eyes burned—relief and gratitude buoyed me. "Thank you."

"You look famished. Sit," Miss Violet said.

I did.

She pulled a small crock from the icebox. She removed the lid and sniffed it. "Chicken salad. Would that suit?"

My mouth watered as the scent filled the space. "Oh my, yes, but I have to get the apples on and boil the potatoes."

Miss Violet took two forks from a drawer beneath the dry sink. "Nonsense. I want you to feel at home, Katherine. You're clearly hungry, so the only solution is to quell your wanting. Then you can work like an ox."

I smiled, still feeling on edge but salivating like mad.

Miss Violet stabbed the chicken salad with one fork and turned the crock, then placed it all in the center of the table. "Eat."

I wanted to devour every bit, but I remembered my manners. I couldn't risk putting Miss Violet off any more than I already had. Miss Violet retrieved the kettle from the pantry. "I'll get that." I stood.

Shaking her head, Miss Violet turned on the faucet, the water making a hollow-sounding stream as the first of it hit the bottom of the kettle. "Unfortunately, we're lacking bread for the chicken salad. The other girls are due to shop, and the bakers in town are lackluster so far anyway. This sandwich would be perfection with a nice leafy piece of lettuce.

Wouldn't it? Nothing like the taste of good, fresh food after having none, is there?"

The way Miss Violet said that made me believe that she must have had times of hunger herself—as much as her current home didn't suggest it.

"That's where you and your mother come in. I can hack up a chicken and boil it like anyone else, but with my finance company and, well, my complete disinclination for kitchen work, I need help."

She put the kettle on the range-top. "In addition to baking and cooking for me, you'll need to blacken the range once a week. I want this stovetop to look as though it's never used, even though you'll be preparing food constantly.

"You've met the other girls, the ones who board here. Two have been trading cooking in turn for their studies with me. Once a week, we take our meals at Huffnaegal's Restaurant, and twice a week we simply eat hot oats for breakfast and cold meats for supper. Perhaps some soup. I take care of those who work for me. But business is changing rapidly, and they've committed to their studies while you take over the kitchen."

Miss Violet sauntered back to the table and sat again, her chin on her fist, looking at me as though I were on display.

She leaned back in her chair, arms crossed, her expression soft. "I wasn't so sure about your family at first. You lost souls trundling up the sidewalk. And that child, your sister . . ." Miss Violet covered her mouth. "I resisted the opportunity, but then I got this feeling it was *exactly right*. I can't remember the last time in my life I felt that way. Even as a babe, my instincts for survival—good, bad, wrong, danger—were all intact, like an animal born ready for the wild, my father used to say. But this was different. I just have a feeling about us."

I drew a deep breath, taken with Miss Violet's admission. Could her father have been the man I'd seen? The one who'd seen me? "Your father? He lives nearby? He's—"

"Dead." Miss Violet scooted her chair forward and pushed the crock and one fork across the table to me. "Fifteen years. I've managed alone, as you can see. But my father's words and guidance stick with me in the worst of times. It's like all the things he used to say come back to me over and over, tethering me to solid ground, like the words are alive somehow, more than just memories of a father."

I had come to understand that to be possible—feeling someone's presence, wisdom from beyond. Without the fear that often accompanied spirits I saw, I was growing more certain that I was experiencing souls of the dead rather than sheer insanity.

I lifted the fork, replaying in my mind what the man had said about Miss Violet knowing I ate and hid apples, and I set the fork down. I wanted my family to have full bellies.

Miss Violet squeezed my hand. "Finish that. There are two more crocks in the refrigerator. Take one to your family when you go." The squeezing reminded me of Mama, the way the two of us would silently say "I love you" with three squeezes. I felt a pang of guilt over enjoying this lovely food and the tender moment while Mama scrubbed the walls next door.

I dug into the crock of chicken salad silently, feeling an ease and comfort with Miss Violet. How lucky I'd become after so much misfortune, to have two women in my life I admired.

Miss Violet's candid, relaxed conversation, the way her eyes lifted to the sky when she recalled meeting my family, that she assigned some sort of goodness—a miracle, no less—to the circumstance, peeled away some of my defenses. This magical, self-reliant woman. And what did Mama always say? *We'll enjoy the sunshine all the more if we've had a few shadows first.* We'd been buried in shadows, but we were reunited. And now Miss Violet? She revealed the sunshine.

I shifted my chair and tried to tamp down my enthusiasm.

No, not enthusiasm. Calm. There it was. The calming, the goodness surrounding me, like when I saw angels or when kind spirits came with people in danger was too much to ignore. I couldn't see the golden glow of angels around Miss Violet that I normally did when I felt this way, but I told myself the angels were there, protecting.

Or perhaps Violet M. Pendergrass was simply a good, fine woman accompanied by no angelic protectors. My fork butted against Miss Violet's as we dug into the crock. We giggled. I tried to eat slowly, to enjoy every morsel, relishing the lunch as though it sealed the beginning of a relationship, as though my craving and Violet's delivering of what was needed had instantly bonded us. It reminded me of when we lived on the prairie, the small, good moments with my mother, enveloped in her love and attention, between all the hardships.

Having Miss Violet pay attention to me this way made me smile, showing me all was well in the world.

Warmth filled me, something similar to when my brother James would appear to me. I scanned the room for golden forms or a flash of color filling out invisible energy that would allow me to intuit a feeling or the actual words and thoughts of those who had passed on, or those who had never lived on earth at all. Perhaps I needed to welcome the presence rather then turn from it.

No, it wasn't James after all. The glorious, quiet moments of sharing a meal was what gave me a sense of peace. "The calming" was how I would think of it. I thought about the spirits I'd encountered and how they evoked different feelings. Mrs. Mellet had brought a chill, a darkness, and it was something I would turn from if it happened again. My experience with the unseen others all started with the fire on the prairie. That was the first time I saw a spirit, my first encounter with a young boy who'd been buried there. Then there was the time I was ill with a high fever, quarantined at the Zurchenkos'. Angels started coming to me later. Most of the time they ushered in comfort or some bit of information I needed.

Excitement now pulsed with my heartbeat. I wanted to explain all of this to Miss Violet, to tell her that, yes, my family showing up when we had was a miracle of sorts. So much had happened to bring us to her doorstep. I wanted to confide that I'd felt the same rush of goodness that she had when we met. And that *must* have been a sign of fortune.

I should trust Miss Violet.

"So good," she said. "I didn't realize how hungry I was, too."

I nodded. Even with all the goodness around us, I knew better than to confide. I was no longer naive. Not everyone wanted to hear that I had a guiding hand from the beyond. I had no doubt now that I had seen Miss Violet's father in the kitchen, but I'd learned that few were ready to accept such things; even fewer found it comforting.

I thought back to the day we were planting corn in Storm Lake, Iowa. Mr. Christoff had driven the rig, and his wife and I had followed behind, dropping and covering seed. It had been a stunning cornflower-blue day. No sign of a storm or even rain. Yet as we'd worked, dread came over me like invisible fog rolling in, noticed by no one but me.

And then James had begun to appear to me in the field, warning me to run. With no sign of a storm, the Christoffs had not listened to me until nearly too late. Finally safe in the cellar, the tornado had ripped past the house, missing it by mere feet, devouring other homes and anything not bolted down. And as the realization had settled over us that something otherworldly had guided us to safety, I'd felt calm, loved, serene.

The Christoffs had been petrified, convinced the devil was working through me. And they hadn't wasted time seeking a way to remove the devil in me. A revival had been planned, and from what I'd seen at those before, I understood what they intended. It would be a violent laying on of hands. Until they could do that, they'd locked me in the cellar. One day their daughter Hannah had come to me, curious, knowing I was far from evil. She'd tried to busy her father while I ran, but he'd overtaken me and attacked. I'd thrown a pocket watch and hit him square between the eyes, knocking him out long enough to tie his and Hannah's hands—to make it look as though she was innocent of helping me—and stolen a horse to run.

No, I wouldn't tell Miss Violet or Mama or Tommy, *anyone* about the calming. I would keep it close, let it soothe me, keep it for times when I had nothing and no one else to depend upon.

Violet popped an apple slice into her mouth, relaxing into her seat. "Your mother's classy, pretty," she told me. "Her dresses belie her current station in life. I can tell she's added some found lace to the hem of a dress and the cuffs. The cut is out of fashion, but her carriage—oh, the way she moves—well, I can see her breeding a mile away. And smart, too. If she wasn't saddled with children, I'd bring her into my business in a heartbeat."

I flinched at the thought of being a burden. That was the last thing I wanted to be seen as by Mama or Miss Violet.

Miss Violet took another apple slice and pointed it at me. "What are your views on women's rights?"

I laughed and laid my fork down. I'd been given orders and ultimatums, pushed aside and used, and I'd been thinking about women's rights ever since I could remember. No one had asked my opinion on the matter in quite some time.

"When you used the word 'saddled,'" I said, "in regard to my siblings and me and Mama, I felt a pinch." I clasped my thumb and forefinger together. "But when I consider the ways of the world and the places women fit in it, well, I can't say I'd be happy depending on a man or having children to tend."

I thought of Miss Violet's paintings in the dining room, her trip to France and references to the way the French live. "I'm going to attend school between my duties for you, and I don't know after that, but I intend to fully exercise every right I might be granted. Women must be close to earning the right to vote by now . . . sometime soon." I shrugged, thinking of how I escaped from the Christoffs, liking when I was able to feel strong in having finally done so. "I suppose sometimes you have to wrest your rights from the powerful."

Miss Violet raised her eyebrows, and I couldn't tell if she was pleasantly surprised or horrified.

Even my own father had made life difficult for us. He'd dropped obstacles in our path as though rolling boulders from the mountaintops. Deep inside, I felt love for him, but it was hard to reach that place now. And the way Mama had been treated since the divorce? Women couldn't easily find independence once missteps were taken. Marriage and children made independence difficult, an illusion if someone were lucky, but divorce obliterated it. Would I want to live the life Mama had? Seeing Miss Violet not subjected to the scorn Mama was made me certain: marriage was less reliable than life without a man.

I shook my head. "If marriage and my existence were to be boiled down to only home-keeping, well I'm certain I'd suffocate." The words were overly dramatic, I knew. But, at the moment, they felt true to me.

Miss Violet put her hand over her heart. "We're of like minds, Katherine Arthur. I'm glad you're here. Kindred souls, it appears."

I smiled and picked up the fork again, stabbing at a chunk of chicken at the bottom of the crock.

"But mind my rules," Miss Violet said. "No skimming, no nosing around, no *anything* except what's in this kitchen or in the cellar when I send you there. I take care of those who return the favor. You'll be compensated fairly."

Violet offered me an apple slice, squinting at me as though trying to decipher my thoughts. "I'm trusting you. Now don't go making a fool of me."

"I won't," I said and hoped I wouldn't betray Miss Violet's confidence in me. "I won't do any such thing."

Chapter 10

Old Friend
Katherine

The rains finally let up. The umbrella Miss Violet had loaned me did its job for the most part, but a few gusts of wind pushed rain like bullets right under the dome, soaking me in odd, blotchy spots. The sun finally poked through the thinning clouds, warming my chilled skin. I stood at the carts outside the grocer's, but knew I had to complete my list of things to do so that I could surprise Mama with the crock of chicken salad Miss Violet had promised.

I inhaled deeply, absorbing the sweet scent of oranges. Someday, I'd have bowls of them in my kitchen all year round. A pink-and-black butterfly fluttered by, landing on an orange. Its velvet wings with blue eyespots pulsed in synchronicity with my breath. I gently dislodged an orange adjacent to where the insect was roosting. It lifted into the sky, then landed on the back of my hand, its tiny feet tickling me.

In seconds, it had fluttered back to its perch on the pile, and I smiled, rubbing my fingers over the orange. I inhaled its scent. *Heaven on earth.*

The butterfly took off again, looping past me, making me giggle. The hair on my arms stood up, and I felt someone watching me. I shifted my shoulders, turning away from the man I saw out of the corner of my eye, the grocer. I wedged the orange I'd been smelling back into the crate between two others.

Someone tapped my shoulder. I didn't turn back. "I'm going." I pulled my list of errands out of my sleeve. I shuffled along but caught my boot on a crevice in the walk, and the grocer stepped in front of me, blocking my way.

I straightened but didn't make eye contact. I let go of my skirt, the hem brushing over the tops of my boots with a heavy *whoosh*, stirring the dust that covered the sidewalk.

"I knew it," the grocer said to someone else as I stepped around him.

I was relieved he didn't mean me and wasn't going to scold me for sniffing his oranges.

I kept walking, searching for the addresses on the buildings as I went.

"Hey, you," a voice came from behind. "It *was* you."

I hastened, weaving in between two women strolling along, and a man's voice shouted from behind, "Katherine!"

I stopped and turned, my eyes tracing a broad man's form, right up to his face. But the sun was in my eyes, and I could only see his outline.

Someone else gripped my arms. The grocer was shoving me toward the store door under the awning. My heart was racing.

"You leave her alone," someone said, and the grocer let go.

I wiped my watering eyes while my vision adjusted to the shade. When I finally focused, I saw *him*, and I stopped. Ocean-blue eyes, blond hair, a hulking build, the massive hands—all told me this person was my old friend, though now he was a man. Taller, thicker, but the same warm eyes.

"Aleksey," I said. It *had* been him the other day.

The grocer grabbed my arm again, and Aleksey gripped the man's shoulder. "Leave her be."

The grocer let go of my arm. "She stole. It's my right to hold her until the police can be summoned."

"She didn't."

"I didn't take a thing," I said. Aleksey's rescue made me feel safe, but I didn't want him to think I was a thief.

"I saw you with the orange to your nose," the grocer said.

"I did do that, but I put it right back."

"She did," Aleksey said.

The grocer reached for me again. "I don't believe you."

"I saw the whole thing," Aleksey said.

The grocer looked Aleksey up and down. "Who are _you_? No one I know."

The man grabbed for me again, and Aleksey blocked the man's arm with his, cuffed his wrist, and twisted his arm behind his back.

"She's lying," the grocer said. "I saw her with the orange."

"I'm not lying," I said.

"She wouldn't lie. Ever. And if you keep this up, I'll see you in court."

I drew back at hearing Aleksey threaten to take this man to court. Same old Aleksey. Always watching out for me.

"I work for Mr. Stevens at the courthouse," Aleksey said. "He'd be more than happy to vouch for me."

"Yeah, right. You a lawyer?"

Aleksey pushed the man away. "Don't bother her again."

A mix of gratitude and humiliation gathered inside me.

When the grocer left, I exhaled.

Aleksey adjusted his hat, smiling like I remembered. "I knew it was you the other day at the alley."

I nodded. "I thought it was you too . . . but . . . well, it seemed impossible."

"I know." He smiled and silence came, making me feel awkward.

"But I didn't take anything. I swear I didn't. Please believe me."

He stepped toward me, his gaze tight on mine, holding me in a way that was far different than I remembered when we were younger. "Of course, I believe you. I'm just so . . . I knew I saw you the other day," he said. "I wasn't sure but . . ."

"I wasn't sure, either. But then, I sort of was." Our conversation felt strained yet right at the same time.

He stepped back, nodding. His attention flicked over me. "Look at you. Tall now, and . . . well, when I saw you at the alley, the way you moved, your hair, and then just a minute ago at the orange crates, I saw." He glanced at my hand, at my little finger that had been amputated more than halfway down.

I snatched my hand from his gaze and hid it behind my back. A ridiculous thing to do. If there was anyone who I didn't need to hide my disfigured hand from it was Aleksey Zurchenko. He'd kept Yale and me alive during the blizzard by warming us between his body and a cow that had sought shelter with us. And Aleksey had held one of my hands when they removed the dead, infected part of my finger. I was overwhelmed with a mix of self-consciousness, an unexpected thrill at seeing him, feeling simultaneously at home in his presence and completely unfamiliar.

"I can't believe it's you," he said.

His words, his rich voice, tumbled over me. I studied him as he beamed at me.

"You are a sight," he said.

I touched my warming cheeks as I felt this tall, handsome man's attention.

He shuffled his feet, appearing as unnerved as I felt. He dug into his pocket and produced a watch, flipping it open, then snapping it shut. "I can't talk long," he said.

I nodded, thinking of his mother and siblings. How I would love to see them all. How Mama would love to see Greta. "How's your mama?"

"Wonderful," he said, "but she's not here. None of them are. Believe it or not, I'm here to read for the law. I work on a farm in exchange for room and board. Mr. Palmer's place, just a ways down the river."

My mouth fell open. Law exams? I subtracted dates in my mind, what I knew of his education, calculating how this could be possible.

"You thought I was lying to the grocer about court, didn't you?" He bent into me and took my hand, holding it to his chest. "Well, you're right. I'm not a lawyer. Not yet. I owe my path to the law to you teaching me to read all those years back. I've been telling the fellas for months about you and what you did for me way back when."

I smiled, remembering when he had read his first word. *Cat.*

"That's amazing," I said. "I haven't gotten very far with my studies." I couldn't get the rest of the words out, the story behind it all. How would I explain all the ways the past few years had robbed me of everything he believed to be true about me? He would never want to know such things. No one would.

He drew his thumb over my fingers. I leapt at the sensation, and he dropped my hand, probably realizing it wasn't proper. He wiped his hand on his trousers, and I wiped mine on my skirt.

"I sent you letters," he said. "Explaining how I came to be so educated."

Letters? I hadn't much luck getting anyone's letters the past few years. "I'm sorry, I never got them. I was . . . *where* did you send them?"

"Yankton. Where I thought you were. Some of my letters were returned; the others must have been lost. I suppose that's why you didn't get them."

I bit my lip, my mind rifling through all the events and moves and homes that I'd experienced since leaving the prairie, feeling as though I was being wakened from a years'-long slumber.

He took off his hat, wiped his brow with his forearm, then crushed the lid back on his head. He looked over his shoulder, clearly done with the conversation. I touched my hair, knowing I must look awful with the rain and gusty winds. Self-conscious of both my appearance and my past, I suddenly didn't know what to say.

I opened my shopping list. "I have a full day ahead." Drops of rain splashed on my paper, and I startled. "Oh galoshes! My umbrella." I looked back by the orange crates where I'd set it earlier.

"Galoshes. I forgot that you say that. I love that," he told me.

I started toward the grocer's carts, and Aleksey said, "I'll get it." He bounded away and returned with it. "Can't lose your umbrella with the amount of rain we've been getting."

"Thank you," I said, unable to stop from smiling. Being with Aleksey, even for a short time, had done something to me.

I read my list but felt his gaze still heavy on me. I lifted my eyes, absorbed by him, as though tethered by more than simply our shared past.

He pulled the watch from his pocket again and flipped the cover open. "I'm late. I wish I could stay and talk. But, oh, if you knew my position! I have a wagon to catch and two stops before that."

I nodded, and he shifted his feet but didn't leave. He turned back and grabbed my hands. "I'm so glad to see you, Katherine. So glad."

He leaned closer, like he was going to kiss my cheek, but then pulled away. "What's your address? I'll call on you soon as I can."

"Ten Mulberry Road," I shouted as he was sprinting away. Chunks of mud kicked up with every stride he took. I replayed the sensation of his hand on mine.

I started down the street and realized I was heading the wrong way. I wheeled around and enjoyed the quiet thrill that shook my insides like a thousand butterflies taking flight, making me think of Aleksey in a way I never had before.

Chapter 11

Fraud
Katherine

I took thoughts of Aleksey Zurchenko's hands with me when
I went to finish the errands. I replayed the way they
swallowed mine, his voice, the scent of rain and grass that he
carried, filled my mind as I checked the items off my list of
things to do. I wondered if I would run into him again, if he
would ever call on us. Mr. Palmer's farm? There were many
along the river, and I wondered which was his. Studying for
law exams? It didn't fit with the boy I'd known back on the
prairie, and though neither of us had had time to linger, the
delight of seeing him again was enough for the moment.
Mama would be so pleased to hear news of Aleksey and that
her dearest friend, Greta Zurchenko, was well.

I refocused on the errands I needed to complete.

That morning I'd made four apple pies, three dozen
patty shells and lemon curd and apple filling to go in them,
carrot pudding, six loaves of bread, applesauce, and an
onion-potato pie. There was no meat available, but I'd
planned to inquire about the possibility of making a creamed
chicken filling for some of the patty shells, get some cleaning

items, and find someone who'd be willing to trade for my homemade bread in exchange for helping Mama till the garden.

I had suggested to Miss Violet that I purchase fresh rosemary, thyme, comfrey, lavender, lemongrass, and more so I could hang and dry the herbs in the far corner of the kitchen. Once dry, I could shelve them in the kitchen and cellar. I'd mix sand and lavender to use while sweeping to bring the scent of spring inside. Miss Violet and I had discussed how Mama would grow these things in the kitchen garden, but until then we'd have to buy what was needed.

A deep-voiced man yelled for his friend, making me think of Aleksey yet again. His name whispered in my ear like a butterfly's soft feet brushing over my skin. *Aleksey. A lawyer.* I shook my head, pride pressing me, knowing that I'd taught him to read in the first place. My current list of chores and accomplishments wouldn't cause Aleksey to think of me the way I was marveling over his achievements, but I was satisfied for the moment that my family was together and we could eat.

There were several places in town that Miss Violet and Mama suspected would have the names of men interested in trading services for bread.

As I walked farther and the older section of Des Moines went from run-down to vibrant, my attention was piqued by beautifully designed storefronts boasting the season's finery and haberdasheries displaying hats that were equal parts artwork and protection from the elements. I touched my hat, digging one finger under the ribbon that hid a hole that had opened clear through. I adjusted the hatpin and straightened my shoulders.

I stopped on the corner, waiting to cross the street, when the crowd around me began to grow tense, people murmuring and moving closer. Shouting came from down the street. "Repent! Turn your feet in the direction of the church and move them posthaste!"

I shuddered, the sense of peace I'd been enjoying shattered by this man's virulent voice calling on religion, creating a familiar clawing at my skin. It was as though the entire Christoff family and their church had risen around me, their hands tugging, pulling me into the cellar, where they felt safe above with me stowed away below.

I knew right away that he was one of the purity pushers I'd read about in the paper. As Des Moines citizens felt increasingly unheard by politicians and police, there were many who thought they could help by screaming scripture, damning people to hell, and warning that the world was ending.

This one wore a suit that had once been fine but was worn down to a flimsy shine. His weedy beard, like thorny brambles, grew out and down to the middle of his chest and provided width to his narrow, gaunt face. He stalked toward the bunch of us waiting to cross the street. His stovepipe hat shaded his piercing black eyes; his hard gaze sent chills up my spine.

I cowered as he strolled closer, knowing he had no idea of my ability, of my past experiences, but fearing him nonetheless. Instead of passing us, he stopped and grabbed my wrist, his fingers burning my flesh as he twisted. I tried to wrench free. "Don't be lured down hell's half acre," he said, spitting as he spoke. "*She'll* come cloaked in all you desire. *He'll* offer what can't possibly be given."

With my free hand, I dug my nails into the skin below his palm. He froze, wincing.

"Let me go," I said and dug harder. Finally, he released me, backing away, holding his hand to his belly.

He kept me in his view but didn't shout more at me.

The whole episode called to mind the revival I'd attended with the Christoffs, the way they dragged a girl to the front of the tent, accusing her of luring a married man into her arms, knowing that men did the luring, the pulling, the roping in, not the young girls who were often accused.

I shivered, the fear I'd felt for the girl, for myself, returning. The crowd waiting to cross the avenue parted to let him pass.

"There's heaven and hell! You choose your destiny." His voice sliced into my ears as he shouted. I hunched, wanting to dash into the road despite it being cluttered with wagons and carriages.

"Hell and heaven!" he yelled again.

Shaking, I moved on with the crowd. The man swung back in our direction. I ducked behind an older couple right beside Miller's Bakery. The storefront held tiers of breads and cakes. One cake made me think of the lemon cake I had often made for the Christoffs.

"Repent!"

I crouched, my nose up against the glass. I wished I hadn't had to leave Hannah Christoff behind. But she was their daughter. Both parents had been cruel to me, but they had been kind to her, so when I ran, she helped me escape but stayed behind.

The couple who had been shielding me from the shouting man stepped back, pushing me even closer to the glass. I walked my hand down my side and touched my skirt where the crystal pendant was hidden. *Please, bring my calming.*

At the Christoffs', I'd survived by blocking out the pinches on the back of my arm by Mrs. Christoff or Mr. Christoff's hot breath on my ear as he whispered his desire for me. I tried to do the same now, hidden between the couple and the bakery window. *Please, James.*

In the midst of the harshest treatment, James would appear and draw my attention to the shifting clouds, as he did when he was alive. Back then I hadn't been interested in James's attempts to predict the coming weather. Now I found solace in boring shifts in the atmosphere and came to see James as a guide. He and a woman would appear together often. Her face was always obscured by a scarf or shadow as she cradled a baby. The woman reminded me of how Mama held Yale in her arms after she'd been born that year on the prairie. The two souls comforted me, taking away the sense of aloneness I'd felt since my family was torn to shreds.

I pressed the crystal against my leg, the street sounds— shouting man, murmuring crowd, old couple—all of it receded, and I was left with a sense of wellbeing, the sense my James was near.

The purity pusher moved far enough away that the crowd, like a giant exhale, dispersed, freeing me up to move down the street. I picked up my pace. At times, it was as if James had never died, he felt so present to me. At times like this, that was everything.

**

No luck. I ticked off the list of possible vendors who might have had a man willing to trade for tilling. One more store was on the list, but I prepared for the idea that I might be doing the tilling myself.

I checked the next address on the list against the store in front of me. The number must have been wrong—the building looked abandoned but for the glow coming from inside the grimy windows. I rubbed a spot clean and peered inside, realizing I'd been in the store before. It had been a jewelry store, with three narrow rooms that marched from the front to the back of the building, wedged in between two larger buildings.

I'd been there countless times to choose a birthday or Christmas present. My favorite visits had been the ones with my father, selecting just the right jewels for Mama. The sapphire necklace had been the one Mama had most loved, the one Elizabeth Calder had taken from her as partial recompense for my grandfather's and father's misdeeds.

Through the crusted dirt on the windows, I saw the furnishings were still opulent. I couldn't resist entering, pushing open the door. Its lavish chandelier still hung in the entry, but the foyer was barely lit. It was so dark I thought it was empty. Then my eyes adjusted. Where were all the jewels? The cases were dusty and empty. There was a set of wooden chairs around a table and a velvet davenport off to the side. The scent of spice and vanilla was so strong it made me sneeze.

This startled two women sitting across the room, hidden by the shadows. "What do you want?" Was this the jeweler's wife? The kind woman with the tiny fingers, who easily worked the most delicate clasps?

I squinted into the darkness, moving forward to get a better look. A woman whose face was painted like a circus clown sneered.

"Oh," I said. "I thought this was . . . I used to come here before."

"Wait your turn," one woman barked.

I was about to ask her what was it I might be waiting for, but her crisp tone kept me quiet.

I scanned the room, wanting to light another lamp, but the second woman's quiet sobbing at the table gave me pause. I immediately knew I should leave. I stepped back, still focusing on the ladies, and I realized what they were doing. The table was draped with pink, red, and yellow silken cloths; a smooth crystal ball the size of a large cantaloupe sat on a wooden perch in the center. The woman with the painted face placed one hand on the ball and tapped her long curling nails, clicking along with the other woman's sobs. I'd heard and read plenty about these operations since the Christoffs decided I was evil or crazy. A fortune-teller, a seer.

"I don't want an audience," the weeping woman said.

The seer shushed the crying lady. "Your Norman will come. He has much to tell you."

It was then I saw the man off to the weeping woman's side. I was riveted. "Tell her to leave," the man said. I waited for the seer to relay the information to the weeper.

The seer didn't glance at him, listen to him, nothing. She rubbed both hands over her crystal ball, tapping her nails, and murmured some indecipherable words. Then she shook her hands above her head, her gaze on the weeper. "Nothing. I'm getting nothing. Norman's not coming today."

The bereft woman turned her gaze on me and pointed. "It's her. She's why he won't come."

I felt the room temperature shift. I rubbed my arms as a chilly breeze cooled me through my wet clothing. I pointed to the man. "But don't you see—"

"Out!" The seer pointed toward the door. She spit on the floor, startling the weeper. "You ruined it." The seer turned back to the woman in tears. "You'll come back tomorrow. And bring another fifty cents."

"But I can't—"

The seer grasped the edge of the table. "If you care about Norman's soul, you'll find a way."

The distressed woman nodded slowly, dabbing at her tears with a handkerchief. "I'm not sure." Her voice was calm, as though something had cleared her, erased the upset that had just wracked her a moment before.

The seer sighed with her whole body and turned to me again. "Out, I told you!" She snapped back to the weeper.

"I'll try again now."

I suddenly wondered if my presence was keeping the seer from seeing the husband and helping the poor customer. "I think I know what's—"

"Out!" the seer shouted again. "Or I'll summon the police. You won't be the first person I've helped the police send to jail."

Call the police for what? Her dark eyes stabbed me. Frightened for the second time that day, I dashed from the building, confused. I stumbled out from under the awning, back onto the sidewalk and turned to more closely examine the storefront, obscured by filth. "Diamond and Sage" it read, and "Madame Smalley" was written underneath.

Madame Smalley. Was that the woman I'd read about in the paper? I couldn't remember the exact name. I patted my leg where the chandelier pendant lay against my thigh. I certainly had my own palm-sized ball that I found comfort in just by touching it, that aided in bringing helpful spirits my way. But my crystal ball had chosen me; it was real. *I* was real. I felt suddenly protective of this gift of mine. I knew there was a difference between me and that angry woman inside.

Madame Smalley? Maybe it *was* my presence that barred her from doing her work. Who was I to call her a fraud?

A train whistle blew in the distance. I turned and hurried right into a woman laden with shopping bags, knocking them out of her hands. Stunned, we offered apologies as we gripped each other, steadying ourselves.

"Katherine?" the woman said.

I looked into her face, studying it, reaching back for a name to go with the familiar, friendly smile. My mind wound back in time until I put the name with the fine clothing, the creamy cheeks and bright eyes. This woman had always been kind. "Mrs. Hillis." I exhaled and reached down for one of the parcels she had dropped.

"Oh my, how grown up you are. I saw your mother at the Mellet home a while back and, well . . ."

I didn't know what to say about that, not wanting to tell her how badly it had gone.

Mrs. Hillis patted my hand. "I'm so sorry how that unfolded." The woman's gentle voice and warm expression comforted me. Mrs. Hillis had always had small gifts in her bag for the children at women's club events. Or she had a story to tell them or questions to ask. She never whisked by us like we were bloodless dummies, like most of the women did.

Mrs. Hillis looked at the name of the store on the window. I followed her gaze. "I thought it was still the jewelry store . . ."

Mrs. Hillis narrowed her eyes on me. "Definitely not."

I realized how odd it was that I might enter a jewelry store in my family's current financial state. "I couldn't afford a hat pin, even if it was still—"

Mrs. Hillis shuffled her parcel to her other arm. "I used to love that store, myself. But now it's different, isn't it? I just hate to see people taken advantage of. It just bothers me to my core. Vulnerable people." She shrugged.

"Taken advantage of?" I said.

Mrs. Hillis's gaze slid to the name of the store again. I was getting very good at sensing a person's honesty, understanding if they were being truthful, just by seeing a flinch here, a flicker of a scowl, a hidden smirk, nervous hands. Mrs. Hillis simply appeared to be thoughtfully considering my question. "Faith is mysterious, you know. I believe in many unseen things, but I'm not sure that what Miss Smalley is doing is kind. Faith, belief, spiritual matters . . . they're all very tricky to label and box up like," she lifted her bags to Katherine, "clothes from a store."

"So she's selling her spirituality? Like a minister, but for money?"

"That depends on whether you believe that a woman can convey the comings and goings of the spirit world, that she sees something the rest of us don't. Many have put their faith in her to no good end. Others find comfort with her."

I thought of the male spirit who was right there and how Madame Smalley hadn't seen him, at least I didn't think she had. Perhaps she *was* a fraud?

Mrs. Hillis cleared her throat. "I try not to judge. When I think of your mother, what faith she has to simply, well . . . *That's* the kind of thing I find easy to believe in. Survival. I'm so glad she's back in Des Moines. I wish she'd come call."

I smiled, relieved to not talk about Madame Smalley anymore. "Mama's doing well. We're boarding at the property of Miss Violet Pendergrass. Mama plotted out the garden—a children's garden, kitchen garden, social garden. There are some issues with the tilling and the garbage under the soil. I'm not sure how she'll grow a single carrot back there . . ."

"Sounds like an enormous undertaking."

"Oh, the garden's not a worry to Mama. She can see it blooming and lush already. All I see is the dirt. Oh, I'm prattling, aren't I?"

Mrs. Hillis set one load of bags down and slipped her gloved hand over mine. The blush kid leather was buttery against my cracked, borrowed gloves. "I understand, really." Her touch was sincere.

A man came up beside Mrs. Hillis and drew her attention. "Reed Hayes." Mrs. Hillis dropped my hand, shook the man's hand, then gestured toward me. "This is Katherine Arthur. She's the daughter of the woman I told you about, Jeanie Arthur."

Mr. Hayes turned to me, gave a small bow, and shook my hand. "The writer, Jeanie Arthur? She's your mother?"

I smiled and nodded, pleased at hearing my mother spoken about in such a way.

Reed Hayes adjusted his hat. "A pleasure, Katherine. I understand you and your brother are fine scholars. And I read some of your mother's work. I'm impressed."

"Well, she hasn't written in a while. With my little sister, Yale, and, well, there's not much time for writing anymore."

Mr. Hayes and Mrs. Hillis smiled and nodded along as though I was their peer more than a child of a formerly wealthy woman. I became aware of my position as I rambled. I thought of my list, only one more option to secure a tiller. "Oh galoshes. I need to finish my list." I pulled it out and read the name of the final place on the list.

"Can I help, Katherine?" Mrs. Hillis asked.

"I'm looking for a store, but the address is wrong. I need to find a man who'll trade tilling services for bread. Mama's so tired with all she has to do. We really need some help turning the soil so we can plant." I looked away. I shouldn't be confiding any of this. It wasn't polite, and it wasn't necessary. These were nice people, but they weren't friends.

"You're a good daughter," Mrs. Hillis said.

I was about to thank Mrs. Hillis for her kindness when three policemen barreled past us, pushing through the front door of Diamonds and Sage.

In seconds, they were rushing back out with Madame Smalley in hand while the distraught woman who'd been crying when I arrived followed behind them. I sidestepped toward Mrs. Hillis to get out of their way.

"You're a fake, Beda Smalley, gypping people out of their last pennies," the weeper screeched. "I'll be there for your trial. I want my money back!"

They dragged Madame Smalley right past us. The weeper stopped, and Madame Smalley shouted over her shoulder while being hauled away, "Your path won't be less rocky for throwing stones at me! I'm Madame Smalley, and I am truth!"

The weeper glared at Madame Smalley until she disappeared. She backed away, looking at Mrs. Hillis and me. "Keep away from the likes of her unless you have money to burn and your own match to do it."

The woman's voice chilled me. I put my hand against the brick wall to steady myself.

"She'll spend the next ten years in jail if I can help it," she said, hurrying off in the opposite direction.

Mr. Hayes shook his head. "Poor woman. I'm sorry she experienced such a thing." He pulled his newspaper from under his arm and flapped it open. "I'm not surprised they arrested her. Says right here the cacophony surrounding Madame Smalley has been escalating each day. A month's worth of stories on the matter. This accuser isn't the first."

Mrs. Hillis bent her head to look at the article.

My shoulders tensed. I couldn't swallow my rising bile. The energy shifted, the lightness I'd felt in talking with Mrs. Hillis and Mr. Hayes was changing to a heaviness, an unsettling inside my bones.

"Katherine?" Mrs. Hillis squeezed my arm. "What's wrong?"

"You all right?" Mr. Hayes asked.

I forced a smile. "I need to find someone to trade for tilling or we'll never get that garden growing. I've wandered off task enough for one day. Nice to see you, Mrs. Hillis. Nice to meet you, Mr. Hayes." I walked away.

"Wait," Mr. Hayes said. I looked over my shoulder to see them coming after me. I stopped and turned, wanting to hear what they had to say.

"We have an idea," Mrs. Hillis said.

Chapter 12

Accused
Aleksey

The thick, humid air sat in my lungs like field dust, making my chest feel as though someone were standing on it. I craned my neck, looking up Locust Street in one direction and then the other. I reached the alley where I was to meet Harold and Palmer, and I felt proud when I saw the wagon round the bend and approach me. I jabbed my fist in the air. I was early!

After dropping off a brief to Mr. Stevens, going into court with him, and collecting my next assignment, a surge of accomplishment hit me. Mr. Stevens was masterful in court, causing even the great Judge Calder to take note of the argument for Mrs. Landman's property line encompassing the well, even though it hadn't originally been part of the property.

I prided myself in having dug out the signed contract from the city files, much to the dismay of Mr. Jackson, who argued on behalf of himself.

Wouldn't Katherine be proud? I couldn't wait to talk to her and her family and get reacquainted. As the wagon slowed in front of me, I hopped over the side. Harold turned from the front and greeted me.

"What took you two so long?" I said.

"Funny guy now, are you?" Harold said.

"Just an early bird today, is all," I said.

"For once." Harold doffed the front of my hat.

I straightened it and let out a laugh, still feeling inspired and satisfied with my day in court.

"Thresher's coming tomorrow morning," Mr. Palmer said. "You finish the wall, and Fat Joe can work with Harold."

"Yes, sir."

I thought of the book we'd found in the wall with the stones. I was intrigued by it and Palmer's reaction to it. Though it seemed to be an ordinary recipe book with notes about some rocks, every time I worked the wall I thought of Mrs. Palmer and her book.

"If we get the stone led in today," I said, "I can work quickly to finish, Mr. Palmer."

He nodded. He took the reins and lifted them, poised to get the horses going, when a ruckus caused all three of us to turn toward a woman being dragged down the sidewalk.

"I'm not a thief!"

The woman stumbled but didn't fall, two officers holding her under her armpits. I recoiled at the rough handling. I felt fear for her, wondering what she'd done. She was dragged across the road right in front of us and turned in our direction. Her painted face conveyed anger and defiance, not the fear I felt at seeing how she was handled. She looked at the three of us, then fixed her gaze on Palmer.

He stiffened and drew back.

"Andrew!" the woman screeched.

Palmer flinched. Was she talking to him? Her boldness softened at the sight of him.

"Andrew Palmer," she said. "Tell them I'm not a fraud! You tell them about Winnie."

The policemen tossed glances our way but kept moving. "Stifle it, Madame Smalley. No one wants to hear your mouth."

Harold looked from me to Palmer. "What's she talking about?"

Palmer shrugged. "No idea."

But it came back to me now. *Winnie.* The name in Mrs. Palmer's book.

Palmer's jaw was tight, but his face had paled three shades. We'd seen the articles about Madame Smalley in the newspaper. I had no inkling what she meant about his wife, Winnie, but I could see from his blood-drained face that he knew exactly what she meant.

Palmer's face seemed to droop, the lines near his eyes deepening right before my eyes. I was left with a quaking belly, an odd sense of unsettledness I didn't understand. "Should we go help her?" I leaned forward.

"Nah," he said, offering nothing more to explain.

I reached into my pocket and wrapped my fingers around the butterfly-shaped stone I'd found in the wall, the smooth faces and jagged edges fitting into my palm as though it had been made just for my hand.

Finally, Palmer said, "She's insane. Clear as the rain that drenched us this morning. She belongs at the asylum."

He shook the reins. The horses whinnied. I pulled the stone from my pocket and turned around to face out of the wagon, sitting with my back against the front seat. I pulled one knee up and set the stone on it. Daylight worked through clear parts of the stone, obscured by the milky parts. An amazing thing—that a stone could be ripped from the earth in the very shape of a living thing.

It reminded me of the dying walnut tree, the lifelike image of the mythical Medusa, the face mysteriously, accidentally rendered in the trunk. I enjoyed the wonders of mythology, stories and fables, but I felt fortunate I had the law to ground me. I appreciated rules written into books that moored us to life. Fantasy intrigued me, but the law kept me tethered and sure.

As we pulled away, the sound of Madame Smalley's voice carried between the buildings, haunting the air, making me wonder what exactly she'd done this time.

Chapter 13

Secret
Katherine

I trundled home from completing the errands with a pencil line through each item. Arms heavy with a box stuffed with Gold Dust Washing Powder, flour, baking powder, and yeast, I was grateful that Mrs. Hillis and Mr. Hayes had stopped me before I ran off. I was even happier he was willing to run the tiller for Mama if I baked him bread for the next two weeks.

I hoped Mama wouldn't be upset that I'd confided in Mrs. Hillis and a strange man, but I had to ask a stranger to do the work either way. Still, I felt as though my disclosure might deepen the shame that shadowed my family.

Upon reaching Miss Violet's home, I pushed through the picket gate; it screeched as the hinges stuck. I followed the walkway around to the back gardens. I stopped at the wall of hedges separating Miss Violet's business and residence from the small home my family was boarding in. I could hear Mama talking to Yale.

"Beans here, your children's garden there. The kitchen garden near the door."

Mama paused as though waiting for Yale to respond. My sister offered something verbal that I couldn't make out, but Mama's voice grew more animated. "Yes, darling Yale, this is your garden."

I moved along the barrier of hedge until I found an open space, poked my hands through, and separated the greens. "Mama," I said.

I could see her worn hem sweep the dirt as she turned toward my voice.

"Here, at the hedge."

I pushed my hand through and wiggled my fingers. Mama rushed over and grabbed my hand. She squeezed my fingers, then let go. I pushed my head into the greens. "I found a tiller. A Mr. Reed Hayes will trade his services for bread."

"Oh, Katherine. You're already working so hard for Miss Violet. Now you have to make extra?"

"I'm fine, Mama. You can't get that garden in fast enough for her."

Mama's expression looked surprised, then worried. "In a good way or a bad way? I'm working hard to clear the debris to prepare for the tiller. She doesn't—"

"Oh no. Only in a good way. She's just excited to have fresh food at the ready for her meetings and such. Oh, wait until you see the meals I'll be preparing. The leading citizens of Des Moines trail into the house for meetings like—"

"I know! I read about it just this morning," Mama said. We grinned at each other.

"You'll never believe who I saw in town," I said.

Mama looked over her shoulder and reminded Yale to stay near. "Who?"

I widened the hole in the hedge. We'd have to cut through it a bit so we could go back and forth. "Aleksey Zurchenko."

Mama drew back. Her hand went to where her long neck met her collarbone. "Greta?"

I shook my head. "Just Aleksey. He's studying to be a lawyer." My voice carried excitement and pride.

"The law?" Mama's face bore the same satisfaction I felt. She sighed, smiling. "He was a smart one. Once you taught him to read, it changed everything about him."

I nodded. "He'll call on us, he said."

"He'll be most welcome."

We looked at each other, lost in our own thoughts.

"I better get these things into the kitchen," I told her. "I have a meal to get on the table." I thought of how the girl named Olivia had scowled at me before I left today. Miss Violet had assigned her to watch over the oven while I was gone, and she'd protested. Miss Violet had returned the complaint with a sharp look, and Olivia told me, "Just this once. I don't work in the kitchen anymore." My apology to her hadn't made a difference. She'd only turned her back to me, mumbling about losing study time, time to prepare for her very important clients.

Mama must have picked up on my change in mood. "What is it?"

"I don't think the girl, Olivia, who's doing Miss Violet's financial education program, likes me very much."

Mama's brow creased.

I stepped closer to the hedges and reached for her. She took my hand, the sharp stems of the boxwood scratching the back of mine. Mama's eyes glistened. "I'm proud of you, Katherine. We'll be careful with our earnings, and soon we'll have enough money to move into our own little home, and we can put an end to our worries for good."

My throat was thick as my own eyes burned. This was not the life my mother had planned for me, for any of us. But things were better, we were together, and that was what I would focus on. "Keep your manners," she said. "Mind yourself roaming around town."

I knew what she was thinking—a young lady should not traipse around Des Moines unattended. But we both knew things had changed. Our circumstances no longer afforded us chaperones and leisure time. It didn't matter what others thought if we weren't angling for invitations to the Moonlight Ball.

I exhaled deeply. I told myself it didn't matter beyond my vanity. At this point, we Arthurs were so far outside of society that most of the rules that had shaped our days in the past mattered very little. There was no more humiliation attached to the scandal that had sent us running. We'd already absorbed every ounce of shame hoisted our way related to that situation. Now was the time for rebuilding.

The sound of Yale weeping caused Mama to yank her hand from mine and rush away, the hedges closing, shielding my view. "See you later, Mama. Mr. Hayes will stop by with the tiller soon," I said. "Be good, little Yale." I backed away from the hedges and picked up the box.

**

At the kitchen door, I thought of all the stops I'd made that day. *Aleksey.* I shuddered at remembering he'd heard the grocer accuse me of stealing, and I felt shame. I'd stolen in the past, yes. But it had been necessary.

Once inside, I heaved the box onto the worktable in the center of the sapphire-and-lemon-walled space. An image of Aleksey reaching for me came to mind, causing my face to redden. I touched my cheek, thrilled at the thought of him.

Seeing him again was wonderful, a champion emerging from the crowd to take up for me. He was grown, burly now, very handsome, still gallant. I'd felt safe just being near him when he defended me this morning, so sure I wouldn't have stolen the orange. And yet . . . the thought I wasn't the same girl he knew four years ago darkened my satisfaction at having seen him.

As I emptied my box and recounted the day's errands, Mrs. Hillis's words about Madame Smalley taking advantage of people with what amounted to a psychic crime came back to me. I shook off the dread at witnessing that today.

I opened the oven and checked the custard. The carrot pudding and apple patty shells were cooling near the screened window. I lifted the lids and inhaled. It looked as though Olivia had kept watch since everything was perfectly done. I fitted the lid back on the crock and heard someone weeping. It came from the direction of the butler's pantry. The crying grew in intensity, swelling to a wail. I set two empty crocks into the sink to soak, crept to the butler's pantry, and peered around the doorjamb. Olivia stood there, head bowed into her hands.

I began to back away, wanting to give her space, but my heel hit the doorway and she turned. Her eyes were swollen slits, her face stained red as though splattered with paint.

I froze.

She sobbed harder, her shoulders shaking. She leaned toward me instead of away. I felt her sorrow as though it were my own. She stepped toward me again. I opened my arms, and she collapsed onto my shoulder.

"What is it, Olivia?"

She cried hard, her mouth open, her teeth grazing my shoulder. I attempted to peel her away, but she just fell harder against me. So I held her and let her bawl, taking on the grip of her sadness as much as the weight of her body.

I closed my eyes. *Please help her, God,* and when I opened them, I jerked at the sight of an older woman standing with us. At first I wasn't sure who she was, but I realized quickly that this woman had come to do for Olivia what I couldn't. Still, I reached out to touch her. There was nothing to touch, nothing fleshy or alive.

"Shush, shush, now. I think . . . well," I said over her sobs. I needed to be calm, soothing, if I was to inform Olivia that someone had come to see her, but her crying was so loud that I couldn't get the words over the howls.

"I just want to die," she said.

I knew how much work Olivia had to do later that day, and Miss Violet would not look softly upon her shirking responsibility. I had my own responsibilities, and Miss Violet certainly would not allow me an afternoon off for no reason.

"Now listen," I told Olivia, wiggling out of her grip. I latched onto her arms, squeezing tight. "This is important."

Olivia's sobs thinned, and her shoulders stopped bucking as I studied the kindness on the older woman's face. Her head was cocked, studying Olivia. The older woman glanced at me and smiled, nodding as though she understood that now was the time to let Olivia know.

"Someone's here for you, Olivia. But you need to calm down or you won't be able to hear what she has to say."

Olivia dropped a hand over her face and snuffled. "I told Miss Violet I can't see any clients. Not after this. Please go tell her again for me, please, Katherine."

I pulled her toward the table and sat her down. I took a seat across from her and pushed a linen cloth toward her. When Olivia didn't take it, I stood and gently dabbed the tears streaming down her cheeks. I knew how odd it was to have this conversation.

I paused, considering not mentioning it all. There was nothing that said I had to tell who I was seeing. I sat back down, resigned to keeping my silence, as it was the only way to ensure my safety, possibly even my family's.

Olivia grew silent, staring past me, her eyes vacant. And as though I'd been pushed back with a strong wind or a hand on my shoulder, I felt deep sadness inside my own skin. I'd known plenty of grief, loneliness, loss, betrayal, but this sadness, though heavy, was not mine. It was Olivia's.

"Please tell Miss Violet I can't see anyone. I'm serious, I can't."

I tried to swallow the sorrow. I rubbed my arms and shook my shoulders, trying to throw it off, but it stuck. The woman opened her hands to me, pleading that I help her and let Olivia know she was there.

Without anything more, I was certain if I didn't connect these two, I would carry this with me. I could not afford to stow away anyone else's pain. It was then I realized that this ability to bridge the past and present was necessary for my own peace as much as it was for the spirits who came to call on a loved one.

"No, no," I said. "You misunderstand. It's not a client here to see you."

Olivia sat up straight and took the cloth from me and blew her nose. She shifted toward the butler's pantry, looking around. "A gentleman caller. Not today."

"No." I took her hand. Suddenly, I wanted to make her tea to help calm her. I went to the canisters in the cupboard and pulled the one with chamomile down. I felt the side of the kettle. Still warm. I put the leaves in the kettle and inserted the long-tongued end of the tea basket into the spout of the kettle, letting the tea steep.

I took the honey pot to the table and put my hand on hers, wanting to comfort her. "This will sound strange, I know. But there's a woman here."

"Well, I can't see her either. Miss Violet discourages socializing with other women outside of the house."

I shook my head. "It's not some woman from down the road. She's right here already."

Olivia looked over her shoulder.

"She's standing to your left; her hand is on your shoulder."

Olivia jerked her head to the left, then the right, her swollen eyes narrowed on me. "Why are you teasing me?"

Panic caught in my throat as dread flooded me, reminding me of the Christoffs and the minister's plans to cleanse me of my evil. I could hear her thoughts in my own head, sense her fear at what I'd said. She couldn't see the woman, so the woman needed to talk through me.

Please tell me who you are.

And then I knew it was Olivia's mother.

"I'll tell Miss Violet you're rude and not worthy of our kitchen if you continue this."

What was I doing? I had no idea what Olivia's religious beliefs were. What if Olivia ran to Miss Violet to reveal this as lunacy, sending my whole family out the door because she thought I was evil?

Another wave of anguish shook me.

Olivia's mouth quivered, and she began to cry again, swept away by her tears, no longer attempting to puzzle out what I'd meant. "I can't stop crying." She rapped her chest. "It feels like my heart's been torn from my body."

Olivia's pain moved through me as if it were mine. And all I wanted to do was make it stop. I pulled my skirt up and slipped my hand into the pocket where my chandelier pendant was cushioned away. My fingers slid over the smooth facets. Calmer, I stood and poured her tea, bringing a piping-hot cup to the table. "Your mother is here."

Olivia's head snapped to me, her gaze confused, then hard on mine. "My mother?"

I nodded.

"You're a cruel girl." She pushed upward. I pushed her shoulder, and she sat back down.

I used the honey dipper to swirl the amber sweetness into the liquid. "I'm not being cruel."

"You are! I just received word that she died, and you're telling me she's at the door waiting to see me?"

So that's it. "No, no. It's not that. It's that she's here."

Please tell me what to say.

Olivia pushed away from the table, knocking her chair over. The tea splashed out of the cup.

I flew to my feet. "No." I suddenly understood her mother's intention and knew what to say. "She got the crops in."

Olivia's mouth fell open.

"She's here." I gestured to the space between us. "Right here. Her soul or spirit or whatever it is, but she, the essence of your mother, is here, and she doesn't want you to worry."

Olivia stared at me.

"She's holding up a yellow hat."

"Yellow hat?" Olivia looked to the left and right again, shaking her head.

"Yes."

Olivia began to shake. She grasped my hands. "How could you know that?"

I sighed, relieved. "It *is* her." This knowledge settled in my bones. I needed to trust these experiences, needed to believe in them.

Olivia stared at me, her expression angry and fearful.

"Please don't be scared, Olivia. I can't explain how this happens. I don't know why—"

"But how?" Olivia said, her red eyes now lit with hope. "She's really right here?"

I nodded. "She is. Her spirit—I suppose that's the best way to say it. I don't even fully understand it."

Olivia smiled. "Really?"

I nodded and guided her to her seat. I handed her the tea. She sipped, her shoulders relaxing.

"To your left," I said. "She has your chin in her hand. You know how mothers do when they want you to look at them or when they wipe something from your mouth. Did she used to do that to you?"

Olivia closed her eyes as though feeling her mother's presence. She touched her chin. "Yes, she did. But I can't feel it, her. I can't. I want to, but I can't."

"I'm sorry you can't feel it."

Olivia rubbed her chin and whispered, "I believe you."

My eyes burned, relieved.

"She loves the hat," I said.

"Oh my." She took my hands in hers.

"Says it's fine and lovely, like you. Spirited? That word keeps coming to me."

Olivia choked and coughed into the linen cloth. "That was her word for me. I sent her that hat a few weeks back. When I left to play the piano in Chicago, she warned me not to go, said I'd be sorry. She was so angry. I told her that I was permitted to play the piano here, but she hadn't been impressed. Even when I told her about the financial work I was doing."

Instead of the sadness I'd felt so deeply before, I now felt contentment. "I don't get that from her—anger or disappointment. She misses you."

Olivia nodded. "Is she in . . . is she all right?"

I waited for something clear to convey to Olivia. "She's smiling and patting your head. I think she wants you to be okay with her . . . you know."

"How can I be okay with her being dead?"

I could see Olivia's mother backing up a little bit.

"She'll always be with you. She wants you to know she'll watch over you. She knows you had to leave."

Olivia's mother moved toward her now. I closed my eyes, waiting for more information.

"I feel that," Olivia said. She looked toward her shoulder and put her quaking hand there.

"I'm warm."

I nodded, now as stunned as Olivia. "She's proud." I watched the woman back away again, leaving the room, but her presence was very clear still. Olivia laid her cheek where the hand had been on her shoulder and closed her eyes.

"I could feel her. Not see her, but feel her," Olivia said.

I sat straighter in my chair, exhilarated that I'd salved this wounded gap for them. "I'm so glad for you," I said.

"It's amazing that you can do this. Let me go tell—"

I grabbed her hand and held her so tight she couldn't move away. My sense of wellbeing was quickly taken over by regret. "No. Please. Don't tell a soul about this, Olivia."

She winced, and I realized I was hurting her. I let go.

"Why not?" Olivia asked. She rubbed the spot I'd been holding tight.

"It's not something I can control. I don't even want it."

"But it's so . . . healing."

I shook my head, thinking of all that could go wrong. "People don't understand it. It's not a good thing to many people. I'm not even sure that . . . *Please*, not a soul."

Olivia looked at the table, then back at me. "I wouldn't even know *what* to tell someone." She pulled my hands to her lips and kissed them. "Thank you."

I nodded, drained and exhilarated at the same time. The idea I could comfort someone in a time of loss was as much a gift to me as it was to the suffering person. Now that the event had passed, I wished I hadn't told Olivia what I'd seen. But I hadn't been able to stop myself. The discomfort had become mine in those moments, and all I had wanted to do was put an end to it for her and me.

"What you just did was—"

I stood. "You can't tell. Please."

She drew back, studying me. She took the chamomile tea and sipped it. "Okay. I won't."

For all the insight I'd had into the sadness between Olivia and her mother, I couldn't gather a bit of surety that she wouldn't tell everyone she saw what I'd done.

Chapter 14

Useful
Violet

"We're done here," Violet told Judge Calder. She rolled back her shoulders, swallowing her frustration. Colt glared. She knew he expected her to be softer toward the judge. The two men left, but not before Colt shot her another look, hiding his alliance to her from the judge but letting Violet know he was not pleased with her action. It didn't matter what Colt thought. He wasn't privy to the complete picture, even if he thought he was.

The judge's interest in Violet had been lukewarm. His interest in her business was even colder than that. She had many years experience with finance, but even more with men in general. She knew how to rope a man into doing what she wanted with a smile, and excitement was to turn him away.

And, she told herself, it didn't matter if her coolness to him didn't ignite his passion for her ideas; she would locate another partner, an investor who understood her mind and body were of equal value. She'd find another judge.

Though the turn of events did leave Violet discouraged, she'd learned that other than a woman's father, there was always another man around the corner. To be certain, she jotted down a note to be delivered to La Reine's Fine French Couture. Three more dresses were required, and she needed the waist smaller by an inch and the bust line lowered just a hair. A man's mind was deeply rooted in his groin. She was confident in her intelligence but less so in that of the men she encountered. Even the smartest, most successful of them.

She scribbled a note requesting fabric samples in the hues of watery blues and pale greens, all the best to set off her golden hair and dark eyes. She demanded the fabrics be delivered in every texture La Reine's had available the next day.

Violet had no trouble letting Judge Calder turn away from her offer, but she needed to be sure she wasn't making it easy for him to shoulder on without buying into her plan. While there were other judges, something about this one interested her.

She had several potential clients coming that evening and needed to be sure dinner was prepared as she liked it. She swept down the wide hall toward the kitchen to let Katherine know the final count for the meal. As she neared the butler's pantry, she heard sobbing from the kitchen. The last thing she had time for was weepy women. Yet something gave her pause. She edged her way to the doorway between the pantry and kitchen and listened, for the second time that day, spying in her own house.

The crying continued, and Violet second-guessed her hiring of Katherine. A girl of fifteen, mostly woman, partly girl, was a risk. Yes, Katherine had shown great maturity in avoiding Colt's attentions. She worked hard, was a master in the kitchen, but tears in Violet's soup was something she would not entertain on a regular basis. Was it her father? A fight with her mother? Worse, a boy? The reasons a girl cried were endless. Violet would tamp this down right now. She was about to enter the kitchen when she heard Katherine's calm voice. The younger girl was *not* the one crying.

Katherine's voice was calming, gentle, yet somehow authoritative. Violet couldn't see who Katherine was speaking to, but most of their conversation was clear.

"Your mother is here," she heard Katherine say.

Violet drew back and pressed her spine against the wall. Of course, it was Olivia crying. She had received word that her mother died earlier that day. But what would Katherine know of it?

"My mother?" said Olivia.

". . . she doesn't want you to worry," Katherine said.

Violet stiffened and leaned closer to the opening. Had she heard right? She waited for the two girls to laugh. But the conversation stayed serious, and Olivia finally calmed, believing whatever information Katherine offered had meant something more than what Violet could imagine.

Violet stopped herself from bounding into the kitchen and accusing them of nonsense, of wasting time and her money. As she listened, the words that Katherine used, the calming effect, reminded her of things she'd seen in the past. *Victoria Woodhull. Cornelius Vanderbilt.* She'd seen the woman read for him, offer him celestial guidance in his work. Violet had never decided whether what she'd seen was true or a scam. Victoria had been accused of it more than once. Although when someone like Cornelius Vanderbilt believed it to be true, it was harder to be skeptical.

Violet listened, and it now sounded as if Katherine was convincing herself as much as she was Olivia that what they were experiencing was somehow real.

Could it be possible that this girl, a girl with a tremendous gift, had fallen into Violet's lap? Perhaps Olivia was simply desperate to believe something just to salve her wounded soul? Violet certainly couldn't assign any special intelligence to Olivia.

Olivia wasn't dumb, she was smart enough but gullible at times, making Violet think she could convince Olivia the earth was flat and stars were diamonds she loaned the sky from her very own tiara.

But Olivia was savvy in other ways—a talented pianist, a good conversationalist due to her ability to lubricate a man's tongue like fresh oil on tight gears. Violet didn't have to worry about Olivia's lack of intelligence, she was that good in getting their clients to disclose their thinking on various monetary matters.

Olivia, full of sniffles, finally started toward the butler's pantry. Violet, hearing Katherine swear Olivia to secrecy, was not sure how she would handle what she had witnessed. Violet pretended she had just entered the pantry as Olivia came through the door, dabbing her eyes. She stopped short, shock widening her eyes. Violet studied her, this beautiful, usually sanguine woman. "You all right, Olivia? I really need you tonight. Your piano playing, your work with Alderman Blake. I know you've received devastating news, but you're very good at what you do."

"Yes, Miss Violet." She looked at her feet. "Just the news of my mother . . ."

Violet put her hand on Olivia's shoulder. "Sometimes it feels better to work. But for now, get some air. Why don't you take this note to La Reine's for me?" Violet handed her the note for her dress order and squeezed the young woman's hand. She wanted to ask her what exactly had happened in the kitchen, but she held back. "Dismissed, then. Go on," Violet said.

Violet turned toward the kitchen. Katherine was at the table arranging plates. Her shirtwaist was worn at the cuffs; a small set of stitches closed holes in the plain brown skirt. But the collar of the blouse was appealing, and Katherine's complexion bore some pink color, highlighting her bone structure in a way that made the girl look more like she was ready to sit for a portrait than run Violet's kitchen.

Violet was long past the days of yearning for the type of beauty Katherine Arthur had and did not yet realize she possessed. This young lady's beauty, her presence, her intelligence, was something special. And now this, this thing

Katherine had just done with Olivia. That changed everything, Violet thought, about this whole situation.

**

"Good afternoon." Violet sauntered toward Katherine. She grasped Katherine's shoulders.

Katherine's eyes met Violet's.

"Was *that* what I think it was?"

She realized how hostile her approach seemed and loosened her grip on Katherine's shoulders, smoothing the fabric.

The girl's eyes darted around the kitchen, and her hand went to her leg, rubbing her thigh. *The chandelier ball.* Violet had observed her touching her leg where her hidden pockets were at times when she appeared nervous.

Katherine drew herself up. "Excuse me?"

"What was all of that?" Violet flung her hand through the air. "With Olivia."

Katherine backed up a step.

She sighed. "I'm so sorry. I got back from the store, and she was crying, and I tried to comfort her. I shouldn't have neglected my work."

"That's not what I meant."

Katherine looked to the ceiling, then met Violet's gaze again. "She just received word she lost her mother. I was simply listening. I shouldn't have shirked my duties."

Katherine wiggled past Violet, hurried to the sink, and filled a glass with water. "I just need a sip and I'll get right to the rest of the baking. I bought all the items on the list and secured a man, a Mr. Reed Hayes, to do the tilling in trade for bread. Just like you—"

"You told Olivia you saw her." Violet's voice was sharper than she wanted it to be.

"Her?" Katherine sipped her water.

"I'm not green, Katherine. Victoria Woodhull told me I had angels. Straight from heaven, she said. I thought it nonsense, of course. But it was through Victoria's connections that I learned finance and women's rights, and, well, though I was grateful to her, it didn't change the fact I didn't believe in angels, and if I did, what would it help? They just sit there invisible to all. What would it matter to have angels or not? But what you just did with Olivia . . . that was . . . useful."

Katherine's forehead glistened with perspiration, and she drank quickly, her eyes squeezed shut as if she had to force the water down. This conversation was causing a great deal of tension. Finally, she spoke. "Useful? Of course. My concern was genuine. Olivia is a nice woman. I don't think she cares for me much, but she was so sad."

Katherine's hand shook as she set the glass into the sink and went to the pie safe. She pulled the flour tin and a mixing bowl from the bottom of it. "I don't know of Miss Woodhull. Vanderbilt . . . I once met Cornelius the second, I believe it was the original man's grandson. I assume that's whom you mean—you met the first? The whole lot of them were duller than I imagined they'd be."

Violet nodded and laughed. Katherine's use of poise to hide her anxiety surprised and impressed Violet yet again. Another piece of the picture that was Katherine Arthur and her family. Wealthy enough to have visited with the Vanderbilts, smart enough to recognize their limitations.

"Victoria Woodhull was quite accomplished in matters of finance and relationships," Violet told her, "and some would say otherworldly connections. I didn't believe any of that. But the evidence for her success in plumping up the wallets of more than a few well-heeled women and very powerful men was clear."

Katherine nodded and measured water for the bread dough. She spread flour onto the worktable with the palm of her hand.

Violet clamped her hand over Katherine's. "You see them? My angels?"

Katherine raised her gaze to meet Violet's. "I don't . . . no. I don't."

Violet released Katherine's hand and crossed her arms, disliking the unsettling sense she felt.

Katherine added a pinch of salt and flour to the dough. "You don't mind if I make cinnamon bread this batch, do you?"

Violet shook her head. She needed to get a handle on Katherine before she became a liability for her.

"And more patty shells," Katherine said, "for the luncheon you are having tomorrow?"

"Of course," Violet said, her voice thin.

Katherine turned to the range and lit wood in the belly of the stove. She put the kettle on to heat water.

"How do you do this?" Violet said. "*What* can you do with this?"

"It's for the yeast. The water has to be warm."

"I mean *this*, this *knowing* you have, this gift. You can deny it all you want. I don't really believe this kind of thing myself, but what you did for Olivia . . . Whether you saw her mother or not, the result is the same. The hat was a nice touch. I've seen Victoria convince a man his raven-haired wife was as blonde as me. People believe what they need to believe, and the comforting you gave Olivia was as real as me and you."

Katherine turned, her hands on the warming stove at her back. She studied Violet's face, her eyes narrowing as though attempting to decode some secret Violet held deep inside.

"You're right. I'm good at comforting people. I've had too much practice with death and loss myself."

Violet wouldn't let Katherine steer the conversation. She snapped her fingers. "Can you tell me the color of my underthings?"

Katherine chuckled and wiped her hands on her skirt. "Oh, forgot my apron." She went to where they hung and draped one around her neck, tying the strings around the back of her waist.

"Tell me."

"Oh my, no. I can't see *through* things." Katherine pushed her hands into the pockets of the apron.

"Come now, I heard what happened between you and Olivia. Tell me what color."

Katherine sighed, then closed her eyes. When she opened them, she stared for a moment, then straightened her posture. "Butter-yellow chemise."

Violet's eyes widened as she was filled with awe.

Katherine waved her hand. "The material's peeking out at your shoulder."

Violet turned and looked under the cap of her sleeve, saw that her chemise was indeed showing a quarter of an inch at her shoulder.

"Plain as day for anyone to see," Katherine told her. "Like you said. I'm good at feeling people's moods, and I can comfort them. And you're right about the hat. I'm sure Olivia mentioned the hat."

Violet's enthusiasm dwindled as she ground through all of what she'd heard—the way Katherine went along with Violet's request, the way she picked up on something. Her glimpse of a shred of sunshine fabric at Violet's shoulder was as convincing as she needed to be in that moment. And that's all it took with most people, Violet knew. Just a moment to convince someone of what they were already committed to believe.

"Well." Violet tugged her neckline to cover the chemise. She would make sure that Mrs. Haverchek at La Reine's was more careful with her fittings. "What you can do, Katherine, is still a gift. You must have been a great deal of help and comfort to your mother when she needed you."

Katherine looked away. "My brother's death was so painful. Nothing could touch that sort of pain."

"Surely," Violet said.

Katherine sighed. "I better get back to work on the bread for Mr. Hayes and also get dinner on the table, or it will soon be breakfast."

Violet didn't like how the picture of who Katherine was didn't quite fit together. There was more to this than the girl let on. And that alone enticed and worried Violet, and added value to who Katherine was, what she could do for the business. No matter if she couldn't see through material things, when Violet thought of how Katherine was with Olivia, all she could think of was the sort of work that Victoria Woodhull had done for Cornelius Vanderbilt. If the brightest New Yorkers could come to believe in the unseen, surely even the sharpest Iowan could, too.

If she could offer something even more than flesh and intelligent investing to Des Moines, it could change everything. "I'm going to be honest with you, Katherine. I think you saw something that Olivia couldn't. I believe you experienced a presence." What did it matter if Katherine's sense of the world could be described as lunatic by a certain crowd? "Olivia never would have experienced peace if you hadn't been here. So I want you to forget whatever reason it is that you're keeping it from me, and I hope that you can trust me. I can help you in ways you never imagined. Your mother is in dire straits. But if you let me help you, you can help her. But you need to tell me. How'd you do that?"

Katherine shook her head.

"This is important, Katherine. I can see you're scared. Why?"

Katherine turned toward the stove.

Violet's mind spun through every scenario she'd seen women experience that would leave someone vulnerable despite her obvious strengths. The parents' divorce could be enough to do it, but Violet sensed there was more to this story. Her mother boarding the kids out was just the beginning of what had happened to Katherine along the way, Violet could see that.

And this was information Violet could work with. Katherine was many things, but she was also young. And youth gave Violet an advantage that intelligence and beauty could not match. Violet recalled the fury that developed when a woman was too powerful. It was easy to call a woman a lunatic, immoral, dangerous. It was simple to find a judge willing to shut a woman away for the rest of her life.

"Explain yourself to me now," Violet said. "Or I'll have no choice but to look further into your—"

"No!" Katherine spun around toward Violet. Violet's lips quivered as she held a smile at bay. There. That was all it took to bring Katherine to heel.

She rushed across the kitchen and sat near Violet. "I didn't do anything. I just . . ." She poked at the flour with a fork. "Receive information, I suppose you could say."

"Tell me about it."

"My brothers and I were caught in a fire."

Miss Violet pulled out a chair for Katherine and patted the seat. Katherine sat beside her.

"It's all right," Violet said. "We all have awful stories in our past. You can tell me anything, Katherine. You can trust me. I understand. You know how busy I am, the business that I run. And yet I'm sitting here with you, asking you to share something with me. Doesn't that tell you how valuable you are? Doesn't that say something, that I notice that and want to hear about you?"

Katherine looked into Violet's eyes as though she were taking her temperature, assessing her trustworthiness.

Violet was exhausted with a day full of coercion. Maybe she was losing her touch. She leaned in. "But if you can't trust *me*, I can't help *you*. And that's not good for you or your family."

Katherine drew a deep, stuttered breath. She looked at her hands, one thumb brushing over the other thumbnail, and exhaled. "We had to climb the bee tree to escape the flames." She shuddered. "The sound."

Violet put her arm around Katherine. "I've been in a fire. It's bone chilling."

Katherine held Violet's gaze. "The flames were horrid, the way they licked past, howling like wind lit with kerosene. The heat, it was…" Katherine's voice cracked. "But no, it was the sound of the boy that I'll never forget."

Violet steepled her fingers under her chin. "Your brother?"

Katherine pulled her knees in close to her, wrapping her arms around them. "No, another boy. He'd died there at the bee tree before we moved there. He'd been buried there, and there he was that day, screaming as though he were flesh and blood. That was the first time I ever experienced a spirit. Really, it was the only time until the fever near the end of our time on the prairie. It's not something that's useful. Not like you said."

Oh, but it is. Violet leaned back in her chair and recalled things that Victoria Woodhull had confided all those years ago. Violet's connection to religion as a little girl might have opened the door for belief in the unseen, but upon losing faith in religious folks and their churches, she'd lost belief in anything otherworldly at all.

Katherine pushed her chair back and went to the stove and returned with the kettle, splashing a teaspoon of warm water over the yeast.

Violet shook her finger in the air. "Think of what you could do. For others, for your family. Think of the money you could make. Victoria Woodhull was as wealthy as many of the men she advised. And the women. Well, you can't ignore this talent of yours. For the good of the world, of your family. You must share it."

Katherine kept working, going to the table and mixing the dry ingredients with the yeast. Violet could see that the doubt Katherine exuded was also tinged in fear as she begged for questions to go no further. Violet knew better than most that everyone had secrets.

"How old are you again, Katherine? Sixteen?"

She shook her head. "Fifteen."

Ah, fifteen. A tricky age, when a young lady discovered her strengths and how she fit into the machinery of a very male world. A fatherless girl like Katherine might have learned that lesson already in a variety of ways.

She sighed. "It's really nothing, Miss Violet. I'm just good at talking to people, is all."

That wasn't true. Violet balled her fists on the table. "You do understand what I mean."

"I can't share this . . . this thing. What happened with Olivia just happened. I can't force this information to come to me." Katherine glanced at Violet's shoulder. She reached for the material and pulled it for Violet. "The chemise is peeking out again."

"Thank you." Violet adjusted her dress and patted the spot where Katherine's fingers had brushed. She could tell Katherine was unnerved, the confidence that had been in her voice with Olivia, and when she told Violet her underthings were yellow, was gone.

The time wasn't right to push this, not yet. Violet exhaled and pulled her gown down at the waist. "You just let me think this through. This *is* something special, and it's not to be trifled with."

Katherine went back to her work. "How many for dinner, Miss Violet?"

"Six. Just six tonight." The men would arrive shortly after Violet left the kitchen. She headed for the stairs to go up to her dressing room, needing to collect herself and smooth out the edge that had sharpened her mood. *This is good. Don't let it bother you. All of this, all of Katherine, is quite good.* Fifteen was an important time in life. Violet would do her best to be sure that Katherine's fifteenth year would be fruitful, that it would shape her future in all the good ways Violet's had not.

Chapter 15

Love
Violet

Greenpoint, New York
1877

Violet Pendergrass drew her coat tight around her, holding it together under her chin. The wind cut her cheeks. Pressing forward, her breath trailed behind like kite strings. She squinted into the gusts. *Almost there.* She picked up speed, heading to the glassworks, fingertips numb from breaking through the ends of her wooly gloves. She tucked them as close to her neck as she could. Her gaze shot side to side, over her shoulder, watching for anyone who might see an unchaperoned fifteen-year-old and take advantage of her.

She neared the glass factory, keeping her feet light on the crisp snow. The fireman and the night guard spent nearly all night sleeping near the front of the building. They wouldn't check the back of the factory until just before the morning shift.

She reached the door and held her breath, unfurling her arms, shaking them out so she could grip the handles and enter quietly. Edwin had warned her to be careful entering. The watchman sometimes lingered in the back before heading up front. There were three crews working the night shift, but they'd be too busy to notice her if she was quiet. As directed, she lifted the door slightly as she opened it to hush the whining hinges.

With the door open, she looked over her shoulder. Her father, gimping along, would arrive soon. His back had become hunched, and his right foot dragged; his ankle turned sideways as though it contained no bone, trailing like a snail foot. She wondered how he stayed facing forward with his leg so twisted.

She entered the building and skittered to the spot near the furnace where Edwin had told her she and her father could sleep warm and unnoticed until five a.m. Edwin would be working with the second crew as the holding-mold boy. He'd explained that this was merely one rung in his ladder of success, that he had a plan to quickly work his way into a position that would allow him the kind of money to support a household, to make Violet his wife. It wouldn't be long, he'd promised. His father was already permitting him to blow the glass once in a while.

The smell of wood and flame filled Violet's nose as she found the blankets that Edwin had hidden in the back corner to make a soft nest. She warmed her hands near the furnace that had been put on a slow burn for the night. Thoughts of Edwin, his cocoa-brown eyes, his lips warm on hers, the firm grip of his hand over hers, caused her love for him to deepen with each recollection. She pressed her fingertips to her lips, remembering.

Edwin had implored her to keep hidden in the back corner once they were in the factory. But she had to try to catch a glimpse of him just to sustain her until morning, when they met at the food wagon to share a honeyed biscuit. She edged to the opening leading to the other furnaces, toward the two crews working the night shift. The rhythmic sounds of sand being transformed into molten then hard glass drew her farther away from where she should have been.

She held her breath and peeked around the corner. She'd seen Edwin work before, when she'd been hired to pack the bottles in a day shift. To her surprise, right in front of her, just ten feet away, was Edwin's crew. His father, brothers, and some cousins worked together. They were vocal, though she could only make out every few words. "Duck under! Coming back. Hot glass here!" And then laughter. They moved as though waltzing rather than performing the work that resulted in bottles and lamps.

The magic dance mesmerized Violet. One boy reached forward, another stepped out of his way before squatting down to miss being struck by the thick glob of fire as the gaffer headed to the blower. "Coming in!" someone yelled out as he headed to the lehr to temper the glass. *Whoosh*, the blower pressed air into the pipe. *Snap!* He removed the pipe from the molded glass. *Clank!* The molds shifted and rattled as they were reset for the next glob of glass to be blown into it.

Violet observed the ebb and flow of the glassblowing ballet for several minutes before she realized that Edwin wasn't holding the mold. Her eyes darted around the faces of his crew and saw that he had backed away from the mold. Would his father let him blow the glass again?

Just the other day he'd given her his notebook of glass formulas to hold. He wasn't supposed to have it—factory secrets—but he and his father would start their own operation soon. They had formulated hues of green, blue, and opal that the owner couldn't fathom until they had produced it. These formulas were theirs as much as anyone's, he'd declared. "There'll come a time when I'll need it," he'd said. "No, there will come a time *we'll* need it, Violet."

She'd looked into his eyes and asked him if they would go to church. "As a family?" she said. "With spring coats and tulip-colored dresses and winter muffs for all the girls in our household?"

He had leaned in and kissed her, his lips brushing over hers once, then again, and once more. He had pulled away with a big smile. "Can't think of anywhere I'd rather be," he'd said, making Violet feel as though half of her soul had left her body, joining his in some celestial way she'd never imagined possible.

Her mind came back to the present as Edwin got up from in front of the mold at his father's feet and shuffled into position above it. She pressed her hand against her chest. "Oh, Edwin," she said aloud. The gaffer handed him a pipe with a screaming orange gob of molten glass on the end. Edwin had it in the mold and blown to perfection in no time. It didn't take long before the younger boys stopped laughing and whistling and began to groan.

Edwin's father worked the mold and then at one point he took the pipe from his son, lifting his voice above the din. "Enough for a while, Son. You're going to wear those boys out." He slapped Edwin's back. Violet could see her love, her Edwin, smile and shrug as he took his spot back at his father's feet, humble as always.

It took all Violet's might not to rush to Edwin and hold him tight enough to choke out all his air, she was so proud of him. She pressed her lips again and sighed, turning back to where she and her father were to sleep that night.

She kicked one foot out and then the other, her heart swollen with the sight of Edwin, her dream to marry him. A glassblower's wife! She was only fifteen, but it didn't matter. He'd already promised her he'd make her safe and warm. They would have a small home. "It'll be fancy, though, like a ring box, all velvety and nice," he'd said. Violet didn't care where it was as long as they were together. Even above a deli would be perfect. Her father would live with them, his health improving with stable housing; she was sure it would.

But Edwin had high plans. She recalled his eyes lighting up. "The Aster apartment building in Greenpoint. Built so every single apartment has its own bathroom and tiny kitchen," he'd said.

It would be perfect. She would be a queen with a king who made it his business to care for her first, above all others. She believed he would do that because he'd found her places to sleep nearly every night since they first talked. He'd fed her each morning, sharing his breakfast as the sun rose and he headed home to sleep.

As she floated back to the corner where she and her father would sleep, the door where she had entered opened with a whoosh of icy air. She rushed to greet her father, smothering him with kisses, checking him over for frostbite or other injuries he seemed to collect these days. She slipped an arm around his waist and guided him over to their warm nest. Clomp, drag, clomp, drag. Her father's broken gait and his hacking cough bent him.

She roped her other arm around his waist, latching her hands, holding him up, his ribs poking through layers of clothing. "We need to get you into the bed here. Don't want anyone to see us," she said.

Clomping, dragging closer, closer, the heat grew stronger. "Here we go, Father. Almost there. A warm night's sleep."

He nodded, shoulders heaving with every gravelly breath.

When they reached the blankets, she lowered him, cradling the back of his head as he reclined. She stuffed the second blanket under his shoulders and head so the mucus in his nose would drain downward for easier breathing. The dirt floor peppered with small stones dug into her knees as she arranged her father's coat, pulling it underneath him, smoothing the front, straightening the arms.

His eyes were closed, his breath still sandpapery. Swallowed by the blanketed nest she'd made, he appeared childlike. Her eyes stung at the sight, knowing at some point she'd started taking care of him instead of him watching over her.

"Oh, Father, you'll feel better after a night's sleep."

She thought she saw him nod, but even with his heavy breath it was clear he'd fallen into slumber.

She removed his hat and smoothed his gray hair back, re-parting it the way he used to insist it be. Old age, poverty, struggle. She put her hand on his heart. "Hang on, Father. I'll make you the home you always wanted to give me. Doesn't matter which of us makes it happen; it'll be just like you promised. I *promise*."

Violet curled up against her father, the glass factory song lulling her as she counted all the ways that life would soon be exactly the way she'd dreamed it would.

**

The odor was strong, waking her, forcing her to her feet, her mind unfocused. Arms out to steady herself, she fought to see through foggy sleep. Where was she? Under the bridge? The alley near the fire pit? The vacant hunting cabin near the water? Her eyes finally settled on the man in the uniform, his face misshapen in anger, his voice piercing the rhythms of the crews. The glassworks. The night watchman in the blue suit, the fireman. And the stench. It was as if the world had slowed down. She struggled to break free from the watchman. He yanked hard, his grip burning her wrists. She looked back at her prostrate father. The smell was him. His skin, slate gray in color, his mouth half-open, his eyes staring, lifeless. And the odor of waste, it was undeniable.

"I knew that wasn't rat shit," the fireman scowled. "Toss her outside. I'll throw him out after her."

"No, make her clean up his mess. Payment for a night's heat."

Violet wrestled away from the guard and dropped to her knees beside her father. She cupped his cheeks. They were cold under her touch. She wanted to believe that he was merely sleeping. She shook his shoulders. No response. Finally, she laid her forehead on his. "I'm so sorry, Father. I'm so sorry."

The fireman bellowed. At first Violet couldn't decipher what he was saying, that she had five minutes to clean the mess or he'd toss her father into the furnace for the first fire of the day.

Violet looked around, not knowing how she would clean up her father, not knowing how she would get him out of there. She began to breathe so heavy and fast that she didn't notice voices gathering until she turned around.

Her eyes scanned all the faces and settled on Edwin's.

"Thank God you're still here," she said.

And he fell to the floor with her, arm across her back. She crumpled into him, but as he held her as she cried, he was ripped away from her, his father wrenching him right off the ground as though he were made of thin air.

"You get back to work, Edwin. We'll lose everything."

He fought back to the ground, kneeling beside her again. His brother yanked him away a second time, and Edwin struggled to free himself, but each of his brothers took an arm and dragged him back. "Wanna get us all fired?" one of them said.

Edwin struggled against them, his feet kicking. "I'll be back for you, Violet. Meet me at the water. Our spot. Don't fret."

Edwin's father stared at Violet kneeling over her father and spat beside her. "Stay away. He's not for you."

Violet had seen this searing hate over the years. Always when she'd trespassed, always when someone was letting her know she wasn't worthy, that she'd gone where she shouldn't have been.

And she shook her head and refocused on her father. She laid her head on his chest and closed her eyes, bringing back the sound of his voice when it was strong and sure. "My Violet. You see everything, don't ya? Smart as a whip. You'll be something big, sure as I'm standing here." She held her breath for a moment, listening to Edwin call for her, feeling as though her father were still alive, his hand warm on her shoulder.

And she repeated her father's words, hoping they would help stave off tears. She felt his declarations deep, buried in her marrow, as though the truths had been laid there when she'd been conceived. She'd be somebody if it was the last thing she did, and Edwin would be there with her.

No, he won't.

She gasped at the thought. Where had it come from? Edwin loved her, wanted to marry her. *He won't. He won't.* She couldn't stop the words from repeating. The tiny sentence grew thick and long, wrapped her tight, clear up to her throat, squeezing until she could not breathe.

The guards tossed rags at her. "Clean 'im up."

She began to scrub around her father as best she could, trying to keep his dignity for him. *You'll find peace, Father. You can rest pain-free.* She gently pulled her father to clean the other side. Her heart punctured twice that night, paralyzing most of the muscle.

Scrub, scrub, scrub.

The grief and loss left what she came to think was one small chamber of muscle left to do the work of four. And so she imagined a shell, a dome of glass that she could encase that last live part of her heart inside, to protect it, to keep for someday, if perhaps she might want to love again. As if that would ever be possible.

Chapter 16

Butterfly Stone
Aleksey

Des Moines
1892

I sat at the desk in the bunkroom at Palmer's, adjusting the lamp so it was dim enough that it didn't keep the others awake and bright enough that I could see my work. I sipped coffee and turned to the bookmarked spot in the *Principles of Property Law*. It would've been better for me to work in the kitchen, where I could warm up my drink when needed and light the room better. But now that Fat Joe had fallen in love with Mabel, they lingered there late as possible, talking, holding hands, dreaming.

I looked over my shoulder at Fat Joe's empty bed. He was suddenly deeply in love with Mabel. So much so that it seemed to have invigorated his work ethic, as he declared wanting to proceed to the third degree, harvester status, in the Grangers as quickly as possible. Mr. Palmer had explained that the length of the seasons dictated the length of time it would take to fulfill each degree. And shocking all of us, Fat Joe had stood at the table. "Then I shall be the best laborer, the best cultivator, the best harvester until I can become a husbandman. A woman like Mabel deserves a man who carries with him all the morals, manners, and ability of the best Granger."

"All for a woman, is it?" Palmer had said. He leaned forward and gestured with his knife. "Not always the best bet." Then he'd shoveled food into his mouth, his eyes on his plate, telling us the conversation was over.

Mabel had swept past Fat Joe and brushed his shoulder like she used to do mine.

And though there was something in me that yearned for that kind of affection, I was satisfied that Mabel had found it in Fat Joe. For my part, I couldn't keep from thinking of Katherine Arthur. I had my law studies to contend with, but I allowed myself breaks to recall her face, how grown she looked, how breathtaking she'd become.

I shifted in my chair, and the stone I'd found in the wall dug into my leg. I pulled it out of my pocket and set it on the desk. The lamp glow infiltrated the stone's butterfly wings. Thinking of Katherine's lovely face, I wrote to her. The words came quickly, just noting my interest in calling on the Arthur family soon. I indicated my ma was doing well and that she'd be elated to hear I'd run into Katherine and would see the rest soon.

I paused after finishing the letter, my pen poised over the paper, wanting to write more but knowing it was best to keep this first letter short. I added that I hoped she accepted my apologies for running off so quickly and that I'd make it up to her when I called. A dollop of ink dropped onto the paper, spreading wide as it splatted. I blotted it away, leaving a brown splotch. I laughed, remembering Katherine scolding me for my sloppy pen so many years back.

I signed my name, set the pen on the drip plate, and leaned back in my chair. Hands knitted behind my head, pleased with the letter, my gaze slid to the butterfly-shaped stone that sat in front of me, and I examined its crystal striations, its incredible intricacy. The variation in the stone reminded me of Katherine. When we were young, she was straightforward, clear, like certain parts of the stone.

But when I saw her at the grocer's, I'd noticed something different, something behind her eyes. The simplicity of childhood was gone. She still seemed as kind and lovely as I remembered, but there was something else there, hidden behind her smile and bright eyes when she recognized me, a lifetime of things that had happened to her that I couldn't know from just one conversation. Parts of her were opaque like the stone. I sighed. Like the stone which had been shaped by time and trials to come to look as it did right then, Katherine had clearly changed under those same pressures.

Luckily, I wasn't interested in courting or marriage. Katherine and I had been good friends, bound by the horror of a year gone bad in both of our lives. That bond felt as real as the stone on my desk, but our connection hadn't been romantic in the least. Seeing her, the prospect of calling on her family, gave me a sense of excitement I hadn't felt since coming to Des Moines.

It wasn't for me to delve into Katherine Arthur's secret life, the darkness behind her bright eyes. I'd too much work to do. I tossed the butterfly crystal into the air, half expecting it to fly away before catching it.

I went to my trunk and withdrew a woolen sock. I dropped the stone inside it and settled it at the back behind a stack of books. One was Palmer's wife's book. *To Winnie P., Book One, Cures and Cautions*, it said on the first page. I withdrew it and let it fall open to a page in the middle. There were recipes written there, but this page was not for food. These were labeled as cures. I flipped through a few more pages, my eyes drawn to a note that read, "Fear comes in all shapes and sizes, forms and reasons. I feel mine like air, inescapable. I want my husband to understand me, what I do, but he will not listen. I can't help the gifts I've been given. I cannot keep them to myself. For it is that which will be my undoing."

A shiver worked down my spine. Fear? Of what? The vague reference explained nothing. I closed the book and put it back under a woolen sweater, blanket and law books on top of that.

I closed the trunk and stood, Winnie Palmer's writing working through me. Sitting back at my desk, I realized what I'd seen on Katherine's face at the grocer's. Fear. When the grocer accused her of stealing, though I knew she hadn't done any such thing, her face paled; she withdrew before straightening her spine, defending herself, finally. But it had been there plain—fear, the expression of a person who'd been accused of stealing before.

That realization pinched my chest. I rubbed where it throbbed. Katherine. Sitting there, the sensation of thread unspooling inside my chest came, undoing my careful plans to work and study and do nothing else. It was right inside that moment that I knew I needed to see Katherine soon. I needed to know her better, again, whether it was prudent to do so or not.

Chapter 17

Partners
Katherine

Weeks had passed since I'd witnessed Madame Smalley being dragged from a store and accused of psychic thievery. That same day I had encountered Olivia weeping for her dead mother. No one mentioned that again, and I began to relax into my duties. I'd come to love the title of kitchen mistress, and Miss Violet never missed a chance to use it when enticing potential investors into trying some of my baking or cooking as a pathway to their wallets. So far, my work had helped to fatten Miss Violet's purse nicely, and I was relieved that she hadn't inquired any further about my ability to commiserate with the recently or longtime dead. Though I enjoyed my work at Miss Violet's, I was eager for summer to pass and fall to bring the chance to resume my studies. At times, I imagined myself at Drake College alongside other intelligent women and men, up to my neck in library books.

Miss Violet had found a book at McCrady's Trade and Buy that she bought for me in order to borrow recipes from it and add my own. Hefty, it was bound in burlap with a leather spine. It was inscribed, *To Winnie with the magic touch,*

Book Two. It was half-full of recipes and cures, and some had dates indicating they were over a hundred years old. The recipes were beautifully written with perfect script, and there were notations regarding whether a recipe came from Aunt Penelope or Winnie had concocted it or altered it herself and why she had. Some of the completed pages contained cautionary tales and spine-tingling drawings of fungi, like Dead Man's Fingers, that looked like a rotting hand pushing through soil and killed off healthy apple trees on her property in no time. Winnie also carefully noted that the innocent-appearing Destroying Angel and False Champignon mushrooms could quickly do away with a person, too—Mr. Heatherington, 1882, she noted. Her drawings were clear and helpful.

Even though the second half of the book was blank, I still hadn't been able to read all of what was in the first half. Though I was hesitant to write my way into someone else's world, it wasn't long before I found myself lured to the book, adding my cures and recipes, imagining all the wonderful things that must have been in the missing Book One.

Many pages had accompanying drawings for recipes. Other pages held sketches of rooms with what I imagined were her family members gathered around a table at various holidays. There were even sketches of people in their sickbeds beside cures for the grippe or boils or headache.

I worked on my own cures and surprised myself at my intuition when I couldn't remember a remedy I'd used at the Christoffs or it wasn't included in the book. I felt as though I was contributing to my family and to Miss Violet, and pride had begun to gather in me, warming my insides like the first spring sun on winter skin. Oddly, one of the least important cures that I came up with brought the most joy to Miss Violet's household.

A few days back, Miss Violet and Olivia had been in the pantry. Miss Violet was admonishing her for rancid breath, saying the stench was causing investors to put their money clips away.

Hearing this, I'd stood in front of the growing herbal collection I'd harvested from some of Mama's plants that had finally become mature. Most at this point had been purchased from the store. My eyes had flicked past the jars and bottles: basil, marjoram, parsley, thyme, lavender, clove, boneset, and more.

I'd pulled the jar of cloves from the shelf and filled a pan with water to boil. I'd added the cloves and stirred as the water began to fold over itself, keeping the mixture roiling for several minutes before taking it off the stove to cool. As I worked, Miss Violet and Olivia had pushed into the kitchen and gone over all the remedies they'd tried—bicarbonate, saltwater rinses, even scrubbing her teeth with whiskey before meeting with clients. All of these things seemed to only amplify the odor.

As the water cooled, I'd surveyed the jars again, running my finger past the labels: ginger, lemon balm, horseradish, sage, and mint. I couldn't wait for seasons to end and begin, allowing me to harvest more from Mama's plantings.

I'd turned away from the shelf when something made me look back. Mint. That was what was needed. I'd poured the clove water into a mug and added a handful of mint leaves.

"Miss Violet," I'd said. "This might help."

The two of them had come forward, each tight with anger that I couldn't fully understand. What difference did it make if Olivia's breath was harsh if she was good at numbers and investments? Yet I understood it was indeed very important to them. They'd gathered around me and watched as I strained the solution through a cloth.

I'd handed the glass to Olivia. She'd leaned in to sniff it and flinched.

"Gargle," I'd said. "The cloves should take care of anything lingering that might cause odor. I've seen it cure the stinkiest infections on a man's leg—it has to work for plain old bad breath. The mint should freshen you up nicely."

She'd shrugged and we'd watched as she tossed the liquid into her mouth, threw her head back, and gargled loudly before spitting into the slop bucket. She'd straightened and leaned toward Miss Violet, who put her hand to Olivia's shoulder to keep her at a distance. "Again."

Olivia had repeated the process and this time was permitted to lean in, breathing on Miss Violet. She'd drawn back, then relaxed her posture. "It worked. I can't believe it." She'd giggled in a girlish way I'd not heard from her before.

"Let me smell," I'd said. Olivia had leaned toward me and exhaled. I'd detected a hint of the former stench, but there was no question it would take very close talking to offend anyone at this point. "Oh galoshes, it works."

Miss Violet had laughed again. "Oh galoshes is right." She'd pointed at the glass. "Bottle that. And make more. We're going to need it on hand at all times."

Olivia had hugged me and Miss Violet's face had softened. The angry lines that had hardened her were gone, and the two women visibly lightened right in front of me. They'd left to go about preparing for their meeting.

I'd begun the process of making a bigger batch. That moment, I'd felt as though I'd truly earned my title as kitchen mistress. Though I'd never imagined myself content with such a title, I felt an undeniable tremble when something I created was useful. Yes, I envied Olivia her work, twisting and wringing numbers and giving advice for investors, but I was still to attend school that coming fall. My goals were intact, and I needed to stop worrying that they were endangered any longer. Since we'd come to board in the little house next to the massive pink-and-green mansion, everything had changed. Everything was just as it should have been.

**

I sealed four bottles of what I'd named Clovemint Breath Solution and made the bread to trade with Mr. Hayes as he continued to work in the gardens with Mama. As I prepared to make soda bread for Miss Violet's meeting, I found myself with a visitor yet again. Miss Violet's father had appeared at the table, sitting there, watching me as he often did. He didn't frighten me, but it irked me that he didn't simply say what he wanted. When he arrived on a given day, he trailed me through the kitchen, the pantry, the dining room. I did my best to ignore him, and sometimes I managed to shield his presence from my consciousness.

From time to time, I'd try to send him on to heaven, where I assured him, upon no authority at all, that Jesus and God and his very own mother were eagerly awaiting his arrival.

"Just go, old man," I muttered to myself.

"Who are you talking to?"

Miss Violet's voice shook me. I spun around. "Oh. Myself. I'm sorry."

She narrowed her eyes on me, then floated into the room, offering a wink of a smile before she moved from one end of the kitchen to the other, examining my work. She laid her ledger on the table and went to the counter near the window.

"Six loaves," she said, lifting the towel that lay over one of the pans. "Delicious."

"Thank you," I said. "Three of those are for trade for Mr. Hayes and for some of the ginger and seed my mother wanted. One more to go today. It's a soda bread."

Miss Violet was quiet. She went to the pie safe and opened its doors. "Three blueberry? Magnificent."

"I made those yesterday, and I'll whip a nice cream right before you serve it."

She nodded as she opened the final door on the pie safe. "What's that?" she asked.

"Angel cake. I mixed a sharp lemon frosting—a light, sugary one that just adds a pinch of sweet with the tart."

"My mouth's watering." Miss Violet turned to me. "I'm quite pleased. Your dishes are a substantial upgrade from our dear Olivia's cooking and baking. And that gargle you made. I can't tell you how that saved us. I was starting to think I had to put Olivia out to pasture. Or hide her away toiling over numbers, not meeting with clients."

I nodded, preoccupied. "She's fresh and clean now." I poured whiskey over a bowl of raisins and walnuts feeling a splash of pleasure at the compliment. I added five shakes of pepper and stirred. "Thank you for noticing my work, Miss Violet."

"You like kitchen work, don't you?"

"I do." Pride warmed my insides.

"You've had practice, I can see that."

"I have."

"One more week," I said, "and I should be organized enough to add making butter to my list of things to do. No need to buy it." I sliced eight pieces of butter off a larger hunk and massaged the flour, sugar, baking soda, and salt into it. The fine, dry ingredients balled into golden crumbs beneath my fingertips. For that moment, I felt contentment. Mama's gardens were plowed and growing. She took on some plain sewing. Mr. Hayes was an enormous help to the family, and even Tommy was contributing by milking the cows and starting the stoves in the morning.

Miss Violet brought a covered bowl to me. She pulled out a chair and sat. "Don't you need that? I saw you mix it in the other day."

I shook my head. "Not for this one. That's a sponge, old bread. It's for the yeast breads. I'll use it tomorrow when I make the loaf for my mother."

"A sponge?"

"It's just part of the dough that's been allowed to ferment, get flavorful. Mixing all the ingredients without mixing in an older, flavorful portion makes it bland."

"Oh my goodness. That's it," Violet said, leaning back in her chair. "Your bread is rich and can be eaten plain as well as with a jelly or stew or ... You *are* talented, Katherine."

"Thank you," I said, full of pride that my abilities were being recognized by someone like Miss Violet. I'd seen several newspaper articles that praised her business acumen, her early success in Des Moines circles. I'd seen several about Madame Smalley as well. The contrast of both reestablished my thinking that keeping my ability to myself was the safest road for me. I would tread the path that Miss Violet took to success before I ever trod on Madame Smalley's.

I spooned the whiskied raisins, nuts and pepper into the dough and stirred. "This recipe doesn't require a sponge or yeast." I mixed buttermilk into the crumbly mixture, stirring with a wooden spoon.

Miss Violet jerked her head toward the bowl of whiskey that remained after the raisins were added. "I suppose whiskey-infused raisins will take care of the flavor enough."

The dough was moist; the ingredients had come together. I turned the bowl over and worked the dough—pushing it forward with the heels of my hands, then folding it back toward me before pushing it again. Eight times. "It's true. The whiskey mixture flavors this bread nicely." The dough was stuck to the table, so I used a scraper to gather the dough without adding more flour.

Tell her what I told you to say.

Violet's father's voice caused me to startle. I froze at the sight of him, saw that Miss Violet was unaware of him, and just ignored him. I shaped the dough into a round, pinching the bottom to tighten the smooth, shiny skin. I set the fat loaf onto a flat baking sheet and used a knife to cut a vertical line, then two diagonal lines that would make a *K* when it was baked.

"Nice touch," Miss Violet said. She pointed at the knife marks.

Tell her, or I won't leave you alone.

I gasped. Ignoring Mr. Pendergrass again, I refocused on the *K* I'd made in the dough. "I'm sorry. I should have just made the cross the way the recipe calls for. I didn't even realize I'd made a *K*—"

Violet swept her hand through the air. "It's all right, dear. You made the bread. Marking with your initial is appropriate."

Now!

"There's something I want to discuss with you," Violet said.

I slammed my fist onto the table. "No!"

Miss Violet was startled by my reaction.

Tell her to stop.

I turned my back to Mr. Pendergrass, knowing that wouldn't remove his voice from my head but hoping it might block him out a little bit.

"What on earth?" Miss Violet narrowed her eyes on me.

"I'm so sorry. I don't know what made me . . ."

Miss Violet straightened in her chair. She looked me up and down with a confused expression.

"What's wrong with you?"

I shook my head. "It won't happen again."

"What won't? You're not suffering from some sort of," she circled one hand in front of her, "breakdown of sorts? I saw you talking to yourself today, the other day. Monday."

I couldn't find a way to explain my outburst. My silence made me appear lunatic; any explanation put me at risk as well. The last thing I wanted was to draw attention to Violet's dead father.

I changed the subject, hoping she'd overlook it. "I thought that since so many of your clients and partners were men, they'd enjoy whiskey butter to go with the bread—it's delectable but masculine."

"That's part of what I wanted to discuss."

I cut into the butter again. "I'm overstepping, aren't I? I didn't mean to plan something for the menu without asking. I didn't even think. I just—"

Violet put her hand over mine. "Listen."

I pulled my hand away.

I nodded and added the hunk of butter into the leftover whiskey. Next I shook in some sugar and a pinch of pepper and stirred.

"It's that, well, this ability you have—what you did with Olivia that time, the way you intuit what is needed to remedy a problem. It's an incredible skill."

My stomach clenched, and I stopped mixing for a moment. *Keep your hands moving.*

I couldn't swallow. "With Olivia?"

"You know what I'm saying. The way you witnessed her mother's soul, the way the dead woman communicated through you. Or the way you convinced Olivia her mother was there."

You know what she's saying! Mr. Pendergrass's voice beat into my brain. *She knows what you are. Tell her what I said!*

"Stop it!"

Violet's eyes widened. "Are you mad?"

I shook my head and set both hands on the table.

"Are you in need of rest?"

Tell her.

I wanted to ignore Mr. Pendergrass, but his presence was becoming oppressive. I wanted to keep this inside me, but I couldn't. One more deep breath and maybe he'd be gone.

I exhaled and saw that there he was, standing near her.

"Katherine. What on *earth* is going on with you?"

"It's him. He's here."

She looked around. Her face was angry, then amused. "Him? Who?"

I stared at the man. I swallowed hard.

"Katherine?"

He pressed me with his spirit, his mere presence. It was time to do what he needed to release him. My shoulders sank. "Your father. He's here."

She scoffed. I felt a surge of irritation that she did so.

"Really, Katherine? I thought you said you were simply a good listener?"

Tell her.

"I will!"

"You will what?" Miss Violet said.

"Tell you that he knows you've tried hard."

"Why wouldn't you tell me that?"

"He said it's time to stop it now. You did things, he said. And now's the time to stop."

I blurted the words out, hating that I was privy to them, not wanting to say such things to the woman who was singlehandedly changing my family's circumstances.

Miss Violet's face whitened. Now it was she who swallowed hard. Her hand quaked, and she pulled both into her lap. "That doesn't sound like him at all."

Mr. Pendergrass's expression softened. "He said, yes, he's been trying to be polite to me, but I've been ignoring him, and he couldn't delay this anymore, and so he left his manners behind in order to get me to listen."

Violet's mouth fell open. "Now that sounds like him."

I thought for a moment. The clarity of that, what I heard and saw, what I knew at that moment, the wholeness of it, the lack of missing bits of information, stunned me. "Yes. All of that."

"Well. Did he say what things I've done that I should stop?"

I saw the worry creased in her face. Whatever it was, she didn't want me to know it.

"No. He didn't say."

She crossed her arms. Fear crushed me. Was this the end? She either thought I had succumbed to lunacy or evil. I imagined how this would go now, spiraling into me being locked away. She would tell Mama, her fears about me would shatter her and make her send me to an asylum to keep the others safe.

My mind was reeling when I felt Violet's hand, warm on mine.

"It's all right."

I reached for the crystal pendant in my pocket. I wanted to take it out and feel the smooth faces that marched around the orb.

"I know what he means," Miss Violet said.

"You do?"

"I'm not upset. I can see you think I am."

"I'm not insane."

"I shouldn't have said that. I apologize."

"Thank you."

"You've got razor-sharp intuition. The way you decided to make the kind of bread you deem more masculine for the men. Little things like that, things like bringing full, genuine, powerful relief to the grieving Olivia. Those things are enormous advantages in business. Wouldn't you say? And you can see my father and relay information to me that I already knew deep inside. I knew what he would think of my choices."

"Of you being a businesswoman? He wants you married?"

Violet raised her eyebrows. She smiled. "Yes. That's what he meant."

I exhaled. "Intuition. Yes, that's an advantage." I was relieved that Miss Violet was thinking about what she'd seen in a way that didn't put me in the realm of a magician or the devil's playmate, but still she believed me.

Miss Violet took up the spoon and began to press the back of it into the butter, churning it into the whiskey, turning it a toffee-brown hue. "I've been in business for some time now. And today just makes me surer than ever that my calculations and strategy were dead on. I want to position you so that you can bring peace to those who suffer, those who question, those who need a little help in making investment decisions."

I knew nothing of investments. My intuition and ability extended only as far as deciding to bake a darker, denser, whiskey-infused bread for risk-taking men doing business with a woman or to dead people coming to call on their living, loved ones.

"What is it?" I said. "I can tailor more recipes, if that's what you'd like."

"You know that's not what I mean."

I pressed the crystal against my leg. "I don't know what you're saying. I really don't."

"I spoke to Olivia. She is convinced you can see the dead. Now, after what you said about my father, I'm convinced. I *think* I am. But it doesn't matter exactly what the truth is. What I've seen you do is all I've thought about since that day. I want to believe now; I suppose that's enough."

I shook my head. "I can read for people like Olivia or you, when your father appeared and bullied me into hearing him. People happen into my life and need something." I stared at Miss Violet, confused. "I won't make trouble. I promise. I won't have any more outbursts, and I'll find a way to block out people who are demanding I pay attention."

Miss Violet nodded. "*I* need something from you."

I pushed away from the table, taking the bread to the oven, and opened the door and adjusted the flue before sliding the loaf into the oven. I thought of the security my family now enjoyed. "What do you need?"

Miss Violet stood. "I've thought a lot about how to handle this." She smoothed her hand over the leather ledger she always carried. "I've run the numbers and studied all the ways you could change minds, hearts, offer something no one else can. I've a system that will make things easy for you. You won't have to wait for anyone to appear. We'll bring in hundreds of people, thousands of dollars just to see you. To see what you do. That's what that ball in your pocket is, right? That thing you touch all the time? A system of sorts."

A system? I shook my head, unsure what to say.

"I have a chart for palm reading," Miss Violet said, "dice for telling the future and softening the sorrows of the past. You don't have to worry, Katherine. I've managed everything already."

I thought of Madame Smalley, the way the newspapers decried her as a fraud. I couldn't weather that type of experience. I'd suffered when those who actually believed in my abilities had deemed me the devil. I looked at Violet but didn't respond.

"You want to help your mother, right? She wants to own her own home."

I nodded.

"She told me about your father. She gave me a sense of how all of you were left vulnerable. I know how it feels to be alone. You lost your father even younger than I lost mine. I know how it feels to forge a way in the world as a woman. I can help you. And you can help your mother."

I looked away.

"You can help *me*, Katherine."

I returned my gaze to her. "Help you?"

She went to the pie safe, withdrew the cake, and set it on the table. "Put the water on, Katherine. I'll cut us a slice of this divine angel cake."

I filled the kettle and went to the table, unsure but interested in how it was possible that I might be able to help a woman who put together a business and a home that even boasted a modern kitchen.

Miss Violet wiped her eyes as though she'd been crying, and I felt sorrow fill the room, an uncertainty I'd felt whenever in the room with her. "What is it?" I couldn't see her father, but I felt him. Why would he hide now?

"My father," she said with a sigh. "He died over fifteen years ago, but I . . . I can't quite get past it. I feel like I didn't do enough, like . . ."

Violet told her story of never having a home as a young girl. Of a father who was intelligent, educated, savvy, but unable to keep a job. "Whiskey," she said over and over.

I understood the toll that took on a person. I thought of Mama, how she reacted to Grandfather's death and his laudanum use. I certainly saw my father bury himself in a laudanum bottle from time to time. I felt overwhelmed by Violet's sorrow; the darkness blanketed me. It was as though her telling of her story called me into it; like magic, her emotions became mine.

Mr. Pendergrass returned, kneeling beside his daughter. My eyes burned as I watched him, his adoring expression as he watched Violet. The feelings I experienced shifted like little particles whooshing away, instantly replaced with something altogether different. "He loves you, Miss Violet. He's proud. You did everything you could've. You did what you needed to. But he said again, it's enough now. You can stop it. Whatever *it* is." I shrugged.

Miss Violet cocked her head as though this was settling in. Her eyes welled, and tears dropped down her cheeks. Her face was soft, open, then wounded, then vulnerable again, completely different than I'd ever seen her. Clearly, she knew what her father meant. Deep inside my chest warmed. I felt special to witness this gentle side of such a powerful woman.

I dug a handkerchief out of my sleeve and handed it to Miss Violet. She dabbed at her eyes and shook her head. And then she straightened. She cleared her throat. "I'm sorry. I didn't expect that."

"What?"

"That this could be real."

I was safer with people not knowing this about me, but Miss Violet's acknowledgement that what I did was "real" brought a wash of pride and calm at once.

The kettle whistled. I leapt up, removed it from the stove, and took two teacups and the tea canister to the table, letting Miss Violet collect herself. I fixed the tea infusers with leaves and retrieved honey and the kettle. I poured the hot water, then swirled the honey into the hot liquid and cut two thin slices of the spongy angel cake.

Miss Violet dried her eyes and straightened her back, recovering her typical posture and strength. Finally, she took a bite and closed her eyes. "Melts right on my tongue."

I smiled and took a bite as well.

Miss Violet swallowed another bite of cake and cleared her throat. "I did something to get this operation started. I figured if it didn't pan out, it wouldn't matter. But what you can do is worth something to all of us. I can help you, your mother, my own business. You can help me, your mother, your family. I had a feeling this would work, and I've already laid some groundwork. I've laid a trail of bread crumbs in papers leading back here, leading to you."

I heard her words but wasn't sure what she meant by all of this. My throat tightened from fear. I could no longer sit still. "What do you mean, a trail back to me?" I paced in front of the table.

Violet stood and moved with me. "I didn't put *you* out there. I put *Dreama* out there."

I stopped short.

Miss Violet gripped my shoulders. "I told you I knew Victoria Woodhull. I saw her work. Honestly, I didn't believe her, not always anyway. It confused me. She certainly never told me anything my father said."

I looked out the window, wondering if Miss Violet was sincere. She sounded as though she was, but her staccato wording and shallow, excited breathing was in stark contrast to what I'd seen of her so far.

She took my hand. "Katherine. I felt *him* because you brought him. And that kind of thing, what you did with Olivia, too. I underestimated the extent of your gift."

I looked back at Miss Violet. Her face had softened again; the vulnerability was back, making me feel connected to her, safe. I shook my head. "He's always been with you. It's not me bringing him."

Violet drew back slightly, surprised. She nodded slowly. "I know the pitfalls involved in you sharing this exquisite gift. I see your fear, but there's greatness in what you do. I can protect you, your identity. But you know as well as I do that you need to do this. My business is everything to me; it's like having a child. And I want you to be more involved."

I looked at my hands, folded my stubby pinkie into my palm. Miss Violet's belief in me granted a sense of security I hadn't expected or even wished for. Still, Madame Smalley's experience and my own, two sides of this coin, left me shaken at the idea of trying to call upon spirits on behalf of others.

I lifted my eyes to see the almost childlike expression on Miss Violet's face. I focused on her, tried to absorb her energy, to really feel her intentions. I thought of Mama. Fear gripped me again. She wouldn't approve. "I can't."

"Think of what you could do for your mother. Think of the extra money, more than you can imagine. You can make her dream of buying a cottage with a garden happen."

"Extra money?"

Miss Violet nodded.

"But I can't tell her. She'd never allow this. And that doesn't seem right. Does it?"

"No." Miss Violet shook her head. She clasped her hands together, holding them at her waist.

"But in the end, she will be so proud of you. Imagine the money you will turn over to her. Erase her worries. Do something more than simply love her."

When Miss Violet acknowledged the wrong of it but found a reason to do it, I felt my mind hook into her thinking. I'd surely lied plenty to save myself. But to lie for no reason, to lie in the hopes something good came of it? I wasn't sure I could be that kind of liar.

"*Do something.* Trust in her. She'll understand in the end."

I flinched. I'd never thought of life that way. I had taken to doing things for Mama since we arrived back in Des Moines, helping her when she had weak moments. But this. A lie to do something good. Was that really different? All right?

Miss Violet shook my hands to draw my attention back to her. "I've placed ads in papers in other towns. I've written some articles about this woman, Dreama, who brings serenity to those who grieve or need to know . . . *something*. I've littered the papers from Chicago all the way here."

"But I'm not this person you wrote about, this Dreama. And I can't just do this because you wrote some articles."

"Dear Katherine." Miss Violet smoothed my hair back, her hands smelling of sweet rose. "All people know when they see the ads I've placed is that they either missed something grand or that they'll do anything *not* to miss it when it comes to their town."

I stiffened, imagining people swarming, hating, cursing me, like had happened to a girl at a revival with the Christoffs. I belted my waist with my arms. This was what I feared. Jail or some sort of soul-cleansing would await me if this was the plan.

"I saw with my own eyes what you did for Olivia, how all the grief left her. I didn't make up what Dreama can do. I just implied she'd already done it in a few choice towns."

I shook my head.

"Think of all your mother has lost. You can do this for her. And me. It will make a difference in my business if I add this element of entertainment—beyond Olivia's piano and Bernice's singing. *This* will bring in the most influential men in the city."

My stomach turned at the thought. The shame brought on my family by my grandfather's and father's actions worked below my skin like waves of heat rising. The memory of seeing Mama in pain, like she had been back then, was as real as the shoes on my feet. *But if I could change our lives . . .* That would be something she'd never forget. "Mama *can't* know about this. Not until I've made a nice nest egg for her, for the home we want to buy."

Miss Violet nodded. "I've even proposed the idea to her of me taking over your schooling. That way, when you spend more time here, she won't wonder. You can surprise her once you are ready."

I looked down.

Violet swung her arms in the air. "Imagine your mother's face. When's the last time you saw her smile? *Really* smile. Think of it."

I felt an overpowering flood of goodness course between us, like the day we first met. I patted my leg where the crystal pendant was inside my pocket. My fear quieted.

"I'll educate you," Miss Violet said. "You'll know everything I do about business. But in the end you'll know even more because I'll never possess the gift that you do. Think of what I'm saying."

We stared at each other, both with our own thoughts. Miss Violet broke the hush again.

"I've no husband, no children, no one. And I'm trusting you with this piece of my business. You'll be an independent woman in the end. Don't you want to be a part of this? Of something big? Think of your independence. I know we are of like minds on the topic. Partners."

Partners? I smiled at the notion. This was a woman unencumbered by children and marital obligations. Her business was her sole attention, and I knew right then that Miss Violet would protect me as a mother did an infant. I thought of Mama. When she had to board us out, the only one she kept close was Yale, the baby.

If Miss Violet turned even a fraction of the attention on me that Mama put on Yale, then I would be safe. I glanced at Miss Violet's ledger, the tiny writing inside it that I'd glimpsed a few times, the incredible detail between the leather covers, the answers inside, the truth of how she created the life she had. Would I want to be a part of that?

I turned my gaze back to her. "All right. Tell me more about what you've planned."

"So we trust each other." Miss Violet's gaze held me.

Partners. My heart swelled. She needed *me*. "We do."

And Miss Violet swallowed me in an embrace, sealing this union as though I'd been invited into a new family where I could contribute as much as I took.

Chapter 18

Lies for Mama
Katherine

I sat back from the sketch I'd been working on, stretching to the ceiling, pulling my neck in one direction and then the other. I lost track of time whenever I drew. Like a deep sleep, when I finally pulled out of the work, I'd be met with a few moments of opaque consciousness, thought obscured by a creative casing. It had been some time since I'd carved out any time to draw, but since Miss Violet suggested I might try to earn money by bridging the gap between the living and dead, I'd been swept by the urge to get to my drawing.

I turned the paper and shaded the space beyond the figure I'd drawn. The woman in the foreground looked back over her shoulder. A baby rested in the crook of her arm. In the background was the shading and outline of something I thought was an angel, a holy presence there to watch over the woman. She was so familiar, but I couldn't name her. Even though I couldn't see her face, I knew she'd been the woman appearing to me at odd times, often along with my brother James. But when I'd sat down with my pencils and papers, I hadn't even thought of what to draw, yet here she was.

"Katherine?" Mama's voice startled me.

I turned to see Mama, Miss Violet, and Mr. Hayes standing inside the door that led out to the gardens. Mama's face was red from sweat and heat. She pushed her loose strands of hair back with the back of her hand. Mr. Hayes stepped into the kitchen behind the two women.

"Oh, Mama. I'm sorry, I sat down for a moment and just started to sketch and . . . What time is it?" I asked, ignoring the clock over my head.

I didn't wait for the answer. I rose and pumped water into the pitcher, wishing our little house had been fitted with running water like next door. I splashed water into several glasses and set them on the table. "Please sit," I said, still clearing my mind.

The three adults sat down and drank. Outside, I could hear Tommy talking, but I couldn't make out his words.

"Who's Tommy talking with?" I asked.

Mama finished her water and began to pour more from the pitcher. She sighed. "His crow of all things, he says."

I remembered that he found a crow the day he stopped working at the Savery. "He's keeping that thing?"

"It's more of a raven, I'd say," Mr. Hayes added. "Nice bird. Intelligent."

"Well, no birds in the house, please," Miss Violet said. "I'm happy to have Tommy do more errands and such now that he's free from his hours at the Savery, but please, no animals inside the house."

"You can count on that," Mama said.

Miss Violet pulled the drawing to her. "This is stunning. It's like she's alive. The woman you drew."

My cheeks warmed. I'd had my share of compliments, but this was different. To watch Miss Violet absorbed in my drawings—a woman who possessed a half dozen oils done by a famous Frenchman—sent chills through me. It wasn't her words so much as it was seeing her reaction, her expression, speaking a library of thought with a moment's jaw drop.

"It's only a sketch. I'm going to save money for paints so I can develop some of the drawings."

"There're more?"

My breath caught in excitement. I lifted the bottom of my satchel and gently shook papers from inside it onto the table. Mama spread them apart while Mr. Hayes and Miss Violet shuffled them between each other.

"You did these?" Miss Violet held one at arm's length and pulled it back in to examine closer before glancing at me over the top of the paper. "All of them?"

I nodded.

Mama held one for all to see. "This looks like Aleksey. And little Anzhela."

I had purposely drawn Aleksey, but I hadn't realized I'd added Anzhela into the background. I eased closer to Mama to see better.

"Did you do this after you saw him at the grocery stand?" Mama asked.

Seeing him that day had thrilled me. And while working, I found myself thinking of him.

"I suppose I did."

"Who's Aleksey?" Miss Violet reached for the picture. Mama handed it over.

"Oh, he's a wonderful boy," Mama said. "He's the son of one of my most cherished friends. They lived on a nearby homestead during our year on the prairie. He kept Katherine and Yale alive in the blizzard. He brought a cow inside the dugout, and they curled up with it, just Katherine's little finger sticking out in the cold. The rest of their bodies were warm until the weather cleared." Mama sighed as she pulled the drawing of Aleksey back from Miss Violet. "I'm forever grateful to him for saving my daughters."

"Seems to me Katherine's the type to save herself," Miss Violet said, her sharp tone cutting through the hushed moment.

"Oh." Mama pressed her hand against her chest. "She *is* that kind of young woman. But Aleksey. He's different from other boys."

Miss Violet leaned onto her forearms. "Well, lucky for Katherine, she'll have plenty of work for me and schooling with me as we were discussing. There'll be little time to worry over boys. Even the heroic type has his limitations. I'm sure you know that, Jeanie."

I smiled at this knowledge Miss Violet carried as though she could see into the Arthur family past, see our struggles, and take us on nonetheless.

Mr. Hayes smacked the back of his neck and jostled the table, making his water glass spill over. "Mosquito," he said, showing us the corpse on his palm. I grabbed a rag and blotted at the spilled water. Mama, Violet, and Mr. Hayes shuffled my drawings and the newspapers away from the water. When I'd mopped up the water, everyone set the papers back down. "Well, look at this." Mr. Hayes held up yesterday's paper. "Madame Smalley'll have some competition soon."

"Madame Smalley's out of jail?" Miss Violet strained to see the article.

Mr. Hayes tapped the paper. "This Dreama woman I've been reading about is supposed to be the real McCoy."

Mama sipped her water. "Oh her, yes. I've heard."

I let the tone of my mother's voice settle onto me. Was she mocking? Interested? Hostile? Mama leaned closer to see what Mr. Hayes was pointing at. Miss Violet glanced at me, but I couldn't tell what she was thinking. I was suddenly frightened that Miss Violet would tell Mama what we were planning. I wanted her to know, but not yet. I wouldn't know how to explain it.

"Dreama brings peace and joy to all those who suffer," Mr. Hayes read aloud.

Mama shrugged. I shifted in my seat and stole a glance at Violet. She was watching Mama and Mr. Hayes, looking as relaxed as ever. I, on the other hand, wanted to dash away, sickened by all the talk, the secret plan.

"Bunk," Mama said. "Same as the potions that claim to cure everything all at once but do nothing. A good chamomile tea is one thing, but these outlandish purveyors of . . . well, everything, are not to be taken seriously."

"And all for a steep price," Mr. Hayes added.

"I don't know," Violet said. "I've seen people comforted this way."

Mama lifted her eyes from the paper and narrowed them on Miss Violet as though determining whether she was serious.

I couldn't take it. I slid to the edge of my seat nearly blurting out that it was me. I was going to be Dreama, that I could do these very things. No matter that this article, touting the arrival of the now popular Dreama, was full of lies about the towns she'd worked in, her actual ability to communicate with the dead was real. But no. The words jammed in my mouth. I'd sound lunatic, like the rantings that got a young woman stashed away in an asylum or hidden in a basement. Until I actually did a reading as Dreama, I could not report to be her. Not to Mama anyway. I slid back in my chair and forced my breath to calm.

Still, the article intrigued me. I wiped a bead of sweat from my brow as I stared at the discarded paper. The words were positive, as to be expected since Miss Violet wrote them, but there were no angry rebuttal articles. The only scathing talk was directed at Madame Smalley.

I recalled being with Mr. Hayes and Mrs. Hillis when Madame Smalley was accused of fraud. I couldn't tell what his perspective on the matter truly was. Of course, if Madame Smalley was a fraud, they should have a right to be appalled, but what if she wasn't? I wasn't a fake. That should have been all I needed to know. But their reactions to the article said it all. For now, Mama couldn't know of our plans.

"Jeanie," Miss Violet said. "I thank you for allowing me to take over Katherine's studies for the year. You won't be disappointed, and I think you'll find her knowledge of the world, finance, and even history will flourish under my guidance."

"I trust that it will." Mama stood and scooped Miss Violet into an embrace. "I can't believe how our fortunes have turned upon meeting you."

Miss Violet's expression was one of confusion, as though not accustomed to affection; her arms appeared stiff as she patted Mama's back. "I think you'll be pleased to see what your daughter learns and earns this year."

Mama stepped back but still held Miss Violet's arms. "I believe that, Violet. Thank you for taking Katherine under your wing. Every single article I read about you reveals another example of a woman's work in a man's world, and I'm thoroughly impressed. Astonished even."

Miss Violet nodded, backing away from Mama. "Your trust is well-placed." And she floated out of the kitchen, taking my breath with her.

The lies were heavy in my chest. These new ones. Not the ones about my past, the lies that I held secret because they kept Mama from feeling guilty that she had to board us out. Those were noble deceits, the kind that saved a mother's soul from crushing sorrow. These new tales turned my insides. I wondered if Mama could feel the fabrications like I could—heavy, dark, pulsing inside her, leaving her confused about where the mass of them came from. I prayed not. I could hold the falsehoods if only I knew Mama didn't have to.

And it was only with Miss Violet's confidence in the operation that I thought I might come out with something good for Mama, for us. Seeing Mama working her garden, Yale alongside of her, happy, Tommy working several small jobs, living in the shed at the back of the property. I could not renege on Miss Violet and risk her turning us out with nowhere to go.

No, I forced air back into my lungs and reminded myself I was in many ways a woman. It was time for me to stick with a difficult decision and take charge of the life path I found myself on at that moment. It was time.

Chapter 19

Settling In
Katherine

I inhaled the clean lemon, lavender, and rose scent that filled the bedroom. I'd combined fresh and dried flowers and herbs and used the mixture to sweep the room and then strategically placed it around the space. It made being upstairs and going to bed pleasurable. Yale, Mama, and I shared a bed, and while the room was stuffy and sticky with summer heat, small details like the flowers made it welcoming.

"That's a nice letter from Aleksey," Mama said. "Thank you for sharing it."

I nodded as I organized the hairbrush and mirror on the old dressing table.

I finished writing a quick reply to Aleksey and reported to him that Mama said hello and sent her best to his mama. I let him know that we looked forward to the time he would come calling. Each night since I'd seen him, I'd fallen asleep thinking of him, wondering if he would actually seek us out.

But as I fell asleep each night, my last thoughts of him were of his good looks—his broad shoulders, strong handshake, his instinct to protect me from the accusing grocer. I couldn't have expected to find my mind so frequently resting on him, on the feel of his palm against mine, on the sense that we might actually see each other soon. I couldn't wait for that to happen.

I rearranged the bundle of magenta peonies Mama had put into a vase. I folded back the precious quilt Mama had made just for our new home. I smoothed it, this treasure. She'd traded some of my bread for cast-off material at McCrady's. Though none of the scraps had been matched in the usual systematic pattern for a quilt, Mama had pieced together the covering in a way that combined a flurry of blues, greens, and every shade of white imaginable, creating an English garden effect. The pieces were laid in circles, squares, rectangles, triangles, all manner of raised wale— thick and thin, water-hued silk that changed color when the light hit it, cotton, calicoes, and even velvet were stitched together with thick wool thread. Mama's eyes lit up every time she looked at it, and her expression made me smile.

Before, Mama would've shunned these loose designs, these crazy quilts, only using them when we lost our home, and the risk of frostbite during the coldest prairie nights were untouched by the hottest of fires. But now the pride in Mama's face when she had presented it to me, every time she looked at it, showed how much she'd changed over the years.

Mama and I got into bed, me with my sketchbook and Mama with her newspapers and garden journal. Yale slept on her side between us, her body curled like a seahorse I'd seen drawn into a fairy story about creatures in the great blue sea.

Mama spread the newspaper over her legs, and set her garden journal open on top. She jotted notes and made drawings. My pencil scratched away as I sketched, the side of my hand growing black when I blended dark strokes into softer shades that brought my figures' expressions to life. Yale yelped in her sleep, pulling me from the drawing of a little girl wandering through fields, her hands swiping past the tall grasses, a serene smile on her face as she looked off to the side.

Mama patted Yale's back and leaned into me. "Beautiful. You've grown so much more sophisticated in your renderings."

I smiled, bolstered by her quiet kindness. "Thank you. I can't wait to paint again, though." Yale yelped again and flopped to her other side, her hand landing on Mama's belly. I took Yale's plump, dimpled hand and pressed each tiny indentation at the base of her fingers. I laid my head on Mama's shoulder. She slipped her arm around me and squeezed.

"You're sure Tommy's all right sleeping out in the shed?" I asked. "I can't imagine he really wants to be out there."

Mama nodded. "It's hot for sure. But he's fashioned it into a home of sorts. I have a feeling that when winter settles in he may change his mind. When he couldn't take the promotion to elevator boy at the Savery and he lost the room there, he said he still needed his space."

"They couldn't allow him to stay on as a bellboy?"

Mama shrugged. "He said no. And he couldn't handle being closed in working the elevator. Said it's sure to fall soon with its frayed wires."

I smoothed a piece of eyelet that formed a thin ruffle at the neck of Mama's nightdress. "I still don't understand why he doesn't want to sleep inside."

Mama sighed. She adjusted her book in her lap, her hand flat on the pages, holding it open. She kissed my temple. "It's not us he's keeping away from by staying out in the shed. It's . . . well, really, I don't think he slept a full night with us in the hotel either or the boardinghouse, and he seemed content in the barn at Mrs. Mellet's home."

"I suppose."

Mama drew corkscrews across her journal page. "I tried to talk to him when he quit the Savery. He wouldn't say much. He was more interested in that crow he found."

"Said it found him, didn't he?" I giggled.

Mama stared off. "That bird consoled him in a way I could not. Can you imagine?"

I laughed. "I know, Mama. He has always sought his calming somewhere else. Even on the prairie. He'd just disappear for hours."

"He named it Frank. The bird."

I shook my head, not completely surprised that Tommy would name his pet in honor of the father he adored.

Mama poked her pencil on the page. "I don't know how things were for him while we were all apart. He won't tell me." She took my hand. "You don't tell me either."

My breath froze as I recounted various homes in which I stayed. They were each awful in their own way, but I especially didn't want to tell Mama of the horrid experience with the Christoffs.

She pulled my chin so that I had to meet her gaze. "Were you all right? *Are* you all right?"

My eyes stung. I thought of the lies, my stealing, the desperation that still dropped over me when I wasn't expecting it. I did not want to sully this fresh contentment with such things. I didn't want to see Mama's new smile falter. Someday I'd confide in Mama small things that wouldn't hurt her like they hurt me. Eventually, I'd tell her, but when I told her the bad, I needed to reveal the good that came of it, my calming, the gathering of spirits at just the right time. When I had money in hand, pride in my heart, with the right explanation for what I was going to do as Dreama, I'd tell her. "Yes, Mama."

Mama reached over Yale and held me tight. Her clean hair, the scent of apple rinse along the neckline of her nightgown, the coziness in being close, made my eyes tear-up. And so I tucked the moment away in my mind for safekeeping.

"As far as Tommy goes," Mama said pulling away, forcing lightness into her voice, "I'm just happy he didn't head back to the woods, for goodness' sake. He seems to have a little of your father's melancholia in him. Perhaps I pushed your father too much when we were on the prairie? I don't know. I don't want to push Tommy away. Not after all we've been through."

I wiped my wet cheeks and adjusted the pillow behind me. "Tommy's not like Father. Not really," was all I could think to say. Father would retire to bed during the day so often on the prairie. I stretched my mind to recall if he'd done that when we lived in Des Moines, when we had everything. Perhaps I'd been too young to notice until we took our shame to the little home dug into the side of a hill in Dakota Territory.

That I remembered. He took to the bed much too often. It had saddened and worried me to see him like that, pained me on behalf of Mama, even as I often feared that we all might die there if he didn't get up and do something. Not that anyone asked me what I feared at that time. Well, Aleksey had. Looking back, he appeared nearly as often as Father disappeared under his covers. Aleksey couldn't have known Father's failings. Or had he? Could he have repeatedly, accidentally shown up at our dugout requesting I help weed his mother's garden at just the time when my Father was hiding away, causing tension? Had his family known? I wanted to ask Mama more about what happened that year between her and Father, but I couldn't. It would only stir up pain and recreate trouble that had already passed us by.

"Tommy said he got a letter from Father saying he's coming."

Mama shook her head, making spirals across the top margin of her garden journal, the pencil threading round and round. "Do you miss your father like Tommy does?"

I thought of him, letting the love for him gather deep inside. "I miss him. But not like Tommy. No." Honestly, I didn't have the time.

She exhaled deeply. "Let's think of something cheerful. Our future. This garden, your studies."

"We'll keep our feet turned to the future," I said.

She kissed my forehead. "Yes."

I turned to my drawing while every so often Mama made a heavy line through an item on the list in her journal. *Weed kitchen garden, children's garden.*

There was writing next to Mama's notes in a different hand. I traced the rolling cursive with my finger. It said: *I'll fashion a cozy for your winter plantings.*

Mama tapped her pencil on the journal. "Reed Hayes wrote that."

"A nice man," I said. He'd seemed friendly when I met him with Mrs. Hillis, and I'd seen him alongside Mama in the gardens. The man went beyond his share of the trade for loaves of bread from me. He was a teacher at Drake University—a doctoral student in science—working to finish his dissertation.

Mama leaned back against the wall and closed her eyes. "He's helpful, polite, hardworking. Assisting with our gardens helps with his dissertation study."

"No wife, then," I said.

"Oh my, no." Mama laughed.

I studied the small smile on her face as her mind had clearly partitioned off her thoughts from me. Mama touched her cheek, her hands, reddened and chafed from dirt, catching my attention. *That* would be the first thing I bought her—gardening gloves.

"I'll make you a salve for your hands." I took her chapped fingers in mine and studied the cracks that webbed across her skin. "Rosemary, comfrey, calendula, maybe some yarrow. I wonder if we could plant that next year. Could you ask Mr. Hayes to get us some yarrow seed?"

Mama looked content in a way I'd never seen her. "Yarrow. Yes. Let's add that to the list of plantings."

We squeezed each other's hands, and I turned to a fresh sheet of paper and began to sketch Mama writing in her journal. I jotted down the ingredients I would use to make her a salve. I couldn't deny how important I felt in being able to contribute to our household, to Mama.

Something told me her contentment was rooted in us being together, but the smiles I saw, the tender mention of his name, assured me that some of her happiness had to do with Mr. Hayes working with her in the gardens. This saddened me and gave me pleasure on her behalf.

Even unmarried, a man like Mr. Hayes, associated with a school like Drake University, could never take on a woman like Jeanie Arthur. Still, I saw the enjoyment Mama was experiencing in working the garden, in having an ally. I looked back at his exclamatory note in the journal. *We can do this!!* Beside that, she'd written a note about salve and yarrow.

She glanced at me and smiled. "A yarrow salve would be nice. I know you're quite good at finding just the right combination to heal."

"Tell me again how you've laid it all out," I said, snuggling into Mama, pleased to have these moments of ordinary closeness, extraordinary contentment. *I can't wait to tell you how I've laid out my work with Miss Violet.*

Mama flipped back to the front of the book where she'd sketched the quadrants. "Here we have the children's garden, where your sister just delights in digging and weeding and communing with the garden fairies. Oh, how she loves a fairy story."

I patted Yale's arm. "She surely does."

"And the kitchen garden in the same area. The rosemary and dill and basil are just flourishing under your sister's companionship."

I laughed. "Oh, Mama. I guess you're right." Yale didn't communicate clearly with anyone else.

Mama licked her finger and turned the page. "We have the tomatoes and the spinach behind that. And then beyond the rosebushes and hydrangeas, we have the blueberries stretching nearly to Tommy's shed. The social garden behind Miss Violet's is coming along. She allotted some extra funds to bring in rosebushes in full blossom, and we transplanted peonies that are blooming wild. I can't believe they did so well after being moved! Even Mr. Hayes is astonished at the sight."

There it was. A flash came to Mama's eye, her cheek pinked, her hand going there as though recalling a touch or just a memory of a grand day in a small garden behind a tiny house.

"And then the orchards," Mama continued, "behind that on Miss Violet's side of the property. The apples and pears. The cherry trees, blueberries, raspberries. Soon we will have everything we need for nearly every meal."

I squeezed Mama's hand three times, and she turned to me. "I love you, too."

Mama scratched a few notes and flipped more pages. At the top of one, it said: *Must sell these to the paper. They're dying for your take on small yard gardening. They just don't know it yet.*

"What's that mean, Mama?"

Jeanie shut the book. "Nothing."

I opened it and pointed to Mr. Hayes's note. "That." Mama had drafted what appeared to be an article with some narrative elements. "You're writing again?"

Mama's lips quivered before pulling into a grin.

"You are? Oh, Mama. That's wonderful. Your words in print again."

"Oh no, no. Let's not leap ahead of things. I'm simply recording observations."

I snatched the newspaper from her legs. "Do you read the gardening articles in here? Readers are asleep after the first sentence. 'Plant your seeds, water your seeds, weed your garden, pull your crop.'" I let my head drop off, and I made snoring noises. Mama giggled, and I opened my eyes. I pointed to her journal. "*You* wrote a story. I agree with Mr. Hayes. The *Register* needs your writing again."

"Oh, Katherine."

"Think about it."

Mama nodded. I set the paper down but noticed that an article in the paper had been circled. I picked the paper back up and skimmed the article.

"Look at this hideous article by Mrs. Calder. Death by household instruction. They need less of her voice in there and more of yours again."

I tapped Elizabeth Calder's article. "Deadly boring."

It detailed how to entertain for summer soirees. The photo showed Judge Calder and the Mrs. with their dogs in their gardens, surrounded by every variety of rose.

Mama's eyes went to the empty space in the room again. "I saw her the other day."

I grunted, thinking of how rude Mama's dearest friend had been when we left Des Moines.

"I'm ashamed to say that I found myself wishing her ill will."

"I'm ashamed to say I might have bopped her on the nose if I'd seen her," I said. "She deserves ill will. I know she was your friend. But something about her was always dark and awful. I never really gave it much thought, but now, picturing her, I feel it clear as the breeze through the window."

Her mother nodded. "I know." She sighed. "There are many times I doubted God, and well, now, just the fact we all survived our separation and we're back together, we have this home . . . why, I can't help but think there is a God. Tommy and his prayer selling for Reverend Shaw gives me pause. But he's driven about it, and so I'll let it go for now. My point is, Elizabeth Calder will find all her nasty deeds turned back upon her. I don't trust religion, but I trust that."

Mama turned a page in the paper. "Poor Madame Smalley—out of jail. I'm sorry she's come to be this person." She held the paper up to me.

I shrugged, more interested in what she'd said before that. "You talk like you knew her."

"I did. Way back. She's the daughter of one of our maids. And, well, she was never satisfied with her station in life."

"You always say one's station in life is only temporary until made better. Isn't that good that she found her way?"

Mama closed the paper in her lap and closed her eyes for a moment.

"I wish her all the success in living the life she desires. I simply hate to see pained souls searching for peace and understanding be exploited by a woman who takes their money with nothing to give in return. That's wrong. And dangerous."

I moved to my side and smoothed Yale's hair. "What if she's real? What if she could soothe tormented souls? What if she could put you at peace with James?"

Mama stiffened. "I've always thought James is with me. With the shifting clouds, I watch the weather, feel the winds, and remember how he worked to predict what was coming. That's him being with me. But I don't need Madame Smalley to tell me that."

"I watch the clouds like that, too," I said. Mama smiled at me.

I opened the paper again and pointed to the large advertisement with thick, ornate lettering: *Dreama will put your mind and heart at rest. Sit with her to find your peace . . .* "I've heard she's real. She can do that."

"No one," Mama said, "understands grief like we do."

I wanted for James to come right then, to provide guidance, but he didn't.

"You miss James deeply, I know that," she told me. "But don't think that if you spend your hard-earned money on someone like Madame Smalley or Dreama that you'll find peace. If all it takes is someone in a room to say, 'Your loved one is at peace, you should be happy again,' why, I could say that. Why, I've said that to myself a thousand times since the blizzard. But it took action, our move here, the lure of getting our life back from Mrs. Mellet, to pull me from the depths of sorrow. To prey on that type of desperation is the worst of crimes."

Mama's words pierced me deep, making me wonder if my temporary secret would remain with me forever.

"Oh, Katherine." She slipped a lock of my hair behind my ear. "I didn't mean to upset you. You're a sensitive soul, like James. All I was saying was if this Dreama comes to town, she may find herself in jail along with Madame Smalley. Mrs. Hillis says the aldermen are trying to clean up the town. And in doing so, police officers are running all over the city, screaming and hating, snatching people up."

Mama's shoulders shook as though casting off a burning cloak. "Regular citizens with a loose grasp on reality are following the politicians, hissing and taunting, passing out cards with naked women's pictures on the front. Vilifying women who have no alternatives. Some of them may be cons, but not all. Some are just trying to survive. But what you don't understand is that it doesn't matter the reason a woman does what she needs to; powerful men use them to make themselves richer. It's frightening to see."

Heat filled me from the inside out. Being in the bed with Mama and Yale suddenly felt suffocating. I admired Miss Violet but now felt heavy with guilt that I was sharing a secret with her, keeping Mama in the dark. Yet I knew that in order for us to continue toward our future, my decision, my path, had been laid. My stomach growled. I should have eaten more at supper.

I went to the dresser and pulled open a drawer, taking a cracker from it.

Mama sat up, crinkling the newspaper. "Don't keep food up here. You'll draw rodents."

I shrugged, engulfed in loneliness. I could've been hundreds of miles from Mama again at that moment, the guilt separating us without her even knowing. I would fix that. Just as I would create a salve for her hands, my honesty would salve our relationship. I just needed time. That wouldn't happen until I settled things with Miss Violet so she did not throw us out. She was reasonable. Certainly, she saw I was valuable in a number of ways. The Dreama operation hadn't gotten too far. We could place an ad saying she moved past Des Moines without stopping. No one would notice her absence after a day.

Mama came to me and pulled the drawer back open. I watched her gaze as she inventoried the contents. It was filled to the brim with fruit and baked goods.

Shame spread through me. "I was just trying to save some in case there's ever none again."

She stared at me. I waited for her to scold me or holler. I rubbed the back of one arm as though she'd pinched me, like Mrs. Christoff always had when she wore that expression.

Mama grabbed my arms. I flinched and squeezed my eyes closed. She shook me. I opened my eyes.

Now she wore a frightened expression. I held my breath, waiting. But instead of abuse from Mama, she wrapped me tight in her arms, her embrace filling up all the empty spots inside me, at least for those moments that she held me close.

Chapter 20

The Bridge
Aleksey

Each footfall in the soft sod made me reevaluate going with Harold, the rest of the boys, and Mabel to the river. A dance was held there twice a week, down a ways from the wall I'd been working on for Mr. Palmer. Another stride over the expansive green land, another burst of water through the hole in the side of my boot.

Harold patted my shoulder as we hit the crest in the land where we could see the wall, Medusa, and the other trees that led the way to the river. "Never saw a fella in such need of a dance as you," he said.

I rubbed the back of my neck and agreed with that much. I'd been working hard, my neck pulled tight from bending over my books, the small of my back pulsing from bending over the wall.

"Oh, the ladies that will be there tonight. That fiddle player is coming, I heard. Oh, I sure hope so," Matty said.

Fat Joe slipped his hand into Mabel's as they walked ahead of me. She looked at him, grinning.

"I saw you got a letter from Katherine," Harold said as the other boys began to express their romantic hopes for the evening.

"She's happy to have me call. Katherine's working a lot. A kitchen mistress, she said she's called. Just until school starts for her, I guess."

"That sound fancy," Harold said. "I'm not sure you're a fancy kind of fella."

"Any work in a kitchen can't be classified as fancy," I said.

"Hey!" Mabel turned around and shook her finger at me.

"Didn't mean offense, Mabel. Hard work and fancy just don't go together you know."

"Well, I think it's wonderful you found her after all these years, after you've been talking about her," Harold said.

"Like you conjured her right up out of the crust of the earth," Sledgehammer said.

I chuckled at the thought. I too marveled at seeing her at the alley and then running into her at the grocer's.

"So why the long face?" Harold said. "This could be big for you, finding her."

I shrugged. "I am happy to know I can call on them. And I'm definitely interested in her in some way."

"But?" Harold said.

"Just preoccupied with the briefs I'm working on and an investigation Mr. Stevens needs."

"Finders, keepers?"

"Yeah. It's ending up more complicated than I thought it would be."

As we got closer to Medusa, the rest of the fellas and Mabel crowded around her, staring at something near the bottom of her trunk.

"That's . . ." Mabel moved closer to Fat Joe. "What *is* that? It's grotesque." She turned away.

The rest of them squatted down. When we got there, I looked over their shoulders. Sprouting up from the ground was a set of hands; the charcoal fingers were bent and straight as though wiggling, reaching up out of the earth, begging to be helped up from under the dirt.

Harold touched one of the fingers. He shuddered and backed away. "Looks like someone got burnt to a crisp right here under this tree."

I squatted and studied the area around the tree. The root system had been exposed even more by the recent rains. I looked upward to see the branches waving in a wind that I could not feel but could see in Medusa's snake-hair.

Harold leaned over my shoulder. "What on earth?"

Sledgehammer laughed and stood. "Oh, come on, fellas. Just a little fungus is all. I've seen it a million times around dying trees like this."

Harold looked closer, sniffing, as though he could figure something out by doing so.

"So there's not a man attached to those crispy mitts?"

"Nope. Just a fungus," I said.

"Just a fungus. I should say not," Mabel said. "Bad omen. That's what that is. I've heard of Dead Man's Fingers. That's what that is?"

I had to admit the sight of this particular fungus caused shivers to climb my spine. And though I'd become enamored with Medusa, I couldn't help thinking this would be the end of her. I pressed on the trunk. Even with the sodden soil and greedy, grasping black-fingered fungus, it didn't budge. "Old Medusa's holding strong. Let's get rid of this and see if she gets better." I brushed away some leaves. "The fungus is attached to the debris around the trunk, not the bark and roots."

Harold kicked at the fingers, and they gave up their grip, flying into the darkening night. Once we'd amputated the finger fungus, we carried on toward the dance. I looked back over my shoulder at the massive, spindly tree. I had a sense of foreboding, a sense that maybe I ought to just go back home and finish the work that awaited. I stopped, and Harold turned.

I pushed my thumb over my shoulder, ready to explain that I was heading back.

Harold stalked back to me. "Oh, no you don't. You begged out last time. Not today. You're gonna dance, and you're gonna have a sip of whiskey. You need to loosen up."

A breeze pushed past us as the sky turned from turquoise to sapphire. And I decided Harold was right. What would one evening enjoying the warm air and dancing with the ladies hurt?

We made our way down to the river where it normally narrowed nearly to a stream. Still a slim section of rushing water, it was higher than usual. "We'll have to cross at the bridge. Mabel will be a sight if we cross here."

We studied the frothing water.

Sledghammer shook his head. "Bridge is out down near the pavilion. Saw it just yesterday while I took my break."

"Too late to ask Mr. Palmer to use his wagon."

"Home, then, it is."

"Home, nothing," Fat Joe said. "There's a rope bridge down a little that way on Mr. Heatherington's property, just between this land and his. Mabel deserves a night to frolic."

"Mabel'll never get across a rope bridge," Harold said.

Fat Joe jerked his head in the direction he wanted us to follow. "Let's just see. Mabel's dainty but strong as wire."

We all stared at Fat Joe as he watched Mabel. Her cheeks turned cranberry at hearing his compliment and she covered her face.

"Like ivy, beautiful, strong ivy."

Mabel peeked between her fingers and finally dropped her hands. "I love ivy. Prettiest plant I can think of."

Fat Joe nodded once. Sledgehammer cleared his throat, but it was as though the loving couple didn't see anything but each other.

We stood looking at our feet and into the treetops, anywhere but at them, unsure of how to break up this private moment they were sharing right in front of us.

"So . . ." Sledgehammer said, "can we skedaddle so I can get my own lady or do I have to stare at Mabel, who is in love with someone else, all night?" Sledgehammer started toward the spot Harold had described.

We laughed, and Fat Joe offered his arm to Mabel. When we reached the part of the river where the rope bridge was strung across, the water was wider and faster.

I stood near the edge, the water lapping near the toes of my boots, looking up at the rope strung across the water. "You think she can get across that?" I said.

"I'll carry her if I have to," Fat Joe said, making Mabel blush all over again.

"I'm going to have to carry you both, I think," Sledgehammer said.

"Give it a go, Fat Joe. If you two get across, we'll come, too," Harold said.

We climbed up the bank that led to the bridge.

Fat Joe gripped the two ropes that were waist high and stepped onto the braided rope. He started walking across, one foot directly in front of the other. Fat Joe wiggled and bobbled as he made his way across, lurching left and then right as he went. When he got to the other side, he turned to us with his hands in the air. "Nothing to it! Come to me, sweet Ivy," he said.

"Aww, enough of the love talk, Fat Joe, you're making my stomach hurt from all the sugar," Sledgehammer said.

"Your envy is sweet as honey, Sledge," Fat Joe said. "I like it."

Sledgehammer and I each helped Mabel onto the rope. Luckily, she was not dressed for a ball or she might have been stepping on her hem as she crossed. She shook and fell to the right. I heaved her back up. "Press the ropes out as you go."

The rope under her feet swung to the right and upright she went again. "I don't think I can keep it steady. I'll be in the drink in no time."

I looked toward Fat Joe. "Pull the bottom rope tight. That'll make it easier."

Fat Joe pulled his end, and Harold pulled the end near us, making the bottom rope taut. Mabel gingerly placed one foot farther out, and when she felt it had less give she swung the other foot in front of that. When she got out of the range of Sledge and me holding her steady, we both helped pull the rope tight from our side. She got to the middle and looked back over her shoulder. "I can't do it, I can't go." And she began to try to swing around.

"No!" we all yelled in unison.

"You're halfway, same distance either way now," Fat Joe said.

She nodded and turned back, moving slower than before. My hands burned at holding the rope.

"You can do it, Mabel, that's it, one foot, then the other. Just like making a pie. One thing, then the next." Fat Joe's voice was kind, full of something I can't remember ever having heard in a friend's voice. Every word was infused with something loving, something meant just for her.

"Well, I'll be," I said, realizing just how in love these two had fallen.

She got to the other side and fell into Fat Joe's arms, knocking him back a few steps.

The three of us made our way across quickly, easily, and all the while I kept thinking of how this love that had bloomed between Fat Joe and Mabel gave me a sense of hope, a sense of the future, of something I couldn't imagine for myself but recognized was there, seeded, something that maybe someday would rise and meet me when I was finally ready.

Part II

Chapter 21

Dreama
Katherine

I stood in front of the hulking, carved mirror in the room at the tippy top of Miss Violet's house. It was tucked in the back, overlooking the gardens, near a luxurious washroom. I'd never been granted access here before and the sweet, clean smell of lilac, violets, and lemon filled me with excitement. The white, peach, and green sorbet color scheme that graced the walls and every fabric in the room made me want to leap on the bed and roll in the frilly, airy pillows and blankets. It was a room for the kind of lady Mama used to be, the kind of girl I'd been.

Earlier that day, Miss Violet had rushed to me, red-faced and huffing, telling me she had an emergency and I was the only one who could remedy it, that it was time for me to be transformed into Dreama and give the whole thing a whirl.

My reflection pleased me. I turned from side to side, examining every inch of myself. Downstairs, Olivia played the piano, her fingers lifting the notes of Beethoven's "Fur Elise" into the air, sending them up the stairs flavoring the day, making me feel as though I'd been transported into another world.

I caressed the dress I'd been given. Wearing the immaculate creamy-white muslin dress almost made me forget that I didn't have the crystal ball tucked inside my secret pocket. I didn't love the high, frilly collar on this dress, but the flounced hem was appealing, and I lifted it and spun on tiptoes, my too small but still lovely silken shoes squeezing my toes. The curvy heel was reminiscent of those Mama used to wear, the ones I'd been too young for as a ten-year-old.

I closed my eyes and recalled a time when my family had donned entirely new wardrobes—over three hundred new garments for each of us each season. We relegated the "old" from the prior year, even if barely worn, to the attic. I'd been a little girl the last time I'd worn a dress this clean, light, and airy. It wasn't made of silken threads or luxurious satin, but it was as close to an indulgence I'd experienced in a long, long time.

"You'll need to read a thousand palms to pay Miss Violet back for that dress. Not to mention the others she is having made for you."

I gasped and swung around to face a woman I'd seen at the house several times but never spoken to.

"I'm Helen," she said, staring at me, standing there in nothing but her chemise. Her toes wiggled against the flower-splashed Aubusson rug. She folded her arms, her lips drawn tight, her ice pick gaze piercing my skin. I looked down and realized I might have been given a dress that had been intended for someone else, Helen.

"This is yours?" I said.

The raven-haired woman rolled her eyes. "My word, no. My dresses are always fashioned in deep pinks. Satins and wools, a slew of velvets ordered for the winter season. Muslin? No, my dear. My gowns aren't cut for a virgin nun. Those billowy sleeves will inflate like a balloon at the fair if you catch the breeze the wrong way."

I lifted my arms and looked down, suddenly embarrassed, unsure of what I'd done wrong. My mind wound around what Helen had said about reading palms. As I opened my mouth to ask her what she'd meant, Miss Violet's distinct, staccato gait echoed down the hall.

Helen came closer and whispered aggressively in my ear, "Be sure to fulfill your potential. You'll be gone before you blink twice if you don't. You'll be ruined, like the others."

Her words hit me like buckshot, unnerving me further. I hadn't felt this fear since running from the Christoffs. "My potential?" I reached for my leg where the crystal ball should have laid against it.

Helen sighed. She pulled my arm. "I'm supposed to let you know that the Archibald Chamberlin stock is about to rise like the morning sun. Make sure you tell Judge Calder that exact thing when he fishes around for information on investments."

My mouth went dry. My tongue stuck to the roof of my mouth. "I don't understand."

Helen went to the dressing table and drew a stopper out of a crystal perfume bottle. She dragged its wet pointed end along her jawline. "You're supposed to be a real smarty girl. Sure don't hit me that way."

I narrowed my eyes as I strained to sort through the confusion that swept me.

"So smart, so intuitive, so this, so that. You seem a little dense in my estimation—"

"*Hel*-en," Miss Violet's voice blasted through the room. The unfamiliar tone sent a chill twisting up my spine.

She pointed at the woman beside me. "Finish dressing in Olivia's room, please."

The black-haired woman looked away from me; the smirk only tightened on her face as she held Miss Violet's gaze. "Fine. I was just giving her the information you said—"

"Enough," Miss Violet said, her voice now low and thick.

Helen sauntered out, her hips swaying as though she was using them to sass back.

Miss Violet blew out a breath. She put her hands at her sides, fists balled, and came to me. She took my hands and smiled, the cold expression warmed, the strained tendons in her neck softened again. "Now let me see you."

She smoothed my hair and tucked some strands behind my ears and stepped back, putting her hand to her chin. "I'm just not sure yet. Not sure this is the look we want."

I spread out my hands and bounced to my toes. "The dress is beautiful."

Miss Violet waved her hand. "It's fine. But I just don't think . . . angelic, yes. But, well. Let's see how tonight goes, and we'll adjust."

"I don't understand, Miss Violet. I'm getting nervous about this. I don't even know what you want me to do. Helen said I'd be reading palms? I can't do that. I *won't* do that."

Miss Violet straightened. "Trust yourself, Katherine. You've been successful in reading for each of the girls in the house and me. Don't let Helen rattle you. She's provisional. An old friend who I want to keep happy now that she's arrived in Des Moines, so I promised her a chance to work with us. Don't mind her a bit. She's not boarding here."

"What did she mean about Mr. Chamberlin and my potential and . . . it was as though I had done something to offend her."

Miss Violet handed me a silver hand mirror and turned me by the shoulders to see the back of my head. My bun was loose and off-center.

Miss Violet leaned closer and sniffed me.

"Did you bathe?" she asked.

I drew back. My hands shook. I juggled the mirror, dropping it. I hadn't had time to bathe with all the baking and preparation for the meeting tonight. I didn't want to disappoint this woman or her guests in any way.

I covered my mouth and dropped to my knees to get the mirror, fear coursing through me. "I didn't have time. You saw all the food I prepared? And when you came in and said I needed to do this, I didn't think of it."

Violet bent beside me and gently took the mirror from my hands. "You smell a little bit like bread. We'll need to be sure you have time to prepare next time. We need you smelling like flowers, not flour. Certainly, not yeast."

"I'm so sorry," I said.

"It's all right, Katherine. I shouldn't have said that."

Miss Violet petted the back of one of my hands and gazed at me with the same expression Mama often did. As though she loved me. *Love.* I felt it like my heartbeat. Being the center of her attention, her generosity, and mostly, her belief in me, I felt more connected to her each day.

"You can do this," she said. "Think of your family. You want to help them. Your mother works so hard, and *you* can change her life. Most of the women who stay with me never have a chance to make a good life for themselves. Most aren't smart enough to head their own firms. Others don't really want to. As soon as they meet a man, well, it's over."

My fluttering stomach began to settle. "I just worry. What if I can't gather the voices? What if I don't hear the right ones? What if my calming won't come?"

Miss Violet squeezed my hand. "Nonsense. What you can do has been nothing short of a miracle. Your ability to comfort is like nothing else. But today you'll pull from these men something I need. You'll plant seeds for these men, giving them something they need. Remember that Mr. Fink will be very curious to know that Mr. Hampton is selling shares of the construction company. And the bit about Archibald Chamberlin, that will come in handy for Judge Calder. The spirits will gather, you will be calmed, and as long as you remember these bits of information, to seed them, well, we will all benefit greatly."

I nodded. As important as I felt, I didn't like to remember even small bits of information for this purpose.

The bitter dishonesty played on my tongue. I thought of Madame Smalley. "Is it wrong to give information as though the spirits offered it?"

Miss Violet pulled me to standing and curled a tendril of my hair around her forefinger, placing it along the side of my face. She sighed and squeezed my shoulders. "Wrong? No, of course not. We're helping a man to understand his partner is bilking him and all the while offering peace about his relatives who've passed on."

"What if I forget? I'm not in control of this, Miss Violet. I can't control who comes, and I don't always remember what I say once it's over."

"Don't you worry about remembering anything. We'll take care of that. There's a record being made of what's said." Miss Violet's neck tensed again. A vein popped out, scaring me. Still, I didn't want to disappoint Miss Violet.

She exhaled and smiled. "You're safe. I believe in this gift of yours, I do down to my very heart and soul. But, I'm a businesswoman, and I know how the world works. People are afraid of women with gifts, women who are special, who buck convention. I understand your worry, and I can protect you. Only those with invitations are permitted to call on you. No one knows you live next door or that you work for me. And no one knows where Dreama is staying."

I nodded, but I wasn't sure how she could protect me if people got especially nosy. And what if the callers recognized me from somewhere and asked questions?

Violet turned and walked toward her painted bureau and pulled out the middle drawer. She lifted a piece of lace from it. "This is the finest Belgium lace. Olivia sewed it onto this beautiful silk and added some beading, and it's just beautiful."

I traced the intricate curves of lace and tapped the beads at the centers of small daisies and sloping leaves.

Miss Violet coaxed me toward the mirror and stood behind me so we both could see in the mirror. With a fluid motion, Miss Violet floated the fabric over my head and attached it around the back of my head, over my mouth and nose. Only my eyes could be seen. She pulled a glittering tiara and a second piece of veiling from the drawer. "This will shield your stunning eyes just enough. The moody lighting will protect your identity, too."

I touched the lace, seeing if I could breathe through it. The veil was thin enough to allow airflow, but thick enough to conceal.

"I told you I know what happens if people grow unhappy with a woman who walks with spirits. I'll keep you safe," Miss Violet said.

I thought of Mama. Once I netted enough money to help the family, and earned the reputation for helping others, Mama would be proud. Mostly, I agreed to this to fulfill a part of me that was only satisfied in this way. Giving someone peace and contentment and the resulting affection for what I did for people filled me up, made me feel worthy.

"Let's not forget, Katherine."

Miss Violet went back to her drawer and returned bearing summer gloves that bore the same lace pattern as the veil. "We need to keep your missing finger hidden." Miss Violet pulled the gloves onto my hands and held them in hers.

I closed my eyes and drew a deep breath. *Could I do this? Please, God, please calm me, please let the right spirits come.*

"Now you're Dreama," Miss Violet said. She pulled open another drawer and removed a perfume bottle. "This blend is just for you." She pulled the stopper from the bottle and dabbed behind my ears, dipped again, and drew the liquid along the insides of my arms. Marigold.

"Thank you." I felt so grateful. Miss Violet saw my gift and allowed me the chance to explore it, to be the person I was meant to be. For now, that was enough. No, it was so much more. With the Christoffs, I was mistreated and abused by roaming hands, scarce food, for my ability to see the dead, and forced to wear gowns removed from corpses. What Miss Violet had given me was a true gift—her belief that what I could do was heavenly, not of the devil and his fiery hell.

I was nervous about what she wanted from me, but I would try, for her. I thought of how she let me stash an apple where I could find it at any time. She understood me, my needs, better than I could have imagined. If I failed at this, I would risk Miss Violet sending us packing. She appreciated me, but I knew my performance was attached to that.

A flicker of fear pulsed through my chest, snatching my breath. *I can't fail.* Then I caught a glimpse of myself in the mirror. At the sight of me, beautifully attired, cloaked in the mystery not even I fully understood, I felt I could do what was required. And in that moment of internal quiet, I heard the word *trust.* James arrived with the energy I had come to associate with my brother, and I no longer doubted if I would succeed in reaching the spirits.

And with that, Miss Violet and I left the room and headed downstairs to the parlor, to my fate and lost souls and business secrets that powerful men longed to know.

Chapter 22

The First Time
Katherine

I sat at the table Miss Violet had arranged near the fireplace in the parlor. I exhaled deeply, trying to expel my nervousness. I glanced around the room. Mr. Fink and Mr. Hampton smoked cigars and drank whiskey, laughing at jokes I couldn't hear from across the room. Bernice brought me a glass of water. She bent close to talk to me. "Miss Violet said don't worry about Fink and Hampton today. The other girls will manage them. Just Calder for you."

She straightened and sashayed across the room, slipping under the arm of Mr. Fink as though they were old friends. The others milled about the room with men I didn't recognize. Each woman wore a perfectly fitted gown with braided trim around the neckline, waist pinched small, sleeves puffed at the shoulders, and each of their bottoms bustled in the latest fashion. Olivia wore a deep plum shade of satin, her cleavage spilling out at the silken neckline. She played the piano, her fingers dancing over the keys, and as she leaned into the music and pulled back, half the males in the room watched her, moving closer.

Bernice wore an emerald-green silken dress with a V-neckline trimmed in a darker pine-hued fringe. Abigail was dressed in a more modest high-necked, bright pink-and-blue gingham divided by ribbons of black. Her waist was nipped with a watery-blue silken sash. Their high fashion caused me to feel childish in my frilly muslin dress. Each woman's hair was topped with a curly fringe and decorated with flowers or strands of glimmering stones.

Helen wasn't there. This helped to relax me as I did what I'd been told—to sit demurely at the table and wait to be approached. All those women exuded strength and something utterly absorbing, something I clearly did not possess.

The confidence I'd felt upstairs with Miss Violet dissolved at the sight of the mingling men and Miss Violet's employees. I touched my leg where the crystal pendant normally sat. I should have demanded to wear my old underskirt since the new one hadn't been outfitted with a pocket. I wouldn't make this mistake again. At the very least, I'd carry the ball in a pouch.

Judge Calder sauntered toward me, his face red from whiskey, his piercing eyes examining me. He plunked down his tumbler, the dark liquid inside sloshing upward, leaving a thick sepia haze on the glass when it sloshed back down. He scratched his jaw near his ear. I'd been in his home before with his wife, Elizabeth, Mama's old friend. I worried he'd know me. But with years between us, the shedding of my childhood shape, and this lace disguise, there was no way he could guess Dreama's true identity. Still, his eyes bored into mine, scaring me.

I am safe. I am safe. I wished my body would listen to my mind's insistence that all was well. My mouth went dry, my tongue thick, my chest tight with worry.

Miss Sally, a new girl hired just for this event, emerged from the kitchen, her lemon-yellow organza gown brushing over the red Persian rug as she waltzed by with a tray of puffed pastry. Judge Calder took two from the silver tray. He jammed one into his mouth, leaving a crumb on his bottom lip. I counseled myself to breathe deeply. *Please, God, please, James, please send me what I need to know.*

The judge jammed the second puff into his mouth, swallowed and grinned, cheese lumped between his teeth. He tossed back his drink and swished the fluid in his mouth. When he smiled again, the debris was gone.

I closed my eyes and opened them, hoping that someone, anyone from Judge Calder's past, would be there beside him, waiting to connect with him through me. If he would have asked a question, it might have helped. But he simply stared, picking at me with his sharp gaze.

He shifted in his seat. "So this is it? We stare at each other? I could do this with my stupid wife."

My throat began to close. Nothing was coming. No spirits, no feelings, no information, no voice from behind me or inside my mind, nothing. My breath caught as it grew shallow. I clasped my hands in my lap. *Please.*

"Well? I'm waiting." He smirked and pulled his thick ankle up onto his knee. His lip curled, mocking.

I felt as if I were falling out of my chair. My lungs were heavy against my chest. I squeezed my eyes closed. *Please.* When I opened them, Judge Calder was looking over his shoulder. Miss Violet was ten feet away, staring; surprise mixed with worry washed over her face. I couldn't bear this failure. I rose and began to move past the judge, wanting to run out of the house. But as I passed him, he grabbed my wrist.

"Wait."

I stumbled backward but kept my balance. I straightened my veil with my free hand.

My fingers were numb under his iron grip as we stared at each other.

"You were raised better than that, Jeremy Harry Calder." I flinched.

He swallowed, his Adam's apple lifting as he did. He glanced over his shoulder, his expression flashing with uncertainty.

"Enough, Slim Pickens."

Judge Calder's eyes widened.

I fought the urge to cover my mouth, afraid he wouldn't understand my scolding tone came from his mother, not me. I knew it was his mother who'd spoken, but I couldn't see her. I looked around the room and listened intently for something that would indicate I had indeed created an opportunity for his mother to converse.

"Sit," he told me. He continued to bear the expression of someone thrown off balance. "No one knows that name. Harry."

My gaze went over his shoulder to Miss Violet. She looked as though she was about to spring across the room at me. I still wanted to flee, but I knew I must sit, that I finally had something to say.

Judge Calder leaned his ham-sized forearms on the table, his unsure expression contrasting his massive size. "I smell her," he whispered. "Marigold and bread. You've conjured her. Like a witch, haven't you done exactly that?" He slid his gut into the side of the table, trying to get closer to me. He inhaled deeply. "I can *smell* her. I can't believe it. It's like I'm back there, coming home from school and she'd spent the day with the bread."

The perfume Miss Violet had put on me must have mixed with the scent of my own kitchen work. He wasn't smelling his mother. He was smelling me. I wanted so badly to have my pendant with me. If I could gaze into it or just brush my fingertips over it, I was sure I would have something more to convey. I couldn't find the calm that came when I was open to the spirits of people's loved ones. I had to please Violet. *The name.* What was that name Helen had said?

I leaned forward and wiggled my fingers to bring him closer. Just one more word from his mother was all I needed.

Something to give him. Still, nothing came. Maybe I was a fraud? What if I'd been a charlatan all along? Perhaps I'd known his middle name from back when our families spent countless hours together socializing?

He leaned forward. His lips parted, and his whiskey breath bridged us. It was all I could do not to bolt. Finally, Helen's words came to me. "Chamberlin. It's rising up."

That wasn't exactly what she'd told me to say. *What was it?*

He clenched his jaw. Then after drawing a deep breath, he fell back in his seat. He knitted his fingers together over his belly, fat like the cinnamon rounds I'd made earlier that day.

He came forward again in his seat, his midsection knocking the table into me. "Mother said *Chamberlin?*"

I didn't want to lie to him. But what was another lie? *Just go with it.* I nodded, and with my surrender, Helen's words came rushing back. "It will rise like the morning sun."

He scratched his face again, his fingers brushing past his long earlobe with every swipe. "Well, I'll be. She always did have a way with the stocks."

Suddenly, his mother's words were back with me. "Trust your instincts with the company you're considering for investment."

He narrowed his eyes and rubbed his stomach as though he could coax his thoughts from his midsection. He looked around the room before leaning back toward me. "Does she mean Pendergrass, her company?"

I felt a smile tug my lips. Yes, this one last piece I was giving him, that was not grounded in anything spiritual or magical. But it was a chance for me to help Violet in a way I hadn't expected.

"Yes. She says yes."

He sank farther in his chair and stared at the ceiling.

I exhaled and sat back, hoping this bit would be enough to send this man away, satisfied. I watched him mull over what he'd heard. Though happy to have given him the nudge to invest with Miss Violet, I couldn't stop the spread of fear, of disappointment that much of what I revealed, his impression that I *did* anything at all was rooted in the fact I spent the day with my hands buried in bread. And beyond that, Helen had planted information about a company in my mind. That left me drained and worried, wondering what exactly I'd done in letting him think Dreama knew anything at all.

Chapter 23

Alliance
Violet

Violet couldn't breathe. Judge Calder seemed to fluctuate between being mesmerized and confused. Normally, the men who attended her meetings circled the women, talking business, small bits of chatter about nothing, about investments, about their lives. The women typically kept their attention on the man at their side, facile with just the right compliment on his appearance, just the right query about his work, just the right brush of her fingertips over the back of his hand or down his arm to communicate her willingness to do business.

But not this time. All attention was on the girl in the frilled collar with the veiled face and tall, delicate figure. Katherine had faltered, her nervousness obvious. Violet had shared Katherine's panic like an animal in the wild knew when another was about to be devoured by a predator.

And then, as Violet was headed across the room to rescue her, already pulling Olivia over to read the prophecy chart or the judge's palm or tea leaves or whatever, everything turned. She didn't hear what the judge said to

Katherine when he grabbed her wrist as she was bolting, but she could sense what was said was good.

Within seconds, Katherine was back in her seat, and the reading went off without another hesitation. From that point, the judge and Katherine exchanged a few more words, and he was out of his seat, grinning, heading right for Violet with his hand extended.

Violet stole a final glance at Katherine, who had relaxed into her chair and was smoothing the golden damask tablecloth in front of her. The judge nodded and offered his arm to Violet. "My lady," he said, his voice syrupy and kind, like the first day she met him when she arrived in Des Moines. He'd been sweet that day and a few times since then, but she knew he had a bitter streak that sharpened his tongue. Violet laced her arm through the judge's and let him whisk her away to discuss his future plans for investing.

Once inside Violet's office at the far end of the first floor, Judge Calder paced. He stopped and stared upward at the top shelf of books and ran his finger along the spines of the ones in front of him. He paced again, a lion in a circus cage. She poured him a whiskey, and he tossed it back. He pointed his finger at her.

"What *exactly* is being run here? You don't think for a second you can sweep into Des Moines, this fine town, and sully it with anything untoward? We're cleaning up the filth. If you haven't noticed the vagrants and imbeciles and corrupt aldermen we've been putting away lately, I can show you the records. This isn't a game. What exactly are you asking me to invest in here?"

Violet shook her head, stunned—all the honey in his mood had crusted over and blown away. He paced back to her. He stood so close that his toes pushed her dress, the hem lapping at the tops of his shoes. It had been a long time since she'd been in the position to feel threatened.

She straightened farther. She would not be pushed around by a man who was pretending to clean up a town for the good of its citizens but was actually being paid to place people in asylums and work farms, as she'd heard he was. The girls in the house did their job in collecting gossip whenever they went to town, and she felt safer knowing it.

"I furnished my letters of reference," she said, "I'd say Corneilus Vanderbilt is as fine a recommendation as one could garner. My references speak for themselves. I allowed you a view of my portfolio and investment strategy. You've seen my results." She felt attacked, as though his moods swung on a trapeze, washing her with his glee and now his anger. She didn't have interest in working with a man who blew like a reed in the wind. She wiggled away from him and went to her desk, leaning back against it, ankles crossed in front of her, trying to convey ease, trying to cover up that her heart beat so hard it dizzied her. "I don't need your business, Judge. It's quite fine. Mr. Fink is salivating to—"

He rushed to her, his face suddenly full of passion. She couldn't tell if he wanted to hit her or kiss her. He leaned past her and grabbed the bottle of whiskey on the desk. She caught a musky cologne scent that stretched somewhere deep inside her and softened her toward him.

He took a swig. "I don't know how you made it so I thought my mother appeared to that Dreama person, to me, but you did and I can't—it's unsettling. It's . . . I'm . . . stunned."

Violet was confused. She rested her hands against his chest. She could feel his heart pound under her hand. He towered over her, yet she was sure the threat she'd felt just seconds ago was gone.

His body relaxed against hers, and he leaned forward, his arm looping her waist as he pulled her hips into him. His midsection was thick, but feeling him pressed against her, she discovered him to be muscular, hardy rather than jelly-like. Was he going to push her into something right here? She would not scream for help. She did not want help. She did not need help. This was what she had wanted for weeks.

"Thinking my mother was communicating with me gave me a sense of joy I haven't felt in ages," he whispered, his awe dissolving away his typical bravado, leaving behind the countenance of a younger man who had not yet found his identity in the real world. His sudden vulnerability fascinated Violet, made her want him.

He looked down at her. She waited for the inevitable, his lips on hers. But instead, he backed off. He stalked to the door and came back. "I don't know what just happened out there. But you're right. I've seen your numbers in the books. I don't doubt your mind for investments. And now I've just seen that—whatever *that* was—and all I know is I want to work with you, Violet Pendergrass. My mother consulted me on the matter, and with *that* kind of recommendation, I can't turn away without feeling a dumber man than I want to be. Screw Vanderbilt. My own mother just recommended you."

She leaned against the walnut desk behind her, her fingers gripping the edge.

"Did you hear what I just said? The insanity," he hissed. "Yet something about what happened was real, down in my very bones, real. And I'm jovial . . . I can't explain it."

Violet had had men force themselves on her before. She'd had men afraid to even speak to her, but something in the way he fell on her and then drew back was odd beyond anything she'd experienced. What on earth was happening? She knew this was not the time to question. She thought of Katherine. *Was she real?* She certainly was sure something happened in the kitchen that day with Olivia, that day Katherine communicated information supposedly from her own father. Consultation with her heart told Violet those moments were genuine in some way, very real. But it wasn't as though Katherine knew what her father might be disappointed in. Everyone can guess a person's father has disappointments. But the girls in the house had been coached to go along with whatever Katherine said. To give her a chance to try to intuit reasonable facts, to see if Katherine could read body language enough to present herself to the world as Dreama. Whatever was "real," Katherine was gifted in communicating it.

"This could make us a fortune, Violet Pendergrass. You're cleverer than your financial success suggests."

She pressed her hand to her throat. She was flattered at his enthusiasm for her skill, for wanting to do business with her, but she was put off by his deciding there was to be an "us." She wanted his body in her bed, his money in her purse, his power clearing the way in the courtroom if necessary, but there was no "us" as it pertained to her work.

Violet reached behind her and lifted the whiskey bottle toward him. He must have misspoken. He had much to lose in life, including his wife, and she knew the last thing this man wanted was a melding of each of them into an "us." She would let it pass and count on it being an excitable utterance. She splashed the brown liquid into two glasses and lifted one to her lips.

He strolled back to her, hands in his pockets, smiling with the abandon of a young man who'd worked his hand into his first bodice, in a way that reminded her of when she'd first met Edwin.

He took the glass and clinked it with hers.

"We've got a lot to discuss, Judge. Much to define."

He drank the whiskey. "We do, little lady, we do."

Violet finished her drink. She told herself not to worry about Katherine, that Olivia knew to take her upstairs, have her change her clothes, give her the small pouch of coins, and head down the back stairs so she could leave unseen. No one outside of three girls would be the wiser about who Dreama was. And she would let the judge have his "little lady" comment a little bit longer.

She would unfold herself for him a layer at a time. Like a rich, aged whiskey that bit the tongue before its flavor delighted and it numbed the soul and made one yearn for more. For that moment Violet would swallow the bile that came with letting him believe she would ever be anyone's little lady.

Chapter 24

Distraction
Aleksey

I couldn't concentrate. I rubbed my eyes and took another swallow of black coffee. At the table in the kitchen I shifted, staring at the books splayed on the table before me. The pencil rested beside my notebook, like my tired mind. The crystal butterfly stone was perched on the spine of the open *Laws of Mergers and Acquisitions* textbook. I slumped back in the chair, stretched my legs, and looked out the window above the sink. Clouds kept the full moon from lighting the space, but I knew from the past months I'd been living at Palmer's place that at midnight, if unveiled, the celestial face would show itself in the window, and if it had been visible, I could squint and see the mottled gray splotches that covered it.

I picked up the butterfly stone and held it into the lamplight, turning it slowly as some striations captured the light and others obscured it. Ice—the thought that I was the owner of a chunk of ice that never melted kept me mesmerized by it.

I thought of all the stones I'd found while working the section of the wall near the Medusa tree. Tiny fragments of purple, clear, shimmering blues, and matte greens found their way into my pocket and then into the trunk with Mrs. Palmer's journal and the first specimens I'd found. I put the butterfly stone off to my left and lifted one side of the textbook. I slid out Winnie's cure book that I'd hidden under it, calling me to read it.

I opened it somewhere near the end, reading the book out of order yet again.

> *Beef Stew—hardy winter meal for healing*
>
> *The farmer down the way, Mr. Sterling, came calling. His wife was shrinking in front of his eyes, he said, her skin disappearing right off the bone. I made him this stew and took it over with Beda. I took one of Andrew's agates—the one he'd been given when he completed his journey to be a full Granger—to her for strength. Also took smoky quartz, turned up near the walnut tree that separated our property from theirs. Finally, a purple amethyst to quiet her mind and allow the spirit to enter her body and do its work in healing her aggressive illness. Note—I told Andrew the agate fell and shattered and that he should not look for it, that I would replace it. As anticipated, he wasn't pleased. He suspects my involvement next door and with Madame. I don't like to lie, but he won't listen to the truth. Wants to protect me. Foraging for the right mushrooms is becoming harder as he keeps me under his thumb.*

What was that all about? There was a sketch of different rocks below the text. Winnie had added dyes to make some of the stones blue and purple, shading with a pencil to turn the others smoky. None of it made sense, and I surely didn't have the time to decode the secrets of a recipe book that had nothing to do with me, yet I was drawn to it. The mystery of it kept me reading. I kept waiting for a page in the book to reveal something about the butterfly stone that was now my constant companion, but so far—nothing. I'd only allow myself a couple pages a night at most. Otherwise, I would have no excuse for why I couldn't pass my exams or complete the work for Palmer.

And tomorrow I would visit the Arthur home, finally. Something about it moved me deep inside. I admired Mrs. Arthur so much. My ma counted her as one of her dearest friends, her best friend, really, to this day. I was eager to see Tommy, too. And, of course, Katherine.

Katherine, Katherine, Katherine.

Her name tumbled through my mind regularly now that I'd seen her. It didn't make sense, I knew. But I needed to see her again. I needed to hear the story behind the new darkness in her eyes. I thought of the dance at the riverside the other night. I'd danced many times with pretty girls, and it had been fun. But even as I'd held this woman or that in my arms, my mind returned to my old friend, wanting to know all the things her eyes had hidden from me the other day.

Chapter 25

Remembering
Katherine

Yale's feet pushed against my legs. She tossed and turned, rousing me from sleep completely. I waited for her to fall back asleep but instead she straddled me and started to climb down from the bed. Not wanting to wake Mama, I took Yale downstairs and whispered fairy tales and myths to her as I walked the floor, her head on my shoulder. I stopped at the window and slid the muslin curtain aside to see the full moon emerge between two massive clouds before hiding away again.

The stories I told Yale reminded me of the reading I used to do with Aleksey—Zeus, Athena, fairy tales, science, and history. I read small sections at a time and then he would read to me as he got better and better. I'd taught him cursive and how to write a proper book report. There was something safe in that remembering. Even in one of the hardest years of my life, there was that joy, that sliver of something precious for me, something I'd largely forgotten about until I saw him at the orange crates at the grocer's.

"She would not steal!" his protective bellowing brought it all back to me. I thought of Judge Calder and how poorly the reading went. Was that stealing? Had I done the same thing people accused Madame Smalley of last night?

Too tired to think clearly about whether I was an accidental thief, my mind wandered back to Aleksey. His bravery during the blizzard kept Yale and me alive that night. He used to look up to me, amazed by how smart I was. And now he was studying the law. What would he think of my life now? Would he still be amazed by me? I couldn't share what I was with him. Not with how things had changed. How noble he was. How lost I was.

No matter. Neither one of us had time for the other. Our friendship would be crippled by the amount of work each of us had to do. He'd never have to know that I was anything other than what he remembered. For wasn't that the best part of one's past? All that was stays the same, true, perfect in its own way.

Chapter 26

A Solid Plan
Katherine

We're not crying people. I inched toward consciousness and Mama's weeping, the same I'd heard every morning since I'd been back with her. My silence, pretending to still sleep, lent her privacy. A quick glance toward the front windows revealed the navy-blue light of night was turning turquoise bright. Had I wakened earlier, I would be downstairs now. Had I slept longer, I wouldn't hear Mama's private, grief-filled moment.

We're not crying people.

Yet after all this time of her swearing she wasn't, Mama was just that kind of person. To let those tears fall must have been like a great mountain range that eventually "allows" a river to run through it. The rock has no choice but to give a part of itself up.

I remembered the mama who had spoken so strong and sure back before all of this. And I would've believed it was so, that Mama never shed a tear, if not for these daily moments. She would sit up in bed, shift to the edge, putting her back to Yale and me, her shoulders slumped.

The mattress would quiver as she shuddered and attempted to keep her cries quiet. I'd hold my breath and resist the urge to offer comfort. My interference wouldn't be a solace, but instead would mortify Mama. Always, at least one audible sob would come. It didn't last long. I imagined a mythical creature, like Medusa or something the Greeks never envisioned, who crept into people's dreams and poured from a great pitcher a stream of liquid pain that Mama would have to uncork and let flow away each morning in order to go on.

After just moments, Mama would draw a deep breath, wipe her eyes, and go about getting dressed for morning as though a wave of turmoil had not just coursed through and out of her. Only then would I begin to stir, pretending to just waken. This morning, I knocked my sketchbook to the floor. Mama squatted down and picked it up. She put her finger to her lips and jerked her head to the door. "Tea," she said, and we crept downstairs while Yale slept after being up in the night.

On the way to the kitchen, the events of the night before came rushing back. Judge Calder's reading. From my vantage point, it had gone terribly but, apparently, he thought it went just as he wanted. When I'd left Miss Violet's, I had been given a small linen pouch of coins for my work. The payment left me with mixed feelings—I didn't want to do that work, that way, offering information that hadn't come from my conversation with the judge's mother—for Miss Violet. But the money. I had stowed it in an empty tobacco box in the front parlor until I could decide whether to give it back and refuse to read again or submit to being Dreama and give it to Mama.

I pulled the doll I'd been making for Yale off the settee. We reached the kitchen, and Mama lit the fire while I inventoried the tea selection, jars and tins of chamomile, lemon, and black teas. More herbs were hanging to dry in the warm kitchen. This kitchen was rustic with a stone fireplace surround, wooden planked walls, cedar floor, and plain pine furnishings, but I was pleased to decorate the space with many of the spoils from Mama's garden. While stocking Miss Violet's kitchen came first, I made sure Mama had fresh flowers on her worktable and at least the basic herbs and canned fruits and vegetables to ensure enough to eat when times were leaner. Though Miss Violet's kitchen was bright with expensive tiles, new gadgets, and matching place settings, Mama's smelled just as fresh and alive as Miss Violet's did. For that, I was very grateful.

Our stove had been lit already.

"Wonder where Tommy got to," I said.

Mama straightened and adjusted the flue. "Probably at Violet's lighting her stove," she said. "And he got another letter from your father."

"Another?"

She nodded. "More of the same."

I didn't know what I thought about this. I didn't know what to say, what Mama might want to hear from me on the matter.

She shrugged and busied herself at the pump. "The potential disappointment is too great to entertain such ideas."

"The letter Tommy had before," I cleared my throat, my voice shakier than I wanted it to be when discussing this matter, "read like more empty promises, the kind that—"

She startled and jerked toward me. "Oh, I'm sorry, Katherine. I didn't mean to upset you."

"It's all right, Mama. Father wasn't clear about coming. Not in the letters I read, anyway. I know that."

She looked defeated. I hadn't meant to squash her interest in my father if she had entertained him coming back. If he did return and contribute to our family, I wouldn't need to worry about earning extra money being Dreama. No, no, no. There was no use wishing or wondering about something that wouldn't happen. I knew neither of us wanted to further explore any what-ifs related to my father.

I held up the half-made doll. "I'll paint the face onto the fabric and add the hair just as soon as I can."

"It'll be beautiful, Katherine. She deserves a real doll, not just that wooden spoon she drags around. Thank you."

Mama opened the stove door and stirred the cinders. When she stood and turned to me, I saw that she was surrounded by a warm light. Awed by the sight, I froze. The presence was lovely, kind.

"You have an angel," I said, pointing with the doll.

Mama straightened, her eyes darting. "She is an angel, isn't she?"

I smiled. Why couldn't this kind of thing have happened last night when I was with the judge? Yes, his mother had given me information, but it didn't feel like this—warm, loving, natural. I wouldn't have felt like a fraud if it had unfolded like this. I thought of my plan not to disclose my work with Violet to Mama. I thought of the Christoffs and the church members who believed me to be the devil's companion. Mama deserved to have peace, didn't she? I didn't have to tell her everything. Just enough to give her comfort.

"No, I mean you have an angel, someone watching over you."

She stared at me. "You're spooking me."

"I don't mean to."

Mama smoothed her skirts. "Like the angels you've been drawing?"

I hadn't realized Mama had seen those.

I shrugged, hoping this opening might be what I needed to explain once it was time. "Sort of. Yes, I suppose. The images come to me like a faucet brings water. I don't force it. It sort of comes. When it wants to, I mean. Like, well, I believe we all have energy around us we can't see."

"You're paying attention to science class, I see," Mama said.

I hated this lie, this one in particular because school was something I had wanted as much as Mama did. "I'm talking about the drawings, what I see when I draw and—"

"You're a talented artist. I've always said so."

I stiffened, my shoulders tight. I rubbed the back of my neck.

"How do you find the time to draw with all your work? And a doll for Yale? How do you find the time with your work and studies with Miss Violet?" Mama came closer, visibly nervous. "You okay?"

I pushed a cuticle back with my nail. I hadn't been doing much studying between baking and cooking and preparing to work as Dreama. Oh, how the lies were piling up. And yet seeing this angel this very morning, I was reassured that my secret work was my biggest truth. That I could trust it. "Why don't you want to have an angel, Mama? People want to know these things, want comfort from God and—"

Mama smoothed the shoulder of my dress. "It's a lovely thought." She kissed my forehead. "And I thank you for it. I know when the fires came on the prairie you took great comfort in such ideas."

"You don't believe in me?"

"Of course, I do."

"Then trust me. You have angels."

Mama flinched. "It's not a matter of trust in a general sense—it's specifically the kinds of things one should trust. Look at me. I had everything. Now, I'm just barely scratching a life together. I trust that if you study and go to college, you will hold your riches in your mind and never be without. When you talk like this and spend an inordinate amount of time drawing angels and whatnot . . . it's true, I begin to worry that you're not building the life you'll need to survive. Maybe Miss Violet isn't the right teacher. East High School doesn't even open for a couple of weeks. We can still get you in there."

"No!" I startled myself at my response.

Mama's eyes widened. She cocked her head at me.

"I mean, look. Hold on a moment." I ran to the front room and dug the pouch out of the tobacco box.

"I've earned this money. Extra so far."

"Baking?"

Don't tell her yet. "I bake *a lot*, Mama." I handed her the pouch, the coins clinking. She stared at the linen, running her thumb over the fabric.

"And as far as the doll goes," I said, "I've added lavender and boneset to the stuffing for peace and protection. I think Yale can use a little of that. Miss Violet found this wonderful book of recipes I'm using along with what I already know. There's a whole section that describes how the very herbs you grow can help all of us. I'm learning so many different things, Mama."

She nodded. Her eyes met mine as they filled. I didn't want to cause her to cry, so I continued to talk, upbeat, trying to convey my excitement and investment in the idea of success. "Every man who does a deal with Miss Violet takes home loaves of bread to his family. And we sell it to the grocer. I'm doing really well for us, Mama."

She opened the strings and peered inside at the nickels and pennies. She shook her head. "This is a nice sum. But I don't know about straying from our original plan—the basics required to graduate. I love your heart's intentions, your kindness. But I feel like you're going several different directions all at once. I don't want you distracted by things like angels and recipe books and—"

I took Mama by the shoulders, making her meet my gaze. "Think of it this way. My working with Miss Violet is important to me. And I can see you think the idea of angels to be fantasy. But I feel like I have them near me, that maybe James is one of them, that you have one. I know it sounds—"

She stepped toward me. "It's a nice thought, a soothing idea. But I've never felt as though James has been far from me. Why, the thinning and graying and bluing of the sky has me forever looking upward. So, I understand you might find comfort in thinking this. But I want your feet grounded, turned on a solid path, like the one that education provides. I worry when you say these things and then I see how much drawing you've done or the time you spent on the doll. While the gesture for Yale is precious, and I love that, I have to wonder how you can manage all of that, work for Miss Violet and study?"

I sighed. This was not the time to disclose anything beyond what I already had. "Think of this. You planted that garden from nothing, from utterly unusable, clay-clumped dirt. You added sand and loam and tilled and worked that land until it burst open with all that we need to eat to live. You trusted that planting those seeds would yield something useful, something completely unseen until the sprouts showed themselves as healthy. I'm doing the same thing. My education is held in a seed in rich soil that consists of many layers and pieces. You trusted the earth to produce what you needed. Please trust me."

Mama pulled the strings on the sack closed. When she looked up, her eyes were still watery, but her expression was now unreadable. She forced a smile. "This money is extra beyond our room and board?"

I nodded. She swallowed hard, leaving me unsure as to what she was thinking. "We'll talk when I get back from the store. Don't forget to check on Yale. She should sleep for at least two hours, but now that she's up and around on her own so much—"

I backed away. "I know. Luckily I woke up when she was climbing out of bed in the middle of the night. "

"It's good that she's finally exploring, but—"

"I know, I know." I moved the kettle to the hottest part of the stove.

Mama was quiet behind me and slipped her arm around my waist and held tight. "I'm proud of you for working so hard. This money's a gift. Thank you."

And she was headed back upstairs to get dressed for the day, leaving me to make the tea.

I took three mismatched plates from the shelf near the door. Mama's creased face revealed her worries. I didn't want to add to her burden. I needed to balance what I knew could help us with what she might think if she found out about it. I pulled one of the tins from the shelf and stared into it, the aromatic scent of bergamot, black leaves, and lemon grass rising into my nose.

I swallowed hard. I wanted to flush away my lies. I wanted to prove to Mama that I was capable, that we could soon buy our own property. I drew a deep breath. Though I didn't feel confident after what happened with Judge Calder the night before, that moment, seeing Mama's face, reignited my determination to make Dreama work.

If I could earn a few pouches of coins a week, then I could take Mama from here. I could remove the worry of room and board—we could be self-sufficient, and if Father decided to come back, it would not change our position.

It might be a welcome thing if there was no pressure to depend on him for our livelihood, if he could just be with us. And so as I scooped the tea into the strainer and pushed the arms into the kettle to ready for pouring, I resolved to find a way to bring my angels, bring the dead into the room when I needed them as much as when they needed me.

I thought again of Mama's folded brow, her daily tears, of all the things that happened to her that I hadn't even been witness to the past few years. I hadn't even considered what she might have gone through while we were separated. My pain had pinched off my worry for her. I pulled the honey pot toward me and pushed the dipper into the golden thickness. Mama had enough to do. I would free us all from worry, and being Dreama was precisely how I'd do it.

Chapter 27

Back and Forth
Katherine

Back and forth all day long. In Miss Violet's kitchen, I kneaded the bread, working as fast as I could. Then I'd rush to check on Yale, bringing her to Miss Violet's for a few hours while I made several pies and also tried my hand at starting the process of making parmesan cheese. This particular group who was coming to meet with Miss Violet and the other ladies consisted of what Miss Violet called "leading citizens." And they didn't request a large meal, but instead she'd decided a combination of egg pies and fruit pies along with teas, coffee, and chocolate would offer a sense of calm and open them up for good dealings without overstuffing them. She'd requested various breads, jellies, and mustards for the evening as well.

It didn't take much activity for Yale to be ready for another nap. I considered setting up a place for her out on the porch, but I worried about her waking and wandering into the gardens or beyond. Then I'd made a small nest for Yale near the back wall but decided that Yale would be safest and most comfortable in our own bed next door.

I raced back and forth several times, in between the baking of one loaf and the rising of another. With every push and pull, the dough squashed between my fingers, emitting a fresh odor. I worked fast; my forearms were relaxing and contracting, nearly cramping.

The monotonous movement gave my mind space. I thought of all the things Mama wanted in our cottage and garden. I imagined a kitchen, cozy, like the one at our house, but perhaps with happy yellow walls like at Violet's. Perhaps I could bring a little bit of the magic I saw in Violet into my life, to keep long after we Arthurs were gone from here.

Chapter 28

Just Business
Violet

Violet couldn't breathe. Excitement sizzled in her bloodstream at the thought of having the prominent Judge Calder support her establishment, to run interference if necessary. The minute she'd met him, she'd felt a stirring. She appraised him standing across from her. He wasn't good-looking in the delicate, fine-featured, perfectly coiffed hair way that some men were. He was massive in size, but his barrel chest and thick belly grew smaller at the waist, drawing her gaze downward, at least for a few seconds each time she saw him.

His thick curls called to her fingers, his coffee-colored eyes alternately warm when he looked at her and detached when he discussed matters that others were softhearted about. She often flinched at his sharp tone when discussing wayward children and derelict adults. The casual way he mentioned shuttling this man or that woman into Glenwood Home for the Insane brought back thoughts of her father, the way the world had seen him but hadn't known him.

Different from other callous men she'd known in her life, for some reason the idea of softening Jeremy only made him all the more attractive to her. It was dangerous, but she didn't care. She had no intention of falling prey to him, and because she saw the risk in being with a cold, calculating man, she thought she could manage him. She was excited by the challenge of making him a better man than he was when she found him.

The reward of turning a problematic beast soft inside and hard in all the places a man should be enticed Violet like nothing else. His money and standing in the community added to her need for conquest as much as her raw attraction to him. Violet didn't let the idea that it had been Katherine performing as Dreama that finally tipped his interest in her business bother her. No. She could appreciate Katherine's value without having to overplay it in her mind or undermine her own importance. Instead, Violet congratulated herself on recognizing Katherine's greatness and making it work. The coincidence that Jeremy's mother happened to love and smell like marigolds, and so had the perfume Katherine was wearing, only lent more mystery to what had happened.

Violet struck a match against the stone fireplace. She leaned in enough for him to glimpse her cleavage, inhale the scent of her rose perfume, the musky French blend that was far different—sophisticated and thick—from the light scent he associated with Dreama and his mother.

Violet stepped back from him and waved the match to put it out, the smoke circling her hand. She glanced at the table, at the book she'd lent him to peruse the details of the business—a ledger that did not include the same narrative about all the girls and the men that her personal records did. "Did you have a look at this week's transactions?"

He nodded, his gaze lingering on her mouth, flicking over her waist and back up to her eyes again. "Of course. You run a fine, tight business. Robust," his eyes fell on her breasts, "I would say. Robust. I've said that before."

She nodded. "Of course." Heat built between her legs as she watched him watch her. They'd been dancing around each other for weeks. When they worked, she would swipe her fingers across the back of his hand as they bent over a contract. She might brush his backside with her hip as she passed him on the way to her desk. She'd catch his glance working into her cleavage and revel in the warmth his hand brought to the small of her back as they walked to the door when it was time for him to go. In response to his hand on her, up until this point, she had always pulled away just as he was turning closer attention on her. She would bring up some part of her business, giving him the sense that she had other things to muse over than him.

The effects of the dance she'd lured him into had been positive. Violet could feel lust take hold of him and see it flash across his face as he licked his lips, his cheeks flushing as he garbled his words. And she'd direct him back to the papers. His desire was for more than her mind. That was always her plan—to seed their relationship with layers of need and desire. The other girls had been successful with the men who frequented her business, and Violet could see that she had finally made real progress in preparing fertile ground with Jeremy.

She'd been patient, knowing she needed to reel in this particular man more than any of the others. She'd done fine by him with his investments, but it was his position in the community that would allow her to grow the business of Dreama with little interference by the police, nosy housewives, or zealous religious folks.

It hadn't been an accident that she'd selected Des Moines as her next home. The men she knew in New York had connections with other wealthy, powerful men all over the country. They spoke often about Des Moines, its strength in coal and steel. It had wrestled—or stolen, as many said—the honor of state capital away from Iowa City and asserted its influence in politics and culture. Des Moines's population ballooned, and with it came the scramble to create local government that worked for its people. But of course, in a town where its inhabitants grew with every stiff wind, it was wide open for the smartest, bravest, and wiliest of men and women to find their place at the top of the town's heap.

Violet didn't care for society in the way that most women did. She didn't search for a man to hide her away under his arm, protecting her from the world only to become her worst oppressor.

She certainly didn't believe in love. But she understood the power of a woman who could use her feminine prowess along with her very sharp mind. She knew in choosing Des Moines she'd find risk-takers. She'd find progressive thinkers. And because the town was rapidly changing and growing as she came on scene, there were fewer historical ties among men, women, and families. She wouldn't have to claw past every woman in town to make her way. She would simply step over them when they'd retired for the night, exhausted from trying to replicate the society living common farther east.

It had only taken a week for her to identify Judge Jeremy Calder as a potential ally, open to breaking rules, but with the aura of pristine character. Violet wiggled her ledger onto a shelf between a dictionary and a Bible and turned as the judge puffed on his pipe, eyes closed as though the act of smoking brought him religious peace and contentment. He opened them, sleepily gazing at her through the sweet haze.

"Violet." There was something thick and wanting in his voice.

And she wanted him, ready to move things past the point of teasing. She lifted her eyebrows, deep breaths pushing her breasts up. His desire emanated from across the room.

He cleared his throat. "You know, my wife—"

She waved her finger at him. "No, no. Jeremy. _We_ don't include _her_. No need to mention her. Ever."

He stepped closer. His eyes blazed with the hunger she'd seen on many a man. He sauntered toward her, finally close enough for her to feel his yearning as waves of desire rolled off his body.

"Nothing to discuss on the matter of my wife?"

He's not quite ready yet if he's mentioning her.

Violet shook her head and stepped away, their eyes still on one another.

"You make me lose all sense," he whispered, then shoved his pipe into his mouth, teeth clicking onto the stem. All the hard edges in his tone dissolved.

She smiled and brushed her hand over her stomach slowly.

He pulled his pipe from his mouth. "You're well aware of your allure."

She stepped back and put her arms up, gripping the shelves behind her. "I am."

"It's time we capture the nature of our relationship on paper." He came to her, pressing against her just enough that she could feel his excitement.

"Our relationship is set in stone already. *This*," she ran her hand up his leg and cupped him, "is different. I don't run a whorehouse. And I don't mind you having a wife. But there's no need for anything to be recorded in regard to . . . us."

She drew her hand up and down. He shuddered under her touch. He took her face in his hands. "Understood," he said. "You understand me, Violet Pendergrass. Like no other woman. Better than most men."

She walked her fingers upward and undid the buttons on his coat, pushing it over his shoulders. He tossed it to the side, and she unbuttoned his vest. He took one of her hands and nibbled her fingers, causing her to push her hips into him, marveling at how off-center she felt, her desire familiar but not frequent with most men she'd laid with.

She worked her fingers into his waistband, his skin radiating heat through his shirt. She lifted the shirttail out of his trousers, her palm against his belly, warming her.

He set the pipe on the shelf over her head, his sharp mask completely melted away. He leaned in, kissing her hard. He wrapped his arms around her, arching her back. There it was—the surrender she'd been waiting for.

His was evident, and she'd known it was coming, but it was her own submission—the lust she felt for him—that shocked her. She fell fully into his arms, and he scooped her up like a feather and was at the settee in three strides. He laid her down and got onto one knee. Then, with unexpected deftness, he caressed her hair, kissing her gently, his eyes watching hers, connecting with her far deeper than their skin allowed. She'd expected him to tear away at her clothing— she wanted him to—but he studied her, followed his fingers with his eyes as though wanting to savor her, not conquer her. He traced every rise and fall of her face. She almost told him to get on with it, but the pleasure in his slowness left her dumbstruck. He got to the end of the settee and lifted her skirts, drawing his fingers up her legs, nearly sending her over the edge as his touch reached her knees, circling them. He gently lifted and bent her legs and untied her garters. He unrolled one stocking, his lips following the fabric downward while his hands kneaded her thighs.

She pulled on his shirtsleeves to coax him upward and pressed her hips toward him, wanting to feel his weight on her. But all he did was chuckle, moving even slower, much more controlled than she expected. He removed her second stocking with the same care and then massaged his way up her legs, kissing her all the way, pausing between her legs, sending her heart nearly through her chest.

And even though knowing better, knowing that this affection meant nothing more than simple lust, she couldn't stop her heart from opening a little more. And as he disrobed and finally lay with her, his body warm over hers, when she felt the unexpected swell inside her chest, she pushed him away. She scooted onto her bottom, her hand pressing into his chest to keep him at bay as she caught her breath.

"What is it?" he said.

She gasped and pressed her hand to her own chest, trying to stop the sensation that had bloomed there. What was this? She shook away the thought that the feeling was leaning toward something deeper than lust.

He took her hand and kissed her fingers. "Let me ravish you, Violet. For these moments, let me take you the way you swallow me whole every blessed time we're in the same room."

She looked into his eyes. There was something in them that had changed, like the feeling in her heart had. *It's business, it's a contract, it's nothing.* She'd learned again and again over the years, in and out of many beds, that this trespass she allowed was, in fact, survival.

But as he cupped her breasts and kissed them, she gave in to something else, reclining, not sure what was happening, but letting it occur anyway.

Chapter 29

Precautions
Violet

Violet entered the kitchen to find Katherine with the cuffs of her dress caked in flour, her face splotchy from the oven's heat, hair splashed with doughy ribbons that had dried onto the strands. And she was heading out the back door.

"Katherine." The girl turned to her. "Where are you going?"

"To check on Yale. It's been a while, and Mama's late. I'm sure she'll be home any moment."

Violet nodded, but she knew her irritation showed.

She swiped her hand at Katherine. "Hurry back. We've a lot to do before tonight's reading."

Katherine looked panicked. Violet knew her protégé felt more pressure to perform and had experienced some anxiety after her reading for Judge Calder. "Don't fret. I've thought a lot about helping you with your recent worries."

"And I'll bring my crystal. Not having it made me unsure. I think that was part of the problem."

"Please do. As a matter of fact, I insist you bring it."

Katherine nodded.

"Well, go on and check on your sister."

"I'll be quick." She dashed out the door.

Violet pressed the button that rang the bell in other rooms to call the girls downstairs. While she waited, she considered what had transpired with Jeremy Calder. She wouldn't let that happen again. Not that way. She'd never allowed a man to control the way sex went. All those lingering kisses, attention to every square inch of her. She fell inside the recollection, the power of a simple memory shocking her. She never put herself underneath a man if she could help it. If she was on top or standing or even bent over a desk, she felt she could escape if needed.

Certainly, she'd not allowed a man to map her body from head to toe as she had allowed Jeremy. The pleasure of it had been unmatched, but it left her vulnerable, unsure. It had allowed the sex to wrap itself around her in a different way. The usual tumble of arms and legs, mouths searching, breath gasping, quick finishing before anything had the chance to become meaningful had been absent. She would stay in control from that moment on.

Olivia appeared in the kitchen, wrapped in a silken robe and wearing shoes with feathery toes and no backs.

Violet held her hand up. "Two things."

Olivia's eyes widened, responding to the sharpness in Violet's tone.

"One. Prepare the solution—and the pills. Make sure they're in the bathroom. We can't have anyone turning up with child. A woman is most vulnerable when she becomes a mother."

Olivia counted off on her fingers. "Alum, vinegar, rainwater for down below."

"The apothecary sent over the pills?" Violet said.

"He did—pennyroyal and black cohosh. But Miss Helen took the last two pills."

Violet searched her mind for the pill count. She looked to the table for her ledger but realized she'd left it in her office. That number seemed off. "Last *two*? There should have been twenty."

Olivia swallowed hard. "There were. Some fell into the commode. I knocked the bottle over. Five fell into the water."

"But still. Who took the other pills? I just ordered them."

Olivia's face went gray. Her lips quivered.

Violet stepped closer. "Did you have relations with Colt?"

"You said it was all right if there's something more to it than just . . ."

Violet rubbed her forehead. "And Mr. Tate and Mr. Carnasty?"

Olivia swallowed hard. "It's not the way it sounds. We aren't whoring."

"Shush." She gripped Olivia's arm. She looked frightened. Violet couldn't blame her for indulging with the men. Still, she was angry. "Don't ever use that word in this house."

"I won't," Olivia said, barely getting the words out. "These men, their desire for us is like . . . I don't know. Fire? Twenty minutes into a consultation, he's panting and pressing me. And the truth is, I like it. Working like this on the numbers is exciting, just the way you said it would be and more. Much more!"

Violet released Olivia's arm. She'd told them to expect that. But she'd also instructed them on how to handle this desire. "How many men?"

Olivia looked to the ceiling, her lips moving as she recounted what she knew.

Violet's heart sped up. "Oh my god. You have to *count*?" She'd dressed the women beautifully, taught them the art of seduction, not for bodily purposes, but for the mind. To get the men to confuse their physical arousal with the desire to allow the offices of Pendergrass, Inc. to manage their money. Sexual arousal was a natural pathway through and past this kind of thing. She had to allow her employees the same discretion she gave herself. Free love was important to Violet, but she didn't intend to besmirch her business with an overlapping reputation for whoring.

"I'm just nervous, that's all," Olivia said.

Violet covered her mouth. Would this turn wild and uncontrollable? "Listen, Olivia. It's a fine line, I know. But we need to draw it. Every man is not worthy. Free love is important, but men can get possessive. Even if they have no intention of making a woman his wife. We can't afford a fist fight between clients over the women who are controlling their money. And when a man grows bored of a woman's body, he'll turn away. In this case, he'll turn his money away. We can't afford that. Judiciousness. You must employ it."

Olivia's eyes filled with tears.

Violet sighed. She'd made her point, and she didn't need Olivia acting strange for the meeting. "Don't cry. It's fine. Just keep your focus on the big money, the investments, not something he might leave on the side table—turn *that* back to him every single blessed time. And most of all, don't fall in love. You can't sleep with all of them. Pick wisely, but remember to keep your heart protected, utterly separate from your body when taking him to your bed."

She nodded. "I assure you. My heart is boxed and bowed and tucked in the side-table drawer. But my body? Oh, Violet."

"Colt's attentive, is he?"

Olivia's gaze shot upward and then she closed her eyes. "Oh my, yes."

"Write down everything related to these men and what has transpired between the girls and them. I need every bit of information in order to—" Violet wanted to say *keep us safe*, but didn't want to indicate they weren't. "In order to be sure each man gets what he needs."

"I will," Olivia said holding her hand up as though taking an oath.

"The other reason I called you down is to let you know you need to take on the baking and cooking again."

Olivia's face scrunched up.

"Don't be sour," Violet said.

"But I'm finally making headway with the railroad investment. I can't possibly add more at this point."

"I'll hire a new girl just as soon as I have time to find one with discretion."

"What about my piano?"

"You'll still play at some point each day. We depend on it to create beautiful atmosphere. But I need Katherine freed up to focus on her end of things. That's important."

"Important?" Olivia's jaw tightened.

"Don't be envious." Violet was growing tired of assuaging the girls' egos. But it was necessary. Unhappy, unappreciated people ran their mouths. She waved Olivia to her and took her into an embrace. She rubbed circles into her back, rolling her eyes at the amount of work this end of things took. "The money Katherine will draw at the auditorium will outdo all of us. With a healthy, let's call it an *endowment*, we can invest like never before. The rich get richer."

Olivia pushed back. "The poor?" She puckered her lips.

Violet put her arm around Olivia again. "Don't even pretend that you are one of the poor. I've a book full of numbers saying otherwise. There are men who sit to hear you discuss their portfolio and pay a fee just to do that, just to be allowed to consider investing with you. But a large sum of money invested at once? Why, we'd be set for life in no time. Don't allow envy to jeopardize our work."

Olivia nodded. "I understand. And maybe I can find a new kitchen mistress for you."

"That's my girl," Violet said. "But don't give any information to any candidate for the job. Only I will decide what to reveal when and to whom."

"I understand."

Violet pushed Olivia's hair behind her ears. "I knew you would. Now go on upstairs and do as I said."

**

Katherine entered the kitchen, making Olivia and Violet jump.

"Go on," Violet said.

"I am," Olivia said, heading up the back stairs.

Violet put her hands on her hips and studied Katherine.

"You're a mess with this baking and tending to your sister."

"I'm sorry. Don't be mad, please. Everything's upside down today. I still need to feed her and settle her in for a nap. Tommy'll be there shortly after to take care of her when she wakes. Mama got behind getting you the plants you requested. After this, no more back and forth today. I promise."

Violet shook her head. The garden Katherine's mother was growing with that man, Reed Hayes, was flourishing. If it had shown any signs at all of failing, Violet would have sent Jeanie and the little one packing. But for now, Jeanie Arthur had taken on sewing for some of her old friends, and combined with the gardening she was far too busy to notice Katherine was doing anything different than what they had disclosed and that helped the whole operation work.

Eventually, Dreama would become so successful that Katherine could tell her mother what she was doing without fear. Her mother might be put off to begin with, but Violet knew that wouldn't last. Money had a way of easing doubt about the path a person walked in order to earn it. Violet wouldn't give Katherine too much money—just enough to keep her mother satisfied but not enough to raise suspicion.

"Let's get you upstairs and clean you up for the reading. I have a new dress for you—*five* new dresses, in fact."

"Five? That's too many. I'll never be able to repay you and—"

"You'll need them. Dreama's path to the auditorium, to *A Night for Mothers*, will mean it's necessary to have more than one costume."

For some reason, Katherine's face clouded over.

"Come. Enjoy what I've prepared for you."

Katherine looked over her shoulder. "Thank you, Miss Violet. But the bread needs to come out of the oven. Five more minutes."

"All right. That's reasonable."

"And then I need to feed Yale, take her to the privy, and put her down for a nap. It won't happen again. Mama must've got hung up."

Violet cringed. She looked at the clock. She did have things to do—she needed to do her own rinse for one. She couldn't afford to become pregnant of all things. She should have taken more control with the judge and should have just put her mouth on him until she was certain her fertile time was completely over. Shortsighted. She scolded herself. She replayed her encounter with Jeremy, how she had been orchestrating their communion and then, when instead of him just dropping on top of her and pushing inside like a soulless animal, everything changed. She lost her grasp on everything, allowing him to manage the course they took. She threaded an errant hair behind her ear, suddenly wondering if she appeared completely disheveled.

"Fine, fine, Katherine. Just hurry and meet me upstairs in the dressing room when you get back."

Chapter 30

A Letter Comes
Katherine

Yale and I wandered back from the outhouse through the gardens to the house. She gripped my hand hard and smiled up at me. With her free hand, Yale clutched the doll I'd made her against her chest. My heart thrilled at the sight of her loving that doll as much as my chest pounded hard when I provided someone with comfort from the beyond. When we reached the children's garden, my sister stopped and pressed her palm against her chest. "Me-me."

I pulled up my hem and knelt in front of Yale. Was it possible that Yale was actually communicating with words? I laid my hand on hers. "Yours?"

Yale nodded. "Me-me."

I pulled her onto my lap. "Can you say *mine*?"

Yale leaned back and looked at me. She pressed her lips together. "Mmmmm."

"Say mine, mmmine."

"Mmmiiine." Her dark eyes were soulful, knowing, even though it was clear she was not developing the way most young children did. Her soft gaze on me as she finally said it filled me with love, making me so grateful I had a sister.

I pulled Yale close. Her hair smelled of lemons from the scrubbing we'd given her the day before. "Good girl. That's it. Mine. Keep practicing."

"Miiiine," Yale said as she wiggled out of my grip and moved from the peas to the lettuce.

Yale squatted down and pressed one hand into the soil for support and used her other hand to pull some weedy sprouts that grew beside the lettuce, but not the actual plant. I shook my head, awed that she knew which were weeds and which weren't. When she pulled a few, she laid back, arms spread, and yawned, mouth gaping as sunshine drenched her. Peaceful. It seemed to me Yale was especially luminous under the sun's rays, like a sweet-faced, nearly silent angel had descended, bringing with this little, slow girl unexplained contentment, lending me the sense that that there was nowhere else Yale wanted to be.

She balled her fists and rubbed her eyes.

I stood and dusted off my skirt where I had kneeled on it. I went to Yale and swept her up, covering her face in kisses. "Let's get you down for your nap, little angel. How about that?"

Yale curled into my body, plunging into sleep in seconds. I got her upstairs into bed, only a thin cotton layer over her legs in the stuffy room. I hoisted the window to let in some more air. As I looked her over one last time, I could hear Olivia's piano music as it floated from next door into the room where Yale laid. I hummed along softly and knelt beside the bed and kissed the back of Yale's hand. "Sleep tight, little one. You're safe and sound in your bed. Mama will be back before your eyes flutter even once."

**

I was on my way out, heading back to Miss Violet's, when I noticed an envelope on the table in the kitchen. The way the writing flowed across the envelope drew me to it, telling me it was another from Aleksey even before I read the return address. I stared at the way he'd written his name, the first thing I'd taught him. His writing was now tiny, legible, mature, but his *K*s still bore the awkward legs he'd struggled in making all those years back. I dragged my finger over his name, thinking I could pick his writing out of a million others. I smiled. This time it was only addressed to me, not Mama and the Arthur family.

A flutter came to my stomach, making me recall seeing Aleksey at the grocer's. I remembered looking at the butterfly, perched on the orange, then on my hand, then back on the oranges. Now it felt as though the butterfly had found its way into my stomach.

I'd never felt an excited sensation this way, deep inside.

I carefully slid my finger under the flap and worked it open without ripping any part of it.

> *Katherine,*
>
> *Please forgive my not calling yet. I intended to have been there several times by now, but my work at the farm and in my studies has tied me up tight. I hesitate to send this to you. But I wrote it and then as it sat here, beside my Mergers and Acquisitions book, I couldn't help but think to send it. You may burn it immediately if it offends you. I confess I can't quite explain how all of this has risen out of nowhere upon seeing you that day at the orange crates. But alas, like one of those fairy tales or myths you used to teach me, I feel as though our friendship instantly came alive upon seeing you.*
>
> *Do you feel the same surprising connection and interest in rekindling our friendship?*
>
> *No. Don't answer that. I rather think this is not at all what you've been thinking. But if you've read this far, please allow an old friend to tell you some of the thoughts that have been my constant companion since seeing you last.*

As I write, I recall your hand on mine as you taught me my lettering all those years ago. Do you remember that? Remember how you would scold me for letting my mind wander away from our studies? Your quick assessment of my performance and abrupt rebuke used to make me grin, and that made you even madder. You said if you were a man that I would not have snickered at you one bit. You said someday I'd see what an important person—not man, not woman—you would become. Person, you said. The dreams you held for yourself lent me the daring to imagine my own hopes and then to leap at the chance to make them happen when an opportunity arose.

Remember when I read to you when we were quarantined? You were so, so sick. Though I tell the fellas about how you taught me to read all the time, I hadn't recalled these exact things (I never forgot the blizzard, of course!) until I stood near you at those oranges, until I saw your face again. Then it all came back, as if by magic. It was as if we'd seen each other every single day of the last four years. This is all so strange. Forgive my writing if it offends and permit me to start again when I finally come to call.

Thinking of you,
Aleksey

I reread the letter three times to be sure I was seeing it right. He'd thought of me since the grocer. Repeatedly, reaching back into our past and grasping at memories that shaped the way we used to know one another. A sweet friendship, it had been. I sighed, realizing I was now late for Miss Violet. I tucked the letter into the dry sink drawer and ran next door, carrying with me Aleksey's sweet words, excited with the idea he just might come calling very, very soon.

Chapter 31

The Ritual
Katherine

I reached Violet's with thoughts of Aleksey's letter, the shape and slope of each word he'd crafted, still turning in my mind and heart as though there was a tangible connection between scribbles on pulp and the sensation in my chest. I couldn't wait to hear his tale of how he came to be studying the law in Des Moines.

But no. Maybe not. My former dreams had inspired his, and I swelled with pride. But when I thought of how my dreams had been hobbled, I worried perhaps he'd see me as less once he knew how my life had turned since I last saw him.

Perhaps we should leave the last four years tucked away in our separate minds and simply tread this new path in front of us. I couldn't imagine how I could possibly fill Aleksey in on all that had happened, all the things I'd missed and done, how I was no longer the person I used to be, not in the least. Perhaps it didn't matter. Maybe our paths were merely crossing for a moment, like the butterfly that flickered near us when I saw him, it was gone, long passed away, and that would be how I viewed our renewed acquaintance—as short and pleasurable, but lacking permanence.

Get to work, I told myself, knowing that no one had use for a lollygagger. I checked over the bread. The cuts in the top of the loaves that I'd made before baking had turned golden brown and resembled the outlines of angels with wings more than the *K*s I'd intended to make. I also checked the doughnuts that had cooled and were awaiting their powdered sugar. Mama, Tommy, and Yale would appreciate that I'd made an extra dozen for us to share—a real treat. I hoped that there was still enough powdered sugar at our home to dust them. Even if not, they should be delectable.

Miss Violet stepped next to me. "I like that. Nice touch."

I went to the refrigerator and pulled out the chicken salad stirring it with a fork. "The way those came out reminds me of my sister, Yale. Sweet little angel."

Miss Violet nodded. "She's a gentle soul, that one."

I saw a flicker of warmth cross Miss Violet's face. It made me smile. "You like her. You like having a little one around, don't you?"

Miss Violet crossed her arms. She shook her head, then shrugged.

"Admit it. I saw that look on your face when she hugged your legs the other day."

She waved her hand at me. "Don't be silly."

I challenged Miss Violet with my gaze, my smile, my knowing.

"Oh, all right. I like her. A smidgeon."

I scraped the fork against the side of the bowl to clean it. "How could you not?" I knew I was pushing my position with Miss Violet, joking with her but I felt we'd become more casual since getting to know each other.

An odd expression came over her. Had I been too presumptive? Or maybe she wanted children after all, deep down, in the place inside where people didn't push too hard to find their truths when they weren't sure they could fulfill what a particular need was demanding.

I stopped my inquisition. I put the fork into the sink and fastened the lid back onto the crock. Miss Violet took it from me and put it into the refrigerator. "Everything looks and smells wonderful," she said, "but there are going to be some changes going forward."

"Changes?" I was just getting accustomed to things as they were, and I didn't want anything to change at this point.

"Don't be worried. Olivia will take the kitchen work back. I need you to have more time to prepare when it's time to be Dreama."

I must have looked confused or shocked.

"You didn't do anything wrong, Katherine. I came to realize, though, you might need some ritual to coax your spirits. I know you were dissatisfied with how things went with the judge, even though he was quite pleased. I want you to feel strong and powerful in this role. Just like you do as my kitchen mistress. I understand that you're not a carnival act. The idea that you might use gimmicks is an insult to what you can do."

I smoothed my skirts, feeling my crystal against my leg. "Thank you." I was relieved, knowing Miss Violet recognized that I could not in good conscious "perform." I needed to be able to be open to my gifts, not replace them with hackneyed tricks that landed people in jail.

She took my elbow and led me spiraling up the stairs to the third floor. Once there, she guided me into one of the rooms that had been converted into a washroom, where a porcelain tub sat full of steaming water. The scent of lemon and lavender filled my nose, relaxing me immediately.

"Part of your preparations should include bathing. Submersion in a proper aromatic bath should help you be as calm as possible. I think if you do that before readings, the big ones especially, it would help."

I nodded, but I was unsure. Baths were normally fast and purposeful, an attempt to finish getting clean before the hot water turned cold.

"Skeptical?" Miss Violet said. "I did some reading and thought a lot. You can add to the ritual as you see fit, but this will get us started. Blakeslee's *Book of Knowledge* recommends a sunbath each day for the highest health, but I figured we'd begin with water and see if that helps you gather your spirits."

It's true I was most receptive when I either desperately needed help from the beyond or when I felt little pressure, like when I saw Olivia's mother or Violet's father—they simply arrived along with a sense of calming, a knowing, a peacefulness. Perhaps if we worked it in the opposite direction, courted them with my calmness, they would come when bidden?

Violet took my hand and led me to the tub. "I've been perusing the recipe and cure book I bought you and have learned that certain herbs and flowers can bring desired states of mind. In addition to that, I corresponded with the doctor at Bedford Springs. He insisted that if we didn't have access to natural springs, then rainwater would be superior to piped water in attempting to create the experience we desire."

I nodded. "Thank you."

"Go on and get into the tub," she said and left the room.

I started to unbutton my blouse. A racket outside the door was followed by a knock.

I opened it.

"Tommy?"

He grimaced, holding a sloshing bucket of water.

He drew back as though I'd punched him. "You? I'm hauling water up these stairs, my back half-broken, so you can have a day-break? There's a faucet right there, for goodness' sake."

"Well, that's not nice at all, Tommy. Why *wouldn't* you do it for me?"

He glared at me. "What's the kitchen mistress doing taking a bath in the middle of the day?"

I tensed. I didn't know what to say. Miss Violet swept out of the room across the hall. "Now, Tommy. Your sister's congested and has a cold coming on. I need her hands busy in my kitchen, not her body flat in bed." Miss Violet shook a glass bottle. "Some eucalyptus will clear that right up."

Tommy squinted at me.

I knew what he was thinking—that I looked just fine.

"Move along, Tommy," Miss Violet said. "You've two more errands to run in order to collect your full fee."

Tommy rolled his eyes and hoisted his bucket up, lumbering into the washroom.

"You take that bath and get back to the kitchen, Katherine," Miss Violet said. "Tommy's right about one thing. There's no time to waste."

Tommy dumped the water into the tub and exited the bathroom, metal bucket in hand.

"Dripping," Miss Violet said, gesturing to the bucket.

Tommy looked down to see the wet floor. He turned the bucket upright. He tried to glare at me, but a smile overtook his face as he shook his head. "I sure hope you feel better, Katherine."

"Don't worry your mama with this, Tommy. You hear me?" Miss Violet said. "She's got enough to think about."

"I surely won't," he said.

"And check on Yale," I said. "She should be dead asleep, but just be sure. Mama will be home soon."

"I will," he said and cruised away, shooting a last look over his shoulder at me.

Once he was completely gone Miss Violet pointed at my feet. "Off with those." I untied my boots and stepped onto the tile floor that cooled my toes right through the stockings.

"Undress," she said.

I began to unbutton my shirtwaist again, fingers shaking. I couldn't stand the thought of Miss Violet seeing the condition of my underthings. And then my nakedness beneath it all. She began to remove items from a carpetbag. One, two, three candles. A large book. She held it up and blew dust from it before setting it on the small wobbly table next to the tub. She put some bottles of perfume with French labels next to the candles and book, then wiped her hands three times.

She turned to me. I stopped midway through unbuttoning my shirtwaist.

She popped her fists on her hips. "I've seen a naked woman before. I *am* a naked woman underneath my own clothes. We're not in church."

My fingers slipped over the next button, barely getting it through the hole.

Miss Violet came to me and flicked my hands away. She finished unbuttoning the shirtwaist and pushed it off my shoulders. "Well, you certainly need fresh undergarments. These are yellow, for heaven's sake."

"They're clean. My mother and I just—"

"Hush. It's not criticism. You were a child the last time you had proper undergarments. We'll fix that. But most importantly, what we're doing here is ritualizing your preparations, every little step you take away from Katherine, the kitchen mistress, toward Dreama the heart healer, coaxing your muse or whatever it is into the light." Miss Violet opened her arms, palms up. "From what I read, it sounds like you can learn to open up to messages and be ready the moment you step in front of clients."

I pulled off the corset cover, exposing a loose, grayed, frayed-edged corset, a gaping hole showing the bottom layer of fabric over my rib. Miss Violet pressed it, shaking her head. She slid each hook out of each eye in the front, and I stood in only my chemise and underskirt. My hand fell right to the pocket where my crystal ball was suspended. Miss Violet reached into it and pulled the ball out.

"It's a fine piece, isn't it?" she said, turning it to catch the sunlight streaming through the window.

I nodded.

"Tell me again how this crystal ball came to you," Miss Violet said.

I repeated the story of how I kept noticing it shudder and shake as it hung from the Christoffs' decrepit foyer chandelier. The fixture was in need of repair and wasn't in working condition. Yet I noticed the pendants and the center ball again and again, gathering in and reflecting light even when there was barely any illumination, quivering above my head even when there was no wind coming through the front door, as though demanding I look at it.

I held out my palm, my fingers wiggling. Miss Violet put the orb into my hand. "Then one night, it nearly glowed every time I passed it, catching only moonlight and lamplight from the dining room, but golden, white, warm blue light radiated from it. At one point, I just stopped and stared at it. It shook and simply dropped into my hand, like it had been waiting all along for me to stand there long enough to catch it."

Miss Violet ran her finger over the hexagon faces that were cut into the ball. She closed my fingers over it and clasped her hands tightly over mine. "Then you must have it with you each and every time."

She understood. Here was someone who recognized my journey. I thought of Madame Smalley, the grapefruit-sized glass ball she'd had sitting on the center of her table at her place of business. The newspaper headlines I'd seen about her flashed to mind. People believed the crystal ball was evidence she was a hoax. I recalled an article describing how a dissatisfied customer had returned to Madame Smalley and smashed the ball on the sidewalk outside. I felt like I might choke, fear taking hold. I closed my fingers over the ball, wanting to keep it hidden, just for me. "I'll need to wear this underskirt with the hidden pocket. I can't risk losing this—"

Miss Violet took the orb and set it on the table next to the book she'd brought in along with her ledger. She picked up the carpetbag and removed an organza sack. Something inside it jiggled and clicked. "Come," she said. "Take a look."

She loosened the strings at the neck of the sack and gently turned it over, shaking it, and crystals littered the table. "I know your concern. I've studied the matter—Madame Smalley here in town as well as other famous and infamous seers. You keep your precious rock close. I've had a pocket sewn into your new underskirt. But I thought in pursuit of adding theatrics to what is your gift that having these on the tabletop might help."

I leaned in and brushed my hand over the clear pendants that would have hung from a chandelier at some point. They were pretty, but I felt no real draw to them. There were others, round ones that must have hung at the bottom of chandeliers. One was perfectly smooth with a cloud of what looked like a snow squall inside it, the same size as my precious faceted one. I lifted it and felt the heft in my palm. I closed my hand around it. I liked the idea of mine in my pocket, but this one felt good, too. An urge came to me to secret it away as well.

"I think that will help," I said.

"Good." Miss Violet took the ball and put the entire stash on the dressing table beside the other things she'd brought with her. She turned me away from her. "Arms up."

She pulled the chemise over my head. A warm breeze from the open window lit over my nude torso, making my skin rise like gooseflesh. I crossed my arms over my breasts while Violet's fingers worked at the string that held up the underskirt. It fell to the floor, and I stepped out of it.

"Drawers," Miss Violet said.

I nodded. I undid the string and stepped out of them. Miss Violet stood back, fists jammed on her hips again, her gaze moving over my body as though cataloging it or studying an old bone just unearthed in the backyard. I shivered as another breeze whipped through the window, racing over my skin, moist with summer heat.

Miss Violet pressed her fingertips against my belly. "Arms out." She turned me around and ran her finger down my spine. She turned me back toward her. "There's running water up here for when your brother isn't available to fetch rainwater, but that's the standard for us. Rain-washed hair, rain-scented skin, beauty sent down from the heavens, like your spirits and angels and whatever else it is that visits you."

Miss Violet pulled my hands away from my body and pushed her thumbs into my shoulders. "Shoulders back." She stepped back and studied me, hand on her chin. "You're perfectly shaped. Lean and long but with all the curves a woman should have."

My body folded in again. Being called a woman when standing naked caused a sting of shame to come along with excitement at the idea I might be seen as such. Either way, I wasn't accustomed to being appraised.

Miss Violet pressed her thumbs into my shoulders, harder this time. "You don't know your worth. Not one bit."

I didn't know how to respond, so I kept quiet.

She covered her mouth, studying me again. "That will change. But for now, into the water."

I stepped over the side, the water warming my toes. With the perfect temperature calling me, I slipped into the bath, the warmth and depth of the water enveloping, like a thousand angels suspending me in heaven. Lavender and lemon filled my nose, and instantly I felt as though I'd been sent away to be reborn, to return myself to who I was before meeting with such pain and turmoil. I drew a deep breath and exhaled.

"Right there, Katherine," Miss Violet said. "That's it." Her voice was urgent.

My eyes snapped open, and I sat up, splashing water over the side of the tub. Miss Violet stood frozen in place, her hands in front of her, fingers spread.

"What?" I asked.

"What were you just thinking? The expression on your face when you submerged. You were instantly . . . blissful. Yes, that's the word. You appeared open, and well, something. Something more than just beautiful. Blissful."

I turned toward the side of the tub and put my hands on the edge, my chin resting on them. "I was thinking—no, *feeling*—as though I were floating on a bed of clouds. I was transported."

"You called on your angels," Miss Violet said.

I looked the ceiling for a moment. "I suppose."

She scrambled to her bag and pulled out her ledger. She flipped to the back of the book and scribbled on the paper. "You'll record this ritual in your recipe book, but I'll write it in here so we don't forget. *That's* number one—well, that's really number two—call on your angels. One is to prepare your waters." She rushed to the table and brought two of the bottles I'd thought were perfume. "This is oil, lavender, and this is lemon." She added a dash of each to the tub. "Bathe in it; rub it over your skin so that even hours later you'll still smell of it. Perfume is fine, but this will become part of who Dreama is. Every time you smell it, you will instantly begin to transform, to become."

Miss Violet held the oil under her nose. "Heavenly. French. Very expensive. Oil, not scented water. It's only for Dreama."

I felt a twinge of disappointment that I wouldn't be able to use it any other time.

"So, one. Scent the water." Miss Violet jotted something in her book. "Two, call your angels. Whatever you did that brought that look to your face, do that."

"All right," I said.

"Three," she said and then poured some oil into my hand. "Massage that into every bit of your skin. Except your face. It's too heavy for your face."

I sat in the tub, knees bent. I began at the nape of my neck and rubbed the oil into my flesh, working down to my shoulders.

"As you do that, just listen to what I've discovered."

Miss Violet grabbed the thick book she'd brought with her. She licked her finger and paged through it. "Here it is. People who can—" She lifted her eyes from the book and met mine for an instant. "People who are gifted the way you are need to be receptive and open to the spirits. I realize now that feeding you information and having the prophecy cards and the palm reading for you if you got stuck was gimmicky and whatnot. That isn't what we want you to think about, ever. I see that now."

I felt a sense of relief work into my skin along with the oil as I fully absorbed Miss Violet's words. *She understands.* She, a respected businesswoman, admitted she'd been wrong about something and could see what I needed in order to be successful.

"In a pinch," Miss Violet said, "if things just go completely flat, I may have one of the other girls read a palm or roll some dice. They've been studying up on how to read one's fortune and use their intuition better."

I flinched.

She sat on the commode. "Don't fret. I realize the world of difference between the other girls studying the how-tos of making invisible energy work for them and what you do. It's the difference between me studying how to draw and what my friend Claude can do. I simply don't possess his otherworldly ability. It's the same for you. You have a gift."

I leaned back in the tub and poked my foot out of the water, droplets streaming down my skin as I rubbed the oil into my ankle, calf, knee, thighs. "Thank you, Miss Violet. It helps to hear you say this."

"And just to give you a little incentive, I've gotten you some paints. I think if you paint at some point after doing readings, we could possibly sell them."

I dropped my foot back into the water with a plop. I extended my other leg upward, droplets tickling my skin as they streamed down my leg. Then I repeated the circles starting at my ankle. "I haven't painted in ages."

"Your mother told me how talented you are. And I've seen what you can sketch. They're prophetic or knowledgeable about the past as well. That man you drew, the one by the furnace, a girl bent over him?"

I couldn't remember what she was talking about.

"In the pile of drawings you had at your house that day Mr. Hayes spilled the water?" I squinted, trying to remember. I'd made so many drawings, usually just half-finished sketches. "I think so."

Miss Violet's silence made me sit up. She was wiping tears from her eyes.

"What is it?"

Miss Violet kneeled beside the tub. Her lips quivered. Even after seeing her vulnerable when I told her that her father had come to see her, this was far different. "My father's death. It reminds me so much of . . ." Miss Violet's shoulders shuddered, and a sob choked her. I reached out to her and grasped her hands.

"It might not be that. I might have seen an article in the paper or something that made me draw that."

Water trailed down my arms, plummeting off my elbows.

She swallowed hard, eyes squeezed shut. "Saying that aloud to you really hit me. It was like being there again."

Her feelings radiated toward me like heat shimmying off a tin roof; her sadness was heavy between us, filling me. "I feel it," I said. "I'm so sorry that happened to you."

Miss Violet nodded. "It's long ago, but . . ."

Her pain was woolen in my throat. A sharpness to the pain, a stabbing through the dull loss was clear to me. I thought there was more to what happened. Perhaps Miss Violet felt responsible? The anguish I sensed right then was different, like two separate streams heading into the same river. For the first time, I thought what I was receiving about a person or experience was specific in its loss—not just sadness, but sadness at losing a parent. I could relate to that loss. My father was gone, but he was still alive. And then came another thread of pain, something different, a kind of loss I had not felt myself before. It nearly turned me inside out.

Miss Violet took her hands from mine, sniffling. I looked up and saw she had gone back to her carpetbag. "I forgot. This is important to help you open up in front of an audience." She took out matches and candles and held them up.

"From now on, especially when we do a big event, I want you to light these candles. I want you to absorb the scrape of the match, the hiss as it lights, the scent of the vanilla and lavender and citrus as the match lights each candle and heats the wax. Each little action should comfort you and coax the spirits toward you at the same time."

Miss Violet lit the first candle. I focused on all the elements she had suggested. The confluence of the oils and the candles and fresh water were like heaven descending right there. I closed my eyes and settled back into the water, allowing the water to lift me all over again.

"You're doing what you have to," I heard and looked up to see Miss Violet's father at her side as she set the candle on the table and reached for another match.

I sat up. "Your father's here," I told her.

Miss Violet stopped just before striking the match, her eyes meeting mine. "What?" I pushed my chest against the side of the tub, as though Miss Violet's father might be interested in seeing me naked.

"He's here."

Miss Violet followed my gaze to just beyond her shoulder. She shook her head. "I don't see a thing."

I smiled. "He's proud of you. He wanted you to really know that."

Her breath stuttered as she inhaled. "Thank you."

My eyes began to burn. I suddenly realized that Miss Violet had been correct in having me create a ritual. These quiet, soothing moments seemed to have guided the necessary spirits right toward me. This would help me to do what I'd been put on this earth to do.

Miss Violet lit the other candles. "I think this has worked very well, hasn't it?" She turned away from me, but I could see her dab at her eyes with a handkerchief she'd stashed in her cleavage.

"Yes," I said.

She started to the door. Her posture had straightened, and I could see the strength and tension return to her neck. I wanted to comfort her.

"It's all right, Miss—"

She gripped the doorjamb as she was leaving but did not look back. "Finish with the oils, then rinse and dry off. I still need you to try on the dresses so we know that everything fits."

I felt the chill of her returning to the very staid woman she normally was. I felt special that I'd been part of seeing Miss Violet like she'd been. I felt empowered that I'd given her something that she would thank me for. The importance of what I could do set around my bones like casting. I knew this was what I was meant to do—provide people with information they needed to heal and go on living.

I leaned back in the tub, floating. I worked the oil into my legs, belly, arms, letting the luxurious moment fill me. I pushed away the thought that I should be down in the kitchen, busy with Yale, or studying for the courses I had told Mama I was taking.

This wasn't the person I'd planned to be—my schooling had been delayed years; my family had been torn apart. But compared to my circumstances just a short time ago, this was heavenly. My fingertips trembled over my skin, tickling, bringing thoughts of Aleksey to mind. The oils softened my skin as I worked them in, causing the water to make soft notes.

Aleksey. I thought of the lovely letter he'd written. Was he thinking of me right then? I imagined him working at the farm. Was he harvesting? Building something? Milking cows? I pictured him hunched over his books, his enormous hand holding up his head as he read, his bright eyes following the words that unfolded in a thick law book. Was he thinking of me just that very moment, like he'd said in his letter?

All of this made me long to push my fingers into his thick corn-yellow hair. I wanted his eyes on me, holding my attention, making me feel special, as he'd done at the grocer's. And as the water turned cool and a chill came over my skin, I thought life had turned good, nearly as quickly as it had once all gone bad.

Chapter 32

Call on Your Angels
Katherine

I dried off and wrapped the damp linen sheet around me. I blew out each candle, attempting to recall each step of my ritual in order. One, prepare the waters. Two, call on my angels—or was it candles first? It would make more sense for me to light the candles first. What were the other steps? I glanced at Miss Violet's ledger, remembering that she'd written the steps in it.

Number four . . . Oh, what had number four been? I closed my eyes and inhaled, feeing the openness that the ritual had created. Repeating the ritual would be important going forward. I could trust Miss Violet's protectiveness; her belief in me and her careful discretion made me feel as though nothing could go wrong. All the clumsy experiences so far—even with Judge Calder—now seemed locked away in a place where I didn't have to return. I exhaled. This ritual would make all the difference.

What was number one? How could I forget already? The bath had deeply relaxed me. Thoughts of Aleksey had distracted me. Surely Miss Violet wouldn't mind if I looked at the page in her ledger where she wrote the ritual notes? I wanted to be prepared and make my own list of the ritual steps in my book, but first I needed to remember them. I looked at the ledger. I shouldn't snoop, but the ritual ... Miss Violet had made that mine as much as hers. I wanted her to be proud of me, not disappointed that I couldn't even remember the steps soon after performing them.

I began to panic. What if I failed after Miss Violet went through all this trouble of helping me create a ritual? No. She'd already caught me stealing an apple when I first began working for her. I couldn't risk getting the pages wet and getting caught. Besides, it was time for me to pare down the number of lies I roped myself into over the course of a day. I was no longer running for my life and fending off male advances. She trusted me, and I could trust her.

I loosened the sheet and dried one arm and then the other. As I reached down to get my toes, I lost my balance and caught the table, knocking the ledger onto the floor. It flopped open. I stared at it and bent down to pick it up. I started to close the book, but Olivia's name caught my eye.

As I stood up, I noticed that underneath her name were numbered items. Even as I was closing the book, my eyes were skimming. A list of the dresses she'd been granted as part of her work for Miss Violet. Some client names I'd heard over the weeks of working as kitchen mistress. Words like *selling off, reinvestment, loss, gain,* and *home for collateral* trailed across the page. My eyes continued down the page and saw different types of words filling the page: *stockings, shoes, lovemaking, from behind.*

What in Hades did that mean? *Put it away. It's not yours.*

I shut the ledger and set it back on the table. Miss Violet's quick gait, heels hitting the wooden floor, began coming my way. Even though I hadn't intentionally opened the book, I felt a twinge of guilt. I then remembered the first time I'd seen Miss Violet's father. He'd seen me steal the apple. I whipped around, expecting to see him watching.

But he wasn't there. I exhaled as Miss Violet entered. She stopped short at the sight of me. I pulled the sheet around me, hoping it would hide my fear that she might know I'd seen a few pages of her ledger.

She squinted at me and looked at the table. She picked up her ledger and the book she'd read from. "Leave those crystals and things there for now. And enough with the shyness. If we have to stop every few seconds for you to cover up, we'll never get this fitting done."

I nodded, relieved that she didn't suspect.

I followed Miss Violet to the room where I'd been dressing before each reading. "To put your mind at ease, our clients have been directed to keep the destination for their particular reading a secret. Sometimes they'll be here, most of the time they'll be elsewhere. The idea that the information should be kept quiet adds a layer of mystery that increases the allure of having Dreama read."

"Thank you," I said.

Miss Violet patted a brocade stool that sat in front of a dressing table and mirror. "Sit. Stockings first."

She peeled away my damp sheet, and it draped over the seat, cascading onto the floor. I covered my breasts again, but when Miss Violet handed me a white silken stocking, I had no choice but to put away my anxiety about being nude. The stocking was buttery between my fingers and easily unfurled up my leg. Miss Violet handed me a silken ribbon, a barely there tangerine hue, to tie the stocking at the thigh. I did the other, drawing my hands up one leg, marveling at the decadent feel of silk on my skin.

I bent over my thighs, feeling the silk from my toes up to the ties. "Oh, what heaven," I said.

Miss Violet laughed. "I thought you'd appreciate finery."

She shook a set of split drawers—darker tangerine-colored cotton. I stood and stepped into them and tied the waist. I couldn't bear the thought of having to relieve myself and possibly splashing anything onto these gorgeous underthings. A pristine chemise came out of tissue paper next.

Over my head it went, the scent of new linen filling my nose. Next Miss Violet reached into the box and pulled out an orange sorbet-colored corset, setting it aside while she helped me into a pale pink underskirt. She pressed my leg. "I think you'll find the pocket was sewn exactly where you like it, right near your fingertips when your arm is extended."

I nodded, awed by the care that Miss Violet had taken. With each garment slipped on, my sense of importance grew, my confidence swelled, my heart opened, preparing for the wisdom that should come, the information from the dead and from my very own angels. I closed the corset in the front, and Miss Violet tied the back. I ran my fingers down the front of the corset, the silken threads luxurious. Next came a corset cover and a white satin evening gown. The neckline was flounced with gauzy, snow-white organza, my arms and shoulders covered with the same airy material. I pressed my hand against my bare skin just above the place where my breasts began.

"It's not as modest as the one you've been wearing," Miss Violet said. "But that frock was for a girl." She pulled a tangerine silk sash from a box and wrapped it around my waist, tying it in the back. "This dress, the lower neckline, is for a *woman*. The satin is worthy of the gift you bestow on others. The muslin frock was for practice. Now let me add some color to your face."

I held my hands up to her. "Oh. No. Surely I'm glowing enough with the gratitude that comes with being allowed to don such attire." I couldn't imagine painting my face.

Miss Violet opened a drawer and pulled out a small glass pot. She unscrewed the black lid. "First of all," she said, "the dresses aren't gifts. You're going to pay for them with your earnings. A women's rights advocate wouldn't have it any other way."

"Well, yes," I said, though I wanted to protest needing to buy them. I wanted the money I would earn to go to a house for my mother, not a dress for me.

"Secondly, I would never, *ever* put anything on you that made you appear to have been painted. I would merely shade you a little, add a little hint of depth to your skin, deepen your red lips just a bit. You'll be hidden under your veil, but I want you to *feel* the power of your beauty. You are exquisitely, unusually beautiful."

I drew back and turned my head to see myself at various angles. Was she right?

"I'm not telling you that so you'll spend your hours gazing in the mirror. I tell you that so you will fully access your power and use it. A woman has many sources from which to draw power." Miss Violet took a charcoal pencil and brushed it lightly on my eyebrows.

"You're fortunate to have breeding, intelligence, *and* beauty." She took a brush and drew it along my lips with the edge and then, with the soft bristles, pulled color over the plump skin. "Like the angels," Miss Violet said, "kissed you upon birth."

"Thank you," I said.

"Close your eyes."

I felt the pencil swipe over my eyelids at the base of my lashes.

"A woman must take inventory of her strengths and bolster her weaknesses. I can see plainly that I am not a beauty."

"Oh no, Miss Violet," I said. She hushed me and told me to close my eyes again.

"It's all right. I've much to compensate for that. You see, pretending wouldn't help me; feeling sorry for myself wouldn't help me. Girding myself does. Your limitation may lie in your heart, Katherine. You must guard it; keep your work, your goals for your independent life in mind. Do not allow anything to draw you from it."

"Yes, Miss Violet."

"Now open your eyes," she said.

When I did, Miss Violet stepped back, her hand at her throat.

"Oh no. It's awful, isn't it?" I stood and pushed past Violet, leaning into the dressing-table mirror. I jerked back at the sight. My mouth fell open.

She took my hand and rubbed the back of it. "Come to the full-length mirror."

We went to the end of the room near the back windows, and I saw myself with daylight splashing over me. "I can't believe I look like . . ."

"A beautiful woman?"

I lifted the skirt and let it puddle over my feet. "It's amazing. I can't . . ."

I turned to Miss Violet, eyes burning. "I know I'll be buying my dresses, but I can't thank you enough for getting them for me." I knew Miss Violet thought I was intelligent and capable, but seeing myself like this, the way she imagined I could be, changed the way I saw myself. She'd turned me into the beauty she claimed I was. "How did you see this in me?"

"It's not that I saw anything *in* you. It's that I actually *saw you*. What you can do for you, your family, me. It's incomparable. I just had the instinct to pay attention."

Overcome with the realization that Miss Violet truly had my interests, my family's interests, at the center of her world, I threw my arms around her. "Thank you, thank you, Miss Violet. I'll make you proud. I'll work harder than you can imagine."

Miss Violet patted my back and pushed away. "Get this dress off and finish up in the kitchen. Olivia will help, and I'll hire another girl as soon as possible."

I reached behind me and released the sash, the satin falling like water through my fingers. "I'll check on Yale. Mama should be long back, but just to be sure. Please?"

Miss Violet cringed before nodding.

"Yes, check on her. But keep in mind that it's not time to share this with your mother."

I touched my cheek. I hadn't intended to say anything, but I would have loved to show Mama what I was becoming.

"Soon," Miss Violet said. "I know you're excited. But not yet. For your sake, for hers, for Yale's and Tommy's."

"I know."

"Now let's wipe you down with some fresh water to reduce the perfume. You can just tell your mother you were making some lavender water for cooking if she asks."

I would keep the secret, the telling of the tale of this wonderful day would wait. It would be all the better to reveal when I came bearing great treasure. "All right. Lavender water."

Miss Violet helped me out of the clothes. With each garment removed, she prompted. "Remind me of your ritual. The first thing you do when you begin your transition is . . ."

I hesitated, then reached for where the crystal ball lay against my leg. I called up the feeling in the tub. I didn't even need the ledger to remember at that moment. "Prepare the waters." And so we went through the process, adding the lighting of candles at the beginning. "And call on my angels," I said. The most important part.

Miss Violet stepped behind me and brushed my hands away, loosening the corset ties for me. "Yes, you summon them with all your being."

I exhaled and recalled the sensation in the tub all over again. "I will, Miss Violet. Oh, I will."

Chapter 33

Disbelief
Katherine

Back in my own dress, face washed and hair in a low bun, I checked the shelf for more powdered sugar at Miss Violet's, excited to treat everyone to sweet doughnuts. I thought there'd been another canister of sugar already powdered, but there was none. I checked the tray of doughnuts for the guests, and they were nicely dusted. I wished I could trade a couple of those for the plain ones I was taking home, but I knew that wouldn't be wise. There was still a small amount of sugar at home from the last time I'd made doughnuts, and I'd use that.

I backed through the hedges to keep the doughnuts from being knocked off the tray, grateful that Tommy had widened the hole so we could easily go back and forth. As I emerged from the hedge, a bird swooped in front of me. It landed on a rock in the children's garden. "Food," it croaked.

I stopped and stared at it. Tommy's crow. I knew the bird could talk, but not that it would know I was carrying something that was labeled food. "Not for you, Frank," I said.

It stamped its feet as though marching or having a tantrum.

"Oh, all right." I tore off a piece of one doughnut and tossed it. Frank caught it and swallowed.

"Thank you."

It flew off toward Tommy's shed. I shook my head, glad that Tommy had something to take care of. "You're welcome," I said.

Up on the porch, I balanced the tray with one hand and reached for the door leading to our kitchen. I heard something crash to the floor inside, and Mama let out a scream. My blood chilled. From the tenor of her voice, I knew this was not over a rodent.

I yanked the door open, half the doughnuts sliding off the tray, plopping at my feet and rolling away. Mama stood there holding Yale, both of their faces white as the satin gown I'd been wearing an hour earlier.

"Mama?" I set the tray near the sink. Behind Mama was a woman, leaning over, rubbing my mother's back. Soothing her. I couldn't see the woman's face, but I'd seen her before. In her other arm was a baby—the same baby I'd seen her holding in the Christoffs' kitchen and at other times. A spirit was watching over Mama and Yale. Had Mama seen her? Is that why she screamed? I stood there as though watching actors in a play. Fear pulsed through me, telling me something was terribly wrong, and it wasn't about the faceless spirit woman.

"Help me! Get some water!" Mama finally got her words out.

I spun around and knocked the tray to the floor, the clanging sound echoing as I pumped water into a glass, and Mama forced some down Yale's throat. As she drank, Miss Violet stepped into the kitchen, grasping the doorjamb. "What is it?"

Mama held the glass. "Katherine was to watch her. Now she's eaten rat poison."

"Mama, no!" I said.

I looked closer at Yale, taking her face in my hands. My heart beat so fast I thought I might pass out. I wiped the powder from her cheeks. I never should have hidden food upstairs. If I hadn't done that, we wouldn't have to worry about mice. I couldn't breathe. I'd felt this clutch of dread and horror before. It was as though I'd been flung back through time, feeling the pain I'd felt when James died, when I'd seen *him* cradled in Mama's arms, the quaking in her voice even as she screamed like a thunderclap.

"She was under the dry sink." Mama pointed. "You should have watched her. How could you have let this happen, Katherine?"

Miss Violet bent down in front of the cabinet. She pulled out empty pie tins and gelatin molds and several unlabeled canisters. She opened each one, sniffing them while Mama and I monitored every breath Yale drew.

She held up a tin of poison and a tin of sugar next. "The lid on the poison's on tight. It's the sugar. Please let it be the sugar."

Mama used her finger to swipe some of the powder from Yale's cheek and tasted it. She nodded, and a great smile covered her face. Her shoulders relaxed, and she lifted her hand in the air. "Powdered sugar!"

"Sugar?" I swiped some powder from the corner of Yale's mouth and tasted. "Oh, thank God."

Mama's shoulder's sagged as she hugged Yale even tighter. I grabbed her under the arms and helped her to the table. Yale wrapped her legs around Mama's waist, and her hands tightened around her neck. Mama rocked her, rubbing the back of Yale's head.

I'd never felt such an incredible swing of emotions. I collapsed into a chair beside them. "I'm so relieved." I patted Yale's back. "The poison's supposed to be in the cellar."

"I don't know how it got under there with the kitchen things," Mama said as Miss Violet slipped out the kitchen door.

I tried to retrace my last use of the poison. Could I be so distracted as to have not returned it to the cellar? The thought petrified me.

"How long were you gone, Katherine?"

I shook my head. No longer than usual, really. And Tommy was to be back to sit with her before she wakened. I didn't want him in trouble any more than me. "Yale was exhausted today, sleeping extra. I checked her regularly. We ate, used the privy, and played a bit in the garden before she went back down to sleep. Tommy checked, too. I know he said he would. I don't even remember using the poison lately."

"I know. We have to be more careful. Yale's so quiet," Mama said, "and when she takes to wandering . . ." Her voice trailed off. My heart nearly stopped, and I felt pain grip my chest. I knew what Mama had stopped herself from saying. "I remember using the poison. I can't believe I didn't put it back downstairs. She's just so quiet. Wandering away, into the . . ." Mama's face whitened all over again.

"Into the grasses. Like Anzhela."

Mama drew a stuttered breath, as though she had to push the air into her body, as though the air were thick and solid. I did my best to push that day from my mind, when Aleksey and I watched his sister while playing chase in the grasses. We had only turned our backs for a moment, and the two-year-old disappeared. The guilt was suddenly fresh and painful. I couldn't find the right words. Whether I was the one who left the poison upstairs or not, I had not watched Yale close enough, and that was the truth.

I wrapped my arms around my family.

"It's not your fault," Mama said, gripping me tighter. "We all need to keep careful watch. All of us. We're all so busy. We'll keep the poison in the cellar. I didn't even consider it could be sugar. I just saw her white lips, and she was sleeping . . ." She shook her head as if to clear the image from her mind. "I'll speak to Tommy. He should have been here. It's not just you. Yale has progressed so much in a short time that we take for granted that she wouldn't move about very much before."

I nodded, relieved. Still, guilt swelled inside me. I imagined me in the bathtub, luxuriating while Yale was wandering, fortunate she found her way into sugar and not poison. "Tommy'll be devastated to know Yale was up and around. He must've checked on her, too."

Her mother sniffed. "I know." She drew a deep breath and exhaled with her whole body, as though releasing the tension that had gripped us all. "Katherine?"

Mama pushed away from me.

"What's that smell?"

I lifted my wrist and sniffed it.

"I made lavender water for bread."

Mama gave me a look that said she didn't understand.

"Please don't be mad, Mother. Yale's fine. Tommy told me he was checking on her . . ." I almost launched into the entire story but stopped myself as Miss Violet's voice came to mind, warning me not to confide yet. Now was definitely not the time. "But I checked on her constantly. We played in the garden, and she was so tired and—"

"She's vulnerable," Mama said. "We have to be extra careful."

"I know."

"It's more than her just being a child. I just came from seeing Cora Hillis. The mayor, the preachers, the judges, the businessmen—they are all looking to clean up Des Moines, and part of that involves punishing delinquent children."

"But I'm not delinquent. Certainly, Yale isn't. She wouldn't hurt a soul."

"It's that she is slow, Katherine. Going to these meetings and seeing how they label children—morons, imbeciles." She shuddered. "I've had to face this. And children like Yale are more likely to be stuffed away in an asylum or die in accidents, like poisoning . . ."

I drew back. The word *die* was sharp, slicing at my heart. Did Mama think I'd put Yale in danger on purpose? The scent of lavender and lemon came rushing back. The heavenly sensation of floating in the tub reminded me again I'd been so absorbed in becoming Dreama I didn't give Yale a thought after Tommy said he'd check on her. "I'm so sorry, Mama. I didn't do a good enough job by her. You're right."

Mama put her finger to my lips. She pulled it back and narrowed her eyes on me. "Did you paint your lips?"

I stepped away. I'd removed all the paint. I thought I had anyway. "Of course not."

"They're so red."

I touched my lips. "Strawberries. I was eating them as I prepared supper." The bitter lie turned my stomach. *A bit longer and then I can tell her everything.* "You know I love strawberries."

I tried to contain the panic welling inside. I wanted her trust. I didn't deserve it. Dreama was for her, for us. The money would change everything. I watched Mama work a hard swallow down her throat, as though my cottony lies were stuck in her throat as much as in mine.

She stood and drew me into her arms, Yale stuffed between us. "I'm sorry for getting angry," Mama said. "I was just so frightened. It was like . . ."

I held her tighter, squeezed my eyes to keep the lies tamped down, and forced away the guilt curdling in my gut. "I know, Mama. Like James all over again."

"Could have happened when I was here," she said. "I get lost in the gardening or my sewing and, well, once I turned around and she was under a cow. It got through the gate, and there she was. I nearly died on the spot."

I was grateful Mama shared that with me, that she wanted to help me feel less guilty.

"I know how this can happen. But you have to be more careful—we all do. I couldn't handle losing any one of you. And Yale is silent and all over the place now. She's changed so much since we arrived, and yet she's too young to grasp danger. Maybe she never will."

"She has an angel, Mama. She has someone watching over her." I stiffened at the sound of my words tumbling through the air; the words were out before I could stop them.

"Someone or something had a hand in her safety today," Mama said, "and I don't care if that someone is labeled God or Jesus or just plain old luck. But she was fortunate."

I wanted to say so much more. Soon I would. "I have to go back to Miss Violet's. I don't want to lose pay." I thought of the dresses I had to pay off. I scooped up the doughnuts that had rolled off my tray. "Sorry about these."

As much as Miss Violet's plan for me and my family was enticing, I wished Mama would forbid me to go.

"Everything all right over there? You stay out of their way, right? Just do your work and lessons and come home?"

Mama's face was earnest, her eyes bright and hopeful after being flushed with horror moments before. Her faith in me twisted at my heart. I wanted her to know someone was watching over Yale.

I pulled Mama into a hug again. "Everything's fine there. But, Mama, we do have angels. When I came in, there was one watching over you as you were holding Yale."

She pulled away, her gaze hard, confused. She brushed back my hair. "I'm not surprised if you thought you saw something unusual. I was frightened to death myself. I even jammed my finger down her throat to make her throw up."

"No." I squeezed tighter. "The angel was here, watching with a protective hand on your back, like she knew you. I couldn't see her face, but she had brown hair and white light surrounded her, like a painting in the museums we used to go to in New York."

Mama cupped my cheek, staring. I held my breath, waiting for her to tell me I'd gone lunatic or yell at me for inviting the devil into our home. Her face softened. "Like the fire. Remember you said you saw a boy there at the bee tree?"

"Yes, yes," I said, relief rinsing through me. "You believe me?"

"Fear is powerful. I swore I saw James get up and walk a second time after he died, when I couldn't let him go. My arms so numb from holding him in that snow, the ice collecting between our bodies. I would have sworn I saw him get up and tell me he would be fine."

"Yes. Yes. That was him, Mama. I see him myself."

Mama's eyes filled. She straightened one of the cuffs on my shirtwaist. "I need you to listen carefully. You can't go around talking like this. I'm serious about what I said about a project to push morals, to rid Des Moines of crime—and things that aren't even crimes. You've seen the articles. People are looking for a cause to elevate themselves in the eyes of voters or lawyers or whomever, and they've grabbed on to this. Just the mention of angels or ghosts or whatever it is you're saying could get you in big trouble.

I shook my head.

She squeezed my wrist. "You don't know how bad it can be when people decide you've done something illicit. You don't remember how we were treated. You don't know how easy it is to call a woman evil or insane and just tuck her away into an asylum where no one will see her again. You don't ever want people to think you're crazy." Mama's breath grew fast, her face reddening as she spoke. "Having an experience in a dire time of stress is something that probably everyone understands. But that doesn't mean—"

I stiffened and wiggled my wrist out of her grip. "I'm not afraid, Mother. But it's not what you think. If you're talking about that Madame Smalley, she isn't seeing angels, as far as I've read. She is up to no good, it sounds like." I felt the crystal in the pocket of my skirt. *Yes. My crystal could put me in the same category as Madame Smalley. But I was different.* Still, I wanted to explain. I wanted Mama to see that I wasn't insane. "Don't you feel comforted with the idea someone's watching out for you? James? He comes to me."

Mama looked away. "That scares the life out of me to hear you say that, Katherine. I comforted myself many times with James's presence, convincing myself he was there, hoping the thought alone could conjure him up like a spell cast. I watch the clouds pretending he is sending me messages with the weather. I understand."

"So you believe me? You don't think I'm lying?"

"I don't think you are lying. I think you might be . . . grieving. People don't take kindly to things like . . . well, Madame Smalley and such. You're smart enough to understand."

Mama's hands shook. She tried to still them by clasping her waist. I didn't want her to worry. "It's not that, Mama. I'm not like her." I covered my mouth to keep from telling her the whole thing with Miss Violet. Mama's gaze went to my pinkie finger. She took my hand and kissed my fingers. "You've been through so much. You have a constant reminder of that year on the prairie and all it wrought. I'm not surprised you're comforted by thoughts of the good things, your brother James. That Aleksey brought that cow into the dugout. That you saved each other and Yale. Those are real things that should hearten you when you're frightened. Don't think about nonsense like Madame Smalley or that Dreama. That's not useful to anyone."

A bell began to ring next door. Miss Violet was calling all the girls to their meeting before the clients arrived. I couldn't push this matter now. "I have to go, Mama."

"*Katherine.*" Mama's voice stilled me. "I understand the need to find peace. I really do. I love you and I know how hard it's been. But, you can let go of all that brought you sadness now."

"I'm doing that. I am. But I have to go."

I leaned in and kissed Yale's forehead. "Stay where you belong, little one."

Mama said, "Same goes for you, Katherine. Same goes for you."

Chapter 34

The Lies Tighten
Katherine

Time passed, and like clockwork, when I went to Miss Violet's to become Dreama, guilt and regret about what happened with Yale and the sugar would wash in. The thought of sweet Yale possibly dipping her fingers into rat poison, the pain that would have followed as it burned her tongue and seared her esophagus if it hadn't been sugar, clung to me like a disgruntled spirit. I was extra careful to return the poison to the cellar each and every time I used it. She was safe, but still, I couldn't shake the dark feeling that grew from the event.

One day as I pushed through the hedges to go to work, I could hear a cow with its bell in the distance. That was it! An idea came to me. I dug through the drawer in the breakfront where Miss Violet kept odds and ends. I located twine and two small metal bells that I knotted onto the string. I would loop the string through a buttonhole at the back of Yale's dress or tie it around her wrist. Her silent movements would be made audible to whoever was tasked with watching her.

I tucked the bell necklace into the drawer under some buttons and thread to retrieve later. I grabbed my recipe book that I'd recorded the ritual in and raced up the back stairs to the third floor. I no longer needed it, but liked to have it near. The gathering ritual Miss Violet and I had developed had helped me more than I could have first imagined. There were four full buckets of hot rainwater standing near the tub. Taking the time to string the bells had me rushing, and as I added the lavender and lemon oil to the tub, I reminded myself to slow down, that none of this would help if I didn't relax into the process.

Something was off. I checked the ritual list and saw that I'd skipped lighting the candles. So as I lit each one, I took deep breaths, allowing the strike of the match, the hiss, the pop of the wick lighting, to draw me in. I asked my angels to gather.

The bath, the scents, the dressing, the lighting of the candles—every little action submerged me in a place suspended, apart from normal life. In this place, there was a gathering, an opportunity to welcome deceased loved ones, almost as though they themselves poured through a faucet that led from the afterlife into the parlor.

Clean and relaxed, I met Miss Violet in the dressing room. "This gown's a little sweeter than the one I tried on you the other day. Tonight requires a little less skin."

Working quickly, Miss Violet had me into the underthings and then stepping into an apricot silken dress that tied with a sweet, thin bow in the back. The sleeves were short and decorated with ruffles that resembled flower blooms. She worked my hair into a simple braid she secured with pins around the neckline.

In a few more minutes she had me veiled and gloved and then moving toward the front staircase.

I pressed the ball that was tucked against my leg. Miss Violet picked up the small bag of extra crystal pendants she'd found for me and gathered the candles.

From below, Olivia played the piano and Bernice accompanied her on violin.

"There have been some changes. Reverend Shaw is the man you'll read for. He's skeptical, but open."

I blew out my air, more confident that Miss Violet anticipated this constraint. "He's acquainted with cons and psychic acts, so we will *not* employ the girls to read palms or throw dice tonight under any circumstances. We need this man to stay out of our business. He has been sworn to secrecy that he is meeting Dreama here. We can trust him. Judge Calder assured me. But you need to come through tonight. It's that important."

I nodded, unsure, but buoyed by her putting so much responsibility on me.

She sat me at a small table with a gold damask cloth draped over it. Then she signaled me to light the candles. With each scratch and hiss of the flame taking hold, I felt more and more receptive. The scent of the candles and the burning match lulled me into a place where I receded from the people around me. I could hear Olivia playing, but everything else had blurred away.

As the reverend settled into the seat across from me, I lifted my gaze and studied his face. Angular and narrow, his features were hard, his expression irritated. I knew he had hired Tommy for all manner of things, including the selling of prayers. Most of what I'd heard of him was that he was generous but strict with the boys he took in.

Nothing was coming to me yet, so I opened the sack that Violet had given me. I spread the crystal pendants and balls around the table, running my palm over them. Nothing. I pushed in closer to the table and lifted my skirt to retrieve the ball I kept in the hidden pocket. I needed it out with the others. I set it in front of me and ran one lace-covered finger over the hexagonal faces.

As I did this, a feather tumbled down between the reverend and me. I picked it up and studied the fluffy white plume. I blew it away and ran my hand over the crystals. A tabby cat meowed from the corner of the room, barely audible over Olivia's playing. I squinted in the direction of it as it moved closer and closer to us.

No one else saw it, and I knew, though it was an unusual experience for me, that this animal had come for the reverend. When I looked back toward him, the feather had floated back onto the table. He picked it up.

"Your cat's here. A tabby?"

He stiffened, his close-set eyes widening. "Is it a gaunt, ugly thing?"

I studied it as it came across the floor. "Fat." I shrugged. "Adorable."

His mouth dropped open. "Fatty. He's here?"

I sighed, relieved. "Yes."

He rubbed his mouth as though attempting to keep something back.

"What is it?"

He pushed farther into the table toward me. "He disappeared. Is he . . . okay? I found some fur but nothing else, and I just didn't know . . ."

I closed my eyes and tried to get a feel for what had happened to cause Fatty to leave one world for another.

I shook my head. "I think he simply died. Was he old?"

"He was, but he never left my side."

Fatty mewled and stretched backward and then forward. "He's fine."

Reverend Shaw leaned forward. When he shifted his hands, I saw the feather stuck to his cuff.

"This feather has been following me all day." He brushed it off the table.

I reached down and picked it up. A realization settled in me, something I'd read in the book Miss Violet had bought. "The feather appeared before?"

He scratched his chin and looked to the ceiling. "All day."

"It's a sign. Fatty wanted you to know he's near."

The reverend smiled and folded his hands on the table. His features had softened, and we spent the next ten minutes discussing all manner of his losses: his parents, his brother, his horse. No one besides Fatty the cat showed himself to me. Reverend Shaw's eyes began to well, then tears fell. I felt a deeper understanding envelop me.

"Maybe the feather isn't a sign that Fatty wants you to know he's with you, but instead it's the others you mentioned."

He looked at me with a curious expression, as though it was worth considering.

"Like tiny prayers raining down."

He shrugged. "Or a sign of my bad housekeeping." He sighed, and I could tell he was pulling away from the gathering as though something I said about other family members and the feathers didn't sit well with him.

As Olivia's music came to an end, I felt myself drawn back into the room, noticing Helen and Bernice and Abigail. Judge Calder had arrived, and he and Miss Violet were deep in discussion across the room. When she saw that Reverend Shaw was getting up, she took Bernice by the hand and brought her to him to attend to him.

Miss Violet gently guided me to the kitchen where my sketchbook, some thick oil paints, and canvases were arranged. She slipped a large smock over my arms, closing it in front, and tied a sash around my waist. "This will keep your dress clean. I don't want you to waste time changing clothes because I can tell you gathered an awful lot with the reverend. Express it in your art. Let it all out."

I nodded. Instead of my sketchbook I was drawn to the paints. And, as though my hand were guided by an unseen force, I added brushstrokes to a pristine canvas. It had been so long since I had the luxury of paint—the blazing gold, azure, deep gray, rose, pine-tree green. Again, it struck me how Miss Violet seemed attuned to me in a way that couldn't be explained. We hadn't known each other well enough, and yet she gave when I needed, she provided what I lacked. And she revealed what I couldn't see for myself.

I didn't know how long I'd been painting, but in the same way my new ritual opened a portal for the deceased to visit, the portal funneled creative inspiration for hours. There were only two canvases stretched over wood, but when I finished those, I painted white over newspapers and used them to make more scenes. It would be days before they dried, but I couldn't stop from wanting to do more.

Olivia joined me in the kitchen with her books and sat at the table, studying the practice investments Violet had assigned to her. It didn't take long for her to fall asleep at the table, head resting on her arms.

"Katherine."

I jumped, turned, and the brush hit the canvas, leaving a trail of pine green where I hadn't intended.

"Mama," I said. I rubbed my right eye with my fist, my vision blurred with fatigue and the warm haze that I could only attribute to falling deep into this creative spell after being in the space between the present and the hereafter.

Mama moved gingerly toward me, her gaze slipping from one painting to the next. I hadn't stopped long enough to inventory what I'd painted tonight. *Is it still night?* I squinted at the door where Mama had entered. The sun was pink beyond the apple trees in the far garden. *Have I been up all night? Is it yesterday still?*

Mama stopped at the painting to my left. It was nearly complete—like one of the sketches I'd done before. A boy knelt over a dead deer, weeping, gun at his side, face skyward, his hands on the deer's body as though begging God to bring it back to life. A girl stood off to the side, watching.

"Katherine?" Mama's hand warmed my arm.

I turned slowly, my eyes finally pulling into focus at the worried expression on Mama's face.

I wiped my forehead with the back of my hand, nearly swiping my head with the brush.

Mama took the brush from me and began to loosen the sash that held the smock closed. It fell open and Mama's expression grew dark as she studied me. "Why on earth are you dressed like this? Where'd you get this dress?"

I felt as though I'd been knocked unconscious and was just coming back to awareness. "Miss Violet gave it to me."

She stared at me and then looked me up and down again. "Even naming you kitchen mistress doesn't rate a fine dress like this." She scanned the kitchen. "Painting? Have you been painting all night?"

I didn't know what to say. I'd no idea what time it was. I licked my lips, having no answer. I looked to my side, where Olivia was just waking, yawning and stretching, and saw her books and papers over the table.

"I was studying, Mama. And then I painted a little, yes." I gestured to the books on the table. I felt exhausted and could have fallen asleep standing there.

"Jeanie." Miss Violet moseyed into the kitchen with an armful of cut flowers. "These cheery sunflowers are simply divine. We must grow them in the back next year."

I yawned and sat down. Mama stared from me to Miss Violet and back again. "Katherine's exhausted. She needs to sleep."

Miss Violet pushed the blooms into Mama's arms and took the brush and paint from the table, setting them onto newspaper spread near the dry sink. She lined the brush up with the others. "She's taking a break during breakfast, Jeanie. That's all."

Mama glared at me, disbelieving. "You got up before first light, before I even noticed? I waited up for you, but I must have fallen asleep."

Sleep? She hadn't slept. "I came in late, yes. I thought I'd wakened you at one point, my tiptoeing not being as quiet as I would have liked. I should have told you I was home."

Mama looked at Miss Violet and back to me. "But that dress?"

Miss Violet sighed and pulled two glasses from the cabinet. She set them on the worktable and poured water into them. "I gave it to her. It's an old frock. I do apologize if I overstepped. Such a uniquely beautiful girl needs a dress that measures up."

Mama seemed to be considering the idea. I knew she was deciding whether our family was needy enough to be given clothing. Mama looked at the papers and books on the table again, and I hoped she was satisfied that I must have been studying most of the time.

"You'll go back to studying?" she said.

I nodded.

Mama looked back at the paintings, her eyes fixed on the one with the boy and deer.

"Katherine?"

"Yes, Mama?"

"Everything's all right? With your studies?"

The wiry lies stuck in my mouth again, making it difficult to swallow. "Of course. I'm learning so much." I couldn't keep this up. Pushing Mama to the fringes of my life after it'd been so long since we'd been close made it nearly impossible to breathe.

Mama stole a glance at Miss Violet putting water on the stovetop.

"She clearly has your intellect and know-how," Miss Violet said, turning to face us.

Mama smiled. I felt odd, as though Mama knew something had shifted between the two of us. I saw it in her face, in the split second that her shoulders dropped. *Just a little bit more time, Mama. I'll tell you everything very soon.*

I put my hand to my chest as though vowing to myself that this would not go on much longer. I'd continue living this lie just until I paid off what I owed. Then I'd give Mama the rest of my earnings. *I'm so sorry, Mama.*

Mama smoothed the back of my hair. "I'm glad Miss Pendergrass agrees with what I've known since you were born."

I looked away, knowing that she used the name, Miss Pendergrass, rather than Violet as a means of separating herself from her, a reminder to me that this was a formal relationship. A sob caught in my throat. I forced a smile, Mama's words magnifying her worth, my unworthiness. *I want to be the great woman you are, Mama.* The plan that had been so clear before was now muddied, feeling absolutely wrong.

Miss Violet pulled out a chair and signaled for Mama to sit.

Mama stepped toward the door. "I need to get breakfast for Yale. Normally, Katherine brings it to us by now."

I flew to my feet. "I'm so sorry, Mama. I just got lost in my work and . . . I'll get it now."

I opened the refrigerator door and pulled out several crocks. Mama was at the door, hand on the knob. She looked back over her shoulder, watching Miss Violet stare at the paintings, her head cocked to the side.

Miss Violet pointed to one of the paintings. "Jeanie," she said. "We can sell these paintings. They're quite good. And my clientele would greatly appreciate this work. And I know you want to buy your own home. This may well get you there faster than you could have imagined."

Mama joined Miss Violet at the easel.

"You like them, Mama?"

"Of course. But you and I both know formal schooling, diplomas, degrees—those are the papers that will ensure your future success and independence. Art is soft, unreliable. Even with gifts like yours."

My heart grew heavy.

She walked over to look at one painting drying up against the wall. She stared at it as though it had sucked her right into it. There was a mother, a baby on her lap, and the father set back away from the pair, his outstretched hand draped with morning glories. There was a second woman kneeling at an open grave, wailing in pain. I hadn't even remembered painting it.

Mama looked at me; her skin paled, gray like winter sky.

I went to her. "Mama?"

"I have to go," Mama said and started toward the door. It was as though the painting frightened her.

"Wait," I said, and Mama stopped.

I opened the drawer where I'd hidden the bells on the string. "Here," I said, putting it in Mama's hand. "To put on Yale's dress or wrist so we don't lose track of her. You'll hear her when your back is to her in the garden or when you're sewing." Mama stared at me as though I was unrecognizable and then she opened the door. "Thank you. This should be very helpful."

I could hear someone calling her from outside. "Who's that?" I said, heading toward the door.

Mama shook her head. "That crow, Frank. He calls to me nearly every time I step outside." She laughed.

Another voice came from outside. "That must be Mr. Hayes," Mama said. She visibly exhaled as she left. The relief that swept over her face when she heard Mr. Hayes's voice reassured me. I was nearly as grateful as Mama that he'd taken an interest in her.

I selected an empty crock from the butler's pantry and saw that Miss Violet was still absorbed in the paintings. She was sucked into the same one Mama had been earlier. I wondered at its allure. It was incomplete, the subjects' faces not yet detailed.

"I need to get out of this dress."

Miss Violet nodded. "I need you to oversee the new kitchen mistress when she arrives."

"Of course." I felt an odd distance forming between us, like a river that splits around land. I couldn't manage if both Mama and Miss Violet were cross.

"Did I do something wrong?" I asked.

Miss Violet walked forward. I could see her jaw clench and then her deep inhale as though she was trying to cleanse away her sour mood. "Not on purpose, no. But now that dress. You've got to take it home and hang it there. We can't use it for Dreama now that your mother's seen it."

I looked down. "I'm so sorry. I didn't sleep a wink last night. I just couldn't stop painting. It was as though I was working with a different mind, a different body. Like a dream. You were pleased last night? Now, with the paintings?"

Miss Violet sighed. "Well, yes. Definitely with last night. The feathers were a little overkill, and I didn't expect you to pull out a gimmick, I must say, but it worked and I was pleased with your initiative."

"But I didn't do that."

"You're saying feathers just materialized out of the air?"

I tried to piece together the reading in my mind. When I become so absorbed in a reading, I don't always remember every little thing. But I knew I hadn't brought the feathers with me.

"Look, you painted a feather into this. Surely you remember."

I looked at the scene, a man with his pipe, feet up, and a cat on his lap. It was clearly Reverend Shaw.

"I remember. Sort of. But I know I didn't bring feathers. Unless they were inside the sack with the pendants and they came out when I emptied it?"

"No, I'm sure of that," Miss Violet said.

"Well, it made sense at the time," I said.

She shook her finger at the paintings. "We need to keep any paintings that we might sell as Dreama's away from your mother. We can't have some satisfied customer going to the press with Dreama's insightful artwork only to have your mother see it in the paper."

A chill crept up my spine. I hadn't even thought of someone seeing me or my painting and then seeing it again with my "Dreama" signature.

"Maybe no one'll want them. Just because you thought I sketched your father dying ... maybe that was just a one-time thing. Maybe it was just the way you saw it."

Miss Violet looked back at the painting that Mama had looked at so long, turning her bloodless. "Yes, yes, I've considered all of that. But it's not the point."

I didn't know what she meant. "Do you believe me or not?"

"What I believe is we need to be careful," Miss Violet said, "until we earn the money we know we can. Don't sign the paintings at all. Maybe draw a little angel in the corner of the ones that you know are connected to a specific reading. But no signature, Katherine Arthur or otherwise."

I nodded. Mama. I wanted to allay her suspicions until I could tell her about Dreama on my own terms. "Allow me to pay Mama again. She was very pleased with that bag of coins I gave her. The mere sight of it put her mind at ease. And I want to tell her the truth soon, Miss Violet."

"No."

"She won't fault me."

"She doesn't understand your gift, Katherine. I can see that plain."

"The money will help. I'll make sure she knows I'm not like Madame Smalley."

Miss Violet tapped her chin with her forefinger, her brow creased. "It's too risky at this stage."

"It'll make it easier. Please. These lies ferment into worry and fear, and then I get a little blocked. It would be easier if—"

"After *A Night for Mothers*," Violet swept her hand across the air as if sweeping away chalk on a board. "Then Dreama will be solid in her work. This one special evening is all it will take. We'll gather grieving, worried mothers and you'll rustle up their deceased loved ones and show the public how you soothe a mother's despair like no one else in the world. And Dreama's fortune will be set to bloom like your mother's garden."

The evening was still two weeks away. "Then please," I said. "Give me money. It'll help. If Mama could pick up food at the wagons on Main Street when she's running errands, she might not pop in here like today. I don't like lying, but perhaps I could give her some more money even before I pay off the dresses?"

"If I give you more, the others will say I'm playing favorites. I can't pay you before them."

I felt a surge of strength course through me. I straightened. The others were clearly book smart, but I could tell by Miss Violet's treatment of me that she knew I was different. If I had to lie, I needed to be compensated. "I'll keep the coins you give me to myself. I've no need to wave my treasure under their noses. You have my word."

"Each person is equally important here. You're exceptional, but so are they. In different ways, ways you can't fathom, Katherine. There's much you don't understand about my work and the girls. Don't begin to feel as though you are above anyone here."

I held my breath. "The others don't support a family like I do. Mama works the garden and trades the eggs and milk. Tommy works hard, too. And Yale—" I immediately regretted mentioning Yale. Miss Violet might recall her initial inclination to turn us away because of her.

Miss Violet's posture softened. She fussed with the bottom of her jacket that made a ruffled plume around her shapely waist. "I do fancy Yale. From afar, of course. But . . ." Her gaze slid off to somewhere else. Then she came back to me and gripped my shoulders. "I'll grant you extra pay. But I expect that you spend your time and energy on being Dreama, her rituals. That's all you need to think about. Find a way to spend less time babysitting Yale."

"Thank you," I said.

"Your mother's hardy. Clearly so. You told me she's been through much pain. She's told me herself. She's managed to convince Mr. Hayes to help with heavy work, right? She'll be fine. You do what I need you to, and soon you'll have all the riches you can imagine. You'll free your family from its disgrace and poverty once and for all. But you must promise to continue to keep this between us until the time is right. I trust you with much of my business. You *must* continue to trust me. Or this simply won't work. And you'll be out on your own before you have a chance to fulfill any of your very lofty goals."

A thick mass coiled in my belly. She was doing what I asked, yet I felt worse about it all, as if she'd said no, as if I was being chained closer to my work as Dreama instead of ensuring I could move away from it altogether.

Chapter 35

First Blush
Aleksey

I stood at Katherine Arthur's door and knocked. No one came. I waited and knocked again and again. When no one answered, I went to the sidewalk and surveyed the grounds. I followed a small walkway around the tiny house to the back. The fenced area was a narrow but long and lush garden. It was sectioned off with paths and trees, and I could see there was a shed way in the back behind tall hedges that formed a gateway, giving way to a row of rosebushes and fruit trees.

I knocked on the kitchen door. No response. Surely, they'd be inside preparing meals, sewing, doing whatever it was that they did each day. I leaned forward and cupped my eyes to cut the glare as I looked through the window. At the kitchen table, a woman sat slumped over, her arms pillowing her head. I thumped the door again. "Mrs. Arthur?"

But before I finished saying her name, the woman turned her head, nesting it back on her arms, eyes never opening. I stared, taken aback. Her face in slumber. Beautiful.

Katherine.

My heart sped up. My reaction to the sight of her caught me off guard. My feelings for her seemed to deepen just at seeing her.

I rapped on the window this time, hard, but not wanting to frighten her. Was she sick? What was she doing?

I knocked again, harder. She didn't stir, so I turned the knob and let myself in.

She didn't flinch. I crouched, my hand on her back. "Katherine."

She leapt up, stepping away from the table. Her gaze was unfixed as she struggled to understand what was happening.

She backed into the wall, gasping for breath, her hands at her temples as if she could clear her mind that way.

"It's me," I said. "Aleksey."

She nodded and pressed her hand to her chest. "You scared the daylights out of me."

I stepped gingerly toward her, hands out. Her beauty dizzied me as though I'd been the one startled awake.

Finally, she relaxed, hand still at her chest.

"I'm so sorry. I knocked. Several times." I stepped closer; the scent of flowers filled my nose. "Are you all right?"

She waved me away and bent forward, hands on knees. I turned and saw a sink with a pump, and I drew water. "Here. Your cheeks are red as cherries."

I gave her the glass. "Are you sick?"

She shook her head, regaining composure. "Tired, is all. Please," she gestured toward the seat, "sit. Let me get *you* something to drink. I don't know how I fell asleep like that. I feel like you yanked me out of a rushing river or something."

I was already headed to the pump for my own glass of water. "You sit." All I wanted was to take care of her, to take away whatever was ailing her.

I came back toward her with a full glass of water. She stared, an odd expression on her face. I guided her into a chair. She smelled of lavender and lemons. That was it. The scent made me want to bury my face in her hair.

As she drank and seemed to become more lucid, I sat beside her and dug into my pocket. "I wrote this to you."

She squinted at the envelope I pushed across the table.

"I know what you're thinking," I said.

Her expression was pleasant but curious.

"You're wondering why on earth I didn't just post the letter rather than show up with it myself."

She grinned. "You know me well. Somehow, still." Her voice was thin, but her gaze adhered to mine. My breath stuttered again. I realized that she felt it, too, our connectedness despite the recent and long distance between us.

"Well, I could have posted it and then waited for your reply to ask when specifically I should call. But then I thought perhaps your mama would be the one to read it and then reply, and what if she didn't ask me to call or what if something came up at the farm with all the rain? Or with my studies."

"You know Mama would have suggested you call anytime." She gave me a sly smile, something that reminded me again how grown up she was.

I nodded. "Yes. But still . . ."

She raised her eyebrows. "What?"

"What if I lost the letter when I went fishing with the fellas? And then if I got distracted at the dance by the river?"

She leaned in, jaw dropped. "Dance by the river?"

"Twice a week, just about. The heavy rains have canceled some of them, but pretty regular, yes."

She leaned back in her chair as though imagining it.

"So," I said, "when we finished our work earlier today than usual, Mr. Palmer said he needed to come to town. I turned in some briefs to Mr. Stevens, and here I am. I couldn't see the sense in waiting any longer to call on you. But I apologize for my dusty clothes."

She smiled, a little smile, the half smile with closed lips, her eyes doing all the work of communicating. She was amused. My stomach flipped.

I'd had Mabel in my lap more than once, her lips on mine, my body on fire with desire . . . but never this. Mabel had touched me every chance she got, and yet here was Katherine, exhausted, sections of her chestnut hair falling down the side of her face, unkempt yet utterly mesmerizing. Parts of me that I hadn't known existed came alive without even a touch, just by being near her.

She yawned and covered her mouth, her cheeks reddening, embarrassed that I caught her mouth open like a cat. I shook my head to communicate—*No, don't be embarrassed. You are stunning.*

She kept her mouth covered, but I could see her smiling behind her hand.

My attraction to women had never been more than skin-deep. This—what I felt taking hold like a vice—was unexplainable, unimaginable. I'd fallen into something completely different with Katherine Arthur—after a year of daily interaction with her and then nothing. Like earth barren for years and then water comes, and suddenly it's green, end to end, thick with life. That was me in those moments. My entire being was springing to life.

I couldn't have been more skeptical of such a thing. Until this. I kept her in my gaze, trying to capture every bit of her to keep in my mind for later.

"What?" she asked.

"I don't know."

She gave me a teasing smirk. "You always had a way with words, Aleksey Zurchenko."

"So I'm not impressing you?" How could I with my words tying up my tongue?

"Oh, I'm impressed, surely." She winked at me.

Now my cheeks warmed. I leaned back in the chair, trying to give myself an air of nonchalance, trying to get my thumping heart to slow itself down. "Tell me what you're doing. What brought the Arthurs back to Des Moines? Where are Tommy and your mama and Yale?"

She shook her head absently, her eyes looking to the ceiling as though she was trying to decide where to start. "That's, well . . ." She shook her head more deliberately now. "Tommy must be running errands or selling prayers or what have you."

"Prayers?"

"Yes."

I crossed my arms, calling up the vision of Tommy wandering the plains, Bible in hand, scripture on his tongue. "That fits with what I remember about him. Always quoting the Bible."

"Oh galoshes. Those verses. On and on he droned."

Oh galoshes. I was taken back years hearing her using that phrase. I could not have been more content at the sound of simple words tumbling from her plump lips. I leaned forward, arms on the table, hands open, hoping to gather up everything she uttered.

We stared at each other, both lost in thought, the silence warm and inviting, and so for some time neither of us intruded upon it. In the distance, someone's supper bell began to ring.

She shot up out of her seat and put her hand to her forehead. "My manners must have been put to sleep when I dozed off," she said. "Let me feed you. You must be famished."

And though I started to protest her offer, I stopped when she began to forage behind doors and in drawers, disappearing into the cellar and reappearing with a Dutch oven. "Stew," she said, setting it on the stove to be heated.

She uncovered a loaf of nutty, golden bread and set it before us. When the stew was hot, she portioned it off and slid two bowls onto the table.

My belly growled and my mouth watered at the sight and smell. Still, I took a tentative sip, remembering that the Arthurs had been brilliant and cultured and mannered, but they hadn't been great cooks. I braced myself as the beefy liquid hit my tongue. I thought I was tasting a little bit of heaven.

I closed my eyes momentarily. "What's in this? You know my mama cooks something wonderful even in the worst of times, but *this* . . ."

Katherine's face glowed at the compliment. She straightened her shoulders as though this was just what she needed to hear. "Just some sweet herbs—"

"Rosemary." I held up my spoon.

"Yes. And parsley, sage—"

"And thyme."

She nodded and tilted her head. "But if you think I'm disclosing my secret ingredients, you're in for a long, long, hungry wait."

I drew the last hunk of grainy bread around the inside of the bowl. Suddenly, I thought of Mabel. I recalled her admonishment that I had been so complimentary of her cooking that she had no choice but to interpret that to mean I was in love with her and would want to travel east with her. I wouldn't want to make Katherine upset that way. I started to silently repeat the idea that I'd no time for love, for women. But then the clink of her spoon on her bowl drew my attention back to her. She sat there like an angel descended from the heavens. I'd thought I wasn't ready for love or anything it required, but something, someone else, had changed all that. My chest constricted. I pressed it and tried to draw a deep breath.

"What's wrong, Aleksey? Did I give you heartburn?"

I shook my head, unable to speak. *More like love.* Her cooking caused me to fall in love right there in this kitchen. She started to get up. I held up my hand.

"No, no. Just tell me. What's the secret ingredient? Mr. Palmer would die to eat this. Mabel would love this, too."

"Mabel?" She rested her chin on her fist and raised her eyebrows again.

"Just a girl at the house. She cooks for us, is all."

She studied me, and I felt as though I could see the question form in her mind. *And do you fancy her?*

"She's quite taken with Fat Joe. One of the fellas."

"Fat Joe?" She laughed, her head falling back.

"Quite plump, yes," I said.

"Well, I'm glad you have nice associates. It can be quite lonely to be away from family."

She would have known that very well. I rubbed my full belly. "I remember when you left the prairie. Your mama said you'd be separated for a bit."

She jerked as though she'd been punched in the belly. The life in her eyes snapped away, and she gazed off. "Longer than that."

I tore off another piece of bread. "How long?" I felt like we'd never left each other's sides. Still, there was so much I didn't know.

She shook her head and shifted in her seat. The easy silence we'd shared, the meal, her quick smile and enchanting way disintegrated right in front of me. Gone as though a spell had been cast to remove all the wondrousness we'd experienced. That darkness behind her eyes that I noticed at the grocer's was back.

"Tell me. Where'd you all go? What'd you do?"

She got up and took my bowl and bread plate to the sink. "Oh, Aleksey. No, no. The tale of your magical journey from prairie farmer to young man studying the law would be so much better. To think of where you started as a student, and now you're studying for law exams and working on this Mr. Palmer's farm with fellas named Fat Joe and girls named Mabel. Tell me about all of that."

I was pleased she wanted to hear about me. It might ease her into sharing if I did so first.

"Well, I admire Mr. Palmer."

Katherine rolled up the sleeves on her white shirtwaist. The rounded collar met where tiny pink flower buttons marched down the cotton. She pulled a scrubber from the windowsill and began to scour the crock the stew had been in. Her waist was a wispy thing, her arms slender. She was tall like my ma, but graceful and slight, unlike Ma. As she scrubbed, her hips moved, making her plain maroon skirt rustle, drawing me in.

I joined her at the sink and rolled up my own sleeves. I took the bread plate, dipped it into the water. My hand brushed hers. She stole a glance, and my stomach fluttered. I could've disappeared into her glistening round eyes, disappeared into this very moment for eternity.

"I certainly have the highest regard for my farming parents. Mr. Palmer has the fellas, Mabel, and me learning the Granger ways. And I admire that, too. But what you gave me all those years ago sprang my mind open to all the other possibilities besides farming. I just can't see the world in the same way since I've learned how big it actually is."

"Farming's a big job, though," Katherine said.

I shrugged. "Anyone can farm."

Katherine froze mid-scrub. For a moment, I thought she was angry. Her body tensed. But then she looked at me, her face full of confusion, and she simply burst out with a laugh that filled the room.

She dropped the scrubber and, with the back of her hand, wiped her hair from her face, still laughing, her eyes filling with sad tears.

I didn't know what to do. "What?"

She stopped for a moment, then was taken again with nearly maniacal laughter mixed with crying.

I took her wet hands in mine. "I didn't mean to make you cry and laugh . . . and . . . are you crying or laughing?"

"Anyone can farm?" she sputtered the words in between her laughter.

My family had managed to produce crops and do relatively well in the worst of times while the Arthurs seemed to turn their entire homestead into barren land. My mind spun, tumbling back through time to the prairie failures. The fires, the locusts, the blizzard, the death and destruction of families.

"I see what you mean," I said, loving the sound of her laughter, her crying, her everything. I laughed along with her, glad she could see humor in what wasn't her family's strength, despite it all.

Her laughter dissolved; only trails of tears remained. I knew it wasn't proper for me to touch her, but I couldn't allow her to stand alone like that inside her pain—experiences I, too, shared. And so I ignored what I knew was expected behavior. I took her face in my hands and dried her tears with my thumbs. She grasped my wrists and closed her eyes, accepting my trespass.

She squeezed my wrists. "I'm so exhausted I don't know if I'm crying or laughing."

Energy tore through me, the warmth of her hands on me took me somewhere else. "I'm so sorry, Katherine." I couldn't help but look at her hand, the amputated finger.

She shook her head and pulled her hands away from mine and plunged them into the water, scrubbing again. She exhaled deeply. "You didn't do anything, Aleksey. You saved me."

I nodded, not sure what else to say.

We fell into the calming silence all over again and finished the dishes, even did some that I suspected didn't need washing. Neither one of us wanted to move away from the sink, from each other. Finally, she said, "Tell me what you're doing on the farm, Aleksey. Tell me about the law. I want to hear it all."

I told her about the finders, keepers cases, the fellas, the wall I was tasked with fixing, and the book and the mysterious rocks I'd found.

"I have a book of recipes, too," she said.

"Obviously! You use yours. Mine sits in a trunk."

I reached in my pocket to pull out the stunning butterfly stone to show her and remembered I'd put it in the trunk that day while my trousers were being washed and forgot to take it back out, so I didn't mention it. She invited me to sit back at the table for some coffee, and the door flew open.

We both startled. A woman burst in, dressed in what I could only define as a dress made for a woman of incredible wealth and leisure—the gold material shimmered and danced like it was alive.

She was an attractive woman, but her beauty was hard, not like Katherine's. "*Katherine.*" She gritted her teeth.

Katherine slapped her hand over her mouth and moved toward the woman.

"Miss Violet's about to drop over dead, fretting about you and why you aren't—"

The woman glanced at me, then turned her body so I couldn't see her straight on and mouthed something to Katherine.

"I'll be there in a minute," Katherine said.

She turned to me, her posture straight, and she talked to me as though we were strangers. "Thank you for the visit, Aleksey. But I'm late for work. Another kitchen awaits." Her words were cold and clipped.

I stood. "Oh, yes. You mentioned kitchen work in your letter."

"*Now.*" The woman pulled Katherine's arm.

Katherine wiggled free and glared at the woman. "Just a moment, Olivia. Tell Miss Violet I'll be there in just a moment."

Katherine stuck her hand out to me to shake, formal, unfamiliar. I was too stunned and confused to do anything other than take her hand. "I'm the kitchen mistress," she said. "Next door."

"Kitchen mistress." *That's* what the letter said. "You work in her kitchen?"

She shot a look at Olivia. "Well, Miss Violet's actually. But Olivia lives there, too."

"After tasting your stew and bread, I'd say they're the luckiest people around to have someone like you working for them."

She nodded.

"*Now, Katherine,*" the woman said.

"Your letter." I swiped it off the table and handed it to her. Katherine smiled at it and then at me. She pressed it against her chest. "I look forward to reading it, Aleksey Zurchenko. I can't wait."

And she waved me out of the kitchen. She and Olivia followed and went down the steps toward the hedges along the border of the garden.

"Isn't it late for kitchen work?" I said from the porch.

They reached a small opening in the hedge. Olivia lifted her skirt, glared at Katherine, and disappeared through the greenery.

"It's always time for kitchen work, Aleksey."

She gave me a nod and a smile and bent into the hole in the hedge. I went to the spot where they had disappeared. The hole was too small for me to fit through. I poked my fingers through another section and spread the branches. I could make out the back of another house, the enormous pink one I'd seen when I found this one.

I hoped Katherine would turn back and give me a wave, but she didn't. I certainly understood a demanding boss. Mr. Palmer and Mr. Stevens were both particular, especially about timeliness. But something about this Olivia, her clothing, the expression that teetered between angry and frightened, left me with a sense of dislike. My skin rose in goose pimples, and I heard the back door of the pink house slam shut. The chirping of crickets filled my ears, and I felt as though my insides had been sucked away.

I turned and pushed my hand through my hair. It was then I noticed the sun had fallen behind the shed at the back of the property. I didn't know what time it was, but I knew I was late. A crow sat on a rosebush where another set of hedges made a gateway to the rest of the yard. I would have sworn the bird was watching me.

It squawked and took off flying as I broke into a jog. Katherine wouldn't be the only one getting a scolding from her boss that night. I'd be lucky if Mr. Palmer and his wagon waited for me at all.

Chapter 36

Vapor Bath
Katherine

A week passed since Aleksey had stopped by with his letter. Though I still helped in the kitchen when Miss Violet's new kitchen help floundered, much of my afternoon time was devoted to sketching, painting, and vapor bathing. Miss Violet had become well-versed in all the ways Olivia, Bernice, Helen, Abigail, and I were to maintain a glow of health that matched our blossoming intellect. According to Blakeslee's *Book of Knowledge*, sun and vapor bathing were central to achieving that result. While we bathed under the sun's rays, Miss Violet held private meetings in her office downstairs.

After a week of sunbaths, I was just beginning to become comfortable with the process. Skeptical of such a thing, Miss Violet had us read about the methodology behind it.

Miss Violet laid several duvets of feathers covered in silken threads on the floor near the floor-to-ceiling windows at the back of the house near the washroom when I needed to become Dreama. At bath time, we were to disrobe and recline under the rays of the sun that spilled through the windows. At first I couldn't relax and finished each vapor bath stiff and tension-filled. But around the third day of this activity, when I laid down, my body splayed, uncovered, and the sun kissed my skin, caressing me, the rays would drag me into slumber. Like we'd read, the experience lured me into oblivion with heavy eyelids and even breaths, taking me to the cusp of sleep, where I only felt pleasure.

After short but deep sleep, we wakened and turned onto our stomachs. Nearly every moment of this time was spent in conversation about the men each of the women longed to call husband. I hadn't expected to join this conversation since I was years younger and certainly hadn't indicated I was interested in marriage to anyone.

"Oh no, you don't, Miss Katherine." Olivia turned her face toward me, her eyes closed, a sweet smile on her face. "I saw that Aleksey Zur . . . Zir . . . whatever you said his name was with my own two eyes. And I saw you hang on every single one of his sugary words like you were hanging on for dear life."

This perked up the other ladies, and they turned onto their sides, heads resting on elbows. "Maybe he's not *that* handsome," Helen said. "Leave it alone."

I peeked at Olivia through my arm. She closed her eyes. "Oh, he's that handsome. In the way that makes him every woman's type." Olivia sat up, her breasts exposed. She pulled a sheet over her lap as she sat cross-legged. She bent her arms and made fists. "Big and strong as a bear. But fair-haired and blue-eyed and . . ." she looked up at the ceiling, "attentive." She shook her finger. "That's the word. Even as I was getting more insistent that Katherine come back to Violet's, he never took his eyes from her for more than a moment. Never looked me over. Even with half my bosom out." Olivia put her hands under her breasts and jiggled them up and down. The others laughed along with her.

"I thought he was an ordinary farmer, Katherine," Abigail said.

Olivia jumped in before I could answer. "Oh my, no. This one's special."

They badgered and prodded me with, *Did he kiss you? Are his hands full of calluses? Are his lips as sweet as his words?* until I admitted that although he'd never kissed me in the way they were thinking, I did have two letters he'd written me in my art satchel. When I refused to retrieve them, Olivia rose and sauntered to my bag, her hips swaying as she moved, unencumbered with any of the shyness I felt at being naked. I got on my elbows to see her dig the envelopes out. She came back toward us, and I noticed her hip-sway was partly the result of her limping from when she'd twisted her ankle the other day.

She smacked an envelope against her palm and settled back on the duvet, pulling a linen sheet over her lap.

I sat up, hoping to turn the conversation away from the letters somehow. "Let me see your ankle."

She lifted her foot and twirled it. I could see purpling and bluing covering the top of her foot and her outside anklebone. I drew in my breath at the sight.

She waved me off. "It's fine. Just a little twist. I had to weave away from Alderman Meyers the other day when he got a bit too handsy for my liking."

I moved toward her. "I could make a comfrey poultice. It'll draw the bruise away, to stop the swelling."

"That will be wonderful. But for now, this is much more interesting." She pulled a letter from its envelope and began to read. I buried my face in my arms. "You're going to be disappointed," I said, knowing the way they talked about love was not at all like Aleksey's letters.

"Dear Katherine," Olivia read with a breathy voice, "the day has ended and night has moseyed in and brought with it the stars, the moon, and thoughts of you."

The girls hooted. "Oh my," Helen said. "Go on."

Miss Bernice fanned herself.

"I think I will," Olivia said.

She read silently for a moment and then spoke again. "Farming, walls, digging holes, big tree that looks like Medusa, Harold and Fat Joe working harder, blah, blah, blah." She bugged her eyes out at me. "You may be right, dear Katherine. This letter had such promise."

Olivia went quiet again and then pointed her finger. "Ah. Here we go. The golden god writes, 'And so as I ready to sleep, I'll close my eyes and see your face and hope that the next time we see one another you bring me your smile, like daybreak brings the sun.'"

"He's smitten, Katherine," Helen said.

I shook my head. "He's an old friend, is all. From way back."

Olivia flicked the paper. "P.S. I can't wait to hear more of your work and studies." Olivia squeezed my arm. "You haven't written to him about your work. Your real work?"

"'Course not," I said.

"Well then, good."

"Bring the next one when you get it. I think the letters are lovely, boring as they may be." Helen laid back down, catching the rays as the sun poked through a thick cloud.

"Tell me what Aleksey looks like. Sounds like a mythical hero," Bernice said.

I was glad that Olivia only found one of Aleksey's letters in my bag as the other was more flowery than the first. And so I started from the beginning, back on the prairie, teaching him to read and write. I didn't get very far before all of us were sleeping again, the sun blanketing us with warm rays.

Someone jostled my arm, and my sleep came to an end. "Katherine."

I opened my eyes, groggy, my vision blurred. Still, I knew it was Miss Violet shaking me awake. I sat up and threw my arm across my chest, legs tucked under me.

The other girls stirred and wakened as well.

Miss Violet shook Aleksey's letter at me. "What is this?"

I reached for a thin cover and pulled it over me. "A letter." It was the other letter from my bag that Olivia hadn't noticed when she got the first one out to read.

"Who wrote it?"

I pointed to his signature. "Aleksey."

"That boy you and your mother were talking about?"

I was surprised she'd remembered his name. I nodded, confused at her anger.

Miss Violet ran her finger down the letter, reading it. She exhaled, her breath smoothing out. "Isn't he full of interest and affection for you?"

Her tone was more accusing than questioning. I reached for the letter. "He's a friend of our family. That year was . . . Well, of course he has an interest in me. We went through a lot. He's a friend."

She pulled it out of my grip, bent down to me, and read from the letter. "Your slim, soft hands dance when you talk, mesmerizing me. The stew you made keeps my mouth watering to this very moment. All the while I farm and study, thoughts of you come with every breath and heartbeat."

Miss Violet shook it again and narrowed her eyes. "Friendship? You're not *that* naïve. It's clear as this window pane this man desires you."

I flinched at the word *man* to describe him. He was indeed, but the way she said it, with a sneer, it felt insulting rather than a simple fact.

The other girls nodded. I looked at each of them and then back to Miss Violet.

"He's a good person."

"But you have big plans, do you not?"

I pulled the sheet against me but straightened up to show her I wasn't some child. "You know I have plans."

"You spoke of women's rights when we first met."

Why would she press this? Of course, women's rights were important to me. She knew that. "Yes. You know that I—"

She moved closer to me. I could feel the gazes of the others on me. "You understand that the first step in handing over every *single* right you own is to give your heart to a man."

I winced. I did have feelings toward Aleksey. How could I not? After what he did for me? And I wasn't blind. I saw his handsomeness. I saw it reflected in Olivia's eyes, the way she described him to the others. I felt pulled to him, so very proud to have taught him to read and to love learning. But I resented Miss Violet's assertion that I might trade away my independence just because someone, even someone I liked very much, sent me complimentary letters.

"I'm as independent as you, Miss Violet." I rose and wrapped myself tighter in the cover, heading to the mirror to brush my hair.

She followed me. "I understand he's a family friend, a close one. That you have a history. But there are two things you should understand—one: I've met many women who appeared naïve and were far less so in actuality. That type of trickery does not sit well with me. That kind of woman can't be trusted. Two: women who find their hearts in the hands of a man, even a good one, lose their senses, their direction, and often the riches that had once been intended for them."

I felt devoted to Miss Violet for all she'd promised me . . . *promised.* The word stopped me dead. I thought of the home I should have been saving for. Promised. Not yet delivered. I continued to brush my hair.

Perhaps I had been naïve, but in more ways than Miss Violet suggested. I wasn't sure why she was so angry about the letters, exactly, but suddenly I knew I needed to keep my true feelings on the matter to myself. I needed to sort through my thoughts, pay more attention to what I owed and earned by being Dreama.

"I'm not either woman you described."

She studied me a moment, as though she thought her steely gaze could crack open some layer of truth I wasn't telling. Aleksey was a fine man and a good friend. But I wasn't in danger of handing over my hand in marriage to him or to anyone.

Finally, Miss Violet nodded and took my chin. "I trust you'll keep your head straight where this young man is concerned."

"'Course." I held her gaze, but drew away so she had to release her hold.

Miss Violet scowled and stepped toward the door. "Put up your hair. Your bath has been drawn." She left the room, and the other girls, who were wrapping themselves in silken robes, came to me.

"You're shaken," Olivia said.

I covered my mouth and realized my hand was quaking. "I'm fine. Miss Violet need not worry about my feelings toward Aleksey."

Olivia wrinkled her nose. "Here. Have a sip of this before your bath ritual."

I was about to down the whole glass of water when a woody scent caught me off guard. I pulled the glass back and looked at the clear liquid.

"Gin," Olivia said. "Sometimes it's the only thing that gets the rest of us through the day. Maybe it'll help with your dead people."

Bernice leaned into the mirror, trimming her eyebrows with tiny scissors.

"What does that mean?"

They passed a glance, and Bernice shrugged. I knew immediately that they were questioning my ability.

"You doubt me?"

Olivia tilted her head and then patted my shoulder. "'Course not, silly. We just understand . . . well, performance anxiety."

Bernice snickered and leaned against the wall, picking at one of her cuticles.

"We believe you, Katherine. Just drink up. We're trying to help, that's all."

I tried a sip but choked it right back out. "That's awful. I could make you a nice tea or hot chocolate if you need soothing."

Olivia let out a giggle. She took the glass from me, tossed the gin down her throat, and lifted the glass. "You really are naïve, aren't you?"

I shrugged. "I don't think so. No."

Olivia poured more into her glass and handed it to Helen, who threw it down her throat in one gulp. Bernice handed a charcoal pencil to Olivia, who began to stroke color onto her lashes and upper lids. A mix of confusion and gratitude hit me.

I wouldn't be comfortable wearing such dark color on my eyes, and I hadn't been asked to. I stalked toward the door and then turned back to see the three women readying themselves. I thought of them, of myself, strewn about the room, nude, all afternoon. I wouldn't have supposed I'd do that either. Perhaps I couldn't trust myself at all. Maybe the lies I told everyone I knew paled in the light of the fibs I told myself.

A door slammed downstairs, jarring me back to the task at hand. I went to the bathroom, where I would sink into the fragrant water that brought my angels calling almost the second I submerged.

**

The day Miss Violet discovered the letters Aleksey was writing to me, the readings had gone well. Nothing more was said on the matter, but in the days following, her gaze would linger on me, her expression probing. I felt her questioning me through queries she asked the others. "You're not becoming soft toward Reverend Shaw, Olivia? That won't help your business grow. We don't have time for men outside of the work we do." And Miss Violet would steal a glance at me, telling me it was a reminder for me as well. She even pushed Colt Churchill away, saying that his saloon was causing more trouble than it was worth for investing. I didn't know what she meant by that, and she didn't explain.

Of all the guilt I felt in lying to Mama about how I was making money, I felt no guilt in allowing Aleksey the run of my mind and lying to Miss Violet about that. The way the girls had talked about him had sown seeds in me, and the way I envisioned him began to change. While I'd always felt connected to him, it was through their eyes that he truly began to grow in heroism in my mind. While we took our vapor baths, they would nearly always circle back to Aleksey.

"Men like him are fascinating. Tell us again how he saved you and Yale," Olivia would say.

I would tell the story again, deepening my admiration for him each time.

"He's a hero. But he's not for the likes of us," Helen would say.

"Barefoot and pregnant. I'm sure he'll have his pick of the litter," Olivia would say.

"I don't need a lifetime with him. Just a few evenings would suffice," Helen would say.

"He's not like that. He's heard of women's rights. And I'm sure someday his wife will be . . ." I didn't even know what I wanted to say, but I wished they would spend less time imagining courting him for any amount of time.

"He's awfully busy with his studies. I highly doubt he has time for more than that."

And they would roll over to warm their bottoms and chuckle at me. "I'd love to feel his arms around me," Olivia would say.

"I bet his lips are as soft as his heart," Helen would add. "Those letters . . ."

And I would close my ears to their words and imagine the same things. The difference was I could recall his strong hand on mine, the warmth that emanated. I swam in the memory of the quick embrace he'd given me when I'd seen him at the grocer's, the scent of work on him that day. All of these things were mine alone, and I hoarded the thoughts like the coins they hid away in their lingerie boxes.

Chapter 37

Cat
Katherine

After a stretch of several evenings and an afternoon of profitable readings, Miss Violet excused me from working. I took my sketchbook and spent a few hours in the garden with Yale, helping her weed and sketching her as she found absolute bliss in having her hands in the dirt.

I walked her around the garden, allowing her to decide on what we would have for supper. It took some time, but after several tries at saying the word *tomato*, she pulled me toward the flourishing plants. She pulled a few of the plumpest, reddest from the vines. I chose cucumbers, and as we were clipping basil, Mama entered the yard with Mr. Hayes.

Their arms were laden with seeds, a special fertilizer blend, and an antique rose plant, root-ball and all. Inside, I left Mama and Mr. Hayes to discuss the meeting they were to attend with Mrs. Hillis. I changed my shirtwaist and freshened up before making the meal. I was excited to make food for just my family, taking care of them that way. I came down the stairs and headed toward the kitchen.

As I neared it, I could hear the low rumble of Mr. Hayes's laugh. Mama's laugh moved inside his like the layered notes Olivia played on the piano. I stopped at the doorway and drew a deep breath. Of course, I'd heard Mama's laugh before, but this was different. Whatever it was that caused them to chuckle, it felt private, soft, yet deeply intense and full of secrets I'd never be told.

Hearing this caused an ache to curl and pit in my stomach, making me think of my father. As much as I second-guessed Mama for making him leave us, I also knew he had not been useful when we were so close to death so often. She had not said it aloud to me, but I knew she blamed him for James's death.

I didn't like admitting that, thinking of Father as useful or not, like a kitchen implement that had broken or rusted beyond using. But Mama deserved a moment of joy, laughter laced with something special. I pressed my stomach to ease the ache. *It's all right. Mama should have this.* It wasn't mine to share, just as my relationship with Miss Violet held secret dealings, an intimacy that excluded Mama in every way. That, I'd change just as soon as I could.

As I entered the kitchen, Mr. Hayes and Mama moved away from the sink, from each other, silenced. The sound of the bells tied around Yale's wrist and the clank of her spoon against the cup of hot chocolate filled in between the ticks of the kitchen clock.

Mama drew me into a tight embrace. "You'll never believe who stopped by today and helped Mr. Hayes and me before we went on our errands."

The word *our* struck me. I let it sit there in the middle of us all, careful not to flinch away from it.

"Who?"

"Aleksey."

I gently brushed at the tomatoes, removing the dirt. "Aleksey?" My voice cracked. I couldn't believe I missed seeing him.

"He was disappointed you were working."

"Yes."

"I told him to go next door to see you. I guess he never made it?"

"No," I said. A chill ran through me as the knife slipped from my grip and onto the floor.

"Katherine?" Mama picked it up, wiped it off, and handed it to me.

I began slicing the tomatoes and cucumbers. "I'm fine," I said. But I suddenly wondered what Miss Violet would have told me if she heard him knocking. I envisioned the girls and me upstairs basking in the sunrays, naked, lost in inane conversation about men and life.

What if he'd come inside and found us like that? Shame flooded me. He wouldn't ever enter someone's home uninvited, of course. But then I remembered him letting himself into my kitchen when I was asleep at the table, worried.

I imagined sharing this part of my life with Aleksey. It was far too private to share with anyone, even someone like him. This was not to be my lot in life. This was just a stopping point, a pause, and it wasn't something I would tell anyone because it was no one's business and it would be gone before I could count to ten . . . ten weeks? What was I doing?

I tried to imagine divulging my work with Miss Violet to Aleksey. Maybe I wouldn't have to tell him. I could quit working for her after paying off my dresses. I stopped chopping. Could I quit? If it brought me this much unease at telling people about it, was it the right job? I started to chop again. I'd come to feel my ability to bridge the worlds between the living and the dead was part of me, like the nerves that came alive when Aleksey touched me. Maybe he *could* understand? Would he laugh? Run? Drag me to the police?

Mama sighed. "He helped us for a bit and went on and on about the meal you gave him. The stew, the bread. He was quite emphatic."

This made me smile. "That's nice."

Would he rave about my ability to bring peace and understanding to those who mourned? His family was so practical, literal, people of the land. He was studying to be a man of the law. As open as he was to my ideas of women's rights, this was different. There was a real chance he wouldn't appreciate my ability. He might think I was a fraud. I imagined having to call him to help me out of jail, like Madame Smalley.

Perhaps he'd believe in me and know that I was not conning anyone. I was real; I *was* helping people. He would see my press to get us into our own home with a small garden for Mama, just big enough to provide for us all, as being noble, not crooked.

It was too late for me to pretend I didn't have this gathering of angels and spirits. I felt its power. And it was mine. There was nothing I could do to change that. And as much as Aleksey Zurchenko enjoyed my stew and bread and wanted to know more about me in the intervening years since we'd lived near each other, I was sure I would not be able to tell him what he wanted to know or needed to hear.

He'd have to find the love of his life in someone else's kitchen. For a moment, I thought that might be too shortsighted of me. Perhaps I should leave room for him to grow in understanding, to try to broach the topic like I did with Mama. But as I played the conversation forward, I was left drained, unable to even imagine saying the words, "I have a calming, a gathering that comes when I need it..." No, I couldn't imagine forming those words, sending them into his ears anytime soon, if ever at all.

**

Mama set her fork down and settled back in her seat. Her head dropped slightly back, and she got a funny smile.

"What is it, Jeanie?" Mr. Hayes said.

She shook her head. "This simple salad tasted so good, didn't it?"

"I'm so glad you liked it, Mama," I said as I stood to clear the table.

"You have a real sense of blending herbs and vegetables in just the right way, Katherine. A real art form, I'd say."

Mr. Hayes leaned forward, resting his chin on his clasped hands. "I'm not surprised Katherine's so good in the kitchen, with you as her mother."

I pumped the water a few times to fill a bucket to wash the dishes. I was struck by the memory of Mama the first time she had to prepare a meal at Mr. Templeton's house on the prairie. I started to giggle thinking of the feathers and fur flying. Mama had retched repeatedly as the realities of her former life as the *Quintessential Housewife* and prairie housewife collided.

I turned to see Mama looking at me, covering her mouth, laughing.

"What is it?" Mr. Hayes said.

"I told you plenty of times my ability to write about running a home and actually having to cook and keep a home were two different things," Mama said.

"I thought you were exaggerating," he said, keeping his gaze right on her. She seemed to glow under the warmth of his easy way.

She slowly shook her head. "I wish I was."

"Well, every meal you've prepared for me since we started working together has been wonderful."

Mama cocked her head at him. "You're so kind, Mr. Hayes. I just don't know how else to put it."

"Well, we better get going to that meeting, or Mrs. Hillis will give us the evil eye."

"What meeting?" I said.

"Another one with the aldermen and judges and the leading citizens in town who want to funnel children to asylums, with women of strong mind and the courage to voice an opinion right behind them. Say they want to clean up the town, but they don't see themselves as part of the problem."

"Sounds important."

"Mrs. Hillis wants your mother to help her write about the matter. Too many children being neglected."

Mama looked down at her hands.

"That's wonderful, Mama," I said.

Her cheeks reddened, and she looked at me. "Thank you."

"Well, go on. I'll clean up and watch Yale."

"No, no. She's coming with us. It's important for all those blowhards to see that a child belongs with her mother no matter what her problems are."

Mama stood, and I saw her old gumption light the room like the old days. My eyes burned as pride welled inside me. I was so happy for her, that she found this confidence again, that I could literally feel her strength radiating. They gathered their things, and Mama scooped Yale into her arms. They were walking out as Tommy came up onto the porch, his crow, Frank, perched on his shoulder.

He thrust his chin up and pushed past Mr. Hayes and Mama. He began to look among the jars of herbs and spices that lined the shelves near the back wall.

"Tommy." Mama went to him, kissing his cheek. "Where are your manners?"

He laid a flinty glare on Mr. Hayes, then me, then Mama. "I forgot them, I suppose."

"Please get the bird out of the house," Mama said.

Frank began to spread his wings, crowing at Mama.

Mr. Hayes stepped forward. "Hey now, let's all calm down."

"Calm down, calm down," Frank squawked, leaping up and down on Tommy's shoulder.

Mama flinched away and Frank began to fly around the kitchen. We covered our heads while Frank demanded "Calm down, calm down all while he sped up his wings.

"Out!" Mama said. "This instant, get him out."

Tommy sighed and put up his arm that Frank dropped onto and tucked his wings up, finally quieted.

"Some forget their family ties. I forgot Frank wasn't welcome here."

I recoiled at Tommy's tone as much as his words.

Mama looked as though her breath had been knocked out of her. She smoothed her hair back and glanced at Mr. Hayes. I knew she'd try to dispel the tension. "Katherine's made a fine salad and bread, of course. And apple pie."

Tommy went to the door and threw his arm up, signaling to Frank to take off flying. He landed in the tree closest to the back porch.

Mr. Hayes moved forward and stuck his hand out to Tommy. Tommy wiped his palm on his pant leg but didn't shake.

"Tommy, *please.*" Mama's voice wavered. I knew how badly she wanted us all to get along and be loving.

Tommy shook his head, then accepted Mr. Hayes's handshake.

"Mr. Hayes," Tommy said. "Nice that you're helping with the heavy lifting to prepare the garden for winter. Oh, and just to let you know, my father's coming back. He wrote it right here." He pulled out a letter and waved it in the air. "He's busy sewing up some unfinished business, but he'll be back. He'll be wanting to make your acquaintance, of course."

"Tommy!" Mama yelled.

Tommy's shoulders slumped. He removed his hat. "I'm sorry, Mama. I came for a cure for Pearl's cat. You know Pearl—you met her a couple of times."

"Yes, yes," Mama said.

"And I just wasn't expecting to have to deal with—" He glanced at Mr. Hayes. The man didn't register any emotion at what he was hearing or how he was being treated.

I just wanted the tension to dissolve. "What cat? What's wrong with it?"

"Something with its belly. I came for some of that boneset infusion you made for me that one time. I figure it'll help her cat if it helped me."

Mama squinted at Tommy, and I knew she wanted to ask why he was so concerned about that. But I think she wanted out of the room as much as I did.

"Katherine can surely help you with that. I need to go."

"Where?" His tone was accusing again.

"Town hall. The meeting about delinquent children, the city falling apart at the seams, criminals."

"He going too?" He lifted his hat toward Mr. Hayes.

"He is."

Tommy looked away. "Well, I'll see you later, then."

Mama took Tommy's face in her hands and kissed his forehead. She whispered something in his ear that I couldn't hear, and he shrugged, his face chagrined.

"When I'm back we'll talk," Mama said as she pulled away.

She and Mr. Hayes disappeared out the door.

Anger had welled inside me as I watched the exchange between Tommy and Mama. I heard the gate squeak shut, and I knew Mama was out of the yard.

"That man better keep away," Tommy said.

I smacked the countertop, startling myself as much as Tommy. "Don't you do this, Tommy."

He drew back and scowled at me. "You're on her side?"

"I'm on your side, my side, her side."

"Well, that's sweet of you to be so easy about her new love."

I stalked across the floor, fueled with unexpected anger. I took him by the shirt collar and felt as though I was watching myself outside of my body.

"Treat Mama nice. She deserves a moment with someone who helps her and thinks she's smart and—"

It was then I heard a meow come out of his coat pocket. Tommy dug inside his coat and produced a fluffy black kitten, holding it toward me.

"Help him, please?" he said, and my heart melted right that second.

**

I took the kitten from Tommy, its fur sprouting from between my fingers. The tiny male rolled up, tense, and he mewled when my fingers probed his belly too hard. I brushed his cheeks. "Okay, sweet boy, let's take a look." I grabbed a towel from the countertop, laid it on the table, and put the cat down.

I glanced at Tommy and saw his worried face. "He's little, Tommy. Shouldn't get attached."

"Too late. Pearl thinks she's its mother. She's at work, and with him getting worse, I figured I better do something."

I could see that he not only cared about the cat but about Pearl as well.

"All right. Let me think."

He nodded.

"Since you have him here, let's try something different than the tea. Hold him while I get this ready."

I stretched to the top shelf and pulled down a glass jar of powdered slippery elm bark. I measured some into a pan, added milk, and stoked the fire. "Once this is just the right thickness, I'll add some honey. It will coat his belly, and the milk will give him some nutrition to help with the weakness."

I stirred the concoction, making figure eights in the pan.

"Thank you, Katherine," Tommy said.

I looked over my shoulder at him as he cradled the kitten.

Once it was ready, I fished a baby spoon out of a drawer, and Tommy squeezed the corners of the kitten's jaws to open them. I drizzled a bit of the porridge into his mouth and watched as the taste registered on his tongue. His tongue moved a bit, and Tommy released his jaw.

We let him fully swallow and then we tried another four drops.

I sat in the chair across from Tommy. "Let's wait a few minutes, and we'll try another bit."

Tommy shifted in his chair, and I noticed him flinch as he did.

"What's wrong?" I asked.

He shook his head. I stood and took the cat from him. "What is it?"

He sighed and pressed his side. "Just my ribs, I think."

I got closer to him and pulled up his shirt. His skin was marbled with purple, black, and shots of pale peach where his normal skin color poked through. "Oh my god, Tommy."

He pushed his shirt down. "I'm all right."

"I don't think so." I went to the shelves and pulled down a jar that held slippery elm bark that hadn't been dried and powdered yet.

I rinsed the porridge pan and added fresh water and the bark until it boiled and curdled to make a thick poultice. "What happened to you?"

"Disagreement is all. Nothing but a little fight at the saloon."

"Over what?" I applied it to his side and wrapped him with a dry towel and went back to feeding the kitten the porridge.

Part of me didn't want to mention to Tommy that I'd noticed he smelled boozy. "Business. Nothing I want to talk about, Katherine. Please. Just let it go for now."

I stared at him for a moment. I thought of all the things I wanted to keep to myself.

"Like your midday bath," he said, smiling. "I'm sure you don't want to discuss that."

"It was nothing."

"This was nothing either."

I felt safe in what I was doing, protected by Miss Violet. I wasn't being hurt. "But you're injured. It's different."

"I promise it won't happen again. I'm fine."

The cat mewled. I put the spoon to the kitten's mouth, and this time he opened it on his own. "Look at that, Tommy. He's taking it easily now."

Tommy leaned in to get a better look and smiled.

Liking to see him smile, I almost didn't press him further on his bruises, but I couldn't stop myself. "Tell me what happened."

"Nothing but a little misunderstanding."

Misunderstandings like this normally happened to people who were at the wrong place. "At a saloon?"

He stared at me for a moment and finally nodded.

"Tommy. Please. You can't go to places like that. Mama'll worry and then—"

Tommy clenched his fist on the tabletop. "I can't stand him, Kath."

"Who?"

"That man. Reed Hayes. Him."

I exhaled. I understood Tommy's perspective, but I also knew he should start to take a closer look at how our father had behaved when living with us on the prairie.

He pulled the toweling away from his skin and then positioned it again. "He's always here. Always helping, always giving her things."

"Tommy." I shook my head.

"You don't care? How does this not bother you?"

"It's not that I don't care, Tommy."

"Then what?"

God only knew what else he was actually up to besides fighting in saloons. I spooned another bit of porridge into the cat's mouth. It was time for him to move on from his wishful thinking about our father. "He's not coming back, Tommy. And so we need to let Mama have a moment of peace with—"

Tommy's face reddened. "He *is* coming back."

"He loves you, Tommy. I know that. You should know that. But he's not coming back." I couldn't believe I'd gotten the words out. Tommy's eyes filled.

He looked away, jaw clenched.

"You're wasting time and energy. You could be doing important things, like Aleksey is with studying the law. Think of where you and he started in life. Aleksey couldn't even read when we met him."

"How can you say that about our father?"

"If he was truly coming back, he would already be here. That's what people do—follow through on their word."

"Are you saying I'm not a man because I don't just go get him? That because I haven't saved enough money to send for him—"

"That's not what I said at all."

Tommy stood and gently removed the towel. At the sink, he wiped off the poultice. I could see his anger tensing his shoulders.

"Talk to me. I'm not saying you're not working hard. What I meant was that *he* needed to—"

He whipped around, and I could see the pain on his face. "Well, if we're going to dole out advice to each other, here's mine to you. Watch your step over at Miss Violet's if you don't want to find yourself without the independence you want. Maybe even ruined if you don't watch it."

I laid the spoon down and brushed the kitten's face. "What's that mean?"

"You're not being courted over there, are you? All those men traipsing through?"

I quickly saw the line of men that filtered through there day after day in my mind. I wondered if he had heard that some of the girls were interested in the men they advised and invested for.

"I'm not sure everything happening there is right," Tommy said.

"Well, you can ask the judges and ministers and aldermen who invest with Miss Violet and the other ladies if they think something isn't right, Tommy."

"Baths during the day?"

"I was sick, Tommy. You heard Miss Violet. It snapped me right back, though, didn't it?" The lie burned my tongue.

"And the others?"

"What others?"

"Bathing during the day. Dressed as though headed to a ball half the time? And . . ."

"And what?" I said.

"Nothing. I just need to know that you aren't doing something . . . something that might . . ."

He stared at me, and I felt as though I might cry.

I couldn't speak. It sounded like he knew something about Miss Violet's that I didn't. Perhaps he'd heard the girls talking about the men they liked, that they wanted them to hold them, to kiss them?

"None of those men are courting you, right?"

I drew back. "What?"

"I read the papers. People question Miss Violet . . . her motives at times."

"What does *that* mean?"

He came to me. "You're not up to anything but cooking and baking and cleaning, are you?"

"Studying," I said. "Learning a lot," I whispered.

He took the cat from me and nuzzled it for a moment, then he sighed as though he'd decided not to push me further. For a moment, I almost told him about Dreama. But there was something too hard behind his softness for the cat.

"Thank you for fixing him," Tommy said.

I stood and studied the kitten's now serene face. "He does seem better." I lifted one of his legs and saw that the tension had subsided a good deal. No mewling, no interruption of his sleep.

"Thank you," Tommy said.

I nodded. We looked at each other for a moment. I felt the inches of distance between us like they were miles. I was sure he felt the same. I wanted to make him tell me exactly what he was doing. I wanted him to let Mama be for a while. I wanted him to pinch back his fantasy that Father was on his way to get us. But with every word I might say to him, he would have something to say to me. My inquiries into his risky behavior would invite inquiries into mine.

And so we parted with questions lingering, accusations smarting. I watched him disappear into the yard and was left grateful that we had the warm connection between us around the kitten.

It was then I realized I hadn't even asked what the cat's name was. I ran to the door.

"What's his name?"

Tommy turned and looked into his arms. "Doesn't have one yet. Pearl's thinking on it."

I nodded. "Well, I think he'll live to hear it now, Tommy. He's gonna be all right."

He smiled and started toward the shed again. I wasn't sure I should have said such a thing. It wasn't as though God had descended with news of the kitten's long life ahead. But in that moment, I felt he would live, and though I saw so much wrong with Tommy's direction in life, I wanted him to have something good, something soft to hold in his heart as we went our separate ways.

Chapter 38

Betrayal
Katherine

With Tommy gone and Mama, Yale, and Mr. Hayes off to their meeting, I headed to Miss Violet's to turn some of my sketches into paintings. When I pushed through the kitchen door, I saw a woman standing near the pantry wearing Dreama's lace coverings.

I froze. "What are you . . ." I lost my words. The woman turned, but I couldn't make out who it was beneath the veiling, *my* expensive lace. The height and build of the woman and her blonde hair made me think it was Abigail. But why would she be wearing my things? I strode toward her awash in confusion and anger.

She drew back as I approached and lifted the lacy covering, revealing her eyes. *Olivia.*

Anger filled me, but I was frightened for her as well. Miss Violet would be enraged at the thought of the dress and veil being worn around for no good reason.

"Let me explain," Olivia said.

"You better get that off. Miss Violet will—"

"Olivia." Miss Violet's crisp voice and clicking shoes coming down the hallway startled me.

"Hide." I pulled Olivia toward the cellar.

She tripped forward and hissed through clenched teeth. "My ankle," she said.

"You'll have worse than that if Miss Violet catches you in my things." I pulled her firmly but gently, supporting her weight to help the pain. "Quick. Down the stairs. I'll tell her you went out."

Olivia wrenched her hand away. "Stop."

"She'll kill you," I said, and Olivia smiled, shaking her head. She let out a heavy sigh.

Miss Violet came into the kitchen and stopped short, a shocked look on her face. I didn't know how to help Olivia. I couldn't find a single thing to say. Miss Violet was stern with all of us and knew none of us wanted to disappoint her. I wished I could vanish and not have to witness the coming exchange, or worse, have Miss Violet think I encouraged this.

I tensed and wrapped myself in my arms, waiting for the tirade. Miss Violet would never forgive her. "Olivia. Wait in the parlor."

Olivia didn't move. I stared at the two of them, marveling at the fact that Miss Violet remained calm. I was sure her anger was boiling deep inside her. I wanted to dispel it before it came firing out.

I stepped forward, touching Olivia's arm. "She didn't mean it, Miss Violet. She was just—"

"I know."

I looked from one to the other again; the words *I know* took hold in my mind.

"Know what?" I said.

Miss Violet gestured toward the hall. "Olivia, please."

As Olivia pulled away from me, limping off, she looked over her shoulder and mouthed the word *sorry*. Then it hit me. I couldn't find the words to express the strangeness that had settled over me.

Miss Violet was dressed in fine silk, her waist wasp thin, her hair glossy and tight against her scalp in the front but woven with elaborate braiding around the crown and back— I knew this meant she was soon going to accept visitors.

My mind tangled around disparate thoughts. "Wait. I thought we had tonight off."

Miss Violet moved toward me. "I said *you* had the evening off."

I pressed my temples. "What's Olivia . . . surely she's not . . . *What* is she doing in my veil and dress?"

Miss Violet drew herself up. "You know I am fastidious about my business. It's important that we have a secondary plan in case something goes wrong. I need to protect my investment."

"What does that mean?"

Miss Violet stiffened, to me appearing oddly uncertain, for the first time having to fight to maintain her typical awe-inspiring poise. "Just a little experiment. Every smart businesswoman has a backup plan."

I felt a twist in my chest. "Olivia dressed as me is your backup plan?" I pressed the spot near my sternum where it tightened. She was going to allow, to attempt, to have Olivia mediate between the living and dead? I thought back to times that the girls alluded to my gift not being real. A butt of a joke. How could they? "You think Olivia can just *pretend* to be *me* and people will believe it?"

Miss Violet swallowed hard, again an unusual reaction for a woman I saw as unbreakable. "Dreama. Not *you.*"

My hands shook. I balled them at my side. It didn't make sense. The ritual, my success—how could Miss Violet spend so much time helping me access my calming, my gathering each time if she didn't really believe that I was destined to be Dreama, that it mattered that the woman in the ads was truly a seer? Could she really think Olivia could pull this off? "You're saying you think Olivia can walk into a room—no *limp* into a room—throw some dice, turn some cards, make things up, and fool anyone?"

My words seemed to land on Miss Violet like punches, her face showing the shock at being hit by someone who'd only been deferential to her. But then a calm came over her as she drew a deep breath, and the moments that had made her appear vulnerable, like seconds on a clock ticking by, passed.

She pushed me into a chair at the table, took my hand, rubbing the back of it, her eyes catching on my stumpy pinkie. "You're a woman in many ways. I don't need to mince words with you, insult you by simplifying what I tell you, do I?"

Feeling a bit as though in a trance, I shook my head.

"It's imperative I protect the investment, Katherine. Dreama is bigger than you. Especially when you have so many outstanding bills. We simply can't risk anything going wrong. And you love being Dreama, don't you?"

I shifted in my seat, my heart racing. I closed my eyes and told myself to calm down. I thought of all the dresses I had yet to pay for, of my mother. The riches I was going to earn for her. All the lying. Was it for nothing? Still at the heart of my unrest was the thought that she might think any woman could take my place. I couldn't stop the sense of betrayal from leaking between Miss Violet and me like spilled ink pooling at our feet.

I worked my hand out of hers. "The world will recognize a fraud. If you try to pass Olivia off as me, this could ruin everything. Only I can be Dreama." I was surprised at my possessiveness. It wasn't as though anyone knew I was Dreama. I thought of Madame Smalley, her tricks and the way people despised her. "I *am* Dreama. Olivia in a dress can't suddenly be me. It'll end in disaster. Everyone will find out. I can promise you that."

Miss Violet gripped my arm. "Is that a threat? You'll reveal Dreama's identity? Put your family in peril?"

I hadn't thought of it that way in a while, but exposure seemed to always be my companion when it came to this. I hadn't meant to imply that I would tell anyone anything. But it would be obvious to anyone that they were being played a fool if Olivia went through with this. Then we'd all suffer.

Miss Violet's face softened as though she could will her anger away. "You're right. You *are* special, my young friend."

Friend. The word softened the edges of my anger, even though I felt as though she was molding her pitch to fit my responses rather than simply telling me the whole truth.

"Calm down and hear me out."

I hadn't realized how hard I'd been breathing. I wiped my brow with the back of my hand. I was sure I could convince her not to attempt this. She got me a glass of water and brought it to me. The betrayal clamped my throat.

She sat beside me and brushed a strand of hair behind my ear. "I didn't say this right. What I meant to say was that having Olivia pose as you is to protect *you*. People who don't understand your gift . . . well, they can be very, very harsh. Sometimes even those we love most aren't ready to give us our freedom, aren't ready to see our greatness, and diminish us. We are intertwined until the time comes that you've paid your way and are satisfied with the purse you've presented to your mother. We must work together."

"But it won't work, and then what?"

Miss Violet went to a drawer near the sink and pulled out some newspapers. "Have you seen these?"

I went to her and looked at the headlines. "Dreama Heals Grieving Soldier's Soul. Dry Well Gushes Next Day."

I couldn't help but smile, remembering the gentle, broken soldier. But I couldn't understand the connection between his grief being eased and his suddenly wet well. Something told me I didn't have to grasp the connection to know something very good came out of my reading. Miss Violet pulled another paper from underneath, pointing at the headline, "Dreama Contacts Dead Matriarch—Reunites Disgruntled Family." I certainly remembered the matriarch of a large family that had splintered since her death, but I was not witness to the reunion. Still, this news filled me with pride.

"They're wonderful," I said.

"They are." Miss Violet pulled another paper from the bottom of the pile. "But this is why I'm protecting you with more than a veil and gloves." She pointed to another headline, "Dreama Conjures Spirits: Questions Arise in Legitimacy."

I gasped.

"And this one." Miss Violet pulled another paper off the bottom. "Evil Walks in the Form of a Beautiful Woman."

That headline rattled me. I sank into a chair at the table. "I see." I felt as though I was thrust back into the Christoffs' basement, where they were hiding me away until I could be pinned on the altar at the next revival to have my demons exorcised.

"You're upset. I can see that. I didn't want you to see these articles. I don't want anything to interfere with what we've created, the ritual that works for you. You've been very successful so far. People are clamoring for the paintings. So to be safe, I've taken more precautions—to have any readings with people whom I'm not already in business with occur away from my home. The fewer connections to this house, the better. The men who we work with are discreet. They can be trusted. But random clients—we will be very careful. You have two more small readings, and then we have *A Night for Mothers*. I want Olivia to dress as you tonight, to do some cards, yes, throw dice."

I crossed my arms.

"Don't scowl, Katherine. It'll age you."

I sighed.

"This precaution, Olivia dressed as you, most importantly, could be the only way to keep you safe if we need a decoy some time."

I still didn't like this idea. "That'll only feed the idea that people like me are frauds. I don't want Olivia or anyone else dressing as me. I'm paying for that dress."

"You haven't paid on one dress yet, let alone that one that Olivia is wearing."

Miss Violet pulled her ledger from the counter. "I have every number in here. Remember? We didn't charge for the initial readings. That was simply to see if we could manage the operation, if there was a market for it here."

I was starting to feel as though I were being harnessed and led in circles. I eyed the ledger in Miss Violet's hands, recalling the page with Olivia's name on it with the details of her work and the money paid for it. I would start to keep careful watch on what was charged and the exact amount of money coming to me.

"I need to give my mother some more money. I can't keep working like this and not give her anything."

Miss Violet nodded. "Of course."

"And if Olivia wears the dress, I want a cut of the money. The only reason you can use her to be Dreama is because of those headlines you showed me. I am the reason they come."

"Now, Katherine. I think I'm being reasonable."

Suddenly, all the things that Miss Violet had said to give me confidence and encouragement came back to me. I did have the power. I was central to this part of her business. "I demand it." I straightened, my hands clenched in my lap, under the table where they would not betray my fear at having said those words.

Miss Violet's jaw clenched. She drew deep breaths. Her eyes were piercing.

"And I need an accounting of how much each dress costs and what I owe on each item." I gestured toward her ledger, knowing every detail was in it.

She sat up in her chair as though to match my newfound strength. She finally nodded. "You go and rest tonight. I'll expect you back with a softer demeanor in the morning. When the evening is over, I'll pull together more money for your mother and some numbers for you."

I was being dismissed, but I understood my value better.

"Then I get a cut. Right?"

Violet nodded, her mouth tight, as if she had to keep back something she didn't want to say. Finally, she spoke. "But remember this, though you're exceptional, your success is mine, too. I put forth the risk up until now. I'm still casting the bugs out of the operation. When you read at *A Night for Mothers*, you want to be brilliant. You want to be relaxed and not have a thing to worry about. I'll worry for you. But you have to let me work things out. Money and all of the logistics are for me."

I nodded, and suddenly an image of Olivia in the tub with my oils and lotions came to mind. "Did Olivia use my ritual?" As soon as the words were out of my mouth, I understood how odd it was to even care that she might have.

She shook her head. I studied her face for sincerity. She appeared truthful, but it was clear now that she kept what she wanted to from me when she deemed it necessary.

The doorbell rang, and she began to head through the butler's pantry. "Now go on. Don't squander your evening off."

I exhaled, not able to imagine just how I'd spend my time. I turned to leave when I noticed the edge of my art satchel sitting on one of the chairs. Maybe I'd make some tea, curl up and do some sketching. As I grabbed the bag another newspaper headline caught my eye. "Dreama Limps into the Hearts and Minds of Des Moines." I quickly scanned the rest of the article. *Olivia's* limp. Was it possible? It must be true. She'd worn my dress before. My stomach clenched. I stared at the butler's pantry where Miss Violet had just disappeared, another wash of betrayal splashing over me. I realized then Miss Violet and the girls had been keeping things from me much longer than just this evening. I held my satchel tight against me and headed for the back door. As I walked into the cool night, heavy loneliness settled in, reminding me that I hadn't felt it in quite some time.

I'd thought I was a central part of Miss Violet's business, that I occupied a much more important role than I apparently had. Torn between what I now knew was true about me—I was special and could offer peace in a way that others could not—and the reality of the situation—I was in too deep to just walk away from Miss Violet—I set to thinking about just how I could make things right and live the life I knew should be mine.

Chapter 39

Friend
Katherine

Into the night I went. The scent of eucalyptus filled my nose. It was time to cut it and store it for when winter illness began to settle upon us. Upset at what had happened at Miss Violet's, but feeling as though I'd been infused with energy since sticking up for myself, I wasn't sure what to do with this free time I'd been given. Sharp wood dug into my palms as I passed through the hedge opening. It mirrored how I felt when I realized that Violet and Olivia had betrayed me. Emerging into my yard, I saw the crescent moon glimmering, its ladies-in-waiting shining just as bright that night.

I rubbed one of my smarting palms and felt the sting of Miss Violet's lies. *Think of what you did, though.* I dismissed the sting with the idea that I demanded to know what I owed exactly so I could better plan to pay off my bill as quickly as possible. I thought of the dress I had to bring home once Mama saw me in it. I owed for that one for sure. Perhaps I could decline the ones I'd never even worn. What I knew for sure was there could be no more mistakes.

Tommy leapt to mind again, his concern for Pearl's kitten and the way he'd smelled of alcohol and been so mean to Mama. I was happy she had someone to occupy her time, even if she couldn't allow her heart to rest on the promise of him being in her life for long. It was good for Mama to have someone to talk to, share her ideas with, and to distract her until I could pay our way into a sweet garden house somewhere we could all start over again.

I noticed swirling smoke rising out of the pipe on Tommy's shed. I should apologize to him for being impatient with him and try again to convince him that Mama deserved to have Mr. Hayes around for as long as possible.

I pushed open the shed door and entered. The space was tidy and fragrant, and a girl sat near a fire that breathed deep, lusty flames.

"Hello, Katherine." The girl stood and dug a thick stick into a pot of boiling water.

I moved closer. She wore a dingy cotton dress with a graying scalloped collar. The sleeves were too short, but the waist fit her slim shape nicely. As I neared the fireplace, her red hair was lit with golden highlights, making it very clear just who she was.

I set my satchel down. "Pearl." The bubbly girl who called Tommy *Prince Charming*. She'd been a delight, filling me with warmth and an odd contentment rooted in nothing I could determine. Instantly, I felt that again.

She mumbled something I couldn't understand and then turned to me, stick in hand, and as though taking diction lessons, she said, "It's a pleasure to see you this evening, Katherine."

I could tell she was attempting to speak in a manner that didn't come easy for her.

"Is Tommy here?"

Pearl shrugged. "Working."

"You're waiting for him?"

Pearl dug into the pot again and I resurveyed the room. A dog sat by the fire, then lay down, comfortable with my presence.

"Just boiling the stink off Tommy's things."

I thought of the grubby shirt Tommy had been wearing earlier.

"Nice of you," I said.

"He's a nice fella."

I studied Pearl as she stirred, the orange flames glowing, illuminating her, bobbing and weaving and making her look as though she'd sprouted a set of angel wings.

Pearl shifted her gaze to me and jumped as though I'd frightened her with my stare. She lifted her hand. "He knows I'm here. It ain't gonna be for long, but . . ."

I saw the girl's knapsack off to the side, open, the dog bowl beside it.

"You're staying here?" I said.

Pearl opened her mouth and closed it. "He's real generous, your brother."

"You stay with him?" I asked.

"Please don't tell your mama. I was in real dire straits. And . . ." Her brow furrowed, and she straightened her bony shoulders. "Tommy was sweet as butter and summer peas for letting me stay here."

"But Pearl—"

She put her hand in the air. "Nothing improper. Honest Abe. Tommy's a gentleman. A prince."

As nice as it was that she thought that about my brother, I still wanted to protest. I didn't want Pearl to suffer from a ruined reputation or lend one to Tommy. But then I thought, what reputation? Pearl certainly didn't tread the paths that led to a seat in society life, and Tommy's greatest connection to the upper crust was selling prayers to wealthy folks and running errands for Miss Violet. And I believed Pearl without question about the innocent nature of her relationship with Tommy. Something about her was pure and trustworthy even as her skin was splotched with dirt.

She stopped working and stared, pleading, panic radiating off her skin. "Please don't tell your mama," she said again. "It's just until I can find a place where no one'll paw at me half the night."

A flash of Mr. Christoff came to me, his groping hands on my skin. I shuddered. I understood Pearl's plight more than I wanted to.

"I won't say a word," I said offering a smile to reassure her. We all have our secrets, after all.

"Thank you," Pearl said. "I can't say thank you enough." She roped me into an embrace, her head against my chest, her arms choking off my breath.

I patted her back. "It's all right."

She nodded, released me, and turned back to her stick without making eye contact with me. She lifted the shirt and shook water off its end. "Needs to boil a bit more."

She leaned the stick against the fireplace stone and took up a poker.

"How's the cat?"

She nodded and gestured toward the dog. I got closer and knelt beside the dog and saw that the kitten was tucked into his belly. I ran the back of my finger from his nose over the back of his head. His mouth pulled into a smile as he slept, showing his eyeteeth. He seemed relaxed and pain-free for the moment. I couldn't believe the little thing had survived.

"Thank you for saving Teddy," Pearl said.

"You named him."

"Couldn't believe when Tommy showed up, Teddy tucked in his coat, still breathing, sleeping, but soft and snuggly instead of rolled into a tight ball.

I smiled. "Tommy watched me make the remedy so he could make another batch tomorrow if I'm working."

"Mighty, mighty kind of you," she said. "You Arthurs are top-notch folks. Wasn't sure he'd make it. Tommy wouldn't let me name him till now."

"I'm so glad Teddy seems better."

Pearl added another log and pushed at it. The flames breathed, filling the room with light, brightening her, making her appear to have wings, the flames sprouting out of her back. Golden light from the fire surrounded her, waves of warm brilliance outlining her whole body, casting a golden glow over the ramshackle room as though the fire existed outside the fireplace as well as in it.

I inhaled and shut my eyes. When I opened them, Pearl was still aglow, stuffing newspaper against the logs. "Just a smidge hotter," she said, "need a good rolling boil to be sure Tommy's things are fresh."

I watched her and realized that Pearl was surrounded by light in a way that looked to be both of her and around her, like an army of angels had descended, clustered to protect.

Pearl came toward me, the golden light shimmying off her back. I squeezed my eyes closed and shook my head to clear my vision. When I opened my eyes, the flames were back in the fireplace where they belonged.

"You all right?" Pearl asked.

I traced my hand around the shimmering white aura that scalloped Pearl's body once the flames had drawn back.

She grimaced, her face confused.

"You can feel that?" I asked.

Pearl's gaze followed my hand, her face creased in confusion. She pushed her thumb backward toward the tub. "The fire?"

I took her hand in mine, expecting it to be especially warm to the touch. "No, no. The light. You can't see it? Feel it?"

"No . . ."

I was mesmerized by what I saw. I'd seen spirits and what I somehow knew to be angels, but this glow around a person was different. I liked Pearl the first time I met her. But seeing this, I realized Pearl was more than a rough-around-the-edges girl. I didn't know what it meant, but if Pearl was paying special attention to Tommy, then it was a good thing. There was an undeniable sense of goodness about her, and that was heartening.

The calm that Pearl brought to me felt so much like when James came that I had to touch her just to be sure. Her forearm was warm where the fire had been licking at her.

"Can I pay you for some comfrey?" Pearl asked.

I thought of the cat. "I have something else for Teddy."

"No, for Tommy."

The bruising. "His ribs," I said.

She nodded. "Got himself a bruise in the gut. Sore all around. A lady come to call at my workhouse once. Real, real nice, gentle lady came to help the wife. The husband beat the wife to purple. He wouldn't call a doc to explain how she got so bruised. Wrapped the wife in comfrey and took away every bit of bruise."

"Bad bruising?" I said.

"Head to foot, that wife. Tommy's just got himself into a little rumble. A little comfrey would do. I'll pay over time if I can."

"I gave him a treatment with slippery elm when he had Teddy at the house. But comfrey's good, too, yes."

"Well, good. Maybe comfrey tomorrow." Pearl seemed to have taken to mothering Tommy as much as her pets. I felt something between Pearl and me, something threading the space between us, through us, around us. I appreciated her caring for Tommy the way she clearly did.

I thought of how I hadn't confided any of what I could see and feel to anyone other than Miss Violet and the girls next door. I'd crept up on the topic with Mama and Tommy a few times, but Mama was frightened or simply disbelieving, and Tommy, well, he was disinterested. I was overwhelmed with the feeling of wanting to confide in Pearl. But I sealed my lips. I understood that she wanted to pay me for services, for comfrey, but I knew she didn't have anything extra to spare. What I wanted from her most at that moment was to be able to draw her.

"Do you mind if I draw you, Pearl?"

"Draw?"

"Could I? I'm quite good, I've been told. In exchange for the comfrey."

Pearl's shoulders softened and then she scooped up the kitten and cradled it in one arm. "Draw *me*?"

I nodded.

"My, oh me. I ain't nev . . . I have never been . . ." A broad smile broke across her face, making me giggle. "No one ever done a portrait of me. I mean look át me. I . . ."

I stood and opened my bag and sat across from Pearl. I worked fast, capturing her innocence, the delicate ruggedness in her features, like crystal rock I'd seen in a museum once. The specimen had been made of crusty, umber-colored, egg-shaped hardness on one side and a lightning-bright display of clear, purple, and blue spikes on the other.

I sketched as she stood every once in a while to stir the clothing and set a log on the fire. She would lean into the kitty and kiss its nose like a mother doting on her child. I was pleased with what I'd captured and knew I could add paint when I had the time. I made some notes about what I'd seen with the light around her so I could recreate it in color. I didn't know Pearl's full background, but I knew she was alone in the world. Still, she brought with her these angels, very protective ones. Pearl was special, and I was sure that although I hadn't seen the angels the first time I'd met her, they were what I'd felt, the goodness, the brightness beneath the rough shell.

"Can I see?" Pearl said, nodding toward the drawing.

I turned the paper and moved toward Pearl. She sat at the edge of her seat and reached for it with her free hand. She held it close, surveying the work. "Lordy be. I think you drew the wrong girl." Her voice was barely a whisper.

I knelt beside her so I could see it, too. "It's you."

"That's me like some fairy-tale princess. I love fairy stories. Tommy bought me my very own copy of Madame d'Aulnoy's tales."

I smiled at the thought of Tommy doing that. "You're beautiful, Pearl."

She stole a glance at me and then looked back at the drawing.

"Who's that there?"

"Where?"

Pearl pointed.

I'd drawn subtle figures feathered into the clouds.

"Angels."

"Well, that's sweet of ya," Pearl said, looking confused. "They sure do . . . well . . . why on earth did you put those in there? I mean, I like them and all. And you made me . . ." It was as if she had trouble saying the word. "Beautiful."

I put the drawing down. "I didn't make you that way. That's how you look."

"But why the angels?"

Because they're there.

I studied her face and once again felt the deep connection between us, like a bridge underfoot. I knew I could trust her. I could see that she took people as they were, didn't want them to be something they weren't. She took Tommy with all his shortcomings after all. "Can you keep a secret?"

Pearl nodded. I searched her face again and felt distinct *goodness* in the room, and I knew it was Pearl's angels. I could trust her.

My mind told me not to say anything, but Pearl was surrounded by such utter decency that I couldn't help but confide. "The reason I drew the angels is because you have angels. I can actually *see* them. You have so many, all around, protecting you, that sometimes, when they're gathered around you, like when I came in tonight, it's like you nearly have wings yourself. It's amazing."

Pearl looked stricken. "I don't understand."

I stood and took the stick to stir the pot.

"I suppose it's hard to fathom."

"It's impossible. Angels in storybooks I love, but—"

Suddenly, I couldn't keep it in. I needed to confide in someone who didn't want anything from me, who I knew wouldn't change their view of me. "Have you read the papers lately?"

Pearl nodded.

"Seen the articles about Dreama?"

"Who hasn't?"

"Well, Dreama can see angels and see the dead, and she helps people."

"But that's not—"

I pushed the clothing down deep in the pot and turned. "Pearl, *I'm* Dreama."

Silence followed, but I let it sit, let her process what I'd revealed. I didn't know what she was thinking and so did not know what to say next. I kept plunging the stick into the clothing.

She hugged herself as she looked me up and down. "Sweet heaven and hell." She looked away.

"It's true." Had I made a mistake in telling her? I set the stick aside and waited.

The quiet, the unsaid began to cause panic to rise in me. How could I have made this mistake?

"I believe you," she shook her head, "yet I can't believe it."

Pearl looked around, unable to look me in the eye. How could I have been so wrong about telling her? Had I interpreted our connection wrong? Had I wanted a friend so badly that I'd invented it?

My heart sped up even more. If I had been wrong about her openness to the idea, to me, I'd just risked it all for no reason. "Please don't tell anyone. I need to tell my mother and Tommy, but I'm not ready yet. They aren't ready to hear about it yet, I can tell. I know you won't tell. Please. *Don't* tell. I had to let it out to someone other than Miss Violet."

"Miss Violet?" Pearl said.

"She's the one arranging the readings and the advertising, and, well, we're making a lot of money."

"Tommy and your mother will appreciate that," Pearl said.

"I only have a little bit of the money so far. I'm paying off the gowns that I have to wear as Dreama, and, well, I let Miss Violet invest some since that's what she does. Soon I'll have a chunk of money, and I can't wait to give it to my mother. But she doesn't know I quit school—"

"You quit school?"

"Sort of . . . not really, well, yes, in a way."

Pearl let out a slow, loud whistle. "Holy *cow*, she'll kill you. Sheesh, I'm dying to go to school."

"I'm studying and learning so much at Miss Violet's about finance and business. But it's not the kind of education my mother thinks it is. I just need to be able to show Mama how much money I can make for her to understand. We could buy a house with a little garden and a safe place for Yale to play."

"You really think that can happen?"

"It *is* happening."

"I ain't gonna lie. I feel all tied up inside not confiding in Tommy about his own sister, but I won't tell. If it means you keep everyone close like your mama and brother want. That's special. A family."

Pearl drew a deep breath and closed her eyes, looking relaxed. My secret was safe. I was relieved to have someone to talk to who wasn't asking me to do something longer or better. Pearl was a person who actually needed the most from the world, yet she didn't ask for anything. I felt a deep connection to her, as if we were sisters.

"Well, I'm going to go. You or Tommy can get the comfrey anytime you want. Heat it and lay it on his body like the woman did for the wife you mentioned."

Pearl stood and looked at me directly for the first time since I'd told her I was Dreama. "So it's not a con?"

I felt a surge of warmth stream between us, hoping she'd had a change of heart.

"It's not a con."

She plunked her fists on her hips. "Well, *I'll be.*" She exhaled deeply. "Dreama."

She swallowed me into another suffocating embrace. I felt like she wanted to say something else. I wished I had more words, a better explanation, but I was certain at that moment that I didn't need them. We pulled apart, and she held her hand out, her pinkie finger extended. "Pinkie promise."

I gave her my good pinkie and we shook, a silly thing that felt weighty and important to me, as if we'd signed an oath in blood.

As we said goodbye, Tommy's crow, Frank, swooped down from the loft and stood beside the dog and the kitten. The dog lifted its head and sniffed Frank before resuming his sleep. The crow nudged Teddy with his beak as if determining if he had managed to live another day.

"We're a strange group of travelers, I know." Pearl shrugged.

That they were.

Chapter 40

Free Love
Violet

Violet had come back into the kitchen as Katherine was leaving. Part of Violet wanted to call her back inside to try again to explain her reason for using Olivia the way she was. She thought perhaps she shouldn't upset Katherine, that she might turn her toward her mother and it would ruin everything. But she'd learned much over the years and knew how important it was to keep everyone in her life at arm's length in order to stay protected. And as much as she wanted to protect Katherine, she wanted to protect herself most of all. Still, she'd grown so fond of Katherine. She saw greatness, beauty, intelligence, and kindness that might have been Violet's if she'd grown up in different circumstances.

Violet had to admit she liked that Katherine looked up to her in a way. She'd never wanted the entanglement that children brought, but having Katherine around, a female caught between girl and woman, brought out a maternal instinct that had shocked Violet. She told herself that her plan, her lies, would keep them both safe, like a mother made choices that might seem bad but were made for the right reason. With that, she'd protect them all.

She watched the girl step into the night and become engulfed by the hedges that divided Violet's home from the tiny house next door. Once she was sure Katherine was gone, Violet opened the cellar door and lifted her skirts, the hem of the fine lavender silk brushing the soot-covered stairs as she rushed downward. She swept past the room where the new girl had done laundry earlier that day, past the coal cellar, and toward the workroom. At the entrance, she stopped to steady her heaving breath. Tommy Arthur was crouched over the workbench, a lantern lighting his work.

"Damn." He sucked his finger, then shook it and sucked it again. She waltzed over to him, pulled his finger from his mouth, and saw a bead of blood form where he must have stabbed himself with the needle. She wiped the crimson bubble away with her thumb. "You'll be all right."

"It's the fifth time today."

Violet rolled her eyes. "Listen, Tommy Arthur. I just wasted time cleaning up your mess upstairs with your sister."

He sucked his finger again, his eyes narrowing with confusion. "What did I do?"

Violet pulled his finger from his mouth. "You were supposed to remind her that she had tonight off, that she should not come over here."

"She's here night and day and for the occasional bath. What difference does it make if she comes over on her night off?"

"It so happens that I needed to address some important issues that she's not privy to. And now I'm going to spend time and worry on whether her being in the right place at the wrong time will cost me more than I can fathom."

Tommy wiped his hand on his trousers. "I'm real sorry. I got to making these lambskins for you and lost track of that one thing to do." He gestured to the edge of the workbench. Violet counted seven new prophylactics. She sighed. "Yes, your main concern is stitching this lambskin up tight enough that nothing gets through. That first one you made had Olivia mixing an abortifacient solution for two days after. But when I add an errand to your list, I want it done. Tell me you delivered the note to the reverend."

"'Course I did."

She felt relieved. She picked up one of the lambskins, pushing her fingers inside it, feeling the seam stitching.

"Tight as drums." He pointed to the one over her fingers. "I even brought a bucket of water down here to test them as I make them. But I might have to charge extra for all the injury."

She shook her head. "Dramatic young man, aren't you?"

"You told me not to ask questions, but I'm not stupid. I know what these are for. And I think you're making even more money than the papers report. More than investments might bring."

Violet gagged. "You're not one of those self-righteous, moralizing hypocrites, are you?"

"No."

"Because I pay you enough to wash away any sign of moral high ground."

"Except for the needle injuries."

"I feel you judging, Tommy. And I don't give a single care what you think you know about me or this business. People who spend too much time judging others can lead to them feeling guilty, and they unburden themselves to all the wrong people. Or they want to ingratiate themselves, and these God-fearing people start to point fingers at people like me. The papers indicate most people in town understand my work, my business acumen. But I'm aware others misunderstand, and that can be harmful if it's not managed properly."

Tommy flinched as though she'd punched him. "I understand."

She studied his face. He'd been gambling and drinking lately. She saw the way his gaze went to the floor or off to the side when his father was mentioned or his mother was disinterested in her ex-husband's return. This boy was trying to make his way, like everyone. "You do, don't you?"

Now he looked confused. "You know what free love is, Tommy?"

He shrugged. "I've heard of it."

"It's the way of the world—even for those who try to pretend it's not. But there's a lot of time and effort spent on resisting it, covering it up, feeling guilty for following nature's course."

Tommy scowled.

"Ugh!" She pointed at him. "There it is again. Don't sit in judgment as you stitch those sheepskins. Those women upstairs are fine, intelligent women. Free love is the way of nature."

"But my sister?"

Violet stared. She'd reassured him when she'd taken him into her confidence that his sister's work was found in the kitchen only. "You're thinking of the bath, aren't you?"

He nodded.

"Not one thing Katherine does in my place of business requires anything made of sheepskin. But as far as the other ladies, they're good women. Someday you'll understand the connection between beauty, intelligence, and intimacy."

Tommy squinted at her.

She didn't have time for this, but she knew it was important to have Tommy's loyalties intact. She stepped closer to him. "Don't act like you're not hiding a girl away in your shed."

Tommy's face reddened, his eyes hardening with anger. "That *girl*, Pearl, is nice. She and I are not . . . we do *not* . . . she's been hurt by . . . someone. She just stays there. That's all. She has no need for sheepskin either."

"But you keep that information from your mother, don't you?"

Tommy nodded.

"I hear you've been spending much of your earnings at the saloon. Gambling? You like that whiskey burn on your tongue?"

He looked at his feet.

She put her hand on his. "I'm not judging either, Tommy. But you want to keep yourself protected. Gambling can lead to risky choices. It can lead to people angling for information if they know you're privy to something important. You just do your job and tie all this information you know about me and my work tight inside your mind. It's not for taking out for a stroll anywhere. My business is finance. My girls need to be protected. You don't want me to feel betrayed, Tommy. Not ever."

He nodded, his jaw still clenched. "I saw the judge here the other day. Calder."

"You know him?"

"You could say that."

Violet thought for a moment. "Before you went to the prairie?"

"Yes."

She saw there was more to it. "Recently, too?"

Tommy sighed. "Yes. You better keep your eye on him. How can you trust that he won't find out your girls engage in free love and tell his wife? She works for the newspaper, you know. Writes articles and fiction, too. Telling awful stories about my mother and pretending it's just made-up fiction."

Violet felt a smile come to her. He was still a boy, naïve in many ways. She thought this confirmed that Tommy had spent time in Jeremy's courtroom and was still smarting from it. "I'm assured the judge won't hinder my work or harm the girls. I trust *you*, don't I? I have a good compass for whom to trust. Perhaps I can protect you from what you think he might do to you in the future as well?"

"Not sure you can manage that. He hates us—me."

Violet smiled. She imagined the judge's enemies would not feel secure in his presence. But she couldn't imagine why he would hate them. It would be a waste of his energy to entertain such a grudge. The Arthurs had no power to use against him. "No, no. Discretion. It cuts all ways with me. I trust you, and I trust the judge."

She reached up and took his chin in her hand, cupped his cheek, a few whiskers pinching her palm. His jaw was cut strong. His size was manly, even though his mind and experience were boyish. She imagined he was telling the truth about the girl in the shed, that nothing physical was going on with her aside from him giving her a place to stay. Yet his protectiveness hinted at something developing for him— something of the heart rather than the flesh. It made her think of Edwin. Young love, one hand grabbing another, the titillation that came with that sweet, pure contact was powerful.

"As long as we understand each other, Tommy. I can't pay you well for your work if I don't trust you."

He nodded. "I understand."

Violet turned and exited the workroom, heading back toward the stairs. She felt a pang of guilt at knowing that the good money she paid Tommy went right to the saloon. This made her think of the girls, their wages, the way they went right back to Violet to fund the clothing they wore to lure the men. She put one foot on the stairs and paused. She had the momentary thought that she should forbid the women from sipping gin, that she shouldn't charge them for the dresses and every little mistake they made so that they could fund their lives as they saw fit.

She shook her head. Nonsense. She'd tried that before. She'd truly trusted before. Her "trust" in the judge, in Tommy, in every single person who lived in her orbit meant control over each and every one. They needed her to survive, and so they did what she wanted. That kind of thing had felt wrong to her at one time. Now it was just the answer to providing the life she wanted to live.

Chapter 41

The River
Katherine

I left the shed as Pearl headed out to deliver some prayers that Tommy had finished. The naked mid-fall gardens struck me—every bloom had gone from Mama's prize rosebushes. Oak trees, maples, cedars, all stood unclothed under the moon, their bones fully exposed, beautiful even in dull shades of walnut, coffee, and syrup. Only the evergreen hedges and stray pines were boldly dressed against the sapphire night.

As I walked, the sense of drifting deepened in me. It stopped me from walking another step. Being released from nonstop work should have brought me peace, but instead I felt unmoored. I didn't want to go home; I couldn't go to Violet's. I turned and looked back at Tommy's place. It was the perfect time for me to be with my thoughts, to invite the calming that used to be just for me.

I sat on the small bench that Mr. Hayes had made and set underneath an apple tree. Overhead, the great oak limbs curled and canopied me, a light wind rustling the brown papery leaves that refused to fall. I sat back, drew a deep breath, and closed my eyes, fully feeling my loneliness mixed with peace.

Deep breaths in and out, I laid my hand over my crystal. I concentrated on the chill that prickled my cheeks as the breeze brushed over me, how the wind carried the scent of meat cooking over a fire, coming from somewhere I couldn't see. I wondered if it was James's wind and weather patterns that brought the spirits with it. I closed my eyes and quickly felt my brother's presence as my calming settled in. Wanting to see him, I opened my eyes. I leapt when I saw what was in front of me.

My heart pounded, dizzying me. I gripped the bench. Aleksey stood four feet away, just looking at me. Had something awful happened to him since he stopped by? I stood, keeping my gaze on him. Had he died? I tried to say something, but nothing came out. I moved toward him, reaching, but before I could touch him, he removed his hat and took my outstretched hand, squeezing it.

"Hello, beautiful," he said barely above a whisper. "You look like you've seen a ghost."

Beautiful. I replayed his words and stared at our clasped hands as though the sight of our skin touching would help my mind register his aliveness, which I felt coursing through him. I struggled to speak. I wanted to jump into his arms. But I held myself back. "Oh my goodness. You're a . . ."

He smiled down from his great height. His white shirt gleamed against his brown trousers. "A what?"

Alive. "Here," I said. "You're here. I was just thinking of you and . . ."

"Well, I was worried I might miss you again. So I decided to just wait for you this time. I was on the porch and heard someone back here."

"It's me." I exhaled, my body shivering at the sight of him, the feel of his hand on mine. We shifted our hands so that our fingers laced together, thrilling me more.

He smiled. "I ran into your ma at the Committee for Healthy Des Moines meeting. Had to attend part of it when my boss spoke. But your ma said you were home. I got here, and you weren't. So I went next door, and the one girl said you'd left, and when I couldn't find you, I thought maybe you'd gone with a beau for the evening."

My cheeks warmed as I registered his concern for me. We looked down at our hands at the same time, and an awkwardness settled between us. I pulled my hand from his and thought of what Miss Violet had planned for the evening. What if he'd seen Olivia dressed as Dreama? I imagine he would've said that first if he had.

"No beau." I stole a glance at him and looked away, shy at meeting him under night's cover. His gaze felt warm but probing.

"So I'm not too late to lasso you in?"

"Lasso me in? I'm too . . ." I didn't know which reason to give him.

He leaned against the naked oak tree and crossed his arms, giving me a half smile. "Too what?"

Too busy, too young, too tired? All would work as reasons for me not having a beau.

"Busy," I said.

"Then you need a break to spend time with a good friend, someone who's nothing but fun."

"Who said such a thing?"

"Mabel. The girl who works with us at Mr. Palmer's place. Palmer's kitchen mistress, I suppose we could call her. If we were being fancy."

"Oh, I see." Now I gave him a teasing look, our easy conversation coursing, like rushing water. "You have your own kitchen mistress? Fun and fancy." I thought of the stoic Zurchenkos and wondered who could think of this serious law student as fun. "So the kitchen mistress thinks you're fun. Didn't you mention her once before?"

"Is that curiosity or jealousy?"

"Neither." His sweet teasing made me smile. "I've too much to do to think of you and your kitchen mistress at Mr.

Palmer's." Yet a stab of jealousy had hit me. It must have showed on my face.

He put his hand out. I stared at it. He reached farther toward me. "Let's go."

"Where?"

"To eat."

"I'm not hungry."

"You're not?"

I shook my head.

"Well, you look like you could use some cheering up and *I'm* starving. Surely, you're done baking the bread and you're free to go now."

How did he know I could use some cheering? I did want to go. I swallowed hard, my eyes filling. What on earth was happening with this grip of emotion? His way with me was so natural, as though he'd never been away from me. His confidence and ease softened me, made me want to be with him. He didn't want a thing from me, and I felt instantly cocooned in his presence.

"Mama won't approve."

"She already did."

I raised my eyebrows at him, shocked.

"I obtained permission at the meeting."

I drew back, surprised. "She said you could take me to supper?"

"When I promised to help in the garden and I reminded her that I'd already saved your life once, she couldn't say no."

My mouth fell open. "You didn't say that."

He chuckled, looked at his feet and then his eyes met mine again. "Oh, Katherine. You are so . . . sweet."

"Oh galoshes."

"How I—" He kept my gaze. I couldn't look away, even though my insides tumbled like a frothy cream shaken and stirred. I felt as though I might dissolve right there, and yet I stood.

He pushed his hand through his thick, short hair. "How I love when you say that."

"Why?"

He pushed his hands in his pockets but never stopped looking at me, holding me simply with his presence. He finally shook his head. "I just do."

Aleksey created the same feeling in me that my calming did. I'd never experienced that with a living, breathing person other than Pearl, and that was completely different. This evening, it was as if I'd been visited by some magic, something unexplainable meeting me at every turn.

Aleksey drew a deep breath and then motioned toward the gate. "This way to supper."

For once in my life, I wasn't hungry, as if Aleksey's presence fed me instead. I looked down at my old skirt and shirtwaist. They were clean, but the hem was frayed and grayed, the cuffs threadbare. I wished to be wearing something finer for dinner with Aleksey, something closer to what I wore as Dreama. But I knew his friendship looked far beyond things like clothing. My insides were full of unfamiliar sensations. I looked into his face, his smile beaming, and all I wanted was to be with him, no matter my dress. In his eyes, I saw me the way I used to be: untarnished, untouched, clean. Tonight, in this moment, I could be the person he thought I was, the person I still was deep inside. He knew I needed cheering, delivering it without my even asking. I needed to be with him. "All right," I said. "Let's go."

He held out his hand. I looked at it for a moment.

"The ground is muddy by the back gate," he said. "I'll guide you past it."

I took his hand, energy lurching between us. He looked as startled as I felt. We reached the back gate. I patted the cow's rump to get her to move aside. Aleksey lifted the handle and swung the gate forward for me to pass. He steadied me as I lifted my skirt and hopped over a muddy section of land. How long had it been since I'd left Miss Violet's property? The navy-blue night sky fell around us, and suddenly I was rejuvenated.

I realized my hand was still clasped inside Aleksey's, and another thrill corkscrewed up my spine. I slowed my stride, and he did also. We swung our hands and strolled. I recorded every second with him in my mind like notes in Miss Violet's ledgers.

Aleksey glanced up at the heavens. "Over the years, I've thought of how your hand felt against mine a thousand times."

I looked at our hands, the way his dwarfed mine. I drank in the warmth of his palm, the row of calluses tickling my skin. As children, we'd never held hands, not like this. At first while teaching him to write, I put my hand over his to help him form the letters of the alphabet and then words and sometimes full sentences, but this was different, yet so incredibly familiar. "You mean when I taught you to write?"

"Of course. And that night. You know."

I nodded. The blizzard. "I remember."

Back on the prairie, he'd always viewed me as the smarter one, the one with the teaching ways. But it was his idea to bring the cow into the dugout to keep us warm and that's what had saved us that night. We ambled along, neither of us talking, and I considered how it was that I wouldn't have remembered such a thing—the way his hand had felt— but he had. I was younger than he by three years; perhaps that was it? Survival had definitely taken all my energy the last few years.

Aleksey had become heroic to me during the storm. Instead of him admiring me for the things I *knew*, I looked up to him for the things he could *do*. But when we'd moved away, when I'd been separated from my family, it was all I could do to simply survive. My thoughts of the past, of anything that could make me yearn for the way things had been, were sealed away in my mind, cordoned off from my heart, where they could not cause it to ache more than it had.

"Look at that sky." He shook his head. "So many stars. That moon."

I looked into the jeweled heavens. "It's so clear tonight. I love it like this."

I realized how little time I'd spent outside at night. I remembered my escape from the Christoffs' home, the way the horse that carried me flew across the land, a night I couldn't wait to end. Now I had a sense of wonder about the darkness, here with Aleksey.

We walked in silence, stealing gazes at each other and then tumbling into short snatches of conversation. "There's the Milky Way," he pointed.

"The North Star," I said before we fell back into quiet. Our deep comfort shocked me in its peacefulness, like the first time I'd realized that someone I had seen was not living any longer. Our feet crunched over the dry grass. I stopped and swung my hand out against his chest to keep him from going ahead. "What's that?"

He cocked his head. "What?" A slow smile spread over his lips.

I closed my eyes and listened. "Music. A violin. A *piano*?" I strained to hear better. "Drumming?"

He pulled my hand and tugged me forward. His smile was infectious. My mind spun back through our last conversation. "Wait a minute. Is this the party you mentioned the other day? You're taking me to a dance at the river?"

He pulled my hand again, guiding me along the path. "I'm taking you to supper at the river, yes."

The eagerness I felt stopped abruptly. I did, too. I looked down at my clothing, spreading my arms wide. "Look at me."

He threw his arms open and looked down at his clothes, then winked. "Look at *me*."

My mind flashed back to the dances Mama and Father attended when I was a child, the parties I'd gone to. "A dance requires the proper clothing, certainly a bustle. I mean, *look at me*. I'm not fashionable at all."

He tilted his head, studying me some more. He scratched his chin, his evening whiskers making a sifting sound.

"You're right. You're not fashionable right now, Katherine."

My heart sank further at the acknowledgement.

"But thinking that you require fashion to be beautiful is like suggesting the sun needs the moon to be yellow, that the night sky needs the sun's daytime shine. It wouldn't be fair if you were fashionable *and* beautiful. It's like having sunshine and moonshine at the same time. No one would know where to look first, and they'd miss it all, trying to see your beauty all at once."

My throat tightened, and my eyes burned. I couldn't talk; I didn't know what I would say if I could. I hid my quaking hands behind my back.

"A woman like you doesn't require fashion. Your intelligence, your beauty. All of it is worth more than anything in the world."

A wave of . . . well, something—I had no idea what this was I felt in my heart—spun through me, causing me to nearly break into childlike tears. I could feel the sincerity, the honesty. His words, uttered under the bright sky, had fallen over me like magic dust, transforming me in some way I could not articulate. His presence, his sentiments, his kindness felt like the calm that came with my crystal.

"Thank you," was all I could say.

He stepped toward me and brushed the side of my bonnet. "Spider."

I caught his hand as he lowered it. Again, words escaped me. I couldn't explain what I felt, the desire to be closer to him right then. I wanted to tell him what his words meant to me after feeling cast off for so long. I felt gathered in, fitted into his heart, safe.

There was a pause in the far-off music and then a violin started again, a fast-paced song I hadn't heard in ages. "Oh!

Susanna" came to me. I followed his gaze in the direction of the woods.

"Let's go," he said. "I want you to enjoy every single moment of this night."

"Let's," I said. I grabbed up my skirt and we ran toward the music.

**

A surge of joy filled me as the music and laughter grew louder and more layered, as though a symphony had risen out of the very earth on which we stood, like the voices that came to me just when someone needed comfort or I needed help. He tugged my hand, and I lifted my skirts with the other hand, and we darted toward the party. A rumbling laugh pulled through me, happiness consuming me. Aleksey seemed energized by my happiness.

We reached a bend in the Des Moines River, where a clearing of grand, hovering elms watched over a roaring fire. The flames lapped at the wood that fueled it. Dancing, laughing couples circled it with intricate three-steps. Under a pavilion made of tree trunks and twigs for a cross-hatched roof, fiddlers bowed violins, drummers kept time on wood blocks, a guitarist seated on an old tree stump strummed away, a flutist, a trumpeter, and a pianist played while a man with a banjo picked away. Lanterns hung from the pavilion roof and gave soft light to the revelers, making them appear mysterious and at the same time so very gleeful. Laughter rang out between hoots, and the scent of chicken cooking over a small fire on the other side of the pavilion made my mouth water. Aleksey pointed toward the pavilion. "That's the direction that we come from when the fellas and I come here from Mr. Palmer's. There's a bridge just beyond these trees that leads right to his property."

I nodded at what he said, but I couldn't take my eyes off the action around the fire. "What *is* all this?" I said.

"Just people who came from back east. Rumor had it Des Moines was looking to build a symphony, and turns out there's a store of pioneering musicians looking to start a new life."

"I didn't know," I said.

He surveyed the party. "My friends from Mr. Palmer's are here somewhere. We'll find them later."

As "Oh! Susanna" came to an end, the notes of a song I'd never heard before started.

Aleksey leaned down, the shape of his words, his breath on my ear, sending sparks through me. "It's an old Russian folksong," he said.

I tapped my toe, watching the dancers.

Aleksey's hand closed over mine. "Let's dance."

I resisted his pull. "I don't know this one."

He responded by grasping my waist and gathering me into him. A jolt knocked away my breath. His muscular body was hard against mine. I looked into his face as he led me into the path of circling dancers. A flicker of thought came to me about being in public, being anywhere like this. I pushed away, moving out of the circle of dancers.

He took my hand again. "We can go. Or sit and have something to eat or—" Listening to Aleksey's words, thinking of how I'd just felt safe in his arms, I drew a deep breath and put my hand on his shoulder to show I was ready to dance. I patted him and lifted his other hand into position. "I want to stay," I said.

He smiled down on me. "Then we'll stay." The broadness and strength of his shoulder, the muscles contracting under my hand, sent tingling through me. The music picked up pace and grew in volume and intensity. He drew me into him again, his hand pressing the small of my back, warming me from my center outward.

Aleksey looked over his shoulder for an opening in the circle and then stepped into it, leading me at breakneck pace. My feet flew, following him, the momentum causing my head to fall back, making me laugh as we blurred by the river, the pavilion, the food tent, the trees.

I couldn't have guessed at Aleksey's dancing prowess as there was never occasion for dancing during the prairie year. As we moved, the music continued to expand, filling the night like feathers lifting a mattress.

"You can dance," I said over the music.

"Yes, I can, my sweet kitchen mistress," he said.

A female vocalist entered into the arrangement, adding richness and even more tempo. Aleksey pressed his hand more firmly into my back. The music sped up, and so did his feet. I couldn't believe our feet weren't tangling, that we weren't falling into the fire or the couple in front of us. We rounded the fire with the force at each turn lifting me off my feet, each step like dancing on clouds.

I felt as though I had sprouted wings, the night, the orange flames blurring as we spun by. The singer's voice bit through the atmosphere, haunting and tight before she lowered it to a whisper that ended the song. The dancers slowed, clapped, and cheered.

"What *is* this again?" I cheered, the group whooping as everyone dispersed.

"A musical gathering," he said. "Can't you see?"

I looked into his face as though he was suddenly foreign to me. Who was this Aleksey? Not the boy I'd once known, the serious, pack-mule, farmer boy. A woman came up to Aleksey and patted him on the shoulder.

Aleksey turned and the two grinned, excited to see each other. My shoulders tensed as I realized the ease between them showed this woman knew Aleksey well.

"Mabel," he said, pulling me closer. "This is Katherine."

She put her hand out. "Katherine? The reading teacher and kitchen mistress you've told us so much about?" She looked me up and down.

I offered my hand.

"Nice to meet you, Katherine." She finally smiled warmly at me, and I relaxed.

"Wonderful to meet you, Mabel," I said, remembering Aleksey mentioning her before.

A young man came up and took Mabel's hand, swinging it. "Katherine? You must be." I shook his hand. "So glad to finally meet the girl who changed this big lug's life."

I drew back. Again, their comfort with each other and with mentioning me demonstrated an intimacy between them.

Aleksey punched Fat Joe playfully in the arm. "Let's not scare her off before I've a chance to show her I'm not just a big lug anymore."

Joe rubbed his arm, exaggerating pain. "Watch it, friend. You don't want a bloody nose, do ya? She won't be impressed with that. All that saving of lives you did was years ago after all. Today's a new day!"

I looked at Aleksey to see if he'd been teasing me behind my back. But he smiled and then shouted as Fat Joe and Mabel danced away. "Yes, a new day."

I pressed a hand to my chest, still catching my breath from dancing, from hearing from Aleksey's friends that he'd been talking about me. The female vocalist started humming, and the guitarist joined her along with a male singer. The woman sang the first words to "Hard Times Come Again No More."

The slow, moody tune had been laid down inside my skin as a child. When was the last time I'd even heard music? Church with the Christoffs—dire, plodding, dark songs. But this one, sad but somehow equally hopeful, flooded the silver-moon night. I suddenly remembered it as though I'd heard it every day for the last ten years.

My nanny had sung it repeatedly.

"Dance with me, Katherine." Aleksey took my hand and pulled me against him again, the fire lighting him, giving him the golden hue of a mythical being. This song was slow and sultry giving me the chance to feel every inch of being held, of his body against mine.

You are so handsome. The darkness forced me to see him differently, to notice others staring at him, at us.

Other couples were already locked into a slow three-step, cheeks against each other as they rounded the fire yet again. I could tell by the way the men held the women against them tight, the way the women laid cheeks on shoulders and chests, closing their eyes, that they were comfortable with such displays. This wasn't their first dance, and I didn't have to worry about the condition of my dress. Seeing the intimate way the couples held one another for this slow song, I suddenly felt the weight of this situation. I imagined Mama seeing me dancing in the dark with a man's hands holding me like the other men were holding their dance partners. But this wasn't just some man. It was Aleksey.

I began to step away. He pulled me toward him. He brushed hair back from my forehead. "I won't hurt you, Katherine. Not ever."

I couldn't breathe at his declaration. I'd known that since he chased the grocer away that day in town by the oranges. "I know," I said.

He roped his arm around my shoulders, and I surrendered to the dance, to his embrace, to his leading me back into the hypnotic circle, my body molded against his—improper, but feeling so good. He leaned into me, and his lips brushed my ear, sending tingles throughout my entire body again. "There's a fair young maiden who toils her life away . . ." He straightened and began to three-step slowly, making me feel every bit as light as I had when we were whipping around as though our hair had caught fire.

The singer stretched the lyrics long and full, slowing the tempo to the point we barely moved. Our bodies pressed together, my head against his chest, his heartbeat pulsing against me. Our intertwined fingers moved against each other, lighting every nerve in my body on fire.

I could tell the song was moving to its conclusion, and all I wanted to do was prolong it. A couple in front of us stutter-stepped, and Aleksey lifted me out of the way, moving around them as though rehearsed. Lifted in his arms, we could see eye to eye. I looped my arms around his neck, curling the hair at his collar around my fingers. My insides quaked, something deep inside was changing yet again, becoming . . . Before I could even think, I closed my eyes, and his lips brushed mine.

He pulled back, and our eyes met before he kissed me again, gently, his tongue parting my lips, his warmth filling me, causing heat to emanate from between my thighs, and all I wanted was more closeness. He responded with a deeper kiss. Another couple bumped past us, and he set me down.

Flushed from head to toe, I gazed up at him, my hands on his chest. I knew what it was that I felt right then—love. How could this have happened in this short time, since I'd seen him in Des Moines, in the space of a song? *Love?*

I shook my head as though I'd said the word aloud. Aleksey held me tighter, his fingers caressing my spine as he led me back into some semblance of a three-step. The music trailed off, and Aleksey tucked a lock of hair behind my ear.

"Did you feel that?" he asked.

I knew he felt the same shift in our friendship. How could he not have?

His hands shook as he took mine and held them to his chest.

"I felt it."

"I meant what I said. I'll keep you safe."

Heat rose up my neck and into my cheeks. For the first time in my life, words like that spoken by a man didn't feel constricting, didn't make me want to argue independence or women's rights or lay down my life plans, which included a fat purse of my own. In that moment, I recognized what it meant to *feel* beautiful, to feel safe. For the first time in my life, those words, "I'll keep you safe," were given to me from someone other than family or the leering Mr. Christoff, or even Miss Violet.

The music stopped and we stepped apart, even though the other couples remained arm in arm, holding hands or swaying to the silence.

"Let's eat," he said.

I remembered he'd been hungry way back at my house. "You must be famished. I was rude not to remember that you were coming here to eat."

I would delay our leaving this dance as long as I could. I wanted to protect this sliver of heaven that had descended like a mystic's spell. I couldn't fathom experiencing a similar moment of perfection ever again.

As we walked toward the tent where the food was spread, the musicians starting up again, playing a rendition of the William Tell Overture. I was fully in the moment, inside my own life, feeling nothing but pure joy at hearing music that moved my feet and sent my heart soaring. I would not forget a bit of it, of that I was sure.

**

We sat under the lantern-lit tent where a banquet was offered. Red-and-white checked cloths covered long rustic tables. Roasted chicken, fresh greens, and a sharp-scented cheese drizzled with pear-vinegar dressing. There was zucchini, just soft enough in the middle, combined with mushrooms, chives, and rosemary. Several different breads were arranged for the taking, and there was crisp lemonade and the iciest water. Near the end of the spread, there were tart lemon bars and cherry pie.

One of the women who'd been performing came by with a small tin cup. Aleksey reached in his pocket and added a few coins to it. "Thank you," they said to one another.

"Thank you, Aleksey," I said.

He smiled. "The musicians bring the food and we all contribute to the cost," Aleksey said. "They want an audience and so we all benefit."

"It's magic," I said, looking around, taking it all in. "Pure magic."

Each bite, the flavors on my tongue, made me feel like a queen, pampered and cherished.

Aleksey wiped his mouth with a napkin. "This tastes wonderful, Katherine, but I have to say that the meal you made me at your house was even better." He held up a piece of bread. "And your bread is way more delicious."

I swallowed a bite of salad and thanked him. I eyed the plate he was sweeping clean with a heel of bread.

I laughed. "I'm not so sure I can trust your assessment. I'm getting the idea you toss around food compliments like acorns fall from an oak."

"I'm hurt, Katherine. I am judicious with my compliments. I mean it. It's true, I am nearly always hungry, but I happen to be a discriminating eater."

I thought of the meals we'd eaten as children on the prairie, sometimes that were made of prairie grass and what passed as gritty grains I wasn't so sure most people would feed to animals. "Discriminating?"

"I am."

"Since when?"

"Oh, Katherine. The meals I've had since arriving here. Mr. Stevens treats me once a quarter to a fat, juicy steak. And, well, I dream about those meals, meat that dissolves in my mouth, gravies and potatoes. And wine. He gave me wine. He's traveled in Italy and seems to think there will come a day in America that wine will be drunk at every dinner."

I couldn't help but smile, listening to him gush over food, something I yearned for so often, but I was lured by what was near and easily pocketed. And sweet. I did like my sweets.

Aleksey glanced at my plate, still overflowing with chicken and vegetables. I pushed the plate toward him. He pushed it back. "You're skin and bones."

I flinched. He reached for my hand and squeezed it. "That sounded wrong. You know—"

"I know what you meant." I pushed the plate back to him. "Please eat."

He shook his head, and I cut a piece of chicken, forked it, and put it to his lips. He sighed and opened his mouth. And with that, he ate the rest of my plate, and I never felt so fed as when I watched him fill his belly.

When he finished eating, he took both plates to where some women were washing them. I watched as they patted him on the back and gestured toward me, smiling. He returned with two lemon squares and sat on my side of the bench, his leg warm against mine. I was worried that he might feel the crystal ball in the pocket of my skirt. I shifted it so I could enjoy the sensation of his body against mine without worry. We ate dessert, and I felt the evening winding down.

The dancers were ramping up, but the tent was emptying. Instead of him suggesting we dance again, he took my hand and opened my palm, spreading my fingers under his. He smoothed my fingers open, brushing them, and then he focused on my palm. He traced the lines that mapped my skin, giving me the shivers.

"See that?" he said.

I pulled my hand away. "What?" I was uncomfortable with playing at this, knowing that Miss Violet sometimes used it to accompany what I did for readings.

He took it back and traced the lines. "It's an A."

I looked at the shape and nodded. "It is."

"It's meant to be, then, isn't it?"

I stared at path of the A he'd etched into my hand and thought that every woman probably had an A on her palm. He traced a line that ran parallel to one of the sides of the A. "Surely this line means that you will live a long, long life, fully loved."

I let him continue, the feel of his finger tracing my skin causing tingles and swells of heat to race from every corner of my body.

"I see you in a large home—brick, probably. There'll be a room stuffed with books so you can teach our—"

He stopped tracing my hand and cleared his throat. "Your children. You'll be something spectacular. A teacher, a professor, I don't know. But I see your life so full of wonder that you'll barely have time to sleep; you'll barely want to. People will come from all over to be with you and hear what you have to teach them."

I suddenly felt exposed, thinking of all the people coming to see me as Dreama. I pulled my hand away.

He coaxed it back. He laid his palm over mine and then lifted it off.

He turned his palm toward me so I could see it. "Look."

I peered at his palm, taking his strong hand in mine. "Same *A*," I said. I traced his *A*, and he smiled at me.

"I'm sure there's lots we don't know about each other at this point, Kath."

"Kath," I said.

"What?" He narrowed his eyes.

"Nothing." *I just like how that sounds on your lips.* He was right. There was so much we didn't know about each other. So much I could never tell him. He clearly held strong affection for me, but who knew what that would bring? I had certainly learned that nothing intangible was dependable. A vow, a love, a promise did not always bring its truth along for the ride.

"You'll have a great life, Katherine. I know you're independent and so smart. And I think you can find a man who understands that, who wouldn't take that from you. Think of the way you study. The way you taught me. Tell me what you're learning from Miss Violet. I know she's quite famous with her investments. I hear that as far back as Chicago people are talking, wanting to give her their money."

I shook my head, a small seed weighing in my belly. The lies. Aleksey was a kind man, an old friend who had grown up and was gentle and sweet. But that didn't mean he'd want to hear the truth. I couldn't tell him about my studies or my work. The lying seed in my belly pushed its sprout and stem up my esophagus, making it impossible to speak at all.

"Tell me about your work?" He prodded as he drew his finger down each of mine.

I tasted the shame and regret. It wasn't fair to this person who seemed to have stepped into my mind, my heart, and knew exactly what I needed to hear. How could I tell him what I was doing with Miss Violet? He read my palm in jest. I thought of the newspaper articles. He'd see me differently if he knew what I did to make money.

No, he wasn't aware of the things that I had done, the lies I've told, the double life I led, the things I did to survive. The tenderness, the simple caress of his fingers on my palm, made me want more, made me want to allow myself these moments of joy. A short time of pure happiness—everyone deserved some, and I wasn't going to ruin it by telling him things I was awfully sure he didn't even want to know.

Chapter 42

Watched
Aleksey

Katherine and I strolled back to her home under the midnight stars. She tucked her arm into mine. Each moseying step that took us closer made me want to stop time and speed it up. I wanted this night, this moment, to last forever. I also wanted to have passed my law exams and have my own practice so I could show Katherine I would take her back to the lifestyle she once enjoyed.

I still couldn't believe I felt this way. There was so much to know about her, and she about me. But the prospect of it felt like Christmas morning was just around the corner.

Katherine's stride shortened as we got closer to home, she squeezed tighter into me, and I knew she didn't want this magical night to end either. Something had shifted—the ground, the earth, the sky—perhaps changed by the hot flames of the fire, the magic that had materialized inside of me when I took her in my arms and felt her body against mine. It was as though this one night had broken open something that had been in the making, laid in the stars for us for years without us knowing until now.

I'd do anything to prove myself to her, to show her I understood she was a modern woman, one who was to be valued for her mind as well as the homemaking she'd clearly mastered serving as Violet Pendergrass's kitchen mistress.

As we neared the front steps of Katherine's home, we stopped. I couldn't take my eyes from her. I cupped her face, she leaned into my hand, and I pulled her into me. "Thank you for dinner, Katherine."

She gripped me, her arms tight around my back, her cheek buried against my chest. "Thank you." In seconds, she stiffened. I released her, longing to kiss her like I had at the dance, but knowing it wouldn't be proper. And I didn't want to risk Mrs. Arthur regretting that she'd entrusted Katherine to me.

I shuffled my feet, unsure about how to end this night. I took her hand. The moonlight splashed over us. I brushed her fingers with my thumb. "When can I call again?"

She swallowed hard. She opened her mouth to speak, then stopped as the front door began to rattle, interrupting us.

"What time is it?"

I pulled my watch from my pocket. "Midnight."

Katherine covered her mouth, seeing her mother's shape emerging from the doorway, a lamp overhead. "Oh no."

I took Katherine's elbow, positioning myself nearly an arm's length away as I guided her up the front stairs.

Mrs. Arthur flew toward us as we reached the top stair. "I was so worried. I knew you were together, but I thought maybe you got caught up in the saloon crowd after eating."

Katherine looked at me as I removed my hat, offering me an encouraging smile. "I think Aleksey could handle anyone we encountered. And we weren't anywhere near the saloons."

Her mother glanced at Katherine and then at me. Her shoulders relaxed, and she smiled. "You're right about that— Aleksey could handle anything that came his way. I know that, but as soon as you're both gone from sight, I imagine the younger boy and little girl you used to be."

"My ma says the same thing, Mrs. Arthur." I hoped she wasn't angry with me. I realized that we did stay at the dance too long, but I wanted to be sure she knew I wouldn't allow any harm to come to her daughter. Still, bringing her home later than expected might not demonstrate my care for her wellbeing. "When Katherine's with me, she'll be safe. And I apologize for the late hour. We started talking and then . . . well, four years is a lot to catch up on. My ma will be so happy to hear you're all well."

"You'll remember to let her know she's welcome anytime?"

"I will."

"So this is the hero, is it?" A woman stepped out from inside the Arthurs' house. I squinted into the darkness that surrounded her, trying to determine who she was. Katherine tensed and stepped farther away.

She pushed a smile on her face to replace the surprised look that had first taken over. Something about this woman set Katherine on edge, far more than arriving home late had done. "Aleksey Zurchenko, ma'am." I offered my hand.

"This is Violet Pendergrass," Mrs. Arthur said. "She saw the light on and came by with your pay, Katherine."

"I'm her kitchen mistress," Katherine said with a quiver in her voice.

"Ah, the beneficiary of all that wonderful baking and cooking," I said. "It's a pleasure to meet you."

Miss Pendergrass shifted, her hips swaying as she moved closer. The woman was short, but she was a large presence at the same time. She seemed to steal all the air for herself. She looked me up and down. "Aren't you handsome? *This* is the boy who saved you and Yale, Katherine? In that blizzard that killed all those people, the Children's Blizzard?"

Katherine nodded, her eyes dropping to her truncated finger before shoving her hands behind her back. "Yes. This is Aleksey."

"Well," Violet said. "It's wonderful to finally meet a living legend."

Something inside her words didn't fit her message, as though she was mocking me, challenging me, more than believing I did anything heroic at all. I ran my hand through my hair. "I'm afraid luck had as much to do with our survival as I did. The cow who kept us warm is the real hero."

Miss Pendergrass cocked her head and pressed her hand to her breast. "A *modest* champion. How very rare."

Her gaze penetrated mine, making me feel as though she were digging inside me for some bit of information I didn't want to give up. The hair on the back of my neck rose.

"Well," Miss Pendergrass said, "I've some work to do before the night is over." She finally took her eyes from me and brushed her hand over Katherine's shoulder. "I trust your flushed cheeks aren't a sign of illness. I've given your mother some extra with your wages, and you know we have a busy week coming up."

"I feel wonderful." Katherine stole a glance at me. "Refreshed. Thank you for the evening off, Miss Violet."

Katherine seemed closed off, her words stilted and forced. But it wasn't because her mother scolded us or that we worried her. There was something about Miss Pendergrass that had unsettled Katherine. I remembered when one of the girls who worked next door came to get Katherine when we were in her kitchen. She had responded in a similar, tense way.

"I'll be ready to go bright and early. As always," Katherine said.

"Yes, as always. You're a fine worker bee, Katherine. You are."

Miss Pendergrass's words rushed over me, giving me again the sense that she was more displeased with us than even Mrs. Arthur had been.

"She's headed to bed right now," Mrs. Arthur said, pulling Katherine toward the door. Katherine looked over her shoulder at me. She wiggled her fingers in a wave, a small smile coming at her lips. I realized I was touching mine, remembering how hers had felt, how she tasted.

Miss Violet cleared her throat, startling me. I smiled at her and wiped my hand on my leg. I was being dismissed. I pulled my hat back on. "Goodnight, all."

"You go right up to sleep, young lady," Mrs. Arthur said as she was closing the door, the hinges whining. I jogged down the front stairs and turned back to look at the house. A knocking sound drew my attention to the second floor.

Katherine stood, her hands holding back both sides of the drapes. She waved to me, grinning before her mother pulled her away, offering me a wave as well.

I began my trek back to the farm. It was the first night that wouldn't end with me studying. I'd climb into my cot, curl up, and wrap myself in every detail of this night. Just the thought of Katherine's name sped up my heart. I turned once again and looked at her house. A flash of light caught my eye next door. A woman ducked back into the doorway, her lamp going dark as she did.

Violet Pendergrass had been watching me. A shiver crawled up my neck, spreading along my shoulders. And as I neared the corner where I would turn to head into town, I shrugged off the sensation that something was just not right.

Chapter 43

Limp
Katherine

I stood at the easel, my arm growing heavy and knotted from painting for so long. The sun shifted, no longer framed in the window, lighting my work. Miss Violet had set me up near the window in the parlor, one on the side of the house so no one would see me from the street. I shifted my feet, and the scent of lavender, lemon, and rosemary from the freshly swept rug filled my nose. Olivia perched at the piano behind me, playing "Moonlight Sonata" in nine different ways, as though she could hear it unfolding in her head at different tempos, with different emphases that made each new version fresh but recognizable. I squeezed my eyes closed, then opened them, ready to finish the painting.

Someone stood beside me silently, and it wasn't until the sound of a teacup rattled against a saucer that I realized I was in need of something to drink. I stopped painting, noticing that Miss Violet was sliding a second palette aside to make room for a flowery china cup.

"Thank you," I said.

She nodded.

Perhaps the painting was done already? I lifted the cup and saucer and stepped away from my work to get a broader view of what I'd done. I couldn't say how much time had passed since I'd begun painting, but the canvas in front of me had come alive. Thick strokes in shades of blue and gray combined to make a moody sky that drew me right into the painting, as though it were not of my own doing, as though I'd been asleep while making it. In the foreground, a woman stood, her dress and hair wind-whipped, one delicate hand trying to pull tendrils back from her eyes. I'd painted a child beside the woman, holding her other hand, gazing up at her mama. The wind pushed their hair over their faces, hiding their facial features. Off to the side, I'd painted a board-and-batten home. Sea-foam green planks held up a cross-gabled roof.

"These colors. You made them all from that basic palette I bought you?" Miss Violet said.

I sipped the tea and glanced at the palette, seeing the result of mixing numerous paints, recalling my combining them like a cottony dream threatening to disappear once fully awake. I nodded.

She let out a soft whistle. "I didn't believe the man when he said any artist worth her salt would make every color in the world from this set of five."

I'd certainly proven my value in that department.

Miss Violet pointed to the horizon on the painting where I'd added a honey-pink coloring. "Is the sun rising or setting?"

I studied it, thinking that it wasn't the sun at all. "It's an angel. Watching over them."

Miss Violet held my gaze for a moment as though deciding whether I was serious. She pointed to a flower basket set off in the background, then her finger trailed through the air toward the porch I'd made. "Who's that?"

"The husband," I said and flinched. "I mean, I suppose it is. I just paint what comes to me."

Miss Violet leaned in closer. "How did you know that address, 231 Allen Street?"

I bent in beside her, looking at the numbers I'd added to the planks on the house near the front door.

I shook my head and followed Miss Violet's gaze back to the woman in the painting. She gestured at the woman and girl's clasped hands.

Miss Violet took my elbow, her hand shaking as she pointed. "And that?"

"What?"

Miss Violet straightened and squeezed my forearm, forcing me to look at her. "Were you listening in on my meeting with Mrs. Atwood?"

Olivia's playing stopped.

Mrs. Atwood? I drew back, trying to fit the puzzle pieces of the earlier happenings into a recognizable picture. I searched my mind for the person she was talking about. "Who's Mrs. Atwood?"

The silence was vibrating until Olivia said, "Katherine wasn't here. It was the two of us and Mrs. Atwood."

"Did you tell her anything that—"

"Nothing," Olivia said. She rose from the piano bench, hitting a key. With her ankle fairly healed, she glided toward us, head cocked, regarding me as though studying a caged carnival attraction. She and Miss Violet surveyed the painting.

"See the woman's bracelet?" Miss Violet said.

Olivia nodded. "Fleurs-de-lis."

They turned their attention back to me.

"We did talk at breakfast and dinner the other day. Perhaps she heard then?" I stepped away from them, a new sting of betrayal that I'd been dismissed from even more important meetings. I'd tried to forget about the idea Olivia had imitated me, that Miss Violet has wanted her to, but this brought the sensation back again.

Miss Violet pulled me to the settee near the piano. She flapped her hand toward the piano. "Play some more, Olivia. It's time to let Katherine know about the shoes."

Olivia flashed a pout before she sighed and went back to drag her fingers across the piano keys.

"Play something *different*," Miss Violet said. Olivia shot me a glare before she began to bring an upbeat, circus-type melody to life, making me think she was mocking me with the tune.

**

Miss Violet explained that I'd painted the very scene—a story, really—that Mrs. Atwood had divulged during a meeting when she agreed to invest with the company.

"Here is this painting you've made. It depicts what she told us." She seemed angry for some reason I didn't understand.

"I didn't listen in on any conversations. At least not on purpose. I could have heard something, but I don't specifically remember . . ."

She shook her head. "Whether you're picking up bits and pieces of information as you work and don't even realize it or we discussed it and don't remember you being here, or perhaps you imparted this in some other way, I don't know. But beyond your paintings being very well done, there is something more to them. And I think we could really make a killing if we sold them *along with* your other services."

I sighed. It took so much energy to call up spirits on demand, if I had to add making prophetic paintings to my workload, I didn't know if I could manage.

"This will change everything. Think if the clients could *see* you painting, how powerful that would be."

I looked at the canvas. "I can't allow people to know who I am. We both know that."

"If you paint in the disguise, no one will know."

I shook my head. I couldn't imagine having the energy for that on top of readings. Not in front of people. In the kitchen was different.

"They don't have to be elaborate. Just something to take with them, a hint of what you've told them."

"They would have to be simple. Maybe charcoal outlines with color highlights."

"Or go where the spirits take you."

I thought for a moment. "What if someone doesn't like the painting, then what?"

Miss Violet shook her finger back and forth at me. "No. It's all about suggestion. For the people whom you don't read for, I'll converse with them and provide you with enough information to create a painting that captures something meaningful to them. Perhaps the reading you do beforehand, if that's how we work it, will give you more than enough."

"I don't like the idea of a client being able to watch me. What if they figure out who I am? It's hard enough in your kitchen when I'm alone."

"I've thought of that. Besides dim lighting and wearing your veiling, I want you to change a simple thing . . ."

Olivia sat beside us, holding something concealed under a linen sheet.

"Actually, we have to make this change whether you paint in front of clients or not," Olivia said.

"What change?" I didn't like that I wasn't part of deciding changes to Dreama's work.

Miss Violet patted my hand. "Turns out the papers have taken to mentioning Dreama's, er, *Olivia's* limp."

"She's not limping anymore," I said.

"Well, the papers seem to think the limp is more than a sprain, and something about it is sympathetic, interesting to readers, apparently."

I stared at Olivia, remembering the newspaper article. That could be explained away by saying she had a sore foot.

It certainly didn't need to be a permanent part of her persona. "So tell them it was a temporary limp."

Miss Violet clenched her teeth. "I agreed to some of your demands the other day. I didn't hold your gallivanting with that Aleksey fellow against you or that moony look you always have on your face when you think of him or the time you spend penning letters to him. So this concession is required of you."

I didn't think all those things she listed meant I owed her more than I'd already been giving her. But I would hear her out. "So I just need to limp around a bit when I enter the room?"

"Not quite." Miss Violet drew the linen back to reveal a pair of boots, beautiful white leather boots with over a dozen pearl buttons marching over the front and up the ankle. Miss Violet normally put me in silken slippers to do readings, but these were certainly pretty enough.

As though Olivia could hear my thoughts, she turned the boots so I could see the soles. One boot was beautifully heeled with a short, delicate, hourglass shape. And the other, she held up and turned over, was heeled with a chunk of wood painted white.

I took the shoes from them. "I don't understand."

"We're going to give Dreama a gimp. Permanently," Miss Violet said.

Olivia's lips twitched, and she covered her mouth, trying to hide her amusement at this thought.

"What?"

"Here, put them on."

I pushed them away, noticing my missing pinkie, knowing that we covered the stump because it was a giveaway to my identity. It made sense to help hide me with a feigned deformity. Yet it seemed to be too much. "I don't know."

She covered my hand. "You float like an angel, Katherine, tall and magnificent, even all covered up. You're distracting from your work with your elegance."

That made no sense to me at all. "I could wear an old dress," I said.

"No, no. It's not the dress, and it's too late to start with the Dreama-as-an-angelic-pauper thing."

She stared at me.

"Try to shuffle," Miss Violet said.

I dragged myself to the middle of the room and tried on all manner of limps, stumbles, and saunters, but I could never do it the same way twice. The last attempt, a combination foot drag and clomp, left the three of us bent over, laughing so hard we couldn't breathe. And when I collapsed back between the two of them, each took one of my hands, and I felt connected again, like I had when Miss Violet first asked me to be an important part of her business.

Miss Violet shifted to face me. She smoothed my hair back. "Like everything I do for you, the boots are for your protection." I started to shake my head, but she squeezed my hand so hard I gasped. "With the press watching so closely, we need—no, *you* need to wear these shoes. If you get nervous or fall into deep concentration, you might forget to limp or forget which limp you did the last time. We can't have the papers suggesting that Dreama's limp comes and goes or changes like the almighty wind."

This all seemed like too much that had nothing to do with my actual ability. I thought of the awkwardness the boots would bring. "Painting in gloves, standing in shoes that shorten one leg?"

Miss Violet covered my hands with hers. "Try. Just once."

I shook my head, staring at the beautiful boots they'd turned into hideous sideshow shoes.

"Through the accidental limp," Miss Violet said, "when Olivia was reading, we discovered it lends Dreama an air of vulnerability. That adds another layer to Dreama. You'll have to walk across the stage at *A Night for Mothers*. It will put everyone at ease, on your side."

I appreciated that. But if we simply stuck with readings, it would be enough. "I can't afford to pay off another pair of shoes. Mama and I have plans."

She nodded. "I know." She began to unbutton the boots.

I shuddered. "They're atrocious."

Olivia giggled again.

"I'll pay for this pair of boots," Miss Violet said. "But I think you'll see we make back the cost of them and more in only a couple nights."

She knelt on the floor, removed my worn work boots, and slipped on each of the white ones. Olivia handed her the buttonhook, and they fastened me into them.

They stood and pulled me until I rose with them. As I stood, my left hip jutted back, knee bent to an awkward angle. Each step brought an uneven gait that made my right knee ache. I certainly wouldn't have to pretend or forget how I walked the last time. I fought the urge to correct my steps as we worked a path into the carpet, arm in arm.

"Step aside and tell us how this looks, Olivia," Miss Violet said.

We started back across the room again.

Olivia watched, hands on hips. "It's perfect. It looks like she was born defective. Brilliant." She clapped her hands, almost as awestruck as she'd been when I mediated between her and her mother that first time.

Something felt constricting to me about this new development, as though I was allowing them to tie my hands behind my back. Their excitement at the authenticity of my limp drilled an odd depression into me. Miss Violet turned me, and we started walking back across the room. I looked down to see my feet kick my skirt forward, one by one, feeling fraudulent inside my realistic limp. "Absurd," I said.

Miss Violet turned me toward her and cupped my cheeks. "No, no. This is it. You'll disarm them even further with your physical vulnerability. They'll open up, the spirits will gather, and you, my darling Katherine, will soar. Dreama will be greater than we ever could have imagined."

Chapter 44

Let Me Make You Dinner
Katherine

Exhausted, I returned home with a crock full of egg salad and a hunk of bread. The days had been exhilarating and too full at the same time. Miss Violet had introduced this new limp wrinkle to the readings and insisted I paint in front of clients, but working with paints was significantly more difficult than if she allowed me to sketch. It was true, I loved the act of painting, the dreamlike sensation that came with it when I gathered the spirits and my angels.

But painting with gloves, even thin ones, standing in my mismatched boots, and staying veiled took its toll. Painting itself could drain or invigorate me depending on the mood of what came to me. So on this evening, after three days of painting for clients, I was tired and hungry and wanted to eat and fall into bed.

When I stepped onto the back porch, a voice startled me, and the crock slipped from my grasp and right into the hands of Aleksey Zurchenko.

He laughed, lifting the lid of the pot, and inhaled. "Scrumptious."

I smiled at the expression on his face, touched at his kindness. "Hardly. It's a day old."

"You made it?"

"Yes."

"Then it's delicious, I'm sure."

I took it back from him, our fingers brushing, bringing heat to my cheeks. Seeing him loosened the grip of fatigue.

"All done working?"

I nodded. "All done." I stifled a yawn.

He removed his hat and gave me a dramatic bow. "Put aside your yawning, dear lady, I've come to ask you to dine with me."

I returned his bow with a small curtsey. "Another dance?"

"Nope. River's too high."

I pulled open the kitchen door and waved him inside. My heart beat heavy in my chest. With the mere presence of Aleksey, I'd been reinvigorated.

"Sit, then," I said. "I'll share my egg salad."

"Nope. We're going out."

My heart sank at the thought of not being able to get permission to go to supper. "Mama's gone. Another meeting with Mrs. Hillis."

"I know. Mr. Stevens is at her meeting. So we'll leave her a note," he said. "I'll take full responsibility for transporting you to and fro. She won't be angry. I promise. She trusts me."

I smiled. "*Should* she trust you?"

Aleksey's face reddened. This made me laugh.

He rubbed his chin. "I'll have you back before she can get the least bit angry or worried, or even get home."

"I don't know, Aleksey." I thought of all the lies I'd been telling Mama. I didn't want to add another.

"I know." He brushed the hair out of my eyes. "You've been working so hard. I see it on your face. Let me do this for you."

I patted the twist that held my hair at the nape of my neck, realizing how disheveled I must appear. He took my hands from my head and held them, his thumbs grazing my skin, sending waves of pleasure through me. "It's time for you to have some fun. You can't be the perfect daughter every single moment of your life."

I scoffed. "I'm far from that."

"Sure you are."

I felt a twinge of guilt that he so readily assumed I was the daughter he remembered from so long ago, but then the excitement I felt in being near him pushed away the apprehension.

He jotted a note on a scrap of paper for Mama and pulled me out the door, around the front of the house, to a wagon waiting. His friend Harold sat in the front of the wagon, ready to drive us. Cotton and wool blankets outfitted the back of the wagon, keeping me and my clothes safe from the mud-caked planks underneath. It was a sweet gesture that made me feel as though I'd stepped out of one life and into another.

Aleksey sat across from me. Though it was proper—if I could classify any of this as proper at all—that he put such space between us, all I wanted was to move closer, to feel his warmth, to hold his hand again, to feel his lips on mine.

Enthralled with Aleksey and excited to be out, I didn't pay attention to where the wagon took us.

"Now close your eyes. I want this to be a surprise," he said.

He slipped nearer and took my hand, and my stomach fluttered. "Trust me."

"I do," I said, enjoying the sensation of not seeing anything but feeling our hands together, both of his around mine.

The wagon lurched to one side, then the other, letting me know that we'd turned off the road. When it came to a stop, I nearly opened my eyes.

"Don't cheat. A little longer. I'm going to carry you while Harold finishes up a few things for me."

I could barely keep my eyes shut. "What are we doing, Aleksey?"

"Something special for a woman who deserves it."

Woman. The word, the thought that he saw me that way, made me float. He stood in the wagon and drew me up.

"You stand here while I get out." Then he took me by the waist and lifted me over the side of the wagon as if I were made of feathers.

He set me down beside him, his hands on my waist, the warmth melting through my skin.

"Lace your hands around my neck," he said. I worked my hands up his arms, over his shoulders and around his neck.

"Don't open your eyes."

"I won't."

He reached down, his arm behind my knees as he lifted, carrying me as though I was his bride crossing the threshold of our new home. With each step, I bounced a little and put my head against him, my cheek close to his neck, inhaling his clean, soapy scent, wanting to remember every bit of this moment.

When he finally set me down, I couldn't wait to see what was happening.

I turned in the direction I thought I could hear Harold in the wagon. "Thank you, Harold."

"You're so welcome. Enjoy your evening, Katherine. I'll be back in time to get you home."

I smiled, feeling strange with my eyes still closed.

I could hear Aleksey exhale, his hand at the small of my back. "All right. Open up."

I surveyed the space in front of me. Night had fallen. We stood inside a familiar walled garden. Candles flickered on the ground, in the trees, everywhere I looked. The apple, pear, and plum trees were leafless, but the smell of fermenting fruit that hadn't been picked was just past sweet and all the stronger. I could see myself climbing them when they were full green in summer. The once manicured flowerbeds were skeletal and overgrown at the same time. My mind kept trying to make sense of what I was seeing, but it just didn't. Still, the magic of the moment kept me from asking questions. I looked at the stars sparkling, the full moon fat, pulsing light. Along with the candles there was more than enough light on this clear, autumn night.

I couldn't imagine why he had brought me here, to my old house.

A light wind blew, making me shiver.

"I don't understand."

He pulled me into him, close against his side, and guided me down a candlelit path. I swallowed back tears. I stopped before we reached the summer kitchen where all our meals had been cooked when it had been too hot inside the house. I turned to him.

"Tell me. What are we doing here? Do you know what this is?"

He pulled me close to him again. "Come on, I'll explain, but I want you to see."

We walked among the candlelit trees along the stone path. Aleksey had created a magical, separate world just for the two of us. As we approached the outdoor kitchen, I saw that a fire had been lit and there were supplies.

"You thought we were headed to Mrs. Huffnaegal's restaurant, didn't you?" he said.

"I don't know what I thought." Suddenly, I was swept with fear. "But we have to go. Do you know—"

He took my shoulders. "No one lives here now."

"But I—"

"I know. It's your old home."

I couldn't fathom what we were doing, but I knew we had no right to be there. "We should go." I pulled him back, fully realizing we were trespassing.

"I'm making you dinner, like I said."

"But why here?"

"It all started because I wanted to see where you used to live. And so, I looked it up and came to see it, and it's for sale. Did you know?"

I shook my head, unsure of what that had to do with us.

"But what about the owners who are selling? They can't possibly think it's all right for us to be here like this."

"No one's lived here since . . . Well, the area has gone downhill a bit, and with all the people who lost money through that—"

I held up my hand. "I'm aware, Aleksey."

"I just wanted to let you know that I know what kind of woman you are. I want you to know that I understand the kind of life you should have."

I shook my head. "I don't know that my past life as a child is what I hold as a model of hope for my future."

He looked hurt. I had let go of all that was associated with our first life in Des Moines. Of all the pain I'd felt in being separated from my family. It was only an occasional yearning to once again have all the trappings of a large home and all it required. He looked down, and I felt sorry for not being more excited about what he'd done even if I didn't really understand why he did.

"I'm sorry," I said. "This is . . ." I looked around the space, at the glittery sky, the flickering candlelit ground. "A fairy tale."

He grinned. "Well, if you think the scene I've set is fabulous, wait until you taste what I'm making you to eat."

"I could have brought the egg salad or made some bread or . . ."

He stepped close to me, the air vibrating between us.

"Your ma said you never stop baking and working and . . . well, I want to wait on you tonight."

My eyes burned with rising tears. No one had ever said such a thing to me.

The emotion was too intense. I had to move away from him. I went toward the windows at the back of the home. I cupped my hands and peered inside. He came up behind me with a candle. I shifted to see past the glare. Floor-to-ceiling bookshelves were empty, the floors were bare, its soul was gone. I drew a deep breath to keep myself from falling into the despair that had visited my family so long ago.

He wrapped my hand in his and pulled me away from the windows. "I've prepared a spot for you to sit while I finish making the meal."

Aleksey led me to a tuffet made from stacked blankets. His hand brushed my waist as he settled me on it. Bricks contained the fire, but it warmed my skin even at a distance. He stood at the flames, the golden glow washing over him, as he examined the roasting chicken, held by nothing more than roping. The scent made my mouth water.

"I thought chicken would be nice tonight."

I nodded and folded my hands in my lap, watching. Anything would have been wonderful. "You did this?"

He squatted down in front of a pot and smiled back at me. "You sound doubtful."

"Well, a man studying to be a lawyer, working as a farmer, is also a cook?"

"Why, yes. Exactly."

I stood to help him.

He shuffled me back to my perch. "You're right to be concerned about my culinary prowess, my lady. Everything I do for the first time goes badly. Lucky for you, I took that into account and tried these recipes out at Palmer's."

"I don't think you have much trouble doing anything, Aleksey," I said, wanting to be near him. I reached for a spoon. He took it from me. "I'm just not comfortable sitting and watching."

"I guessed that might be the case." He took me back to the tuffet again. "I know you're not a laze-about woman in the least."

He sat beside me and pulled a small burlap sack from behind the tuffet.

"Open it."

"A gift?"

"I'm no oaf, you know."

I looked at him, the urge to kiss him so strong. I'd never felt such a need before; my body tingled in places I didn't know had an ability to ache. But as he was leaning toward me, one of the logs rolled out of the fire, and he hopped up to push it back in place.

He knelt in front of me again. "Open it."

I loosened the neck of the bag and reached inside. I removed a rusty-looking tin that was just a few inches wide and a few inches long. I wiggled the hinged lid open and gaped. I moved toward the fire to see better.

"Watercolors?"

He nodded.

"I had them mixed just for you. The fella at McCrady's does it for all the kids in town, and, well, he upgraded the formula for you. But I told him you didn't need many colors, just some with great pigment and you could create any color you wanted from just a few."

I'd never felt such an incredible sense of being understood in my life, beyond even the feeling I'd had when Miss Violet seemed to understand my needs.

"And I told him no oils. They take too long to dry. And I thought you could carry this small tin wherever you go and paint whatever it is that captures your imagination. I brought you some brushes. And I thought you might want to paint while I cook and we talk."

I didn't know what to say; my words tangled, becoming useless, my emotions caught in my throat.

His shoulders slumped, waiting for me to say something in appreciation. "I hope you like them. I brought some paper, too. In the sack, on the bottom. The man cut it down from these big slices of hard linen. Said he uses it at the college to teach."

When we were young, it was he who was short on words, never me. And now, faced with this great act of kindness, I couldn't get my words to work. So, I leapt up from my seat and threw myself at him. I knocked him back a bit, but he stood as I wrapped my arms around him, holding tight, wanting to let what I felt, the thanks I desperately felt, to seep into his skin, hoping it made up for my lack of words. And it worked. I was sure. I felt him as he realized it, as his arms tightened, his hands gently caressing me. There were no words or explanations or bumbling thank-yous. Only our embrace.

**

The cozy nest Aleksey made for me was warm as he cooked and I sketched and added some of these beautiful watercolors to the linen paper. I drew a loose rendition of Aleksey at the fire. Several times I got up to help him prepare the meal, but he sent me back, chasing me with a giant wooden spoon at one point. "I'm pampering you, doggone it. Now allow yourself to be pampered."

I smiled and finally followed his directions. I jotted down the recipe for what he was making on one sketch.

"Blackberry pudding. Sound good?"

"Wonderful," I said.

He laid out a linen cloth. "Nice, tight weave is very important." After a bit, he said in a funny voice, narrating his work, "I'm going to need some assistance, my sweet."

He snapped the linen cloth in the air and handed it to me. I held it to create a vessel while he added ingredients to it.

"Some of the best cornmeal around, this is. And," he reached for a glass container beside him, "thick, delicious molasses, fresh milk, pecans, and these fine eggs. And some of the best sugar ever made."

I held the linen while he turned to gather more and came back with a carton of blackberries. I opened the pouch so he could add them. But, instead, he held one blackberry to my lips. Our eyes locked, and I opened my mouth. He slid the fruit past my lips, his fingers grazing my skin, sending me nearly through the stars.

He put his hands around mine. "Now I'll tie this off and we'll get the pudding boiling, and soon we'll enjoy a scrumptious meal."

**

Our meal was absolutely delicious. Not the taste. The chicken was dry as it had hung over the fire too long while we waited for the pudding to finish. The pudding turned out mealy with the eggs somehow under and overcooked at the same time.

But I ate every bite, unwilling to critique a bit of it. He could have fed me dirt that night and I would have thought he'd hidden a chef behind the fire to coach him along. We ate slowly, the evening more full of quiet than talk. He'd brought one of his law books to read as I painted and drew after dinner.

After a while, my sketching turned to making lines and shapes, shading them, unable to focus on anything except how it felt to be close to him, alone, how much I wanted to feel him next to me for the rest of my days. Rest of my days? How very dramatic. Yet every single worry or thought seemed to have left me in those moments. Only the warmth of his body, his arm moving against mine as he turned a page, or my leg brushing his as I shifted the paper in my lap, drew my attention.

I was so overwhelmed with contentment that I nearly burst into tears. It wasn't joy, it certainly wasn't sorrow or anything bad at all, it was sheer appreciation and peace, as if I'd died and found heaven waiting. How odd that this sensation could leave me breathless yet at peace at the same time. I held my tears back as long as possible, turning away so that Aleksey couldn't see when the wetness began to fall. In that moment, inside the time that I spent with him, I wanted so much for Mama to be here experiencing the same happiness I was feeling, to see that there would be a day when she felt whole again. Whole. Yes, in that moment, I felt as though I'd been thrust back in time, and the sensation of goodness, wholeness, my true self, was upon me for the first time in years.

He patted my shoulder. "Katherine?"

I wiped my eyes.

"What's wrong?"

"Nothing at all," I said.

I waited for him to press me to explain the things that were swirling inside, but he didn't. He slung his arm around my shoulders, his fingers drawing circles on my arm. And as I sat in his comfort, I captured images from the night on the paper so I could fully explore them later—the moon, the stars, the fruit trees and candlelit garden.

He closed his book and set it aside. "I wanted to bring you here to show you that I will be the kind of man a woman like you deserves."

For the first time in my life, it wasn't me explaining, hiding, trying to show my worth just so I could be left alone or chosen for something safe. *He* was courting me.

"I realize we aren't really in the house, this massive, luxurious home you used to live in, but someday . . ."

I turned to look right at him. My insides jellied. What was he saying?

"Someday you'll have a house like this again. And you'll have someone cook for you . . ."

"Not you?"

He wiped my wet cheeks, smiling protectively. "Well, I'll have to show up at the courthouse once in a while. We can't live on . . ."

I met his gaze. Live on what? Love? He smiled at me.

He shrugged. "Well, they won't pay me at court to be a cook, will they? And then children will starve, people will be cranky." He raised his eyebrows as though he was as surprised as I at what was coming out of his mouth.

Children? I giggled at the thought. "Well. My goals are less concrete, I suppose. Independence doesn't always come with a mansion. I aim for lofty but perhaps less obvious trappings. So you are free to work. I shall cook."

In that moment, I thought I would be satisfied living outside, cooking in a summer kitchen . . . if he was with me. But as soon as those thoughts crossed my mind, I was suddenly struck by other thoughts I'd had so many times— that I had no interest in marriage. I'd read my father's love letters to Mama and saw how sweet love words could dissolve into the ether.

My back began to ache, and I stretched, pressing my fists into it.

"You're stiff?"

I thought of how I'd been walking crooked on the uneven boots and painting like that for hours. I nodded.

He shifted toward me, pulling me close, but pulled back suddenly. "What's that?"

I realized my skirt where I tucked away the crystal pendant must have pressed hard against him.

I couldn't speak.

I shook my head. He pressed the spot, layers of my clothing between it and his hand. I couldn't tell him that I carried around a crystal ball, that it comforted me in a way that nothing ever had, that is, until him.

He didn't let my gaze go.

I had to say something. "An apple. I carry one in my pocket in case I get hungry. Miss Violet allows me to take one when I want." I rubbed my belly as though I were hungry that moment.

"She does?"

I nodded.

"So she's nice to you? I wouldn't have guessed she was so generous."

I nodded, feeling as though the Miss Violet part of my life was intruding in these lovely moments. I didn't want to think of any of that. "She is."

"I'm sorry you get hungry." He took my hand and drew shapes in my palm.

I didn't know how to respond. It was something I didn't want to confide, the times I was so hungry I stole, how I still hid food just in case. He knew my family had fallen on hard times, but scavenging, stealing?

He cocked his head. "Do you see any of her clients when you're there?"

I stopped breathing for a moment and pulled my hand away, picking my pencil back up. "Sometimes."

"Hmm." I could feel him staring at me. "All the women there are smart? Investors, too?"

"Oh yes. At this point, they're giving as sound advice as Miss Violet for all the clients each of them has."

"I've heard that," he said. "Mr. Stevens mentioned he was interested in investing, but even though your employer's results are miraculous—too miraculous—he didn't think he'd go there for advice."

"Why?" I asked.

He studied me for a moment, then shook his head. "It's that she's . . ."

The thought came to mind that perhaps Mr. Stevens was one of the men who didn't trust her because she was a woman. "A woman?"

He chuckled, his eyes creasing at the corners. I studied him and saw that he was sincere. "No, although I know that's the reason many people give in the newspaper."

I felt defensive of Miss Violet. "Her numbers beat any man's, in half the country, I think I read the other day. Think of what she's doing by teaching the women she tutors—and me. Everyone she meets she gives something to. She's a prime example of how to be independent."

He took my hand in his. "But, Katherine, none of those women live on their own."

It was as though he'd lifted a veil from my brain that I hadn't even been aware was there, clearing my view of Miss Violet. His words fell over me like the burning, rolling log had when it came out of the fire. I recalled Miss Violet saying they didn't want to live on their own. That was different. I got up. I hadn't really examined what Miss Violet said further than filing it away. It was true—all the women, like me, owed Miss Violet far more than they'd earned.

Surely Aleksey couldn't know their arrangements. Truthfully, I'd never heard any of Miss Violet's students express the desire to live on their own. They did want to earn enough to pay her back for the money she spent on their gowns, but most were more enthralled with the idea of men than financial independence. When we had free moments or took our daily sunbaths, they'd say as much. Thinking about this dampened my mood. Had I fooled myself into believing independence was possible?

I gently closed my paint box and wiped off the brushes with the rag he'd enclosed in the bag. I added the pencils and papers and pulled the drawstring closed.

"Katherine?"

His brow was creased. He appeared worried. I set the sack down and walked toward the gardens, and he followed me.

"Don't be angry."

"I'm not."

"I want you to be safe," he said. "That's all. You're smart as blazes. I'm not questioning you."

I didn't want to discuss where his concerns might be rooted. I didn't want this night made smaller by such big talk. I didn't want to ask him exactly what made his boss decline investing with Miss Violet.

I wasn't angry. But I couldn't allow this conversation to burrow further into my work with Miss Violet than it already had. He slipped his arm around my waist. I looked up at him. His eyes were lit with something I'd never seen in a man's eyes before. Not directed at me, not like this. "I'm glad she treats you nice, that she allows you to stow apples away in your skirt pocket. I've just been thinking about how much you work, is all. And what Mr. Stevens said just gave me pause."

His words were soft. He slid his hand behind my neck, his fingers lighting my skin under them as he played with the hair that had freed itself from its twist.

I closed my eyes for a moment, feeling alive under his touch. "She's good to all of her employees and her clients," I said. *But this, this with you is what I want to experience. No more talk.*

His gaze held me and made me want to be near him for the rest of my life.

I could see him processing what I'd said. And his chest rose with heavier breath than before. "As long as I'm near, you won't have to worry about food. Not ever."

I felt his sincerity like a presence, like its own spiritual being. And mixed in with an absolute knowing that his sentiments were loving and true was also the worry that he, nor any other man, could ever really deliver on such a promise. I'd learned the hard way that it was simply the way the world worked. Still, I wanted to let him try.

And because of that, I knew that somehow I had to let him know the truth about me. Just not yet.

**

Aleksey pushed me on the swing that had hung in the garden since my birth. I leaned back, feet up to the crystal heavens, head thrown back, wind working its way through my hair like Aleksey's fingers had. With my eyes closed, I felt as though I was weightless, the silent push of his fingers into my back every time I swung toward him felt otherworldly, sacred.

It wasn't until he jerked me so hard that I nearly flew off the swing that I realized the moment had been shattered.

Feet on the ground, I turned to him. "What on—?"

He grabbed my wrist and dragged me. Voices came from the back of the garden where we entered earlier that night.

"We have to go. Now."

Back at the kitchen area, he scooped up the sack with my paints and papers. He surveyed the area, picked up his law book, and grabbed my hand. "Leave everything else."

"I thought you said—?" I said.

"Not now."

He yanked me toward the fence that lined one side of the house. Though I hadn't been at this house in ages, and it certainly looked run down, I knew there wasn't a gate there. The fence was too high to climb.

"This way," I pulled him back and jerked my head toward the other side of the house. He hesitated.

"You there!" One of the voices rang out over the mumblings.

Aleksey followed me, and we moved in the shadows until we reached the gate. I jiggled it and lifted it just the way the old latch used to require, and it popped open.

"Oh, thank God," he said.

We dashed to the front of the house and saw that Harold hadn't yet returned. And so we locked hands and bolted. At a safe distance, we slowed, and relief came that we'd escaped. It was then laughter took us as we walked to the trolley and hitched a ride to Main Street. On the trolley, we sat improperly close, my satchel on my lap, his arm around me. In the darkness, the two other passengers near the front paid us no mind.

"At least we left them blackberry pudding for their trouble," he said.

This caused me to bend over laughing.

"Can't you picture it? Those fellas relaxing, enjoying a tasty treat," Aleksey said.

I shrugged and continued laughing.

"What?" he asked.

I drew a deep breath trying to stave off my laughter.

His eyes widened. "It *wasn't* tasty?"

I slowly shook my head.

He laughed, too, shifted in his seat, and adjusted his hat. "I thought maybe you didn't notice. How awful was it? I'll eat just about anything."

"Oh, Aleksey," I said, my laugh smoothing into a sigh. "It's the best meal I ever had in my life."

He cupped my cheek with this hand. I eased closer, letting his lips come to mine. My fingers trailed into his hair, the softness curling around my fingers. The little groan he let out when we pushed as close together as possible made me want to tunnel into his coat and live inside his warm, protective arms. We kissed until the trolley slowed to a heaving stop. Another man got on, and we moved apart to a more appropriate distance.

And as the trolley took us toward my house, every single thought that threatened to ruin the evening was easily swept aside and replaced with the sound of Aleksey's voice as he told me just how it was he came to Des Moines to learn to be a lawyer, his fingers weaving in and out of mine, our breath synchronized like a single organism, each second laid down in my skin, in my heart, in my soul.

Chapter 45

Secrets
Katherine

Toiling, consulting the dead, painting. And wedged in between each and every moment I owed Miss Violet, Aleksey lived. The night that we'd stolen away in the garden had changed me. Instead of my thoughts going to him intermittently, my mind saw him in everything around me. In lighting the stove for Mama in the morning, I saw him tending the fire, checking the roasting chicken. In the scent of fresh-baked cobbler, I smelled the berry pudding he'd made. In an unexpected wind brushing past the back of my neck, I felt his fingertips exploring, so real I often spun around thinking he was actually there.

The night in the garden had awakened me and brought thoughts that were improper, suggested by conversations the girls had had during our vapor baths. I never revealed our secret garden dinner, but they offered all manner of details of the men they'd been with. How male hands caressed bellies, lips explored necks, hands slipped into bodices. And so I listened to their tales and imagined Aleksey's hands moving from caressing my back, him daring to move his hand to the front of me. I imagined being locked in an embrace, kissing for hours, more . . . our bodies pressing against each other, yearning for him to touch the back of my knee, of all things. That yearning appeared out of nowhere, leaving me imagining things I should not have been. But mostly when I thought of him, and the life he described for my future, I stopped myself before too long. Had he really meant he wanted a life with me? Or just that he would be there to help me as he'd done before, then move on to something else in life? I shook off the thought. It was no matter at that point. I had much to do before I could ever consider hoping Aleksey would want to be with me in the future, before I seriously— beyond a vapor bath fantasy—considered wanting such a thing.

I yawned and entered the kitchen. There was another new kitchen mistress there. Miss Violet had found several before this girl, but one had been fired for nosing around the parlor, getting too close to Miss Violet's office. Several others had come and gone since then. This new one was incurious and seemed to not want to leave the kitchen for any reason. Gertrude was busy with the dough. I resisted the urge to push my fingers into it and pull the mound toward me, flipping it over and pushing its ends toward the middle before pounding the top with my fist.

Gertrude was a freckle-faced, mousy brunette from Idaho. The girl did her best to punch the dough, flour rising. She wiggled her nose and turned to sneeze away from the table, and I handed her a hanky. I set the dough on a tray and covered it with a tea towel and lined the tray next to the other twelve loaves fresh out of the oven.

I sighed and put the back of my arm to my forehead, exhausted. I was trying to focus on my responsibilities, but Gertrude's first few days in the kitchen had been disastrous. She killed the yeast, and her attempt at my trademark angel I carved into each loaf came out looking like the troll who guarded the billy goat's bridge. Gertrude's patty shells were soggy, and somehow she managed to take sweet, canned blueberries and turn them sour.

When Miss Violet discovered the state of the pastries the other day, she'd simply sent Gertrude to the Hodgkiss bakery with a fistful of coins and had everything they needed delivered.

I offered to go back to the baking. I wanted Miss Violet to be happy. She had given Mama another installment of coins recently, and this satisfied me, kept me going strong even when I felt as though I wanted to pull away from Miss Violet and just find work that didn't require the use of my gathering of souls.

I was grateful Miss Violet had loosened her purse and given Mama more money. I knew Miss Violet had been pleased with my artwork recently. I glanced at the ones she'd lined up around the kitchen to dry.

Though I was relieved to have the bulk of the baking siphoned off to a bakery or this girl or that, I found making bread, every step in the process, relaxing and an easy way to connect to my guides—James and the woman with the baby. Recently, the face of the woman had become clearer, but just when I was on the edge of grasping who she was, the information vanished. But I was learning to trust my ability.

Sometimes a spirit would flash in front of me, as though made of flesh. Other times a shadow would catch my eye, and a feeling of knowing something would grow inside me. Information would just sprout out of me, for whomever it was who needed or wanted to hear. I knew for sure at some point the woman's face would be clear to me and I'd know who needed that information. Other times spirits came lit by moody, bright, or clear colorings that told me all I needed to know.

"Katherine?" Tommy stuck his head into Miss Violet's kitchen.

I startled and turned to him, my hand across my chest as I breathed deeply. "You scared me to death."

He smiled and snatched a doughnut from the table. I swatted the back of his hand with my paintbrush.

"Hey," he said. "Doesn't the brother of the kitchen mistress have special privileges?"

"I share the title with Gertrude now, and it took her three batches to get twelve decent doughnuts. Miss Violet will have my head if there aren't enough for today's clients."

He forced a smile and winced.

"What's wrong?"

"A little mishap."

I ran my hand down his arm and was struck by a moody darkness surrounding him, giving me a chill. "Another fight at the saloon?"

He rubbed his shoulder. "Nah, just ran into a door as I carried a load into the house for Miss Violet."

I didn't believe that. I uncovered the plate with all the deformed doughnuts and offered them to Tommy. "I suppose you do have Pearl." Her warm glow and angels might help keep Tommy safe.

He shrugged as he ate.

"But you need to be careful. Mama and I need you to be healthy. Stay out of the saloons."

He popped another piece into his mouth and smiled. "Oh, this is good."

"I'll tell Gertrude you approve."

He swallowed and washed it down with a glass of water. After he finished, he said, "What do you mean, you suppose I have Pearl?"

"What do you mean, what do I mean?" I stared at him, and when he didn't answer, I took his hand. "You have Pearl. And she's special. She's watching over you. Don't make her want to leave you."

Tommy lifted his eyebrows.

"She's a good soul."

"She is," Tommy said.

"I mean *really*."

Tommy shrugged. "Suppose so."

"Be gentle with her."

He nodded as he walked toward the paintings scattered around the space, each with its own easel. He moved to look at one. "How'd you pay for all these supplies?"

He was changing the subject. "Miss Violet."

"She paid for seven easels just so you could paint?"

I nodded, relieved that I hadn't signed any of them as Dreama. Instead, I'd marked them with a small angel in the corner of each, blending it into the scenery, only noticeable if someone really looked.

"You're good, but—"

His eye caught one painting tucked behind the others. He inched toward the one of a boy kneeling over a deer, a gun to the side as the boy wept, his face upturned, appearing as though he'd lost a friend. In the back corner of the painting was a healthy deer, somehow appearing protective of the dead deer and the boy. There was a bundle of daisies near the gun, and a girl in the foreground, barely in the frame.

His finger shook as he pointed. "That one is . . ."

"I love that one. The shades of brown are gorgeous, aren't they? Mr. Hayes bottled up some walnut stain for me. It's been a godsend."

Tommy glared. "I've had enough of that Mr. Hayes interfering with our family."

I felt his anger course between us. He needed to let this go. "He's helping Mama. And he helped me with that paint color."

He shook his head. "Never mind that. How did you know about this? Why would you have painted this, this *exact* scene? The girl there in the corner. Everything."

I'd seen this reaction before—when someone realized what I'd painted came from somewhere other than my own mind.

"Did I tell you about it?" Tommy said.

I didn't know what "it" was, but it had clearly been troubling for him. Was he ready to hear what I could do? Maybe it would comfort him. It had for so many strangers.

Tommy shook his head as though it would straighten out his thoughts.

I pulled Tommy's hand, directing him to sit at the table again. I took the kettle from the stove and poured some water for tea. "Why are you so upset at a painting?" I spooned in some honey, stirring. I brought the cup to him and set it in front of him.

Tommy leaned past me, staring. "It's as though you saw me watch a deer die and you painted it. You captured everything about it." He sipped the tea. "All those people died on the prairie. James, the Zurchenkos, Lutie and Ruthie Moore. I felt sad then, but I didn't feel *them*. And then I shoot some deer and I feel as though . . . well, as though my brother just died. How crazy is that?"

I nodded, pulling my chair closer to the table.

He closed his eyes. "The look on that deer's face was as human as you looking at me now." He opened his eyes. "When I stood to end her life for good, I aimed and felt her sadness as though she had a soul, and it passed right through me. I couldn't do it. I . . ."

"She did have a soul."

"It was a deer."

I pushed back, arms crossed. "I know, Tommy."

"What does *that* mean?"

"It means I know things about people who die, and people who live with those souls still connected to them. I just *know*."

Tommy put his palm up.

I pushed his hand down on the table. "I tried to tell you before. When I first got back to Des Moines."

He looked me over as though determining my seriousness. "They'll put you in Glenwood talking like that. Or jail. You *don't* want jail."

"Don't say *that*."

"Why? You tell me to leave Mr. Hayes alone. So I'm telling you it doesn't make sense, what you just said. And you know what happens when people stop making sense."

"Look at the painting again." I pointed to it.

He turned.

"Can you look at it and doubt me at all?"

Tommy stared at it for a minute before turning back to me, his face full of questions he wasn't asking. "Pearl told you, didn't she?"

Miss Violet appeared in the kitchen. "I need to speak to you, Katherine."

Tommy stood, appearing confused.

"Are you finished with your errands, Mr. Arthur?"

He shook his head and left the kitchen, slamming the door behind him.

"Well," Miss Violet said. "He looked like he saw a ghost."

She laughed, and I forced a smile and told her, "It surely looked that way."

"Just a few hours and then you're on, Katherine dear. Don't be late getting ready."

"I won't," I said. I pulled some eggs out from the container and some cheese that had been shredded earlier.

"Not too many eggs. We're giving half to the needy folks down the way."

I held the egg over the bowl and looked at Miss Violet for a moment. *Half? Needy people?* I felt the old sensation settling over me that I had at the Christoffs' when food was rationed—the food I was permitted anyway.

I wondered if this was Miss Violet's way of showing me her continuing disappointment that I'd taken up corresponding and visiting with Aleksey. The girls in the house continued to talk about him, to question me about him, my dreams as they related to him. Miss Violet would interrupt such conversations and steer us back to our goals at hand—making money.

"This is your biggest night so far, Katherine. After this, it's *A Night for Mothers*. You'll reunite the grieving mothers of Des Moines with their dead children. I simply want your attention, you focused on the work at hand. Don't worry about Tommy, Yale, or your mother. She's as capable a woman as I've seen. And I've seen plenty of women in my day."

"She is," I said, searching Miss Violet's face to be sure her expression matched the sincerity of her words.

"I have an extra special gown for that night. These mothers are waiting to salve their souls. That's the only thing you need to worry about. Not your family, not some boy."

Aleksey's face flashed to my mind, and I pushed the image away. I had let myself recall the delicious moments when we'd escaped the men who found us at my old house. In fleeing with Aleksey, I'd felt alive and protected at once. A secret. This one was between us, adhering us rather than pulling us apart as the secrets I kept from him did.

"You're not seeing Aleksey, are you? Not since the night of that dance?"

Without a heartbeat's time going by, I responded, "No."

She stared at me, delving for the truth. I grew hot under her appraisal. A bead of sweat formed at the nape of my neck.

"I do understand," Miss Violet said. "First love. Everyone has one. But none of them last. I understand your attraction to him."

I thought back to the apple, when she seemed to know I'd taken it and she'd given me the path to either lie or tell her the truth.

"I'd understand if you confided in me. I simply need the honesty between us, that has been there since we first met, to continue. A winding, continuous river of truth. No jutting off into streams of lies."

She paused. Her mouth twitched, and I saw a hardening beneath her invitation to trust her, to prove she could trust me. I felt the urge to tell her the truth about Aleksey, about our secret garden, about how I could not stop thoughts of him flooding me all day long. But just as I almost spilled it all to her, I saw the hardness again, something darker, something that made me keep the whole thing to myself. Her secret with Olivia. That was the first stream to break off from the coursing river, whether Miss Violet admitted it or not.

Aleksey was to be kept clean and safe in my heart. He wasn't part of this. Another bead of sweat formed in front of my ear. It dripped down the side of my face. I wiped it away.

Miss Violet stepped forward, offering a handkerchief. Again, her gaze penetrated me, silently pressing. She ran the back of her fingers over my forehead. "You're hot as Hades. You sure you don't have something to tell me?"

I shook my head and cleared my throat. "A little under the weather today, is all."

Miss Violet gave me a pitying look. "Well, you must ready for tonight. Rest up, dear heart."

This lie. It revealed itself in my beading sweat. Violet would never know this particular truth, but I wasn't so sure that mattered. My lies were spreading, tangling, leaving me strangled rather than freed up, as it always felt when the lie first popped to my mind. A tool, most lies were, a means of protecting myself or someone else. Yet now they all seemed alive, like snakes, spreading, weaving, coming back and lashing themselves around my neck, my chest, spiraling down to my ankles until I wouldn't be able to turn and run in the direction of anyone who knew the whole truth about me at all.

Chapter 46

Between Us
Katherine

One more day until I took Dreama from little, intimate reading venues to an auditorium for *A Night for Mothers*. After a few details Miss Violet wanted me to work out, I headed home. Entering the kitchen, I smelled stew simmering on the stove. Mama was at the kitchen table, stitching a collar to a shirtwaist. I leaned in to see her hands darting over the fabric, her fingers deftly working the needle in and out. "You need more light, Mama."

"Stir the pot, please," Mama said.

I did, and then I opened the cupboard door and pulled out a lamp. I wound the wick and lit it. "I'll clean the wick this week. Should be okay for now, but I'll do that soon."

Mama glanced up with a smile. "Thank you, sweetheart."

At the table, I began to pick up the newspapers that littered the space that wasn't covered in the material she was sewing.

"Much better." Mama pointed her needle at the light. "Hadn't even realized dusk was settling in."

I pulled the papers toward me and saw that the articles weren't attached to the larger paper but had been clipped out over the last month or so. On top was an article about three children who were snatched from Third Street, then found at a workhouse when one of them escaped and reported to a widow down the road from where they were. The article stated that a pattern of sweeping the streets for kids who were idle, dirty, or in some way neglected by their parents and then turning them over to workhouses for a fee was becoming commonplace.

"That's awful," I said. "Who would do such a thing?"

Mama focused on her stitches. "People will do all sorts of things for money."

The next article was about Dreama. A rush of excitement filled me at the thought of Mama wanting to cut out articles about Dreama and her successes. But then I saw it was the same one Miss Violet had shown me about Dreama's skeptics. The next was about a group forming that wanted to take measures to "manage" Dreama and her ilk. It didn't explain just what that meant. Reading it made the air in the room thin.

I reminded myself that Miss Violet had planned for this. I was perfectly safe from even the loudest skeptic. The next article was about a brother and sister whose parents requested they be sent away to a workhouse. Suspicion was that the parents collected a fee for handing over able-bodied children. The next was about Madame Smalley, and the next about the plight of frontier children whose parents failed at homesteading.

"What are you doing with these, Mama?" I spread my hands over top of the articles.

She glanced up, put the needle in her mouth, cut off another length of white thread, and began to poke it through the eye. "Mrs. Hillis and I are collecting data on who's in need but not getting assistance and who's being targeted by certain very important people."

I felt a surge of protectiveness toward Dreama. "Well, I've read many articles about how Dreama is doing very well for herself and for people who need her. Why didn't you include those articles—the good ones?"

"Believe it or not, Dreama is serving as an epicenter for this push to clean up Des Moines. Her presence, along with Madame Smalley, has generated this hum from which tentacles of delinquency have spawned. Or so *they* all say."

I stared at her. "So Dreama arrives in town and . . ." I paged through the articles. "Dreama, skullduggery, burgling, robbing, and vandalism. Each is up sixty-six percent?" I skimmed farther in the article and saw Judge Calder's name. *He* certainly trusted Miss Violet. Perhaps I'd have to tell her to talk to him about trying to tie these two matters together.

"I can't believe Judge Calder would say there's a connection between Dreama and crime."

Mama stopped sewing and narrowed her eyes on me.

I squirmed in my seat. "I mean, he's a judge. A reasonable man."

She set her sewing down and rubbed her eyes. "Someday you'll see that being a judge doesn't actually mean you've been granted any real insight or intelligence. It's about power, Katherine."

"But the judge? He—"

She picked her needle and shirtwaist back up. "He's misguided. He doesn't understand the plight of people who choose such paths as this Dreama or Madame Smalley. And don't get me wrong. Con artists should be punished. But many of these women are simply mothers without husbands, vagrants who haven't settled yet, children fending for themselves and their families—all are being targeted. It's not fair to them. And for some reason, the real push to remedy these problems came with the appearance of Dreama."

I didn't know what to say, so I sat quiet.

"Between Dreama, Madame Smalley," Mama stopped sewing and laid her hands on the table, "and that saloon! That's getting its fair share of barbs as well. As it should. But that's the problem. It's now clouded just who is causing trouble and who is merely a victim of it."

I turned the paper over to see what Mama was referencing.

"These women are going to find themselves tossed into jail or worse if they don't find their way to the straight and narrow. And it's like these men, these leading citizens of Des Moines, some judges, some businessmen, some policemen and aldermen—it's as though they'd been waiting for something to come to town to cull all the angry energy they'd been waiting to spend. And in walks this Dreama to centralize it all."

Mama shook her head. "I'm going on and on. We're just trying to separate all this out so that children don't get shoveled up and sent away. Do you know they sent thirty-three children to Glenwood in the last three months?"

I'd never thought of such a thing. It was as though I'd been living in a dark closet, aware of only myself and what Miss Violet allowed me to see. Were others in danger because of Dreama?

"This Dreama is just now becoming fully visible to the community. And people love what she's doing or they hate it. Fortune-telling is no way to earn a living."

I couldn't speak.

"Not to mention this Dreama person could be in danger herself," Mama said. "Groups forming, women talking nonstop about this *Night for Mothers*."

I grimaced.

"People coming from all over the area to see her help grieving mothers."

I wanted to shout, "That's good, isn't it?" but I couldn't talk.

"I've heard she leaves the impression of someone young and vulnerable, sickly. People want to pay her more now that they think she's sickly."

My mouth went dry. Miss Violet's plan to create a sympathetic figure, at least in the eyes of some, had worked.

The sound of Yale's bells coming down the hall drew our attention. I welcomed the chance to move away from Mama, to hide my upset at what I was hearing. When I got to Yale in the hall, I saw the glint of something in her hand. I rushed to her. She was clasping a penknife. I gasped and took it from her, scooping her up. "No, no, no, Yale. You can't play with this. It's not for little girls."

When we reached the kitchen, I dropped the knife on the table. "Where'd she get that?"

Mama stared at the knife and shook her head. "I don't even know. See, that's the kind of thing that gets a mother and her babies in trouble." She took Yale from me and cradled her on her lap. "Mama would simply shrivel up and die if something happened to you. No sharp things for Yale." She kissed her head and hugged her so tight she looked as though she was trying to impart all her love right into the little girl.

I took Yale back and sat down. Mama began sewing again.

"I've also heard," Mama said, "that Miss Violet had Dreama to her home for entertainment purposes?"

I froze, glad I had Yale in my lap to shield me from the question.

"I said that's impossible because my daughter would certainly know that. I surely would have been told."

I still couldn't speak. I wanted to tell her not to worry, that I was safe, that Miss Violet was looking out for all of us. I swallowed my fear. After *A Night for Mothers*. I'd tell her and hand her overflowing pots of money. She wouldn't be as angry at my lying. At least I hoped she wouldn't.

"Must have been when I was off work." The words were thick and scratchy in my mouth. One more night and I would tell her the truth.

Mama stopped stitching. "I knew you would've mentioned such a thing. And this is exactly why I want you to study hard, get your diploma, go to college. I don't feel cozy toward Miss Violet, but she's smart and she runs a business that all the leading citizens of Des Moines are investing in. I don't even like some of the men who are her clients, but I know they understand finance. At least that's what the papers say."

That was all true. That was the one thing her mother could know about Miss Violet that wasn't a lie or the hedging of a truth.

"That's what's important," Mama said. "A woman needs to carry her wealth in her mind before she carries it in her purse. It's the only thing we can be sure can never be snatched away."

I bristled and pointed to an article. "I know. But Dreama doesn't seem to be telling fortunes at all. Says here that she's comforting grieving and lost souls."

Mama began to stitch again. "I don't begrudge anyone finding their way in the world. I of all people can't judge on that matter. But not at the expense of others who might have even less. If not for the articles, and the mighty, leading citizens who swear to Miss Violet's acumen, I might even wonder about her. I might even take you out of there and put you into a kitchen on Grand. I know you believe in angels and such, and I don't want you taken advantage of with people like Dreama. Keep your pennies close."

Mama pushed her sewing aside and reached across the table for my hand, squeezing three times. I returned the "I love you" with three more.

Shame curdled inside me.

"Keep your attention on a sure path, going straight and forward."

"No one loves a garden path more than you."

Mama paused and looked up from her sewing. "A real garden path, yes. But not ones that lead astray in life. Sometimes what seems exciting, fascinating, and unpredictable isn't good. You'll learn that solid people, solid men, family members, all of that is what's important. Look at Violet. She works like a—"

"Man?"

"Yes. But we all work like men. We just don't get compensated like men. I want your mind pliable and full of important things."

"Yes, Mama."

I exhaled, relieved to move away from the topic of Dreama.

"And I bet you've been thinking of Aleksey. He's quite taken with you."

I couldn't hide my smile. "Oh, Mama. Yes. I think of him all the time."

Mama smiled, her gaze softening before her brow furrowed. I knew she was worried about my independence. What if she knew how Aleksey made my heart leap, how he brought a smile every time I saw him? I wanted to be with him every second, but my workload and his studies seemed to prohibit it most of the time.

"Don't worry, Mama. I intend to forge my own path. I understand how love can go wrong. I will shape my own future. That much is true."

Mama sighed. "As I said, having an education and some assets of your own would be desirable in my view. It's all about reliability."

I nodded.

"I still believe your strength is within," Mama said. "But I've changed my tune a bit on men. The right man is . . ." she gently stabbed the needle into the wooden table, "well, a good thing. I want you to be educated, but someone like Aleksey . . ." Mama went back to her stitches. "He's different."

My cheeks warmed.

"Have you been writing to him?"

I sat down. "I have. But don't tell Miss Violet."

Mama drew back, put the needle in her mouth, and cut off another length. "Why in heavens not?"

I shrugged. "She doesn't want me distracted."

"That's none of her business." Mama finished a few stitches. "I'll tell her not to—"

"No! Please. Don't say a word."

Mama looked up, startled.

"Just between us," I said, glad to have a secret with Mama instead of another kept from her. "Please."

"If you promise to stay your course and keep your head about things, I'll keep this between us."

I couldn't wait to see Mama's face, to feel her pride wash over me, when she knew the truth about what I'd been doing for us. That would be a great day for both of us indeed.

Chapter 47

A Cure
Aleksey

I had to promise Harold, Mabel, and Fat Joe that I'd replace the pots, blankets, and time they'd lost when Katherine and I scrammed from her former home as the angry owner, or whomever was entrusted to keep an eye on the house, investigated who was trespassing.

My friends were kindly, not terribly angry, but they teased mercilessly that this future lawyer had indeed broken a bigger law than any of them ever had and all to show a girl he was worthy of her affection. I'd written Katherine upon returning to Palmer's that night.

I'd been charged with energy and couldn't sleep. So I wrote her a letter, toeing the line between proper, polite words that also conveyed the depth of affection I felt.

That night, after reading a letter from my ma, writing to Katherine, and attempting to dig into another case of finders, keepers for Mr. Stevens, I headed to the kitchen for coffee. So deep into night by then, I surrendered to the idea of not sleeping at all. I didn't seem to need anything as ordinary as sleep. I seemed to be existing on thoughts of Katherine, who would hopefully join me on my path through life.

I entered the kitchen to find Mabel bent over a cup of tea. She looked up, her eyes tired slits, her lips dry. She rubbed her temples.

"What's wrong?"

"Sick," she said, her voice scratchy and weak.

"Did you try—?"

"I tried everything. If I don't get some sleep, I don't think I'll be able to cook a thing tomorrow. And you fellas have a big day with all that work in the barn."

I stared at her in this weakened state and knew I wasn't the one who could comfort her. "I'll get Fat Joe."

"No," she said. "Let him sleep."

"Not one remedy I know worked," she said. She bent over the table, grabbing at her belly.

She moaned. "Bring me something, anything."

"I don't know what to—" I stopped talking as I remembered that Winnie Palmer's book listed cures, ingredients, and people she'd helped. "I'll be right back."

I ran to the bunkroom, dug through the trunk, and uncovered the book I was supposed to have burned months before. I pulled it out, and the rock in the shape of the butterfly slid off of it and hit the bottom, clunking against the wood. I picked it up and rubbed my thumb down the center that divided the ice-like striations that formed its wings. I pushed it into my pocket before heading downstairs.

At the table, I turned the wick up on the lamp to get a better view of what Palmer's wife, Winnie, had written. I paged through it as Mabel groaned.

I didn't know how to put this delicately. "Is it that you *can't* go or you've gone to the bathroom *too much*?"

She raised her gaze. "Don't you tell Fat Joe. I'd die of embarrassment."

I realized the sensitive nature of a person's bowel activity. "I won't."

"Can't go. Three days."

That was a long time to have things clogged up.

"Don't make that face," she said, a small smile covering her pained grimace.

"Sorry. Just know that can be uncomfortable."

"I feel like I swallowed linen, I'm so stopped up."

I ran my finger down page after page looking for where I'd seen that someone had been cured of their headache and plugged-up belly.

"Here," I said, pushing the book so she could see. "Jalap-senna infusion."

She stared at it as though she didn't think anything of it. I pulled it back to get a closer look. "Says don't use mercury. Or Rush's capsules. Too harsh." I shrugged. "Does Palmer have any of those pills? Maybe we could halve them?"

She groaned again. "Don't care. Give me something."

I went to the pantry and dug through some items. Nothing that resembled cures or herbs. "Do you have a store of herbs and spices and things?" I said.

"Palmer likes plain, you know that."

She groaned again, laying her head on the tabletop.

Judging from what I saw in Winnie Palmer's book, I thought there had to be stores of dried plants somewhere. Had he tossed them out with everything else of hers?

"Cellar." She raised her head to inform me. "Maybe there."

There was access to the cellar outside through a storm door. But Palmer had made an entrance to a small section of cellar storage leading right from the kitchen. I took the lamp and headed into the darkness below. There was a small room, more like a wedge of space under the stairs than a room. I moved along the shelves, raising and lowering the light. Winnie's handwriting on the labels was smudged with use. At one end of the shelving, I found jalap, and at the other, at the bottom, I found senna.

I took them upstairs and made an infusion according to the book's instructions.

"I'm no expert, Mabel. I hope this works," I said. She responded with a groan as she forced the liquid down.

As morning light was breaking, Mabel was heading to her room, wanting to lie down until the medicine did its work. "I won't mention your . . . problem to Fat Joe. But don't mention the book to Palmer," I said.

"Promise," she spit the word out as she lumbered away. I wasn't sure the infusion would work at all, due to not knowing how old the herbs were.

I was about to return the herbs to the cellar when I heard Palmer's footfalls coming toward the kitchen. I stashed the glass containers and book under the dry sink and explained to Palmer that Mabel had fallen ill.

Three hours later, she emerged from the privy with the brightest smile I'd ever seen on a person's face. I removed my hat at the sight of her, and she smiled at me as she explained to everyone that her illness had left her and she would be ready to resume her duties by suppertime. I couldn't believe the cure had worked.

Palmer seemed to be in the kitchen every time I planned to return the herbs and the book to their rightful places. I dug my hand into my pocket and rubbed the seams of the butterfly rock. I felt as though I'd had a little bit of Winnie Palmer with me that night. Helping ease Mabel's illness made me feel proud, like the older brother I'd been when I was back home. And though silly, having the butterfly rock in my pocket made me feel connected to the work I did that night as though somehow it led me where I needed to go to find the herbs. Having it in my pocket made me feel connected to the earth it came from, to the woman who first claimed it. And for some reason, that mattered to me even if I had no idea why.

Chapter 48

A Night for Mothers
Katherine

My *Night for Mothers* had finally arrived. In a small, musty room backstage at the Bagley auditorium, I fussed in the mirror, spritzing myself with the lavender perfume that clients loved. The scent appealed to everyone, somehow recalling childhood warmth that relaxed minds and opened hearts.

I smoothed the front of the white satin dress. It was the most exquisite gown Miss Violet had the seamstress make for the readings to date. The material appeared delicate yet was thick and fine and smooth, moving like water as the braided empire waist fell into a column that skimmed my hips.

Ocean-blue threads were woven throughout it, making the dress seem nearly alive as the light hit it from different angles. Golden threads ran through though the blue, luring the eye, leaving me to wonder whether the material had been peeled from the inside of a seashell. I lifted the sides of it and practiced a curtsey in front of the mirror the way Miss Violet had suggested I do.

Oh, how I wished Aleksey could see me dressed like this. I kept his generous, sweet words close. More than that, it was the way he looked at me, his gaze caught by mine, the affection for me as clear in his eyes as in his gentle touch. But if he could see me like this, so fresh and pink-cheeked, lips just red enough, my eyes highlighted with a hint of charcoal, he would see me fully as a woman. Olivia had roped my hair into a smooth luster of braid. I was a princess, like we'd read about so many times as children.

Spending that time with Aleksey in the garden, our narrow escape and huddled, whispered conversation as we sat on the trolley convinced me that after *A Night for Mothers*, I would confide in him and Mama about what I was doing with Miss Violet. Mama deserved to know first, and from there I would introduce Aleksey to the whole of me, invite him to appreciate all of me, not just what he thought he knew. If he saw me looking like this, perhaps a lie would not matter.

Miss Violet swept into the room, swinging the ugly boots from her fingers, Olivia and Bernice following. Oh, how I wished I didn't have to don those awful things.

"Oh my," Miss Violet said. "You *are* a beauty." Awe covered her face as she drew close, her specially made violet perfume wafting along with her. A gift from Judge Calder, she'd said. A thank-you for their work together. Sounded like an odd business gift to me, but I let it slide as her rambling about gifts gave me another opportunity to think of Aleksey, to imagine his body close to mine, the heat of him warming me.

In front of the mirror, Miss Violet stood behind me and tucked sprigs of baby's breath into my hair. She finished the buttons marching up the back of the dress. "Angel Whispers. That's what the dressmaker named this dress," she said.

I drew myself taller. "I like that."

"You like the waistline?"

"Oh yes. Like a princess."

"The cut of it lends a sense of romance to the affair, yet it's still innocent. The color is like angel wings. The quality would turn Queen Victoria green." She took my shoulders and turned me toward her. "You're giving mothers and their children a gift that no one else in the world can. You reach into their hearts and souls and still the throbbing grief that grips them, healing them in a way that time alone never can."

My breath caught. The responsibility of it all settled in, making me stiffen.

"Don't be scared."

I thought for a moment. I wasn't afraid at all, just excited. I rubbed my neck, trying to ease the tension that belied my confidence.

"Think of that," Miss Violet said. "You open up the seam between here and the afterlife and salve their wounds. You give them a sense of understanding they can't get from their minister or spouse or anyone else in the world. You are *that* powerful. You are *that* great. You *are* . . . Dreama."

Miss Violet's words rippled through the air, embedding themselves under my skin, filling me. Yes. This was exactly what I did. This was exactly why I'd been born. I was sure of it. "Yes."

Miss Violet opened a flat, rectangular box, moved tissue paper aside, and pulled out the veiling. She turned me back toward the mirror and lifted the lace over my head, tucking the ties behind my ears, securing the bottom piece above my lips. "Tonight is for the mothers. There may be some children with them as well. But you don't have to worry about Olivia running a dice game off to the side or Bernice engaging businessmen in her prophecy card—no palm reading. It's a simple, enormous night."

Miss Violet lifted the top tier of veiling over my head, covering my eyes. She fastened the back and tugged to be sure it was secure. She pulled some pins from the drawer and began to press them into my hair.

I pushed my shoulders down and back, lifting my chin. "A great night."

"Yes." Miss Violet pulled out the lacy gloves and began to work them onto my hands. "I almost wish you were unveiled. Your beauty is like no other. I think we might be able to charge—"

I shook my head.

"No, no. You're right. The mystery is worth far more."

She helped me into the limping boots.

I drew a deep breath and exhaled. Boots or not, I was ready. "My bag!"

"Your crystals?" Miss Violet opened the carpetbag she'd brought with clothes for me to change into afterward. She removed a satin sack. It was made from the same silk of the dress, with golden threads woven through and hints of ocean blue, the same allure that the dress had. As if it had descended from the heavens to be plucked from the sea.

I clasped the bag to my chest. I tapped my leg where my most special crystal always lay. Suddenly, I didn't want it hidden. I thought of the crowd and how I might become anxious. I needed to be able to feel the hexagon facets under my fingertips. I drew up the dress to expose my underskirt and took out the crystal. I added it to the bag. "Thank you," I said, feeling as open and capable as I ever had since Miss Violet suggested I could earn money from the very thing that had saved my life two years before.

**

I stood in the wings of the stage. Cigar and pipe smoke scented the air, making me realize there must be at least as many men as women in attendance. I inched toward the curtain and pulled it aside to get a look. Miss Violet snatched it shut. She pushed the bag's drawstrings over my hand so it would dangle from my wrist. She then pushed five small white candles into my hands.

"The selected guests are in the opposite wing," Miss Violet said. "You'll work with each set of guests by themselves, and when you finish with them, they'll exit and

Olivia will send the next set out to the table. You don't even have to look at the audience if you're nervous."

I ran my fingers down my parched throat.

Violet snapped her fingers at Bernice. "Water. Fast."

She took my shoulders. "The matches are inside the bag with the balls." She brushed something from my shoulder. "Bring your ritual to the stage; the hiss of the matches, the scent of lemon and lavender, deep breaths, your sweet perfume. *Take your time.* There's no need for you to look beyond the table. You'll be everything the clients need you to be. You'll be brilliant."

Pride licked at every bit of my heart, inflating my mood. In those moments, I was Miss Violet's equal. She recognized me fully right then, and I accepted myself as I was.

Miss Violet exhaled, her relief evident at seeing my strength. It was time. I cleared my throat. Bernice handed me the glass of water. I drank it down. *Just go.* I pushed through the curtains and started to dart toward the table. The uneven boots forced my gait to slow, and the audience hushed, leaving room for the full weight of my limp to fill the space. My foot caught on a floorboard, and I tripped. Catching myself, I held my breath, thanking God I didn't actually fall. A collective gasp came as I steadied myself. *Slow down. Remember your ritual.*

I glanced beyond the table at center stage and was relieved that the lights were so bright I couldn't see anyone's face in the audience. *Clomp, drag, clomp, drag* echoed throughout.

I set the candles on the table near the middle and gently loosened the silk drawstrings and turned the bag over, letting the crystal balls scatter onto the wood tabletop. I palmed the precious one I normally kept in my pocket and pulled it toward the seat where I would be for the reading. I picked it up and ran my thumb over each of the thirteen hexagonal faces that belted the ball. One, two, three. I spun the ball in my gloved hand and caressed the glass again, its coolness seeping through the lace.

Calmed, I set the ball with the others. We'd decided against using a table covering of any sort so no one could proclaim Dreama had hidden anything or anyone under the table. I ran my hand over the other orbs and swept the smooth one Miss Violet had found for me right next to the faceted one, feeling deeper calm in touching them.

A cough from the audience broke the silence. A muffled cry from a baby filled the air, lifting to the great ceiling. Next, I lit each candle with its own match. Just as I'd practiced, each swipe of each match, the hiss, the scent, the flame as it rushed upward upon lighting the wick, all of it opened me further to what I was to do next. I paused, breath caught.

"Get on with the show!" someone yelled from the back of the auditorium, startling me out of my calming.

For a moment, I questioned what I was doing. I looked toward the wings of the stage, searching for Miss Violet. She stepped forward just enough for me to see her. She nodded reassuringly. My head began to feel light, dizzy, and I considered the idea of bolting. My stomach turned, and I closed my eyes, hands clasped at my waist. *Please, God. Help me.* I straightened and pressed my hand to my belly.

Stay open. Stay calm. I drew a deep breath, filled with what I knew as God's grace. I was awash in peace and confidence once again. I opened my eyes. I was no longer drawn to gaze at the audience, the idea that anyone other than the people coming to the table were present was gone. I was ready.

I sat, closed my eyes again, shifted my bottom, and gently held the sides of the wooden table. My lace-covered thumbs tapped the top, and my fingers were underneath, tracing the ruts and jagged ends of wood and nails. *Please, God, help me see the people who need me, please keep me connected to my guides. Please let James help me.*

I opened my eyes and looked ahead, where a round, dark-haired woman had just sat down with two ladies—her daughters, I supposed. I felt a small smile come to my lips as

I watched the girl closest to her mother squeeze her hand and offer a look of reassurance.

"Hello," I said, nodding at each one of them. "I'm Dreama."

The woman put her hand out toward me, then drew it back, stuffing it into her lap. "I'm sorry. I don't know how these things work."

I reached for her, knowing I might need her as relaxed as I needed to be. "Tell me your name."

"Penny Catwall," she said. "This is Eunice and Phoebe. My daughters."

Genuine warmth emanated from the family, like an invisible river rushing between us. The daughters looked to be older than me, but not by much. "Pleasure to meet you."

"It's ours," Penny said. I could tell she'd relaxed when she slumped back in her chair and took her daughters' hands, all of them visibly released from the tension. I drew another deep breath and felt the presence of a male who appeared at Penny's shoulder.

I leaned toward them. "There's a man with you. Right beside you."

Penny raised her eyebrows. "Conrad?"

I wasn't sure, but I had the distinct feeling of a male who loved her. "I think it's your husband."

Her face whitened, and she slid closer to the table, her eyes telling me I was correct.

"Penny, I'm getting a sense of . . . well . . ." *Lightness* was all I could think to say, and that didn't quite seem to fit. But I remembered that it was up to the client to interpret, not me.

The man began to laugh, his shoulders shuddering. I didn't feel comfortable at that, seeing that he'd arrived to alleviate their grief. But instead of asking for more from him, I simply said, "He's laughing. Bent over, can't stop himself."

Penny and the young women grew wide-eyed.

"I'm so sorry," I said. "I don't—"

"Laughter," Penny said. Eunice and Phoebe fell into their mother, chuckling. The man grabbed his belly and laughed along with them. "He's laughing with you."

I tried to grasp what it all meant but reminded myself again that it wasn't for me to interpret.

Penny covered her mouth, and tears wet her cheeks. "He'd be gone on the railroad for so long and then he'd come back and set us to laughing the instant he came in. Oh, the stories! He mocked the passengers, his boss, himself. We were never short on laughter when he was around."

One of the sisters grasped my hand. "Can I ask him something?" Their laughter died away, and their faces grew serious again. "Ask him what he was just laughing at.'" Her voice was meek, but her eyes were light, glistening.

I was about to say that I wasn't sure when three lights behind them on the stage went out. Someone screeched in the audience. Then someone else laughed, and soon the room was roaring. "He heard you." I watched as the man nodded. I crinkled my nose. "He's showing me a pig. Pig."

All the Catwalls bucked forward, hilarity gripping them. This made the audience laugh all over again, even me. I was filled with joy as though I were part of the family and their jokes.

Penny drew a deep breath and exhaled. "We were so worried he was in pain. Still in pain. When he was sick, we would tell stories about mishaps on the farm, and this story of the pig was particularly funny. This pig knocked me right into the mud. I had been sobbing at the idea of losing him and then just full of laughter at what a sight I was. He nearly died laughing so hard. Right then, I mean. He did die a day later, but that laugh. It was the most robust thing he'd done in a month." They began to laugh again, shoulders shaking. Conrad's too. The love I felt swirling around us was like nothing that had happened in a reading for me before.

"He watches over you all. No more pain."

The Catwall ladies joined hands, smiling. I was relieved that even in front of the large audience I could connect with the spirits who wanted to be heard, that it was a light, joyful experience.

Mr. Catwall raised his hand, refocusing me on him. "He provided for you, the children, a long time ago, when they were babies. He wants them to pursue the highest calling they can. He said you already know where *it* is."

"It?"

I waited for more information. The audience was hushed.

I shrugged. "Provisions. I keep getting that word from him."

She wrapped herself in her arms and looked upward.

"Chicago," I said. "Does that seem familiar? Provisions, Chicago?"

Mother and daughters looked at each other, faces confused.

"I keep hearing the word *note*."

Penny fell against the seat back, and a smile spread over her face. "The letter. The letter that arrived from Chicago after he died. I never opened it."

She sighed and pulled her daughters close. "Tell him we love him."

"He heard. He knows."

The three women kept hold of each other's hands, Penny kissing Eunice's hand, shaking her head, relieved and so joyful, filling me with utter relief.

∗∗

Penny and her daughters were whisked away, and another family was seated. The baby with the haunting cry at the back of the auditorium wailed again, causing me to flinch. With so many people present, I was beginning to feel the presence of spirits connected to any number of people who were observing, but I told the encroaching bodies to keep back, to let me do my work.

I brushed my hand over the two crystal orbs closest to me and picked them up, feeling their weight in each palm. I wanted to take off the gloves to feel the smoothness of the plain one, to better feel the hexagons on the faceted one.

I closed my eyes to clear my mind of Penny's reading. The chairs at the table were pulled back, scraping the floor as the clients bumped the table, settling in. I opened my eyes and set the crystals back on the table in front of me, focused on a gray-haired woman. Her arm was around a younger woman whose head was bowed, her shoulders shuddering, her hands fisted on the tabletop.

In the same way that joviality and lightness characterized the spirit of Mr. Catwall, a redheaded woman carrying two babies emerged from the left, bringing with her heaviness, blackness. She stood behind the younger woman, and I felt the grip of deep sadness, the kind that strangled some, the kind I'd felt myself before.

A wave of agony coursed through me below my belly button, cramping my insides. I squeezed my eyes shut, the slow-gripping spasm causing me to shudder. I buckled and pressed my belly, knowing the pain was important to what I needed to communicate.

I forced my eyes open and gasped at what I saw. The two ladies followed my gaze behind them. They looked back to me, their expressions questioning.

Six more spirits, women, had appeared around the redhead, all holding babies of various sizes. I swallowed hard, waiting for one of them to offer something to say. When nothing came, I decided I should reveal what I saw.

"They're holding babies. Infants, a couple of toddlers."

"They?" the young woman said, her eyes narrowed on me. This stilled her mother, and they both stared at me.

"There's a red-haired woman in the center, holding two babies. They look like newborns. The other children look tinier and some—two of them—look to be one and three years old, about that."

The younger woman sobbed so hard she couldn't speak. I pressed a hand to my chest, just above my heart, wanting to find the right thing to say that would give her comfort. I wondered if she could breathe because I couldn't. The gray-haired woman pulled her close, patting her head. "The redhead with the babies. That's my other daughter. She died birthing twins . . . could that be her?"

With those words, a name came right to me. "Jenny."

The younger woman wailed louder, and her mother nodded. "It's her."

"The other ladies," I said. "I can't see them clearly—their faces, I mean—but they're all holding babies. A teeny one who looks impossibly tiny, a toddler, a newborn, another infant." There were so many that I wondered if perhaps these women were attached to audience members, not the two women sitting in front of me.

The younger woman sat up. "The toddler. Is she a redhead?"

I drew a deep breath and tried to zero in on the details of what was in front of me. I swallowed hard. "No. Yellow-haired, golden, all of them."

The young woman nodded, her eyes starting to swell from crying. "They're mine." Her voice was tight, the words rasping out of her mouth, drifting toward my ears.

That made sense. I'd read that in the book called *Angels, Guides and Saints*. It had said that older spirits tended to escort young children, to watch over them. Although there was sadness in these spirits, the darkness they'd originally brought had lifted. The sister with the twins stepped forward, bringing a burning sensation in my throat.

My hand flew to my throat. The force of these two readings were different than any other I had done. "Throat," I croaked.

"My two-year-old died last year," the grieving woman said. "Scarlet fever. And I had many miscarriages over the years. It's them. I know it. I can feel it." She lifted her hands, the shaking radiating down her arms.

The daughter shot to her feet, leaning over the table toward me. "Are they okay?"

I drew back, frightened by her raw and recent pain, like when my own brother died.

Be brave. It's not your loss.

I took her hand. It was hot as a boiling pot. I forced my breath to be calm and forced my mind to clear, to slow my heartbeat so I could comfort her rather than increase the smarting loss.

With my free hand, I reached for the faceted ball, hoping the cool glass would seep through the lace glove and allow me to draw my calming from it. A few moments passed, and I began to feel the heat in her skin, the trouble, recede.

"Your children have people watching over them. They miss their mother. Love. I feel the distinct sensation of love."

The young woman nodded. The audience murmured.

I finally realized that these women carrying the babies were indeed guides, just as I'd read about and now here they were, right in front of me. "The guides are all holding the babies up. They want you to see that the babies are peaceful. They all have soft expressions. Like they're sleeping."

The woman covered her mouth.

"But your sister is begging for it to stop. *It.*" I shrugged.

The mother appeared confused. The younger woman looked frightened.

"Does that mean anything to you?" I said.

The mother shook her head.

I began to feel nauseated, and a piercing headache settled in. I cleared my throat. The adult spirits gathered behind the young woman as though protecting her, and I knew the message was for her. I stared at her, hoping to get more. Murmurs and movement in the audience drew my attention. I could see, even with the stage lights, that the audience was leaning forward in their seats. The woman at the table who'd lost so many babies was vulnerable. Her slight build now seemed fragile, not simply thin. Her eyes were wide, her face bloodless. I should have said what the spirits were telling me, but I couldn't.

The young mother leaned toward me, reaching across the table, her fingers outstretched, jostling one of the candles. I steadied it and wanted to tell her what the spirits were communicating, but it would embarrass the woman. I couldn't do that in front of all these people.

I got up from the table and walked around it so my back was to the audience. The audience grew even more silent; their desperation to hear was thick and heavy.

I ignored the audience members shifting in their squeaky seats and leaned into the woman's ear so only she could hear. "Your sister said to stop with the laudanum. You won't have babies until you do."

"Come on!" a male voice shot from the audience. The force of the angry voice sent chills down my spine. I straightened and turned. "Enough," I said to him, glaring through my veil, knowing he couldn't see my piercing gaze. Something in my voice must have settled the man, who was right up front. He looked down, clearly ashamed. I wouldn't be bullied into hurting this woman in a public manner.

"We paid to hear this!" another voice came from the left and farther in the back.

I pushed the audience members' escalating murmurs away and focused on the young mother. I closed my eyes tight and sought out more information. The woman turned toward me. I took her hand, squeezing it.

"She said the women she's with, they all want to see you have a healthy baby. That there's a soul waiting for you to be ready."

The young woman stared at me. I could tell that her searching gaze was mining for truth, for something that would indicate that what I said was real. "Are you sure?" she said.

I nodded. And with that, the woman fainted against her mother. This caused the audience to rise, mumbling, pointing, craning to get a closer view, and I fanned the woman back to consciousness.

I allowed the excitement to feed on itself while the woman settled down. She looked at me. "Thank you. Thank you," she said, and her mother began to take her toward the wing of the stage from where they'd come. The younger one broke free of her mother and dashed back, swallowing me in an embrace that took my breath away. As we clung to each other, the pain in my stomach and throat gave way, and I felt a surge of energy return me to the lighter mood where I'd been before this very sad reading.

I suddenly felt as though I could go on forever without stopping to sleep, to eat, to do anything other than bring these souls to the people they needed to see. I rubbed the uneven wood of the table with my gloved fingers, moving them back and forth on the splintery pine, knowing I'd found my calling, no matter the discomfort it brought me. I had relieved someone else's, and that was important.

**

I drew a deep breath, waiting for a fresh surge of my calming to return. I reached for the crystal ball, and my glove caught on a rough table-plank, jarring me, reminding me to be careful. I covered up my unease and reestablished my calm. Finally, I opened my eyes and focused on the woman.

I felt as though I'd been stabbed in the chest. I blanched and closed my eyes. It couldn't be her. I exhaled and looked over my shoulder to where Miss Violet was standing. Was this a trick? I hadn't seen the woman who sat in front of me in years, but it was her. I stared at her and knew from how she looked at me that she didn't recognize me. A ruckus in the middle aisle drew me away from this client.

"That's my ma," the man's voice said somewhere near the hubbub. I straightened in my seat.

No, no, no. I stole a glance at the woman seated across from me. I looked back at the mountain of a man who was now striding across the stage. The woman rose to greet him. He embraced her. "If you're doing this. I'll be here with you, no matter what I think."

My heart stopped.

No, no, no.

I looked toward the wings again. Miss Violet was gone. So was Olivia.

It was him. I saw him every night in my mind, felt him every day in my heart.

Oh, Aleksey. No. My blood rushed loud in my ears. But not in the way that thrilled me when we were alone. This time it was fear that sent my heart running.

I reminded myself I was veiled. They wouldn't recognize me—certainly, Mrs. Zurchenko wouldn't. I would disguise my voice. I held their gazes one by one, testing to see if they recognized me. And when neither of them showed a flicker of recognition, I prepared to proceed. Aleksey Zurchenko and his mother, Greta. The sight of them choked me. Though I knew I needed to go on, I wasn't sure I could.

I pulled the faceted crystal ball into my lap and felt its weight, hoping it would help with my calming as it had just moments before. I closed my eyes again and took full breaths. I couldn't allow the appearance of Aleksey and his mother to throw me off when there were so many watching.

I opened my eyes and saw that a crowd of familiar spirits had gathered around Aleksey and Greta. A smile came to me at the sight. Anzhela.

I set the crystal ball down and leaned back in the chair, flattening my hands on the table. I shivered. All the pain I'd experienced right along with the gathered spirits on the homestead years back pushed over me like a gust of prairie wind. Their pain was as much mine as theirs. Images of my brother James, dead in Mama's arms, came to mind. *James, help me.*

The same blizzard that took him had frozen to death Aleksey's brothers Artem and Adam. And then there was Anzhela. Anzhela, his youngest sibling.

I dug my fingers into the wood, moving them back and forth, the uneven splinters poking through my lace gloves. The pain of that one prairie year filled me. They were all there, the Zurchenkos, James standing with them. Lutie— one of the sisters who'd lived near us—was also present along with the woman and baby I'd seen so often.

I slid my hands back and gripped the edge of the table, preparing to speak.

I strained my voice, pulling it lower and quieter than normal in order to disguise it. "They want you to know they're warm." It all came out as a whisper, barely enunciated—saying as little as I could so that Aleksey would not recognize my voice.

Aleksey and Greta leaned in, their faces conveying they couldn't hear.

I held Greta's gaze and swallowed hard. I'd known the lot of them, Artem and Adam and my brother, and Anzhela, and Lutie. "Under the tree, they're warm."

Greta's face whitened, and she grasped on to Aleksey. His lips tightened, appearing skeptical even as his mother clearly grew relieved.

"The toddler, a blonde girl, is up on a young man's shoulders. A brother."

Greta grinned and grasped Aleksey's hand.

"She's reunited with them, smiling, laughing. Her wispy blonde hair blowing in the wind. They're warm, and they want you to know they know you did your best. It wasn't your fault. None of it."

I'd forgotten how stoic the Zurchenkos were. Even their spirits were reserved. I hadn't expected to feel my own rush of relief. Seeing Anzhela with her brothers and with James, released me from guilt I'd experienced over the years. But I couldn't revel in it because Aleksey was right there.

Greta's eyes shone with tears, but her posture was steely, as usual. I recalled even in the midst of their worst losses, they were nearly always dry-eyed and even-keeled. I couldn't stop the memories flooding back. Staring at them, knowing the love they had for each other, I felt the calming leave me, being pulled from my path, back to where I was processing thoughts as I would normally. I was suddenly heavy with exhaustion. My shoulders slumped. Bridging the living to the dead allowed them to cut a path right through me. Panic was beginning to grow.

"They love you, and it wasn't your fault." I needed to finish this and leave. "No one could have known the weather that was coming. No one could have known a girl could disappear into the grasses just feet from her brother." I kept waiting for a reaction like the other clients gave when I offered the words that comforted in just the right way.

"And someone is sorry. Someone. One of them who is with them is saying she's sorry. I don't think she's related. Dark coloring?"

Greta's brow furrowed as she seemed more perplexed than relieved or disbelieving.

One of the hot lights at the end of the stage blew out, and my attention was drawn into the audience. The hundreds of people who sat in the seats were beginning to rise and move toward the stage, with spirits who wanted their attention following along.

"We can't hear you!" they yelled.

My mouth dried, and my belly ached. I began to shiver. "They're safe. They love you," I said as clearly as possible to Greta. I couldn't live with myself if this woman didn't leave as relieved as the others, whom I didn't even know.

Her lips quivered. I had to get out of there. My stomach roiled. Bile was rising up my esophagus, but this time it wasn't simply a message from the afterlife. I was about to vomit. The crowd had begun to come down the aisles, yelling things I couldn't make out.

I stood and snatched my hands from the table, and when I did, one glove caught on a splinter again and was pulled right off my hand.

The splintering wood had caught my finger, too, making it bleed. I tried to pull the glove away from the wood, but it just caught on the lace harder. Men and women were climbing the stairs on the side of the stage, growing louder. I pulled the glove again, but it wouldn't budge. I glanced at the Zurchenkos. Greta was leaning back in her seat, eyes closed, with a serene expression across her face.

But Aleksey was staring at my hand. Watching as I struggled to pull away the glove. It had slid down on the splintered wood so far that I'd be better off letting it stay. Clusters of people were swarming toward me. I had to leave the glove. I covered my mouth to stem the rising bile. I turned to run offstage. Aleksey met my gaze with wide eyes. I froze as he looked back to my hand, to my deformed pinkie finger.

I bolted from the stage, leaving the glove behind, only looking back once I was in the wings of the theater, seeing Aleksey rise from his seat and bending over the glove, pulling it from the wood.

Chapter 49

Escape
Katherine

Limp, run, drag, limp. I rushed back through the stage wings, slipping through Miss Violet's outstretched hands, wanting to escape the shadow of Aleksey's narrow-eyed gaze, his angry, hard-drawn mouth. This wasn't how I wanted him to find out. What would he do now? Maybe he hadn't realized Dreama was me at all. He'd looked surly throughout the entire reading, really.

I hiked up my skirt, running as fast as my uneven boots would allow. I tore open the door to the dressing room. I lifted my old dress off the rod where it hung, scooped up my old weathered boots, and poked my head into the hallway. I could hear the men Miss Violet hired for security keeping the audience corralled beyond the hallway.

I poked my head out the door and expected to see Miss Violet stalking toward me, rage vibrating right off her body. But nothing, no one. Except for security barking an order here or there, only silence echoed off the wooden floors and dingy plaster walls. No Olivia, no Bernice, no one.

I undressed quickly. Off with the boots, the veils, the remaining glove. I paused, held up my hand. It shook wildly. Was it recognizable as my hand because of the missing finger? I turned it back and forth. *Yes, he would know.*

My breath came in forced spurts. I reached behind my neck, my fingers working at the buttons, tearing at those I couldn't reach, the sound of pearls skittering across the floor increased my panic. I wiggled out of the dress. I was scared to death at the anger and confusion I'd seen in Aleksey's face. I'd seen it before when I was boarding at the Christoffs', when they recognized my gift and thought me to be evil and dangerous. I slipped out of the beautiful new undergarments and dressed in my old clothes.

I imagined Miss Violet in front of the crowd explaining Dreama's departure. Had she sent Olivia and Bernice to run dice games and prophecy charts? I pulled the old dress over my head and buttoned the bodice.

I pulled the baby's breath from my hair and loosened the intricate ropings and braidings. I used the hem of the inside of my dress to wipe off as much of the lip stain and cheek color as I could.

My heart drummed deep in my ears. I moved through the shadows of the dark halls that led out the back, where the wagons dropped off their wares. At one point I had to wait, holding my breath for Miss Violet and Judge Calder to pass by as they blocked my exit.

"Just be patient, Jeremy." Miss Violet took his hand and brought it to her lips. "I promise you, this will only light the town's interest in Dreama on fire. Did you see what she did with those families?"

Judge Calder took Miss Violet's chin in his hand. "There were hundreds more who were unsatisfied."

"Nonsense. They want her more now. This is what we were waiting for."

He let out a sound that was more growling animal than human breath. It sent a chill right through me.

"I don't buy it." He backed Miss Violet into the wall.

Should I help her? He was married. Miss Violet didn't suffer disloyalty of any sort. I nearly stepped out of the shadows to stop him from pushing her when I saw her hands work their way up his back, and she let out her own moan indicating she wasn't resistant to his pressing her into the wall in the least. To my surprise, Miss Violet managed to get him turned back into the wall, her hand working the outside of his trousers.

I didn't know which reality felt worse—that Miss Violet might need help from a trespassing man of great power or that she didn't.

Please stop, please stop. I looked around for another exit I might use but saw no way out but past the two of them.

Miss Violet laughed. "Let's see to the receipts first?" she said, her hand still working. His head rolled back against the wall, his eyes closing, lips parting with a lost smile. I covered my mouth and squeezed my eyes shut.

"And after that, I'll do my best to further explain the value of Dreama and how her particular worth is very, very different from other business dealings. But you have to trust me."

He groaned. "Oh, I do, I do."

Miss Violet pushed away from him, wiping her hands on her skirt. "Good." She brushed her palms together as though wiping away dirt.

"Wait," his voice was thin, weak. He reached for Miss Violet. She wormed her hand out of his grip. "Finish, please," he said.

"Later. How you feel right now, that's lesson number one in why an aborted show might just be better than finishing things off first time around."

He rubbed his chin and grabbed at his pants. "Oh, you, Violet."

She smoothed a lock of his hair away from his forehead as casual as I'd ever seen her. "Yes. Me. Now let's go count the money."

She turned and started toward the auditorium, the judge trailing behind her like a hungry pup.

Once the hallway was clear, I made my way to the back of the building, exited through the service entrance, hopped off the loading dock, and ran home, my feet slapping over the dirt roads. I reached my house and stopped to catch my breath. Everything would be fine. Aleksey probably didn't recognize me. I climbed the stairs and entered the house, wanting to hide away in bed.

I had one foot on the first step of the stairway that led to our bedroom when I heard my name called from the parlor. I turned slowly, stilling my quaking hand on the banister, not wanting to know why Mama's voice bore her "We have visitors" tone I so rarely heard these days.

Please let it be Mr. Hayes.

I walked toward the room. Mr. Hayes leaned against the fireplace mantel, puffing on a pipe. I felt a smidge of relief, but as I got farther into the room, Greta Zurchenko came into view. And sitting on the settee, sipping a drink and staring right at me, was Aleksey, his blue eyes fierce and cold, not at all the eyes I had come to know so well.

Chapter 50

The Guests
Katherine

Mr. Hayes remained at the mantel, nodding hello. Greta came and swallowed me into her arms. She hugged me so tight I coughed. Her honeycomb-scented hair took me back instantly to the year we lived near her. I relaxed in Greta's embrace, remembering how loving she'd been when we were quarantined at their home.

Mama patted Aleksey's arm. "Isn't this a lovely surprise, Katherine? Aleksey and Greta popped in after their evening out."

I looked from Greta to Aleksey, who was sitting on the settee his mother had been sharing with him, next to Mama in her chair with Yale squirming on her lap. It was clear Aleksey hadn't revealed anything, but my nerves continued to fray. I wiped my forehead with the back of my hand, telling myself to calm down.

Mama stood with Yale on her hip and came to me. "Were you painting again?" She looked at my hand and took it in hers, studying it. "Is that blood?"

I pulled my hand away and put it to my side, trying to be as natural as I could. "It's nothing."

"A kitchen accident?"

I cleared my throat. "Yes. That."

Mama looked at our guests. She pulled my hand, examining it. "Just a scrape. She's been working so hard. Violet Pendergrass next door has given her the position of kitchen mistress. Katherine's baked goods are quite in demand."

Every word Mama spoke punctuated a lie, twisting my insides. "My hand's fine."

Mama looped her arm around my waist and guided me to a chair by the settee.

"Just a scrape," I said, stealing a glimpse at Aleksey, who was still glaring at me. I stiffened.

Greta sat beside Mama. "As I was telling you, Jeanie, the medium, this Dreama woman, was *wonderful.* It was a miracle." Mrs. Zurchenko's voice was fuller than I remembered, her English more fluent than when we first met four years past. "Have you had a session with her?" Greta took Mama's hand. "With James gone, you should. It was magic. I can't find the right words, enough words to say what it was."

Mama's forehead wrinkled as though considering the suggestion. I knew what she thought of Dreama, and I wasn't looking forward to this discussion.

"Amazing," Greta said. "I feel so calm now, as though I've been touched by God himself."

A flicker of pride ran through me. But then I caught Aleksey's penetrating, still angry gaze, and shame streamed in, dampening the goodness.

"More coffee?" Mama poured more into Aleksey's cup. Yale wiggled to the floor and crawled toward Greta. She climbed onto Mrs. Zurchenko's lap, making me smile.

Mama put the coffeepot aside and seated herself in the chair, hands in her lap. "I'm glad it gave you peace, Greta. There are times I'm sure I feel James is with me. When a breeze shifts or the clouds change form, darken and splash down buckets of rain, I swear it's James calling my attention. He and Mr. Templeton could predict the weather so well. Except for . . . well, you know. That once."

Mrs. Zurchenko squeezed Yale tight, eyes shut. She looked her best, serene, with a baby in her arms. "Go see this Dreama. The serenity . . . You wouldn't regret it. I promise."

Mama cocked her head and appeared to be considering Mrs. Zurchenko's words in a way she hadn't considered mine on the subject.

Mrs. Zurchenko patted Yale's back. "You know I have sense. I'm not schooled, but I'm not a fool either." She slid to the edge of the settee, her face lighting up. "This Dreama knew everything. She said the children are warm. I know what she meant."

Every word Greta spoke made me withdraw further into myself. Aleksey was studying his mother, then he'd look at me, then back to Mama. I could see he was considering the matter of whether to reveal it was me who had brought Greta the peace she'd sought. I don't think I drew more than three breaths that whole time.

Mama glanced at Mr. Hayes. He smiled at her and then bit down on his pipe. "I'll bring you that storm glass I told you about, Jeanie. Works on air pressure or something, water and crystals floating in it. Not sure, but seeing how you love to gauge the weather. Sailors used them forever."

Mama leaned forward, her expression soft. "I'd like that, Reed. Thank you." I knew she wouldn't want to hurt her dearest friend and so she continued to explain herself to Mrs. Zurchenko. "It's painful and mysterious, isn't it? People die or leave without explanation, and life goes on—James left me his clouds, his changing weather to watch, and that's enough for me at this point, I suppose."

No! James is with you. He visits; he comes to you, Mama.

Aleksey cleared his throat, making me look at him. His glare was cold and made me keep my mouth shut. I couldn't bear revealing what I could do, who I was, only to have him reject me in front of everyone. I wished I'd never promised Miss Violet to keep Dreama a secret. I should have told them all right from the start.

"We're left looking forward, not back," Mama said. "I simply won't—I can't."

I saw pain sweep across Mrs. Zurchenko's face, and Mama's face mirrored it. Mama flew out of her seat and knelt in front of Greta, taking her hands. "I'm so sorry, Greta," Mama said. "I didn't mean to sadden you. I just . . . I can't put my faith in something I can't see—something like Dreama, I mean. There's so much talk about her—people thinking she's telling them the truth, but when they get home, when they have distance, they're not sure. All this anger and handwringing over her." Mama's voice cracked. "Something inside me tells me James is at peace. I don't need anyone else to tell me so."

She released Mrs. Zurchenko's hands, but Greta grabbed Mama's right back, fighting away tears.

I felt sorry that Mama had gone so long without a friend like Mrs. Zurchenko.

Aleksey rubbed his eyes as though he couldn't believe what he was seeing.

"I'm glad you have faith like this," Mama said. "I wish I did, too."

"No," Greta said, squeezing Mama's hands. "It's you who has faith. You don't require consultation with dead children. You trust much more than I."

"Perhaps our faith is just unique for each of us."

"Yes." Greta sniffled.

Yale went to the floor and crawled to Mr. Hayes. He scooped her up, and she laid her head on his shoulder.

Mrs. Zurchenko pulled her bag onto her lap and dug through it. "I have something for you, Jeanie." Mama sat back in the chair across from the settee.

Greta pulled a wooden cylinder from her bag. "Aleksey told me you were gardening, and I wanted to bring a gift." She handed it to Mama.

"It's beautiful, thank you," Mama said, holding it up to the light.

"There's more. Inside."

Mama twisted the lid and lifted it off. She peered inside. "Seeds."

"Yes. Coneflower. It reminds me of you. When we first met, the land was full of them. Remember?"

"Oh, Greta." She kept staring into the container. "I can't wait to plant them."

"That takes a leap of faith, doesn't it?" I said. "Even a garden requires belief in the unseen."

She studied me for a moment. "I agree, yes."

"I've been using the flowers when I get sick, too. I didn't realize at first all the ways this one flower could be used," Greta said.

Mama stood, returning the lid to its spot. "Katherine's quite good with remedies. Maybe you could add this one to your book?"

I nodded.

"Let me make more tea," Mama said.

I sprang to my feet. "I'll do it."

Aleksey shot to his feet. "I'll help." He clenched his jaw. No one seemed to notice his mood but me. This was not the way I had wanted things to go with us.

I pointed to the settee. "Stay. I can manage." And I started toward the kitchen without checking to see if he obeyed my command.

**

I raced toward the kitchen, glancing over my shoulder. There he was. Lumbering, his face twisted in anger. My throat grew thick with unshed tears. I dashed through the kitchen and flew out the back door.

My breath was heavy, heart pounding. There was no escape from facing Aleksey. I balled my fists and waited.

The back door opened, and the lantern he carried pierced the darkness. Heavy footsteps on the landing, then two, three, four squeaking stairs as Aleksey descended and took his place on my right, his arm brushing mine.

He set the lantern down on the step behind us. "How could you do that? To my ma, to me?" His voice came soft, bearing none of the anger I'd seen on his face.

There was no explaining my ability to anyone who didn't experience it. He had. He'd seen the relief his mother received, that should have been enough.

"I offered your mother relief. How'd I do it? I can't explain that. I simply can't."

"Katherine," he said.

"Don't *you* do that."

"What?"

"Say *Katherine* like that, like you don't believe me, like you think I'm a rotten person. I saw the look on your face."

He scratched his face near his mouth. "You're right. I think that's bunk. Of course you know what to say to my mother. You were *there* for all those deaths! I couldn't believe it was you orchestrating this ridiculous . . ."

My eyes burned. I swabbed my tears with the cuff of my dress and swallowed my hurt. He didn't believe me. The crushing sorrow stopped my breath.

He pushed his hands into his pockets. "When you ran from the auditorium, I got up to get the glove and follow you. I swear I'd have just . . ." He threw his hands into the air. "But when I was pulling the glove away from the wood, I looked at my ma, her face . . ." He shook his head and shrugged. "I haven't seen that kind of peace in her in, well, *years.*"

See?

"I was set to tell your mother to make you stop, that you can't run a con like this. No matter how hard up you are. *She* should know better, I was ready to tell her. It's better to live right and poor than criminal any day. I would have said it all, but again, my ma, years of tension swept away. I can't ruin this for her—this peace she thinks she found."

Seeing his anger, his sneer, my heart shriveled like dry summer skin. I imagined it would soon be a hard walnut shell, useless for giving and receiving love. He may not believe me. Aleksey may not like me anymore, but he was wrong about me. I straightened and cleared my throat. "I'm *not* a fraud. You can believe what you want, but don't you dare tell anyone about me. I'm helping people, not hurting them, and you know it. People believe, and they feel better after it."

He took my arm and turned me toward him. "Have you seen the papers?"

He looked worried, less angry for the moment.

"I've seen them. Everyone wants a reading with Dreama."

"Tell me you've read the *other* articles. The ones calling for people to mobilize against Dreama." His chest heaved, his face full of worry. "Against you, Katherine. *You.*"

I pulled my arm from his grip. "No one knows it's me. Just you. If you keep quiet, I'll be safe."

"Oh, I know. I figured it out before you got back to the house. Your mother has no idea you're Dreama. Sure as I couldn't hurt my ma, I couldn't hurt yours either. But a raging mob won't care about your ma or you. They'll rip off that veil, reveal you to everyone and toss you in Glenwood or jail. Don't you understand?"

"There's *no* mob. Did you see those people tonight? Hanging on every word? The articles are nothing more than simple gossip. The paper's chock full of hateful articles. It doesn't mean a mob is actually forming. It's talk."

"They plan to expose everyone in town who's involved in fraud, debauchery, delinquency. Look what happened to Madame Smalley."

I clenched my teeth, full of anger. "I'm no fraud, Aleksey Zurchenko. And people like Miss Violet believe in me."

He squatted down and picked up a stone. He whipped it into the darkness, hitting something in the distance. He met my gaze with an unreadable expression. He didn't seem angry anymore, more like he wanted to boss me around. He picked up another stone and tossed it against the fence, making a ping.

"There's no *ability* for you to protect and keep secret. You're just smart. Twenty people just like you made their way through Yankton last year, doing just this thing. Taking people's money, offering vague promises of hope. One woman was tossed in an asylum for six months right before I left. You want to spend time locked up? You?"

Anger snapped open inside me.

I took a step closer to him, wanting to scream but keeping my voice to a taut whisper. "I don't care about some lady you heard about last year. People come to me. Some dead, some alive. But I assure you, I don't make up a single thing. I see their souls, and they let me know what they want their loved ones to hear. I understand their wishes as clear as I know yours. And you were there the second time it happened to me . . ." I paced away and spun back. "How could you be there when the fever came during quarantine and doubt me now? You were there, and you know I saw your brothers that day."

He closed his eyes and then leveled his gaze back on me. "That was delirium. If everyone who ever had a high fever thought they could really see the dead, we wouldn't even call them dead anymore, it would just be other people." Aleksey removed his hat and hit it against his leg.

"Yes. Exactly."

He shook his head.

This dismissal of my truth was suffocating. Especially coming from him. "How can you of all people treat me this way, like you don't care at all?"

"I don't care?" He put his hat back on his head and walked away before stalking back.

"You lied to me," he said." You're lying to your ma. You're the one that doesn't care. If this . . . this thing that you can do was so real, you would have told me about it. You'd have told your ma."

He had no idea what he was suggesting. He'd never been threatened, stuffed in a cold cellar.

He took my shoulders. "You have to fix this."

I pushed his hands away. "Fix what? Just tell Miss Violet *no more*? Pretend I can't comfort people, such desperate, needy people?"

"Yes."

I drew deep breaths, my mind whirling. I didn't know how I thought he'd react when I revealed this to him, but I didn't think he would be so unwilling to understand, to even try. My lies, so many, so varied, old and new, piled up in my mind. I straightened and lifted my chin at him. There was no way to unravel it all. "*That* would be the biggest lie of all, Aleksey. I'm sorry if my life turned down roads that left me grasping at lies to stay alive. But my ability to do this thing, whatever it is, isn't the lie I've been telling."

One side of his mouth pulled up. "Stay alive?" his voice carried an exasperation that infuriated me. He didn't believe me.

"Yes."

He looked away, and I thought he rolled his eyes.

I stepped forward and poked his chest. "You're so perfect, aren't you? I know that. Don't throw it in my face. You don't do anything wrong. But I promise you, you don't want to know the things I've been through. I promise you. The lies I've told are so much better when I set them up against the truth."

He looked at his feet, then back at me. "I'm sorry things have been hard. But it's not an excuse."

I scoffed. The loneliness, the utter despair in going without meals, without clothing, without my dignity as male hands attempted to map my body and female hands pushed me to work beyond reason. The fear at never again being loved swamped me, forcing me back in time as though I were still somewhere else, somewhere away from here.

I dropped my face into my hands, legs quaking. Aleksey steadied me. Finally, I looked up at him, the fear giving way to anger at his assumptions. "You're right, Aleksey. Trying to survive on my own and all that it took is no excuse for lying. It was a necessity. You were with your family, learning to read, plowing fields, your mama there with you every blessed day. While I ran for my life."

I stepped away from him trying to force myself to swallow, but my throat clamped down on the emotion that was stuck there. He watched me, finally listening. I pushed my shoulders back, trying to convey confidence that hadn't been mine when I'd lived in danger. "I kept myself alive. Me, this ability, this thing I can do. But I'm not stupid. I see what you think of it, and something kept me from telling you the truth because I knew exactly how you'd react."

"Kath—"

"No. You're right about one thing. It's my fault. I shouldn't have kept this from you. Would have been much easier if I'd told you right off that I wasn't the person you thought I was."

He reached for me.

I stepped farther back. "Just go, Aleksey. Revel in your honesty and integrity. Every tangled bit of my being is knotted in one lie or another. And that won't change just because you want it to. I'll never measure up to who you thought I was, what you want me to be. That year on the prairie…" I shrugged. "That girl's no longer me."

The kitchen door swung open, flooding the space with more lantern light. "You two!" Mama said. "I made the tea." She rubbed her arms, and her breath showed in the cold air. "Come in. You'll both be sick as the devil standing around like this. And I want you to visit with Greta."

I nodded, glad she didn't hear our conversation. "One more minute." I tried to lighten my voice.

"Just one." She disappeared into the house.

The strength I'd just felt left my body with a *whoosh*. I collapsed onto the bottom stair, waiting for him to go inside.

He sat beside me, our bodies touching, shoulders, hips, and knees. I clasped my hands in my lap to warm them. He removed his hat and turned it by the brim in a circle.

"I don't know what to think, but—"

"Don't tax yourself. You've got the law to study."

He shook his head. "I want to protect you, not hurt you."

"Really?" I said.

He narrowed his eyes on me, studying me as though he wasn't so sure. Finally, he nodded.

I looked away. "Then keep this to yourself."

"You have to tell your ma."

"I know that." I'd tell Mama everything soon, all of it: what happened when we were separated, the Christoffs, the chandelier—the chandelier pendant! My heart raced. The crystal balls.

I jumped up.

"What's wrong?" he said.

I could never divulge this to him. "Nothing."

"Tell me, please."

"Just go. Tell Mama I'll be right back."

"You're not leaving."

"I have to go back to the auditorium."

I started toward the path that led to the garden gate, and he pulled me back. "You can't go back there."

"I have to."

"No, you can't."

"Trust me. If I don't, I can't imagine making this work, or—"

He grabbed my wrist. "Probably still swarms of people there. They were angry you left. It's not safe."

I yanked away. "I need my crystals."

I reached the gate, fumbling with the latch. He covered my hands with his.

"I need them," I said and struggled to get away. He turned me toward him and wrapped me up tight.

"Let me go."

"Please don't," he said.

I pushed against him, trying to wiggle away. "You don't understand."

"They're gone," he said.

I froze in his arms. A cold breeze cut through the back of my dress in all the places not covered by Aleksey's arms. I shivered and spoke into his chest. "Gone?"

"When you left and I got your glove, others from the audience rushed the table and started taking things. Wild-eyed, they snatched every single crystal. Even the bag you brought them in."

I deflated as though my bones had liquefied. I collapsed into him, letting the tears finally pour out of me.

I shook my head against him. My tears wet through his shirt.

He brushed the back of my hair with one hand and held me tight with the other. "You can get others. I've seen the exact same ones in a parts bin at McCrady's. They're just spare chandelier parts."

I shook my head. "Two of them were special. They actually *came* to me. One of them, from the Christoffs' home . . ."

"Christoffs again?"

I shook my head, dismayed. How could I tell him all that happened there? How could I explain just how badly I needed something otherworldly to save me, that something angelic, holy—whatever its label—had?

I pushed away and wrapped myself in my arms, heading back toward the porch. I imagined the crystal balls scattered among the audience members, sitting on someone's kitchen table, a bedside stand, tossed in a junk pile.

Aleksey followed me, stopping me from going up the stairs and onto the porch. "Wait." He reached into his pocket. "I have this." He pulled something out. He opened his fingers, and in his palm was what looked like a chunk of ice.

"What on earth?" I inched closer. "What is that?"

He shook his head and brushed his finger over the jagged chunk. "Stone."

I moved his hand to catch the moonlight in the piece of crystalized earth. I pushed it with my finger, and when it turned over fully, I drew back at what I was seeing. My breath left me. I pushed words out in a whisper. "Angel wings."

"What?"

"Angel wings," I said again.

He lifted his hand toward me, offering it. "It doesn't shine like diamonds or the sparkly glass, ones you had, but—"

I reached for it, drawn to the mystery, the allure of the muted, snowy wings as though it had been chiseled for someone who would see it this way, someone like me.

I held it up to the moon. It looked like a winter river—cloudy in some spots, clear in others. The moonlight caught on its feathery edges, looking satiny-soft even as my fingers told me it was hard rock.

"It's beautiful."

"Selenite, I'm pretty sure."

I pointed to what appeared to be silken threads and ice and moon all at once. "I can't stop looking at it. It's impossible, like it's ice and water and rock all at once. Where'd you get this?"

"Inside that wall. That one I fixed at Mr. Palmer's. It's not the same as your others." His quiet voice drew my attention to him. "But if it helps you feel better."

I looked back at the angel-winged stone, turning it to discover a new layer of magic on every surface. "It's like the angel I saw with the woman. I mean, it was a flash of something I thought was an angel, the sense of angel wings was with me, like this."

He stared at it with me. "I've kept it with me nearly every day."

I clutched the stone and pressed my hand to his chest. The crystal warmed my palm, and I realized how important this moment was. "You brought it to me. It's like the other two that came to me. Only this time *you* brought it."

"The others we found were so colorful and pretty," he said, "but something made me keep putting this one in my pocket. It fit my hand just right."

"Others?"

"Well, yes. There were a bunch along with the book I found in the wall, the recipe book. Didn't we talk about that the one time? Apparently, the stones and the book belonged to Palmer's dead wife."

A chill shook me. He rubbed my arms, warming me.

"Palmer told me to burn the book and re-bury the stones. He wanted them out of sight and mind. He was livid when I showed him the things we found."

"Burn? Bury?" My heart leapt to my throat.

"But I didn't. I keep it all in my trunk."

"Except for this one." I held the stone up, turning it in the light again. "My eyes tell me it will melt in my hand—but it doesn't. Angel wings."

"I was calling them butterfly wings, but yes. I see that now."

I was overcome with emotion that Aleksey had just handed me this precious rock. "Can I keep it?"

"Of course."

"But you'll take me there, to the wall and show me, right?"

He shrugged. "I can. But nothing to see now. I patched it up nicely."

"Please."

He sighed. "All right. I will."

I pulled up my dress and tucked the rock into the skirt pocket. I would never remove this one like I had the other.

"What are you doing?"

"Keeping it safe. So it can keep me safe."

He shook his head. "Then you'll stop with the Dreama thing, right? You understand it's dangerous."

I couldn't speak. I thought something had changed for him, that he understood.

"I'm glad you like the stone. I love it, too, for some strange reason. But don't think it's going to keep you safe. The others didn't. You've been lucky. That's it."

I crossed my arms and stepped back. "So you still don't understand."

"If you get caught, you're going to jail."

I thought of Miss Violet in the corridor with Judge Calder. I immediately understood how I was even more protected than whatever the veil, glove, and limp had offered. The judge wouldn't hurt me as long as he held such lusty affection for Miss Violet.

"That won't happen. Miss Violet has measures in place."

"Miss Violet doesn't seem to suffer fools."

I stiffened. "Fools?"

"I don't mean you. I mean she doesn't seem the type of woman who would allow someone to jeopardize her business, the financial part."

I told myself to keep my words inside. But my anger boiled up, and I felt patronized. What made him say that? "I *am* her business, Aleksey."

He squinted at me.

"I work for her."

"In the kitchen."

"That's how it started."

"So she isn't a financier?"

"She is. But she's also the person who gets Dreama where she needs to be."

"You need to stop this now. She'll toss you in front of the first wagon that roars by if she needs to. People save themselves first. If there's anything I've learned in working for Mr. Stevens, it's that at the end, and in court, people save themselves."

His disapproval was thick between us. I struggled to keep my confidence. "Tonight's receipts will cover the cost of my dresses and then everything else is pure profit. She'll invest our take, and we'll all be sitting on mountains of cash."

"My god. You really believe that?"

I stepped forward. "Yes."

"You're so much better than this. You're meant to go to college and live in a home with a library and children scattered at your feet and . . ."

I saw the shame he felt for me in his eyes. My heart folded in on itself like a letter being tucked away, secreted for later.

"You'll be reduced to a circus sideshow, humiliated in front of everyone. How could you fall into such a thing? You need to stop this."

"Stop what?"

"This. This fortune-telling."

I glared. I drew several breaths, giving him the chance to change what he said, to decide he didn't really mean that. But he stood silent, the distance between us growing by miles. "You'll never understand."

"Understand what? That you're asking people to pay for something that's not—"

I shook my head.

He took my shoulders. "You're brilliant and talented, and you need to trust me. We'll tell your ma together."

All the events of the past three years tumbled through my mind at once. "I can't do that."

I needed to be strong. I needed to shield myself from the hurt that would come with the idea that Aleksey would not be mine. I needed to tell myself right then it wouldn't matter. And then he could go on his way, not needing to yoke himself to someone like me.

Trust him with my past? All that happened? Cold cellar nights in Yankton, slaps and pushes at the Roth's, Mr.

Christoff's probing hands, my endless sewing in late-night light, famished nights, complete despair, the threat to force the devil out of me. I'd worked hard to bury it all and I wouldn't dig it up now.

"You don't need to worry about me or my family, or my first job in the next circus that pulls into town."

"I didn't mean that. I'm sorry."

I turned and started up the stairs to the back porch.

His fingers brushed the back of my dress. "Please."

"You're better left with my lies than the truth, Aleksey."

I could hear his feet coming faster as I moved away. "Don't—" he said.

I spun around and pressed my hand against his chest to keep him from getting closer. "Let's get this evening over with. The sooner. The better."

He reached for me again. His fingertips caressed mine, sending sparks up the length of my arm. I ignored the voice inside that told me not to turn away from him. I had learned enough from my time with Aleksey to know better than to listen to the voice. Most of all, being with Aleksey that night simply reminded me that life for some people was meant to be spent alone.

Part III

Chapter 51

Without
Aleksey

After putting Ma on the train to Yankton, I did my best to reorient my life. I made it through the evening at the Arthurs without revealing Katherine's secret. I wouldn't hurt Ma or Mrs. Arthur, but that didn't do much for the pain that gripped my chest with every breath. Knowing Katherine was Dreama as our mothers talked nearly killed me. I wanted to shake her, hold her until she trusted that I cared. But none of that happened, and I found my own convictions about the matter taking hold. I wouldn't hurt her, but I couldn't stand by and watch her be so foolhardy, to play games with her safety, with the hearts and minds of strangers.

At my desk in the bunkroom at Mr. Palmer's place, I was back at my books, attempting to turn my notes into a usable brief that was due the next day. Thunderclouds dropped troughs of rain onto the tin roof above, the hollow pinging pulling me away from my work.

A flash of lightning startled me. The clouds grew coal-black, blotting away daylight. I lit the lamp. *Focus on the case, Aleksey.* I traced the words that I'd written on my pad again:

finders, keepers. The legal arguments over goods that were lost, abandoned, or set aside for later were as ancient as the Romans and Greeks. I read through the deposition responses listed in my notes from the week before, and it became clear that the problem with a certain Miss Hawthorne and a particular Mr. George was not the meteor pieces she'd taken from his property the night she left his home for the last time, it was that he still wanted her hand in marriage, and she had pulled hers back with stinging surety.

Love lost.

I'd made that notation days before, but now it seemed to draw me into thoughts of Katherine and the lies she'd told her family and mine. I tried to reread the case law, but only for a moment. The abstract problems of clients I'd only met once couldn't keep my mind from the very real puzzle I'd found with Katherine.

I turned the lamp wick up and down, making the light surge and recede, as though it were breathing along with me.

How could I have been so stupid? How could I have thought that our childhood bond could have sustained over the years, swelling into something deeper? Katherine's beauty, the fresh lavender and lemon scent of her hair, the way she felt pressed against me as we danced, her face as she concentrated on sketching the night I'd made her dinner, her soft, full lips—all of it drew me into another world.

Focus on your work!

I set the lamp to a moderate level, dipped my pen into the silky ink, and proceeded to write out the rest of the brief. Mr. George claimed that a portion of the meteorite that Miss Hawthorne had removed from his property hadn't been abandoned, lost, or set aside by him. It simply had not been found by him yet. It was his property, so it was his meteorite. Just because he hadn't seen it yet didn't mean it wasn't his. "I loved her. She can *not* have the meteorite if she does *not* accept me along with it. That's only fair. That's the way things work."

I exhaled. Even the flat letter of the law lured me back to Katherine. Rain needled the house. I loosened my collar. Katherine's face, the tilt of her head as she considered a new idea or listened to me talk about what I was learning, came to me again and again.

I wiped sweat from my brow. How could she have gone from the studious, ambitious girl who'd once taught me to read to this person trading in utter nonsense?

As angry as I was at her for lying to me, it was her expression last night when we argued that really tore at me. When she declared that I didn't know anything about our years apart, her eyes were full of hurt and questioning. I'd suspected those years hadn't been good. She didn't trust me enough to explain even for my sake, even if it would help me understand. I leaned back in my chair and scratched my chin. I'd known since seeing her at the orange crates that first day that something shadowy veiled her. I thought I'd been prepared to hear what had brought that darkness. Was I? Was she right to not confide? It seems as though neither of us wanted to fully trust in the other.

My eyes burned as I remembered the way we danced by the river, how she tossed her head back as we rounded the fire, laughing, all sense of that darkness gone for those moments.

I pictured her dressed as Dreama, comforting Ma with information she made up and facts she already knew, and all the goodness I felt for her was snuffed out like a flame in a sudden storm. Acid crept up my throat. I turned back a page in my book to reread the case and accidentally tore the corner of it. Mr. Stevens would be angry. It was no use. I couldn't sit any longer.

I pushed to my feet and headed downstairs.

Harold called out as I passed the kitchen. "We could use your hands, Aleksey."

I stopped and went to him and Palmer.

"Lift the stove. Flue's all to crap." Palmer got down on his belly to see underneath the stove. He leapt up. "Now both of you heave it forward so I can see behind it."

Harold lifted the other side with me.

Palmer fussed behind the stove. "Harold says you're melancholy."

I glared at Harold. He shrugged but held my gaze. My fingers slipped on the stove. I re-gripped with a grunt.

"Says it's about the girl who taught you to read. That kitchen mistress of yours."

I told Harold things hadn't worked out with Katherine, but I hadn't offered too many details. I glared at him. Harold looked away.

Palmer wiggled something behind the stove and dropped down, reaching underneath again. Finally, he stood and gestured for us to settle the stove back in its place.

Palmer brushed his hands on his pants. "Women cause nothing but pain, Aleksey. Even when they're not trying to. It's natural that things don't work out. Not worth it for someone with goals like yours." He put his hand on my shoulder. "Put her from your mind. And someday another girl will saunter on by and catch your eye at the right time. You won't even remember this one."

I knew that was a lie. I saw his loneliness at the loss of his wife as plain as I saw the nose on his face.

He cleared his throat and stepped away from me. "Life'll be better without this Katherine."

His mention of Katherine, as though we'd talked about her all the time, sent chills over my skin. I couldn't bear to hear her name aloud. My heart raced, each beat heavy and painful. I couldn't breathe. I pushed past Mr. Palmer and Harold.

"Aleksey!" Harold's voice nearly roped me back. But I burst through the kitchen door and ran out into the rain. My feet pounded over the land, sinking into the ground, muddy from endless rains, temperatures a smidge above freezing.

Blinded by the downpour, I went full speed until I found myself at the Medusa tree, by the wall Fat Joe and I had repaired all those months ago. Heaving for air, I leaned back against the tree. Freezing wind whipped the rain and lashed at my chest and thighs, stinging my cheeks.

I stared at the wall, the section where the secret book and stones had been hidden. Palmer's disgust when I presented him with his wife's book came to mind. I remembered the way Katherine's face had lit up when she saw the angel stone I pulled out of my pocket. I could feel her warm palm as I placed the winged stone there, could envision the way she calmed at the very sight of it, held it up, marveling at the way moonlight poured through parts of clear stone and was obscured where it was opaque. Her face looked innocent, awed, as though she'd just discovered the solution to a complicated, enduring problem.

Katherine evoked so much emotion. Dizzy with desire, anger, confusion . . . love? I nearly toppled over. I turned toward the Medusa's trunk and dug my fingers into the massive, once great tree. I pushed against it, fingers digging into the peaks and valleys of the bark. My feet slid in the mud as I pushed, wanting the action to release the feelings rushing through me. I couldn't keep it inside any longer. I opened my mouth and released a bellow from deep in my gut, the anger at her lies streaming out of me with every burst of my voice, catching on the wind, exploding as gusts carried my voice to the river.

And when I had expelled it all, I was left with thunder rolling over the land, my breath heavy, the only heat against the dousing storm.

The throb came back to my chest. This aching, like when I hit my thumb with a hammer, was not because Katherine had lied. I pressed my chest, trying to still the pulsing. I looked into the dying branches above me. Why was this happening? This awful thumping that spread through me wasn't inflamed anger, it was regret because all I wanted to do was ease Katherine's pain. Instead, I'd done nothing but hurt her more.

I turned my back to the tree and leaned forward, hands on my knees, heaving for breath. I wanted to protect her. I wanted to get past all the awfulness I'd felt since I saw that glove slide off her delicate hand. But how that would be possible, I couldn't say.

Chapter 52

Aftermath
Katherine

Lying in bed with Mama, struggling to find sleep, every bit of my body screamed. I struggled to keep my pain quiet because waking Mama with crying wouldn't have helped me forget Aleksey and the way he'd carelessly tossed my heart aside like an apple core. After we talked in the garden and went back into the house with our families, I kept thinking he might take me aside before he left with his mother and apologize. I understood his shock would need to burn off before he could view me as he once had, but he made it clear that he'd no intention of even trying to quell the hurt that choked my heart. It was plain to see that he was finished with me.

Edging toward morning, the realization that I wouldn't sleep rose in me like the sun. I left Mama and Yale in bed and went to the kitchen. Tommy should've been there to light the stove that morning, but he hadn't arrived.

My throat burned, raw from the chilly evening, from swallowing silent sobs. My stomach rumbled. Hungry, nauseous, I readied the ingredients for chamomile tea. It should soothe my throat. If only it could coat my broken heart. Rain pelted the house. The steady, thick sound of dripping drew my attention to the back corner of the kitchen. A bubble had formed under the plaster, allowing a little bit of water through at a time. I set a bucket under it to catch the flood when it finally broke open. My actions that morning were lifeless, heavy.

I pressed my leg where my crystal chandelier ball normally sat. It was gone, I remembered. But I'd been given something new. At the window, I drew the angel stone that Aleksey had given me out of my hidden pocket. My eyes watered at the sight of it. I was grateful for his gift, but I'd have to work extra hard to block out my feelings for him every time I touched it.

My connection with Aleksey had been mysterious. In the way that fairy tales unfolded, I marveled at the way I hadn't longed for Aleksey, for any boy all those years, yet when he appeared at the grocer's that first day, it was as though his presence answered questions I hadn't even known my soul had been asking. His presence had been a salve, bringing months of wonder to my life, where all the pain I felt over the years seemed to be funneled away, absorbed by his great strength. I pressed the stone to my chest. Not even my ability to gather protective spirits could compete with the calm that Aleksey had brought. Now that I saw that, it was too late.

Morning light lifted the night sky, but not in a dazzling, yellow-sun way. It was as though the sun wasn't so sure it was ready to rise any more than I was ready to face life. I reminded myself it was not long ago that I had staunchly protected my desire to remain single and independent. And here I was puddling like the water plopping through the ceiling into the bucket below.

Enough. I rubbed the stone wings with my thumbs and tucked it back in my pocket. Outside, clouds formed and fell apart, making me think of James. *Help me, James. Let me forget Aleksey.*

I lit two lamps and filled the kettle with water, letting the heavy, dark day blanket me. I adjusted the flue on the stove and settled the kettle on the stovetop. Something about this simple action reminded me of Aleksey, the night he cooked for me. I sighed and let the thoughts have their way. The memory wrenched my insides like someone wringing a washrag. I couldn't deny my affection for him, the way it had sprung open as though it had been growing for years without my knowing, without even having thought of him for stretches at a time.

But what the past four years had taught me was that I could isolate my emotions from the things that were happening to me. *I could forget him. I had to. He didn't trust me. He didn't believe me.* I'd blocked out things much more unpleasant than that. Yes, I hurt because Aleksey thought I was a con, no better than people like Madame Smalley.

But Mr. Christoff's rough hands had trespassed. I made *that* go away. His groping, his sour breath, his sloppy lips searching. No. That did not happen. I had found a way to replay these things in a way that didn't re-harm me, like watching it happen to someone else. Soon I'd forget Aleksey and push our relationship out of my mind, out from under my skin. I'd survive this. I would.

I'd cry quietly if I had to and stitch my soul back together in my spare time, when no one was looking. Aleksey had humiliated me the night before. The look on his face— what was it? Anger? Fear? Revulsion? It surely wasn't understanding or compassion.

"Morning, Katherine." Mama glided into the room, Yale in her arms.

I was relieved they'd interrupted my thoughts. I kissed them both. "Kettle's on," I said.

She settled Yale into a chair, handed her the wooden spoon dolly and the stuffed one I'd made her, and sighed.

"What's wrong?" I said.

Mama waved her hand through the air. "Just dividing my workload in my mind. Elizabeth Calder hired me to make her coats. It was so nice to see Greta and Aleksey that I almost forgot all the work I had waiting."

I thought of how much Mama was already doing and what it would feel like to sew for her former best friend. "Coats? Now? You're already working so hard," I said.

Mama lifted her chin, hands on hips. She looked the way she used to way back when. "Extra money for our cottage savings. I can manage. Elizabeth thinks she's doing good deeds by paying me a pittance for work. I'll let her think it if she keeps the coats coming."

I took the kettle off the stove and poured, straining the tea. I thought of how Mama used to be Elizabeth Calder's equal, how now the woman went out of her way to humiliate her by wearing Mama's sapphire necklace around town, reminding everyone that they were no longer friends. "Let me help you with the material," I said, even more determined to pay off my dresses and get the money owed me to help us buy our tiny little haven.

Mama smiled, and we went to gather the material from the front room. It made me cringe the way Mrs. Calder held Mama responsible for the mistakes my grandfather had made when investing the Calder family's fortune. It wasn't as though they'd lost it all. They didn't have to run from town, they didn't lose everything that made them whole, the way we had. Yet they acted as though they had. I was grateful that Miss Violet never told the judge I was Dreama, that he never paid me a bit of attention if I happened by him in the hallway.

I added the last few yards of lemon-yellow brocade to the pile. I helped Mama ready the thread and needles and poured her more tea. "I'm due at Miss Violet's."

Mama waved me to her. She cupped my cheeks and kissed my forehead. "You look pale. Sure you're all right?" Her thumbs brushed my swollen glands, making me flinch. I pulled away.

"You're sick."

I shook my head. "Throat's sore. That's all."

"You and Aleksey were outside too long last night."

It's just my broken heart, Mama. It's made my whole body burn and ache. It'll go away soon, I'm sure. I'd had a headache since the argument. My eyes were swollen from not sleeping. This time when I thought of Aleksey's reaction to my revelation, it made me resolute. Nothing had changed. Nothing had made it so I couldn't be independent. My brokenness hurt like nothing I could have imagined, but it gave me clarity. I was reminded of the importance of helping to build our coffers.

I grasped her wrists. "Just a scratchy throat and a headache. *You* look tired though, Mama. Soon we'll have more than enough money, and you'll never have to sew for someone else again. Especially not for old friends."

I almost told Mama about Judge Calder in the hall with Miss Violet, the way they talked and touched each other. I wanted her to know that Elizabeth Calder wouldn't escape the sting of a wayward husband, even if she carried on as though her husband was above such things. I looked at Mama smiling at me. She kissed my forehead again before she went to her sewing basket. She pulled the lamp closer to where she would work. "This rain's wild, isn't it? Winter thunder never ceases to surprise me."

"James?"

She nodded and gazed out the window, her eyes looking as though she were reading the sky like a book. "Almost like he's right here, telling me to pay attention to something, to him. Something's brewing."

I wanted Mama to have the comforts she desired. I wanted to be part of what made it possible. I could feel her loss right then, the dead son who would never return, and right then I swelled with forgiveness at her having torn us apart before. She'd never have allowed us to be separate if she'd been in her right mind.

I picked up Yale from her seat and patted her bottom; the little girl's arms circled around my neck. "I'm proud of you, Mama," I said.

She cocked her head and gave me a half smile, her eyes full of questions.

"I don't know how you've done it since . . ."

She pulled me toward her, Yale between us. I breathed in the scent of Mama's hair, her freshly washed face.

"Thank you, Katherine." She said this so quietly I had to strain to make out the words.

We separated, and I saw her eyes had welled up. Yale yawned against my shoulder.

"He's with you," I said.

She looked away, out the window before looking back at me, a tiny frown forming. I knew it wasn't the time to explore the idea of spirits and angels and sons who stayed behind even in death. Last night was enough of that for the time being.

"Thank you for wanting to help with the finances," she said, ignoring what I'd told her about James. "But let me," Mama said, "do the heavy lifting of wrenching us out of this situation. You keep up with your studies in trade for kitchen duties, and soon enough riches will come. With the money Violet gave me for you the other day and this coat money, we'll be getting close to having a little something that matters. Tommy needed to borrow some, so that took us down a little bit."

I shook my head. "Tommy?"

"Needed shoes. Worked a day in the steel mill and melted his soles right off the leather. Don't think about it again. We're making progress."

And though I wanted to ask more, I went with the idea that we were indeed making progress toward the day we would have our little home with the sweet garden that burst with every food imaginable. The skies darkened further and thunder clapped, shaking the windows. I adjusted the wick on the lamp to give Mama more light to work by. I settled Yale back onto a chair. I made the lavender doll I had sewn "walk" across the table and nuzzle into my sister's neck. "I love my Yale," I made the doll say.

"Love," Yale said, squeezing the doll along with her wooden spoon. She smiled up at me, easing the sorrow that had sunk into me the night before. My family was together, and I told myself that was all that I needed. That was what I would tell myself from that point on.

**

The rain continued, but the temperature dropped. I bundled up, holding my remade wool coat tight at the neck. I ran out into the icy rain, my cough forcing me to hunch as I made my way through the hedges and into Miss Violet's kitchen. My cough bent me over, the dry hacking causing Miss Violet and Olivia to turn away from the stove. My desire to make demands of Miss Violet was weakened by the aches and pains this cold had brought. Miss Violet and Olivia stood staring into the stove, brush and pan in hand. Tommy must not have made it to light their stove either.

I didn't want his forgetfulness to color my argument for why I was owed more than I had been getting. I took the brush and pan from Olivia. "I'll get the cinders. I can't fathom what has happened with Tommy today."

"Forgot your stove, too?" Miss Violet said.

I nodded and began to sweep the cinders, not wanting her irritated before I had a chance to say my piece.

I drew a deep breath, holding tight all the confidence I could. "I'd like to talk frankly, Miss Violet."

She was silent.

I paused in working, my head throbbing with the ache that had chased me since I'd started crying the night before.

"Well, what is it?" she asked.

I brushed the remaining cinders into the pan. It would be easier to get the words out if my hands were busy.

I kept brushing, even though I'd swept them all out all the way to the back corners of the stove. "I . . . well." I cleared my throat again. *Be strong. For Mama.* I emptied the cinders into the pail, set the brush and pan beside it, and wiped my palms clean. I stood tall, channeling Mama when she issued orders. "I've been working the numbers, and I was hoping . . ." I cleared my throat again and took an apron from the hook and put it over my head. "I believe that I'm owed more money for my services than I've been paid."

I tied the apron and held Miss Violet's gaze, wanting to convey strength, looking for a sign she took me seriously.

"Our agreement . . ." she said.

I didn't know if it was the pain in my temples or the fact that Aleksey made it clear that even he couldn't accept me for who I was, but I saw clearly that while I was grateful to Miss Violet, I also understood I brought value to her operation that no one else did. She herself had told Judge Calder in the hallway of the auditorium that my leaving early had created more interest in me, not less.

I smoothed the apron front. "Yes, our agreement. It needs to be altered."

Once the words were out, I realized I hadn't yet heard what the final take was on *A Night for Mothers*. That shouldn't matter. I knew Miss Violet's purse grew fatter with the auditorium full to bursting. *Please let that be so.*

"Your hands are shaking, Katherine."

I looked down to see them quaking. I balled them at my sides, wanting to contain my waning confidence. My scratchy throat made me cough. "Just fighting something off. Tired."

Miss Violet jerked her head at Olivia. "Make some tea. Gertrude's late, too." Olivia rolled her eyes but fetched the kettle.

Miss Violet pulled me toward the table. I sat, feeling shaky, nausea waving through my midsection. I didn't know if it was the cold settling deep into my bones or simple nervousness at confronting Miss Violet this way. Now that I'd made a demand, I needed to explain my thinking. "I've worked hard. But I need to do more to ensure my family's future. Last night must have brought in a great deal of money."

Miss Violet's jaw clenched. Other than that, her expression was benign, and I couldn't discern what she was thinking. "It did. But you also ran out halfway through the evening."

This gave me pause. Seeing her with Judge Calder, a married man, had unsettled me, but this bit, where she was using his argument against me, had the effect of pulling me out of the closeness I'd felt with her. It was clearer than ever that our agreement was structured to be more one-sided than I'd initially understood. Part of me wanted to blurt out what I'd overheard between her and the judge, but something told me to keep what I knew to myself.

"I was overcome with the intensity of it all. That was Aleksey Zurchenko, my . . . friend. Did you invite him and his mother to the table? I realize running out wasn't professional, but I showed people what I can do, and that was the goal, correct? Each person—around six hundred in that auditorium—paid a fee just to get in, isn't that so?"

She shook her head, and her face went white. She rubbed her stomach and closed her eyes as though staving something off. Had I been wrong? Had she not charged everyone who came to see me? I wanted an answer about why Aleksey and his mother had been seated at the table.

She squeezed her eyes closed and shifted in her seat.

"Are *you* sick?"

She exhaled. "Appears as though the evening took the best out of both of us."

I coughed into my hand, agreeing. Olivia brought us water. I drank half of it down, hoping the fluid would quench the burning in my throat. "And my crystals are gone. I realize that I have gowns I'm still paying on."

"And the bath oils," Olivia said.

I shot her a look and pointed at her. "None of your business."

Olivia jerked as though I'd hit her. She glanced at Miss Violet for support, but when Miss Violet continued to fight off her discomfort with eyes squeezed shut, Olivia turned back to the teakettle.

I didn't mean for my words to cut. But I was proud that something inside was giving me voice.

Miss Violet took deep breaths, and I thought for sure she was going to vomit right there. "And the paints," she pushed the words out and stared right at me. "You owe for the paints."

She drew some more deep breaths and then relaxed against the back of the chair making me think the sickness had passed. She fanned herself with one hand and wiped away sweat at her brow with delicate swipes of her fingers.

"I'd like to consult," I said, "the figures related to my work and know exactly how much I still owe on the dresses, paints, oils, whatever else I'm being charged for. And I'd like to give one of the paintings to my brother, and I'd like to know exactly how many more readings will lift me out of servitude so I can save more money for my family. More than what you give me every so often."

I instantly regretted the word *servitude*, knowing the characterization wouldn't sit well with her.

She glared. "As I said, you left the venue early last night. That will be taken into account."

"I didn't expect Aleksey and his mother. Of course, that added to my distress. What was he doing there?"

"Oh my goodness." Olivia rustled the newspaper, causing us to look her way. "Oh my," she said and lowered the paper so we could see her face.

"What?" Miss Violet said.

Olivia came to the table and turned the paper. "Purveyor of Peace: Dreama Brings Serenity and Laughter to Living and Dead."

She angled the paper so she could read. "Allow me."

Dreama brought the house down as she offered words of comfort from the deceased family members of grieving women and families like the Catwalls and Zurchenkos.

While it was clear that Dreama was able to salve unseen wounds with what she whispered to these families, something made the seer bolt from the theater. This incited the audience as they descended, vulture-like, on the woman's crystals (turns out they were simple pendants found on any chandelier in town), but their unrest was calmed and resulted in citizen after citizen adding his or her name to a list of people who wanted an audience, private or otherwise, with the Great Dreama, purveyor of peace, they began to call her. Surely Dreama's sudden departure doesn't mean it's the last Des Moines will see of this mysterious, missing soothsayer.

Miss Violet snapped her fingers at Olivia, and she handed the paper over to her.

Hearing the Zurchenko name said aloud, being reported in the paper, took my breath away. My question had still not been answered.

"Who invited the Zurchenkos on stage?"

Olivia shook her head in a way that was just barely perceptible. I thought of all the times she spoke about Aleksey, how she admired his looks. I shuddered.

"Did you ask them to the stage, Olivia?"

Miss Violet's eyes swept over the article, her finger drawing down as she read. My heart thumped with every beat of Olivia's silence.

Miss Violet flicked the paper three times. "Impressive results, my dear. Very well done," she told me. "I'll look over the books, and we'll adjust our agreement."

I sat straighter in my seat, focusing despite the hazy headache that was only growing worse, the Zurchenko issue poking me. "And I want to tell Mama what I'm doing. No more lies."

Miss Violet closed her eyes and opened them, her face blanching. "It's not time. I'll concede the money, but it's too risky to reveal such a thing right now."

"I can't keep this up. It's making me sick."

Miss Violet laid the paper on the table and sat straighter. "Not yet. You're a good daughter. You have her future in mind, and I admire that. But I think of you as a daughter, too, Katherine. All you girls," she said, glancing at Olivia, "are my daughters. And so, I ask you for a little more time and then we will tell her together. Don't let a little guilt get in the way of you achieving what you desire for her. Her own home. Think of it."

Miss Violet's face grew even paler, fragile suddenly. Her lips quivered, and her sudden delicateness was as jarring as a slap. I thought of how alone she was. She considered me her daughter. I softened at the sight of her vulnerability.

I started to argue my case further, but Miss Violet had flown to her feet and stumbled through the back door, where I could hear her vomiting.

I followed her with a damp cloth. "Here."

She nodded, already straightening. She spit to clear her mouth, and I saw how hard she was trying to regain her composure. I'd never seen her shaken like this. Seeing how she could barely stand, I steadied her and used my free hand to blot her mouth with the towel.

She grabbed my sleeve. "Promise me. Please. A little longer."

Miss Violet needed me more than I needed her in this one small moment; her desperation was clear. And so, I'd look upon this concession as an act of charity, one that had limits and one I hoped I wouldn't regret. I reached for her and supported her weight as we walked up the stairs onto the porch. Olivia stood near the door reading the paper, biting on one finger. *Zurchenko*. The thought of Aleksey and his mother came back. I helped Miss Violet hobble toward the door. She hung on my arm like an elderly woman.

"How *did* the Zurchenkos get selected for a reading?" I said.

She tilted her head, her eyes watering with whatever this illness was. "Olivia selected her."

"Why didn't you stop her once you heard the name?"

"There was a ruckus backstage just before Mrs. Zurchenko was to be seated. Olivia said at one point Aleksey wasn't even going to sit with his mother. I was busy dealing with some thieves attempting to steal the moneybox, and when I saw Aleksey coming down that aisle to sit with his mother, it was too late. I just let it go. I figured it wasn't so bad if one of the people you read for was a guaranteed success. You would know things even if your . . . even if that calming didn't come."

She squeezed her eyes closed. A new wave of nausea must have been threatening. I felt my own nausea. *That calming.* I felt the doubt in how she said it. How was that possible at this point? I dropped my hand from her arm, and she moved toward the door, reaching for its handle.

She looked over her shoulder at me. "You didn't say anything to him, to Aleksey, did you?" Her normally smooth hair pulled from its bun in brittle flyaways. Her drawn, pale face and hunched posture aged her twenty years. Her scratchy voice turned my blood cold.

I thought of the horror on Aleksey's face as I confided the details of my work as Dreama.

I kept her gaze, careful not to let the truth into my eyes. "'Course not," I said. Her knees gave way a bit. I caught her under the arms and helped her into the kitchen and to a chair. Her manipulation unsettled and ensnared me. The only way out without devastating Mama was to pay off everything as quickly as possible. Then, money for a house or not, I'd beg her forgiveness for telling such lies, for creating a part of me that she knew nothing about.

Chapter 53

Floating
Violet

Violet kicked off her covers, another tide of nausea bringing sweat and weakening her with every retch. Once the worst of that round had passed, she burrowed back under the covers. She rubbed her temples, attempting to coax the throbbing away. Closing her eyes, sleep came and went, and at one point she thought the worst was over.

Her sweat-soaked sleeping gown stuck to her skin as she struggled to sit up and do some work. She pulled her ledger onto her lap and examined the numbers and notes. It was time to put her plan into action. Olivia would assume the role of Dreama regularly.

Though Violet was sure that Katherine had some sort of ability, that she was not a con in the way that the police claimed certain clairvoyants to be, she was also confident that someone else could do what Katherine did just by reading the cues from clients about the things that worried them or they felt guilty over or wanted resolved. Violet still rehashed the two times Katherine "saw" her father. She wasn't convinced that she hadn't told a story about him or led

Katherine to "see" something that wasn't really mysterious at all.

Yet... Olivia was nowhere near the attraction Katherine was. The most enthusiastic, gullible, desperate clients accepted Olivia's clumsy reading of palms and charts and the rolling of dice, but Olivia was as poor at reading people as Katherine was gifted at conveying enough honesty that people were guided along a journey, a very valuable one. Violet knew skeptics would dismantle Olivia's act in no time.

Violet had never intended to replace Katherine with Olivia as Dreama. Katherine's impeccable performances of the fantastical character Violet had created and advertised in the newspapers in towns leading to Des Moines made the idea of losing her nearly unthinkable. But Jeremy had mentioned that a young law student and his mentor were poking around the courthouse, asking questions about Violet Pendergrass's business.

She had asked Jeremy for their names in the hopes that one of them had been a client who could be manipulated with information Dreama may have learned from them. But when Jeremy mentioned the name Zurchenko, fear vibrated inside her like a piano note held to its very dead end.

She'd met Aleksey once and seen him from afar several other times. There was a devastating honesty about the man, something that she could smell on him the same way the scent of outdoor work clung to a man. His gaze seemed to capture a person and hold them, discerning who they were without even asking a question. He wasn't to be managed the way most men could be.

She'd seen the way he held Katherine with a softened gaze, and the way she looked back at him, utterly absorbed. He couldn't be trusted. Not by Violet, anyway. Even if Aleksey Zurchenko had the biggest bank account in Des Moines, she would have wanted him far, far away from her. Damn Olivia for thinking it would be nice to watch him at the table with Katherine.

He'd been attentive to his mother during the reading, not a hint that he knew anything at all about Dreama's true identity. But Violet had seen the cynicism on his face. He wasn't a believer. Still, Katherine's disguise kept her secret. When she tore out of the auditorium and the audience erupted, storming the table, Violet switched her focus from the Zurchenkos to the moneybox and in the chaos didn't see the Zurchenkos leave.

Violet thought again about Aleksey nosing around the courthouse. Surely Jeremy Calder had done his part in keeping her and Dreama's reputations clean.

Yet even as she reassured herself, she couldn't deny she was beginning to feel a tightening in Des Moines, like stays being pulled a little more with each wearing, a little less breath every single day. There were plenty of other places where she could continue her work. Perhaps that was the answer—leaving. She could begin again and somewhere better. Dreama may have been an added bonus to her business, but she reminded herself that she was good with investments. Not just when she was working an angle, but always.

Still, the Dreama money would allow her to invest and build for the future faster. She added to her list of ways that Olivia could be coached to extract information from a client when Violet felt a weave of nausea and vomited again, only clear liquid coming out. She couldn't remember the last full meal she'd eaten.

Katherine had looked to be coming down with something as well. This gave Violet a measure of confidence. She wasn't pregnant after all. Abortifacients were only reliable to a degree, and Violet had become a master of using her mouth to satisfy the judge before he'd the chance to make love to her during her fertile times. Still, she'd seen her share of pregnant girls, and her constant greening hearkened back to what she'd witnessed with others.

Violet lay flat on her back, arms spread. Dizzy again, her thoughts flew in all directions. She recalled her days as the midwife's assistant. The pain she'd witnessed during birth, sometimes even death. She couldn't fathom being the actual participant in a birth.

Put that thought away, she said to herself. She felt feverish, with chills, and she reminded herself that morning sickness normally consisted only of nausea. There was no way she was pregnant.

Under the floorboards right beside the bed, she'd stowed away cash and kept her ledgers when she wasn't using them. She had that at least, and it might be all she needed if Katherine turned unreliable. She thought again of Katherine and Aleksey's relationship.

Could Katherine be pregnant?

No. The girl had a cough and sore throat, not nausea, not the way Violet did anyway. She was quite certain Katherine hadn't even a first kiss let alone lain with Aleksey. She'd know if he'd had her; she'd sense it as she always did with the other girls.

She pressed her belly with both hands. There *was* that time when she let Jeremy inside when she shouldn't have . . . Her stomach lurched and the pain made her teary and emotional, wanting him near her.

She'd let him inside in too many ways, letting him grasp her very heart. This disgusted her, that she might want him to comfort her, that she needed him. She shook her head, but the feeling stayed. She yearned for him the way she used to ache for Edwin. She covered her eyes and let out a small cry.

She'd never felt so weak. She'd canceled the meetings she had planned with Mayor Rothschild, Reverend Shaw, Sheriff Tinsdale, and Judge McCarthy and Jeremy. She'd sent Olivia to each person with a note explaining that she was rescheduling, that the reports on the past month's investments had been delayed.

She was nodding off when the door opened, the telltale squeak pulling her from sleep. She opened her eyes, ready to reprimand whomever it was, but when she got up on her elbows, she saw Jeremy.

Excited, mortified, she flopped back down. No pinked cheeks, hair a loose bird's nest, sour mouth—she'd never presented herself in such a way to anyone. Still, she would have sprung off the bed and wrapped herself around him if she'd had the energy.

He stroked her arms and smoothed her hair, his eyes darting over her as though he were a doctor assessing her fitness. "Oh, my Violet. Olivia tried to hide your illness from me, but I knew. I just knew something was wrong."

She got to her elbows again, wanting to clean up and let out a whimper. She mustered the strength to cover her mouth, wanting to stuff her weakness back inside. He'd never look at her the same way after this.

"Lie back, lie back, my little flower." The kindness brought another moan as the nausea swelled. Jeremy slid his arm under her legs and lifted her, setting her back on the pillows. He covered her with the thin blanket and disappeared into the washroom where she bathed and applied her makeup. She heard him turn on the water, and he returned with a wet towel and laid it on her forehead.

"You need a bath. The water always helps my stomach when it's out of sorts."

She couldn't speak. His care of her took her by such surprise; the shock of it was like the loosening of a corset, allowing her to take a full breath for the first time. She covered her mouth, her eyes burning, and swallowed her rising sob.

He scooped her up, saying, "Oh, Violet, my beauty," and carried her to the bathroom. He set her on her feet and gently kissed her forehead, cheeks, and nose. "I love your beautiful freckles, Violet, each as unique as you. Every one of them deserving a kiss."

He slipped his hands under the straps of her thin nightgown and pushed them over her shoulders, letting it fall to the floor.

His gaze fell over her nakedness, tracing the path his fingers took over her shoulders and down her arms. A knock came at the door. He disappeared and returned with two buckets of hot water and poured it into the cold, making the perfect temperature for her comfort. He helped her step into the tub and sit. She closed her eyes, her body relaxing as she floated, releasing the discomfort she'd felt nonstop for the past few days.

She opened her eyes. He sat on the commode, elbows on knees, hands clasped under his chin, wearing an expression that she could only characterize as worry mixed with affection. No, something deeper than affection, something that turned Violet away from all good sense, from all the lessons she'd learned over the years. A yearning, an aching, a need was sown. She'd once called it love.

"Thank you, Jeremy."

He nodded and gave a small smile, the most genuine thing she'd ever seen on his face. He got onto his knees and reached for a cake of oat-and-honey soap. He dipped it into the water and ran it from her fingertips up her arm, across her collarbone, and down the other arm. "You just get better. I can't have my partner so sick that we can't make magic together. You're everything, my love, everything."

The fragrant water lifted her body while his words sent her heart soaring. Did he just say he loved her?

Love. She was a child the last time she'd felt the romantic kind, naïve, convinced that it existed. The sensation pulsing in her chest made her sit up suddenly, a blend of elation but nausea, too.

"Shush," he said, slipping his arm down her spine, easing her into a weightless lounge.

She watched him run the bar of soap over her belly, seeing Jeremy in a way she hadn't before. He set the soap aside and made circles on her belly, studying her body, enraptured, making her wonder if he'd ever cared for anyone as he was doing for her. Perhaps this was different for them both. She wanted him differently than before, more. It wasn't a warming between her legs or the desire to have him bring her to climax. This time it was a thirsting of the heart.

His shirtsleeves were soaked, water creeping up the material. The sight of him tending her uplifted her and made her forget her sickness, her worry over her possible pregnancy, his marriage, and that her life was suddenly headed in an unfamiliar, uncontrolled direction.

He met her gaze and kissed her forehead. "That's my girl. We have big things on the horizon. No time for illness, is there?"

She nearly blurted that she might be pregnant, but she gripped the sides of the tub, stopping short, swallowing the words, tears burning her eyes again. His nursing was convincing, alluring, lovely. But something told her this moment was best left unaltered. This moment would be one that would sustain her going forth.

He cocked his head. "What it is, Violet?"

And to keep herself from spoiling their intimacy, she answered him with a smile and the shake of her head. He ran a warm cloth down her middle and she closed her eyes, relaxing further into his arm that held her afloat, just below the surface of the water. She knew right then she would keep this sensation, this very moment, close for the rest of her days.

Chapter 54

Digging Around
Aleksey

The wet winter that fluctuated between blinding snow and drenching rain meant extra labor at Palmer's farm. With the sodden terrain and cold weather, the cows required extra attention. I welcomed the work. I'd managed to keep up with my law studies, but the days of preparing in advance were gone. Katherine's face, her laugh, the way she'd felt in my arms, tight against my chest, all those things returned to me, a crippling concoction of desire and pain that I'd thought impossible until I'd felt it myself.

The mindless labor at the barn was reassuring. Breaking my back meant lessening the pain in my heart. Most of the time, anyway. I was shoveling out the soiled hay the animals slept on, and suddenly I'd think of Katherine. Her face in my mind would stagger, then freeze me mid-shovel. Pain cracked my chest, a heavy blow like a sledgehammer. My hand shook as I pressed the area, hoping to relieve the discomfort. How was it possible to feel as though my heart had truly been physically broken? I began to breathe shallow, fast, and thought I might pass out. How would I manage without her?

"All right, big man?" Harold slapped my back as he passed by with fresh hay. I forced a mumbled "yes" out and then compelled my legs to move, taking the load of soiled hay outside.

I forced deep breaths into my lungs. *Just keep moving. It'll pass.*

Shuffling along, I recalled that day at the tree when I'd tried to outrun my despair, to have the rain wash it away, and I'd decided I needed to protect Katherine even if I couldn't be with her. I'd worked even more efficiently at the courthouse, completing tasks and then digging for information on Violet Pendergrass and her business.

I dumped the load onto the pile and leaned on the shovel. There were no legal documents associated with her name except for a complaint to the city's planning committee about her choice of green and pink paint for her massive home. They tossed it aside as unfounded since it was the former owner who didn't like seeing the house "mistreated" with what he deemed garish paint.

I'd asked around, pretending I might like to invest with Miss Pendergrass but wondering if I was wealthy enough to do so, playing naïve bumpkin in the attempt to loosen up lips. Every single lawyer, judge, and secretary I'd spoken with indicated anyone could take their money to her, no matter how small the amount. No one offered anything but praise for her.

Researching the newspapers, I'd found articles characterizing how people were divided on the "realness" of Dreama's work. Other columns indicated Violet Pendergrass was the person who facilitated every single event and meeting between Dreama and her clients. I'd made a list of all the people who might be willing to talk to me about what they experienced with Dreama and Violet.

Katherine. No one had yet attached her to the role of Dreama. I leaned back against the wall, grateful.

"What's wrong with you?" Harold breathed heavy and leaned on his shovel, narrowing his eyes on me.

When I didn't answer, he pointed at me. I looked down to see that I was gripping my chest. The pain had returned and stopped me cold all over again.

Chapter 55

All Those Lessons
Violet

Violet sat at the kitchen table instead of the dining table, still in her robe, reading the newspaper, nibbling on dry toast, sipping peppermint tea that Katherine had made to help with the nausea. Violet wouldn't sully the beauty of her French dining room with her unkempt dress, but after days of illness, she had to get back into the world, at least back onto the first floor of her own home.

Olivia fussed at the stove, and Tommy came up from the cellar and removed his hat.

"Morning, Tommy," said Violet.

He smiled. "Finished the coal and the . . . you know," he told Violet but gestured toward Olivia. Violet knew he was unwilling to discuss making condoms in Olivia's company.

Violet almost told him he'd better go check his work, that she might be pregnant, but in mentally paging back through her lovemaking with the judge, she had to admit there were several times they hadn't taken precautions at all. That was her fault, not the one who made the sheath.

Tommy lingered. Violet looked up at him, eyebrows raised.

"I won't be available until later today," he said.

Violet squinted, not sure why he was telling her that. He did look haggard, nearly as awful as she'd felt the past few days. She felt a surge of relief that another sick person would be evidence that she wasn't pregnant, that her missing monthlies were due to stress and overwork.

"Sick?" she asked.

He looked at his hat and then met her gaze. "Just piecing together extra work. Heard from my father. He's looking to come back, and I want to add to that nest egg for us."

She wasn't sure if Father Arthur was ever returning, but she knew Tommy wanted that more than the rest of them. She wondered what Katherine and Jeanie thought of that news.

"Katherine better?" she said.

"Still coughing quite a bit."

"Grippe?"

"Think so."

Violet realized Tommy was seeing her without proper dress or grooming. Smoothing her hair back, she sat straighter and took up the paper to shield her. "It had me, too. The grippe."

"I have some errands today for Mama. Have to watch Yale since Katherine's fighting that cough. Mama's got some eggs and such to deal with, and something with those indoor garden things she and that man made. Just lots to do."

Violet lowered the paper and studied him over the top of it.

A shock of fear hit. It had been days since she'd seen Katherine. She replayed the conversation, remembering Katherine's facial expressions when she said she wanted to tell her mother about Dreama. She'd agreed to wait and appeared sincere when she made the promise. Surely, she wouldn't suddenly disclose her secret without letting Violet know. Perhaps she should go next door and pay Katherine a visit.

"Well. Carry on, then. I'll see you later this evening." Violet tried to read again, but her mind wandered. She thought of Yale, the way the family always had a hand on her lest she wandered away and got into something dangerous. She was a wee child after all. So slow. But pleasant. Violet imagined holding the girl in her arms, having someone cling to her, slender arms looped around her neck, a little one wanting her, needing her.

She had mixed feelings when it came to children—mostly never wanting to be saddled with such a thing. Perhaps if things were different. She glanced at Olivia, pulling out the chair across from her. She felt as though Katherine and the girls were her daughters. They depended on her like children. Nearly like that. Wasn't that enough?

She thought back to when Jeremy had nursed her through the worst of her nausea, how his tenderness had moved her. She looked out the back window. He hadn't returned, though. It hadn't bothered her at first. The soft recollections of his affection were enough, but his absence in subsequent days brought heaviness to her heart. What was he doing? Who was he with? Were his fingertips mapping his wife's collarbone, trailing down her spine, between her legs, his mouth following every touch?

The kitchen door slammed as Tommy exited, and Violet jumped. *Stop thinking of him.* She bit down on her cheek. *You don't need him. You're not a wife, you don't want that.*

She straightened and focused on the headlines in front of her.

DREAMA BRINGS FOLKS FROM FOUR CORNERS. WITNESS HER MARVELS. SIGN UP NOW!

And another:

EVIL AND DEBAUCHERY FOLLOW DREAMA'S APPEARANCE. STOP HER! SIGN UP NOW!

Violet clutched her throat. *Oh my*. A smile came to her, and she inhaled deeply. "We're getting somewhere, Olivia. Finally, Dreama's a sensation."

Olivia stood and refilled Violet's cup with tea. "What?"

Violet held the paper open for her. Olivia bent to read over Violet's shoulder. "You don't worry about that?" Olivia pointed to the paper. "These people seem determined to see Dreama unveiled and jailed."

Violet exhaled. She was feeling like her old self. Reading the articles brought her mind back where it belonged, set on the goals she'd determined when she set off for Des Moines. "That article?" She shook her head. "No, no, no. That's the very mood that . . ." She set the paper down and held out her hand, palm up, drawing her fingers into a tight fist. "Brings everything together, locking success into the Dreama formula for good. The mob that wants to rid Des Moines of Dreama provides the energy that fuels greatness. No one becomes legendary with the help of fawning, praising, sycophants. No. It's one's detractors, the ever-present handwringers filled with hate and fear that stir things into a frenzy. It's rage and fright that shakes money free from pockets and opens purses. That's exactly what we've been hoping for." She knew Jeremy would be gathering money from the handwringers who thought he agreed with them while she collected fees from those who couldn't see Dreama enough.

Violet reached for Olivia's hand and squeezed tight. "Always, *always* welcome the handwringers, Olivia. They plow the land and turn the soil so the money can grow like summer corn."

Olivia squeezed Violet's hand in return and smiled, though still appearing unsure.

Violet released her grip, sat back, and rubbed her belly. No sign of the nausea that had plagued her. "Now let me finish basking in these articles, and we'll set about dressing for the day. You send word to the judge and the others. We're open for business again, finally."

Violet lifted the paper and realized that she had given too much power to her weakness, the unfamiliar, emotional fragility she'd been experiencing in the midst of her illness. But to her great relief, it had been temporary, like the nausea itself.

**

Violet closed her ledger and set the paper she'd been writing on aside. She felt better than she had in days, but her earlier rally had been cut short with the return of fatigue and intermittent nausea. She ran her finger down the list of items that detailed expenses Katherine had asked to see. But the girl was late, and she was never late. The clock's ticking was steady against the quiet in the house. Katherine had been a stable presence. Until now. Or perhaps Violet was worrying about nothing. Katherine had been dependable and successful as Dreama. Loyal. Perhaps the strange unsettledness Violet was feeling had to do with Katherine pulling away from her. The girl, her kitchen mistress, had touched her heart. She held Katherine close, very much like a daughter. She'd said those words the other day to Olivia and Katherine, but she hadn't realized how deeply she felt protective of them until the words were out, until she saw the expression on their faces that said they were pleased with the thought.

But perhaps Katherine really wasn't ill? Could Tommy have been lying? Violet's insides clenched. *Aleksey.* Katherine might have confided in him. Violet covered her mouth and paced. Was Katherine truly loyal, or had Violet just been hoping she was?

The illness still fogged her mind, loosening her grip on every aspect of her life. Where had her renewed energy and confidence gone? It might have just been four days, but it felt as though she'd fallen off the edge of the earth and was a stranger in her own world. She needed to get a hold of herself and her business, and most especially, Katherine. Yes, she needed to secure Dreama's existence by training Olivia to be her. It was the only way Violet could care for herself, the girls, and Dreama. She'd convince Katherine that it was best for all of them. But she had to be careful to keep Katherine invested until just the right moment.

Violet slipped on her emerald cloak, buttoning the collar. She worked her fingers into her soft black leather gloves, clutched her notebook under her arm, and stepped outside to the porch.

She patted her pocket where she'd stowed a small velvet bag filled with pennies and a few dimes. She'd included one gold coin to give Mrs. Arthur, even though Katherine hadn't worked in days. The shiver returned, the chill telling Violet something wasn't right. The money pouch would help ensure Jeanie Arthur was grateful to Violet, saw her as generous, and would allow continued access to her daughter.

Violet carried with her one of Olivia's notebooks on investment philosophies and practical applications to show to Jeanie in case she questioned Katherine's studies. If Jeanie noticed the handwriting was different, Violet would claim she accidentally brought the wrong one. She felt the tenuousness of her life at that moment and saw it was more important than ever to keep the Arthurs doing what she needed them to until she didn't need them anymore.

She descended the front steps and hurried toward the home next door. As she neared the little house, Violet could see only the top of Jeanie's head, the rest of her hidden by tall, thick Rhododendrons and overgrown evergreen bushes. Violet heard the swish of Jeanie's broom across the wood planks.

Something kept Violet from going up the front steps to the Arthurs' front door, and just as she went to a section of the bushes where she could see Jeanie but remain unseen herself, Jeanie stopped sweeping and leaned over the broom handle. Violet leaned in and saw Yale sitting near the door, bundled in a coat. Jeanie was smiling at her daughter. "Sweet Yale. Be good for Mama."

Yale held her hands in the air, fingers spread wide, grinning, her eyes filled with what could only be described as adoration. "Love!" she said and alternated making fists and spreading her fingers, blinking with her hands.

Violet pressed her belly. An unfamiliar ache gripped her, an odd pulling in her pelvis. The sensation passed, and she couldn't say whether it saddened or relieved her. She'd thought she'd gotten over the yearning for children years before. But with that stabbing in her stomach, she was struck by the sense that something was changing. Jeanie Arthur had nothing but trouble with her children and absent husband, yet Violet was chafed, envy hot in her heart.

She moved closer and heard the tinkling of the bells Yale wore around her wrist. Tommy must have finished watching Yale and was off doing whatever other job he had to do. Absorbed in the scene between mother and daughter, the simple joy as Yale moved the wooden spoon doll across the wood planks in front of her, making it walk, Violet could not move. Yale struggled to her feet and lumbered toward her mother. It was then Violet saw the rope tied around Yale's waist and shoulders to harness her to a lead tied to the front doorknob.

Katherine had said they needed to take more safety measures with Yale, but Violet hadn't realized she meant leashing her this way. A pity the girl's development had been so hindered. She felt sorry for the little one.

Jeanie blew Yale a kiss. The little girl pushed her palm against her lips, her smile showing even with her hand over her mouth. She yanked her hand away, yelling out "Love, love!"

Violet's eyes burned. She was overwhelmed with jealousy, sadness, disappointment—each emotion now distinct inside her. *None of this matters.* She had her business. She had her girls.

A breeze kicked up, milder than the rest of the air, giving her the shivers. She wiped her eyes and was about to move out of the bushes when a man's torso came into

Violet's view. He stood at the bottom of the Arthurs' stairs. The man was too thick to have been Reed Hayes.

"Ahem," the man said.

Jeanie jumped and turned, her face drained of its pink color.

That voice. Violet's blood turned cold. The familiar tenor pricked her skin. She strained to see more of the man but couldn't do so without exposing herself.

"Well," the man said. "I now see how you keep your figure, Jeanie."

Violet covered her mouth and held her breath. She inched nearer, a Rhododendron branch digging into her shoulder. Jeanie, he had called her. Not Mrs. Arthur. *Old friends,* she remembered.

Violet quietly worked her fingers into the branches and spread them to see better. Jeanie's unfashionable A-line dress was ragged at the hem, soiled from top to bottom, the mark of a woman tasked with manual labor.

He went up on the porch. Violet saw him more clearly, his finely cut suit, his wool overcoat slung across one arm. He held a paper toward Jeanie.

Jeanie cocked her head toward the paper, her fist on her hip. "What's that?"

"Why don't you come and see?"

"No thank you, Judge." She stepped around him, working the broom at the ground-in dirt where the riser met the tread.

Jeremy moved toward Jeanie, but she kept sweeping, ignoring him, swatting at his feet with the broom. He moved with grace that belied his size, pressing into Jeanie's back, his lips near her ear, his voice now too low for Violet to hear. She thought she might fall over and gripped the Rhododendron branches for stability, hoping she didn't give herself away.

She wanted to tear them apart, dig her nails into Jeanie's throat. Violet's breath and heartbeat sounded in her ears. Had she been naïve in not suspecting that Jeanie Arthur was up to something more than sewing or gardening? Should she have paid attention and realized that Jeanie might try to burrow back into her old life through the bed of a powerful man? Reed Hayes was a fine person, but powerful he was not.

Calm down. He is yours. He is yours.

Jeremy reached for Jeanie, but she jammed her elbow into his gut. He drew back, and she took the opportunity to step toward the door. Violet shifted her position. Jeanie was sweeping again, hovering near Yale as though wanting to create distance between the judge and the little girl. Violet exhaled and drew a deep breath. It was clear that Jeanie was, at least right then, not interested in Jeremy. Although Violet hated to admit it, Jeanie standing there embodied an elegance that couldn't be turned ragged like her clothes.

Jeremy took a step toward her, and Jeanie stepped away, pushing the broom at his feet, and Violet knew this was no game. She'd known a lot of coy women, and Jeanie wasn't one of them. Still, it did nothing to dampen her rage.

"You do realize," Jeremy said, "how easy it is to shuttle children to Glenwood and the boys' home of Des Moines? Very lucrative for certain people in town. The indigent, morons, tramps, imbeciles, boys who gamble and drink. A great deal of money is made. I'm an important friend to have."

Violet ran his words through her mind. She realized that he hadn't shared that information with Jeanie to make her his confidant. He was threatening her.

Now Jeanie stepped closer to him. "I'm well aware. I've attended many a meeting to address the matter. Leave my children alone. Everyone's children." Her voice quivered. Violet remembered then that Tommy had been in jail before. Violet knew Jeremy was a busy man. She knew his time was filled to the top with her, with his work, with his wife. Why take the time to threaten a powerless woman? Did he want her? Violet didn't like the answer that came to mind.

"My wife's looking forward to those coats you're making for her. Nothing like an old friend's touch on new clothes, she told me. I'm sure you miss your old life, Jeanie. A shame."

Jeanie untied the rope from the doorknob and scooped Yale into her arms.

He touched the harness around Yale's shoulders. "What's this?" his voice boomed.

Violet saw the fear on Jeanie's face as she searched for words.

Jeremy shook his head. "You certainly have your hands full, don't you? Shameful how the world works, unforgiving, harsh. Not just a wayward son who troubles you, is it? In some ways, daughters are more of a burden, especially those who are touched. Those who are most vulnerable are safest when put in a secure place like Glenwood." He patted her shoulder. "I'm so glad to be counted as your friend, someone who can help when you really need it."

"Don't start this—" Jeanie said.

Violet could not stand another moment. She should have walked right back to her house and shut Judge Jeremy Calder out of her life. Competing with a wife was rarely concerning to Violet. This was different. Her thoughts flew, tangled, wanting to blockade her home from him. But it was too late. Too much was invested in him beyond her feelings for him. She had no choice but to tie him closer, not push him away.

She eased back out of the bushes and onto the sidewalk. She wouldn't allow his attention to stray, let his appetite be whetted by someone else.

"Judge Calder," Violet's voice was harsher than she wanted it to be. Jeanie stepped away, and Jeremy dashed down the stairs toward Violet.

He pulled his watch from his pocket. "I'm late, aren't I, Miss Pendergrass? Just having a chat with your neighbor. I'm sorry to keep you waiting. Time *is* precious."

Violet glared and then smiled, unwilling to reveal what she'd overheard.

Jeanie waved at Violet, her face conveying relief as she reached for the doorknob. As Violet led Judge Calder back to her home, she caught a glimpse of Reed Hayes coming down the sidewalk, smile full and open.

**

Violet and Jeremy pushed through the garden gate at the front of her home, and their hands found each other. Seeing him pursuing Jeanie had stunned her, and yet it lit every nerve afire.

"Come with me, Judge."

They took the steps, her pace quickening as her desire grew.

He opened the door for her. "The railroad investment," he said. "It must have been a haul."

She met his gaze as she passed him, waiting before answering, making him suffer.

"It was."

"You're feeling much better, aren't you?"

She stalked through the parlor, tugging her gloves off, casting a glance over her shoulder to him, and stared, thinking about how to rope him to her permanently.

"I am." He trailed her into her office, and she unbuttoned her cloak, tossing it onto a chair. He watched her every move, a slow smile appearing. She reached around him and shut the door, pinning him where she wanted him.

"Pleasure first, is it?" he said.

She answered by working the hook that fastened the top of his trousers. The fly was splayed before he could get another word out. She couldn't compete with Jeanie's breeding or his wife's marriage license, but she had abilities she was quite sure neither woman claimed. Jeremy had told her as much many times.

She reached into his trousers, cupping him, sliding her hand up and down his length. He inhaled sharply and took her shoulders. "Violet, you know," his breath quickened, "I do like a little seduction before we—"

She dropped to her knees, pulling his pants down. She took him in her mouth and glanced up. His head lolled back against the door, his eyes half-closed. Sometimes during lovemaking she'd hold him away to control him. This was not what the situation required. She pushed her free hand upward, under his shirt, his skin warming her palm. He was already shuddering. "Oh god, Violet. You . . ."

And she didn't hear another word.

Chapter 56

Taken
Katherine

Miss Violet dismissed me for the day when she saw me still struggling to keep my cough under control. Since what she considered her near-death illness had passed, she was fearful of recontamination. Back at my house, in the tiny, sparse kitchen, I readied tea. Mama and Yale were out, and I hoped that the latest infusion would finally clear away the fatiguing illness that had been coming and going at me like the ocean tide.

I sliced several pieces of ginger from the root and slid them into boiling water. Next I ground more ginger in the stone mortar, losing my grip on the pestle, my strength sapped from the persistent cough. Grateful the nausea I'd experienced earlier in the week had dissipated, I wished I could get rid of the congestion in my chest and soothe the burning in my throat. Despite my stuffed nose, the scent of ginger hinted at the comfort that would follow this tea.

I removed the pot from the fire to let the mixture steep and took my recipe book to the table to sit. I turned to the original recipe that Winnie had created and added a note about the extra amount of ginger I used. It had been months since I started working for Miss Violet and she bought me this book of Winnie's cures and recipes from McCrady's. As I used it and added my own recipes, homemade medicines, and a section for my notes about serving as a conduit from the living to the dead, I began to feel connected to Winnie, our worlds coupled through words on a page. I couldn't help wondering why she would have gotten rid of a book that contained so much of her hard work and a chronicle of her life.

I coughed, eyes watering; the act of expelling whatever was ailing me seemed to just make my coughing worse. I wiped my eyes and refocused on the book. My illness hadn't been bad long enough for me to take to my bed for extended periods of time, but it had slowed me down, providing more than enough time to review Winnie's book. While I had waited for an infusion to steep, or in between sessions as Dreama, I found myself yearning to meet Winnie, wanting to find and read *Book One*.

I'd attempted to make my own lozenges as directed by Winnie after reading the recipe. It was in making notes regarding my failure at the task that a notation caught my eye:

For Mrs. Johnson—Sore throat: Slippery elm tincture. Morning sickness? See Book I. Lozenges may be safer if with child.

I must have left out a vital ingredient for the lozenges because, though they were sweet, they were largely ineffective.

Now I paged back through the section that mentioned the lozenges to verify if I'd missed an ingredient but saw that I hadn't. I turned the page and read further.

This one I hadn't noticed before:

Cure for broken heart—literal, figurative: magnesium waters (resupply Bedford Waters), two hours sunshine, oranges, turkey stew—Book I recipe (turmeric—B. Smalley source)

Pink stone held by sufferer or laid on chest

Andrew balks at use of stones, even though the agate sample he holds dear is symbolic for Grangers. Doesn't want to believe. I fear I may need the broken heart cure for myself. Sometimes I feel with every beat of my heart my chest shrinks a little, ruining what was once the saving of my life. His narrowed gaze pins me, paralyzes me. He tells me it's worry I'm seeing, but I see the truth: it's disapproval he wears plainly. I want his love again. I want him to understand who I am and love me still. Please, please, please.

I drew back. Waves of sadness lifted off the pages, seeping into my skin, causing me to grip my chest, to think of Aleksey and my own broken heart. I traced Winnie's words. *B. Smalley?* I hadn't seen any mention of her on other pages, but up until I was sick I'd mostly looked for recipes. I stared at the writing. This Winnie knew a B. Smalley? Could it be Madame Smalley?

I turned the pages, looking closer. There were several other notations regarding stones, and a page that included drawings with added coloring of blue agate, geodes with outer, rocky earth-toned shells that when split open were full of purple crystals, blue, clear.

The ginger had steeped enough, and I poured the concoction into a teapot, the fragrant aroma filling the air. My raw, swollen throat barely allowed enough room for my cough to leave my body.

I added a pinch of ground cloves, drizzled in some honey, and stirred the liquid, remembering Aleksey that night in our secret garden dinner, the way he had taken care to treat me like a queen, even stirring my chocolate for me.

The memory made me smile, then the reality of Aleksey's absence, the look on his face when he struggled to make sense of what he'd seen at his mother's reading, made me fold over, coughing as though my body were trying to release every bit of Aleksey that had filled me up. His absence caused an aching similar to being held under water, wanting so much to breathe but knowing it was impossible. I pushed the honey dropper back into the pot and took my tea and spoon to the table.

Back at the table, I sipped the tea and read the second page that had drawings of stones.

Fluorite—blue, green, pink—selenite—like angel wings. The sketch beside that notation stopped my breath. I drew back, then looked closer. How had I missed these pages before? I pulled out the stone Aleksey had given me when I lost the glass crystals at *A Night for Mothers.* I ran my fingertip over its wings of stone, the smooth and rough edges cool and warm at the same time across my palm, and my fingers curled around it as though it had been carved just for me. I set it next to the drawing in Winnie's book to compare. Perhaps the rough drawing just accidentally looked similar to the stone Aleksey had given me.

I leaned back in the seat and crossed my arms. What had he said again? A book in a wall, right? He'd worked on a wall with Fat Joe, and they'd found stones and a book. He'd said Mr. Palmer ordered him to burn it. I compared my stone to the drawing in the book again.

Uncanny. Not accidental. It was exactly the same—the striations, clear spots, and wings—as the one I held. I held the stone to my chest, chills scrambling through my body. I thought back to the day that Miss Violet brought me this book from McCrady's. Winnie must have sold Mr. McCrady this book and hidden the first from her husband. Could they really be a set?

I stared at the book again. Impossible. He'd brought me this stone that was drawn in my book and he had another book—Winnie's *other* book? I exhaled and paged through it, looking for a notation that indicated Winnie's last name was Palmer. *Andrew, Winnie's husband.*

Aleksey never mentioned Mr. Palmer's first name. My skin tingled again. I was excited at the thought that Aleksey may still have the first book, that I might be able to retrieve it. *Winnie.* Her desperation wafted off the pages. I reread what she'd written about the way Andrew looked at her with disappointment. I placed my palm on the book where she'd written about her broken heart. *We're the same, Winnie. I understand.*

**

My cough shook me again, and I jostled a second cup of tea, the liquid splashing onto the table. The spill ran toward the middle where Mama had stacked newspapers and I'd put the small paint set and papers that Aleksey had brought for me that night in the garden. I would use the paints, as much as it pained me, reminding me that we weren't "us" anymore, but when the paints were used up, I would throw out the tin and be done with him once and for all. No. Somehow, I knew I'd never be rid of him.

I wish you could love me, Aleksey. Please, please, please.

I dipped a brush into water, moistening the brilliant sapphire blue that Aleksey had chosen for the tiny palate. I added it to the sky of the scene I'd sketched for Mama the night we'd supped in the garden. I smiled at what I'd drawn—Mama and Yale as I so often saw them, in the garden, kneeling beside one another, their hands in the soil. I'd painted them looking at each other, depicting a loving pause in their toiling. They were smiling, emanating utter contentment. I couldn't wait to make it perfect and give it to Mama.

I swirled the brush over the paper, watching the color fall in between some woven threads of parchment and rest high on the plateaus of others. The color was stunning. How could the man who I'd believed had peered into my heart and soul, the man who I'd believed loved me deeply, just turn away, disgusted, so cold? I thought the connection between us had been unique, as otherworldly as my ability to mediate, as enduring as the stars. I'd been so wrong.

I set down my brush and leaned back in the chair. I sipped my tea and moved the papers aside and noticed the front page of *The Des Moines Register*. "Political Labyrinth—Judicial Questions—Religious Answers?" I scanned the page, seeing familiar names. Judge Calder, Judge Harbison, Reverend Shaw, Alderman Feeney—all of them making promises of stopping crime, even the crimes of Dreama if it turned out she was a con.

I squinted at the paper. I practiced nothing untrue, but Judge Calder's words about Dreama made my blood run cold.

The jury on the phenomenon called Dreama is out. Being a measured man of the bench, I'm hesitant to begrudge the grieving women she helps or deny that Dreama provides some sort of salve for the soul. But I will commit to the idea that an investigation by the law, aldermen, and our very own religious men is in order. That, I support.

All the men commented on Dreama with none of them indicating any support for her. This angered me. I'd read for each of them quite successfully. The judge was especially partial to Miss Violet. That *must* mean something. She would protect me, wouldn't she?

I made a note in my book to bring this up with Miss Violet. At this point, if I hadn't even revealed to Mama my identity as Dreama, I needed reassurance that despite this investigation I was safe.

I closed my paint tin and gathered the other papers on the table, feeling as though I could use a rest. I bundled up the papers and clutched them to my chest. Heading toward the pile of discarded newspapers, an envelope fluttered out from between the pages. I set the bundle down and picked up the envelope. I recognized Aleksey's writing and could feel him as though he'd mailed himself inside.

I saw the postmark. He'd mailed it the day of *A Night for Mothers*. I set the letter down, not wanting to open it. He'd written it before he knew I was Dreama. I stared at it and shook my head. No. I tossed it into the garbage. Why would I read it? It wouldn't have anything I wanted to hear. Not after all he'd said in the garden.

I poured more tea and stared into space, ignoring the letter I'd tossed away. Trying to, anyway. Its presence just feet from me was powerful. Maybe I'd feel better if I read it. Maybe it would allow me to move on. Perhaps it would be comforting, hopeful somehow. Perhaps his letter would allow me respite, entrée into another world where we'd once been hopeful, in love. I wondered how long the letter had been in the house. It had gotten lodged between newspaper pages, nearly lost to the fire or to be used in the garden come spring.

No longer sleepy, I rushed to the trash can and snatched the envelope. I slid my finger into the flap and opened it.

Dear Sweet Katherine,

We just parted. My lips are still warm from yours. Though we are now apart, I'm positive our hearts still beat in partnership, same pattern, same pace. My being is intermingled with yours, our breath, one.

I couldn't wait to write this down by chance I wake tomorrow and not remember some part of the evening in the garden, some aspect of how it felt to have you so close, to feel as though we might have passed from one realm of earth and sky into another.

For someone like me, who appreciates the practicalities that anchor my mind to the law, the words that shape it, and the arguments that play out in court, I can't believe how deep and strong my feelings are for you. Until recently, great distance lived between us. We only knew one another as friends, as children, and now it's as though we'd never been apart.

It was odd to take you to your old home, I know. But as you've seen the sparse living quarters I'm accustomed to back on the prairie, I wanted you to understand that I've seen how you lived from the beginning of your life and wanted you to know I aspire to bring that back to you. A large home with books. A home that has an artist's studio befitting your talents, with high ceilings to let your laughter breathe but keep it close enough to hear it up and down the halls, to look out my library window and see you on the

garden swing, your head back, hair flowing behind you . . .
I'll save this talk for when we're together again.

My life, always simple, straight, narrow, my feet on the sure path, I thought I had everything. But I didn't know I was only half-alive until we met again. It was then I knew I was put in your path to protect you yet again. I can't believe what I feel, but I promise to bring you love and light and provide safety from all that threatens you. That, I can say for sure. I don't expect that you feel all of this for me as common sense advises that it's much too soon. As for me, it's as though magic has been worked over me, like those stories you used to read.

I understand now that although I wrote to you a few times since you left the prairie, I didn't realize I was searching for you all along. I am sure we are intended to grow in friendship and affection. Though our lives right now are on different paths, I trust our paths will join someday. Someday, yes, I know it.

It's important for me to tell you something I've learned since coming to Des Moines and reading the law, writing briefs, and observing Mr. Stevens in court. Those with the least have no representation and are taken advantage of at every turn—their enormous deficits in education, finances, housing, and health are rarely addressed. And yet those with the most, those who have everything, will fight for the smallest crumbs, not even recognizing their wasteful ways, their own small hearts. I want you to know that though I wish to own a proud home with an abundance of, well, everything, I intend to be a person who will defend the least of us, protecting those I love like a warrior keeping safe the nation's treasure. I will be that person.

So, until I see you again, know that I've tucked away the memory of the night in the garden like a page torn from a fairy tale, folded and kept for later.

When I arrived home, I found a letter from Ma. She's coming to visit. I'm pleased. She wants to call on your family. There's so much to say on the subject of her visit, but

I want to talk in person as her reason for coming is a bit sensitive, something that might make you unsure of her faculties or question my own sanity for entertaining her whim. The subject is not something to discuss in a letter. More soon.

Yours always and forever,

Aleksey

My hands shook. I pressed the letter onto the tabletop. Finally, I understood. His magical sense of attraction could so quickly be tamped out because his letter made it clear that even he saw our connection as unexplainable, clearly fragile. Hardly enduring. And his mother and her visit. Her reason for coming, what he could not tell me, was that she planned to see Dreama.

I want to talk in person as her reason for coming is a bit sensitive, something that might make you unsure of her faculties or question my own sanity for entertaining her whim.

But now it made even more sense. His reaction to me being Dreama was partially due to my lying but also clearly rooted in shame that his mother might have been seeking solace in someone he saw as a con, an embarrassment, a shame.

I folded the letter and slid it into the envelope. I tucked it into my bag with the paints. This letter revealed Aleksey's feelings for me as I had experienced them before he found out who I was. That girl, the one who made him remember the way his fingers felt on her skin, the way his heart sped up being with her . . . But that girl didn't exist for him anymore.

Sitting there, reading his words, knowing they were no longer meant for me, well, I didn't think sunshine, oranges, turkey stew or any other concoction could cure my broken heart as Winnie's book had suggested.

**

I sat at the table, tea cold, heart numb, blood rushing, pulsing through me. I couldn't think about it any longer, about him anymore. I ignored the worsening cough. I needed to busy my hands, my body. I went to the cellar to gather some rosemary and thyme. I took my paints, papers, and the painting I was doing for Mama to hide it away until it was dry and ready to present to her.

Winnie had written, *Sometimes I feel with every beat of my heart my chest shrinks.*

I know what you mean, Winnie.

I visualized that happening, wishing to close off one's heart and feel nothing, no reminders of what once was. Family was the most important thing in life. I had Mama, Yale, Tommy. That was where I would set my mind. I'd work even harder to secure my independence, to raise the funds to buy a little cottage. And I'd find the right time to confide my hidden self to Mama. She'd be angry, but not in time.

I sprinkled some thyme and rosemary into six beaten eggs and poured the liquid into a crust to make an egg pie for supper. I was closing the oven when the kitchen door swung open and knocked into the wall.

Pearl tripped through the doorway, hair springing out from under her hat, crystal-green eyes wide. She dove for me, grabbing my forearms tight as a vice, and drew deep breaths. "They took her," she said.

My mind flew past the names of every "her" she could mean. "Who?"

She released me, pushing her hat off her head, knitting her fingers into her hair. "Yale."

I couldn't fathom what she meant. "What?"

Pearl went to the coatrack and grabbed my coat. "Hurry."

Pearl was helping me into my coat since I was too stunned to move on my own account. "What happened?"

"At the children's party in town. Tommy and me took her. She climbed a tree, and we turned away for a moment, *just a moment*, I swear, to see the juggler. *Just a moment.* And that was it. She fell. Some doctor was there, and some woman working for the courts. Judge Calder was there. Judge Smython, two officers. That greasy alderman O'Hara."

I shook my head. "Mama?"

"Running errands."

I ran the list of names through my head and the fact it was a party for children. "Was Mrs. Hillis there?"

Pearl buttoned my coat. "No, no, not her. I didn't know this woman with Judge Smython. But it was just seconds that we turned, Katherine . . ."

"Where's Tommy?"

"He's trying to undo this. He sent me for your mama."

"She's not here. I thought she was with Yale."

"She was supposed to come to the party, but she hadn't gotten there yet."

I covered my mouth. "We can't let someone else tell her this."

Pearl nodded.

"Why would they do this?"

Pearl's eyes filled with tears. "Oh, Katherine. Judge Smython. He skedaddled with Yale in tow as though he were saving her from the fires of hell. Can't piece it together why."

I pictured Yale, her sweet countenance, the way she must have been petrified, and still would be.

My legs buckled at the thought of her being at the mercy of strangers.

Pearl kept me upright. We had to get Yale back. I took a towel and removed the raw egg pie from the stove.

"Let's go. We need to find Mama."

Chapter 57

Strength
Katherine

Pearl and I ran as fast as we could. The mild air had turned sharp, cutting into my skin. I squinted into the wind and coiled the scarf tight around my mouth. My legs turned numb as I fought against the illness that weakened me. At the corner of Hurst and Hamilton, I stopped running, my cough bending me over. I pulled my scarf down to get fuller breaths in between hacks and lifted my head to see Pearl, looking over her shoulder, realizing she'd left me behind. She barreled back and took me by the shoulders, straightening me.

"Little farther," she said.

I pictured Mama, her empty arms, and desperation surged through me. I imagined the fear Yale must feel at being torn from her family's embrace. I certainly knew that misery, but Yale was so young, so backward. I imagined hands reaching for her, pinching, prodding. I'd been able to fend much of that off. But Yale would never manage. I choked, memories swarming me, paralyzing me.

Pearl squeezed tighter, her breath warm against my ear, my stomach churning with worry. "Almost there," she said. A stiff gust came up and knocked me forward, calling me back from the past.

And before Pearl had to nudge me again, we were off, pounding through the streets.

**

We reached the house where the party had been and found it empty. My heart stilled, dizzying me. Pearl took my hand. "Courthouse. That has to be where they are."

And so we headed back into the cold. Swirls of snow, like miniature tornadoes lifting into the air and sweeping across the sidewalks, pushed us back as we ran again.

In the courthouse, our footfalls echoed. We went into the first three offices we saw but had no luck. Finally, we were pointed in the direction of Judge Smythton's chamber. I tore open the door to find Mama being held upright by Tommy. I caught a glimpse of the judge's robe as he disappeared into a doorway at the back corner of the room. A man began to usher Tommy and Mama toward us. "The judge will see you in court. Not here, not like this."

When Mama lifted her gaze, her eyes glistened, filling with the tears she'd always kept private. I ran to her, pulling her into my arms, sheltering her from the sorrow swallowing her whole. "We'll get her back, Mama. We will." And as I held Mama tight, her body quaking against mine, I thought I'd been transformed. All the weakness I'd felt over the years, the way I'd been pushed one way and pulled another, all of it disappeared, and I knew Yale would come back to us. I would make it so.

Chapter 58

Taking Charge
Katherine

I stayed up all night with Mama, doing my best to console her. Nothing I said was helpful—how could my reassurances really be trusted? In her eyes, I was still a child. What could I know of the world? But I felt it in my gut that Yale wasn't lost to us. I would do what was needed to get her back. Mama forced a smile at my declaration and let me yammer on, accepting my words and promises though she clearly didn't believe them.

Most of the night she was silent, trapped in her despair, listening to me go on. Tommy and Pearl would come in and then leave, planning yet another way to convince this judge or that to help us. Mama would nod at their latest ploy like she nodded at my promises. For the second time in my life, I didn't shrink in the face of my troubles. What I'd given her at that point might have only been words, but I knew Yale was coming back to us, I knew it in my bones.

At one point, when I couldn't watch Mama's suffering any longer, as her pain began to leach out of her skin, sharpening the planes of her face and shrinking her body right before my eyes, I pulled her into a hug. She let me hold her, softening into my arms as I rubbed her back and whispered, "We'll get her back, Mama, we will." But soon it was as though any comfort she found in my embrace dissolved. She stiffened, drew deep breaths, and moved away from me to stand at the window and stare into her winter garden, eyes searching, I'm sure she was praying and wishing Yale would appear in the back, like spring sprouts. I funneled cup after cup of lavender tea into her, hoping it would have a calming effect. She paced the kitchen, then plopped into a chair at the table, spreading her hands, looking into her lap, making me wonder if she was silently calling Yale into her arms. I tried to fill them with her sewing, with mindless work. But nothing brought comfort. Every word I spoke fluttered past her ears, unheard, definitely unheeded.

I even turned to Tommy to secure some whiskey to mix into the tea as Mama's breath grew so rapid I thought she might lose all her air and topple onto the floor. After two hours of splashing the whiskey into her teacup, the alcohol took hold. At the kitchen table, I watched as Mama cradled her head in her hands, and she fell asleep like that, sitting straight up except for her head bowed into her palms.

The quiet that came with Mama's slumber pulsed in my ears with the ticking of the kitchen clock. The stillness called my aching muscles and sore throat fully to my attention. As I had plied Mama with what I hoped would be healing tea, I had swallowed my own share, replacing the splashes of whiskey I'd added for her with drops of honey to soothe my throat and curtail my cough. I steeped another cup of tea and went to the cellar to retrieve the watercolor I'd painted for Mama. It had dried nicely, and though I might have wanted to add more detail, I thought Mama could use it now more than ever.

At the kitchen table, Mama slept statue-still but for her breath lifting her shoulders just a fraction of an inch with each inhale, and I sank back in my chair, recalling the hollow

that James's death had created in Mama, in each of us. I
stared at the painting I'd made of Mama and Yale in the back
garden, kneeling together at the rose-bed, Mama brushing
hair away from Yale's upturned face. My eyes burned, finally
allowing myself to trace the events of yesterday in my mind.
Could I have helped more?

Should I have told Mama not to allow Tommy to watch
Yale? Had I even been told there was a children's party to
attend and that Tommy would be taking Yale? My throat
tickled and pricked as I fought to keep back sobs. We
couldn't allow ourselves to crack open and empty out, not
like we had after the Children's Blizzard. My head pulsed,
aching worse than I ever remembered.

It's not the same as James dying. Yale's alive. We'll get her back.

I thought of the lies I'd been telling about Dreama, how
Mama could not learn of my identity now. I needed to assure
her that Yale would be in her arms before she knew it. I
thought of Judge Smythton, his demand to see Mama in
court. A shiver spiraled down my spine. I remembered
passing Judge Calder's office. Him. He should be able to help
us.

His interactions with Miss Violet took many forms.
They were close, their lives and limbs intertwined in
inappropriate, intimate ways. Knowing that information
would help me now. I looked at Mama, her face peaceful as
sleep protected her from the pain of loss.

"I'll be right back." I smoothed her hair and kissed the
top of her head. I slipped out the door, through the hedges,
the air temperature seeming to drop with every step. I
entered Miss Violet's kitchen. The silence stopped me. I felt
the top of the stove. Cool. It was as though no one had
baked or cooked since morning. Maybe Miss Violet was sick
again and in bed. I scrambled from room to room. Someone
must be there. Dining room, front parlors, Miss Violet's
office—each one vacant. They must be upstairs, sunbathing,
studying, working? Flying up the stairs, I heard a thump

down the hall near the front of the house, coming from Miss Violet's bedroom. I pushed open the door. "Miss—"

I stopped short, my gaze going directly to Olivia, who was on her knees on the floor near Miss Violet's bed.

Olivia jumped, but when she saw it was me, her face flooded with relief.

"Where's Miss Violet?" I said.

Olivia brushed the boards with a rag and replaced a small Oriental rug over the boards where it belonged. She stood and moved the spindly bedside table over the rug.

"Now," I said, my voice screechy. "I need her now."

She finally turned to me. "She's in town. Don't know where. I just . . ." She adjusted the side table and shuffled some tiny china boxes near the base of the lamp.

"What are you doing?" I said.

"Cleaning. What else? Call me Cinderella."

She hadn't been quite so snappish with me in months. "Under the rug?"

"Dirt finds its way into everything, even under rugs."

"I understand the nature of dirt, Olivia. But Yale's been taken, and I need Miss Violet's help. Please think. Where is she?"

"I *don't* know. But I've ten things to get done before she returns and—"

I balled my fists. *"Yale's gone!"*

Olivia drew back as though I'd pushed her with both hands.

She sighed and tilted her head to the side and said in annoyance, "Glenwood exists for people like Yale. She's better off—"

"What?" I took a step toward her.

She stepped away from me.

"You already knew about Yale? That she's at that *place*? Does Miss Violet know?"

She shrugged and looked down at the rag she was running through her fingers. "You're so very naïve, aren't you? It's not an act, is it?"

Tears burned the corners of my eyes as I dug my nails into my palms. My head throbbed and my throat seemed to be closing, rawness creeping down my esophagus, making me acutely aware of my insides, aware of the illness I'd been trying to outrun. My ears felt stuffed with cotton. I pressed my hand against my head and forced myself to leave. On the way out, I said, "Don't ever say that again, Olivia. No one belongs in Glenwood, least of all my sister."

I fought off the urge to puddle to the floor and cry right there. Olivia's attitude was normal; her nonchalance reflected what most people thought of children, especially those like Yale. I knew that, but we'd kept Yale from all that. Mama needed me, and this time I was no longer a frightened little girl like I had been when we had to go to the prairie, when we left it. I'd bring Yale home. That wasn't naïve. That was simply how things were going to be.

Back in our kitchen, Mama was awake, my painting in her quaking hands. I ran to her and held her. "We'll get her back, Mama. I promise."

Mama let out a choking sob. I moved so I could see her face. I pointed to the painting I'd made. "That will happen again. You and Yale in the garden, smiling, sowing your seeds and your special secrets. But next time, it'll be *our* garden behind our own little cottage with a roaring fire and Tommy will be there, and . . ."

Mama drew the painting into her chest and closed her eyes. She nodded.

"I promise. I promise."

She opened her eyes. "You are so very determined."

"I am."

"But the situation's complicated, Katherine."

I saw a glimmer of the same look Olivia had given me when she called me naïve. "I'm not a child anymore, Mama."

She narrowed her eyes on me for a moment, then looked away. I understood her skepticism. I'd hidden so much of myself from Mama. How could I expect her to fully understand my knowledge of the world when I'd kept it all from her? I couldn't tell her now, not when she was reeling from Yale being gone. I would just have to prove it to her.

I turned away and coughed into my hand. I reached for a square of muslin on the table and covered my mouth as I hacked away. Mama rubbed my back, and I turned to her when the coughing fit passed. "When Miss Violet gets back, she'll help. She has money, Mama—a lot. She'll let us use it to get Yale back. That must be it, right? They want money and will release her when we pay. So you can sleep, Mama. I'll work on your coats for Elizabeth Calder. I sewed so much at the Christoffs' I could do it half-awake. But you need to rest. In bed. I'll fix this. All of it."

Mama's complexion had grayed, and her eyes were unfocused as she looked as though her thoughts took her miles from me. She mumbled things to herself, leaving only a few decipherable words here and there.

"Can't. I can't. Can't," were the only words I made out.

"Can't what?" I said, leaning toward her to hear better, holding her hand in both of mine.

She met my gaze with watery eyes. "I never should have let you go. I didn't know it would be so long. Yale's so cold. I know she's cold. I didn't, I can't—"

I squeezed her hand. "It's all right. I'm here. And we'll get Yale back. We *can*."

I went to the parlor to retrieve the material and sewing box to get started on finishing the work Mama had promised Elizabeth Calder while I waited to talk to Miss Violet. She'd built up plenty of influence in Des Moines, and it was time for her to use some of it for my family.

When I returned to the kitchen with the material, Mama was at the stove swirling honey into a cup of tea. Her posture was straight, her face steadfast, not full of fear. She was determined, like me. She swept through the kitchen over to me. "You're the one who needs to get to bed. You're getting sicker," she said. "*You* need to rest."

I exhaled deeply and set the material on the table. Relief. Mama wasn't going to come apart as she had when she'd boarded us out all those years ago. I could set aside my fear that she might disintegrate from the inside out for the moment. "No rest yet," I said. "We'll finish this set of coats and get Yale back. Then we'll both rest."

Mama looked at me, questioning. But then she lifted her chin in that way that she did when she was gathering her strength and pride, and she gave me a smile. A little one, but it was enough. She believed in me, and that was enough. I *could* do this, and she knew it, too.

Chapter 59

Column B
Aleksey

Judge Smythton slammed his gavel. It brought a smile to Mr. Stevens's face, but Miss Hawthorne flinched at the sound as though she'd been rapped between the shoulder blades. She'd wasted considerable funds paying lawyers to fight for her right to call a piece of the meteor shower of 1879 her own. Mr. George looked miserable, too. And he'd won the case. My boss's client had nearly suffered the loss of his chunk of rock, but I knew why his victory made him frown. How could he be happy? He would no longer have a reason to stay in contact with the woman he loved. Appeal? I found myself hoping she filed an appeal just to see the broken-hearted client smile again.

This heartbreak in court reflected back at me like blazing sun, making me think of Katherine. I realized I wasn't breathing and forced myself to inhale, to make my body work again.

Mr. Stevens gripped my shoulder as we headed toward the judge's chambers as he'd requested we do. Opposing council followed behind.

"Tough one, Hazlet," Mr. Stevens said.

Hazlet shoved his papers into his case. "All in a day's work. I knew it was tricky for us."

We entered the chamber, and the judge gestured to a credenza. "Drink up," he said. Our opponent sprinted to the bottles, selecting his glass.

I wanted to leave the courthouse now that the case had concluded, but I'd been given my orders, and until I was a lawyer with full rights, I would do as I was told. I glanced at the clock over the judge's desk. Judge Smythton gestured toward the credenza again. "Counselor, drinks."

"No thank you, Judge," Mr. Stevens said. I exhaled, glad that my boss didn't accept. My buddies had their share of drinks—heck, I'd had my own—but not on the job, not in a judge's chamber, not with a judge.

I squinted at the cut-glass bottles that lined the table. It was my first time in Judge Smythton's chambers, and I was surprised to see that he had liquor there and that our opponent was so comfortable drinking right here.

"Pour me one, Hazlet." Judge Smythton eyed Mr. Stevens and me and sliced his hand through the air in our direction. "Teetotalers. More for us, Haz."

Mr. Hazlet raised his glass. "More for us." He stalked across the chamber and gave a glass of amber liquid to the man who just decided the case against him.

"I've asked you here," Judge Smythton said, "because I need some help with a case. A few cases, actually. Children." He sipped his drink. "It's not like I didn't know you'd turn down my offer of booze. You're a good, wholesome man, and this one, this Mister . . ." He pushed his glass in my direction.

Mr. Stevens glanced at me with a confused look on his face before looking at the judge. "Mr. Zurchenko."

"Yes, you and your student are quite the team. I've heard so for months, and now I've seen what they mean."

Mr. Stevens gave the judge a sort of bow, and I could see that he was confused about our invitation into chambers.

"I'll be frank," Judge Smythton said. He pulled out his chair and sat. "The time has come for us to settle up, Stevens."

Mr. Stevens knitted his brow.

"I've got some women about town squawking about children and vagrants, and when Judge Calder and the others promise to clean up the streets and do away with criminal behavior, the women squeal like pigs about children not being criminals. They cry and bleat about horrid Glenwood and the treatment offered there. On and on it goes. Delinquents shouldn't be in jail, they say. Until one of them is ripping their handbag from their arm while shopping at La Reines. Then I hear them screaming to be saved, to throw the pricks in the slammer."

Mr. Stevens laced his hands behind his back and rocked forward. He was a confident, good man, but I could see from his fingers turning red then white that he wasn't comfortable with this conversation. He cleared his throat.

"Back to Glenwood, Judge. What exactly are you saying?" Mr. Stevens drew out the word Glenwood, and I knew he was agreeing with the assessment of whatever women Judge Smythton was referencing.

The judge opened a drawer and pulled a paper out. He flicked it with his finger and offered it to Mr. Stevens. He read it, clearing his throat again.

"It's a list," Mr. Stevens said, shrugging.

"Yes. These children were either neglected or delinquent, and they were processed and sent to Glenwood or Sheridan Workhouse. Being an intelligent man, no matter what you've said publically, I know you understand the need for places like Glenwood."

Mr. Stevens pursed his lips. I noticed his hands quake as he read the list again, rustling the paper.

Judge Smythton picked up his tumbler and raised it in my direction. "Your man here. He's reliable, right?"

"He's a student. Just learning. He can't—"

"He'll be fine. It's perfect. You don't have to do it yourself, and we still settle up. Twenty years is a long time for a deal to go unsettled."

Mr. Stevens looked at me, staring. I couldn't have been more confused about their discussion—doubly so since Mr. Stevens seemed to understand the vague talk perfectly. The only thing I was sure of was there was a threat in the interaction, and my boss was on the receiving end of it.

**

Once in the hallway, Mr. Stevens tore ahead, forcing me to speed up to keep pace. When we reached his office, he stalked to his desk and collapsed into his chair. He buried his face in his hands. I closed the door behind me but wondered if I should let myself out. Perhaps with a night's sleep, he could explain it to me. I pulled the door back open to let myself out.

"No."

I froze.

"Aleksey. Sit." He pointed to the chair on the other side of his desk. "Please." His voice cracked, and my heart pounded.

I followed his directive, waiting for him to talk.

He dropped his hands onto his desk and laced his fingers together. His hair flopped forward, and it was as if he had aged twenty years.

He exhaled and slid the paper across the desk. I glanced at it, clearly a list of names mentioned in the judge's chambers. "You're going to represent those folks on that list at a hearing at Glenwood—the ones listed in Column A. Column B is never getting a hearing."

"But I'm not a lawyer yet."

He stared at me.

"I don't understand. Even if I do a good job by them, it's wrong. It'll be appealed. I'm not—"

"A lawyer, I know."

"I don't understand."

"He wants you to fail one way or another. It shuts up the screaming housewives who might stop him from getting paid to send children to various work farms and asylums. Some children actually need to be there, by the way. But if kids come back from Glenwood too quickly, the fee isn't paid to the judge."

I drew back. "That place is worse than the streets in some ways. You said so yourself after we met with Mrs. Hillis and the others. I've seen the despair when you had me go to those hearings."

He waved me off. "Just get acquainted with the files. More information to come."

My stomach tightened. I was stunned that Mr. Stevens would want me to do this. It wasn't like him at all. "Tell the judge no. I can't do that. I won't. It's not fair to the children, and I don't want to ruin my chances as a lawyer. What if someone finds out? Not that I'd do it, anyway."

Mr. Stevens shook his head. "You'll be fine if you do it. If you don't, that's where the trouble lives. I promise you that."

I ran my tongue over my dry lips, wanting to down half a gallon of water. "Why on earth would you agree to this? What trouble?"

He stared at me and shook his head. This wasn't the man I'd seen at meetings with parents and leaders in town, the man who stood up for children.

"My god, that judge just strong-armed you. Expose Smythton, and he'll be removed from the bench, then you can run the hearings. You'd win for sure. You understand these cases."

Mr. Stevens's face went white. "Not possible."

"Sure it is. Write this up and go to another judge with the evidence." Even as I said it, I knew . . . what evidence?

"I can't. It would harm my family. You're a good man, Aleksey. But you're young and don't yet understand how complicated the world is. You see the world in stark contrasts, right and wrong."

"Like the letter of the law. The way it's written."

He rubbed his chin. "You know it's not that simple. I won't harm my family, Aleksey."

"Harm how?"

Shame spread over his face. He'd done something that Judge Smython knew and was holding over him. I could feel the weight he carried.

"You can do something about this. Just own up to whatever it is. I'm sure your family would—"

He pounded the desk twice, making everything on it shudder. "Just do this, Aleksey. It's taken twenty years for him to come back to me to ask this favor, as distasteful as it is. Just do the hearing, and no one will know the better. The children on that list . . . most likely, every single one needs to be there. But a hearing will make it appear as though someone was looking out for them."

My throat tightened. No way would I do something untoward. There had to be another way. Mr. Stevens seemed to have shrunk behind his desk. I looked at the list again, each name conjuring up images in my mind—Clara Best— age three, imbecile. I could envision the girl, probably slight with dirt-smudged cheeks and chin. Ned Wright—age nine, vagrant, vandal, thief. I imagined a bruiser, a kid with holes in the knees of his trousers and scraped knuckles, but with fragility in his eyes. I stopped reading.

"Most of those kids actually do belong in Glenwood," he said. "The rest will get out when the administrators realize there's nothing wrong with them. They'll get paid, then let them free." He rubbed his eyes.

"But why do any of this?" I said.

"Money for children. Power. Cleaning up the streets so the papers print that the judges are tough on crime. Why else? The judges, half the ministers, the aldermen. They soap up and bathe in their power every day of their lives."

I couldn't have felt more let down if I'd found out my own mother was stealing from orphans. How could these men of great position, with their credentials and education and supposed morals, behave in such a way?

"In a way, the kids are lucky," he said, his voice thin, clearly not believing his own assertion. "They get fed in jail and housed at Glenwood. There's a chance they'll be helped while there."

I forced myself to look at the names in Column B—the children who would receive no help, no help from me. I scanned down the list and my body temperature dropped when I saw the name Yale Arthur—age four.

I blinked and looked at the name again. It couldn't be right. "Who wrote these names?"

"Smythton's secretary? Who knows?" Mr. Stevens said.

It had to be Katherine's sister, yet it couldn't be.

"You can do this, Aleksey," Mr. Stevens's voice drew me back to the larger situation.

"When?" I said.

"Two days or so," he said. "I'll arrange your transportation and speak to Palmer to make sure you have time off if you need me to. Don't think too much on this. It'll be easier."

Now my hand was shaking. I folded the list and slid it into my coat pocket. I didn't know what this was about, but I knew I had to get Katherine's sister back.

I ran into the darkening day, wanting air as much as wanting to be back at the farm. I chugged to the corner where Palmer would pick me up. The sun was setting; pink and orange swathed the sky as snow began to fall. It had been a balmy forty degrees just hours before. Now the moisture in the air crystalized, snowflakes popping into existence right in front of my eyes like tiny colorless fireworks. Katherine must be insane with grief. I had to help get Yale back.

Chapter 60

Sick
Katherine

Mama and I finished a few coats, slower than I'd have liked. The sickness that I'd kept at bay for so long tightened its grip. My head pulsed, and every time I took a deep breath, it led to a coughing fit. Mama would pat my back. She kept her swollen heart quiet, but every once in a while she would go to the window, peering into the yard, unmoving. The weather had swung in temperature again, and heavy, thick dollops of snow fell, covering the winter garden quickly and quietly.

I didn't know how much longer I could keep sewing as sick as I felt. But I wouldn't go to sleep until I'd spoken to Miss Violet. I pushed my needle into the spool of thread and stood. I put my scarf around my neck. I cleared my throat, barely able to speak above a whisper, it hurt so bad. "I'm headed next door. Miss Violet should be back."

Mama gave a little nod but didn't turn from the window.

"Would you like to come with me?"

"No. I have to be here. In case."

I went to her and hugged her from behind, my arms easily circling her waist. My eyes were heavy. I could've fallen asleep standing, Mama keeping me upright. My goal to finish the coats would have to wait. After I spoke with Miss Violet, there'd be time to rest. I squeezed Mama's hands three times, and she squeezed back to say she loved me, too.

I moved toward the door, glancing over my shoulder, dizziness causing me to stop mid-stride. I rubbed my temples, turning fully to Mama again. Stiff, clutching the windowsill, lost in the scene outside, she exhaled deeply. "Go lie down, Mama."

She didn't reply.

Dizziness shook me again. I held the doorknob tight, steadying myself. If I didn't go to Miss Violet's now, I might not get there. I told myself Mama was fine, that I'd be back in no time and then we'd have a plan and get some sleep.

I wove my way through the hedges, forcing my feet through the ever-piling snow to go where they didn't want to and dragged myself up the stairs to the back porch. I couldn't remember feeling this horrid in years. How quickly my cold had turned from irritating to debilitating. I opened the door to the kitchen. In contrast to earlier in the day when I'd stopped over, this time the kitchen had been occupied recently. Lamps were lit around the room, and my paintings were set up on easels, displayed in a way I hadn't seen them before. All sizes, all manner of scenes and people. I hardly remembered making most of them, but seeing them now, I realized I had. They lined the floor, the table, the sideboard, and dry sink. Everywhere. Wherever there had been any space, someone had displayed one of my paintings. I moved around the kitchen, running my fingers over the oil, most of it dry, some of them still soft and wet.

I heard footsteps coming down the back stairs—Miss Violet's. It was then I realized I didn't even have to ask her for money to get Yale out of Glenwood; we just needed to sell these paintings. From all that Miss Violet had said about my talent and demand, they would surely supply enough cash to get Yale back.

The dizziness that had started earlier was growing stronger. Chills ran through me. I grasped the countertop for balance. Miss Violet entered the kitchen and stopped when she saw me. "I want to sell my paintings," I said. I pulled the scarf tighter and turned to warm myself near the stove. It was then I saw that Miss Violet wasn't alone. Judge Calder stood beside her.

"*Your* paintings?" he said.

Miss Violet's eyes grew large, and she gave a small shake of her head. She then glanced at the judge. She cleared her throat. "Dreama's paintings aren't for sale, Katherine. And if they were, you wouldn't benefit. Of course, you know such a suggestion is—"

I shuffled across the kitchen and steadied myself, gripping the edge of the table. My shaky hand caused a painting to fall over, sending others to the floor. I looked at the canvases and coughed until my tightened chest could hack no more. I bent down to pick up the fallen pieces. On my knees, I rubbed my temples, my brain pulsing hard. I worked my fingers down around my ears and in back of my jaw, pressing, relieving the tension, if only for seconds.

I coughed one final time, a wad of phlegm coming up. Olivia and the other girls spilled into the kitchen and uttered a collective "eww." I ignored them and picked up paintings while Miss Violet helped, the judge watching over us.

I pulled myself up, holding the table with one hand and a painting in the other. I set the overturned easel right and settled the canvas back in place. The judge wandered over, staring at the painting. Miss Violet set some aside, and pulled his hand. "Let's go, Jeremy. You don't want to catch her illness."

"This one," he said. "She did it?"

I'd been working on this particular painting for some time. First I painted the couple, but I couldn't figure out what they looked like. As I returned to it again and again, I'd added more details—a library behind them, an emerald necklace of delicate posies on the woman's neck, and thick golden-brown hair that fell in waves over the woman's shoulders. I still hadn't gotten the features of their faces the way I wanted them.

"But I thought . . ." the judge said, now staring at me.

I forced a swallow down my smarting throat and leaned on the table, feeling as though my breath was no longer coming easy. "I need these, Miss Violet. Yale's been taken and—"

"Shush," she spat.

I flinched and then drew as deep a breath as my heavy lungs would allow. I rubbed my chilled arms, and Miss Violet flew over to me, grabbing my wrist.

"Keep your mouth closed."

"I did all of this, and I . . ." I drew in my breath again. My chest was tight, as though it was refusing air. My head hurt so bad that I couldn't think clearly. All I knew was that we needed Yale back.

"You said," I forced another breath, "we could vary our price depending on the reading and the wealth of the client." My knees were weak, and the dizziness was overwhelming me. "Been patient. Now it's an emergency."

Judge Calder stepped closer to the canvas. I watched his shoulders tense, the tendon in his neck tighten, snaking up from under his collar. If I hadn't been wracked with illness, I would have handled this differently, but I couldn't be diplomatic, not at a time like this.

He reached for the painting. I felt his anger as sure as I saw it, and I stepped away.

He spun and glared at Miss Violet. She squared her shoulders as though trying to prove her strength was equal to his.

"You told the kitchen girl about Elizabeth's—"

Miss Violet shouldered past me. "Nothing. I said nothing."

They whispered to each other, and I shook off my blurring vision, steadying myself, holding on to the kitchen chair. I saw them in profile, the ire in Judge Calder's face, the fear in Miss Violet's. She turned back toward me and pinched my elbow, moving me toward the judge. Anger flashed in her eyes as she tried to control her voice, and it frightened me. The doorbell chimed, and a quiet fell over the kitchen. Miss Violet turned her attention toward the other girls but dug her nails into me.

"Ladies. It's the Johanssons. Please take them up to the offices and begin. I'll join you shortly with the judge."

They looked at each other, unsure of what to do.

"Go, ladies. You're more than trained for this."

I was grateful not to be shuttled away with the rest of them. I didn't think I could make it up a few stairs, let alone two flights. All I wanted was to climb into bed and let sleep take me, to let deep rest heal my burning throat and lungs. I wanted Mama. My eyes burned as I forced another painful swallow.

The judge swung around and glared at me. "What gives you the right? How dare you intrude into my life, and my wife's loss, and paint it? Just because I knew your family at one time . . . Haven't you Arthurs done enough?"

I saw him pointing at the painting, but I couldn't formulate how the concept and the shapes came to me for the painting. I certainly hadn't done anything intrusive, but I remembered Tommy's reaction to the deer painting. I must have painted something that hit him emotionally. The judge turned to Miss Violet, a snarl on his face. "And you. I trusted you. And you told this girl about the inner workings of my marriage. Do you think you have that kind of entrée into my life? You don't—"

"Stop it!" Miss Violet spit out the words. She turned to me, and I faltered under her glare. I gripped the chair, trying to stay upright. "Did you spy on us, Katherine? After all I did?"

I shook my head, confused. I tried to clear my throat, which felt as though it had now swelled to three times its normal size. Miss Violet knew I frequently illustrated events I hadn't witnessed when I painted. Clearly, she didn't want to let the judge know of my abilities. "I don't know what you mean," I said. My voice was pained, hurt with not only the sore throat but with the mean way Miss Violet was treating me.

The judge took me by the wrist with one hand and pointed at the painting with his other. "This scene," he said. "This woman with two babies in her lap, and those two in the clouds. The toddler at her feet? That necklace? Five emerald flowers for her five angels. And that locket you painted, draped over her hand. I gave that to her—a lock of hair is inside it. From our one-year-old baby who died. My wife has never worn it in public. Never. Yet here it is in your painting."

I opened my mouth, but nothing came out.

Miss Violet pried the judge's fingers from me. "*Did* you eavesdrop, Katherine?" Miss Violet looked wounded, as though the possibility hurt her feelings.

"You know I didn't. I've been painting this for months. You saw me. You know—" I pushed the words over my dry lips. "That locket could be anyone's."

"She's right, Judge." Miss Violet shrugged. "You and I had those discussions over months. She couldn't have been listening in on all of them."

"Just like your brother," Judge Calder said.

"What?" I said, not understanding. I wanted to say I had never spied on Miss Violet. The room grew fuzzier, like the paintings in the dining room, and I hung on to the chair.

"Then how?" he said. "Did you have your brother tell you—"

"There aren't even faces on the couple," Miss Violet said, stroking his hair at the nape of his neck.

He shook his head and stared at me.

What did he mean about Tommy?

Miss Violet touched Judge Calder's stomach. She made circles over his shirt, that same intimate touch I'd witnessed at *A Night for Mothers*. "It's coincidence. Pure artistry, imagination," she said.

I felt my face crunch in confusion.

The Judge studied me, his face quivering with fear, awareness. "No."

Judge Calder looked back at the painting and then down at Miss Violet. He held her against him, wrapping her in his arms. He then pulled back. "You've both been lying to me. I know exactly who she is. And this is no coincidence."

A smirk crossed his face as he met my gaze, and chills fell over me in waves.

And then the room turned dark, and I felt as if the world had snapped shut.

Chapter 61

Mother
Violet

Violet and Judge Calder hoisted Katherine to her feet. "Hold tight, Katherine," Violet said. "We're taking you home."

"This ailment of hers best not be catching," Jeremy said.

"Just get her to her mother," Violet said through gritted teeth. As they exited the home and started across the porch, she saw Reed Hayes leaving Katherine's home.

"Mr. Hayes!" Violet shouted.

He paused for a moment, Jeanie coming out onto the porch behind him and then he took the stairs two at a time and was down the sidewalk, using his feet to plow a path through the snow. He pushed the gate, wiggling it to move the snow aside, and finally ascended the stairs to the porch.

"I'll take her," Mr. Hayes said, scooping Katherine into his arms as though she were a young child.

Jeanie burst through the gate, her face flour-white. She flew up Violet's stairs. "Katherine." She wiped at her wet brow. "She's shivering. I knew she should have lain down."

Violet felt panic, responsibility for Katherine being suddenly so ill. She watched Jeanie rub her daughter's arms, her whole body shaking, her face flushed deep pink, her lips dry and chapped.

"What happened?" Jeanie said.

"She—"

"Your daughter should be in bed, not out and about spreading her cough around to the healthy folks in town," Jeremy said.

Jeanie glared at the judge, her face reddening, her lips tightening. She turned her gaze to Violet. "Why didn't you send her home, then, Violet? If she's such a health threat to your clients." Jeanie's voice was high-pitched.

Violet should have recognized this; how could she not have? "I didn't realize it was more than a cough," she said. "She was just here for a moment—"

"I knew she was working too hard," Jeanie said.

"Perhaps a young woman needs more fresh air and fewer lessons in finance," Reed said. His eyes were hard on Violet.

"Perhaps you should take a meeting with Miss Violet and her employees," the judge said, "before you decide good finance isn't as important as good health."

"Take her to the house, Reed," Jeanie said. "Upstairs." Jeanie felt Katherine's forehead. "She's burning up."

Reed eyed the judge and descended the stairs. "Isn't it a little late for business on a Friday?" Reed said. "I heard there was going to be a benefit this evening to raise money for probation officers. I heard you and Mrs. Calder would be there."

"I'm not sure that's your business," Jeremy said. "No, I'm sure it isn't."

"Take her now, Mr. Hayes," Jeanie said. "Put her into bed."

Violet resented Mr. Hayes mentioning Mrs. Calder, as though it was a weapon. It certainly felt that way to Violet. Her anger turned to fear, just as it had that day when she spied on Jeanie and Jeremy on the porch.

Mr. Hayes raced toward the house, Katherine's arms flopping as he went.

"Reed Hayes sure is a godsend to you, isn't he, Mrs. Arthur? Being divorced and all, to have someone to help with heavy lifting," Violet said, emphasizing Jeanie's marital status for the judge's benefit.

Jeanie got a glint in her eye. She knew that Violet was implying that Jeanie and Reed were doing more than just working on seeds and tilling. "Our work's in the garden." Jeanie exhaled and started down the stairs.

"Gardening in the dead of winter, are you?" Jeremy pulled himself up taller and patted his belly. "Mr. Hayes is a good Christian man. Upstanding professor. Dr. Hayes he will soon be, right? Won't have time for digging around in the dirt with a divorcée. Won't be proper."

Violet watched hate radiate from Jeanie toward the judge.

His smirk, the investment he seemed to have in making Jeanie uncomfortable, tightened Violet's belly. *Was* something happening between these two? Had she dismissed her suspicions too easily? Had she banked too hard on her own sexual prowess, misinterpreted his affection for her?

Jeanie hurried down the stairs. "I don't have time for this. My daughter needs me."

Violet scowled at Jeanie's back as she caught up with Mr. Hayes, noting for the millionth time how tattered her finery was, yet her carriage, her bearing, all the knowledge she embodied, would never be made threadbare. And this history with the judge . . .

Jeremy went back into the house, and she watched as Mr. Hayes and Jeanie disappeared next door.

"I'm sorry, Jeanie," Violet said to herself.

Watching Jeanie Arthur and Reed Hayes rush Katherine away brought a sense of loss, of being pushed away from a girl who she'd come to care for.

But Katherine wasn't hers. And truthfully, when it came to the judge, she'd been more concerned over his anger than how he mistreated Katherine. When had she started making such stupid mistakes? She peeled through her memories for a date, a time, an event. It wasn't one thing. In two areas of her life, love had grown, right underfoot, right inside, yet completely unnoticed by Violet until it was far too late.

**

Violet remained outside. Snow piled quickly, covering the tops of her shoes. She could hear Olivia playing "Moonlight Sonata" as Jeremy entered the house not waiting for Violet. She wasn't ready to go back in. She wrapped her arms around her waist and watched Jeremy stand near the window, holding the painting of his wife.

Violet's teeth chattered as she stared at the Arthurs' doorway, unable to move. Was Katherine all right? Before long, Reed Hayes blew through the door, leapt down the steps, and hopped into his wagon. Violet swallowed hard. He must have been going for a doctor. She should have offered to do that herself. She shook her head and laid her hand on her belly. *Mother.* She wasn't fit for the title.

Chapter 62

Tears
Aleksey

Outside Palmer's front door, I buttoned my coat up as high as possible, tucked my scarf into the collar, and squinted into the biting wind. Heavy snow carpeted the land, and the cows were stuck in snow up to their necks. The pathways we'd cleared to and from the barn had been covered again from the new and blowing snow. Evening was falling, and it was time to make sure the livestock made it safely back to shelter.

The fall had been very warm and wet, and the winter swung between frigid, snowy days and mild, drenching ones. The day I was to head to Glenwood, snow made the roads impassable, and I was relieved, but only partly. I couldn't stop thinking of Yale locked away, being neglected or abused. If there was something I could do to help those children, and Yale specifically, I'd do it. With snow piling up, I'd waited for the driver to take me to Glenwood, but he never showed. I tried to make my way to town twice to meet with Mr. Stevens, but the winds had whipped the snow into blinding sheets, keeping me from getting anywhere. Like so many times on the farm, I was grateful to have physical chores to occupy my hands when my mind wrapped itself around Katherine.

Like the unstable winter weather we'd had, I found myself careening between being angry at her lies, at the jeopardy she put herself and possibly her family in by choosing such a dangerous line of work, and understanding that her choice may have been made out of desperation. I jammed the shovel into the snow and tossed a pile off to the side, forming a two-foot wide path. Maybe I had overreacted. *Could* I trust her? The love and protectiveness I felt for her might not be enough to forge a life together. And that crushed me. I shoveled more snow. Harold worked the end of the path closest the cows, protesting their frozen obstacle. I could hear him talking to them, telling them they would be warm in the barn very soon. In my mind, I repeated the same sentiments to Katherine and Yale, though the path to their safety was completely obscured by more than just a winter dump of snow.

**

Back inside, Mabel warmed chocolate for Palmer, the fellas, and me. She'd whipped fresh cream into peaks that she plopped on top of each of our mugs. Fat Joe stood and took Mabel's hand in his. "I'd like to announce that I've asked Mr. Palmer for Mabel's hand."

He grinned at her. For a moment, she appeared startled, and I wondered if he had even asked her to marry him or if this was news to her, too.

She turned toward us and broke into a great, easy smile. Different than I'd ever seen her wear. "And I said yes!"

Palmer backed out of the room, his face stony. We all cheered, slapped Fat Joe on the back several times, and gave Mabel hugs, wishing her all the best. I was last in line to congratulate them. I remembered Joe's crass retelling of the first night Mabel had gone to him with amorous intentions. He'd changed so much since then.

I hugged Mabel. "You've got a good man, Mabel. You've chosen well." When I pulled away, there were tears in her eyes. She cupped my cheek. "Thank you, Aleksey. You've always been a gentleman. Someone will be very fortunate to rope you in."

I shook Fat Joe's hand, and Mabel's words sank in. Would there, could there ever be another? I slipped out of the kitchen and went to my room to organize my books and notes for when the weather broke and I could give Mr. Stevens the news that I hadn't made it to Glenwood at all. Was it possible that the Arthurs had given up custody to Glenwood? Would that explain why she was in Column B? Reading through the files I'd been instructed to take with me, I saw that a number of the children in Column B had been turned over by their very own parents. I couldn't imagine that was the case for Yale, but if it was, I needed to know. Not every child had a file with long notations; many only had their name, age, and date they were processed.

Out of the corner of my eye, I saw a flash of brown scuttle along the baseboard. Mouse. I had a lot of work still to do, but rounding up a mouse would mean more busywork for my hands. I opened the bottom cupboard under the dry sink to retrieve the trap we'd been using all winter.

My fingers brushed the familiar burlap and leather that covered Winnie Palmer's book. I'd forgotten I'd stowed it there after making the cure for Mabel's bellyache.

I pulled it out and set it aside. I sighed, distraction easily drawing me from one task to another these days. It really had been a helpful book. The mouse could wait, enjoy its freedom a little longer. I paged through the book yet again. A section of it I hadn't paid attention to before caught my attention. There was a drawing of a stone, colored pink with a delicate dye or paint of some sort.

Rose quartz: heals a broken heart, imparts healing for illness.

My bear of a husband with his sodden brow. Cool rags helped for a time. I lay a stone on his sternum to heal his fever and infuse his heart with the love he once carried for me, just for me.

Palmer must have been terribly ill at one point. She had listed cures for every illness Aleksey had ever known. Some of them had names beside the cure and dates when people were healed or died. She was always clear in which date meant what. Some notations had drawings of stones along with the words. Often Winnie had included notes on why she thought some cures hadn't worked for some people. In one instance, she referenced the farmer next door, the one Mr. Palmer did not speak to anymore. A few pages later in the book, she'd written more.

Comfrey is needed. Two farms over, it's growing. Get by tomorrow for Mrs. Sterling. I feel her demise coming like it's my own. I see her people coming to welcome her home. Beda S. was to bring the comfrey, but she's been jailed. I warned her, but she does not listen. Firstly, using the name Madame Smalley evokes a sense of theater, not real healing. If only that were the worst of her plan. Perhaps Andrew will go for me to get the comfrey. This one time.

I felt as though there was an actual story being told rather than a simple list of ingredients and results that filled much of the book. Madame Smalley. I remembered that day we were in the wagon with Palmer in town and a woman, Madame Smalley, had been arrested right in front of us on the street. She'd yelled for Palmer to help her, but he had turned away. Later, the newspaper said that she'd been found guilty of theft, conning people out of money with a crystal ball. Palmer would never discuss it with us, only mumble that we were not to mention her name in his house.

I turned the page. It felt thicker than the others, as though several pages were stuck together. I gently pulled apart the first two and scanned them, noticing that the ink was splotchy in places. I knew what the splatters were.

Winnie's tears. I'd seen the same splotches on the letters Ma wrote to relatives back in Russia after so many of my siblings died that awful year of the blizzard.

Mrs. Sterling died. I didn't get the comfrey in time. Andrew wouldn't help. Now Nell Hartly has fallen ill. I won't make the same mistake again. If Andrew won't help, I'll do it myself. Beda's bad judgment shouldn't keep my own husband from understanding I'm not like her. She's a dear, misguided friend, but I have an ability that's not a lie. I'm not a thief. But I won't continue to heal or mediate for others if such action dulls his love for me. He used to love me with all his heart. His face once lit up upon seeing me. No more. My heart breaks as I write this. I've stuffed my underclothes with rose quartz, fending off the pain of heartbreak that bores into my bones. I'll get the comfrey and cure Nell, then I'll bury the stones—hundreds that I cherish—and get rid of the books, as he asked. I can not believe he doesn't love me anymore. I will not believe that as long as I live. Please don't let it be too late.

I moved to the kitchen table and stared at the page. *I'll bury the stones . . . get rid of the books, as he asked.*

I thought back to the day that Fat Joe and I found the book and the stones in the wall, the way that Palmer reacted to it. I wondered if he ever saw this page, if he knew that his wife had listened to his request for her to stop with her healing. Healing, stones, cures . . .

I have an ability that's not a lie. I'm not a thief.

I shuddered as I reread those lines. I'd heard those words before. Katherine. I remembered the angel-wing selenite I'd given her and how it had instantly alleviated her anxiety at losing the crystal balls that night. It was as though my finding the book and the stones in the wall was meant to be, as though she had needed me to do so in order to replace what had gone missing.

Hundreds.

Hundreds of stones? There had been several inside the book, tied closed with the ribbon. There had been a few other stones in the wall that I'd brought back to the house—

blues and purples and clear stones—but certainly not hundreds. I felt a hand on my shoulder, and I jumped, turning, the book tumbling out of my lap.

"What the—?" Palmer said.

His face was twisted, angered. I stood and closed the book.

He snatched it out of my hand and bolted. I followed him into the keeping room. He lurched toward the fire, tossing the book toward it. I lunged and knocked the book away from the fireplace and into the corner of the room.

"What are you doing?" he said. "I told you to burn that."

"You need to read it," I told him.

Palmer raced toward the book, but I dove for it and rolled with it, clutching it, protecting it from him. I got to my feet. He charged me, clasping his hands over mine, but I jerked the book away and held my hand out, pressing hard against his chest.

"She loved you. She—"

He pressed forward again. I pushed back.

"You don't think I know that?" he shouted, sending a great shuddering into the room. "I know what she did."

"I don't think you do," I said. *"Read it."*

He stepped back and clenched his jaw. "I did read it. I read how she promised to stop healing and dealing with the dead and half dying. I read . . ." His voice cracked, and he turned away. When he turned back, his cheeks were wet.

Seeing him like that choked me. He'd read it? He'd read it.

"I read it."

Realization settled over me, and I finally understood. Those weren't Winnie's tears that had stained the pages of the book, but his. I couldn't speak.

Tears fell down his face. "I know she needed me to get the comfrey," he said, "but I wouldn't. That's when she went into the thunderstorm. That's when she died."

He spoke barely above a whisper, each word knifing the both of us as I imagined the lightning striking her, destroying their chance to make amends.

He shook his head. "Do what you want with the book. But understand this: I don't need a reminder of it. I know what I did. And I'll have to suffer it for the rest of my days."

I didn't know what to say. I wanted to tell him she must have forgiven him. She must have felt his love even when he had turned from her. I wanted to tell him not to blame himself.

But I couldn't form the words and make them leave my mouth. How could I say such things when I myself was doing the exact same thing to the woman I loved?

Chapter 63

Distorted
Violet

Violet bit her thumbnail, staring through the kitchen window into the snow-covered yard. The footprints Katherine had made when she arrived earlier, before collapsing, long since covered. The winds finally fell away, and coin-sized flakes settled on the hedges, maples and apple trees. Unlike the quieted winds outside, Violet's thoughts whirled, paralyzing her. Katherine's illness, Dreama, the paintings Katherine wanted to sell, Jeremy's upset at Violet keeping details from him about Dreama, Olivia's growing gin habit, and now this. Jeremy's apparent interest in Jeanie—something was there, but what, Violet couldn't say. Jeanie was preoccupied with her own work, her missing daughter, Yale, and Reed Hayes. She had no time to entertain Jeremy. What Violet witnessed on the porch was simply an innocent conversation between two people who once knew each other. And yet the anger between them was as tangible as the kitchen Violet stood in.

The stirring in her womb came again. She pressed her stomach and closed her eyes. Was this real? Violet had gone from suspicion she was pregnant to believing she wasn't, to just this very morning feeling distinct movement inside the growing pouch, to feeling nothing at all again.

Her breath caught. There it was. A foot? A hand? A bottom? She exhaled through pursed lips. The truth was taking hold like an infant curling her fist around her mother's finger. This reminding, a heightening of Violet's senses, brought the understanding that her life was forever altered from this moment forward.

She spread her hands over her stomach, part of her wishing the convex shape of her belly might pass like a winter storm. The time for such empty hope was long past.

Violet's monthlies were often unreliable, and it made it easy to ignore their absence. But now there was no more pretending her body's cycles were simply off. She was pregnant. And that realization had hampered her ability to problem-solve. All was going wrong at the worst possible time. Or was it? She thought of Jeanie Arthur again, the love for her children that fueled her. Even with one son dead and a daughter having been taken, her love kept the woman alive, gave her purpose. The loss she imagined Jeanie feeling gripped Violet's chest. Perhaps she was ready to experience that sort of love even with the pain that often came with it.

Her pregnancy skewed her emotions and her vision for her future. Run. She should just run. She would start toward the stairs, reminding herself that she'd stowed her suitcases in the attic. But then Jeremy would flash to mind, and she would find herself staring out a window, imagining sitting fireside with Jeremy, nursing a baby as he caught up with his work after a long day in court.

Like a velvet baby blanket, soft and comforting against her cheek, Violet would pull out the memory of the way Jeremy cared for her when she was sick, when she thought she had the flu. Oh, how he had loved her that day. But before she could make any of her fantasies reality, she had to actually divulge her pregnancy to him. But Jeanie ... Was there something there? No, he would not have interest in a poor divorced woman saddled with children, even if he'd known her before. No. It was impossible that he might hold interest for such a woman.

Jeremy had sent word earlier that he'd call later in the afternoon. She was excited and nervous, a swirl of eager anxiety turning with the baby. Whether she ultimately ran for her life or stayed with Jeremy, she needed Katherine to be Dreama at least one last time.

Violet dreaded the idea of Katherine being seriously ill. But for more than just the money she brought. Inside Violet, like the kicking baby, she felt an honest pull of affection for the girl. The notion surprised her as much as the realization she was pregnant. Her body had hidden the baby even from herself for months, in a way that was shocking and awe-inspiring. She could no longer deny it even though her belly wasn't large like other women she'd seen. Like her belly expanded slowly, barely noticeable, she felt a pull in her heart at odds with how she'd viewed Katherine all along. Her illness revealed that she'd grown to really like her. She covered her mouth. In a way, she loved Katherine. Was that possible? She'd lied to Katherine, manipulated her so that her business could grow. Was that something a person did who truly cared for another? Yes. Violet told herself her lies and manipulation were needed to protect Katherine. Perhaps that was the very definition of love?

Violet felt movement inside her again. She pressed her palm against her stomach, wondering what exactly she felt for the baby. Her baby. Just thinking the words brought a fullness to her chest. It was similar to what she felt for Katherine, but now there was more. There was a desire to ensure its safety over any other. She shook her head. For the first time in her life, she wasn't sure how to do that.

Should she tell the judge? It was too late for a doctor to help her. Run away? If so, when? Hide in plain sight and give the baby away upon birth? She thought of the ledgers and the money hidden under the floorboards in her bedroom. It wasn't enough. She needed one more big haul. Whether she told the judge or not, it was imperative she keep her nest egg close. That came ahead of everything and everyone.

**

Violet lifted the lid on the pot and inhaled. The chicken soup smelled . . . not too bad. She had attempted to find the cookbook she'd bought Katherine when she first began working for her, but she couldn't locate it. In a drawer in the pie safe, she'd found the pile of recipes that Violet had used before she hired Katherine. There was a simple recipe for soup that Violet had followed to the letter. She knew it would be missing all the special herbs that Katherine normally added to dishes to heal and cure, but this would have to do.

Hours before, not caring that Reed Hayes may have summoned a doctor, Violet had sent Bernice to fetch one, too. There was still no information regarding the results given to Violet. Though she had decided her own child was primary, she felt an obligation to help Katherine get better. She carried the soup pot to the Arthurs' and rang the bell with her elbow.

Jeanie's face was full of worry when she opened the door.

On sight of her, Violet lost her words. Had she ever had the right words to say in the first place? "I made soup." She held the pot toward Jeanie, who lifted the lid and inhaled.

"Couldn't find Katherine's recipe book, but hopefully it'll help. Somewhat, anyhow."

Jeanie opened the door wider to invite Violet in. "It should help once she can eat."

Violet followed Jeanie down the hallway to the kitchen and set the pot on the stovetop. "She's not eating?"

Jeanie crossed her arms, staring at the pot. "Maybe I should keep this out back until she's ready for it."

"Cold enough for it," Violet said.

Jeanie glanced at the clock. "Tommy'll be back in a few moments."

Violet grabbed Jeanie's hand as she walked toward the pot. "I sent for Dr. Rager."

Jeanie stopped and looked back at Violet, their hands still joined. "That was you? Thank you. He came. And went. And well . . . I'm not sure he did much. But, well, thank you."

Violet's nerves flared. She hadn't felt so unsure about how to behave since she was a child. "She's going to be fine. Just winter sickness, all the strange temperature changes."

Jeanie tilted her head as though considering the veracity of Violet's assurance. Jeanie shuddered, and Violet felt her quaking working its way from Jeanie's hand into hers, like electricity flowed through wiring. The two women held tight.

"I can send for another doctor if Rager wasn't helpful," Violet said.

"Thank you. But Mr. Hayes sent for one who said the same lot of nothing," Jeanie said.

They took the soup to the back porch and set a stone on the lid to keep it tight.

Violet wiped her hands on the front of her dress. The wind was stiff again, cutting straight through the fabric. "And Yale. I'll help with her, too. Katherine told me that she'd been taken from you before she fainted."

Jeanie's eyes began to water. She drew a deep breath and covered her mouth. "Anything you can do would be much appreciated."

Violet choked down the tension between them, but instead of turning and leaving as she thought she should, she swallowed Jeanie into her arms. "It'll be all right, Jeanie. I know it will."

Jeanie was so much taller than Violet that her cheek was at chest level as they embraced. Violet felt as though she'd been folded into the arms of her mother, whom she'd never met.

Someday it would be Violet comforting her own daughter. They pulled apart. And then Violet felt it right there, a catching inside her, something wrapping around her soul. She knew then that a mother moved through the world differently, *felt* the world differently than others, saw the world for all the ways it might take away the very things that made life worth living at all.

Chapter 64

Column A
Aleksey

The day after the blizzard, Palmer allowed me to use his small rig to head to Glenwood. As I neared the fork in the road that would take me in the direction of Yale Arthur, I could see it was still high with packed snow. Even if I cleared the way as far as I could see, it would make no sense to think the road might be passable farther away.

I took the road back toward Palmer's to let him know I couldn't complete my assignment but would need to head into town to report to Mr. Stevens. He grumbled and turned from me, sipping his coffee, tapping his fingers on the table, lost in thoughts he wouldn't share.

He had changed since our argument, since he revealed the truth behind his bitterness. He demanded more from us, delegating those chores he normally did himself to whomever had irritated him most recently. He averted his gaze from me every time we crossed paths and claimed recurring headaches were keeping him from eating dinner with us, preferring to take his meals in his bedroom near the back of the house. I repeatedly tried to apologize to him, knowing my possession of Winnie's book was the source of much of his mood.

Once I got to the courthouse and reached Mr. Stevens's office, I found him bent over his desk, his hair greasy, and his eyes red, narrowed with exhaustion.

"Couldn't make it to Glenwood," I told him. "Your man never showed today, so Mr. Palmer lent me his rig. The road was blocked."

Mr. Stevens coughed into his hand and gestured toward the chair across from him. I sat. "I know," he said.

I thought of Yale. "I'll go as soon as it's passable. Those kids should be released as soon as—"

"I already went," he said.

"How?"

"Before the storm hit. I dealt with the list."

I pulled out the paper he'd given me. "What about this girl, Yale Arthur?"

"What about her?"

"I'll take her back home. I know the family. They must be sick over this. They never would have given over custody. I know them."

He waved me over. "Let me see." I walked around his side of the desk and pointed to Yale's name.

He shook his head. "She's there by rights. Belongs there."

"No one belongs there. She's not neglected or—"

"She's in Column B."

"So what? A mistake was made. What difference does it make what column someone wrote her name in? It's a list on paper that can easily be lost or destroyed."

Mr. Stevens sank back in his chair. He looked as though he'd been wrung through with the laundry. "I did my best."

"What does that mean? What aren't you saying?"

"I arranged for the children who aren't imbeciles or dangerous or intolerable to be released in a few days. Just long enough for the checks to clear."

I shook my head and thought of Katherine and her mother and all the loss they'd experienced. "This is about money? That's it?"

He scoffed at me and rubbed his stubbly chin. This enraged me. I grabbed his shirt in my fists. "You don't care?"

"Problem children are caught up. Deals are made. Payment is transferred upon admittance to Glenwood. Because those who benefit are good, generous men they release children who aren't a good . . . well . . . fit for Glenwood. There're some children who aren't there as part of the —"

"The con job!" I pushed my fists into Mr. Stevens's chest, causing his chair to teeter back. I backed away, pushing my hands through my hair.

Think.

"It's no use. Aleksey. I owe two judges for a favor they did for me twenty years ago. There's nothing I or you can do. And put away your righteousness. If these children are on this list at all, they got there for a reason. They might not belong in Glenwood, and you know I don't agree with tossing little ones there willy-nilly, but they were *not* plucked out of the beds of safe, clean homes of the leading citizens of Des Moines." He spit as he talked, his face reddening. "I'm on the verge of losing my mind over this, Aleksey. I have a family to protect, and I don't need you adding to my burdens."

I stared at him. He was unrecognizable—physically and in character. I shook my head. I'd find another way. I went around the desk and gathered my things. I couldn't believe this man had gone from an upstanding lawyer to this puddle of uselessness in just days. "What does he have on you?" I said.

He looked away. It was then I realized, though I didn't want to break the law, I wouldn't allow the Arthur family another moment of pain. Not if I had a way to alleviate it.

"Mr. Stevens. Please."

He shook his head.

"I want Yale Arthur added to Column A."

His jaw went slack for a moment. "Don't ask me that. I just want this to be over."

"We can go to Judge Calder. Surely he—"

"No!"

I clenched my teeth, ruminating. "So he's involved too?"

"I didn't say that, Aleksey."

"Tell me."

"Don't ask for more, Aleksey. Just do what you need to do to finish your studies."

I felt the threat in his words, the sense that I should back off if I wanted to fulfill my dream of being a lawyer. Still, I couldn't let Yale stay where she was no matter what other information I decided to overlook. And farming. It wasn't so bad. If I was to lose my chance to be a lawyer over Yale, so be it.

"Certainly, you can get one little girl moved to Column A. She doesn't belong there any more than you or me."

"It says on the paper that she is an imbecile. She does belong there."

"She has a family who wants her. I don't care what label they gave her."

He stood, his posture rickety, bent over his desk, resting on his fists. "It's not that simple."

"I'll make up a new list. No one will notice. There are forty names on that paper."

Mr. Stevens stared at the desk.

Please.

"We sat together at those meetings with Mrs. Hillis," I said. "You heard everything she said about children like this. You know she didn't want them there."

He straightened further. "Well, Mrs. Hillis had to go to Louisiana. So, she can't help. You think the timing of this was an accident?" He rubbed his face with both hands, then finally met my gaze.

"You have to help me get Yale Arthur out."

He sank into his chair and straightened his lapels.

Please.

He pulled open a drawer and pushed a blank paper toward me. "Make a new list. But I can't guarantee—"

"Thank you," I said, grabbing his hand and shaking it.

"It'll be days still."

I studied his creased face, his crow's-feet having deepened since I saw him last. "I'll check back in two days."

He allowed me to sit at his desk and complete the new list, adding Yale to the column that would allow her release.

I started toward the door, wanting to get word to the Arthurs that I'd seen Yale's name on that list, to tell them I was doing something about it.

**

Outside Mr. Stevens's office, I nearly walked right past him. Something made me stop and look back again. Tommy Arthur. He stood beside a column near the stairwell, looking one direction and then the other. I went to him. He was out of breath and smelled of stale whiskey. "You all right?"

He grimaced, appearing irritated that I had come to him. I put my hand out to him. He took it. "Katherine's sick," he said.

I pulled back. "Sick? With what?"

"Don't know yet. She's a little better today."

She was better. That was good to know. But hearing this news sat heavy in my chest. "Should I get a doctor?"

"He's on the way."

"Does she need anything?"

He shook his head. "Not unless you can turn the illness away with a magic wand."

His tone was sharp, and I wondered if he'd learned about Katherine's own brand of magic. "You all right? You look under the weather, too."

"Mine's my own making," he said.

I wasn't going to lecture him about drinking right then, not when he was so clearly regretful and worried about his family. "I want you to know that I'm working on getting Yale out of Glenwood."

Tommy straightened and squinted at me as though he was going to jump down my throat. "You know about that?"

I nodded.

His expression softened. "That's my making, too," he said.

I lifted my eyebrows.

"You said you're helping get her out?" His eyes were wide, and I could feel his hopefulness at the idea.

"It'll be a couple of days, at least. But my boss thinks there's a way to move things along."

"I just took my eyes off her for one second, Aleksey. She was sitting on a tree limb, and she fell in a blink, and her arm . . . I just can't . . ."

His red, swollen eyes watered.

I grabbed his shoulder. "Get cleaned up and go to your ma. I'll stop by and check on them."

Tommy looked crestfallen. I knew he wanted to take care of his family, and he must be mortified to have caused this situation.

"If you were standing there, why'd they take Yale away?"

He shook his head and finally gave a big a shrug. "I don't know. I've surely made my own messes from time to time, but this . . . I've no idea."

We stood there thinking, quiet for a moment, and then I knew I needed to check on the Arthurs myself—sooner, not later.

Chapter 65

Veiled
Katherine

I opened my eyes. At least I thought I had. Had Miss Violet veiled me? I felt for the lace over my face but only touched skin. The world beyond my body was blurred, like rain-soaked windows.

"Shush," Mama whispered. Her hands, the soft press of her palm on my forehead, her ear against my chest as though listening for breath.

"My heart's fine," *I say to her, but it's as if she can't hear me. I think my lips are moving. I go in and out of mind and body, the shivering so bad I think my skin might shake off my bones. Mama pulls warm covers up to my chin, and I feel sleep come, pulling me farther from the room.*

**

Prickling heat spreads over my skin. I kick off the blankets. I hear voices somewhere in the house. "Mama?" *I need water, but she isn't near. Mama and a man enter, their words growing clearer as they near my bed. The man comes close, his face over mine; his breath smells* of onions. He puts some tubing around his neck, and I know he's a doctor. His rough hands work over my skin, cold in all the places Mama's hands had been so warm.

His touch is scratchy, painful, and I lose sight of him, lose sight of myself in the hazy, rainy-window view of the world again.

"Katherine?" I think I hear Mama say. "Can you hear me?"

"Was that the doctor?" *I say.*

I force my eyes open. Are they open? A brisk wind sweeps over my skin, setting me to shivering all over again. "It's too cold," *I say, but it's as if neither one hears. Mama and the doctor at the bedroom door, talking, pointing. Arguing? Their voices rise over my fever, my clogged brain.*

He leaves, and she comes back to me, her face sorrowful, her warm, pillowy hands on me again, pulling the covers to my chin. She puts her cheek against mine. "I love you, sweet Katherine. Please, please get better."

I think I'm reaching for Mama, trying to touch her cheeks in the same way she touches mine. I must have done it because she sits up, her face confused as we hold hands. I try to squeeze three times and say "I love you" the way we silently do, but she doesn't respond, so I suppose I couldn't do it.

The love on her face, the concern, gives me a sense of peace, allowing me to surrender to the pain that wracks my head, my throat, my chest.

She looks over her shoulder as though someone is behind her. I point, or I think I do. James. "James," *I say, but I'm not sure I got his name out.*

"James," *Mama says, and I feel a smile come to me. She heard me right. I force a nod. She looks over her shoulder again. She feels him like I do.*

"He's here," *I say.* "Look."

She shakes her head slightly.

"He's right here with us, Mama. Right here."

She shakes her head again. "I don't see him."

"Feel him." *I speak as clearly as I can.*

Mama looks frightened and starts to get off the edge of the bed. But then she settles back beside me. She holds my hand in both of hers and closes her eyes and draws a deep breath.

My vision returned, clear as a sunny day. I was still weighed under with fever and pain, but my mind didn't feel so cottony anymore. Mama, James—they were both as real as me.

"He watches over us, Mama."

Her face grew troubled, as though she could feel the second presence enter the room.

"You see her?" I said. "With the baby? Always, always with the baby. She's holding her out to you, Mama. The baby's for you."

Mama's perplexed expression grew sadder, and she looked as though she would cry. "Yale?"

My heart felt paralyzed at hearing Yale's name. Was the woman carrying Yale? No. Yale had been taken.

"She's lost, she's lost," Mama said.

The crushing pain in my chest, the sadness at Yale being gone, lifted slowly, like peeling away a heavy compress. Calm, peace came to me. "Don't be sad, Mama. She's safe."

Mama's brow creased and then she swallowed hard. She nodded as though she believed me, as though she knew what I felt, this surety.

I tried to reassure her with my words, but as I was telling her to trust me, my feelings, I felt my chest constrict with pain, and the coughing returned, shaking me, each expulsion of air burning my throat.

"You're getting upset." She shushed me. "Rest, rest, rest." She turned me on my side and patted my back. A chill came again, bringing the shivers, my mind fogging all over again. Why didn't someone close the window?

"Soon as I get you warm again," Mama said, "I'll make the poultice." I wanted to say more to her, but I couldn't speak. The pain belted my skull, pulsing with my heartbeat. I felt Mama lay with me, her arms around me, pulling me into her, nestling me into her body, keeping me safe.

Chapter 66

Useful
Aleksey

I drove to the farm as quickly as I could. Mr. Palmer had gone into town in the other rig, and I'd asked Harold to do my chores. I said I'd make it up to him when I returned. Katherine was ill, and Yale had been taken from them. I couldn't waste another moment. No matter what the consequences were.

I changed my clothes and was heading down the staircase when I remembered Winnie's book. It contained endless lists of cures. I ran back to the trunk and put it into my satchel along with the stones that had been hidden inside its spine when Fat Joe and I uncovered it. Silly as it may have been, perhaps even the suggestion of healing stones might help.

Harold stopped the wagon to drop me at Katherine's. He would head back to do both of our chores. I would owe him for such an act of kindness. Even with all that I kept from him about Katherine and the pain she caused me, he understood that she and her family were important.

"Just don't forget your studies, Aleksey," he said as I hopped onto the ground. "I understand Katherine's allure, but . . ."

I nodded to stop him from talking. "I know. I won't mess up." I cringed at the precarious position my relationship with Mr. Stevens was in at the moment.

A gust of wind bore down on us. Harold's hat flew off his head. I retrieved it for him, and he snapped the reins and pulled the wagon into the road, disappearing as he turned down the road that would lead him home.

I held my hat down against the wind and knocked at the door, but no one answered. I went into the street and looked up at the second floor. The windows were open, and I knew they must be there. I knocked again then let myself in.

"Mrs. Arthur? Katherine?" I said. The parlor and kitchen were empty. I took the stairs two at a time, finding the only room upstairs. I stuck my head into the bedroom doorway to see Mrs. Arthur kneeling beside the bed, holding Katherine's hand. The curtains whipped wildly, and from the doorway I could see Katherine was shaking.

I rushed into the room and startled Mrs. Arthur. She sprang to her feet and hugged me. "She's getting worse."

I couldn't breathe at the sight of Katherine.

Mrs. Arthur pulled me closer to the bed. "Sit with her. I need to make another poultice."

I set down my satchel and looked at the windows again.

"The doctor said to leave them open," she said, "to move the pneumonia out of the room, not close it in."

"Pneumonia!" I looked at Katherine, quivering on the bed, the blankets pulled to her chin.

We both glanced back at the windows. "I'm not a doctor, but . . ."

"You're right. Close them, Aleksey. I don't care what that doctor said."

I slammed both shut and wiggled the curtains closed to keep out any drafts that might sneak in through the weathered window sashes.

I shook out of my coat and layered it over Katherine's blankets.

Mrs. Arthur was already heading toward the door. "I hope this works this time."

"Mrs. Arthur, wait." I pulled my satchel open and dug through it. "This book's full of cures and recipes," I said. "The woman who wrote it used to cure everyone in town."

She walked back toward me.

I flipped through the book, more familiar with its pages than I'd thought. "Try this one," I said.

She took the book, and I turned my attention back to Katherine. I tucked the blankets and my coat around every inch of her body. She coughed, her whole body lifting as she did.

I went to the area behind a curtain at the back of the room and rifled through a small closet looking for another blanket and another pillow. I didn't find anything and took off my sweater. I balled it up and set it under Katherine's pillows, lifting her shoulders. Her breath was shallow and short.

She moaned and shook her head as though dreaming and talking in her sleep. I remembered when we were quarantined back on the prairie. She had tossed and turned with fever then, too. It was afterward that she told me she saw my brothers and sister who had died that year. I dismissed it as part of her fever, and she hadn't pushed it further. But with all that I'd learned since *A Night for Mothers*, it made me wonder if she really was made different by the fever. Was that possible? Was she seeing people who'd passed away? Right then she turned her head, shivering, mumbling about James.

Mrs. Arthur returned to the room, moving gingerly, carrying a pan.

I took it from her and strode toward the bed careful not to slosh the water.

"Should be warm enough," she said. "The recipe you showed me called for eucalyptus—luckily, we had some."

I peered into the pan and saw the moist rags, the scent of oil and eucalyptus filling my nose. I rubbed Katherine's arms, trying to get her warm.

"She's worse," Mrs. Arthur said as she readied the poultice. "For a while, I thought she was through it, not so bad, but then she just turned, like going around a bend and tumbling off a cliff."

"What can I do?"

"I need to get this onto her chest, but I want you to keep her as covered as possible or she might shake right out of her skin."

"Turpentine, lard, and eucalyptus," Mrs. Arthur narrated her work. "Lift that side of the blanket. I'll pull the neck of her gown down to spread this on her chest."

I averted my gaze. *Please, God, help her.*

"That's it, Katherine," Mrs. Arthur cooed as though her daughter was a small girl. "Nice and warm." Katherine was silent except for moaning.

"Lower that side," Mrs. Arthur said. "Come on to this side, and I'll do the same over there."

We changed sides and applied the poultice.

"I'll stoke the fire," I said. She nodded, smoothing Katherine's hair back. Her eyes were closed, and her body began to slow its quaking. I couldn't imagine Mrs. Arthur losing another child.

I added wood to the fire and rechecked the window for drafts. "Mrs. Arthur," I said, hoping she was strong enough to talk about Yale. "I know about Yale."

She looked as though I'd kicked her.

I went to her and got on my knees. "I'm working on getting her out of Glenwood."

She gasped.

"I'm taking care of it."

Her lips quivered. "Thank you. Thank you."

And as the day grew long, the natural light dimming, we sat beside Katherine, each on one side, watching as she forced breath in and out of her body. Watching her weakening further, fragile, lost to us while the fever held tight. I couldn't imagine living without her.

She continued to shiver. Any amount of our massaging her arms and legs seemed ineffective in warming her. I got up. "I'll get some of those river rocks in the garden. We can heat them and slip them inside her covers."

Mrs. Arthur nodded, her head bowed in her hands.

I collected a couple of smooth, palm-sized, rocks, heated them, and slid them in between layers of covers. This added heat but not enough to burn Katherine's skin.

Hours passed with us trying to get water into her, her lips losing their natural redness. The skin pulled into dry crevices, the corners of her mouth cracked and bleeding as she moaned. Mrs. Arthur dug through a drawer and pulled out a small tin of balm. She gently worked it into Katherine's lips. "She made this for Yale when her lips were cracked in the fall. Always thinking of her sister."

I nodded.

"Made her a doll, too. Filled it with lavender." Mrs. Arthur froze for a moment and lifted her eyes to me. "Do you think they allowed her to keep her dolly?"

I doubted it. I knew that Mrs. Arthur knew it, too. She'd been there at the meetings where the welfare of the most vulnerable children was discussed. "I'm sure they let her keep her doll. I'm sure they want her comfortable and calm."

Mrs. Arthur smiled, satisfied with the lie. She felt Katherine's head again. "Even hotter. Get the lanolin off the dressing table."

Next to the jar was the stone I'd given Katherine. I picked it up.

"She had that tucked into a pocket in her underskirt," Mrs. Arthur said. "Pretty, isn't it?"

I nodded, setting it back down, feeling awful in knowing the stone all too well, in knowing Mrs. Arthur had no idea why Katherine would keep it close.

Katherine began to labor harder for breath, her chest heaving to take in air.

"Never mind the lanolin." Mrs. Arthur shook her head. "Let me see that book you brought."

I retrieved it from the kitchen. We opened it on the bed beside Katherine. "There's got to be something else," she said. "That doctor was no help at all."

"Here, near the back, there's more about illnesses of the chest." I paged through the book and located a cure.

Pleurisy/pneumonia lingering-worsening: Pleurisy root. Strong cure, careful use. Few ounces of root, boil, cool, boil again—give large glass of infusion throughout day and night. Do not give to pregnant women. In worst cases, when patient can't swallow infusion—try oil. Very careful. Do not use if patient has chronic heart problems.

Mrs. Arthur read the cure again and gripped my arm. "Head to the apothecary. Shano's place on First Street."

I looked at Katherine, her face red and damp. I didn't want to go. "You sure I should leave?"

She nodded. "We have the root in the cellar, but there's no time to make an extraction. We can barely get a teaspoon of water into her, let alone an infusion. Tell Shano we need the extract."

I started to get up.

"There are coins in the coffee tin near the flour." She pulled Katherine's torso up and attempted to adjust the pillows under her shoulders.

I rushed back to help, sliding my arm behind Katherine's back. "Go ahead, fix the pillows." Mrs. Arthur pulled my balled up sweater out from under Katherine. She held it out to me. "You'll need this. It's frigid."

I took it with my free hand and put it behind Katherine again. "She needs it more." We gently laid her back on the pillows, her hair splayed out around her shoulders. She looked angelic, her sleeping face calm for the moment. I backed away, knowing I needed to get the extract before she grew agitated again, but wanting to stay with her. Mrs. Arthur paged through the book again, and I leaned into Katherine, putting my cheek next to hers. "Hang on. I'll save you," I said into her ear. When I pulled away, Mrs. Arthur was staring at me. The awkwardness lasted a moment before she smiled wearily.

"Go on, Aleksey. I don't know how long this calm will last."

I nodded and grabbed my satchel, bypassing the coin tin Mrs. Arthur had told me to use to pay the apothecary. I'd take care of the cost. It was only the beginning of what I would do for Katherine from this moment on.

Chapter 67

Healing Waters
Aleksey

I arrived back to the Arthur house with the pleurisy root extract in hand. I rushed the stairs but slowed upon entering the room. At first I thought Mrs. Arthur was asleep at Katherine's side. But Katherine's head flailed, and I saw Mrs. Arthur grip her hand tight and pray aloud.

"Please, God, please. Pain me any which way you want, but please take hers away. Save her, save her, save her. Please, God, please."

Memories of my own ma's prayers to a god who allowed her children to die came flooding back, and I was overcome with sadness and fear. I didn't want to interrupt this private moment, but Katherine needed the medicine. I inched closer. "Mrs. Arthur?"

She exhaled deeply. "You're back." She smiled, but her eyes went past me. I turned to see a man in the doorway.

"Doctor Rager," Mrs. Arthur said.

He rushed to Katherine's side. "Violet Pendergrass insisted I come back to check on Katherine."

The doctor swung around and ripped his stethoscope from the case. He butted Mrs. Arthur out of the way. "Looks like she was right."

His harshness made me move closer to the bed, protective of Katherine. He stopped and glared at me. "Who's this?" he said to Mrs. Arthur.

"A friend of our family. He's family," she said.

The doctor shook his head, and though I wanted to stay and watch over Katherine, I knew it wasn't appropriate. I didn't want more delays. "I'll wait outside the room."

Mrs. Arthur grabbed my wrist. "Stay."

I backed away from the bed, and the doctor began to explore Katherine with his scope. Mrs. Arthur leaned against me, and I turned to keep from seeing anything I shouldn't. The doctor sighed and grumbled something under his breath. Mrs. Arthur moved away from me and back toward Katherine. She knelt beside the bed opposite the doctor. The fear in her eyes gripped me. I'd seen it on Ma's face when she was coming to terms with the death of one of her children. I shook my head. No. This was different. She had to live. I'd squandered the last moments I'd had with Katherine, and I needed time to make it up to her. *She's going to be all right. She has to be.*

The doctor stood. "Who shut those windows? I ordered them open, to flush away this disease."

"She was shivering so," Mrs. Arthur said, "practically chipping her teeth. How could I keep the windows open? It doesn't make sense."

Dr. Rager wagged his finger. "I'm the expert. When I say open the windows, you open the windows."

He pushed past me and yanked up one window hard, shattering the glass. He hopped back, arms and legs spread as he stared at the fallen shards around his shoes.

The frigid air rushed into the room, freezing my arms right through my sleeves. Mrs. Arthur's mouth gaped. She leaned over Katherine, shielding her from the icy wind.

"Her lungs are full," he told us. "The pneumonia has taken hold. Tight as a pauper's fingers around a dollar."

I swallowed hard. What was the matter with this man? Where was his kindness and understanding? I didn't care what he said, I wasn't going to allow Katherine to freeze to death in front of my eyes. I knew there was nothing warm in the closet, but I went back there to check it again, crunching over the broken glass. A few dresses. Two hat boxes, shoes. Staring into the closet, I remembered seeing fabric in the parlor when I first arrived.

I went downstairs to the cellar, gathered nails and a hammer and all the material I could hold. As I neared the bedroom again, I heard the doctor's scolding voice. Would he speak to Mrs. Arthur this way if her home were still on Grand?

"There's nothing more I can do, Mrs. Arthur." He stepped over the shards and rested his bag at the foot of Katherine's bed. "You have root extract, I see there. That'll do, I suppose. In this case."

That'll do. The way he said that, those little words were tiny knives sinking into my heart.

Dr. Rager stuffed the stethoscope into his bag and loped toward the door, walking through the glass, unfazed by the fact that he had shattered it himself.

At the doorway, I stepped in front of him.

"What did you mean, 'That'll do'?"

He set down his bag and pulled on his cloak. "Keep her comfortable. That's all that can be done once lungs begin to fill."

Lungs begin to fill. As though we were talking about an object, not a person. "They're not filled completely though," I said.

"A matter of time. I've twelve more patients to see," he said, picking up his bag. I stepped aside to let him pass.

A matter of time? It was a matter of time for lots of things, like completing my studies, getting a job, and telling

Katherine I loved her. Did she love me? After what I'd said to her that night we argued?

I went to the window and began to bang nails through the fabric, the swirly golds and pink shapes easily pierced by the sharp nails. I banged layers and layers of the stuff over the window until I was sure the wind had been cut at least in half.

I studied the work and shook my head. That doctor might have been an expert for his other twelve patients, but not for Katherine. That doctor didn't know a thing about Katherine Arthur. Not one thing.

**

For a while the material I'd draped over the window kept a good bit of wind at bay. But when the storm picked up again, the gusts eventually ripped the fabrics clean off. While attempting to reattach the fabric, the weather grew so blustery that the wind toppled a tree a couple of houses away and blew another neighbor's planter down the sidewalk, tumbling it through the snow, crashing it into the Arthurs' front steps. Dissatisfied with the fabric nailed to the window, I stalked to the bed and looked down on Mrs. Arthur and Katherine. Both were shaking with cold. "We're not keeping her in this freezing room."

Mrs. Arthur stood. "Yes."

I scooped Katherine up and cradled her close. "Let's get her into the parlor. I'll bring the mattress down, and we'll warm her when she's cold, and cool her when she's hot. That pleurisy extract will do more than just comfort her. The apothecary swore it would. And I, for one, believe him and that book I brought more than that doctor. Might sound crazy. But I believe it might work."

Mrs. Arthur looked at me, and said, "Okay." She started toward the doorway. "Yes."

And I carried Katherine down the stairs, into the parlor, and settled her onto the settee.

**

Mrs. Arthur sat with Katherine in the parlor while I hauled the mattress and bed coverings downstairs. We tucked our patient in, and I took the fire from a dull glow to roaring. We sat vigil through patterns of fever and relief. We dripped extract into her mouth. Pale, sunken cheeks, sweaty, matted hair, shallow breaths, coughing so suffocating that I swear I felt Katherine's every strain for air in my own lungs. Mrs. Arthur sent me back and forth for cool cloths when Katherine's fever raged, and we tucked every covering we could find around her body when she quaked from chills. And in moments of quiet, Mrs. Arthur brushed Katherine's hair, each chestnut lock smoothed before the fever came again.

At times, Katherine seemed comfortable in her periodic stillness. Throughout the night, her breathing thickened, her cough full of phlegm. Mrs. Arthur and I took turns clapping her on the back to clear her chest, hoping to bring the mucus up. If there had been a way to suck all the fluid right out of her lungs, I would have done it.

**

Deep in the night of the second day I was there, Katherine's cough subsided. Her fever flamed, but she was suddenly calm. Exhaustion had leached into my bones, every inch of my body heavy and sore. I lay down on the floor beside the mattress, her ma on the other side.

"Sleep, Mrs. Arthur," I said.

She shook her head.

"She's calm now. I'll stay up. You've been awake for days."

Her eyes drooped, the color long gone from her cheeks. She looked at Katherine. She lay beside her daughter, smoothing her hair.

Mrs. Arthur closed her eyes and a few times lifted her head, putting her hand on Katherine's chest as if to check for breath.

Drained, I closed my eyes, but they popped back open. As tired as I was, my body wouldn't allow sleep to come. Not with Katherine still so sick, not with Mrs. Arthur finally getting needed sleep. Once she woke, I could take a nap, but for now, this chance to take care of Katherine meant everything to me.

I moved closer to the mattress and held Katherine's hand. Her skin was chapped. Her chest pushed upward, far more labored than a person normally needed to breathe. But her face was placid at the moment, the fire lighting the dark room, washing her in golden light that made me think of the fairy tales we used to read when we were kids. I kissed the back of her hand. "Get better, Katherine. I was wrong. About all of it. I just couldn't imagine that you were . . ." I kissed her fingers. "I'll do whatever you want, believe whatever you tell me. I'll get Yale from Glenwood, and we'll all leave this place. I don't care about my studies. We'll just go. I'll love you—*love you*—no matter what."

She turned her head toward me but was clearly in a deep sleep. I didn't know how much time had passed. Sweat beaded at her hairline, a rivulet streaming past her ear. I felt her head with the back of my hand the way I'd seen Mrs. Arthur do a thousand times. She was warm, but not blazing hot as she'd been earlier. I went to the kitchen for a cool rag and more elixir. I knew before long, she'd begin to kick off her blankets again, the fever agitating every inch of her. When I returned to the parlor, I was shocked at the sight of the other people in the room.

Two girls bent over Katherine, and another stood at the fireplace. Mrs. Arthur had gotten to her knees, her back to me as she bent over Katherine. The girl kneeling where I had been laying just a few moments before placed a cloth over Katherine's brow and was leaning into her, saying something quietly. I couldn't hear, but Mrs. Arthur nodded at the girl.

With Katherine still calm, I didn't approach, allowing Mrs. Arthur this moment with the girls and her daughter. I had no idea who they were, but I assumed they came from next door at Violet Pendergrass's.

I looked toward the front door. I could see the lock still turned to the locked position. The fire glowed brighter as the third girl peered into it as though checking it. She must have stoked it while I was in the kitchen. *Had* they come from next door? Violet's girls? Mrs. Arthur clearly knew them. They must have a key to the house. That would make sense since Violet owned it. I don't know why I didn't burst into the room and demand to know who they were, but Katherine looked so peaceful, her mother, too.

Now all three girls knelt beside Katherine, talking quietly, praying with Mrs. Arthur, hands clasped to their chests. Katherine opened her eyes. Was she waking up? I took a step toward them and stopped. She was saying something to them. I strained to hear. Relief came, overwhelming me.

Someone rapping at the front door startled me. I went to it and pulled the lacy curtain back. Tommy. Arms crossed, he was bouncing on his toes, trying to get warm. I unlocked the door and let him in.

"Back door was locked," he said, blowing into his hands. "Glad you were standing there. How's she doing?"

I patted his back. "I think she's turning a corner."

Mrs. Arthur joined us in the hallway. She took Tommy in her arms.

Tommy squeezed his mother, and they pulled apart.

"Pearl brought eucalyptus water," Mrs. Arthur said.

He shrugged. "She locked me out. Glad she's here. I wasn't sure where . . . How's Katherine?"

"In and out," Mrs. Arthur said. She pulled Tommy toward the parlor. "Aleksey's been a godsend."

I followed, finally understanding how the girls had suddenly appeared in the house. "So Pearl's one of the girls with her now?"

Mrs. Arthur and Tommy looked at me. "Girls?" she said.

"Yes, when I brought these from the kitchen..." I pulled them into the room. Only one girl remained at Katherine's side, turning the cloth on her forehead, singing a lullaby. I looked at the fire, scanned the entire room. No sign of anyone else. The fire grew brighter again, and I thought I saw someone near it. I rubbed my forehead, feeling my exhaustion. I rubbed my eyes. I was more exhausted than I thought. I went to the girl sitting by Katherine.

"Pearl?"

She nodded.

"I'm Aleksey."

She nodded.

"Where are the other two?" I said.

She reached up and gestured for me to give her the fresh cloth I'd brought to put on Katherine's head. "Two what?" She handed me the old one she'd placed there before. "I only brought one cloth to keep dipping in the water. Go on," she told me. "Dip that into the bucket. Full of healing water. Used one of Katherine's recipes, right out of that cure book of hers. I think it's doing the trick."

I dunked the cloth into the water. Lack of sleep took strong hold. "How'd you get in here?"

"Front door. Back door was locked when I tried it. Luckily, I know the trick of getting in the front one, yes indeed."

I shook my head and rubbed my temples. I must have been in the kitchen when she slipped into the house, just missing her when she went to the back door. That made sense.

"Keep it in there for a bit," Pearl said. "The healing water should help when the fever comes again."

I felt as though I'd gone lunatic with fatigue. "I meant where are the other two girls?"

She looked over one shoulder, then the other, and back at Katherine. Her eyes were closed again, but Katherine's breath was steadier now, even, deep. As though Pearl just realized something important, she whispered, "Oh, Katherine."

"What is it?" I said.

She looked at me, then at Tommy and Mrs. Arthur. "Nothing. No one was with me. Just Mrs. Arthur."

Mrs. Arthur knelt beside Katherine with the elixir. "You need to rest, Aleksey."

"Can you get me more cloths, Tommy?" Pearl said.

"I'll go," I said. "Tommy, stay with them."

Tommy sat beside Pearl. She gazed at Tommy and brushed his hair from his face. "She was askin' for ya," I heard Pearl say as I went back to the kitchen, so tired I was wondering if I might sleep for days when I finally had the chance.

Chapter 68

She Brought the Angels
Katherine

I inhaled as deeply as possible before a coughing fit took hold. As it tapered off, I found I could open my eyes. The light burned, and I wondered how long it had been since I had been awake. My tongue was thick against the rough roof of my mouth. My head throbbed, and all I wanted to do was sit up and release the pounding pressure. I pushed up on my elbows but fell right back down. The ceiling was unfamiliar. Where was I?

"There you are, Katherine," Tommy said.

I tried to say his name, but I couldn't get anything out. He pulled me up by the shoulders and pushed some pillows into my back to prop me up like a rag doll.

I looked around the room and realized I was in the parlor, on a mattress on the floor. My head lolled to one side, then the other. "Mama?"

"At the courthouse."

Courthouse? Why would she be there?

Tommy dug at his nail. "She has a hearing about Yale."

"Yale," I said, but I still couldn't fathom what he was talking about.

"She was taken to Glenwood, remember?"

I fought through my foggy thoughts, searching for a memory of such a thing. Finally, I remembered. Pearl and me running, looking for Mama, the courthouse, Mama crying, staring into the yard.

I nodded, looking around the room, feeling as though years had passed since I was last aware of my normal life.

"Remember getting sick at Miss Violet's?" Tommy said.

I struggled to think. Paintings. Wanting Miss Violet's help. The judge. I remembered.

"You're down here because the window broke upstairs," Tommy said. "Wind whipped through like it was auditioning for a role in the next tornado."

"Got the part?"

He squeezed me tight. "Fever didn't take your sense of humor, did it?"

I smiled, feeling good in my brother's arms, wondering how on earth the window broke.

"Mama will be so happy to see you awake. She didn't want to leave you. She nearly missed the hearing, but we forced her out the door."

I felt a pinch in my chest thinking of Yale.

"I'm sorry you're so sick." He pulled away and reached for a small jar of lanolin and applied some to my lips with two swipes. "Your lips are cracked."

"Water," I said, trying to rub the lanolin in.

He poured me a glass and held it to my mouth. I swallowed a few drops and then sucked down the entire thing.

Drinking so fast caused a fit of coughing so fierce it sounded as if a saw was being pushed over wood.

Tommy patted my back.

I heard another voice say, "That's good, Tommy," and he looked over his shoulder to see Aleksey, coming in from the hall.

Aleksey. I was dizzy all over again.

"What's good?" Tommy said.

Aleksey stopped at the end of the settee, holding a bowl. I tried to focus. Was he really here? He appeared in the room as though he'd lived here forever.

He smiled at me. "The phlegm is moving around even more. She can get it out if it's loose. Definitely on the road to recovery."

I touched my hair and looked down, knowing I must be only half-dressed. The blanket was up around my chest; everything but my arms were covered.

Aleksey's blue eyes shone electric and bright. A swell of happiness spread through me.

I whispered, "Hello."

"I heated up some of the soup Miss Violet made for you the other day."

Aleksey knelt beside us.

"You got some sleep," Tommy said.

Aleksey shrugged. "Couple hours. Thanks for letting me use the shed."

"Sure," Tommy said. "Just glad that last night she finally turned the corner on this pneumonia."

Aleksey scratched his chin. "Let's get her to the settee so she can eat."

Tommy shuffled to the side, and Aleksey angled his body toward mine, soothing me with his voice. He pushed strands of hair behind my ears, making my insides flutter. When had I last seen Aleksey? He was so comfortable with Tommy. How sick had I been, how long? The garden. That was when I'd seen him last. He didn't want me. I stiffened.

He swept me up, blankets and all, and set me down on the settee as though he'd been doing this our whole lives. He motioned toward the mattress. "Hand me those pillows." Tommy brought them, and one-by-one Aleksey added each, propping me up until I felt comfortable. I exhaled, tiredness coming heavy all over again. Aleksey smiled and eased himself away, but I followed the movements of his body, folding into the contours of his shape.

He stayed beside me. Nestled in his arms made me want to fall back into deep sleep. Was this a dream? I didn't want to wake up and find him gone.

Tommy leaned over me with the soup. He carefully tipped the spoon into my mouth. The bitter liquid made me flinch. I forced it down and turned away.

"Just a little more," Tommy said.

I shook my head.

"Miss Violet made it especially for you. I suspect it's the first thing she's ever cooked."

A small laugh spurted out of me. My eyes were heavy again, and all I wanted was to sink into sleep.

"We'll try more soup later."

"There's a recipe in the book I brought," Aleksey said. "I'm no cook, but it's got to be better than whatever this is."

I sank deeper into the pillows and into Aleksey, nearing sleep again as they talked.

"I got your ma to the courthouse," Aleksey said. "She'll be in front of Calder, not Smythton. I sent documents with her to bolster her plea. Your ma said he's known her all her life. I can't imagine why he wouldn't help her."

"Thank you," I said, listening with my eyes closed.

He held my hand, and my mind swirled as his warmth enveloped me.

"Yale should be home in no time," Aleksey said. "Especially if they're doing it this way and not . . ."

Oh, Yale. I didn't want to hear bad news. I yearned to feel her little arms flung around my neck. I fell closer to sleep, turning to my side.

"This past year taught me that," I heard Aleksey say, "somehow I know more and less about the world than I thought I had. I'm a dumb farmhand in part, but I aim to make a difference with what I've come to see about the world."

"Something's not right about all this," Tommy said.

"You got that right," Aleksey said.

"Get her back," I said, but I wasn't sure anyone heard me.

Fighting sleep proved too difficult. I wanted them to explain what I'd missed. How had Aleksey helped? What documents? Had Miss Violet visited me? My eyes grew heavier. My white-knuckle grip on Aleksey's hand loosened. I tried to snatch and capture Aleksey's words from the air so I'd remember what was said later, keeping this protected feeling as close as I possibly could.

**

With no progress made at the courthouse, but still trying to find a pathway to bring Yale home, Tommy watched over me when Mama or Aleksey couldn't. He fed me soup, water, and jokes, talking to me as though I was a full participant in our conversations. Finally, I advanced to sitting upright for hours at a time between sleep.

"Try this," Tommy said.

I sat at the kitchen table, eating like a healthy human being again.

Tommy pointed a spoon at a bowl filled with a thick mahogany-colored liquid. "Aleksey got us some beef to make that stock, and there's bread underneath."

"Smells good," I said.

"Should help bring back your full strength. This book Aleksey brought has been great."

I sipped the stew-like liquid from the spoon. It felt as though my insides were rejuvenated. "Book?"

"Some book he found in a wall he was fixing for his farmer."

I stopped mid-spoonful. The wall. Wait, he'd told me about that, hadn't he? Had he? Despite my progression toward health, my thoughts still unraveled from time to time. "Yes. He told me about a book he found."

"Well, it's really helped when you needed it most."

I nodded, making a note to ask Aleksey about it when he came back. I spooned up some broth and admired its mahogany richness. "It's good, Tommy. Very, very good."

**

As I ate, Tommy read most every article in the paper aloud. I noticed him reading a few silently, then he would turn the page quickly when I attempted to look closer.

On one page, I glimpsed the name Dreama. He'd skipped that one for sure—unless I'd fallen asleep without realizing it and had missed it. I set down my spoon and rubbed my head. I leaned over and turned the page back. "Read that one." I pointed. "The Dreama one."

He stared at me.

"What?"

He sighed and looked into my eyes. "Just . . . no."

"Yes."

He looked away. I studied him, knowing he was withholding something. I looked at the paper again. Dreama. He knew. That had to be it. The realization seeped into me the way sunrays heated skin. I simply knew that he knew. I reached across the table.

"How did you find out?"

"I told him." Pearl stepped into the kitchen from the hall.

She came to me and looped her arms around my shoulders from behind, squeezing tight.

"So very sorry," she whispered in my ear. She smelled of lemons and vanilla. She pulled out the chair next to me and sat down, taking my hand in hers. "Our pinkie promise. I ain't never broke one before. But when you got sick and—"

"Really, Pearl?" Tommy said. "You think a pinkie promise means something, like a signature on paper?"

Pearl glared, and he held her searing gaze. The two of them were clearly in the middle of something they weren't revealing to me. "What's wrong with you two?"

"Nothing," they said in unison, startling me.

Pearl gripped my hands. "Never mind him. I'm deeply sorry. From the deepest parts of my being."

"I told you not to." Tommy's voice was icy toward Pearl.

Fear crept over my skin, lifting it into bumps. "Mama?"

Tommy shook his head. "We wouldn't add to her worries," he said, turning the pages of the paper and folding it in half. "I didn't tell Mama. But it's not because I didn't want to. This is serious, Katherine. People are starting to . . ." He tapped the article I had wanted him to read.

"I'm not a con."

"I didn't say that."

"But that's what the headline says."

"Tommy," Pearl snapped. "Tell her you believe her."

He exhaled. "I can't deny the painting you made with the boy and deer is exactly what happened. And I know you couldn't know. Pearl swears she didn't tell you."

"Pinkie swore." She held up her pinkie. I took her hand and held it on the tabletop, smiling at her.

"You just broke a pinkie promise two days ago," he said.

"Enough," Pearl said.

"But this isn't a game," Tommy scolded me, sounding grownup in a way I'd never heard him before. "Law enforcement's involved. Angry people who—"

"Stop it, Tommy," Pearl said.

"I just want her to be safe," he said. "And you thinking you brought angels to heal her the other night won't change the fact that there are mobs forming, that the law is coming for my sister."

I gasped, remembering Pearl and two women who'd been in the room when I was sick. The fireplace, the heat and the cold, all of it at the same time. The women and their soothing touch, comforting words, telling me I was going to be fine. Tommy and Pearl stared at me, waiting for me to react.

I'd been in so much pain at the time. My throat so swollen and burning I could barely breathe, my chest so tight I felt as though my ribs were collapsing around my lungs. I'd simply forgotten about it until this moment.

"She did, Tommy," I said. "She brought me angels."

Pearl's mouth dropped open.

I nodded.

Pearl's eyes filled, tears spilling over. "I thought so!" She wiped the streams away with the backs of her hands. "That night I hoped and wished for them to come, and the whole time I was mixing the healing water I called for them, feeling silly, but you told me I had angels, that they were warm and kind, something like that. Well, when I heard you were so sick, the first thing I thought was I'd visit you, and I suppose . . ." She looked up to the ceiling. "I suppose that in saying the words over the water and in going to you that I brung—I mean, *brought*—the angels with me. I didn't really need them, seeing how healthy I am and such. So, I thought I might lend them to you. *And you got better.* That night." Her face revealed her marvel at what had happened.

I felt the same awe Pearl did at their healing power.

Pearl sank back, covering her mouth. "I couldn't see them, but I felt them. What did they look like?"

"Two women, sort of smallish. Just beautiful, holy, with a warmth. They milled around you and me and . . . well . . . brought their healing."

"It worked. I really have angels." Pearl straightened in her chair.

Tommy let out an exasperated puff of air and stiffened in his seat, arms crossed.

Pearl shot him a cold look and moved closer to me, softening her manner. "No one ever said such softhearted things about me as you did that night we talked in the shed. I mean, other than Tommy here, but boys do that when a certain mood takes hold. But *girls*, they don't compliment easily. Not like you did."

She took my head in her hands, coaxing me closer, and kissed my forehead. "Thank you." She released me.

I felt nurtured. I couldn't think of another person who I liked so much since we'd left Des Moines when I was ten years old. "You're welcome, my friend."

"Friend." Pearl stood, eyes glistening, and said to Tommy, "I'll let the"—she cleared her throat—"dog and cat out and pluck another chicken and start up more soup. Our Katherine needs all the liquid and goodness she can get. She's going to be all right."

I yawned, feeling weighted by fatigue. "She's a good woman, Tommy. You better be good to her."

He nodded and waved my comment off as he leaned on the table. "Don't change the subject. There're more articles. You need to pull away from this Dreama thing. I can say I believe you, whatever it is I'm supposed to believe, but that doesn't change the business you're in. Trust me. I know some of the men involved, and I've heard things around town."

"What does that mean? What kind of things? Are you in trouble?"

He shook his head. "Nothing for you to know except to stop it. Everything I know is in the paper, except I hear it firsthand. And I can take care of myself."

I thought of his bruises and the way he often smelled of booze. "*You* need to be careful, Tommy. Not me."

"Just once, will you listen to *me*? I'm not book smart, like James was, or wise like Mama or forward thinking like Father, but for once, can you just trust me? I know things, and I want you safe. You're my sister, and I . . ."

I leaned toward him. "You what?"

"I love you, Katherine. And I don't want to see anything happen to you. It would be"—his voice cracked—"awful." He shielded his eyes. "It would be awful."

I couldn't remember him ever saying such things to me, not with such feeling.

"I trust you. Of course, I do. I love you, too."

His shoulders relaxed, and he leaned back in his seat, his face releasing the tension that had been pulling his skin into angry folds. "Thank you," he said.

In some families, people would have jumped up and embraced on the heels of such heartfelt revelations, but this, for Tommy and me, the quiet awkwardness following such a declaration, was the equivalent of unbridled hugging. And so, we sat quietly in the kitchen, the clock's ticking filling the quiet space. After I was reassured that our disclosures of love and trust had settled deep into the both of us, I stood. "I should rest."

He smiled. "Yes, rest, get better."

I headed toward the doorway and ran into Aleksey. He looked at me, then Tommy, and offered me his arm. "You've been up for a while. Time for a nap?" I took his arm, and he led me into the parlor. I laid on the settee, and he covered me with fresh blankets.

"I'm fixing that broken window today," he said. "I figure it's about time to get you back into a proper bed."

He sat with me as I fell asleep, talking, narrating the rest of his plans for the day, but I was already slipping into sleep, suspended on the sound of his voice, wishing it were possible I might have the chance to have him lull me to sleep for all the days of my life.

Chapter 69

Seeding
Aleksey

With Katherine snug on the settee downstairs, I worked upstairs in the bedroom to fix the shattered window. Palmer had loaned me the money to buy the glass and was even more generous in letting me visit Katherine when I wasn't due at work for Mr. Stevens. I was putting in as many hours at the farm as I could, getting even less sleep than before. But caring for Katherine and her family this way added meaning to the work I'd already been doing. So far there had been no movement in getting Yale out of Glenwood. Mr. Stevens was secretive, saying that there were holdups he couldn't explain to me. Mrs. Arthur believed she had a good chance of getting Judge Calder to help, but so far that hadn't created any movement. I felt as though there was something between the judge and Mrs. Arthur beyond what I could see. Something kept this caring mother from being given her child back. She denied my suspicions and my digging didn't turn up new information. I told her that she would only have to say the word and I'd break Yale out burglary style, but, so far, she wouldn't allow it. Her fear that she would lose Yale forever if she didn't follow the rules was too great for her to risk.

I finished the window and surveyed the room, remembering how Katherine had looked when I first arrived and saw her here in bed. I noticed the angel stone still on the dressing table, and I knew Katherine must have wanted it near. I put it into my pocket and hurried downstairs.

Pearl and Mrs. Arthur were sitting beside Katherine. The scene reminded me of what I'd seen that night when Katherine finally turned for the better. And I remembered what I'd overheard earlier today when Tommy, Pearl, and Katherine were talking in the kitchen. Hearing their thoughts on Katherine's abilities was heartening. From what I'd learned about Winnie, and the fact that her book came into my hands, that I read important parts just when I needed to, and that I saw Pearl's angels with my own eyes, all of it told me that Katherine was no con, but that I was indeed a jerk.

It still amazed me, as it did when I heard Pearl and Katherine talk about the angels that came that night. I'd seen the golden light wash over them from the fire. It all solidified in my mind now. I had indeed witnessed spiritual beings. And they'd healed Katherine. It wasn't exhaustion or lunacy, as I'd tried to write it off as.

"Come in, Aleksey," Mrs. Arthur said.

I moved quietly but saw that Katherine was awake.

"Short nap?" I said.

"Katherine seems to be wider awake today than she has been in the last ten days put together," Mrs. Arthur said.

Katherine smiled at me, warming me from the inside out.

I'd heard Tommy and Pearl confirm that Mrs. Arthur was still not privy to Katherine acting as Dreama, and though I knew that would soon change, I took solace in Katherine being too ill to perform. Tommy was helping watch over her. When the time was right, I'd talk to Katherine again, and this time I'd do it right so that she understood I simply wanted her safe.

I was happy to be invited into the room, but I didn't want to interrupt Mrs. Arthur and Pearl tending to Katherine. I was content to make myself useful, poking at the fire, adding logs and adjusting the pan of water heating on the grill over the hottest part of the fire.

"Aleksey," she said, "could you pour some of that water into the bowl and bring it here?"

I moved quickly and set the water between Pearl and Mrs. Arthur. Mrs. Arthur was drawn, her shoulders drooping, and I wondered when she'd last eaten a good meal.

Pearl added some oil from a dropper and dipped a cloth into the water. "I once overheard a doctor who was picking up his mail discuss the importance of keeping sick folks extra clean."

Mrs. Arthur dipped a second cloth into the water and helped Pearl bathe Katherine's hands and arms.

"Would you like me to bring you some of the beef broth and bread, Mrs. Arthur? You need to keep up your health, too. I know you're worried and tired."

"After this."

She had made it clear to me that she didn't want me to tag along to her meetings with Judge Calder. I wasn't sure why, but I suspected it was because I wasn't yet a formal lawyer. I couldn't blame her for that.

"I wanted you to know," I said, "I'm waiting to hear when Yale will have a hearing at Glenwood, Mrs. Arthur. Mr. Stevens understands how important this is."

"Thank you. The hearing with Judge Calder wasn't fruitful. Told me to come back tomorrow and he'll meet with me. I was so tired that I scarcely refrained from storming the bench and wringing his neck." Her cheeks flushed, and her voice was shrill, something I'd never heard from her.

Mrs. Arthur massaged Katherine's hands with lanolin, then dabbed some on her lips while Pearl brushed her hair.

"I can go in your place," I said. "I'm sure I can get Mr. Stevens to accompany me." I wasn't sure at all, but now that I knew he had done something illicit, I figured I could use it against him. Much as that tasted bitter, I'd do it for Mrs. Arthur.

"No," she said. "Just leave it, Aleksey. It's a mess. Complicated and . . ."

She was exhausted. She would never be so short with me, with anyone under normal circumstances. So, I didn't push her. I would ask and offer my help later when she was more rested and Katherine was fully recovered. Meanwhile, I'd keep working from my end.

"I just want her back," Mrs. Arthur said. "And this is delicate. It's not something you can fully understand, Aleksey."

Pearl gave me a sympathetic look. "Tell us again about the finders, keepers case, Aleksey." She brushed a section of Katherine's hair. Katherine smiled at me and nodded. She was trying to lighten the mood.

"And tell us again how the couple ended up back together again," Pearl said. "Tell us how love won out even after the fella won in court. I love a good fairy tale. Even if I ain't gonna have my own come true. Not like in the books."

Pearl's voice was filled with a mix of hope and resignation.

"What's wrong?" Katherine said, but Pearl just brushed Katherine's hair and didn't answer.

"Pearl?" Mrs. Arthur said. "Are you getting sick now?"

Pearl stopped and set the brush in her lap.

"Is something wrong at the post office?"

"No, no."

Katherine took Pearl's hand. As I watched Pearl, I got the feeling that perhaps Tommy was at the root of her mood. But I didn't want to push the matter in front of Mrs. Arthur.

"Can we help?" I said.

Pearl exhaled and clenched her jaw before she forced a smile and began to brush again. "I can manage. Thank you."

She looked at me. "Tell us, Aleksey. I love a story with a happy ending."

"Everyone does, Pearl," Mrs. Arthur said. Her voice was short, her appearance haggard. The toll of losing Yale and Katherine's illness was taking hold. "Let's all hope each of us has a magical ending somewhere down the road."

I nodded.

"I need my Yale back." Her voice was so quiet I almost didn't hear her. But her words lodged in my heart, reminding me of my ma. *You'll get her back,* I said silently. *You will, I promise you that.*

"So one day I was in my office," I said, retelling the story Pearl wanted to hear, "and a man walked in . . ."

**

I was pleased to have been so useful to the Arthurs while Katherine was sick. But I was eager to talk to her alone, to express how much regret I felt for having made her feel so bad that night we argued. I got my chance one afternoon a few days later. Pearl left for the post office, and Mrs. Arthur was busy starting a vat of hot water in the kitchen to launder Katherine's blankets. When Mr. Hayes arrived to help Mrs. Arthur with some of the chores, I finally had a private moment with Katherine.

"Don't go," Katherine said as I went to the front door for my satchel.

"I'm not going anywhere."

I sat on the chair that Pearl had been using and pulled the angel stone from my pocket and handed it to her. She stared, running her finger over its wings.

"It was on the dressing table upstairs," I said. "I kept an eye on it when you were sick."

"Thank you," she said. All the awfulness of the night I gave it to her was a mountain between us. She wouldn't look at me. I couldn't blame her. Remembering that night must have felt terrible. It did for me. But now was the time to make it right.

I took a deep breath and told myself to be brave, to tell her all I hadn't been able to say that night, all I hadn't realized. I pulled out a small burlap sack and handed it to Katherine. "I have something else for you." She smiled and loosened the ties that cinched the neck. She met my eyes and smiled again.

She dug into the sack, her brow furrowing as she turned it upside down, dumping the contents into her hand. She pulled her hand closer to get a better look. "Seeds?"

My throat caught as I felt the silliness of it when she said it aloud. "Apple seeds."

She cocked her head, staring at the treasure that wasn't what she expected. I ran my finger over the brown kernels in her hand, making them jump and turn, wishing they were diamonds instead of simple brown seeds. "I know they aren't beautiful or expensive or, well, anything you might have wanted a gift to be."

She stared into her palm, unmoving.

I folded her fingers over the seeds. "But they're a promise."

She swallowed hard. Was she about to throw them across the room? Break into laughter? Ask me to leave? She covered her mouth with her other hand but still didn't look at me.

I took her closed hand in both of mine. "I'll make sure you never have to hide apples in your skirt, your stomach never growls, you never have to worry that you have a safe home. You'll have a house with a garden, and a house with a room filled with books, and a bright room for you to paint. And we'll plant those seeds together so you have your very own apple trees right outside your window. Always fed. In every way possible."

Her cheeks grew red, and I could see that she wasn't breathing. Was she trying to avoid telling me how silly I was being?

Finally, she lifted her eyes and looked at me square, tears brimming. Her hand shook, and I drew it away from her mouth.

I couldn't stop now. "I love you, Katherine. I'm so sorry for the night we fought. I'll make you the happiest woman on earth if only you'll let me try. Let's start all over again. Please."

Her lip quivered, and tears dropped, but she still wasn't replying.

Was she crying because she didn't feel the same or couldn't forgive me for that I hurt her so?

"Katherine?"

She shook her head and waved her hand in front of her face, but still didn't speak. The tendons in her neck pulled taut. I felt like I was losing her.

"I saw the angels Pearl brought," I told her. "I saw them in the room with you, golden, loving. I believe what you can do. I brought Winnie Palmer's cure book here because she did what you do, and I knew there'd be something in it to help you, and it did, and—"

Before I could say another word, Katherine let loose the biggest smile I'd ever seen and flung her arms around my neck, pulling me tight.

"I love you, Aleksey. I love you, too."

Chapter 70

One More
Violet

Stupid, stupid, stupid. Violet fought with the seam ripper as she started on her third skirt. Although she ate less to control her weight gain, she still needed to let out the waists in her skirts. Now she was adding some stretchy muslin that could be hidden under her jackets and shirtwaists to make room for her growing belly. She pulled on the thread, cursing to herself. Still, she couldn't bring herself to hire a seamstress, afraid she'd alert someone to her current situation.

She didn't even trust Olivia to be discreet, not with her gin habit. Two months ago, Violet would have kicked Olivia out of the house for putting their business at risk. But now, she was too fragile to train another girl and didn't trust her own judgment, especially after all the poor decisions she'd been making of late.

Katherine's illness had brought new perspective. Perhaps she'd invested too much in Dreama and Katherine's commitment to playing the part. Jeremy's absence since his devastating reaction to her pregnancy added to her predicament. His snarling words kept playing in her mind.

Surely, you didn't expect me to leave my wife! It wasn't just his current absence that stung so, it was her own misjudgment, the fantasies she'd spun in thinking he could have actually wanted her by his side.

Making a mistake, the same one twice over—depending on both Jeremy and Katherine to ensure her success—was something she viewed as deadly. She hadn't made that kind of mistake since Edwin, and yet here she was. A grown woman, pregnant and suffering morning sickness and feeling lost. She used to think there was always more cash to be coaxed from the purses of the citizens of Des Moines, but now she was grateful she had her private stash of money hidden in the floor of her bedroom. It wouldn't last her years, but it would sustain her if she needed to run, if she had to hide.

Running away. If she was honest, that was her only choice. She thought of all the beautiful furnishings in her home, the paintings, and all the time she'd put into training her charges. She took a deep breath. *Focus, Violet.* Told herself to take the one tiny sunflower painting by Vincent. The rest—good copies, but not authentic—would be left behind.

No. Two paintings. She'd take the one Katherine had done of the girl near a furnace bent over a man. That one grabbed her by the heart every time she saw it. She could manage if she ran. She'd get as much cash together as possible, demand Jeremy add to her cache and then start again somewhere farther west. There were so many ways she could turn her tale, convince people to trust her. Just six or seven towns over would be all the distance she needed. A widow. Yes, her husband died of a weak heart? An accident with the plow? A devoted daughter—her parents, victims of influenza, no siblings. Even though she'd lived high in Des Moines, her gowns the latest in fashion, she'd learn to survive on what she had hidden under the floor until . . .

She set her sewing down and looked at her profile in the mirror. Until, until, until. Until what?

She was exhausted. Should she have the child here and leave it behind with the Arthurs? There was a chance for one more reading, one more haul. If Katherine would only get well enough, soon enough.

She rubbed her belly, the baby stirring inside. No. This baby was the only one who mattered. Her heart leapt at the thought of cradling the newborn to her breast. Her stash in the floor, even that small sum, would allow her to have what the Arthurs were running ragged trying to achieve—a tiny cottage on a quiet street with a sweet kitchen garden. It was all she and the baby needed; it was all she wanted now.

Except for Jeremy. Even thinking his name stung. She relived every detail of the way their relationship had grown from business to so much more. His hands, the weight of him on her, the feel of him in her, the gasp in his breath when he fell under her spell and lured her to love him. How could this have happened? He must feel the same or she wouldn't feel this way for him.

She resumed her sewing. Tedious, necessary. Her stitches were loose and like drunken footprints through snow, but it gave her a chance to plot. Jeremy might not know it yet, but he loved her. He'd want to leave with her once she gave him a chance to change his perspective. And how hard could that be for her to do?

**

Once again, nausea and fatigue had come for Violet. It seemed that for each day that she had energy and clarity, there were two days where she felt as though she wasn't even master of the next few minutes, let alone queen of her destiny. So when Tommy's Pearl knocked at the back door, tomato-red face and breathing fire, complaining about how she couldn't stay with him anymore, it made all the sense in the world to invite her into the house to work.

Pearl wasn't a gifted cook in the way that Katherine was, but she managed to prepare chicken, soup, bland porridge, and crisp crackers that helped settle the acid in Violet's belly. Pearl may have arrived due to some undisclosed infraction by Tommy, but her presence helped fill in the gaps created now that Olivia was often incapacitated.

Pearl was busy making strong coffee for a drunken Olivia, who'd passed out in the parlor just a few moments ago. Violet turned the coffee grinder to help, and the kitchen door opened, admitting Katherine.

She was still drawn, her hair loosely gathered in a tie, the length of it hanging down her back. She moved slowly, but her cheeks glowed pink again.

"Pearl? What are you doing?" Katherine asked.

Pearl shrugged. "Room and board."

Katherine drew back. "Since when? You didn't mention it yesterday when you were over."

She shrugged. "It's nothing. Just time to move on."

Katherine glanced at Violet and then hugged Pearl, whispering something in her ear. Pearl nodded and busied herself with the kettle.

Violet led Katherine to the table.

"I see the soup was helpful in returning you to health."

She crinkled her brow and then nodded. "Yes, the soup," she said. "Thank you so much for making it." She sat straighter in her chair. "But I would like to talk. Please."

"Of course," Violet said.

"Privately," Katherine said.

Violet felt her stomach clench. "In my office, then." Perhaps her luck had changed this afternoon.

**

Violet and Katherine stopped at the settee in the parlor where Olivia was snoring in a drunken sleep. "She's all right. Used to this by now."

Katherine followed Violet into the office, glancing back again and again at Olivia. "Doesn't look all right."

"Trust me," Violet said and gestured toward the empty seat beside her.

Katherine sat, drawing deep breaths, the exertion from this small bit of activity draining her.

"You were missed," Violet said.

"Thank you," she said. "Feels like a year since I've been here."

Violet shifted to face her straight on.

"Have you seen the papers?" Violet said. "There's much to do now that you're back. An important event for you."

Katherine was shaking her head. "I've seen the papers. And I think we should just let Dreama fade away."

Violet swallowed hard, hoping the sensation of panic didn't unleash another bout of nausea.

"Fade away?" Violet clenched her hands in her lap. "Dreama's at her height now."

"Being so ill taught me a lot."

Violet fought to subdue the anger that bubbled inside. How dare she? Didn't she know how worried she was about her? Didn't she know how her illness affected Violet's business? No, this wasn't like Katherine. It must be the illness talking, it must be . . . Violet straightened. She knew what it was. "This is because of Aleksey Zurchenko."

Katherine gasped, then tried to cover it up.

"I saw him at your house," Violet said. "Repeatedly."

Katherine nodded.

"So." Violet flicked her hand at Katherine. "He's promised you love and fidelity and a home, is that it?"

Katherine stiffened. "Well, yes, he's mentioned those things."

Violet shook her head. "You know better, Katherine."

She drew back, injured by Violet's sharp tone.

"What about the independent life you've planned?" Violet said. "What of your own career? Your own business? Your dreams?"

"Well, it's not as if—"

Violet knew what Katherine needed to hear to come to her senses. "Money, a little house for your *mother?*"

"I'll have all those things. With Aleksey."

"You owe your mother more than a marriage to a farmer with the dream of being a lawyer. A man will only ruin what you've started for your mother. Ruin it."

Katherine rubbed her temples. Violet could see the fatigue, the fresh blush of recovery losing its color.

"Aleksey's different," Katherine said, lifting her chin at Violet as if to shield herself from criticism.

Violet felt her own fatigue taking hold. Her breath grew shallow as she saw Katherine's resolve. "He's different. Until he's got some girl's naked legs wrapped around his waist and her hands tight on his bank account. Then he's just like all the rest."

Katherine's mouth fell open. Her eyes welled. Violet could tell the girl was shocked, getting ready to run.

She took Katherine's hands. "I'm frank with you because I care. You deserve to know the truth before it's too late, not after. Your father hurt your mother. Now Tommy's hurt Pearl, and, well, let's just say I've had my own education on the matter."

Katherine's expression was now unreadable. She pulled her hands away and went to the fireplace, poking at the flaming wood. "I'll pay you every penny I owe you, Miss Violet. But Aleksey *is* different from other men. I'll make weekly payments."

Violet couldn't believe what she was hearing. She gathered her wits and went to Katherine. If the play to help her mother and save her independence didn't work, she would have to try something else. She took the poker from her and flipped a log from the bottom of the firebox to the top of the log pile. "I need you to do one more night of readings, Katherine. One. That's the least you can do. For me."

She shook her head.

Violet dug the poker tip into the hearth. "It's important. It's life or death, actually."

"Learned that myself when I was sick. I see it more than ever that my family needs me, especially with Yale gone."

Katherine's gaze hardened on Violet in a way that she'd never seen before. The sight of Katherine transforming, her own ideas crystalizing right in front of Violet, shook her to her core.

"Being Dreama has only led me to debt. I read in the papers that half of Des Moines wants to string me up. I can't risk being accused of being a fraud and a con. I can't go to jail."

Violet felt her resolve weakening with Katherine's increasing resistance. "I'll protect you. In fact, Katherine, Judge Calder can protect us all. *And* I think I can even make sure that Yale is released from Glenwood."

"No," Katherine said, backing away. "Aleksey's handling Yale. I've made up my mind."

Violet's insides turned. She gripped the mantel for balance.

Katherine's face softened. "I won't tell a soul about us. Dreama's our secret if you let me make payments slowly. Just let me be."

Violet was overcome and feeling desperate, angry, weak, rudderless. *Just let me be.* Katherine's words swirled in her head, and her knees buckled. She clung to the mantel to gather herself, but before Violet could think of what to say next, tears came, and she buried her face in her hands, shoulders shuddering. It was as though someone had yanked her out of her own body and she had no control over the sadness and fear pouring out of her.

Katherine was silent, unmoving.

Violet couldn't believe that Katherine could have grown so hard so fast.

But then Violet felt the girl's hands on her shoulders and heard Katherine say, "What's wrong? You'll be all right. You know it. You're rich and—"

Violet knew these things, but she didn't expect them to be used in an attempt to comfort her when she was clearly so broken. She spun away. "Just go, Katherine."

Katherine sighed. "What is it?"

"Just get out," Violet said.

She listened to Katherine's feet padding toward the office door and then there was silence. A suffocating moment of desperation stopped her breath, her thoughts wild as windswept prairie grasses.

That's it. She's walking out.

Violet cradled her belly, wondering if the walls would crash in along with her self-respect. Then she heard it, the sound of feet coming back toward her.

"What's wrong?" Katherine gripped Violet's shoulder, making her turn. Violet couldn't remember the last time she'd felt vulnerable in front of someone, not this way. "Tell me."

Violet swallowed the rolling sobs.

Katherine pulled her toward the settee and gave her a handkerchief from the cuff of her shirtwaist. "It can't be all that bad?"

Violet's mind, still muddled, wasn't sure what to do. Truth, lies, self-preservation, all fought to be in charge.

Weren't they all the same thing? "Oh, Katherine. Only you can help me."

Katherine studied Violet. Violet slid closer. "Olivia's a mess. Everything is falling apart. All I can do is beg you, have mercy, just this once, and then, yes, you can be free of Dreama, and we can pretend we never heard of her."

Katherine blew out her breath. Violet could see she was weighing her loyalties. She shook her head and looked away.

Which tact? Anger, threats, desperation? Which was best right now, this time? "Never mind," Violet stood. "*We'll* be fine."

Violet sniffled into the handkerchief and walked toward the door.

"We?" Katherine said.

Violet turned back. Katherine stood. Violet put on her most pitiful face, partly on purpose, mostly because she felt as pathetic as she must have appeared. "My baby and me."

Katherine's expression changed, her eyes narrowing on Violet before dropping her gaze downward.

Violet massaged her midsection. "Just one more night," she said, patting her abdomen protectively. "Then I'll slink away, all debt forgiven. I just need enough for my baby and me to survive."

Katherine's face grew dark. Violet knew the girl understood exactly how much a single woman with a child would need. Children changed everything for an unmarried woman, crippling even the most capable sort, even someone like Jeanie Arthur.

Katherine finally nodded. "All right, Miss Violet. I'll help you. One last time."

Violet accepted an embrace, and as they clung to each other, her conscience only pinched for a moment when she thought of how she was planning to leave Katherine. But Violet had a baby to worry about, and that was the only thing that mattered now.

Chapter 71

Confession
Katherine

Had I heard that right? *My baby and me.* Violet's words kept repeating in my head. I was left to assume the baby was Judge Calder's, but I didn't want to know more; I didn't want to think about the judge's wife, their dead babies, not any of it.

Violet's tears and predicament combined with my own waning strength to weaken my resolve. Unwed mothers were shunned. Unwed mothers struggled for crumbs of food and slipshod shelter, their children suffering to death. An unwed mother was as vulnerable as the child she bore. I couldn't be party to causing Miss Violet's child to suffer an orphan's fate or worse. I had no choice but to do the right thing. No matter that it angered me, that she taunted me with what she viewed as my lapsed independence in trusting Aleksey. What did I know? The judge had a wife, didn't he? Perhaps betrayal was unavoidable when it came to love. Perhaps Miss Violet was right.

I flipped through the recipe books, book one and book two, a pair reunited like long-lost family. I exhaled. I couldn't imagine explaining to Aleksey why I was going to be Dreama one last time. He would have to understand Miss Violet's predicament, that I couldn't in good conscience not help. He'd have to. Looking at the books, thinking what an absolute miracle it was that Miss Violet had bought me one book and Aleksey had found the other and that they were back as a set. If the universe could allow that to happen, surely Aleksey could understand my plight, my need to help Miss Violet.

As I passed the parlor, I saw Mama standing by the front window, holding the wooden spoon doll. Her shoulders drooped and shuddered, and though she was silent, I saw she was shrunken with loss. Though she had devoted much time to me in the time of my illness, she never missed a day in going to the courthouse, to fight to bring Yale home.

Mama drew a deep breath, pulling up every inch of her height. She went to the table that stood between the windows and picked up a glass tube that stood upright in a wooden base. She moved to the window light, holding it at eye level, scrutinizing it. The glass portion was filled with clear fluid.

"What's that, Mama?"

"Come see," she said.

I studied it. Most of the water was perfectly clear, but white crystal slivers swirled in the middle of the tube rising upward or drizzling down. I didn't know which.

"It's a storm glass," she said, holding it so I could see better. "Mr. Hayes made it for me—sent it from his sister's with the code that explains what the liquid and crystals are telling us. Said storm glasses are old as time for telling the weather for sailors. See, with the crystals spread like this, it means rain's coming."

My mouth fell open at the sight, at hearing her marvel at the power of crystals.

"James would've loved this," she said.

I stared at the flaky crystal slivers, so white and jagged they could have been shaved right off a wing of my angel crystal.

"The past two days, the crazy weather was actually predicted by this storm glass. So odd."

"I love it," I said, lost in the suspended crystals.

"I only wish I had one of these to help me predict the rest of my life. Little Yale," she whispered.

I put my arm around her. "We'll get her back. Aleksey promised, and I think Miss Violet is helping."

She shrugged, turning the glass slightly to catch the light in different ways.

I looked at the crystals. They seemed to corkscrew in the liquid. "Gonna be windy."

Perhaps now was the time to confide in Mama about Dreama. Surely, she'd understand my having to help Miss Violet in her condition and that in doing so Miss Violet would help us? If she believed this storm glass could predict the weather with water and crystals, surely she would believe I could use a crystal to gather desperate souls.

"I'm glad that reminds you of James. He's always with us, Mama."

"That's true. Always on my mind."

"No one really dies, Mama."

She nodded, tilting the glass back and forth. "He's almost more alive in me with his death. And Yale." She sighed. "At least I know James's lot."

"Mama. I have something to tell you."

She set the storm glass on the table and looked at me.

My throat tightened, and I moved my lips, but no words came. I wanted so much to share the truth, and surely this time, with such closeness between us, was the right time to tell her.

"There's a lot that—" I stopped, hearing someone knocking at the door.

"Oh, I hope that's not Elizabeth Calder looking for her coats," Mama said. "I don't think I can face her. Not right now."

I thought of how Aleksey had nailed some of the expensive fabric to the windows when the glass broke. I couldn't imagine how we'd remedy that in a way that would satisfy Mrs. Calder. I thought of how her husband had made Miss Violet pregnant. I disliked the woman, but I felt sorry for her being betrayed.

Mama got up and crept toward the door, limbs taut, shoulders stiff. Once there, she pulled back a corner of the filmy material covering the window in the door. I watched, holding my confession about Dreama in my mouth, waiting for the chance to spill it all out.

I couldn't see who had arrived, but Mama's rigid posture softened like warm butter, and she flung open the door. Mr. Hayes stepped through and roped his arms around her, pulling Mama up off her feet. He buried his head in the space between her shoulder and neck, jarring me. My hand went to that same place on my body, that space was precious and private and certainly not where a man secreted his lips on a woman who was simply an acquaintance.

They whispered, and Mama looked nervously back at me.

She deserved some kindness and affection. It brought strange feelings to me. "Mr. Hayes, hello," I said, moving toward them.

They stepped apart, his face wrought with surprise, then a detachment formed between them, their more formal masks returning.

"Hello, Katherine," Mr. Hayes said. "It's wonderful to see you up and around. Your mother gave me updates as I was finishing my dissertation and defending it and then tending to my sister and her family."

"Thank you, Mr. Hayes."

Mama stepped forward, appearing more self-assured. "It's Dr. Hayes now. He defended his dissertation."

I felt a mixture of emotion at seeing the affection between them.

He removed his hat. "I had to come in person because I need to leave again. I'm due back in Ames."

Mama nodded. "They're still sick?"

"Mighty," he said. "I was told Aleksey Zurchenko and Alan Stevens are doing their best to secure Yale's release. I've forwarded my letters of support to help."

"Thank you," Mama said. "I'm headed to the courthouse now. But first I have to face Elizabeth. With all these coats. All this unfinished material. Ruined. We used it to warm Katherine when she was at her sickest. And the rest is full of nail holes. Aleksey was wonderful when Katherine was sick, but with Yale gone, I couldn't even attempt to finish these coats. I've been running down every way to get her out of Glenwood, gathering information for Aleksey. Meeting with judges. I re-wet and re-ironed the coats that were finished, and the shine is perfect. But Judge Calder saw me wearing one in court. I was so exhausted that I'd put it on without even realizing it."

"Let me do it," Dr. Hayes said.

"Do what?"

"Return everything."

"You can't," Mama told him. "She'll skewer you. You have so much at stake. Your standing . . ."

"I'm not in their circles. That only matters if you want to be included with them."

"Only because you choose not to enter their circles, not yet anyway," Mama said. "But it's when they ostracize you that—"

"It doesn't matter."

"Judge Calder is childhood friends with the president of Drake. It could hurt your career," Mama said.

"They can't hurt me. I'm not looking to sit on a board of anything they're involved with. What does she care about the activity of a post-doctoral student in science and agriculture?"

Mama grimaced as though she knew another answer to this, as though he was not correct in his assessment.

He took her hand. "Let me do this for you." He smiled at me. "For all of you."

Mama's eyes welled, and she lowered her gaze, overcome by his gesture. "Thank you."

I turned away to give them a moment. Although I wasn't sure about Dr. Hayes's intentions, I'd never seen a man offer so much to Mama. I'd never seen anyone take care of her more than she took care of others, and for that little bit of grace on earth, I wouldn't interfere even if Tommy would have turned inside out with anger at the thought, at the sight of any of this. Mama deserved this, every sliver of love I knew she felt in those very short moments. The moment had passed for my confession. Her worry, the load of work she had to take on to get Yale back, made my telling her about Dreama seem unimportant and cruel. I didn't know when the right time would come to reveal my part in Dreama, but I knew it wasn't right then.

Chapter 72

Denied
Aleksey

The judge slammed his gavel. "Denied."

I stood beside Mr. Stevens, in front of Judge Smythton. I looked at Mr. Stevens, then back at the judge, swamped in disbelief. I shuffled around the table and strode toward the bench. Judge Smythton drew back, startled at my approach. "Didn't you hear one word that he said? Those children were moved to Glenwood under false reports of vagrancy. Further, the children in Column A—"

Bang, bang, bang. Judge Smythton hammered the gavel and pointed it at me. "Control your man, Stevens, or you'll both be sleeping in a cell."

Mr. Stevens grabbed my arm.

I shook off his grip. "Yale Arthur's brother was standing right there when she fell," I said. "She was *not* unattended. And she's listed in Column A. Those patients can be released into custody of a responsible adult."

Mr. Stevens pulled me back. "Shut up, Zurchenko. Don't draw attention to this girl or this proceeding. See those reporters back there? They'll sniff out a story, and we'll all be doomed. Your girl Yale, too."

I'd promised the Arthurs that I had this under control, and now it would be another month at least until Yale's case was addressed. I'd had it with Mr. Stevens, feeling he and the judge were playing me for a fool. I wanted to grab the reporters who hung around the courthouse and tell them the whole thing. But something gave me pause. I knew I needed to speak to Mrs. Arthur before I publically used Yale's name.

"I'm going to expose this," I said. Stevens turned his back to me. I stalked out of the courtroom.

All right. What's next? How can I get Yale out before a month passes? I imagined her in the care of strangers, their uncaring hands, worse ... I wove through a clutch of newspaper reporters and bit my tongue to keep from telling them everything right then. "Excuse me." I bounced off one reporter then the next as I made slow progress.

I passed two fellas talking, and had I been moving as quickly as I would have liked, I might not have heard what they were saying.

"Dreama performs tomorrow. Seven at the Savery Hotel."

I stopped.

"And the police will arrest her?" the other man said.

I scratched the back of my neck, pretending not to listen.

"Twenty-three men, locked and loaded. Or maybe they'll just string her up. Heard old Reverend Conway's hot as Hades over his wife's reading. Dreama said she was near death, and the woman hasn't left bed since."

"And those yammering gasbags always pushing leads on us?"

"The devil-did-every-crime ladies?"

"They've already alerted me they're coming with a passel of other angry ladies. And their husbands."

"Husbands? This is getting serious."

"Mob theatrics can be fun for some men. You know how that goes."

I couldn't breathe. I dropped my pencil to make it look less like I was eavesdropping.

"Dreama's harmless," the first reporter said. "Told me my mother was sorry for slapping me silly just before she died."

"Truly?" said the other reporter.

He raised his hand. "Honest Abe."

"Huh."

"Huh is exactly what I said."

"So you're not the least curious who Dreama is?" the second reporter said. "Where all that cash is going?"

I untied and loosened my shoe before tying it all over again.

The first reporter shuffled his feet. "For a while, I thought Violet Pendergrass was pretending to be Dreama."

"Nah," the second man said, "too busy getting her girls into her clients' beds."

I stood and raised my hand as though waving to someone across the hall. I didn't know how much longer I could appear casual to these men.

"Dreama's tied to Pendergrass for sure," the second reporter said, crossing his arms.

I scribbled on my legal pad.

"But why?" said the second reporter. "Plenty of wealthier, savvier men than me claim she's a financial visionary."

The other reporter bit the end of his pencil before circling it in the air. "Haven't seen hide nor hair of Dreama for at least two, two and half weeks. Maybe she got wind of the angry folks and left town? Maybe the crooked politicians and judges are having second thoughts and shut things down?"

"I'd love to print that; wouldn't you?"

"Just need some evidence. Tight operation they're running."

"For now. Something will leak."

"Always does."

The doors on courtroom number three swung open, and all the reporters pushed by me, heading in to take their seats for the next proceeding. When the hall was nearly empty, I looked toward the exit. A woman sped from a judge's chambers, moving quickly. From down the hall, I heard what I thought was a sob, a release of pain.

I squinted at the woman's back. Mrs. Arthur. I yelled for her, but she'd already made it down the steps and out the door. If she'd been there to see about Yale, she would have been in Smythton's courtroom with me. I followed her and looked at the office she'd exited. *Judge Calder.* Old friends, weren't they? Had he declined to help her? Whatever happened, it wasn't good. How much more could Mrs. Arthur take?

My mind went back to the reporters' conversation, the fact that Dreama was to perform tomorrow night. My stomach lurched. Could Katherine have really promised such a thing? She still grew tired after doing simple chores at her home; I couldn't imagine that she'd been to Miss Violet's and had been convinced to work as Dreama again. I rubbed my chin and fought back the fear caught in my throat. Not after the talk we had. Perhaps this reading had been planned for a long time and she'd forgotten about it?

One thing at a time. I didn't know how to keep Katherine safe. Just weeks ago, I would have thought the police and the court system could ensure her safety, especially with all I thought I knew of the law. But now . . . I couldn't trust anyone. If only she'd never left Darlington Township. If only she were safe back on the prairie.

I bit my pencil. That was it. I'd get Katherine out of Des Moines. Miss Violet couldn't be trusted to put Katherine's safety first. Yale was unsafe. There weren't any officials I could trust. Mrs. Hillis—out of town. No, no one.

I had to get her out of Des Moines. If reporters and other people were piecing together Dreama's connection to

Violet, if there was a group forming to confront Dreama, it wouldn't end well. I told myself to stop worrying. Katherine had told me Olivia often replaced Katherine for quick readings. Katherine had promised me she was finished being Dreama. My belief in her ability had comforted her. I knew that was something that would be part of her forever, but we both agreed that monetizing it was dangerous. She promised. No more Dreama.

But as I headed for the exit, I realized there would be records and money and all sorts of things that might leave Katherine in danger even if she was not playing Dreama anymore. *One thing at a time.*

**

I sent a telegram to Ma in Yankton, knowing she would collect it with her mail in the next few days.

We're coming—Katherine, her ma, her brother, and me. *Be there soon. Will explain then.*

Next, I hitched a ride back to Palmer's place as rain began to fall hard. With every mile toward the farm, the temperature kept rising, turning the thick snow to deep mud. Soaked from not having rain gear, I entered the house and found Palmer in the kitchen.

"I need a leave of absence," I said.

"A what?"

I doubted Palmer would give a damn about my dilemma, and I was prepared to take the consequences of my demands, but I knew what I had to do and had never been surer of anything in my life.

"It's Katherine. I need to get her to my ma's place. I need to keep her safe."

He squinted at me.

Palmer came closer. "Safe from what?"

"Something's brewing in town. If Katherine stays here, I can't be sure she'll be safe."

Mr. Palmer took my sopping-wet hat from my head and hung it on a peg. He wiggled his fingers. "Get out of that coat."

I unbuttoned it and shook out of it, water sprinkling the walls.

He reached for the coat and hung it. "You took the book when she got sick, didn't you?"

I stepped into the bootjack and pulled my foot out. "I didn't think you wanted it. I can get it back. The cures worked. They really worked."

"I won't destroy it. Not now."

I removed my other boot and set the pair in line with the other fellas' mud-caked pairs, always set biggest to smallest for some reason. "I'm sorry for not asking permission to take it," I told him. "But Katherine..." I needed to say it out loud to someone. Something about Palmer had softened. His confession that he'd read his wife's book, that he understood that Winnie had done what he asked, had created crushing guilt. The tears on the page had been his.

"I thought I might die if someone ever found out how awful a husband I'd been," he said, looking down at his feet.

"You couldn't have known what was going to happen, that she'd go for the comfrey."

He put up his hand to stop me from saying more. "I didn't *listen*, Aleksey. I let her go into the storm. And I'll live with that for the rest of my life. But in you knowing the truth, something about that just released this massive... I don't know"—he pressed his chest—"clot, the regret."

I nodded, seeing the sadness in him.

"At the time it all happened," he said, "I was so angry. Beda Smalley and her charade. Her friendship with Winnie. I was so frightened that instead of helping Winnie, I just shamed her, thinking she'd stop and be far away from being lumped in with the con artists in town."

I couldn't breathe for a moment. I thought of Dreama, Katherine's part in her mythology. Maybe the release of

Palmer's guilt had more to do with me knowing than he could imagine. Maybe it wasn't just that he confided in just anyone, it was that I specifically was the person who knew the story.

I touched his shoulder, startling him. He met my gaze. "Katherine. She's like Winnie, Mr. Palmer."

He flinched. I thought of how he had responded to Madame Smalley when we saw her getting arrested that day in town. But I had to tell him anyway.

"Like Winnie?"

"Yes. And your Winnie's book saved her. And I'll always be grateful for finding that book, for keeping it, for your wife writing it. But I need to get Katherine out of Des Moines before they take her. And I need you to let me go. Just for a while."

He drew back. "Who would take Katherine?"

I stepped back. I hoped he could handle hearing this particular truth. "Dreama. Katherine is Dreama."

His eyes widened.

"She isn't a con artist. She can do what Dreama does, but she's being used by . . . Look, I just need to get her to my ma's place until this passes. I'll come back to finish my share of work here. I promise."

Mr. Palmer put his hand between my shoulder blades, guiding me down the hallway. "Go on. Get dry clothes. I read the papers. Do what you need to do."

I grabbed Palmer up, squeezing the air out of him. I set him down and thumped his back.

"Just go, Aleksey. Go get her."

**

I reached Katherine's front door, calling for her. I entered the parlor as she was struggling to sit up. She looked groggy. I'd interrupted a nap. I knelt beside her, wanting to be as calm as possible when I talked to her.

Her eyes widened as she curled her legs underneath her. She gripped my shoulders, shushing me, pulling me into an embrace. "What's wrong?"

I pulled out of her arms and held her hands. "We need to go."

"Go?"

"To my ma's."

Katherine swung her feet onto the floor and rubbed her eyes. I could see she was still coming out of sleep.

"What are you talking about?"

I forced myself to talk slowly, to convey urgency without making her panic. "At the courthouse. Reporters were talking. That group of ladies who've been yammering for months about Dreama is finally taking action. The concerned citizens of Des Moines have decided if the police won't take care of Dreama on their own volition, they'll take care of her for them. But police are planning to be there, too. Crooked judges and politicians. You're not safe."

Katherine stared into her lap. I could see she was sorting through what I told her. I was certain she would argue that since she was no longer playing Dreama, this wouldn't affect her. She may have been partly correct, but I wasn't sure that was enough at this point.

"They're starting to put together how Miss Violet is associated with Dreama."

"Well, she introduces Dreama at every reading," Katherine said. "I'm not sure that's so newsworthy."

"But now they're inquiring about more than that. They said Miss Pendergrass is selling her girls to her clients, that she didn't hire them to do their finances. They're prostitutes." I gripped Katherine's arms. "Did you know that?"

She drew back. The surprise on her face told me she hadn't. She brushed at my hands. I released her.

"Prostitutes? Who?"

"They didn't name names."

She shook her head, staring into her lap again. "The girls have relationships with their clients, but not *that* kind. Not what you're saying."

"We have to go," I said, pulling her up. She wiggled out of my grip.

"I can't just leave. Mama and Yale and Tommy are here. This isn't the first mob that the papers claimed would confront Dreama. It's all just fodder, excitement. It brings in money."

"But they're digging. They're searching for records of money going in and out for various things. Surely, you know she must have kept records. Your name could be in them."

She covered her mouth. Her face paled. She pushed me aside and stood, arms tight around her waist. I followed her to the fireplace, where she poked at the dying fire.

"Ledgers," she said. "She has a record of what I owe." She set the poker aside and ticked off fingers. "Lists of the girls' work, their skills—" She covered her mouth as though she just remembered something. "Yes. She keeps them."

"Them?"

"Two ledgers."

"Do you know where they are?"

"With her at all times."

"I'll take care of that end of things. But you need to prepare to leave tonight."

Hardness flashed in her eyes, her jaw set. "Not without Mama."

I paced, pushing my hand through my hair. "You have to listen to me about this."

I stopped in front of her and took her hand in mine. I kissed the back of it.

She sighed. "No one's coming for me, Aleksey. I promise. I'm safe. That reading is tomorrow."

"So you're doing it?"

She wouldn't look me in the eye. "I won't leave Mama like this." She pulled her hand away and went to the front window, pulling a curtain panel back. "No way. You don't know what we've been through since we left the prairie. And now Yale. No way."

I stared at the back of her, the way she stood rod-straight. Her voice reinforced her stance on the matter. Did we have the time to spare if we waited until tomorrow? I didn't want to leave her. I wanted her next to me. I wanted to keep a close watch until I got her back to Darlington Township.

"Promise you won't do any more readings? Even if every grieving mother in town knocks on your door."

She was silent.

"Katherine? I'm not judging you. I'm not angry. I'm not—I love you. I love you so much. Please promise me. I feel this love as surely as I feel rain in a storm."

She turned and smiled weakly. She held her hand up. "No more readings, Counselor. I swear."

"Thank you, thank you, Katherine. Soon you'll be safe for good." I took her hand in mine. "Let me see to Yale. There has to be a way to get her before we go." I wasn't sure how I'd manage it, but the time for polite lawyering, even for a man not yet a lawyer, had passed.

Chapter 73

Stay
Violet

Betrayal. Violet's hands shook. She clasped them tight on the kitchen tabletop. The stillness frightened her. Her breath, her baby inside her, her own heartbeat. For a few moments in time, over the past year and a half, she'd felt as though she could enjoy her life in Des Moines unencumbered. Now her contentment was hindered, attacked.

How could she? Violet had heard Aleksey convince Katherine not to perform. The girl said the words, "I swear." She was pulling away from Miss Violet despite their conversation the day before. Katherine's promise had felt sincere then. But she knew . . . Something had made Violet go next door to be sure that Katherine was feeling well. *Something* had told her to go there to check, and now she was glad she'd done just that. The conversation was ending when she arrived. How lucky that she hadn't delayed going next door even longer. What if she'd missed their entire discussion? Now she realized Katherine was a weaker part of the plan than she'd anticipated.

Damn Aleksey. Violet certainly understood the power of love, or whatever this was between Aleksey and Katherine—infatuation, sexual attraction—especially the first blush of it, but now she knew this was different. Katherine's interests seemed more complicated and involved than a first love. The last thing Violet wanted was to have Katherine discuss the business of Dreama with Aleksey. She slipped back outside, watched for his departure and then sent Olivia to call for Katherine.

Violet's mind cleared, her energy returning as she considered the situation. She stood and paced, thinking, figuring. Jeremy had ignored every note she'd sent via Olivia or Helen. She could let Katherine leave with Aleksey, throw drunk Olivia into Dreama's costume then take the money and be gone before the crowd figured out Olivia was no more intuitive than the kitchen sink.

That could work.

If needed, she'd do it. She held her stomach and exhaled. No. That wasn't the answer. Katherine had moved on in her heart and mind. But Violet was sure that she could appeal again to Katherine's goodness, her concern for children and single mothers. It was clear by what Violet overheard that Katherine was leaving, but what if Violet could arrange the reading for tonight, before the angry masses formed, before Katherine left town?

Violet had watched as Aleksey left Katherine. She'd told him she wouldn't do the reading. He had believed her. He would busy himself with the details of leaving town, and Katherine would be available to do the reading without any harm done to their plans.

That at first had nauseated Violet. But now, now perhaps that very development was the thing that would make it all possible.

Could it work? Violet went upstairs and surveyed her private rooms. She'd created a soothing, luxurious place to rest and dream. She could hardly believe she'd have to leave it all behind. She pulled her carpetbag from the closet and rechecked it; a change of clothes, stacks of money, room for her ledgers and other small possessions. Beside the bag were her sunflower painting and Katherine's painting of the furnace room at the glass factory. When the time came, she'd be ready. She scanned the room and took in her precious belongings. She ran her hand down the silken dresses and said a little goodbye to this particular life.

"Miss Violet?"

Violet turned. "Olivia."

"I told Katherine you wanted to see her. She'll be here soon."

"Thank you. I have a job for you."

Olivia stepped closer to Violet, rubbing her palms together. "Dreama?"

A spur of irritation came to Violet. She grabbed a box from the top shelf of her closet and opened it, pulling out some envelopes. "Not just yet. But soon. What I need now is for you to take the carriage and run these letters to our clients who intended to come to the Savery tomorrow night."

"All of them?"

"It's a smaller, wealthier group, remember?"

She sighed.

"It's very important, Olivia. They must keep this news quiet. That will excite them. Tell them Dreama's spirits have gathered unexpectedly, earlier than she thought, and let them know they'll need to pay another thousand each. For when Dreama's gathering happens early, she's always rife with fruitful information. It will be well worth their while."

Olivia scowled.

A burning sensation crept up between Violet's breasts with her anxiety. She rubbed her sternum. "Oh, Olivia. No pouting. You know your role is *always* most important, even if Katherine believes otherwise. Without you, what would the rest of us do? Neither of us has received the accolades that Katherine has, yet we do everything, don't we?"

Olivia smiled and lifted her eyes to meet Violet's. The acid in Violet's chest receded as she saw Olivia's good humor return.

She suddenly embraced Violet. "Thank you for loving me, Violet. Thank you so much."

Olivia disappeared with the letters, and Violet was left swamped by the scent of gin, saddened that Olivia's usefulness had run its course.

**

When Olivia returned, she brought back some interesting information. Violet grabbed her umbrella. Tommy Arthur had been thrown in jail. Another distraction. Some men had mentioned to Tommy they thought Pearl might be a lady of the night. He'd defended her honor. One of the men there had been Judge Calder.

What infuriated Violet was that Jeremy was involved. Her anger threatened to distract her. She'd deal with him later. Right now, she needed to tie Katherine tight to her plan for one final reading. If Jeremy was going to spend time in saloons with destitute drunks and whores, Violet was going to use his name to get what she needed.

The drenching rain was not letting up, and she'd waited long enough for Katherine to come as summoned. Outside, it must have been sixty degrees, but small patches of ice still held tight in the middle of her yard. She knocked at the Arthurs' front door, and this time Katherine answered. Her eyes were swollen, and Violet knew the girl had been informed of her brother's incarceration.

She waved Violet in, trying to speak between heavy sobs.

Violet expected Jeanie to be home, that she'd have to approach this matter with even more delicacy than was time effective. But she must have gone out.

"Tommy's in jail," Katherine said.

Violet cocked her head, a twinge of sympathy embedding itself. She put her arm around Katherine. "Sit down, you're so upset. Tell me."

They went into the parlor. "Some man," Katherine said, shoulders heaving, "thought Pearl was a prostitute, and Tommy intervened to save her. But there was a big fight, and I guess the police came. Judge Calder and Reverend Shaw were there, and somehow Tommy punched—" Katherine dropped her face in her hands.

"What?" Violet said.

"He punched Judge Calder, and he tossed Tommy in jail."

He deserved a punch, Violet thought, and covered her mouth until she swallowed the laugh that threatened. "Oh my, oh my," she said.

"And I can't do a reading at the Savery, Miss Violet. There's a group of people who want to unveil Dreama and have her arrested. It's not just talk like all the other times."

Violet took Katherine by the shoulders. "Listen carefully. Look at me square in the eye. I can make all these problems go away."

She shook her head and tried to wiggle away.

Violet squeezed harder. "Look at me." Katherine did, and Violet told her, "We'll do the reading *tonight* instead."

"No," Katherine said. "I promised I wouldn't."

"You promised me yesterday you would, and all those months ago in my kitchen. You said you wanted to save your mother. Remember all of those promises?"

"Things have changed, Miss Violet."

Violet dropped her hands. She wanted to move quickly on this, before Jeanie returned. She wouldn't get into what she overheard between Katherine and Aleksey; that part didn't matter if she got Katherine to agree to perform tonight. She got on her knees in front of Katherine. "*I* haven't changed. My caring about you like a daughter hasn't changed. You're my *first* daughter. That hasn't changed. And you know the baby and I—"

Katherine nodded. "I know."

"If you do this reading tonight, the last one, as you promised, I'll get Tommy out of jail and your sister out of Glenwood. Then you can all disappear and live that fairy tale you've been telling me about in a sweet little cottage with a fenced garden in the back."

Katherine stared at Violet. "If you can make this happen why haven't you helped us get Yale out already?"

Violet nearly choked. Her mind was foggy, the pregnancy leaving gaps in her ability to plan and think.

"I just figured the whole thing out now. That's all."

Katherine glared at her. Violet could see her mind wind around the truth—that Violet hadn't done all that she could to help.

Katherine exhaled. "Never mind. How can you make this happen now? That's all I care about."

"Judge Calder and I are close. You know that. I know you do. And if Tommy punched him, you're going to need my help in calming the man down."

Katherine shook her head. "Mama could talk to him. They go way back."

Violet felt her role as a needy woman faltering. "Katherine, your mother isn't who you think she is. And ask her the same question you asked me. If she could make Yale's release happen, why not yet?"

Katherine drew back. "What does that mean?"

"It means your mother isn't that different than me, really. You just see her one way. That's all. Open your eyes. She has priorities beyond you. Reed Hayes, for one. And now you bring up Judge Calder's name. Perhaps there's even more on her plate than we *both* knew. It's time for you to trust me fully," Violet told her. "I've never left you to fend for yourself. Have I?"

Katherine scowled. "That wasn't what happened. Mama didn't leave us on purpose."

Violet ignored her response. "This is your chance to save your family, to show that you're grownup."

Katherine's face reddened. Her jaw clenched and Violet knew Katherine was growing angry. "How do you know you can get them out, that Judge Calder will listen to you?"

Violet pulled folded papers from her pocket. "Here. Right here."

Katherine read the papers. "They aren't signed."

Violet snatched them back. "Afterward."

Katherine put her hands on her hips and bit her lip. "Those papers say Judge Calder will immediately release Yale and Tommy as soon as the event ends. He agreed to that?"

"Of course, Katherine. You're witness to my intimacy with the judge. Surely, you can see how that type of influence is powerful."

Katherine moved so she could examine the papers without touching them.

"It's an easy decision," Violet said. "No one will fault you for one more reading. Just one. For your family's survival. You'll be forgiven. You have new information. Earlier promises are deemed moot in this case. Aleksey will understand. Certainly, your mother will if she was ever to know. This is what you've been waiting to do. And they love you. You know that. This is a gift to them, to your family, present and future."

Katherine's shoulders tensed. "You know what I promised Aleksey?"

Violet nodded. "I overheard. I didn't stick around to—"

Katherine reached for the papers. "Give those to me now, and I'll get the judge to sign them."

Violet scoffed, snatched them back, and folded them up. "A few weeks ago, I would have agreed to that. Not today. You've plotted and planned behind my back. I'm the one taking the risk by trusting you. So think of Tommy in jail, grown men having at him. Yale in Glenwood . . . ."

Katherine jerked as though she'd been hit.

"No, no," Violet told her. "Don't think of that. Just act, Katherine. Save them all."

Chapter 74

Change of Plans
Aleksey

Driving back to the farm, I stopped to let a family cross the street. It was then I saw a woman coming toward me. Her eyes were dazed, her hair mussed, her shirtwaist unbuttoned at the collar. I looked away but then the face of the woman settled into my mind. I shook my head. It couldn't be. I looked again. Her haggard appearance had made Mrs. Arthur look like a stranger.

I called to her, and when she met my gaze, she appeared startled. I pulled over and hopped from the rig, jogging to her. I held out my arm for her to take. Still looking stunned she accepted my arm and followed me to the wagon.

"What's wrong?" I said.

"I just . . ." She looked around nervously, as though someone might be following, listening to what she was saying.

"What is it?"

She drew shallow breaths and seized my arm to steady herself. "I don't even know where to start."

Mrs. Arthur was tall, although slight, like Katherine. The woman had always seemed formidable to me. Now it was as though she'd shrunk right before my eyes, delicate, like dandelion seed.

"I have something I need to tell you, too," I said. "I'm taking Katherine to my ma's tomorrow. You, too, of course, and Tommy. I'll come back for Yale—"

"Taking us?"

"I know this is unexpected, and it must seem so strange to hear. Katherine wants to explain—"

"So you know?"

I drew back. Had *she* known all along? Had she allowed Katherine to risk her safety for money?

"*You* know?" I said.

She swallowed hard. She covered her throat with one hand. "I was made aware that my son found his way to jail today."

"Oh, so you don't mean ..." Relief allowed me to breathe again. She hadn't been aware of Katherine's dangerous work after all.

Her lips quivered. "I was told about Katherine today, too."

My stomach churned. I'd never felt so disgusting, repulsed at myself, in my life.

"You knew?" She looked at me square. "You all knew?"

I didn't know what to say.

Her gaze shamed me.

"How could you keep this from me? This awful game she's playing?"

How could I explain that I hadn't wanted to? That once I found out, I didn't reveal it, that I didn't want to hurt my ma or Mrs. Arthur, that once Katherine got sick, it didn't seem important. My defenses woke at the word *game*.

"It wasn't a game. She isn't pretending or trying to scam people. What she can do is real. And I only found out just before she got sick. At first I was angry at her, too."

"Oh, dear god, Aleksey. Her reputation and safety are at risk, and there are very powerful people who know about this."

"I told her to stop, to tell you. And then she got sick and . . . I know people are inflamed about Dreama and want to arrest her and Violet. And that's why I'm getting her out of town."

"Thank you." She looked dumbstruck, her eyes unfocused.

I could understand how this had taken its toll. But I also knew how hard it would be to see Katherine go.

She nodded. "All right. Tomorrow. She should go."

"What about Tommy? Can I help?"

The mention of Tommy put life back in her eyes. "I have to go."

"Let me help," I said, but she hurried off.

"I have to do this myself," she called over her shoulder. "Just get everything ready for Katherine."

I nodded as she disappeared into the crowd, moving toward her home.

Nausea swept over me again, and I felt her utter dismay. One of Mrs. Arthur's daughters was part of a questionable business arrangement, her son in jail, and her youngest child in an asylum. I couldn't fathom how she'd cope with all of that.

The only thing I could do was get Katherine out of town. That, I could do for certain.

Chapter 75

Revealed
Katherine

I waited as long as I could for Mama to return so I could tell her everything. Miss Violet's allusions that Mama was using men, or allowing them to use her, sickened me. It wasn't true. I knew that. Yet the expression of the idea chilled me.

I considered writing a note explaining how I was going to get Yale and Tommy back by simply doing one more thing, one more time for Miss Violet. But Mama would be blindsided, and I didn't want her learning such a thing about me without my being able to explain it, to see her face as she processed it and finally came to understand I did it all for her, for the family. Did she even know about Tommy yet?

I went next door to get dressed for the evening. There was a note on the makeup table:

Driver to pick you up at six this evening. Costume at Savery, arrive in makeup.

I sat in front of the mirror and glanced at the tub, the warm womb where I'd first felt as though I could actually become Dreama, or that she could be me. I'd gotten so good at calling the spirits that I no longer needed to coax them, to calm myself with baths, oils, and perfumes. I applied a bit of red to my lips, but I no longer needed extravagant paints. Being veiled, no one saw it anyway, and it had been part of my ritual only to boost my confidence when I first began on this path. How naïve of me. How perfect I'd been for the taking. The admission that I'd offered myself up was heavy on my conscience. I thought of poor Tommy, vulnerable Yale. Now wasn't the time to mull over my decisions. I quickly braided my hair, patted the angel crystal in my pocket, and bowed my head.

Please, God, let Aleksey forgive me. Let him understand I don't mean to betray him. I only mean to save my family. Please.

My eyes stung. I stood and saw that I still had an hour before the driver would arrive to take me to the Savery. I went next door to see if Mama had returned. I would have just enough time to explain it all before I had to go.

I sloshed back home through the muddy backyard and arrived just as Mama was leaving through the back door. Her head was down as she dug into her pocketbook. She nearly ran right into me. She secured the clasp and looked up at me, and her eyes went hard. A chill twisted up my spine under that glare. I couldn't remember her ever having looked at me quite like that. She stared, her jaw clenched. The rain lashed us, the wind wrapping our skirts around our legs.

"Mama, come inside," I said, pulling her hand. My insides shook at confiding my secret to her, but it was time.

She let me guide her back into the kitchen, and once inside, with the gusts shut out, I could see her better, the sharpness of her expression, the coldness it conveyed. It was almost as if she . . .

"How could you, Katherine?" She pulled her purse tight against her belly.

"I can explain, Mama. I can—"

"What have you been doing?"

"I wanted to tell you. I tried a couple times, but I couldn't and then I wanted to get us the money for our own little home and—"

"Katherine! Stop."

Her hands shook, the tremors working up to her shoulders, and her disappointment in me flooded the kitchen. I waited for her to speak.

When she didn't, I touched her forearm. "Let me explain."

"I heard it all, Katherine. More than I wanted to. More than I can bear."

Her disillusionment stopped my breath. My lies felt alive, roped around me.

"Who told you?"

"Judge Calder. Then I saw Aleksey, and when he heard that I knew, he filled me in. He told me he was going to take you to Greta's."

"Did they tell you I'm not a con, that I can see angels and gather up the spirits of dead people to set things right with their living family members? Did you believe me when I said James was with us, watching over us?"

She flinched. "Aleksey said that, yes. But that's not the point, is it?"

"I didn't want to lie, Mama. But I couldn't tell you. You didn't want to hear."

Mama shook her head. "It was wrong to . . . I think of Greta and . . ."

"Remember that night when she came over? How she felt? She was relieved, at peace. It's a gift I have, Mama. It's no scheme."

"I just can't imagine how this whole thing got started. I mean, Dreama? How on earth did this happen? How didn't I know? You didn't . . ."

I didn't know where to start, but I saw Mama's hurt. I wanted to take that away. "Miss Violet saw me help Olivia and believed, or at least she said she believed, I could help people. That the money would help you and our family and then—"

"And you let me talk about Dreama as though she were some abstraction, some fictional character in a newspaper story, and you talked about it, too, making me a fool."

"No, Mama. It was for you. I just needed to pay off the gowns and the makeup and the—"

Mama shook her head. I pulled her hand again. "Please. Let me explain more. Please."

As I tried to make her sit, but she jumped, appearing frightened. She covered her mouth. "I have to go. Tommy's in trouble, and I need to deal with that first."

"Miss Violet has papers to get Tommy out of jail and Yale out of Glenwood."

"You know about Tommy?"

I nodded.

"I'll go with you, Mama."

She shook her head. "No. Stay put."

"But Judge Calder gave Violet some papers to release both Tommy and Yale if I do one more reading. Maybe if we go together and confront him with what I know about him, his secrets—"

Mama pushed me down in the chair. "I'm not getting Tommy out of jail. Not yet. I'm paying off the men who want to break his legs when he gets out. He's run up quite the gambling debt at the saloon."

My lungs felt as though they'd been crushed. I thought of all the bruises I'd seen on Tommy over the past weeks. *Break his legs.*

Mama opened her purse, pulled out money, paged through some cash and change, and shut it again. "I have to do this alone."

I stood, and Mama pushed me back down again. "Stay."

She backed away, studying me, as though piecing together all that she'd learned, fitting it with the me she thought she'd known. I felt the same fear I'd felt all those years ago when she left me with that family, the first horrible family.

"I'm sorry, Mama."

She stopped and nodded. "I know. I'll be back once I settle this matter."

She left, taking my ability to think, to breathe, with her. My stomach tossed, and I ran to the sink, dry-heaving into it. Mama's disappointment in me, in Tommy, her loss of Yale, it ate away at her like acid. I looked out the back window. Mama had told me to stay. She was paying off Tommy's gambling debt, using her savings to keep Tommy from being maimed or killed.

I couldn't just sit there and wait. I had to get what was owed us.

I wasn't going to perform. But I was going to get what was mine, what Violet should have given us a long time ago.

**

When we turned onto the street that led to the hotel, I could see that a crowd had gathered in front of the Savery.

"Someone tipped them off," I said.

"'Excuse me?" the driver said.

I swallowed my fear and sat straighter. "Nothing. Around back, please."

When we got to the stage door in the rear of the alley, I hopped out of the carriage and entered the darkened space. It smelled of mildew and dirty feet. I headed down the hallway and could see some men at the far end, barking orders. "Miss Pendergrass requested extra security."

That didn't matter to me. After *A Night for Mothers* and someone trying to steal her take, I knew Violet wouldn't keep the money in the wings this time. I entered the dressing room, expecting to see Dreama's costume and Violet waiting for me. Instead, I was greeted by Olivia dressed as Dreama. She leaned against the back of a chair, a slow smile coming to her as she registered who was standing there.

"Where's Miss Violet?"

Olivia mumbled a few words. I shook her. "What are you doing?"

My shaking forced some clarity into Olivia's eyes, and she plucked my nose with her finger. I smacked her hand away. "I'm Dreama today," she told me.

That was fine with me. But I needed the money and for Olivia to make it onto stage so I could escape without anyone noticing.

"I'm Miss Violet's best girl," she said. "Not you."

She bobbed like a snake rising out of a basket. I steadied her. "You always were, Olivia, yes."

Olivia's head dropped to the side in an exaggerated way. "You knew that? Really? You knew?"

"Where's Violet?" I said. I needed Olivia to tell me where the money was. "She asked me to make sure the money was safe." I stroked Olivia's head. "She didn't want you to have to worry about that. She wanted you to focus on performing."

"She said that?"

I nodded.

Olivia mumbled again, and as I shook her, her eyes rolled back in her head and her legs gave out. I caught her and gently laid her down, surveying the space for anything that looked like it might hold the receipts for the night.

A crashing sound came from the hall. I stuck my head into it and saw men that I knew were hired as security pushing back several others. "Where's Dreama?" The interlopers were punching fists in the air. "She's a thief! She's the devil!"

My breath left my chest, and I ducked back into the dressing room. I looked at Olivia, who hadn't moved. I patted her cheeks. "Wake up."

The screaming crowd was getting louder, closer. I wanted to run, but I knew those angry people would harm Olivia. She wouldn't be able to defend herself. I leaned a chair back and wedged it under the doorknob to keep it shut if someone tried to enter. I snatched off Olivia's veiling and turned her over, gripped the dress at the collar, took a deep breath, and just ripped as hard as I could. The buttons flew in every direction, and I peeled the dress off like a fruit skin, then the boots with the uneven heels. I tossed everything in the corner.

Someone was pounding on the door. I held my breath, but the door held. I hoped whoever was at the door would move along. I told myself to stay calm and dragged Olivia into the closet. Then I opened the window that led into a side alley. I grabbed the lace from Dreama's veil and draped it across the windowsill, as if it had snagged on something while she hopped out the window. I climbed into the closet with Olivia, shut the door, and hid us beneath the old theater costumes and wigs. I heard the door to our room fly open and slam into the wall, the chair smacking into the closet door.

I held my breath, praying. Dust and mildew from the costumes filled my nose. Beside me, Olivia drew in a deep breath as if to sneeze. I pinched her nose and covered her mouth, hoping it would stave it off.

The voices in the dressing room rose and fell as they dug through drawers and tossed things around. I squeezed her nose tighter. *Please don't sneeze.*

Her body relaxed, and I exhaled. No sneeze.

I pulled another layer of costuming over us.

"Open that," I heard a man yell.

Someone yanked open the closet door. Light came in, visible even though we were buried under the clothes. I could feel costumes being pulled from the pile, the weight on us growing lighter.

I squeezed Olivia to me, covered her mouth, and waited.

Someone yelled, "She escaped!"

I peeked through some costuming and saw the mob had gathered at the window.

"She's gone," one man said.

"Check the back hall, near the dock."

"She can't be far," one man said.

"Fine, check the closet again, all the way in the back."

Some of the voices drifted away, disappearing completely with their footfalls. I held my breath again. This was it. When this man uncovered us, I could kick him in the gut and leap out of the window. Olivia would have to fend for herself.

The man grunted as he ripped away another costume. Another. Another. I prepared to kick and bolt. I forced my eyes to stay open, to be strong and attack.

"This way!" a voice came from farther away backstage. I stayed still, waiting for this man to finish his search. But as he got down to just a few more garments covering us, he turned and left.

Were we safe? I waited for perfect silence, still convinced that when I got up someone would be standing there ready to punish me.

Finally, I kicked off the costumes and left the closet. Olivia stirred but wasn't fully conscious. When she rolled onto her side, moaning, I took the chair and set it again under the doorknob, once again wedging the door closed. I grabbed the water pitcher that Miss Violet always set aside for after readings. I tried to rouse Olivia once more, nudging her with my foot and saying her name. Still no response.

"Here goes," I said and tossed the water onto her face. She sprang upward, eyes crazed. I pulled her to her feet, and she seemed to gain some lucidity. She leaned against the door and held up her hands so I could pull her work dress over her head. I put her shoes on her and put my finger to my lips.

I stood at the door. There was silence on the other side. I wiggled the chair and set it aside and pulled the door open to have a look. I held my breath. Nothing. No one.

I shook Olivia by the arms. "Let's go, and go quietly but quick. Pull it together before someone heads back." She leaned on me as we slunk down the hall toward the loading dock. Her head lolled to the side, and I squeezed her cheeks with my free hand.

"I'm sorry, Katherine. So sorry," she said.

"Shush, just keep moving." From back down the hallway, far beyond where I could see anymore, I heard voices again. There wasn't time to move as cautiously. We simply needed out. I pushed open the door that led to the loading dock. A horse neighed. I felt a rush of relief. The driver was there, in his seat, smoking a pipe. When he saw us, he hopped down and came to help. I handed Olivia over to him, and finally we moved quickly enough to escape the encroaching mob.

**

At Miss Violet's house, the driver helped me get Olivia through the kitchen and onto the settee in the parlor. He prepared to leave, saying he'd done more than he'd been paid for. I thanked him and handed him two bottles of Miss Violet's whiskey. He ran off, grinning around his pipe.

I had to find Miss Violet. She must have been upstairs if she wasn't at the theater. I covered Olivia with a blanket, lit a lamp, and ran through the house looking for Miss Violet, heading to the third floor where her private rooms were.

Empty.

I opened her closet. Many of her gowns and dresses were there, but many were missing. I thought of what she'd said to me about her baby, about needing nothing but money. She couldn't have simply left. Could she? Left Olivia and me to fend off the crowd at the Savery?

I stood there getting my breath. The last of the lingering pneumonia tightened my chest. I set the lamp down, and its light cast forward toward the bed. My eyes followed the path of light, trying to steady my breath. I noticed the edge of the rug had been disturbed.

The memory of Olivia fussing with the rug and dusting underneath it came back to me. I stared. I moved the side table and pulled the rug back and got on my knees, feeling around, pressing the boards this way and that. One of them gave a little. I pushed harder on one end, and the other upended. I removed it and then another and another. I moved the lamp closer and held it where I could see into the space.

It was too dark to see, so I pulled the lamp closer and reached inside, groping. I touched something solid but couldn't grab it. I got onto my belly and stretched, my fingers brushing past a leather plane, and I felt the edge of something hard, solid. A book. I dug my fingers in and pulled. I got to my knees. It was the ledger, the green one. I blew the dust off and opened it to be sure it wasn't an extra blank book. The spine cracked open, and I leafed through— nearly every page was full of notations and figures, profits and losses, and who owed what. I couldn't believe it had been left there. I dug around for more, something I could use to pay Glenwood for Yale, but my fingers only brushed thick dust and horsehair insulation. I replaced the floorboards, rug, and table, tucked the ledger under my arm, and headed back downstairs.

I stopped at the top of the stairs, listening. Silence. I gripped the banister and closed my eyes. I'd eluded the mob; no one knew I was Dreama, and I had the ledger. The moment was short-lived because the sound of a door slamming and footsteps startled me back to reality.

I was turning to run when I saw it was Mama who entered the parlor, barely noticing Olivia. Her shirtwaist collar was open, and her hair was mussed. I knew by how she was rushing that she'd gotten even more upset.

She looked up and saw me. "Katherine."

I ran down the stairs, and Mama came toward me, arms open, sending me right to tears as she hugged me tight, smoothing my hair, and when I pulled away, her eyes were full.

"You're all right," she said as she checked me over. "When I didn't find you at home, I—"

"I went to the Savery, but I didn't perform. I just wanted to get what was mine—ours."

"We have to go now," she said.

"I'm safe, Mama. I have Violet's ledger. This has everything Violet had planned and orchestrated while she was here. Probably more. And she's gone. She must have taken the other ledger, but she's gone. She's not going to tell people about Dreama or anything else. I'm safe. I'm fine."

"No. They're headed this way."

"Who?"

She shrugged. "I don't know names. Men and women, all gathered at the saloon when I paid Tommy's debt. They were ready to tear up the town. The winds and rains stopped them, but as soon as those die down . . ."

"No one knows, Mama. I know they don't."

"They know enough. Certain people know, Katherine, and we can't take a chance."

"I have the ledger with the names."

"There must be other records. We can't take the chance they find you here."

I shook my head. "There was another ledger, but Violet had to have taken it. It wasn't with this one. And she won't tell, Mama."

I could see that didn't soothe her panic.

"The papers Miss Violet promised me. If she left the ledger, she might have left the papers for us. We need them to get Tommy out of jail and Yale—"

"We've got to get out of here now!"

I looked over my shoulder to Miss Violet's office door. I'd come back and search the place for the papers. She couldn't have been so cruel as to go off and not leave them. She said she cared about Yale and Tommy. I believed that much.

"We can't leave Olivia," I said.

Mama ran to the settee and grabbed Olivia under the arms. "Get her under the knees," she said. We lumbered down the hall and a ground-shaking noise stopped us.

"What was that?" I said.

Mama listened for more noise or a clue as to what it was. "No idea. Let's go."

We readjusted our grip on Olivia and finally got her out the back door. The rain and wind bore down like a freight train, bringing Olivia to awareness. We got her to her feet, and she clung to us, arms slung around our necks. We neared the hedges and saw a fallen tree blocked our way. "That was the noise!" Mama said.

We half-dragged Olivia over Miss Violet's fallen oak, through the mud-soaked garden and stumbled into the safety of our kitchen where we set Olivia on the floor. Mama and I collapsed beside her, the ledger soaked, all of us trying to find our breath.

Chapter 76

Back at the Farm
Aleksey

I packed a bag with a change of clothes. Palmer and Harold gathered blankets for me. Mabel wrapped some bread and dried meat that would tide us over until Katherine and I could stop and eat a hot meal. I wrote a letter to Mr. Stevens and sealed it. I'd written a brief for an emergency hearing for the release of Yale Arthur from Glenwood, attempting to get one of the judges who didn't seem to be tied into criminal acts to hear me, but he'd refused. Said it wasn't appropriate. He did things by the book. After that, I had nothing left to try that night and headed back to the farm. I'd written to Mr. Stevens, telling him I planned to tell the truth about all of them if he didn't help me get to Yale and also get Tommy Arthur out of jail.

I shuddered as I closed the portfolio and swallowed hard. I straightened my pens, pencils and blank papers on my desk, hoping I would return to finish my studies after I tucked Katherine away at Ma's. But in thinking about how I essentially strong-armed Mr. Stevens into risking his own job for the sake of the Arthurs, I wasn't so sure he'd be willing to help me finish what I started. The absence of Yale in Mrs. Arthur's eyes haunted me. I knew more than ever that getting Katherine out of town was the right thing to do, but something else pricked at me. Was it enough?

**

The smell of freshly brewed coffee filled the kitchen. I poured myself a cup, questioning my plan to wait another day before we departed for Ma's place. It sounded reasonable when I'd agreed to it, a strong strategy when I went over it in my mind. But something in my belly said I should have just taken Katherine with me right then. Something told me it was time to go right now.

I went back toward the hall to go upstairs and gather my things, and Fat Joe came from the parlor. Mabel followed, grabbing his hand. They smiled as though they'd just finished opening gifts on Christmas morning. I looked forward to a time when Katherine and I could spend time together like they did.

"You two are happy today," I said.

"It's an important day," Mabel said.

Had I lost total track of the goings-on in the world? "What is it?"

"Some man at McCrady's gave Mabel a very special present today."

I knew the store. Mr. McCrady traded and sold everything from valuable silver to simple black buttons. "Wedding silver?" I said, having no idea what could make them so excited.

"Nope," Mabel said. "Tickets, very expensive tickets, to something that'll change my life."

I squinted at her. "The circus?" I joked.

"No, no, silly." Mabel patted my hand. "Dreama. I'm going to see Dreama tonight. And I'll finally know if my parents are at peace. I just know she'll pick me."

The blood flushed from my brain. I gripped the doorjamb. "Dreama?" A chill came to me like a winter wind.

"Mr. McCrady said he was supposed to attend tomorrow night but then the date changed, and he had another obligation so he gave us the tickets."

"Mighty generous," Fat Joe said.

I stared at one, then the other. "You're sure? Tonight?"

They nodded and happily swung their joined hands

"I have to go," I said, rushing out. Dreama wouldn't perform today. She couldn't.

Chapter 77

Run
Katherine

We were out of breath by the time we got Olivia to our parlor and settled her on the settee. In the kitchen, I filled the kettle with water. The burden of all my lies weighted me. "I'm so sorry, Mama. I didn't mean to cause all of this. I wanted to give you a house, a sweet garden, a little room all for yourself and your winter seeds."

She stood across the room, arms crossed. We stared at each other. I wanted her forgiveness so badly.

As though she heard my silent plea, she rushed to me and pulled me close. "I know, Katherine, I know."

We held each other.

"But you have to leave. It isn't safe. Aleksey told me his plans when I saw him earlier."

"Tomorrow. He knows to get me when we can all go." I shook my head. "But I can't leave you, Mama."

"I know, I know. It won't be…" Mama's voice thinned out.

"For very long," I finished her sentence bringing tears to her eyes. I'd believed that line so many times before. I knew she didn't want to separate again. We grasped hands.

"Aleksey'll come back for the rest of us once you're out of harm's way. He said he has another path to get Yale."

"I won't go. Not without you. I'll go back to Violet's to search. Those papers have to be there. And we'll all go. Miss Violet and Judge Calder knew each other well. She's pregnant with his baby, Mama. That has to mean something to him. She said he'll do what she wants and help us."

"Judge Calder has his own plans," Mama said.

"But she said—"

"Violet said what she needed to say, Katherine, to get what she wanted. Surely, you see that now."

I did. But it pierced me to hear it said aloud, to know how foolish I'd been. The pain at realizing my idiocy was another knife in the chest.

"Judge Calder will listen if we go to him," I said, "you knew him. Talk to Elizabeth."

"I *am* in talks with him, Katherine. That's what I'm trying to say. But I can't explain it all. Not now. Please trust me." I had trusted her as a younger child, believed without a second thought. Now, after so much time, so much we had experienced, I trusted her because I knew deep inside she loved me. I owed her trust after being part of the reason we were left with nothing but awful choices.

Violet's words about Mama not being the woman I thought she was returned to me, daring me not to believe she was a good, loving mother. But she was. Standing there in front of me, I saw every bit of the love and strength Mama carried for us, plain as day.

I started toward the door. "The papers were unsigned, but we can forge them. I don't care anymore. I'll check her office for them."

Mama pulled me back. She put her fingers to her lips. "Listen."

We heard shouts coming from outside.

"You need to go now," Mama said.

I shook my head. "I can't. I won't. Come with me."

"I have some things in the works myself. You've done your best with this. Now let me get Tommy and Yale back and then I'll join you. We're wasting time. Listen to me, you have to go now."

"I won't leave you. I need to make this right."

"If you want to make it right, you have to go." Mama's voice cracked. "If you go, all I have to worry about are Tommy and Yale. Pearl can help me if I need it."

I didn't like the idea. "I can hide here. No one will bother with this little house. They'll go to Miss Violet's. They won't suspect our home is connected to hers in any way."

Mama tilted her head. "There're people involved who know all of Violet's financial holdings and who worked for her. I don't care what people think they know about us, but I don't want them hauling you off. I couldn't live with that."

"Mama, please."

"If you want to help me, then you need to go now."

"I won't leave."

"People know who you are. And if you stay here, they'll take you, they'll …" Mama's voice cracked and dissolved.

I shook my head. I couldn't believe I'd caused all of this. Mama's words were ripping at her insides, what she knew petrified her.

She turned toward the front of the house. "They're closer."

It sounded as though there were hundreds of people heading our way. Mama began stuffing me into the canvas coat for gardening that Mr. Hayes had left behind. Her fear permeated the kitchen making me ready to listen to her rather than my own flawed reasoning.

"Are you sure, Mama? This is the right thing?"

She nodded and pulled the coat closed on me. "That'll keep you dry. Go to Aleksey at Mr. Palmer's farm. Along the river. You said you knew the way."

My breath caught. I remembered Aleksey saying there was a bridge that led to Mr. Palmer's farm from a spot near the dance we'd attended. I reached for the ledger.

Mama blocked my hand. "Leave it. I need to see exactly what it says. It will keep you safe in the end, I'm sure."

My stomach lurched at what Mama would read. I choked. "Please. No matter what it says in there, I love you, and I did this for you, for us."

She took my face between her hands and kissed my forehead before leveling her gaze on me. "I know. And what you need to know is that I believe in you, what you can do. I believe every single word of it. You have a gift. That's what scared me all along."

I collapsed into her arms. She patted my back and shushed me for a moment.

"We have the rest of our lives to sort this out. But now, you need to go. And you need to know I understand that you wanted to help. I know."

We clung to each other. A gunshot rang out. "Move," she said, pushing me toward the door. "You can do this."

I turned the knob and felt the hairline crack in my heart, the one that had healed in the last year, begin to open back up, the pain taking my breath away. I couldn't go. But as I turned to say I was staying, another shot rang out.

Mama gave me a heave from behind and into the dark, drenching rain I went.

**

I made my way through the gardens toward Tommy's shed. I stopped and turned to see Miss Violet's house lit up with torchlight. Silhouetted men and women were visible in the windows, and I could hear their shouts, things crashing, her house being destroyed. Pearl emerged from the shed and stood beside me, staring, startling me since she'd been gone from the shed for some time.

"I have to go," I said.

"I understand."

"Aleksey'll come back and get Yale and Tommy back to Mama and then back to me."

She nodded.

"Mama needs your help," I told her, and we embraced.

"She'll explain everything," I said.

And then Pearl was plodding through the gardens, heading toward Mama's kitchen, into trouble, ready to help our family like no one ever had.

I exited the gate and exhaled. I was moving away from Violet's home, from all that I'd done and relief flooded me.

"Katherine," someone said.

I froze, fear keeping me from running.

"It's me, Violet."

I started to walk away, but her sobbing drew me back. Her crying made me angry, not sad this time. She was crouched near the fence, sitting on her suitcase, her hair matted under her silken flowered hat. I got closer and could see her eyes were red from crying.

"What are you doing?" I said.

Her teeth chattered. "Judge Calder's coming."

I sighed. "Go to the boardinghouse on Main and get warm. Get away from this place. Send word to him from there. You're going to die of exposure if you stay here. Or worse, from this mob."

"You're being so mean," Violet said between sobs.

"Go get warm, Violet."

"Plenty warm. Rain's letting up."

I shook my head.

"Come with me, Katherine. Think of what we could do now that we understand how to run this."

"That's funny," I said.

She took my hand. "I depend on you."

"You don't need anyone."

She stared at me with sunken eyes, and for the first time I saw her as a tiny woman, barely strong enough to stand.

"My baby. We need you. They took my money."

I started to ask who *they* were, but it didn't matter. I wasn't even sure I believed her.

She pulled my hand again. "Please."

I stepped away. "No, Violet. I'm leaving, and I want you to remember that I know as much about you as you do about me."

I didn't mention the ledger for fear she'd go trouble Mama for it. The sound of a wagon crunching along filled my ears. "If there's one thing I know, it's that you'll be just fine." And I left her behind, feeling free at last.

I moved as quickly as I could toward the river, along the winding bends, toward the direction of Mr. Palmer's farm.

Please get me there. Please. I laid my hand on the pocket where my angel crystal was and felt calmness descend as the rains picked up with the wind.

Chapter 78

Rescue
Aleksey

Driving Palmer's small rig through town the horses were agitated at the noise and number of people who kept running into the street in front of them, drunk from whiskey or high on the energy of the mob that was still out in force. I finally stopped a few stragglers at the Savery. They indicated they would soon be heading for the saloon district to gather forces. One group had already headed toward Violet Pendergrass's home. A second group had headed toward the courthouse, hauling Helen and Bernice along with them. I hopped out of the wagon, took one man by the shoulders and shook him. "Where's Dreama?"

His crazed eyes finally settled on me. "Gone. The fellas headed to Pendergrass's house will bring 'em both in." The man pulled me by the arm. "We could use your help. Sweeping through the white district, the saloons. We're cleaning all of them out in one swoop."

I yanked myself away, hopped back in the wagon and headed toward Katherine's house. Turning the corner too fast, I nearly drove the horses smack into Pearl.

"Pearl!"

I leapt out and grabbed her, helping her regain her bearings. "You all right?"

She nodded.

"Where's Katherine?"

"Gone."

I removed my hat and pushed my hair back. My heart sank at the thought she left with Violet.

"She's going to your farm. Said she knows pretty much how to get there."

The dance. I'd told her how to get there that night. What if she didn't remember the directions? My heart pounded.

"How long ago?"

"An hour, a little less, maybe, but she left from her house." Pearl patted her coat. "I have to get to the courthouse."

Confused, I started to ask her what on earth she was talking about, but she waved me off. "Go get her."

I hugged her tight. "I owe you." And I climbed back into the wagon and turned the horses toward the river.

Chapter 79

Medusa Tree
Katherine

As I rounded a bend in the river, movement up ahead made me stop. The wind screamed and whistled, bending trunks back and forth, bouncing limbs and pushing loose brush past my legs.

Please keep me safe, keep me safe.

I ducked behind a tree, watching. I squinted into the night, listening, cursing the clouds that blanketed the dark sky. The battering rain made my hat useless. I thought I was nearly to where the dance at the river had been held, so not very much farther to where Aleksey said a bridge to Mr. Palmer's farm spanned the water.

The movement came again, and I leaned out to see better. A wagon. It moved slowly, as though the driver was searching for something—or someone. I couldn't believe how close it had gotten without my noticing. Just twenty yards away, it stopped. I held my breath. The driver coughed and turned in his seat, and I froze. He looked into the treetops. Even in the dark storm, I could see blond hair sticking out of his hat.

Was it him? The man's build was the same as his. Aleksey. It had to be.

I stepped out of the tree line and yelled to him, but another burst of wind cut through the river path, keeping my voice from carrying. He snapped the reins and started moving again, faster.

A branch fell in front of me, just a few feet away. I clasped my chest, relieved it hadn't hit me. I looked beyond. He hadn't noticed the falling branch and continued on. I pulled up my skirts and jogged down the riverbank, my feet sucked into the swampy mud with each step, calling his name. Finally, the wind died back just as I was yelling for him.

He pulled the horses to a stop and shifted in his seat, squinting, looking to see where my voice was coming from.

I pushed on despite my lack of breath, my burning legs. "Aleksey!" I drew closer to the wagon and banged on its side. It stopped, the horses neighing.

Finally.

He looked back toward me, eyes widening as he recognized who I was. He leapt from the wagon and scooped me up, holding tight, so tight I thought our two beings might meld right into one. "I love you, I love you, I love you," he said, his breath warm on my ear, neck and cheeks as he kissed me everywhere, as amazed at finding me as I was at being found. His words warmed me from the inside out. He lifted me into the wagon and yelled over the wind as he settled onto the seat beside me. "We have to cross the river and get to Palmer's for supplies."

I sat as close to him as I could, his body heat warming me. He talked loud, but gently to the horses, encouraging them over the soft riverbank. After a time, he slowed the wagon, and I leaned forward to see what he was looking at.

He pointed. "The bridge." He moved the wagon closer. He stood and surveyed the crossing. He hopped down, and I started to join him. "Stay there," he said. "Let me look at it first."

He returned quickly and jumped into the seat. "It's almost washed out again, the road and the bridge right here. Same thing happened a while ago."

I stood to get a better look. "Let's go back," I said.

"Up ahead, there's a rope bridge. We can walk across. We'll secure the horses here, and Harold will come back for them just as soon as we let them know."

He leapt back out of the wagon and reached for me.

I took his hands and jumped down. He pulled me along, allowing me to move much faster than I would on my own.

"A little ways more," he said, tugging at my hand. Before long, Aleksey stopped and gestured. "Right there."

I squinted. *Where?*

He pulled me closer to the river's edge and I saw something, but nothing I would have called a bridge.

We trudged closer still and then three ropes strung across the water came into view.

"That's not a bridge," I said. My stomach clenched at the thought of having to use that to cross over the frothy, racing water below. "We'll get killed."

"We can do it." He took me by the shoulders. "Mabel did it before, and you can, too."

"Another way across. There has to be."

"The rear end of Palmer's farm is right across here." He stepped one foot onto the bridge and wiggled it, getting a feel for the rope. He grabbed the hand-ropes. "Just across the way there. Can't go back now." He stepped fully onto the tightrope.

"Wait," I said, stepping nearer. He paused and looked back at me.

"I can't."

He nodded and I exhaled, thinking he was turning back, looking for another way. Instead, he told me, "You can. When I get across, I'll pull the rope tight, and you'll be able to run across like it's a summer field."

He started across, one foot in front of the other. I shook my head, relieved that he'd told me that but unsure that he could possibly pull the rope tight enough to make a difference.

As he moved across, he weighed that rope down so low that I thought he'd topple in and be swept away by the rushing Des Moines River. He leaned one way and pulled up on the ropes to re-center his weight. I covered my mouth. It was as though his great size did nothing to keep him from gracefully moving across. I'd never make it. He seemed to instinctually know how to use the ropes against his size to balance and move quickly.

I held my breath as he took the last steps across to safety on the other bank. He sat down, dug his feet into some tree roots and rocks, and pulled the rope taut. "Come across," he yelled.

Maybe I could do it with him holding the rope.

"Come on," he shouted over the roaring river. "You can do this."

I took one step onto the rope. The toe of my shoe shot right off, and I lurched forward. Not even off the riverbank yet, I stopped. I backed away, looking back in the direction of the wagon. I could go back and drive it back through town. No one would be looking for me, looking like I did, that late at night. Surely the mob had dissipated.

The wind died down, and I heard Aleksey calling. "Up, Katherine, come this way. River's getting higher." I stared upward. The rain had actually slowed. But I knew the river's rising waters would be coming from upstream as much as from the sky. Water lapped at my feet. He was right. I could do this. I took a deep breath and stepped with the middle of my foot this time. I pulled myself up and felt him tighten the rope by pulling it from the other side.

I wiggled each foot to get the right placement as I stepped, feeling my way as I'd seen him do.

When I got closer, I could hear him. "Look at me, Katherine," he said. "Just keep your eyes on the bank and feel your way."

The rope under my feet was going slack. I heard him groan as he dug in to keep it steady. I wondered if his feet were losing hold in the mud. I kept my eyes on him as he coached me along, encouraging.

I slid each foot past the other, letting the rope push into the arch of each foot. I pulled and lifted the hand-ropes as he told me to, barely taking a breath.

One foot. Other foot. One foot. Other foot.

"Almost there, Katherine," he said.

Please keep me safe, please keep me safe, God, keep me safe.

I reached the other side and fell into Aleksey's arms. He lifted me, and I held tight, face buried in his neck, wanting to just find shelter right there. He squeezed me. "I knew you could do it." He kissed me, and I felt a surge of relief that we were safe.

"Rain let up," Aleksey said. I realized then that it had stopped midway through my crossing. We looked up. "Wind's better, too," I said, thinking how lucky for me that it had died down as well.

"Nearly there." He bent over. "Hop on."

I patted his back. "I can walk."

"We'll move quicker this way. You're exhausted."

I nodded and reached over his back, grabbing his shoulders and pulling myself onto him. He stood and hitched me up, pulling my legs around his middle. He threaded his arms under my knees to keep me easily on his back.

He carried me along that way for some time until we reached a portion of land that was so deep and soft from the constant shift between deep snow and slush and mud that he couldn't yank his feet out of the muck. He set me down, and we pulled each other along. On our right, a tree fell off to the side with a crash, and I jumped. Its roots stuck straight into the air. We stepped around its branches, thanking God it missed hitting us.

"A little farther," Aleksey said. "They'll be waiting at the wall."

There was an eerie stillness that came with the absence of wind and rain. It felt as if we were the last people on earth.

"Listen," I said. We stopped.

"What?"

"The quiet. The wind is completely gone.

"And that crackling sound. Can you hear it?" he said.

We stepped over a long, skinny tree trunk.

The crackling, followed by a sucking sound was similar to when we pulled our feet from the mud. I looked up and saw movement. I squeezed Aleksey's hand. Another tree was falling in the distance. The crash when it struck the ground shook us as though we'd been right beside it, reminding me of the sound the oak made when it fell in Miss Violet's yard.

Aleksey squeezed my hand. "It's the shift in weather again, warm, cold, rain, snow. All of these trees are just falling over. Let's get into the clearing before one of them lands on us."

We came to the open field and looked up to see the clouds had thinned, like cotton stuffing being pulled apart revealing a deep blue sky and the full moon against its velvet. The contrast in brightness between when we'd started across the bridge until that moment was as bright as daylight to our eyes.

"It's beautiful," I said, still staring upward. He pulled me to his side and nudged me along. I shivered, the temperature not too much above freezing. The nearly frozen raindrops that had wetted everything shone like diamonds.

As we got farther into the clearing and the clouds continued to part, I saw clearly the outline of the wall and the massive tree beside it. I stopped again. "That's it, isn't it?"

He stopped and looked in the same direction as I was.

"That's where I found the book and the angel stone."

"The Medusa tree," I said, pointing. I could see the face in the trunk and the wild, naked limbs that made her famous snake-hair against the blue light of night.

"Yes," he said. We started walking again, drawing closer. Then Aleksey was waving his hand and yelling, "Mr. Palmer! Harold!"

I could see the outline of people sitting in a wagon. "That's them. In the work wagon. They came," Aleksey said.

The people in the wagon stood and waved their hands overhead.

It was harder than ever to pull our feet out of the mud as we moved. The wagon began to roll toward us.

One foot, then the other, the sucking noise accompanying us.

In the silence between our steps, I heard something different that the noise we were making. "Aleksey." I stopped squeezing his hand to hold him back.

He froze mid-stride and looked around. "I hear it."

It sounded as if fabric was being ripped in two, and it echoed around us. I covered my head, imagining a tree falling on us, even though I knew there was only one tree in the clearing. I followed Aleksey's gaze toward Medusa. The ripping continued and then Medusa moved. Moaning, she swayed. "Oh no," he said.

Was she moving? I was frozen, staring. I didn't have the chance to discern the movement for sure before Aleksey was pulling me into him and at the same time, still facing the tree, pulling me back from Medusa, moving as fast as we could through the thick mud. The great skeleton tree lurched and then threw herself to the ground, shaking the earth under our feet, her surrender coming like the groans of a thousand men.

We clung to each other, our breath synchronized. The air cleared, and the ground stilled, and I looked down. In front of us was a branch stretched from the trunk, her fingertips brushing the tops of our shoes.

Aleksey pulled me closer. "You all right?"

I nodded. "You?"

"I'm all right," he said. "Mr. Palmer?" Aleksey called. "Harold? You okay?"

"Fine!" they yelled back.

I surveyed the length of the tree, my gaze slipping in between the brittle branches, the thick arms and what had once seemed like snake-like hair. My gaze traced the length of the trunk and that was when I saw it. Them. What was I seeing? Medusa's root-ball stood on its side, upright, a massive brown underskirt, twinkling with dripping water. I pulled Aleksey's hand. "Look at that."

"What on earth?"

Thunk, thunk, thunk. It sounded as though someone was lobbing rocks toward the tree. We moved closer, feet sinking and sucking as we moved. The root-ball glimmered and shone and glistened in the moonlight. My brain couldn't make sense of what we were seeing, but we were drawn to the magnificence. The root-ball stood ten feet in the air, thick with wiry roots. Among the dirt and fibers were jewels, circling, crowning, hiding in every square inch.

"What on earth?" Aleksey said again.

I was lost in the sight of it. "It's not water," I said.

"Well, I'll be," a voice came up behind us.

The older man removed his hat and pressed it against his chest. I looked at him as he stared, his eyes glistening. I assumed it was Mr. Palmer, but I didn't want to interrupt his obvious reverence for what he was seeing. "Winnie's stones," he said. "Those are Winnie's stones. *That's* where she hid them."

Harold came up beside us, removing his hat and shaking his head.

"The book said Winnie buried them," Aleksey said.

"So, this is where," Palmer said, his face folded in sadness. "The tree died when she did."

I felt his grief. I wasn't privy to the full story, but I knew Aleksey was, and I could see that Mr. Palmer was in the midst of a reckoning.

Mr. Palmer looked at me. "Aleksey tells me you're like Winnie, like my wife."

I glanced at Aleksey and back at Mr. Palmer.

"She healed people," Palmer said. "Stopped their grieving like erasing chalk from slate." He snapped his fingers. "I didn't . . ."

Aleksey patted the man's back. "It's all right. She knows you love her. She has to know. If she's like Katherine, she knows."

Mr. Palmer looked at me and then at Aleksey. "Lucky for you two, it's not too late."

"Lucky," said Aleksey. "Yes, I am."

Harold moved closer.

"How'd you know to meet us here?" Aleksey said.

"Fat Joe and Mabel said you ran out when they told you about their tickets to see Dreama. Harold took the rig to Katherine's. Her mother said she'd gone the river way here. We just hoped we were guessing right by coming back this way."

"Thank you," Aleksey and I said.

"You sure you have to go?" Harold said.

Aleksey nodded. "For now. Don't know who I can trust. Until I do, she can't stay."

I was drawn to the root-ball and its magical stones. "Can I take one?"

"Anything you want," Mr. Palmer told me. "We'll gather the rest up once you're on your way."

While Aleksey explained where he left Mr. Palmer's smaller wagon, I went to the root-ball and pulled a few stones from the roots, my fingers brushing over purples and blues and pinks, and others clear as water. The angel stone in my skirt would remain my favorite, but these were special for another reason. Aleksey had admitted to someone the truth about me. He saw me as I was. And for the rest of my life, I'd do anything he needed to repay him.

I got into the wagon, and Mr. Palmer explained what he and Harold had loaded onto it for our trip.

Mr. Palmer stuck his hand out. "You can trust me, Aleksey."

They shook hands then fell into an embrace, each of them thumping the other's back. "I know, sir. I know. Thank you." Aleksey shook his head as though this exchange was more than it appeared to me.

"Me, too," Harold said as Aleksey pulled away from Mr. Palmer. Harold grabbed Aleksey into an embrace. "Come back quick. You've got work to finish."

Aleksey got into the wagon. "When I get back, you can rest for a week while I do your chores," he said.

"A week? How about a month?" Harold and Mr. Palmer stepped away from the wagon.

"A lifetime," Aleksey said. "I owe you a lifetime."

Harold looked away, digging his hands into his pockets.

"Stay safe," Palmer said as we pulled away. I looked over my shoulder and saw the two of them watch us leave before turning and heading toward the river to cross the rope bridge and retrieve the wagon we'd left behind. It'd be a long night for them by the time they got the wagon back to the farm the long way around town.

Aleksey covered my legs with a blanket, took my hand in his and kissed my fingers. I moved closer, and he put his arm around me.

"You're rich in friends, Aleksey," I said, thinking how fortunate he was.

"Rich in love as well," he said, and he squeezed me into him, making me feel more loved than ever before. I ached for Mama, for Yale, for Tommy. Were they safe? Now that I was at a distance I knew this was the right way to proceed, for me to be removed from the ensuing chaos, to remove one variable for Mama to worry over.

Tears fell down my cheeks, freezing on my skin as the temperature dropped yet again and exhaustion settled over me. The only thing that felt stable and sure was Aleksey. And I knew he would stay by my side, just as he was right that moment. That was enough for me, for right then, until we found a way to bring us all back together again.

Chapter 80

Next
Violet

Violet sat on the edge of the bed. She cradled her belly in her arms, wondering just how much longer she had to go before becoming a mother. The coverlet was worn and rough to the touch. The sun from the window lit the dust swirling in the room.

She went to the tiny desk near the windows, sat, and pulled her book from the desk drawer. She dabbed her pen in ink and reviewed her list. She checked off the small pile of knitted clothing made from soft yarn, tiny hats and coverings for her baby. She smiled at the thought of a little squirming newborn, legs kicking, fists balled.

Violet's heart sped up at the knock at the door. Jeremy. She opened the door, filled with anticipation. Her heart pounded, blood rushing, making her feel more alive than she had since the last time there was a knock.

A scrawny, elderly man stood there. He removed his hat. "Ma'am."

Violet stiffened. Not again.

He held a paper out to her. "Said he's real sorry. Got held up with business. Said you'd understand, being a businessman—I mean a businesswoman yourself."

Violet bit her tongue, rage coursing through her.

She thought of the money she had hidden, the money she'd lied to Katherine about when she saw her leaving. Was it enough? Did she need Jeremy? Oh yes, she did. But she would not beg. She began to shut the door.

He pressed it back. "Ma'am. The letter."

"Tell him, no thank you. I'm returning it to sender."

And she slammed the door even as he was raising his hand to keep it open.

"Judge Calder said to tell you the little girl is out of Glenwood," he called through the door. "The boy is free from jail." She felt a twinge of relief. Jeanie Arthur would have her children back. Maybe Violet played a part in their release. But if she was honest with herself, maybe she'd had nothing to do with it at all. She refused to respond and finally heard the man walking down the hall away from her room.

Near the front window, Violet straightened a painting, the one of the girl in the factory. She dragged her finger over the dried oil, absorbed in each careful brushstroke. The other painting brought a smile, the cheerful flower coloring her mood, reminding her new life was on its way. She was so glad she found a way to bring them with her.

Violet drew open the gauzy curtains covering the window and sat at the desk, staring into the sleepy streets of Willow Creek. She pulled a second book from the drawer, one that she'd filled while in Des Moines, most of it records of her success, good luck, good planning.

She ran her pen down the side of a page. Katherine. How she missed her. She shook her head.

No matter. The baby would only make things better. In every way. She put her chin on her hand, thinking of all the ways a baby could work into her plans. As she was imagining, a wagon pulled past her window. Jeremy's messenger, headed back to Des Moines.

She bit the end of her pen. The baby stretched inside her, a foot jammed against her skin, the child announcing it had its own plans.

She rubbed her stomach. "I know, baby, you have big things to do. And so do I. So do I."

She gasped as a pain pulled a wide swath across her midsection. The pain felt good to her. The pain reminded her that soon she'd be the whole world to a little innocent soul. It made her think of her father, the feel of his rough-hewn hand on her back, guiding her through the streets of New York, protecting her, teaching her. She would be that kind of person to her baby. She'd be everything other mothers were not.

Another knock came. She looked out the window, craning to see down one end of the street and then the other. Was Jeremy's messenger back to try again? Violet stormed to the door and flung it open, ready to more firmly turn the man away.

"What?" She drew back. "Oh." She shook her head.

A girl stood in the hall with a suitcase at her feet. She seemed stunned.

"I'm sorry," she said, bending to pick up her suitcase. "I thought . . ."

Violet appraised the young woman in seconds, knowing by her frayed hem, dirty nails, and wind-blown hair under a ragged, flowered hat that she had been expecting someone very different to answer this door.

The young woman lifted her suitcase. A good, solid, new suitcase that didn't match her wardrobe or appearance. "I'm sorry." Her voice cracked, and she started down the hall.

Violet started to close the door but then stopped. She stepped into the hall. "Young lady," she said.

The woman stopped.

"Are you all right?"

She turned slowly. She met Violet's gaze, her eyes full of tears. Violet exhaled at the sight, smelling desperation. She raised her arm to the side. "Why don't you come in? Have some tea."

The woman hesitated and considered the offer.

"Just to get your bearings," Violet said.

As the woman walked toward Violet, a small smile appeared, relief flooding her face.

"Thank you," she said. "After . . . everything, I can't thank you enough."

And so she entered, and Violet sat the woman near the fireplace and readied some tea.

"I see the fortune in your arrival, as well. I'm Violet. It's lovely to meet you."

And the woman fell into tears, telling a tale that Violet had heard many awful times before.

Everything would be fine, Violet knew right then. She drew a deep breath that filled her with the hope she'd been so accustomed to feeling for so long. And so, she told the woman just that.

"Things have a way of working out," Violet said, petting the woman's head. "They always do."

CPSIA information can be obtained
at www.ICGtesting.com
Printed in the USA
LVHW011801131119
637246LV00012B/1251/P